The Da

The bones of the Magi have been stolen from their resting place in a German cathedral. When a dying priest whispers a cryptic clue, Maddock and Bones find themselves in the midst of a deadly race to solve a centuries-old conspiracy. Danger lurks at every turn and no one knows where the clues will lead... or what they will uncover. From ancient cathedrals, to hidden temples, to icy mountain peaks, Maddock and Bones must outrun and outwit their enemies in the thrilling adventure- *Icefall!*

Buccaneer

For more than two centuries the Oak Island Money Pit has baffled researchers and foiled treasure hunters, and when Dane Maddock and Bones Bonebrake take up the search, they get much more than they bargained for. Danger lies at every turn as they search for a treasure out of legend that dates back to the time of Christ. Ancient wonders, hidden temples, mythical creatures, secret societies, and foes new and old await as Maddock and Bones unravel a pirate's deadly secret in *Buccaneer.*

Atlantis

What is the true story behind the fabled lost continent of Atlantis, and what power did the Atlanteans wield? When archaeologist Sofia Perez unearths the remains of an Atlantean city, she unwittingly gives the Dominion the power to remake the world after its own design. From the depths of the Caribbean to the streets of Paris, to Japanese islands and beyond, Join former Navy SEALs turned treasure hunters Dane Maddock and "Bones" Bonebrake on a race to stop the Dominion from unleashing its greatest threat yet in the thrilling adventure, Atlantis!

Primitive

Bones teams up with a television crew to investigate a creature out of legend, but what if the legend is true?

Praise for David Wood's *Dane Maddock Adventures*

"David Wood has done it again. *Quest* takes you on an expedition that leads down a trail of adventure and thrills. David Wood has honed his craft and *Quest* is proof of his efforts!" **David L. Golemon, Author of *Legacy* and *The Supernaturals***

"Ancient cave paintings? Cities of gold? Secret scrolls? Sign me up! A twisty tale of adventure and intrigue that never lets up and never lets go!" – **Robert Masello, author of *The Medusa Amulet***

"A non-stop thrill ride triple threat- smart, funny and mysterious!" **Jeremy Robinson, author of *Instinct* and *Threshold***

Works by David Wood

The Dane Maddock Adventures
Dourado
Cibola
Quest
Icefall
Buccaneer
Atlantis
Ark

Dane and Bones Origins
Freedom (with Sean Sweeney)
Hell Ship (with Sean Ellis)
Splashdown (with Rick Chesler)
Dead Ice (with Steven Savile)
Liberty (with Edward G. Talbot)
Electra (with Rick Chesler)
Amber (with Rick Chesler)
Justice (with Edward G. Talbot- forthcoming)

The Jade Ihara Adventures
Oracle (with Sean Ellis)
Changeling (with Sean Ellis forthcoming)

Stand-Alone Novels
Into the Woods
Arena of Souls
The Zombie-Driven Life
You Suck
Callsign: Queen (with Jeremy Robinson)
Oracle (with Sean Ellis)
Destiny (with Sean Ellis)
Dark Rite (with Alan Baxter)

David Wood writing as David Debord

The Absent Gods Trilogy
The Silver Serpent
Keeper of the Mists
The Gates of Iron

The Impostor Prince (with Ryan A. Span)

THE DANE MADDOCK

ADVENTURES

Volume 2

DAVID WOOD

Gryphonwood

The Dane Maddock Adventures- Volume 2
Copyright 2015 by David Wood
Published 2105 by Gryphonwood Press
www.gryphonwoodpress.com

ISBN-13: 978-1517625382

ISBN-10: 1517625386

Your book has been assigned a CreateSpace ISBN.
Icefall- A Dane Maddock Adventure
Copyright 2011, 2015 by David Wood

Buccaneer- A Dane Maddock Adventure
Copyright 2012, 2015 by David Wood

Atlantis- A Dane Maddock Adventure
Copyright 2013 by David Wood

Primitive- A Bones Bonebrake Story
Copyright 2015 by David Wood

ICEFALL

A DANE MADDOCK ADVENTURE

Prologue

"They are coming for me." Johannes had repeated the words so many times that they no longer held any meaning. It was now a mantra; sounds to ward off the shadows that lurked in the night. He no longer remembered what, exactly, he feared lurked in the darkness just beyond the edge of his vision. Bitter cold and utter exhaustion had driven that from his mind. Now, it was only the memory of fear that drove him on.

Snow crunched under his feet with each frozen footfall, a counterpoint to the steady whisper of the ice-choked Rhine. Each exhalation sent up a cloud of vapor that wreathed his face like an ethereal fog as he stumbled through the frozen night. Up ahead, a faint twinkle of lights beckoned to him. He was almost there!

Hope kindled a tiny flame somewhere deep inside him and he quickened his pace. He tightened his grip on the sack slung over his shoulder. What was inside it? He couldn't quite remember.

By the time he staggered up the cathedral steps, he scarcely had the strength to stand. He fell against the door and managed with only the greatest of efforts, to knock twice. He waited, soft flakes of snow brushing his cheeks like angel's wings. Finally, he heard a voice from inside.

"Who is there?"

"Johannes." He poured all his strength into the word, but it came out barely a murmur. The man inside must have heard him, because he continued as expected.

"And what brings you here at this hour?"

Johannes drew a shivering breath and spoke the one word that would gain him entrance.

"Dreihasenbild."

The door creaked open and he managed to take three wobbling steps inside before he fell to his knees. The cathedral was hardly warm inside, but after days trekking through the snow, it felt to Johannes like summertime. The gloved fingers of his left hand sought the clasp at the neckline of his cloak, but they were too numb to manage the task. His right hand still clutched the sack, and he would not relinquish that until he saw the priest.

"Here, brother, let us get you somewhere you can rest." Strong hands grabbed him under the arms and helped him to his feet.

"Must see the Father," he gasped. "Dreihasenbild," he added for emphasis. That should forestall any argument from the robed and hooded monk who supported his weight as he hobbled down the aisle, stopping before the altar. "Bring the Father."

"I am here." A tall man with a shaved head and amber-colored eyes seemed to materialize out of thin air. He moved to the altar and stood before Johannes. Their eyes locked, and the father's brow crinkled slightly, as if he waited for Johannes to answer a question yet unasked. "I am pleased to see you have returned safely."

Johannes found himself unable to meet the priest's gaze. His eyes drifted to the golden casket behind the altar. As his eyes locked on its shining surface, memories came flooding back. His knees gave way and he slumped to the floor.

"Johannes!" The priest dropped to one knee in front of him and clasped his shoulders. "Forgive me. I was so pleased to see you alive that I did not consider the condition you are in." He glanced up at the monk who had opened the door for

Johannes. "Fetch a blanket, food, and a cup of hot water for our brother."

The monk hurried away. When the sound of his footsteps faded into silence, the priest's demeanor changed. His expression grew grave and his stare hard.

"Did you find it?" There was no need to say what 'it' was.

"I could not get close," Johannes said.

"But it exists?" The priest gave him a small shake as he spoke.

"I believe so, but there is no way to say for certain." Uncertainty crept into his voice. He doubted the priest would believe what he had seen. But then he remembered what was in the bag and why he had brought it. "If it is where I believe it is, death awaits anyone who ventures there."

The priest stood and folded his arms across his chest. "You will have to go back. I will send men with you to keep you safe."

"There aren't enough men to fight the devil himself!" Johannes was surprised at the strength in his own words. "His minions guard it."

The priest cocked his head. "Minions of the devil?"

"Monsters," Johannes croaked. "And I brought proof." With trembling hands, he opened the sack and upended it, spilling its contents onto the floor.

The priest sucked in his breath through gritted teeth and took a step back. "What are these foul things and why have you brought them into the house of God?"

"I needed to prove the truth of my words. It is just like the temple..."

"Are you mad?" the priest hissed. "You are in the cathedral. Remember yourself."

Johannes did remember, and he began to tremble as he recalled the past several days—the fight for his life and his desperate trek back to the cathedral, all the while fearing what might be following behind him. "The devil..." His mouth was suddenly dry. "The devil gathers all the light to himself. They will come for..." He raised an unsteady hand and pointed at the golden casket.

The priest seemed to understand immediately. He once again knelt alongside Johannes and placed a comforting hand on his shoulder. "I will do what needs to be done. You may rest now."

Johannes closed his eyes and let his shoulders sag. Rest would be a welcome thing.

His eyes snapped open as a fiery lance of pain tore through his chest. He tried to cry out, but his breath was gone. He looked down to see a knife hilt protruding from his chest.

"No, don't look at that. Look at me," the priest cooed.

Johannes looked into the amber eyes and saw nothing there. No compassion, no love, only emptiness.

"You have done well," the priest said. "The secrets must be kept. You understand."

"I... don't..." Johannes gasped.

The priest gave a sad smile, yanked the dagger free, and wiped it on Johannes' cloak. Gently, like a mother putting her babe to bed, he eased Johannes down onto the hard floor. The cold stone seemed to leach the remaining warmth from Johannes' body even as his life's blood flowed from the wound in his chest.

"You know much, yet you understand nothing."

The light seemed to dim around Johannes, and a circle of blackness slowly closed in on him. He watched as the priest gathered the contents of the sack, stepped over the altar, and moved to the golden casket. As death gathered him in its arms, Johannes whispered one final word.

"Dreihasenbild."

Chapter 1

This place was cold– a biting, stinging, run home and put your feet up by the fire kind of cold that soaked through every layer of your clothing. Key West this was not.

"What are you thinking, Maddock?" Jade's sleek black hair was sprinkled with the powdery snow that floated down on the vagrant breeze. Her eyes sparkled with the reflected light of the lamp-lined street and her smile outshone the mantle of white that lay heavy on the world. "Don't tell me. You are so glad I talked you into this!"

Maddock grinned. He was glad he hadn't answered the question. He'd actually been wondering how Jade had extracted him from his well-worn holiday tradition of beer and barbecue somewhere, anywhere the only white thing blanketing the world was sand. Not wanting to spoil her good mood, he pulled her close and kept his thoughts to himself. They'd spent too much time apart of late. Jade had been working in the Far East while Maddock had been... too many places to count. She wanted this trip and this time together and he was happy to oblige her.

"Christmas in Germany!" she breathed. "I've dreamed about it ever since I was a little girl. The cathedrals! And..." she drew the word out like a game show host about to announce the grand prize "...the snow!" She swept out her arm, her gesture taking in the city's frosted skyline. "And then we're going to the Alps!" She squeezed him tight and bounced up and down like an excited child.

"Tell me again why we came here so early?" He enveloped her in his arms and they looked out across the Rhine River, the light of the street lamps flickering across its choppy surface.

"Because the celebration of the Christmas season started the evening of December sixth. I wanted to be here for more than just Christmas day! I've got tonight all planned out. We'll have our tour of the cathedral and then I've got a restaurant picked out where they serve some of the traditional holiday treats. "

"I hate fruitcake." He knew better, but it was worth it to see the scandalized look in her eyes, though it passed almost immediately.

"I am not letting you mess with me tonight. I'm too happy." She turned back toward the water. "And for your information, you are going to try Christbaumgeback even if it kills you." She glanced at her watch. "We should probably get going." Her face fell into a frown and she looked up and down the street.

Maddock's eyes followed hers, but he saw nothing amiss. "You never told me how you managed to schedule a solo, nighttime tour of the Cologne Cathedral."

"I know somebody," she kissed him on the left cheek, "who knows somebody," a kiss on the right cheek, "who knows somebody." The next kiss was full on the lips.

"Get a room you two!"

No way. It couldn't be who he thought it was. Jade was going to have a cow.

Maddock turned to see a six-and-a-half foot tall Native American strolling along the river walk. His height and breadth of shoulder drew the attention of everyone he passed.

"You have got to be kidding me." Jade turned her angry eyes upon Maddock. "What is Bones doing here?"

Uriah Bonebrake, known to his friends as "Bones," was Maddocks business partner and best friend since their days as Navy SEALs. He also was not Jade's favorite person, nor was she his.

"I don't..." Maddock was dumbfounded. He'd only told Bones that he and Jade were going away for the holidays. How had Bones known where they were going, much less where they would be standing at this exact moment? "Bones, what the hell?"

"It's Christmas, dude!" Bones grinned. He wore his black leather biker jacket unzipped, revealing a t-shirt featuring a character from the South Park cartoon garbed in a Santa outfit with *Merry Bleeping Christmas* printed above the character's head. The fact that the shirt read "bleeping" instead of the actual expletive was unusually restrained for Bones. It wouldn't help with Jade's mood, though.

"I can't believe you invited Bones on our romantic Christmas getaway." If he'd thought the breeze coming across the river was frigid, Jade's words took it down a few degrees. "Is he sleeping in our bed too?"

"I..." Words failed him.

"You got punked!" Jade's icy expression melted into a warm smile. "I got you so bad, Maddock! I wish I had it on video."

"I got it." A female voice rang out and a young woman stepped out from the shadows a few paces away. "Maddock, you so got owned. Dude, your girlfriend rocks."

Angelica Bonebrake only vaguely resembled her brother. They both had long black hair and mischievous twinkles in their eyes, but that was where the similarities ended.

Where Bones' face was hard and chiseled, Angelica's features were soft and finely formed and, though she was tall for a woman, she was a far cry from her towering brother. She pocketed her camera and hurried forward to catch Maddock in a crushing embrace. She was beautiful, no doubt, but underneath her thick winter clothes she was one hundred forty pounds of solid muscle. When she wasn't working security at her uncle Crazy Charlie's casino, she was a bantamweight fighter in the WFFC. Many a drunken man had gotten too friendly with Angelica and had his shoulder dislocated or jaw broken for his trouble.

"I can't believe this." Maddock was almost dizzy with surprise. He turned to Jade, who beamed up at him. "You engineered this?"

"Did you really think I'd try to keep you away from your best friend at Christmas? It's a holiday for family and I know you guys always spend it together." The joy on her face made her even more beautiful.

He arched an eyebrow. "You're sure you want to spend Christmas with Bones?"

"Definitely." Jade turned to Angelica. "You must be Angelica. I'm Jade Ihara."

"You can just call me Angel."

Maddock cocked his head to the side. "When did this happen? I thought people called you Demonica."

"That was before she became a supermodel." Bones gave his sister a playful punch to the shoulder.

"I am not a model," she said through gritted teeth as she hit him back.

Bones rubbed his shoulder in mock hurt and Angel made an obscene gesture. "Hey chick, it's Christmas. Anyway," he turned to Maddock and Jade, "you are looking at the new female face of the WFFC!"

"It's no big deal." Angel looked embarrassed.

"She's on all their ads and she's got tons of endorsements." Bones clapped her on the back. "Of course, that might just be because all the other chicks are butt dog ugly."

Angel elbowed him in the gut and shoved him away. "I don't know why I agreed to come on this trip. You are such a..."

"Christmas!" Bones held up a hand, forestalling what Maddock was sure would have been one of Angel's streams of choice profanity. She could swear in English, Cherokee, Spanish and a smattering of several other languages.

"Don't listen to him," Jade said. "You're every bit as pretty as Maddock described you."

"Oh really?" Bones gave him an appraising look. "Now you're hot for my sister too? How many babes do you need?"

"What I said was, you must have gotten all the bad genes in the family."

"Don't hate," Bones said. "You've always been jealous of my good looks."

"How about we get going?" Jade said. "We're supposed to meet my friend at the cathedral in ten minutes."

A few minutes later found them rounding the Kölner Dom. The massive Gothic cathedral was, according to Jade, the largest in all of Germany. Maddock had never seen its equal. Its twin columns, square in their lower sections, octagonal in the middle and tapering off to points far above, were inlaid with stone reliefs and towered above them, almost sinister in the darkness.

"It withstood all the bombings during World War II." Jade spoke in a tone almost as soft as the downy flakes that fell harder as they approached the cathedral entrance. "Everything around it was leveled, but the cathedral stood."

Bones whistled, clearly impressed.

"Some think the Allies tried to avoid hitting it because its height made for a good landmark for pilots. Others credit more otherworldly protection." Her eyes flitted skyward for a moment before locking on a man who stood waving to them. He was tall and wiry with thinning brown hair sprinkled with white. He looked to be of late middle years, but his smile was eager and his eyes brimmed with vitality. He gave Jade a quick embrace before turning to introduce himself to the others.

"Otto Döring. I am an archaeologist and an old friend of Jade's." He had only the slightest German accent.

"Otto has pulled a few strings to get us access to the cathedral after regular tour hours." Jade beamed. "He is going to show us around."

Otto nodded and led the way through the main entrance, filling them in on details as they went. Bones snickered at the mention of "flying buttresses," but it turned to a wheezing cough when Angel elbowed him in the gut. Otto did not seem to notice, so absorbed was he in his subject. "The cathedral is nearly one hundred fifty meters long, more than eighty-five meters wide and over one hundred fifty meters high."

Maddock performed some quick calculations. That put the towers at over five hundred feet tall, the nave nearly that length, and the transept almost three-hundred feet wide. As they stepped inside, he fully appreciated the sheer size of the place and what it must have taken to construct it, considering the available technology between the thirteenth and nineteenth centuries. The towering columns drew his eyes up to the vaulted ceiling overhead. This place was an architectural marvel.

"The windows on the south wall were donated by ..." Otto's voice trailed away. "Oh my!" He pointed to the far end of the nave. "The Shrine of the Magi. What happened to it?"

"The what?"

"The Shrine of the Magi," Jade said. "The golden sarcophagus that supposedly holds the remains of the three Wise Men, who visited the baby Jesus."

Ignoring the others, Otto took off at a trot and Maddock ran alongside him as the archaeologist hurried toward the far end of the cathedral. They skirted the transept altar and ran toward the main altar.

Under a different set of circumstances, Maddock would have goggled at the ornate stained glass, the sculptures, and the artwork. Now, however, he had eyes only for the scene around the altar.

Three steps led up to the black marble altar outlined in ornate white friezes. Directly behind it stood the shattered remains of what had been a bulletproof glass container. Nearby lay an upended golden sarcophagus, and behind that were bodies.

Chapter 2

Three men in clerical robes lay around the fallen sarcophagus as if they had tried to defend it from whoever was after it. Maddock knelt to check on the nearest man. He was dead. He'd been stabbed multiple times in the abdomen. Deep slices in his palms indicated defensive wounds. He glanced at Bones, who was examining another man. Bones shook his head.

"This man's alive." Angel knelt over the third man, feeling for a pulse. "But I don't think he has much time."

They surrounded the dying man, whose eyes suddenly popped open. He looked down at the blood soaking his vestments and he let his head fall back. He stared glassy-eyed at Angel, the knowledge of his certain death filling his eyes.

"Engel?" he gasped, reaching up to grab her by the sleeve.

"Angel, yes." She looked surprised. "How does he know my name?"

Considering the dying priest's probable delirium, Maddock thought, the beautiful young woman clad in a white jacket with a few snowflakes still dusting her hair probably looked like an actual angel to him. "I think he believes you're an actual angel." Maddock kept his voice low, as if they sat at a hospital bedside.

"You guys, look at that." Something had caught Jade's eye. Carefully skirting the fallen bodies, she moved closer to the fallen sarcophagus, which lay on its side like an upended house. The top had either fallen or been tossed to the side, and on the floor nearby lay three skulls and a scattering of bone fragments.

Jade slipped on her gloves and picked up one of the skulls to give it a closer look. Candlelight flickered across its surface, lending it a sinister feel.

"Do you think he's a Magi?" Maddock moved closer to Jade, and Bones and Otto followed.

"I don't know what he is." Jade's voice trembled. "But he's not human." Slowly, as if turning over the last card in a losing hand, Jade rotated the skull for all to see.

Maddock stopped short. Behind him, he heard Bones' sharp intake of breath, and Otto's mumbled German curse. At least it sounded like a curse to Maddock.

Protruding from the skull were two small, curved horns.

"What the hell is that?" Maddock could not believe what he was seeing.

"Tuefel," Otto whispered, taking a step back.

The priest's eyes drifted toward Jade, and he seemed to experience a sudden moment of clarity as he saw what she was holding. "Nein!" he gasped. His grip on Angel's sleeve tightened and he rattled off a stream of words. He let go of her arm and pointed beyond the altar toward the apse, where seven chapels formed the cathedral's chevet. The priest was speaking so fast that Maddock could make out only a few words, though he did catch "Mailänder Madonna" and something that sounded like "dry house and build." He paused, gasping for breath, and hacked up a gout of blood. This seemed to take everything he had left. He let his head fall back and his eyes close. "Ewige." His voice was a scarce whisper. "Ewige." He coughed again. "L...." He fell silent as life fled his body.

"What did he say?" Angel's jaw was set and she looked like she was ready to punch anyone within arm's reach.

Otto held up a hand and shook his head. He took out a cell phone and made a call. His voice sounded both grave and urgent. When he finally hung up, he turned back to Angel. "I apologize. I felt I should call the authorities right away." He gave a quick shake of the head as if to jar his mind back on track. "The priest said the skulls must never be seen or people will lose faith. He begs us to take them away." Otto scratched his head. "After that, I think he was confused. He said all the priests were dead and he had to share the secret or it could be lost forever."

"What secret was he talking about?" Bones asked.

"I do not know. As I said, he sounded confused, though he was insistent that I listen to him. I could see in his eyes that it was important." Otto looked around. "He mentioned the Milan Madonna, as you would say it in English, which is back there." He pointed to a statue that stood beyond the altar, far to the right, where the first chapel began. "It is a well-known work of art." Otto shrugged.

"He said something else," Maddock said. "It sounded like 'dry' something or other."

"Dreihasenbild. The three hares." When everyone looked puzzled, Otto continued. "The three hares is a symbol found on many churches, cathedrals, and other sites of religious significance, from England, all the way to the Far East. It depicts three hares chasing one another in a circle. The image is rendered in such a way that each hare has two ears, but there are only three ears in total in the image."

"I've heard of it," Jade said, "though it's not my area of expertise. It's a symbol of the Trinity, is it not?"

"It can be." Otto nodded. "But to the Pagans it can represent fertility or the moon cycle."

"How does fertility connect with the Madonna?" Angel rose to her feet, finally turning away from the priest.

"She got fertile after Jesus was born, didn't she?" Bones said.

"You're a pig." Angel scowled at her brother.

"No, really. I mean, he had brothers and sisters."

"That is true." Otto almost managed a smile. "In the middle ages, it was believed that the rabbit was a hermaphrodite that could reproduce without losing virginity, hence the connection to the Blessed Mother."

"I get it." Bones nodded. "So it's not an Easter Bunny thing." Everyone ignored him.

"Otto," Maddock began, "what was that last thing he said?"

"Ewige. It translates to English as *eternal, perpetual, everlasting.*"

"He didn't get the last word out." Angel folded her arms across her chest. "It started with an "l" though."

"What's the German word for life?" Bones asked.

"Leben."

"You mean like Chris Leben?" Angel grinned. "Chris Life doesn't really suit that guy." When Otto frowned, she shrugged. "Sorry. He and I are in the same line of work."

"If he was trying to say 'eternal life,' that would make sense, wouldn't it?" Bones asked. "He's a priest and this is a church."

"If I was dying," Angel added, "that would certainly be on my mind."

Otto shrugged. "I just cannot believe this. Why would someone kill these poor men, and why would they want the bones of the Magi?"

"Why would they bust open the sarcophagus and not take the bones?" Jade asked. "Unless these skulls were not what they expected to find."

"I do not think anyone expected to find skulls like...that." Otto took a deep breath and as he exhaled, seemed to deflate a little bit. "It is all too much. I do not understand why this has happened."

Maddock chewed on his lower lip. The gears in his mind were turning at a rapid clip. He had a sixth sense about secrets and mysteries, and something told him there was more to the priest's final words than mere confusion.

"As long as we've got to wait here until the police come, we might as well do a little searching. See if we can make sense of what the priest was saying."

"Great," Bones deadpanned. "Another Maddock mystery."

"I'm game." Angel headed straight for the Milan Madonna and looked it up and down. "What exactly should I be looking for?"

"Maybe the three rabbit thing?" Bones said, coming up to join her. "He did make a point to mention it."

Maddock turned and scanned the seven chapels. The priest had said "Mailänder Madonna" but he had pointed to the left side of the chevet– the side opposite the Madonna. He carefully stepped around the shattered bulletproof glass that lay scattered around the altar and moved into the chevet.

Each chapel was a recessed area containing works of art. He inspected them one by one, looking for... he didn't know what exactly. He thought Bones was on the right track in searching for the three hares. It was the sort of out-of-place symbol that might bear significance in a place like this.

His eyes were drawn to a large, busy painting. As he drew close, Otto joined him.

"*The Adoration of the Magi.* It depicts the donors being presented to the Madonna." He indicated the figures in the foreground. "In the back are shown scenes around the birth of the Christ child."

"The title is promising." On either side of the painting, a figure knelt before a draped table, and on each drape a symbol was rendered– a dark background with three shapes. His heart racing, Maddock moved closer but was disappointed to find that the symbols were fleur-de-lis, not hares. He took hold of the frame and pulled, but it did not budge. He gave it a push, which made no difference either.

Jade sidled up to him and peered at the painting with keen interest. "You think there's something here, Maddock?"

"I don't know. Just checking it out." He ignored the foreground for the moment and examined the background images. The world swam in his peripheral vision, and he was about to give up when something caught his eye. "Otto, what is this scene?"

"That is the Christ Child being presented in the temple."

He could clearly make out the scene in the temple, but the artist had slipped some odd images into the scene: a child performing a handstand, a flock of birds, and animal that could have been a cat, or perhaps a rabbit, and..."

"What is this here?" He indicated a brown triskelion-like shape in front of one of the temple columns.

Otto leaned in close and his eyes widened with surprise when they fell on the spot Maddock indicated. "Ja! I think it might be the three hares!"

Maddock wasted no time. He placed his thumb over the image, grimacing at the thought of damaging the work of art. He pressed down gently. There was definitely something underneath, a raised bump or... a button. Before he could change his mind, he pressed down hard.

He felt the raised area give way, heard a click, and a loud scraping sound filled the silent cathedral. He sprang back, putting his arms out to shield Jade and Otto, but there was no need. The portion of the wall where the painting hung slid forward. Maddock stepped around behind it and saw a hole in the floor just big enough for a person to enter. There was no ladder, but he could see handholds cut into the stone.

"Sweet!" Bones was leaning over his shoulder, looking down at the passageway Maddock had discovered. "Me first!"

Otto gaped at the discovery. "I cannot believe this." He gave a sad smile. "It seems I am saying that a great deal this evening." He straightened and looked Maddock in the eye. "Clearly the priest was not confused. There is a mystery here, though I cannot imagine what it is all about." He turned to Jade. "There could be much at stake here, and if there is a secret, it should be entrusted to someone who understands the value of history and of spirituality." He held out his hand. "I trust you."

They shook hands and exchanged a solemn look.

"Go now. Die Polizei should be here soon. I am a regular visitor here so my presence will not rouse suspicion. Perhaps we can keep you and this mystery out of the public eye until you can uncover the truth."

They thanked Otto and, one by one, climbed down into the darkness. Bones led the way and Maddock brought up the rear. As he descended into the shaft, he saw Otto wave goodbye and reach up to press the button on the painting. The section of wall slid back into place, plunging them into darkness.

Chapter 3

Maddock took it slow, careful not to rush Jade and Angel who were not experienced climbers. A faint light blossomed down below. Bones held his latest favorite gadget—a combination ink pen, flashlight, and laser pointer that he frequently used to entertain cats and annoy everyone else. When he reached the bottom, he fished his own keychain flashlight out of his pocket and he and Bones shone their lights all around.

They were in a circular chamber, the stones fitted neatly together with expert craftsmanship. He saw no doorways, trapdoors, or anything that would indicate a means of egress.

"Dead end?" Angel looked around. "I sure don't see anything here."

"Places like this are never as they seem." Maddock hoped he wasn't about to be made to look the fool. "The sign of the three hares is what got us down here, so I'd guess we're looking for something similar."

"You mean like what's right next to your foot?" Jade too had taken out a small flashlight and directed the beam down at the floor where Maddock stood. A manhole-sized disc carved with the three hare symbol was set in the floor.

"Why am I the only one with no flashlight?" Angel stood with her arms folded. "It's not exactly an essential, yet you all have one?"

"We're archaeologists," Jade explained as she and Maddock knelt down to give the disc a closer examination. "You never know when you're going to find yourself crawling into a cave or a dark tunnel." She held her flashlight in her teeth, grasped the disc with both hands, and tugged. It did not budge.

"Maybe it turns. Let's get some extra muscle on it." Maddock found handholds on the raised portion of the carving and was surprised when Angel lent a hand.

"You want muscle? You want me, not Bones. He's a wuss." She flashed her brother an evil grin. He, in turn, flashed her an obscene gesture, which only elicited a laugh. "On three?"

Maddock counted to three and they heaved. The stone circle held fast for a moment, then gave way so suddenly that Maddock almost fell on his face. They continued rotating the stone until it came free, then slid it aside. Damp, musty air, warmed by the earth far below the frozen streets, rose up to meet them. It was a short drop to a narrow passageway down below.

Angel looked at him with questioning eyes.

"In for a penny, in for a pound." Maddock pocketed his light, dropped down into the tunnel, and stepped out of the way. The others followed in short order.

The passage in which they found themselves was scarcely wide enough for two people to walk abreast, and the ceiling was so low that it barely cleared the top of Bones' head. It ran only about ten paces in each direction, each end terminating at a stone door flanked by Doric columns and surmounted by a Roman-style arch.

"So, do we take a left turn at Albuquerque?" Bones flicked his light back and forth, examining each door in turn. "Of course, I don't see any rabbits in here."

The figures of five women were carved in each door. The women on the left held containers and gazed out with expectant expressions on their faces. Maddock marveled at the skill of the sculptor whose stonework could convey such emotion. The women in the carving to the right averted their faces, some looking down, and one even covering her face with the hem of her cloak.

"Weird." Maddock mulled their options. "I know which door I'm inclined to stay away from." He indicated the women with downcast and averted faces, "But I'd like something more solid to go on."

Jade narrowed her eyes and looked like she was about to say something when Angel chimed in.

"I know this story. These are the ten virgins!" She smiled and punched Bones in the shoulder. "Dude! I remember it from vacation Bible school when we were kids."

"I was going to say the same thing," Jade agreed. "Not my specialty, but I felt pretty sure. Angel just confirmed it."

"Ten virgins. Nice." Bones grinned and danced out of the way before Angel could punch him again.

"So what's the story?" It sounded familiar to Maddock, but that was about it.

"It's a parable, also known as the Wise and Foolish Virgins. Ten virgins waited late into the night for the bridegroom to arrive. The foolish virgins," Jade pointed to the door on the right, "were unprepared and had no oil for their lamps. They are left out of the marriage feast. The wise virgins were prepared, so they were rewarded. It's supposed to be a lesson to always be ready for the second coming. To always keep the light burning, so to speak."

"Wise Virgins," Maddock looked to the door on the left, "and Wise Men." He looked upward. "Can't be a coincidence."

"Let's do it." Bones strode to the door.

"Wait up!" Angel said, hurrying after him. "You guys have done crap like this before. I've never gotten to open a big, scary door."

Bones stepped aside. "Be my guest." He motioned with both hands, doorman-style, and shook his head like a bemused parent as she brushed past him.

What had looked like a single door was actually two. A fine line ran up the center, and an iron ring was set on each side. "Here we go. One for each of us." Angel grabbed hold of one of the rings and indicated Bones should take the other. They heaved in unison, and the doors swung outward on unseen hinges. The space behind was pitch black. Angel put a hand out, as if the darkness itself had substance.

"Somebody with a flashlight can go first."

Chuckling, Bones led the way. They entered a room twenty paces long and ten across. Columns lined the walls and arches rose up to support the vaulted ceiling. An altar of white marble stood in the center of the room. At the far end, the figure of a nude man was carved into the wall. He held a cup in one hand and an ivy-wrapped staff in the other, and leaned against a stump wrapped in grape vines with bunches of grapes hanging from the top.

"Dionysus." Bones said. "God of wine and hard-partying. That's the man right there!"

"Bacchus, actually." Jade shone her light on the figure. "He's the Roman version of Dionysus. Subtle differences but, in essence, the same."

"A temple to one of the old Roman gods down here underneath one of the best-known cathedrals in the world?" Maddock shook his head. "This is crazy."

"Maybe not. The Romans came here in 50 AD, long before Christianity took hold in their empire. There are plenty of Roman ruins in, and even under, Cologne. I'll wager this place pre-dates the cathedral." Jade played her light around the temple. "It's interesting that the way down here was preserved and that someone along the way didn't destroy it. You'd think the church would consider this place blasphemous."

Maddock mulled that over as he approached the altar. The darkness in the room had hidden what lay atop it. It was a black figure of vaguely human shape. His first, terrible thought was of a badly burnt child, but when the beam of his light fell upon the crowned head, he knew it was something else entirely.

"Jade, do you see what I see?"

"It's the Milan Madonna!" Jade hurried to the altar and leaned down for a closer look. She glanced up at the confused faces all around her. "The Madonna upstairs is actually the second one. The old cathedral was destroyed by fire in 1248, and it was thought the original Madonna was destroyed as well, but apparently not, because here she is."

"The priest must have wanted us to find her, but why?" Maddock looked down at the blackened figure. Only the head was recognizable. The rest merely a scorched remnant of what had once been a classic work of art.

"I've got a crazy idea." Bones moved around the altar and stood at the Madonna's head. "You've got the three kings. Kings wear crowns." With that, he placed a hand on the statue's head, grasped the crown in the other, and twisted.

Maddock winced, wondering if his friend was going to destroy a piece of history, but the crown came free in his hand.

"It's hollow." Jade reached inside and withdrew a stone disc about the width of a man's hand. She held it up and shone her light on it. The three hares were carved on one side, and tiny writing was engraved in an ever-tightening spiral on the back. "It's German," she whispered, "an old form. We'll need someone to translate this for us."

Everyone jumped as the silence was broken by the sound of stone sliding on stone and a loud crash reverberated through the temple as the doors swung closed. Maddock and Bones hurried over and pushed against them, but the doors did not budge. Jade and Angel joined them, and they searched for a release lever, but to no avail. They were trapped.

Chapter 4

Niklas looked both ways before exiting the treasury. It had been a frustrating search. The American, who had been put in charge of this mission, had said that they were looking for "instructions" and that he would know it when he found it. The man's face had contorted with rage when they had opened the Shrine of the Three Kings and found only those strange skulls. Of course, the man's scarred face, partly hidden by the wraparound sunglasses he wore day and night, always looked like it was twisted into a scowl.

The priests had been of no use. They had tortured them one by one and hadn't gotten a thing out of them. The ensuing search, thorough but careful, had proved equally fruitless. Niklas exchanged nervous glances with Ulrich as they stood in the snow and waited for their leader to give them further instructions.

The American was a bear of a man with a personality to match. Despite his battered body and pronounced limp, he moved with a confident, deadly air, like a caged beast ready to be unleashed at any moment. Niklas had seen him lose control only once, and it was not a sight he wanted to ever witness again.

"I think we're done here." The voice was a low growl. "I've changed my mind about those freak skulls. We'll take them with us. They must be a clue though I can't see how."

Privately, Niklas thought they should have taken the skulls with them in the first place, but the scarred man's rage had been so overwhelming that he had refused to even look at them, and neither Niklas nor Ulrich was about to argue with him. At least he had changed his mind. At worst, they would have something to show their superiors.

They slipped back inside the cathedral, the warm air a welcome after the chilly winter breeze. Niklas moved silently, more out of habit than necessity. It was after hours and they had dispatched the few living men inside the Kölner Dom. There was no danger.

They rounded the corner of the transept, turned toward the nave, and froze. A man sat on the floor alongside the dead priests. His face was buried in his hands and he was speaking softly, the rhythm of his words indicating he was at prayer.

The American held a finger to his lips. He motioned for Ulrich to keep watch at the main entrance and for Niklas to follow him. He moved like a shadow across the floor, impressive considering his bulk and awkward gait. He was on the praying man in an instant, wrapping his thick arm around the man's throat like a python squeezing its prey, and lifting him up off the ground. The man kicked, flailed, and made squelching noises, but froze when the American spoke.

"You answer my questions, you might live."

That was surely a lie, but it wasn't Niklas' problem.

"You try anything at all and you die. Painfully. Understand?"

The man nodded. He kept his eyes squeezed shut, as if he could deny what was happening.

The American sat him down and the man dropped to his knees. He was shaking so hard he could barely remain upright.

"Tell me what you know."

"I... I know nothing. I come here to study..."

Snap! The American broke the man's little finger eliciting a shriek of agony.

"Shut up and listen." His tone was enough to cut off their prisoner's screams. "I can tell when you're lying. I can tell when you leave things out. And I... don't... care... how much I hurt you. I'll cut your eyeballs out and eat a damn Big Mac while I do it. You got me?"

Niklas' limited knowledge of American cuisine did not include 'damn Big Mac' but the words seemed to do the job. He saw the paltry bit of resistance drain from the man as his shoulders sagged and his chin fell to his chest.

Torture was something only an exceptional person could endure for any length of time. He had faced his share as part of his training prior to induction into the Heilig Herrschaft. Maintaining one's focus on the Most Holy was central to the denial of pain. Academics like the man who cowered before them usually broke quickly, for they had faith in nothing.

"Tell me everything."

The prisoner nodded vigorously and launched into an explanation, his words coming in short, disjointed bursts as if each phrase was trying to jostle the others out of the way so it could be heard first.

"One priest was not dead. He made no sense. He said he had a secret. Mailänder Madonna. Dreihasenbild. He made no sense."

"That can't be everything." The American reached for the knife at his waist, but the prisoner kept talking.

"He tried to say something else, but he died. All he said was 'ewige' and then he died." The prisoner stiffened as if waiting for something to happen. Indeed, Niklas expected the American to kill the man soon, if not now. "It is true. I swear it!" The man's eyes remained firmly shut. This might be a bad dream, but it was one from which he would not wake.

The American looked around and froze.

"Where are the skulls?" His voice was velvet soft, and it sent frozen fingers like the touch of a spirit down Niklas' spine.

The man hesitated and, for a moment, Niklas thought the fellow might try to hold something back, but courage apparently failed him.

"The others took them. I was giving them a tour, and they took the skulls."

"Did they hear the priest's words?" Heat rose in the American's voice.

"Yes. They hear everything. Then they took the skulls and left. I stayed here to wait for die Polizei."

So the authorities were on their way. That changed things. Niklas looked around as if uniformed men lurked in the shadows.

"I want names, and fast."

"I do not know them all. They introduced themselves quickly and then we saw the priests." The man was shaking; clearly fearing this lack of knowledge would cost him his life. "One man was a red Indian. A big man, almost two meters tall. There was a woman, also a red Indian. I do not remember their names. And there was another man and woman."

"You'd better come up with at least one name or the remainder of your very short life will be filled with pain."

"Verzeih mir," the man whispered. *Forgive me.* "Jade Ihara. She was a colleague..."

"Jade Ihara the archaeologist?"

"Ja." The man nodded, his body quaking.

"They are here!" Ulrich called. "They did not use their sirens. We have no time."

The American let out roar of rage and frustration and clubbed the prisoner across the temple, knocking him unconscious.

The three men dashed back to the transept and slipped outside, past the treasury, and across the street. Ten minutes later they were in their vehicle, driving along the Rhine. The American sat in the passenger side, muttering to himself. Niklas finally broke the silence.

"This Jade Ihara, you know her?" He bit his lip, waiting for the explosion, but it did not come.

"Oh yes. I know her well, and if I don't miss my guess, I know the men she's with. But they think I'm dead."

Chapter 5

"You have got to be kidding me." Angel's tone was as flat as her stare as she stepped back and regarded the closed door. "I thought you guys were winding me up when you told me about your crazy adventures."

"I wish." Maddock shone his light on the door and ran his fingers along its surface, but felt no switch or lever. "The good news is, there's always a way out."

"How can you be sure?" Angel didn't sound doubtful– only curious.

"You see any remains in here? Obviously, everyone who came in here left again. We just need to figure out how." He continued to search. "Let's start by looking for either the sign of the three hares or the wise virgins. This is a pagan temple, so I think the hares are more likely."

They spread out and continued the search. It wasn't long before Jade called everyone over to the Bacchus frieze.

"I found the hares!" She shone her light over a bunch of grapes.

Maddock and the others circled around behind her and looked where she indicated. He frowned.

"I don't see anything but grapes."

"You won't at first. Step back and squint." Jade turned and flashed a bright smile. "Tilt your head if you have to."

They must have made an odd-looking trio, the three of them leaning to and fro, looking from different angles, trying to see what Jade saw. She moved the side and shone her light across the carving, casting it in long shadows.

"There it is!" Bones' voice was triumphant. "It's like one of those weird posters where you have to let your vision go all fuzzy before you can see it."

Almost as soon as Bones had spoken, Maddock saw it too. It wasn't quite a stereogram, but some of the grapes were raised far above the others, and when seen in the proper light, the image swam into focus, forming a shape that resembled the three hares.

"Give it a push." Maddock held his breath as Jade pressed her palm to the carving. He saw no seam that would indicate that the hare sign was anything other than a clever artistic detail, but after a moment, Jade's hand slowly moved forward as the hares slid into the wall. Something snapped into place and the wall sank slowly into the floor, revealing an upward-sloping passageway, the twin of the one that had brought them here.

The way was long and steep, but uneventful. They finally came to a blank wall. The ceiling here was low, and even Jade had to duck to avoid banging her head. Maddock shone his light on the ceiling. There were no hares or wise virgins here, only two handholds set in a square stone as wide as his shoulders. He reached for it and hesitated. What, or who, would they find on the other side?

"Do you think we're back at the cathedral?" Angel asked.

"No. This tunnel was almost a straight shot moving away from the cathedral. I think we're closer to the river." The air was cooler here and, he thought, just a touch more humid.

"Does it really matter?" Bones stared up at the trapdoor as he spoke. "It's not like there's anywhere else to go."

"True." Maddock nodded. "Tell you what. If we wind up in the middle of someone's living room, you and Angel start talking in Cherokee and Jade can chime in with Japanese. Act confused and get the hell out of there."

"What about you?" Bones eyed him, an amused smile on his lips. "What other language do you speak, Maddock?"

Maddock grinned. He knew a smattering of German and French, and enough Spanish to order drinks and a meal and to ask for directions to the bathroom, but none of those would help. "Pig Latin."

Bones chuckled as the two of them pushed up on the trapdoor. They lifted it up and set it over to the side. Up above, faint yellow light flickered on an arched stone roof.

"Another cathedral," Maddock muttered. He helped the others up and then climbed out with an assist from Bones. Looking around, he knew immediately he had been correct. This was not the Kölner Dom. The interior, though impressive in its architecture, was austere. It lacked Kölner Dom's splendor, the stained glass one of the few sources of color.

"This is St. Martin's," Jade whispered. "It was almost destroyed in World War II and rebuilt afterward."

"You can tell us all about it later." Maddock slid the stone back into place, took Jade's hand, and led the way out.

Just before they reached the doors leading out, a white-robed man appeared. He spotted Maddock, frowned, and opened his mouth to speak. And then he spotted Bones. As was often the case, the sight of the massive Cherokee rendered him speechless. He gaped as Bones took out his wallet, withdrew a twenty, and pressed it into the monk's hand.

"A da ne di." Bones smiled, patted the monk on the shoulder, and led the way out.

"What did you say to him?" Jade asked.

"I told him, in Cherokee, to get himself a happy ending massage."

"He's lying." Angel seemed to have given up punching her brother, and gave him a dirty look instead. "He told him it was a gift."

"It was either that or punch the dude. I figured he has enough problems already. You know, no cash, boring clothes, no babes."

Maddock had to laugh. "Remind me about this next time I complain about your ugly mug."

"Right." Bones feigned disbelief. "Everybody knows I'm the good-looking one."

Chapter 6

The winter garden in Heller's Brauhaus was decked out for the holiday season. Traditional music played in the background, scarcely audible over the talk and laughter in the crowded pub. The cheerful atmosphere was at odds with Maddock's gray mood which had only begun to lighten when Jade had received a text from Otto letting them know he was all right and had been released after being questioned by the police. They had sampled a few German Christmas specialties and were digging into plates of Braumeisterbraten, a pork roast in beer sauce, and drinking Kolsch, a local specialty beer, when Otto wandered in with a bandage on his finger and looking dazed but otherwise whole. He declined Maddock's offer to buy his dinner, but accepted a Kolsch and drank half of it in three large gulps.

"I don't feel right about leaving you there by yourself," Maddock told him. "We should have stayed with you." The others agreed. Excited as they were about the discovery they had made, leaving the man to face the authorities alone felt wrong.

"No, no." Otto waved away their apologies. "The police would have taken the skulls and we would not have had a chance to look for the hidden passage. The place is now a crime scene. There is no telling how long it will be before it is once again open to the public." He took another swallow of his beer, this one moderate, and wiped his mouth on his shirt sleeve before continuing. "I also agree with the priest. If the public knew the Shrine of the Magi held such grotesqueries..." He pinched his lower lip, his eyes narrowed in thought.

"What do you think they are?" Angel asked. "Have you ever seen anything like them?"

"Never. I suspect they are forgeries— a sinister joke left behind by whoever stole the real skulls of the Magi."

"So you think the bones of the Wise Men really were in the shrine at some point in the past?" Maddock had been wondering if perhaps the horned skulls had been there from the beginning.

"If the records are to be believed, the shrine once contained three crowned skulls. This was supposedly verified by priests at Kölner Dom. Of course, everything is in question now." Otto lapsed back into deep thought, then his eyes suddenly brightened and he looked at Jade. "Where are the skulls now?"

"Back in our hotel room. I thought about leaving them in the temple, but changed my mind."

"What temple?" Otto's eyes shone with disbelief as they filled him in on what lay beneath Kölner Dom.

"A temple to a Roman god beneath Cologne's most sacred site. It is difficult to accept. Of course, ours is a tangled history." He smiled sadly. "Why do you suppose the priest wanted someone to know about it? Would it not have been best for the church to let it fall from memory? If he was the keeper of the secret, he need not have passed it along."

"Jade left out the most interesting part." Maddock smiled. "She does that for dramatic effect."

"I was getting there, Maddock." She blushed, giving her almond-colored skin a warm, pleasant hue. "But you go ahead."

"You've got the disc. You tell the story." Maddock took a long pull of his Kolsch, savoring its sweet, almost fruity flavor, something between ale and lager. He glanced at Otto, whose eyes sparkled as he leaned in close, his beer forgotten as he waited for the rest of the story. Bones smirked and Angel grinned behind her glass.

"But you're the one who found the compartment inside the Milan Madonna." Jade played along. "You should tell him."

"Disc? Milan Madonna?" Otto sounded like a little boy, early on Christmas morning, begging to open his gifts.

They all took long pulls of Kolsch, prolonging the moment as Otto's pleading eyes darted around the table, eager for someone to let him in on the secret.

"It was nothing much," Jade said, placing her glass on the table and reaching into her purse. "We found the original Milan Madonna and this was hidden inside of her." She handed Otto an object wrapped in a handkerchief.

He held it gingerly and unwrapped it with care, holding it close to his chest and hunching over as if to hide it from prying eyes. Maddock thought the man need not bother. The place was packed, mostly with young people overindulging in ale and holiday cheer, and no one was paying them a bit of attention.

When Otto's eyes fell on the three hares, he gaped. He turned it in his hands, gazing at the ancient symbol. Apparently satisfied there was nothing more to see there, he turned it over. "Latin?" he asked as he once again turned the disc, his eyes following the writing that spiraled in toward the center.

"That's what we thought." Jade sounded annoyed. "But nothing translates, at least not on any of the websites I tried." She shrugged and made an apologetic face. "My specialty is the native tribes of the southwestern United States, and I've branched out into eastern Asia. My knowledge of this part of the world is comparatively small."

"I think," Otto said, a ghost of a grin materializing on his face, "that it is Latin, but in a cipher."

Now it was Maddock's turn to grin. He had suspected the same thing and had sent photographs of the disc to his friend Jimmy Letson, an accomplished hacker and a computer whiz of the first order. Jimmy had replied with a text that read, *I do have a life, you know*, but if Maddock knew Jimmy, he was already hard at work cracking the code. Like Maddock and Bones, the man relished a challenge, though his specialty was of the cyber realm rather than the archaeological.

"Any idea what kind of cipher it might be?" Maddock asked Otto, who was fixated on the text.

"I cannot say at first glance," he mumbled. "The Caesar shift cipher was commonly used in the church. One simply chooses a number to shift the letters, either to the right or to the left. A shift of one to the right and the letter 'A' becomes 'B' and so on. It is simple enough for a priest who was not a cryptographer to use, but complicated enough to fool the average person."

"Could the average person even read back then?" Angel asked.

"We do not, of course, know the time period when this cipher was written, if that is indeed what it is. If it is more than a few centuries old, you are certainly correct, particularly for a message in Latin."

"Any chance it's a fake?" Angel asked.

Otto tilted his hand back-and-forth. "It is possible, but the temple and the Madonna suggest otherwise."

Maddock nodded. It was the same conclusion they had drawn. He was looking around for a server from whom to order another round of Kolsch when his cell phone vibrated in his pocket. It was Jimmy.

"Why don't you give me something that requires neurons next time, like a ten-piece kindergarten puzzle?"

"I take it you've deciphered our cipher." At those words, all eyes at the table turned to Maddock.

"If you can call it that." Jimmy was clearly disappointed at the lack of challenge posed by the text on the disc. *"It was one of the most common ciphers ever."*

"The Caesar shift?" Maddock asked. Relishing Jimmy's sudden silence, he caught the eye of an attractive blonde waitress and signaled for five more drinks. She nodded and gave him a wink that did not escape Jade's notice. She arched an eyebrow at him, but then smiled.

"You're smarter than you look, Maddock," Jimmy finally said, sounding even more disappointed. *"Want to take a guess at the key?"*

"The what?"

"The number of the shift. How many letters over you count when substituting the new letter." A bit of Jimmy's cockiness was returning.

Maddock thought immediately of the Wise Men. "Three."

"All right, Carnac, which direction?"

Maddock decided not to spoil all of Jimmy's fun. "No idea."

"The right. You should have known that. This is more of that ancient church crap. Right hand of God. Left hand is unclean..."

"True. I'm a little distracted right now. I'm sitting in a pub in Cologne, downing a few brews with a couple of beautiful women."

"You're such an ass, Maddock." Jimmy chuckled. *"Of course, Bones is probably there too, which sucks all the fun out of everything."*

"I'll tell him you said so. Can you send me the translation?"

"Sure. The last word was partially rubbed out or chipped away or something, so I didn't get it all. Emailing it to you right now. And, of course, you owe me a meal... again."

"What would I ever do without you? Thanks, Jimmy."

Maddock ended the call and punched up his email on his phone. Everyone leaned toward him as he began to read.

"As the lion roars for the king, the peacock be your guide into the depths of the well. The kings point the way to the falling ice that hides eternal l..."

It ended just as Jimmy had said— with an incomplete word.

"There it is again," Bones said. "You know, we figured the priest just didn't manage to get the last word out, but if he knew the words on this disc, maybe he was trying to tell us all he knew."

"Maybe." Maddock looked up as their next round of drinks arrived. He found he had lost his thirst, though, and drank mechanically as he pondered the words. "It's a far cry from step-by-step instructions."

"And this should lead us to the missing skulls, you think?" Jade leaned over to read Jimmy's email. She shook her head. "The wording makes it sound like there's something more. But what?"

"Should we go to the police with this?" Angel asked.

"I don't know." Bones spoke slowly, absently spinning his beer mug as he thought the problem through. "What do we really know? The killers want the skulls of the wise dudes. I'm guessing you told them as much." He looked at Otto who nodded. "We could give them this clue but what would they do with it? Can you see a cop who's probably got a ton of cases on his hands taking the time to trying to figure this thing out? That's what *we* do."

"I could share this with the police," Otto volunteered. "I will tell them it is something I found in my research. I suspect it will all be meaningless to them, but at least we will not be holding back anything significant." He frowned as he said the last.

Maddock nodded. It made sense. Still the fact that they were hiding their presence at a murder scene, though they arrived after the fact, felt wrong. He remembered that the killers had left no footprints, and he had a hunch they'd been careful not to leave behind any fingerprints or DNA.

"The safest course would be to go on with our vacation and just forget the whole thing. Then again, my gut tells me the only hope there is for finding the murderers lies with us. Maybe if we can solve this riddle we can figure out who was after the Magi's bones and why. Even then, who knows what we can really prove?"

"I say we go for it." Bones had the familiar gleam in his eyes that Maddock associated with the start of a treasure hunt. "What better way to celebrate Christmas than solve the mystery of the lost bones of the Magi?"

Jade nodded. "You know I'm in. And you," she turned to Maddock, "live for this stuff, whether you want to admit it or not."

Maddock grinned. He and Jade were kindred spirits; both loved the sea, archaeology, and mysteries. That left only one person. He turned to Angel, whose cheeks were aglow and her brown eyes sparkling as she gazed back at him. He was suddenly struck by her beauty, and there was something in her expression that made him uneasy. He was pleased to see that Jade's attention was once again on the stone disc, and she hadn't seen whatever might have passed across his face. He took a quick drink, buying himself a moment to clear his head.

"How about you, Angel? You signed up for a vacation, not a mystery."

"Are you stupid? I'm all over it. Do you know how sick I am of Bones coming home and bragging about wrestling Bigfoot and all the other crap you two get up to?" Her roguish grin was so like that of her brother that it made Maddock flinch. It was one thing to notice Angel was hot. To think that *Bones' sister* was hot— that was something else entirely.

Otto cleared his throat.

"There is something else I must tell you." Not meeting anyone's eye, Otto recounted the time after they had left him alone in the cathedral. His voice was soft, remorse weighing heavily in every word. "I told them about the three hares." He lapsed into silence, but Maddock sensed there was more. "And I gave them Jade's name."

Maddock and Jade exchanged glances. He couldn't tell exactly what she was thinking, but she didn't seem too upset about it. She was tough.

"One of them knew you and he sounded very upset when I told him your name." Now Jade did look surprised, but she kept her silence. "That was when the authorities arrived." Otto finally looked at her. "I am so sorry. I have read adventure novels and imagined myself a hero, but reality is something entirely different. I am not a strong man." His chin fell to his chest and his face darkened.

"It's all right." Jade took his hand in both of hers. "I would have done the same thing."

Maddock knew that wasn't true. Jade was stronger than Otto ever dreamed of being.

"This is really jacked-up," Bones said to Jade. "If you have any rivals in your field, they would have one of your specializations, wouldn't they?"

Jade shrugged. "I suppose."

Maddock looked at Bones and could tell they were thinking the same thing.

There was only one group that was likely to have it in for Jade. If his hunch was correct, they were all in danger.

Chapter 7

"Did he say what, exactly, we are looking for?" Ulrich appeared in the doorway looking annoyed. "I searched the other two rooms and found nothing but suitcases that had not even been opened. It appears Ihara's friends checked in and stayed only long enough to drop off their luggage." He ran his fingers through his wavy black hair. His vanity and legendary poor swimming ability had earned him the nickname Hasselhoff, though few dared say it to the quick-tempered man's face.

"The skulls, obviously, and anything else that might connect to the three hares, the Magi, or the cathedral." Niklas finished his search of the bag. Neither it nor Ihara's luggage had turned up anything. The name on the identification tag read Dane Maddock. The name meant nothing to him, but he committed it to memory all the same.

"Have you found anything?" Ulrich opened the bathroom door and peered inside.

"I have not yet finished." Niklas felt a flash of annoyance. He did not want to leave empty-handed, but he was concerned that Ihara had taken the skulls with her. He searched the dresser, closet, and even the floor beneath the bed skirt, but came up empty. Ulrich poked around, looking in all the places Niklas had already checked.

He was about to give up when he noticed a bulge behind the curtain. Not wanting to give away his presence to anyone looking in from the outside, he drew back the curtain just far enough to see a black backpack resting on the windowsill. Dark, hollow holes gaped up at him from sinister, horned skulls. He had found what they were looking for.

"I've got them! Let's go."

Ulrich's tense face sagged with relief. He cracked the door open and peered up and down the hall before signaling that the way was clear.

They took the stairs down to the first floor and, along the way, Niklas slipped out of his overcoat and draped it over his arm, concealing the backpack. Neither Ihara nor the rest of her party knew him or Ulrich, but there was always the slim chance she would recognize her own backpack, and he did not want to risk blowing things through a chance encounter. By the time they exchanged the warmth of the hotel for the cold December night, he knew he had made the right choice.

Four people approached, talking and laughing. Though he had never seen a picture of Ihara, he knew this had to be her. An attractive young woman of mixed Asian ancestry along with two American natives— one a tall, muscular man with long hair and a roguish face, the other an attractive twenty-something girl with captivating eyes. How many of their race did one see in Cologne? The fourth member of their group was a muscular man with blond hair and eyes the color of a stormy sea. This must be Dane Maddock. Though he smiled and spoke with his friends, his eyes locked on Niklas and Ulrich as if he somehow knew something was amiss with them. Then again, perhaps it was because Niklas was not wearing his coat despite the snowfall that was growing heavier by the minute.

They passed close enough for him to catch a whiff of Ihara's jasmine-scented perfume, and to realize just how tall the Indian was. Niklas was six feet tall, a shade taller than Maddock, but the Indian had him by at least half a head. Tension climbed his spine, knotting the muscles in his back and neck. He had a bad feeling about these two men and, though he and Ulrich were armed, he would prefer not to have an encounter with them.

By the time they reached their car, the group was rounding the corner of the hotel. He breathed a sigh of relief, set the backpack containing the skulls in the back, and slid into the driver's seat. He looked at Ulrich, who was standing on the sidewalk staring back at the hotel. He called his name, but Ulrich raised a hand.

"Wait a moment. I will be right back." With that, he vanished into the swirling cloud of white.

Angel pulled up her hood, lowered her head against the wind and snow, and hurried along the sidewalk. How dumb had she been to leave her purse in the rental car? She wasn't a girly girl by any measure, but her wallet, passport, and phone were inside it and she didn't want to risk it getting stolen.

She was in such a hurry that she didn't notice the man approaching her until he was almost on top of her. They had just passed one another moments before. Great! Another random stranger hitting on her. She pushed back her hood and turned, about to deflect his advances with a polite rejection when he reached out, grabbed hold of her French braid, and yanked her forward.

"Come quietly and you will not..."

His words ended in a grunt as Angel drove a fist into his gut. The average person would have instinctively tried to pull away from the attacker and get loose from his grip, but Angel was not an average person. Her fighting instincts kicking in, she drove the heel of her palm up into her attacker's chin. He turned at the last instant and her strike caught him on the jaw. He took a step back, trying to yank her off balance by her hair. Angel barely noticed the pain; she'd had much worse in the octagon. As he moved backward, she scooped one of his legs and drove him backward. He was bigger than she was, and maybe stronger, but her aggressiveness caught him completely off guard. He stumbled back against a parked car, letting go of her hair as he fell hard to the ground. She heard the whoosh of breath leaving his lungs and the satisfying *thunk* as the back of his head cracked the sidewalk. The snow had probably cushioned the impact a little, but not much.

"Don't you know," Angel growled as she pummeled his face with sharp blows, "boys aren't supposed to fight girls? It's not gentlemanly."

The man flailed about weakly, trying to fight her off and regain his breath at the same time. She should probably get away while he was still too stunned to chase her, but she wasn't known for making good decisions when angry. He caught hold of the front of her coat with one hand and pulled her toward him. She used the added momentum to her advantage, driving her elbow into the bridge of his nose. Her coat was thick, but the padding was not enough to save his nose. Two more elbows in quick succession and it was a flattened, bloody mess.

He sucked in a deep, rasping breath and let out a cry of rage. With a sudden burst of strength, he rolled her off of him. Angel scrambled away before he could pin her down. The man was up on his knees but instead of coming after her, he pulled an automatic pistol from his coat pocket.

Before he could so much as take aim, Angel's roundhouse kick struck him in the temple and he went limp. His eyes glazed and, like a falling tree, he slowly fell forward. Just for meanness, she added a front kick to his face as he went down. She caught him at an awkward angle, and pain shot through her ankle, but she could not stifle her feral grin. "That's what you get," she whispered.

She hesitated for a moment, wondering where the pistol had fallen and if she should search for it.

"Ulrich?" An unfamiliar voice called from down the street. A shadow appeared in the whirling snow. Resolving into the form of Ulrich's companion– the odd one who hadn't been wearing a jacket.

Still pumped from her beat down of Ulrich, Angel entertained a fleeting thought of taking the fight to this guy as well before common sense overrode adrenaline. Reminding herself that Bones was the dumb one in the family, she turned on her heel and ran.

Chapter 8

Jade was already awake when Maddock rolled out of bed. The previous evening's events, followed by the news that Angel had been attacked outside the hotel had kept the wheels of his mind turning until well into the night. When they discovered the missing skulls, they knew why the men had come.

He and Bones had taken turns staying awake, though neither of them expected the men to return. They had the skulls and didn't know about the existence of the three hares disc.

He sat up, closed his eyes, and inhaled the welcome aroma of coffee. Exactly what he needed to start this cold morning.

"It's about time. I've been on the web for hours." Jade did not look up from the tiny screen of her phone which she was using to search the internet. "I've already solved the mystery while you were dreaming about... sand, or whatever it is you dream of."

"Seriously?" He sat up straight, feeling wide awake.

"No." She turned and gave him a coy smile. "But since you're awake, how about pouring me a cup of coffee."

He gave her a playful swat on the hip and rolled out of bed, sparing a moment to work out the kinks from sleeping on a mattress that was much too soft for his liking. He poured two cups of coffee: black for him, two sugars, no cream for her. He sat her cup on the nightstand on her side of the bed, opened the curtains to let in the glow of the snow-frosted city, and settled into a nearby chair.

"I do have an idea, though." Jade took a sip of coffee and regarded him over her cup. When he didn't bite, she made a mocking pout that melted into a smile. "Fine. Don't let me have any fun."

"Tell me, my wise and beautiful queen..."

"No!" She held up her hand. "Too late now. Just sit there, drink your coffee, and enjoy the fruits of my labor." She picked up the hotel notepad she'd use for her note-taking. "Aside from the message on the disc, our clues are the three hares, the wise men, and the wise and foolish virgins. Agreed?"

"I suppose you could add Bacchus to that list."

"Might as well." She made a note. "I tried combining phrases from the message with some of these clues, along with Germany and cathedrals or churches, and using them as search terms. I've come up with one place I feel good about."

"Let's hear it."

"Saint Mary's Cathedral in Hildesheim." She fixed him with an expectant look.

"Never heard of it."

"It's famous for the Bernward Doors— huge bronze doors that depict scenes from the Bible." She checked her notes. "Each door has eight panels, and one of them shows the adoration of the Magi."

"Sounds iffy." Maddock held his coffee close to his nose, savoring the aroma. "There must be tons of representations of the Wise Men all around Germany, and that's assuming the skulls are still in the country. Who knows?"

"You're such a cynic, Maddock." Jade sighed and handed him her phone. "Take a look at this. It's a picture of the Three Kings panel."

The image was impressive. The Magi were sculpted as was the Blessed Mother holding the baby Jesus, and gave the etching a three-dimensional quality. But it wasn't the scene itself that drew Maddock's eye; it was the door knocker in the shape of a lion's head that dominated the lower middle of the panel.

"You see?" Jade grinned. "I thought the mention of the word 'lion' might be figurative, you know, Jesus was the Lion of Judah. But if it's a literal clue, this is a good fit. You've got the Magi, the lion, and the cathedral. The place is filled with works of art. There's even a shrine that includes a depiction of the wise and foolish virgins. I'll wager that somewhere in there is a depiction of the three hares. What do you think?"

"It's a stretch, but I suppose it's worth a try."

"Look, I know it's not a sure thing but, the way I see it, we're on vacation and it's a place I wouldn't mind visiting anyway. What do we have to lose except a few hours in the car?"

"That works for me," Maddock said. "But I'm guessing you've forgotten what a road trip with Bones is like."

Maddock didn't know if it was holiday spirit or the presence of his sister, but Bones was much less annoying than usual on their drive to Hildesheim. Instead of playing his favorite car game— thinking of an obscenity that started with the first letter of every road sign they passed— he contented himself with singing Christmas songs, though his habit of changing the lyrics to make the songs off-color finally drove Angel crazy and she put a stop to it. By the time they arrived at the cathedral, even Bones was focused on the task at hand.

"We'll start by checking out the door and take it from there," Jade said. "Keep an eye out for anything with the three hares or the wise virgins."

"What about the shrine you mentioned?" Angel asked.

"We'll take a look at that too. Anything that looks promising. Just don't draw attention to yourself." Jade directed the latter comment at Bones.

"You know me. I always rise to the occasion." Bones grinned.

Maddock gazed up at the cathedral. In no way was it as magnificent as Kölner Dom. It was smaller and less elegant, and the massive repairs to the damage wrought by Allied bombers in World War II had deprived it of the aura of age that imbued so many structures of its kind. It did, however, have its own charm. The symmetry of the structure gave it an orderly feel that was pleasing to the eye, and the sand-colored stone put him in mind of home.

It was only a short walk to the cathedral's western portal and the Bernward doors. Though impressive in photographs, the sheer size of the doors, which stood at nearly sixteen feet tall, gave him pause. The artistry of these thousand-year-old castings was breathtaking. Assuming the role of tourist, Bones took out a camera and started snapping pictures of Angel. She positioned herself to screen Maddock and Jade, who, in turn, moved in for a closer look at the Three Kings.

The panel was much larger than Maddock had imagined. He had figured the doors to be closer to an ordinary size, and thus scaled down the image in his mind.

"I don't see any hares here," Maddock said.

"The clue mentions the lion. Give it a twist." Jade whispered.

"Seriously?"

"These doors are probably thick enough to hide something inside. Maybe the knocker comes off or releases a panel." She looked around, clearly nervous. "Hurry while we're alone."

Maddock took hold of the handle, feeling the cold bronze through his thin glove, and twisted.

Nothing.

He tried the other direction with no more success. He tried pushing and turning, pulling and turning, and anything else he could think of, but no dice.

"It's just a solid piece," he finally said, rocking back on his heels.

"You didn't expect it to be easy, did you?" Bones pocketed his camera and joined them at the door. "Pretty cool, though. This alone was worth the drive, but let's check out the inside."

They were disappointed to learn the cathedral was closed for renovations, though Bones declared it "no freaking problem" to slip inside after hours, should they deem it necessary, eliciting a roll of the eyes and a vow not to post his bail from Angel.

A break-in proved unnecessary. Angel located a foreman who spoke English and apparently liked flirtatious women with dark skin and big brown eyes, because, five minutes later, they were inside.

Like the exterior, the interior had a feeling of newness about it, though tempered by the classic works of art all around. The construction foreman was eager to give them an impromptu tour, showing them the high points, including the "Christ Column," a millennium-old, fifteen-foot tall cast bronze pillar that depicted scenes from the life of Jesus, and a bronze baptismal font that rivaled the pillar in its artistry.

By the time they reached the Epiphany Shrine at the east end of the cathedral, Maddock was ready to give up. They had found no representations of the three hares, the Magi, or the Wise Virgins. The shrine was their last hope. The golden shrine was reminiscent of the shrine at Kölner Dom. Among the many images on its face was one of the Wise and Foolish Virgins. And, like the Shrine of the Magi, it was sealed in a thick glass case.

"It holds the relics of the patron saints," the foreman explained. "It is very old."

Maddock and Bones exchanged glances. If they wanted to see what was inside, they would have to blast it open like the men had done back in Cologne. The idea did not sit well with Maddock. Also, something told him this was not what they were looking for. The door to the temple had been guarded by only three wise virgins while this shrine depicted all the characters of the parable, both wise and foolish. It didn't look right. He thought back to their sole clue.

"As the lion roars for the king..."

He had taken "the king" to simply mean Jesus, the "King of Kings." But if the allusion to the lion had been literal, why not the king as well? He turned to their guide, who was having trouble keeping his eyes off of Angel. She was playing along, though Maddock knew her well enough to see she was growing bored with the charade.

"Are there any relics or treasures from any kings here?"

The foreman cocked his head, thinking. They all fell silent, and only the distant sounds of workmen going about their business interrupted the quiet. Finally, he nodded.

"In the museum is the Kopfreliquiar of Saint Oswald. He was King of Northumbria."

"A cop what?" Bones asked.

"Kopfreliquiar." The man cupped his chin, struggling for a translation. "This," he indicated the shrine, "holds all the bones. A kopfreliquiar," he held his hands in front of him about eight inches apart, "holds only the head."

Jade beamed at Maddock. A reliquary that held the skull of a king? That was more like it. They thanked the man, who had managed to wrangle a phone number from Angel, and left the cathedral.

"Real or fake?" Bones asked his sister as they headed back out into the cold.

"Sort of fake." Angel grimaced. "I gave him Crazy Charlie's number."

"That's cold, sis. Dude was nice enough to let us in and show us around."

"Nice? You didn't notice his wedding ring?"

Maddock and Bones looked surprised while Jade and Angel exchanged a "that's a man for you" look.

"You two can find gold at the bottom of the ocean but you can't find it on the hand of someone standing a foot from you." Jade shook her head.

"Hey, just because I haven't settled down doesn't mean I've started checking to see which dudes are single," Bones protested. "Besides, we need to find Ichabod Crane." They had arrived at the museum, and he opened the door and ushered them in with a mocking bow.

"Ichabod Crane?" Jade frowned. "What are you talking about?"

"The Headless Horseman. Am I the only educated one here?"

"Ichabod Crane was the..." Jade threw up her hands and stalked inside. Bones winked at Angel, who gave him a rueful look.

"You're such a jerk," she said, "but at least you're pestering someone else for a change."

They paid the modest entry fee and found themselves alone in the museum, save for a lone employee who reminded them that the museum would close in twenty minutes. They made a show of examining various displays, but quickly found themselves at the glass case that held Saint Oswald's head reliquary. The golden artifact was an odd-looking piece- an octagonal base with a domed cover, topped by a sculpture of Oswald's crowned head. Writing ringed the bottom, with etchings in the panels. They circled the case, scrutinizing the piece.

Jade squeezed Maddock's hand and he could feel her excitement.

"Look at the crown," she whispered. "Do you see it?"

Etched in white stone on the front of the crown was the sign of the three hares!

"Okay." Maddock kept his voice level. "So how do we get to it?"

"Leave it to me," Bones said. "You three spread out and don't act so interested in this thing." With that, he sauntered over to the museum docent and struck up a conversation. In typical Bones fashion, he soon had her laughing. The two of them soon headed out to the lobby, Bones returning a few minutes later with a slip of paper in his hand.

"You got a number too," Angel said. "What's your plan, charm her and talk her into bringing you back here later?"

"Nope." Bones reached into his pocket, pulled out a key ring, and tossed it to Maddock. "Museum's about to close," he whispered. "Call us when you're out."

"You'd better take my backpack," Jade added, slipping it off her shoulder and handing it to him, "just in case you find something."

Maddock had to laugh at his friend's resourcefulness. This just might work.

Careful not to be spotted, he slipped around the corner in the direction of the men's room. The door was propped open and a sign with the international symbol for "don't slip on this wet floor and fall on your butt" guarded the entrance. Good! He could hide inside without being found by the cleaning crew. He hurried inside, found an uncomfortable seat atop a toilet and waited for the lights to go out.

Forty long, boring minutes later, he pulled up the hood of his jacket to shield his face—he hadn't seen any security cameras, but better safe than sorry—and moved out into the darkened museum. It had been at least ten minutes since he'd heard a sound. Though he knew only a handful of German words, he was fairly certain he'd heard Bones' new friend complaining about her missing keys. He supposed she'd hitched a ride with a friend because he heard not a sound as he moved through the dark hallway.

It took several failed tries before his clumsy gloved hands found the key that opened the protective case around the Oswald Reliquary. Heart pounding, he reached inside, took hold of the cover, and lifted the lid.

It was heavy, but it slid free easily. He gingerly set the lid aside and peered down into the reliquary. The dim glow of the security lights was more than enough to show him what was inside.

The reliquary contained two skulls.

One was unremarkable, but the other was topped with a bronze crown. Unable to breathe, he lifted it out of the case and held it up so he could take a look at the head of one of the legendary Magi of the Christmas story.

The crown was fused to the skull so perfectly that it looked to be one with the bone. Aware that he should get out while the getting was good, he opened Jade's backpack and made to put the skull inside when a faint glimmer of light caught his eye.

An opaque white gem was fixed in the front of the crown and, though it defied logic, a band of light seemed to glow from within the stone itself. He frowned, turning the skull in his hands. The light flickered but did not go away. He was intrigued, but instinct told him he was fortunate to have gotten this far without being caught. He slipped the skull into the backpack, replaced the reliquary lid, and locked the case. At the front door, the flashing lights of the security system gave him pause, but there was nothing for it but to hurry. He chose what he thought was the front door key, let himself out, locked the door behind him, and tossed the keys beneath a shrub a few feet away. Maybe the owner would find them in the morning.

By the time he reached the street, the tightness in his chest had eased and his heart had stopped racing. Even if he had set off an alarm, what would the police find? The museum locked up tight and everything in order. Even if they found the keys and concluded someone had been inside, nothing was missing as far as they knew. If a security camera showed a shadowy figure messing with the reliquary display, St. Oswald's head was still in its resting place. He wondered if this was what a thief felt like when he committed the perfect crime.

He told himself it wasn't really a crime. The skull belonged to the cathedral at Cologne, and he would see to it that it was returned. But not until they solved the mystery.

Chapter 9

The knock came again, louder and more insistent. Andre sighed and closed his eyes, inhaling a deep, calming breath. This was his time for prayer and contemplation and the church was closed. Whoever was at the door would have to come back in the morning.

He counted to ten in his head, waiting to see if the knock would come again, but it did not. Satisfied that he would not be interrupted he returned to his prayer.

The crash shattered the momentary silence and seemed to rattle Andre's very bones. He sprang to his feet and hurried from his study.

The front door stood open and a veritable bear of a man stood in the doorway. Silhouetted against the moon, he was scarcely more than a shadow blotting out the light, but as he closed the door behind him, the sight of him changed from frightening to horrifying.

Though it was evening, he wore wraparound sunglasses that did not conceal his badly scarred face. He looked like a man who almost lost a battle with leeches. What had done this to him? Some sort of plague?

The man must have seen the horror in Andre's eyes because his pockmarked face split into something between a sneer and a grin.

"This is the church of Saint Victor." The words, spoken in heavily accented French, formed a statement, not a question. His voice was a cold, low rumble from deep within his chest and sounded to Andre like boulders crashing down a hill.

"It is." Andre swallowed hard. "What can I do for you?" He supposed it was possible the man had no ill intentions, and was merely here to see the church. Andre was wrong to judge him by his appearance. He was a child of God, the same as any other. And yes, it was rude of the man to intrude, but entering a church during prayer time was far from the most grievous of sins.

"Take me to the head of Lazarus."

"You can see all of him right here." Andre nodded to the statue of Lazarus of Bethany. The venerated saint stood with his face turned toward heaven. In his left hand, he held a crosier. "You might be interested to know that, beneath this statue, are two stones from the saint's sepulchre in Bethany."

"Don't mess with me. I don't want a statue. I want the real thing."

Andre frowned. "I do not understand."

"The skull!" The man seemed to blot out the light as he came closer. "I want to see the skull of Saint Lazarus."

"The bones of Lazarus are not here." Andre felt the blood drain from his face and his stomach grow cold. "The saint died in Cyprus and his remains were later taken to Constantinople. Perhaps if you look..." The man snatched Andre by the neck, squelching his words in a vise grip.

"We know the truth. The grotto, the three hares, all of it." He pulled Andre near enough that the priest could feel his hot breath. Up close, the scarred face was even more disconcerting. He steeled his nerves, reminding himself that he was a man of God and the Spirit would protect him.

"It is a common misunderstanding," Andre gasped. "Many confuse Lazarus of Bethany with the bishop of Aix, Lazarus."

"You aren't fooling me, and if you waste one more minute of my time, you will die a slow and painful death. I want to see the head of Lazarus. Now!" He gave Andre a shove, sending him hard onto his backside. He opened his jacket to reveal the handle of a weapon. Andre knew nothing about firearms, but the sight of it was all he needed to confirm the danger he was in.

Andre had always considered his own mortality with a serenity grounded in his assurance of salvation. Of course, he had always imagined meeting his maker from his sick bed at an advanced age. The life of a priest was a secure one, at least physically. Now, for the first time in his life, he felt death staring him in the face. This man oozed evil.

"I will take you there." Andre slowly crawled to his feet. "It is not far." His heart pounding and his bowels threatening to empty, he led the man to a door on the south side of the nave. It opened onto a staircase descending down into the ancient subterranean church beneath Saint Victor. This church, untouched after nearly two thousand years, had been built by Cassianite monks in the third century. Behind him, the man switched on a flashlight and Andre began his descent. The cold air chilled him to the bone, as did the feeling of great age and power. While many people found the fortress-like exterior of Saint Lazarus dark and intimidating, it was down underground where the true darkness lay.

Andre did not care that this place had once been a church. Something was wrong down here. Perhaps it was that this place had the feel of a dungeon; or maybe the odd carvings, many of which should not be in a place dedicated to Christ. No matter how many times Andre came down here, he always felt vulnerable and unwelcome.

He passed beneath the high ceiling supported by a few round pillars, the silence broken only by the footfalls of the man behind him. Each step sounded to him like the ring of a hammer nailing the lid on his coffin. He forced himself to keep moving, and soon came to the entrance to the ancient grotto that had been the original first-century church of Saint Lazarus. A tangle of carved vines wound its way around the entrance, adding to the forbidding nature of this dark recess.

"It is in here." Andre stepped back and motioned for the man to enter.

"You first." The man's voice made it clear he would accept nothing less than total obedience.

Andre stepped inside with only the greatest reluctance. It was as if invisible hands held him back. His fear of the crypt, however, was nothing compared to his fear of the man behind him.

"Which one is Lazarus?" The man swept his beam across the two stone sarcophagi. Between them lay a stone rectangle where a third sarcophagus had once rested.

"Neither." Andre hurried on. "These were too large to move. Lazarus is here." He hurried to the back wall, cursing himself for cowardice. Keeping the secret had been a simple thing when it was only a matter of misleading researchers, but an armed man was more than he had ever bargained for. His fingers searched the rough, shadowed surface until it found what he was searching for- the odd carving of three joined hares. Some said it was a symbol of the Trinity, but Andre knew it was an evil pagan symbol. Grimacing, he pressed his hand to the hateful symbol and pushed. The stone slowly gave way. When he heard it click, he turned it to the right once, twice, three times. It locked into place and, behind him, Andre heard a grinding sound. He turned to see the foundation stone slide back, revealing a dark hole the size and shape of a grave.

The man shone his light down into the darkness where the beam fell on a small stone box inscribed with the same three hares symbol.

"Open it."

Andre did not hesitate but clambered inside, turning his ankle in the process. Trying to ignore the burning pain, he knelt down by the ossuary. He had never actually laid eyes on it before. Taking a deep breath, he took hold of the lid and heaved.

It was a struggle. He was not a strong man and the lid was heavy, but fear had his adrenaline pumping and he was able to wrestle it free and slide it to the side. Despite his terror, he could not help but feel a thrill at knowing what was inside. The air in the ossuary smelled of dust and age. Andre leaned closer to see what lay inside.

The shaft of light shone on a perfectly preserved skull. He found he could not breathe, but it was not due to fear– that had been forgotten. He was gazing upon the remains of Lazarus himself, whom God incarnate had raised from the dead.

"Take it out and hand it to me." Despite having found what he sought, the man sounded angry.

Andre reached in and gently cupped the skull in his trembling hands. Though the air down here was cool, a solitary bead of sweat rolled off his forehead, making a crater in the dust at the bottom of the ossuary. Slowly, carefully, he raised the skull to eye level and took one long look at it before handing it over to his captor.

The man turned the skull in one hand, scowling. He shone his light back down into the ossuary.

"There's nothing else?"

"No." The fear was back. "We have only had the skull for many centuries."

The man moved the skull to the crook of his left arm, took the flashlight in his left hand, and drew his gun with his right. He leveled the weapon at Andre's head.

"What was the secret?" The bearlike voice was now a scratchy whisper. "How did he bring Lazarus back from the dead?"

Andre gaped. Did the man not know the story?

"By the power of God. He spoke the word and Lazarus rose from the dead."

A sound like a thousand thunderclaps erupted in the crypt and fire lanced through Andre's leg. He slumped to the ground clutching his wounded thigh. He had never dreamed such pain was possible.

"Last chance to live," the man snarled. "What is the secret? How was he brought back?"

"I only know what the scriptures tell us." Andre's voice was a whimper. "I do not know any secret."

"Are you sure?"

Andre nodded. "I know nothing. Please, let me go."

The flashlight winked out, leaving them in absolute darkness. Pulse pounding in his ears, Andre strained to listen for any sounds, hoping to hear receding footsteps that would mean his terror and suffering were at an end. Silently he prayed, eyes squeezed shut. He heard the soft tread of footsteps and then...

No!

The loud scraping of stone on stone filled the room. He tried to get to his feet, but his wounded leg betrayed him and he fell down hard. Summoning all his remaining strength, he hurled everything he had into the effort, and sprang to his feet.

Pain exploded in his head as he cracked the top of his head on hard stone, and he crumpled to the ground. Head swimming and ears ringing, he tried to push himself up, but his strength was gone. Only a moan of pain and desperation escaped his lips as the stone cover slid back into place, entombing him where the saint had once lain.

Chapter 10

"Let me take another look at the skull." Maddock reached into the back seat and accepted the skull from Angel. He sat it in his lap, its face grinning up at him. The Magi, the Wise Men who visited the baby Jesus in Bethlehem. Could it be true? He had to laugh. How many times in the past few years had he wondered that very thing? Either the world was jam-packed with mysteries and secrets or he and Bones were very lucky– or unlucky, depending on how you looked at things.

"I don't know what to make of it." Jade leaned over his seat to get a better look. A moment later, Angel's face joined hers.

"Hey chicks, we're driving on a snowy highway. Put your seat belts back on!" Bones shook his head. "And they say I'm reckless."

Angel laid a hand on his shoulder. "We just trust your driving ability, that's all."

Bones rolled his eyes but dropped the issue.

"Does that light ever go out?" Angel pointed to the stone set in the front of the crown.

"I think it's just reflecting light from the dashboard," Jade said.

"I'm not so sure." Maddock remembered his first impression when he removed the skull from its reliquary. The light seemed to come from within the stone. "I could see a glimmer of light in it from the very start."

"A stone that generates its own light? Maddock, that's impossible."

Maddock and Bones exchanged a quick glance. They remembered a temple underneath the earth lined with stones that could absorb and amplify light. "I once saw something along those lines, though not quite the same." He told them about what he and Bones had found in the Holy Land a few years earlier. "I have an idea. Bones, can you pull the car over and kill the lights?"

A few minutes later they sat on a dark, deserted stretch of highway. They all huddled around the skull, blocking any ambient light, and peering intently at the opaque gem.

"I see it!" Jade gripped Maddock's arm. "There's a faint sliver of light there."

"It's almost shaped like a triangle," Angel mused. "See how it's narrower at one end?"

"But is it generating its own light, or is it like the stones we saw before, and just using the light it absorbs?" Bones asked.

"This isn't like those stones." Maddock shook his head. "Those took a little bit of light and multiplied it. This is just a sliver that seems to come from within the stone itself. Weird."

Just then, Jade's cell phone rang, interrupting their quiet contemplation. She glanced at the screen and smiled.

"It's Otto."

The conversation was brief, and Otto must have done most of the talking because Jade's contribution consisted primarily of "okay" and "uh-huh." When she hung up, she was smiling ear-to-ear.

"What was that all about?" Maddock asked.

"Otto thinks he's solved another of the clues. Paderborn Cathedral has a well-known three hares window. That by itself wouldn't help us out much, but it also houses the remains of Saint Liborius." She paused for effect.

"This conversation is already feeling laborious." Maddock grinned. "Cut the suspense."

"He was a bishop of the late fourth century during a time paganism was strong in this part of the world. Legend has it, when the relics of *Liborius*," she emphasized the correct pronunciation, "were brought to Paderborn, a peacock led the procession."

"The peacock be your guide." Maddock quoted the passage from the clue. "Well, I guess we're headed for Paderborn."

The west tower of the Paderborn Cathedral rose above the ornate Romanesque-Gothic church like a sentry on the lookout for intruders. At least, that was how Maddock felt as he gazed up at the structure that stood three hundred feet. It was, to him, the cathedral's most impressive feature, though he was also blown away by the many large arched windows that contained within them smaller, narrower arched windows topped by round, highly decorative portals. No matter how many cathedrals he visited, the architecture and craftsmanship never ceased to amaze him.

"So, what exactly are we looking for?" Bones asked.

"There are two key connections to the clue," Jade said. "The three hares, and the peacock. Paderborn Cathedral has a famous three hares window. Let's start there."

They circled the cathedral examining all the windows for the three hares sign. They drew a few odd glances but probably due more to Bones' presence than their interest in the stained glass. They had searched for a half-hour before Jade decided to ask for help. They were directed to an inner courtyard where they found the three hares window and more.

"This has got to be it!" Jade exclaimed as soon as they were alone. It was not as impressive as Maddock had expected. The three stone hares in a circle were set atop a stained glass window and in front of it stood...

"A peacock!" Angel brushed the snow off of the dark stone fountain surmounted by an ornately carved peacock. "This must be what the clue was talking about."

"Could be," Maddock said. "Bones, you keep an eye out in case somebody comes this way. The rest of us will see what we can find."

They scoured the courtyard, paying particular attention to the area around the stained glass window and around the peacock fountain. The window offered no promising leads, so they focused on the peacock, but no amount of poking, prodding, pushing, or twisting uncovered any hidden compartment or passageway, nor did they find any telltale three hares images like those they had found in Cologne and Hildesheim.

They expanded their search, checking the walls around the courtyard and scraping away snow and ice from the ground in any likely spot. Maddock scrubbed rough blocks until his gloves began to tear, but with no success.

"I don't think this is the right place." He looked at Jade, who nodded. "What else did you find out about this place when you researched it last night? You know, hares and peacocks and stuff."

"If by 'stuff' you mean the Magi or the Wise Virgins, I didn't find anything. Nothing else about the three hares either." She screwed up her face in concentration. The expression made other people look constipated but, on her, it was cute. "There is supposed to be a lot of peacock imagery inside the cathedral."

"The clue talks about the peacock being the guide. A peacock supposedly guided the relics. Considering where we found the first skull, I'll bet that's the connection." He'd had a feeling about the relics, but they had wanted to eliminate the obvious first, and thus had checked the area around the three hares window.

Jade nodded. "It's the next best possibility, if not the best. The relics are down in the crypt. Let's check it out."

The Paderborner Dom featured three parallel aisles, all reaching the height of the roof. The stained glass windows that ran the length of the side walls cast the interior in a warm glow. Christmas trees hung with white lights added to the cheer. Jade took Maddock's hand and leaned her head on his shoulder.

"It's nice, isn't it?"

He nodded. It was all too easy to get caught up in the mystery and not enjoy the moment. Bones and Angel seemed to feel the same way. Each was smiling and taking in the beauty that surrounded them. The cathedral, not one of Germany's most famous or popular, was almost empty today, with only a handful of people wandering about.

Angel's face suddenly froze. She ducked behind a column and beckoned to the others.

"The guys who attacked me are here. The dark-haired one is Ulrich; I didn't get the other guy's name."

Maddock didn't need her to point out the two men who stood at the crossing looking around. If he had not remembered what they looked like, the black-haired man's battered face stuck out like a sore thumb.

"What are they doing here?" Bones scowled at the men. "Do you think Otto told them?"

"No way," Jade said. "He told them about the three hares, remember? They're probably checking out any cathedral with a three hares symbol."

"And considering what they did at Kölner Dom, they're probably going for the shrine. You two," Maddock said to Jade and Angel, "get back to the car and wait for us."

"Not a chance." Angel shook her head. "You ain't the boss of me."

"Same here, Maddock," Jade added. "Cut the chivalrous crap. You know I hate it."

"Fine." Maddock eyed the men who were slowly moving toward the east end of the cathedral. "You two keep out of sight and look for peacocks and anything else that might be promising, just in case we're wrong about the shrine. Let's go Bones." His friend nodded and they made their way through the nave, eyes on their quarry. The men were moving faster now, presumably headed for the crypt.

The columns that supported the roof were huge and it was easy to remain out of sight as they stalked the two men. Their quarry disappeared down a flight of stairs where a sign read DIE KRYPTA. A few lines in German followed. He recognized the name *Liborius* and the words *"please do not."* At the bottom, *"Silence Please"* was written in English.

Not a problem, he thought.

At the bottom of the stairs, Maddock peered around the corner, seeking the two men. What he saw took him by surprise. The crypt, Jade had told them, was one of the largest in Germany— more than one hundred feet long, but he still was not prepared for the sight. The ornate columns, arched ceiling, and tiled floor made the place look like a church beneath a church. Indeed, the space to his left appeared to be a small worship area complete with pews, a confessional, and an altar. To their right, a gated archway opened into a dark, gloomy place where the tomb of Saint Liborius lay and, directly across from them, a second set of stairs led back up into the cathedral.

The chamber in which the saint's remains were held had a semicircular ceiling that reminded Maddock of a Quonset hut. The faint light danced off the ornate walls, casting the space in a bluish glow. A representation of the saint was carved on the lid of the stone tomb. Beyond the tomb, beneath a stylized representation of peacock feathers, an arched doorway led into a second, smaller chamber, where a low plexiglass wall guarded a golden shrine.

Maddock was surprised at the lack of security afforded to Liborius's remains compared to that of the Shrine of the Magi, but he supposed the Three Kings were just a bit more famous. As that thought passed through his mind, the two men appeared from either side of the doorway in the back chamber. One of them took a quick look around to see if they were alone, then nodded to his companion. They vaulted the plexiglass wall and approached the golden shrine.

Bones took a step toward the tomb, but Maddock held him back.

"We have to assume we're outgunned. Take up positions outside the door to the first chamber and we'll jump them on the way out."

Bones grinned. He loved a good brawl.

They moved like shadows, eyes never leaving the men in the burial chamber, who were now lifting the lid off the shrine.

"Gottverdammt!" The dark-haired man with the bruised face swore. "Es ist hier nicht!"

Maddock's German vocabulary was sufficient to get the gist of the words— *It is not here.* He looked at Bones who arched an eyebrow and nodded. He'd understood too.

Inside, the men replaced the lid and clambered back over the barrier. "Das grab?" the blond man asked. His partner nodded and they moved to the tomb of Liborius. Maddock moved back from the doorway so he would not be spotted and listened until grunting and scraping told him the men were hard at work trying to remove the lid.

A sudden crash shattered the silence.

"Dummkopf!"

Maddock grinned. These two were having a bad day. He stole a glance into the chamber and saw that the blond-haired guy, apparently worried that someone had heard the noise, had drawn his gun.

His partner inspected the tomb for a long time, moving things around and muttering under his breath. Finally, he let out a long sigh. "Nichts."

The blond man sagged visibly, pocketed his weapon, and indicated that they should replace the lid. They set to the task with angry expressions on their faces.

"Let's go." Maddock mouthed the words to Bones, who nodded. No sense in picking a fight if the bad guys were on their way out. Before they could head up the stairs, though, he heard the lid slam into place and footsteps echoed in the crypt. He ducked into a nearby alcove, hoping Bones had hidden too, rather than let his usual fight response take over. He breathed a quick sigh of relief as the men passed his hiding place without so much as a sideways glance, and mounted the stairs up into the cathedral. His relief was short-lived, however, for it suddenly occurred to him that Jade and Angel were alone and unarmed in the cathedral. He had told them to keep out of sight, but this was Jade and Angel. With a grimace, he slipped from his hiding place and followed.

Chapter 11

"I'm beginning to think this is a dead end." Angel looked down at the English language brochure, searching for any clue they might have missed.

"It can't be." Jade stood with her hands on her hips, scowling at the big stained glass window in the cathedral's east wall as if it was somehow at fault. "The connection is too perfect. The hares, the peacock, this has to be it."

"We've looked at every peacock in this place and found nothing." Angel wasn't sure why Jade got under her skin so badly. She was actually pretty cool– quick-witted and not too girly. She supposed it was worry over Bones and Maddock that had her on edge. "I think we should check on those two."

"They're fine." Worry painted Jade's face, but she shook her head. "Whatever you might think of your brother, neither of them are dumb, and they've been through plenty of dangerous situations before. They won't let themselves get into serious trouble."

"You're sure about that?"

"I have to be. If the bad guys didn't kill us, Maddock would. He knows what he's doing. Let's just keep looking." Jade turned about slowly. "Anywhere we haven't looked?"

"How about this Trinity Chapel? The hares are a Trinitarian symbol and there were three Magi." She shrugged.

"Sounds good," Jade agree. "Let's do it."

There was not much to the chapel. Its most prominent feature was a gilded relief of Liborius himself, set in a niche between a window and a pillar. The saint held a staff in his left hand and a book, presumably the Bible, in his right.

"What are the three things on top of the Bible?" Angel cocked her head to the left. "Rocks?"

"Rocks, stones. They symbolize healing. He's the patron saint against gallstones."

Angel guffawed. "No, seriously."

"I'm not kidding. Think about how bad it must have been to have gallstones back in the Middle Ages."

Angel took a closer look at the odd sight. A saint of gallstones! It sounded like some ridiculous crap Bones would make up. She ran her fingers across the stones and, as they passed over the center stone, she felt something. She frowned and leaned in close. There was a faint shape there! Heart pounding, she beckoned for Jade.

"Check this out!"

"What is it?" Jade's eyes popped when she saw what Angel was pointing at. "The three hares! It's faint, but definitely there." She grinned at Angel. "Want to do the honors?"

Angel put two fingers on the stone and pressed down. It resisted at first, but when she put all her strength into it, it slid back into the wall. The Liborius relief swung forward, revealing a small alcove containing a stone box. It was small, but not too small to hold a skull— even a crowned one. More nervous than she'd ever been before one of her fights, Angel removed the box and held it out for Jade to see. The three hares were engraved in the top.

"This has got to be it." Jade's low voice trembled with excitement. "You found the second skull!"

"We thank you for that." The voice startled them, and they whirled about to see the two men who, two nights before, had accosted Angel, standing with guns trained on them. "Now give us the box." The blond man grinned at her and held out a hand.

"I see your friend isn't smiling." Angel glanced at the dark-haired man's battered face. "Tell you what. I'll fight you for it. Hell, I'll fight both of you. Put away your guns and take me on like men."

"Let's kill them, Niklas," the dark-haired man said, ignoring her. Gun trained on Jade, he moved closer to her. "I'll start with this one. I think I'll shoot her in the gut. Make sure she dies slowly and painfully."

Jade stared at him, wide-eyed, not daring to move.

"Calm yourself Ulrich," his partner said. "If they give us the box, no one need get hurt."

Angel could see the lie in Niklas' eyes. "First, you back away from my friend. Let her leave. Then I'll give you the skull."

"Angel, no!" Jade protested.

"Quiet!" Niklas snapped. "If we shoot you now, we will take the skull and still be away before anyone notifies die Polizei. I would prefer to leave here quietly, but it is not necessary." He tightened his grip on his gun.

Angel saw him swallow hard. She had a feeling the guy wasn't really a killer, but he was still dangerous.

"Fine." She kept her face blank, though her heart was pounding with fear and excitement in equal measure. "Here you go."

She heaved the stone box in his direction. After years of training with a medicine ball, the weight of the box was nothing. She didn't throw it at Niklas but tossed it over his head.

As the men turned their heads to follow the flight of the box, and Niklas moved to catch it, Bones, who had crept up behind Niklas, drove his fist into the man's face, sending him crumpling to the floor. Ulrich whirled about, pistol upraised, but Maddock stepped out from behind a pillar and cracked him across the back of the head with a candelabra.

"Nice job delaying them while we got into position." Maddock wiped the candelabra with his shirttail and dropped it the ground.

"We weren't delaying for you," Angel said. "We were just delaying. I didn't even see you until Bones popped out from between those pews and motioned for me to throw the box."

"We're SEALs." Bones retrieved the stone box and held it up for inspection. "All part of the training."

"You did a lot of in-church camouflage work in the service?" Jade kissed Maddock on the cheek, which sparked an unexpected flare of jealousy in Angel. What the hell? Maddock was like a brother to her. She supposed she'd feel protective of Bones if he ever got serious with someone.

"These guys will be coming to any minute." Maddock scooped up Ulrich's pistol and tucked it in his inside jacket pocket. "Let's get out of here."

Bones grabbed the other dropped weapon, and the four of them headed for the exit. Angel paused long enough to give Niklas and Ulrich each a kick in the groin.

"Two down," she said to herself and chuckled. Skulls or bad guys? It fit either way.

Chapter 12

"There's something weird about these skulls." Maddock had been examining stones set in the matching crowns on the two skulls and the odd phenomenon of the internal lights continued. "The lights are still here and they're getting brighter."

Bones glanced over from the driver's seat. "They haven't seen the light in who knows how long. Maybe they're absorbing the light."

"Maybe, but they get brighter when they're closer together."

"Let's see," Jade said from the back seat.

Maddock held the skulls up and slowly moved them apart, then together again. Sure enough, the light dimmed as they moved away from each other and glowed brighter as they came back together. Maddock pursed his lips. "There's something else, though. You know how we noticed the light looked sort of like an arrow? Well, they both look like that and, get this, no matter how you turn them, the arrow always points in the exact same direction." He demonstrated, first with one skull, then with two held side-by-side.

"Are they like compasses?" Angel asked.

"They seem to work that way, but which way are they pointing?"

"Bethlehem." Bones' expression was serious. "Maybe the star the Wise Men followed wasn't literal."

"I swear I've heard a legend of a compass stone," Jade mused.

"The Vikings supposedly had one." Maddock had always enjoyed reading about early sailors and expeditions, and the Vikings had been among his favorites. "They called it a sunstone because it pointed the way to the sun on a cloudy day."

"But these stones aren't pointing toward the sun." Bones took another quick glance at the skulls. "Looks like they're pointing south to me. My vote is either Bethlehem or a reverse compass pointing to the South Pole."

"Or we're reading them backward and they're just plain old compasses. That would be the simplest explanation." Jade took one of the skulls from Maddock so she and Angel could have a closer look.

"Yeah, but simplest isn't funnest," Bones griped.

"Funnest? Bones, do you even know what you sound like?" Angel sounded exasperated, but her amused smile told a different story.

"I sound like a guy who doesn't have a stick up his butt."

Maddock had to laugh. Bones and Angel were definitely the brother and sister he never had and wasn't completely sure he wanted, but they were fun.

"All right, let's put the skulls away. We're there."

The Catholic University of Eichstatt-Ingolstadt was the only Catholic university in the German-speaking world. Its history dated back to a sixteenth-century seminary, and some digging had produced the name of one of their faculty members, August Adler, as an expert on local Magi lore. They hoped he might be able to provide them with some clues that weren't easily found through an internet search.

"Call me crazy," Angel said, looking out the window, "but even with this crazy mystery, this place sort of puts me in the Christmas spirit."

Indeed, the snow-covered forests and mountains of Bavaria were some of the most beautiful Maddock had seen. It almost made him want to forsake the search and settle down in a warm pub in front of a cheery fire and let the holiday spirit wash over him. Almost.

"I know this isn't the Christmas trip you guys signed up for." Jade bit her lip.

"Nope, this is better." Bones looked as happy as he ever had. Though he loved a relaxing good time as much as the next guy, like Maddock, he was happiest when on the trail of something lost, be it a shipwreck or an artifact.

"I'm cool with it," Angel added. "I'm starting to see why you guys let yourselves get hooked up in these sorts of things. I feel so... alive."

"Facing death does that to you," Maddock said, admiring the campus, now almost empty with students on holiday. "It makes you appreciate the little things." Out of the corner of his eye he caught Jade gazing at him with a strange expression on her face. There would be plenty of time later to figure out what was on her mind. Right now, they had an appointment to keep.

August Adler was a short, stocky man with wavy white hair and a bushy salt and pepper mustache. He reminded Maddock of Mark Twain, if Twain were an aging German professor of theology. He ushered them into his office, where dark wooden shelves sagged under the weight of books stacked double.

"I understand you are all archaeologists?" He settled into his chair and placed his folded hands on his cluttered desk.

"Three of us are," Jade said, not adding that Maddock and Bones were marine archaeologists.

"Odd man out." Angel waved. "I'm just along for the ride."

"Very good." August nodded. "Tell me how I can be of help."

"We are interested in legends surrounding the Magi."

Adler frowned. His bushy eyebrows looked like two aging caterpillars performing calisthenics. "I assume you have heard about the theft of the bones from the Shrine of the Magi from Kölner Dom." A note of suspicion rang in his words.

"We did." Jade nodded gravely and the others followed suit. "That was terrible."

"What is your interest in the Magi?"

"It's really for me. I'm researching the connection between the Three Wise Men and the three hares symbol."

"Aha!" Adler relaxed visibly and leaned back in his chair. "A very interesting subject, but only to me. I assume you have read my paper on the subject."

"I just learned that the paper existed, which is how we found you. Since we were in the area, I couldn't miss the opportunity to meet you, though I would love to read your paper." Jade flashed her smile, just warm enough to melt a man's heart like butter.

"I will give you a copy before you leave." Adler took a deep breath and looked up at the ceiling, collecting his thoughts. "The connections between the hares and the Magi are speculative. The hare has long been associated with mythology and imagery of the divine. It symbolizes fertility, renewal, and new birth. The rabbit was adopted as a symbol of Easter due to its connection with a pagan fertility goddess of the same name whose festival was celebrated in the spring. The three hares are a pagan symbol, though the church adopted it, like so many other pagan symbols, as an emblem of the Trinity. Like the Magi, the origins of the symbol are unknown, but they have been found across Europe and the Far East."

"The Magi came from the east," Maddock commented.

"So it is believed." Adler nodded and went on. "Little is known about the Magi and, to be honest, scholars take little interest in them compared to other figures in the Bible. They appear only in a single gospel. Consequently, many consider them to be a fabrication inserted by the author in order to make the Nativity story better fit Old Testament prophecy. For that reason, a scholar is left to gather rumors and legends about them, nothing more."

"Could you tell us about them?" Jade asked, scooting closer to his desk. "We're interested even in the far-fetched stories."

"The more mundane legends hold that they returned to their lives in the east, or wherever they supposedly hailed from. The most unusual legend I uncovered is actually one I grew up hearing in the small village in Upper Bavaria where I was born and raised. The legend holds that the Magi were not kings, but pagan magicians, and they left the Holy Land on a sacred task set before them by God Almighty."

"What kind of task?" Bones interjected.

"It depends on who is telling the story." Adler grinned. "Some say the three gifts to the Christ child were actually items of great power that had to be hidden from humankind. The gift of gold represented alchemy. Frankincense has been called everything from Magic dust to the dust from which mankind was created. Myrrh was an embalming oil, so it has been rumored to grant the power of resurrection. Other legends are less specific, but all agree they were hiding a great power, perhaps to preserve it until the end of days." He rolled his eyes. "This is where the legend of the Magi crosses paths with the three hares. If the legend is to be believed, the Magi hid their secrets somewhere in the Alps, and the three hares became the symbol of the cult of the Magi. Three magicians, three hares..." He shrugged.

"What about the story of the Wise Men following the star? Any legends surrounding that or is it taken at face value?" Maddock was thinking about the compass-like stones.

"The serious scholars have always tried to connect it to an astronomical event– a convergence of planets and stars. The legends have suggested that the star was actually a light the wise men carried that shone toward Bethlehem. Another story is that the star was a jewel that pointed the way."

"Like a compass stone?" Angel asked.

"Very much so." Adler nodded. "You did ask for the most far-fetched stories. Those hold that the star was taken away from Bethlehem and hidden away. One story claims that the star is hidden in a cavern deep below the Arabian Desert and can be identified by the smoke that pours up from the ground. The local version, of course, places the star in a cavern in the mountains."

"In my research, I uncovered a riddle that I believe is connected to the Cult of the Magi." Jade looked uncertain, probably hoping he would not ask where she found the riddle. Maddock wasn't worried. Jade was good at thinking on her feet. "Can you think of any place this might be referring to? It would be a place connected with the three hares or the Magi. Probably both." She recited a passage from their clue. *"Into the depths of the well. The kings point the way to the falling ice..."*

Adler stiffened. "Are you perhaps playing a joke on me?"

"Not at all." Jade's voice was soft and reassuring. "I take it this means something to you."

Adler's eyes bored into hers and she looked him in the eye. He stared at her for the span of five heartbeats before appearing to make his mind up about something.

"Forgive me. The words were unexpected." He swiveled around and plucked a book off the shelf. Its cover was worn with age, but Maddock could read the title stamped on the cover in faded gold letters.

Drekonhas.

"My home," Adler explained. "Its coat of arms is a triskelion– three connected legs. This was not always the case. Historically, the coat of arms was the three hares." It was as if a veil of sadness was suddenly drawn across his face. "The Nazis changed that when they came to power. The swastika became the new symbol until after the war."

"Why didn't they go back to the three hares?" Bones asked.

Adler took a deep breath. "My village is deep in the mountains. Even today they are a superstitious lot and undercurrents of paganism run strong among its people. The leaders viewed a return to three hares symbol as a return to the backward ways of the old world. The current symbol is more... common." He looked up at them and his face brightened. "I see a connection to your riddle for a few reasons. There is an ancient stone engraved with the three hares. It now stands beside the town hall but, prior to the rise of the Nazis, it was part of the old village well, and had been for centuries." He leaned forward and his voice fell, as if what he was about to tell them was a secret.

"As I told you earlier, Magi lore is strong in my village. The name, Drekonhas, contains parts of three words: Dreis, konig, hasen. The three king hares." He swallowed hard. "Also, there is the eisbruch."

"I'm sorry?" Jade frowned.

"Icefall," Adler explained.

"An icefall is almost like a waterfall of ice," Maddock explained. "They don't move like water, but they move faster than a glacier. They can be climbed, but they form crevasses and are filled with fractures, making them potentially deadly for climbers."

"Exactly." Adler nodded. "Drekonhas is nestled in the mountains near Sternspitze– one of the tallest peaks in Germany. Below and all around it is karst." He looked up at the ceiling and tapped his cheek with his forefinger. "How would you say it? Soft stone... no..." He shook his head. "It is filled with caves. You know limestone caves?" They all nodded. "Legend tells us that a cave beneath Sternspitze is the final resting place of the Magi's secret, and that path lies beneath the icefall."

"Has anyone tried to find it?" Maddock's heart was pounding. The idea of climbing an icefall was as exciting as it was foolish. One look at Bones told him his friend was as eager to climb as Maddock was.

"A few. All have failed. Some have lost their lives on the icefall; others returned having found nothing remarkable. Others still have sought a way in through some of the caves in the karst, but that has proved deadlier." He grimaced. "The caves go on forever, they say. They are like a warren, which is fitting, I suppose. In some places, the way grows too narrow to pass. In others, the ceiling or floor is weak and will give way under pressure. So many have failed to return that few venture there at all anymore, and those who do restrict themselves to the outermost passages." He lapsed into a brooding silence.

"I get the feeling there's more to the story," Jade said.

"Only more foolishness." Adler barked a laugh and turned to stare out the window. "It is said the caves are guarded by Krampus."

"The Christmas guy?" Jade laughed. She saw the puzzled expressions on the others' faces. "According to Alpine tradition, Krampus is a partner to Saint Nicholas. Saint Nick rewards the good children while Krampus warns or punishes the bad."

"The Anti-Santa?" Angel laughed. "What is he? A fat dude in a black suit? Deliverer of coal and fruitcake?"

"No, he's a hairy, horned man..." Jade fell silent, her face ashen.

"Are you all right?" Adler reached out and took her hand. "It must be the heat in here. Open a window, young man." He nodded at Bones and inclined his head toward the window. Maddock felt poleaxed. None of the earlier revelations had been much of a surprise, but having seen the horned skulls with his own eyes, he knew Adler's story had a kernel of truth.

"Do you believe in, like, the Yeti and stuff?" Bones asked. His awkward question an attempt to jump-start the stalled conversation.

"I do not know." Adler shrugged. "But, though I would not admit it to most people, I believe in Krampus for one very good reason."

"What is that?" Maddock's heart was hammering his ribs like a blacksmith at the forge.

"I saw him." Adler paused as if waiting for them to scoff. When they remained silent, he went on. "When I was a young man, young enough to believe in the impossible, but old enough to be a skeptic, I ventured deep into the caves below Sternspitze. I could have died, but something made me turn back." He paled and his voice grew suddenly hoarse. "Something peered around a corner and looked at me just as I am looking at you. A hairy man with horns."

"Could you have been mistaken?" Angel asked. She seemed to be searching for a reason not to believe the skulls came from real creatures. "A shadow on an oddly-shaped rock or something?"

"Does a rock have glowing eyes that reflect a flashlight beam? I know what I saw, and I have never gone back." Adler's gaze turned flinty, and his countenance grew cold. "I fear that is all I can tell you. I hope you will exercise caution if you investigate the subject any further."

They thanked him for his help, and he assured them it was no problem. He spared a minute to print out a copy of his paper on the Magi cult and then saw them out.

Maddock could not stop thinking about the mountain, the icefall, and the mysterious caves below. "Professor Adler, does Sternspitze have a meaning?"

Adler gave him a wry smile. "As a matter of fact it does. It means star spike."

Ubel Karsch heard footsteps on the other side of the door. He hurried across the hall, slipped inside his office, and peered out through the small window set in his door. He watched as Adler saw his visitors out, and what a group they were: two men, one of them the biggest American Indian he had ever seen, the other a blond man whose serene face stood at odds with the danger he exuded with every step. Both of them had a military bearing about them, though the big Indian tried to hide it with his ridiculous motorcycle jacket and juvenile t-shirt. The women were unusual too— one American Indian and one Asian.

It was not the strange visitors he cared about, though. It was the story Adler had told them. In the seven years they had worked together, Ubel had probed him on many occasions for legends about the Magi, and the old fool had never told him the legends surrounding his own home town.

He grimaced. How would his news be received? Would he be praised for finally ferreting out this new information, or would he be treated as a failure for having taken so long to uncover it? It made no difference. There was nothing he could do now except make the call and hope for the best.

He looked up and down the hallway, making certain no one was about. He turned on the radio and turned it toward the door. "We Three Kings" wafted from the speakers. Fitting.

Heart pounding and throat tight, he punched up the number. When someone picked up on the other end, he spoke the two words that would gain him immediate access to his Elder.

"Heilig Herrschaft."

Chapter 13

Drekonhas was the epitome of the classic Alpine village. Nestled amongst the snow-capped mountains, the place made Maddock feel like he'd been sent back in time. The morning sun set everything aglow. Except for the occasional vehicle they passed, the scene was like something out of a picture book.

"This is a pretty cool place. I wonder where the Burgermeister Meisterburger lives." Bones turned toward Maddock. "What's the plan?"

"Make like tourists," Maddock said, pulling into a parking space near a small pub. "Bones, you hit the pub and see if you can meet up with anyone talkative, preferably an old-timer. See what you can learn about the caves and the icefall." Bones fist-pumped. "Two things," Maddock added. "Don't get too pushy with the questions, and take sips, not gulps."

"Dude, I know the drill. When it comes to pubs, this is not my first rodeo."

"Oh, and don't get distracted by any babes you might meet."

Bones rolled his eyes. "Yes, Dad."

"Angel and Jade, you check on lodging and do a little browsing in the shops. Act like normal visitors. I'll scope out the well. If it looks like a one man job and no one's around, I'll take care of it myself and we'll move on to the next phase. I think the stones in the crowns are compass stones and they're pointing the way to whatever is under the icefall." They had purchased climbing gear and warm clothing in anticipation of climbing Sternspitze. "If not, Bones and I will have to go back after dark."

"I don't like you going by yourself, Maddock," Jade said. "Let one of us go with you. It doesn't take two to see if there's 'room at the inn.'"

"No offense, but you three will stand out like crazy in a German village. I'm a blue-eyed blond. The only thing conspicuous about me is my good looks."

Jade rolled her eyes but relented. The three of them left the car and spread out. Maddock waited for them to disperse before heading for the old village well.

Jade checked her watch as she stepped outside of the cozy inn where she'd managed to secure the last available rooms. She glanced at her watch. That hadn't taken long. She'd meet up with Angel, wander the village for a little while. Maddock shouldn't need more than an hour. Then they could firm up their plans.

She ignored the shiver of worry that passed through her as she thought of Maddock out on his own. He was as solid a man she'd ever known—smart, capable, and resilient. He wouldn't get himself into anything he couldn't handle.

Snow crunched underfoot as she wandered through the town, returning the occasional wave. Adler had made Drekonhas sound like a small, secluded pocket of paganism, sort of an Alpine version of *Deliverance*, but it didn't seem to be the case. It was bigger than the "village" she had pictured in her mind, and seemed tourist-friendly. The woman at the inn had been pleasant enough, and there was a warm, friendly vibe about the town. The mystery notwithstanding, this might be a fine place to spend Christmas.

A strong hand seized her by the arm.

"Quit messing around Bones." She turned and what she saw made her jaw drop.

"Hello, Ihara. Missed me?"

Sunglasses and a scarf hid much of his face, but she knew him immediately.

"Issachar!" She froze in shock for only an instant, but that was her undoing. Before she could lash out with a punch or kick, he yanked her toward him and crushed her in a bear hug.

"Isn't this nice? Two old friends reunited."

His warm, damp breath on her ear and his sickly sweet tone turned her stomach. She squirmed, trying to break free, but he held her so tight that she could not move an inch. He held her face pressed into his coat, preventing her from crying out... or breathing.

"Thought you got rid of me out in the desert, didn't you? I'm not so easy to kill. Your friend Maddock will find that out soon enough, but first, I have a job to do and you're going to help."

Jade tried again to fight, stamping down on his foot, but he avoided it with ease. She was already feeling the lack of oxygen and her strength was waning.

"Go to sleep, little traitor. You're going to need your rest."

Maddock, Bones, Angel, somebody help me! Her thought faded as blackness overcame her.

When she came to, she was face-down in the back seat of a car. Her arms and legs were bound. Where was she? What had happened to her? Slowly, as if gluing together the pieces of a shredded picture, she remembered. And when she did, she screamed. At least, she tried to scream, but all she managed was a weak cry. The vehicle backed up fast, sending her rolling forward, and she found herself wedged between the seats, not quite down on the floorboard. They were moving forward now. She must have been out for only a short while— long enough for Issachar to put her in the car and tie her up. She took a deep breath and called out again.

"Help! Help!" This time it was good and loud.

"Keep screaming, Ihara. This might as well be a ghost town— nobody's out on the streets this morning. In about two minutes, we'll be out of town and headed for the mountains."

Jade took him up on his offer, shouting herself hoarse and kicking the door the best she could manage considering her bonds and awkward position. Finally, she gave up.

"About time. You were drowning out my Christmas music." Issachar's wicked laugh sent chills down her spine. "Bet you're sorry you betrayed us now."

"I didn't betray you," she wheezed. "I was never part of the Dominion."

"Doesn't matter. You're going to help us now."

"The Dominion is dead." She wanted to believe that, but knew it wasn't true. Maddock had learned a few things during his trek into the Amazon— enough to know there was more to the Dominion than they'd previously believed.

"The Deseret Dominion is dead, or close to it, but there's more to us than that. Much more. How do you think I found out about this town and the icefall? I even have a pretty good idea what this does." He held up a crowned skull. "I got to the well first."

No ice could have been as frozen as Jade's insides at that moment. "Adler told you? No way." She couldn't believe the kind old man was part of the Dominion.

Then again, she'd misjudged people before on that score.

Issachar barked a laugh. "Heilig Herrschaft has plenty of eyes and ears."

Jade squeezed her eyes closed. Her head was throbbing and she still felt woozy from her lapse into unconsciousness.

"What do you want with me, Issachar? If you know about Adler, you know everything I know." Issachar was vicious enough to kill her out of revenge for what he considered a betrayal of the Dominion, but instinct told her he had a scheme and she was to be a part of it. Either possibility made her want to throw up.

"Let's just say you're going to be a litmus test. I was going to use one of those Herrschaft idiots, but this will be much more satisfying." He smiled. "Santa came early this year. It's Christmas Eve and I've already gotten a present."

Chapter 14

It was gone. Maddock looked down at the stone etched with the three hares, lying on the frozen bottom where someone had dropped it. The space it had once filled was set at eye level. It was easily large enough to have held one of the skulls of the Magi. He took one last look, then reached inside and felt around just to make certain he had not missed anything, but he knew it was futile. Someone had beaten them to it.

Cold and angry, he made the climb back out, the frozen stones slick under his fingers. He lost his grip a few times, but managed to catch himself. Come on, he chided himself. You can't escape armed bad guys only to die falling down a well. When he finally hauled himself out, he was in a foul mood. Were the skulls essential to finding the secret that lay beneath the icefall? If so, would they need all three? He supposed it did not matter now. They would have to proceed with what they had.

"Put your hands in the air." He knew that voice. He'd heard it just a few days earlier in Paderborn.

He looked up to see Ulrich and Niklas standing there, weapons drawn, grinning. Warily, he held his hands away from his body to show he was unarmed. They had taken the skull and then set a trap for him, and he'd walked right into it.

"Give us the skull." Niklas held out his hand.

"What?" Maddock was genuinely surprised. "You already have it."

"Let us have it!" Ulrich shouted. He trembled with anger. Perhaps his battered and bruised face, which was probably a handsome one under ordinary circumstances, and the memory of the two whippings he'd already suffered at the hands of Maddock's group, was the cause of his anger. Maddock looked into his dark eyes, and saw something more; there was a deeper cause for his rage. "We must have it. Time is almost up."

"What do you want with it?"

A wiser man would not have wasted time bandying words with Maddock, but Ulrich had already proved himself reckless, and his agitated state only amplified that trait.

"We must find the Magi! They left the key to resurrection."

"Ulrich, Nein!" Niklas snapped, but the other man rambled on.

"The Fuhrer must live!"

"Wait a minute." He tried to recall what Adler had told them about the Magi legend. "You think the myrrh will bring back a guy who's been dead for more than a half-century?"

The two men exchanged furtive glances, and Maddock's heart skipped a beat.

"No way!" It couldn't possibly be true.

Ulrich clearly realized he had said too much. His face reddened, but his eyes burned with righteous anger.

"It doesn't matter anyway. I don't have it."

"Do not play with us." Niklas sounded stern, but Maddock could see in his eyes that the man knew something was amiss. "Give it to us now."

"It's gone. If you didn't take it, someone else must have." He raised his hands a little higher. "Search me if you want. Heck, look down in the well. The stone that covered its hiding place is still lying there."

The men exchanged looks. Niklas nodded, and Ulrich approached Maddock. Pistol in one hand, he gave Maddock a light pat-down with the other. Maddock breathed a sigh of relief that the man had skulls on his mind. Otherwise, Ulrich might have given him a more thorough pat-down and discovered the Heckler & Koch USP he had lost in Paderborn and Maddock had recovered. Satisfied Maddock did not have the skull, Ulrich pushed Maddock in Niklas' direction and leaned over the edge of the well to look inside.

Maddock wouldn't get a better chance than this. He pretended to stumble forward, then lashed out with a right cross that caught Niklas on the chin. It was a quick, clean blow that sent the surprised Niklas stumbling backward. Turning around and drawing the HK-USP, Maddock clubbed the unsuspecting Ulrich across the back of the head and then leaped to the side as bullets flew.

Niklas' shots tore through the space Maddock had occupied a moment before. Two bullets ricocheted off the old well, but the third caught the slumping Ulrich in the back, and he slid to the ground, leaving a smear of blood on the weathered stone.

Maddock rolled to his feet and pumped two rounds into Niklas' gut. No hired thug could outshoot a SEAL. He would have put another in the man's head to finish the job, but he hoped to get a few questions answered first.

He kept his gun trained on Niklas, but there was no need. The man had dropped his weapon and now held his arms pressed to his ruined belly as if he could hold the life in. He looked up at Maddock, his eyes glassy with disbelief.

"Help me," he gasped.

Maddock had seen enough wounds to know there was no hope for Niklas. He had minutes left, if that. "The only thing that can help you right now is to make things right with your maker if you believe in one."

"Of course I believe." Niklas closed his eyes and let his head fall back. "I work for Him."

"Who do you work for?"

"Heilig Herrschaft." His voice was already fading.

"What is that?"

"The Holy Dominion." He groaned and shuddered. "Hurts."

Maddock felt numb. "Are you connected to the Dominion in America?"

"America." Niklas managed a weak laugh, and bloody froth oozed onto his cheek. "So young a nation and so limited in their vision. The same is true for our Herrschaft brethren there." He coughed weakly.

"Do you have any idea who took the last skull?"

Niklas' eyes sprang open, and for a moment he seemed fully alert. "Issachar!" he hissed.

Maddock could not hide his shock. Stunned, he wobbled to his feet and took a step back. "What did you say?"

"Issachar. That is the name of the American the Herrschaft put above us. He must have betrayed us and taken the skull for himself." The sudden burst of life was already dissipating, but Maddock understood the man's final words. "Kill him." And then he was gone.

He dumped the bodies in the well and tossed in some branches and snow to hide the bodies. He figured it wouldn't take too many more snowy days before they were hidden until the thaw. Considering the well's remote location, it might be longer before they were discovered. His mind spun as he drove back to town. How could Issachar still be alive? It had to be the same guy. How many Issachars were in the Dominion? Or in the world, for that matter?

Bones and Angel were waiting outside the inn when Maddock made it back to the center of town. Before Maddock could cut the engine, Bones had yanked open the door and hopped in.

"Don't you ever answer your phone?" Bones snapped.

"Not much reception up here. What's up?"

"Jade's gone. The innkeeper saw her with some dude. Said he was big and had a messed up face."

"Issachar." Maddock spoke the word like a curse.

"What? He's dead, Maddock. You killed him."

"He's back." Maddock's voice was as cold and flat as a frozen lake.

Shock registered in Bones' face. "If that's true, he's got Jade. The lady said it looked like she fainted and he helped her to the car and drove off."

Hot rage boiled up inside Maddock. He wanted to kill Issachar with his bare hands, feel the life drain from his body.

"Did you find out the way to the icefall?"

Bones nodded.

"We're going after her. The skulls and climbing gear are in the back. Angel, you go back to the inn and call the police."

"No way, man. I'm coming with you."

"No! The police need to know what happened. The lady at the inn can tell them what happened. Show them this." He took a picture of himself and Jade from his wallet and handed it to Angel. "They'll want a picture of her, and the lady at the inn can confirm that the guy she left with isn't me. I don't know what kind of law enforcement they have up here, but maybe they can get some help to us."

"Fine, but as soon as they've heard my story, I'm coming after you." Angel slipped out of the car. "Pop the trunk so I can get my share of the climbing gear."

Maddock looked at Bones, who shook his head. Maddock hit the auto-lock button, put the car in reverse, and backed out of the space. Angel cursed and punched the driver's window, though not hard enough to break it; she was a fighter and knew enough to take care of her hands.

"You two better make it back so I can kick your asses!" she shouted as Maddock hit the gas and shot down the frozen road.

Chapter 15

"I can't make it." Jade lay where she had fallen face-down, the warm, salty taste of blood in her mouth and her cheek stinging from its impact with the ice. Issachar had untied her ankles but left her hands tied behind her back. The icefall was difficult enough to traverse without the added handicap. Already they had slid back a dozen times on the glassy surface, and they never knew when the ice would give way beneath them.

"You'll make it if I have to carry you," Issachar growled.

She was Issachar's canary in the coal mine. He made her walk in front so, if the ice gave way, she would be the one to fall. Considering he outweighed her by at least one hundred pounds, she held out hope that they'd cross a place where the ice would support her but not him. Then again, if he fell, she had no doubt he'd take her with him.

"I need my hands free if I'm going to climb."

"Not a chance. Now get up."

"I'm lying face-down on the ice with my hands tied behind my back. How am I supposed to get up?" Fiery pain burst through her skull as Issachar hauled her to her feet by her hair. He pulled out a knife and she wondered if he was going to kill her right then and there, but instead, he sliced her bonds.

"Don't try anything." He spun her around and retied her hands in front of her. "That's as good as it's going to get. Now move it."

Despite her warm clothing, the icy breeze cut through her and she found herself wishing for a quiet place to curl up and go to sleep. She dismissed the thought as a wish for hypothermia. She didn't know what sinister plan Issachar had in store, but she was determined to find a way to escape before he put it into effect. To do that, she had to stay awake and alert.

The stone set in the Magi's crown glowed brighter the higher they ascended. Following the direction the small arrow of light indicated, they found themselves at the base of an overhang. The moment they moved into its shelter, light exploded in the stone, and it shone like a tiny sun, the arrow pointing directly at the rock. Grinning, Issachar took an ice axe off his back and began hacking away at the frozen ground.

Jade wondered if she could get away now while he was down on his knees, focused on his task, but quickly dismissed the idea. He had a gun, a knife, an axe, and two free hands. Maybe she should try anyway. What other chance might she have?

Just then, Issachar broke through the ice, and warm air, at least warmer than the outside air, flowed up from the dark passageway that ran at an angle down into the mountain.

"You first." He stood, grabbed her by the back of the neck, and pushed her toward the hole.

Dropping down onto her bottom, she slid into the passage and scooted forward until the way leveled out enough that she could get to her feet. Issachar followed behind. He held the skull, gazing down at the compass stone. The light in the stone pointed straight ahead. Issachar gave her a shove and she led the way.

The glow from the stone was sufficient to light their way for a good fifteen paces up ahead, allowing her to avoid several places where the floor had broken through. She glanced down at the blackness and wondered how far a person would fall should they slip through.

As he had done on their trek across the ice, Issachar kept a few feet behind her in case she fell through. She considered running away but, assuming he didn't shoot her immediately, she'd only make it forty feet or so before she'd find herself immersed in total darkness.

They picked their way through the warren of twisting tunnels that split, rejoined, and crossed one another until she was completely befuddled. Had it not been for the compass stone, they would have been lost within minutes. Each time they came to a fork, Issachar would consult the stone and tell her which way to go. They kept going, always another turn, another passageway, and always down.

It went on that way until she found herself wondering if they'd been fooled. What if there was no secret down here? What if they wandered these passageways without ever finding their way out? The thought of dying down here in the dark with no food or water was even more horrifying than her fear of Issachar.

"What do you think you're going to find down here, anyway?" The darkness had seeped inside her and she longed for the sound of a human voice, even if it was her own... or Issachar's.

"The treasures of the Magi. One in particular."

"Gold? Magic dust? Embalming oil? What does the Dominion want with any of that?"

"Idiot! It's much more than that." He paused. "The Magi were true magicians. They had power we can only dream of."

"Such as?" She actually did want to know what Issachar believed waited for them, but she also wanted to occupy his mind as much as possible. Maybe he would make a mistake.

"The power to bring someone back to life." His hushed voice rang with reverence and wonder. "How do you think Lazarus was brought back to life? Or Jesus?"

"I thought God did that."

"It was myrrh. The little bit the Magi left as a gift was enough to resurrect two men, perhaps more! Think what I can do when I find their entire store!"

"What *you* can do?" She frowned. "What about the rest of your Heilig Herrschaft friends?"

"Heilig Herrschaft has its own plan for the myrrh, and it's an idiotic one. I don't think it would work for what they want to do and, even if it did, it's a bad idea. It goes against what the Dominion stands for."

"You're nuts." Jade meant it. She'd expected this mystery to reveal something unusual. She thought the compass stones might point toward a deposit of the stone from which they'd come or something with at least some grounding in science, but an embalming oil that restored life?

"You had better hope I'm right."

"What do I care if you're right or not?" Up ahead, she spotted a sunken place about the width of a man. Cracks ran across it like cobwebs. Could this be her chance? She needed to keep him talking. "Take your oil and bring back whoever you like. Just let me go."

Issachar laughed. "You still haven't figured it out? I thought you were smart, Ihara."

Ten more steps.

"I have to make sure the oil is going to work before I take it back to the Herrschaft."

Jade missed a step. She turned and gaped at Issachar. He'd taken off his wraparound shades when they descended into the tunnel, and his scarred face was even more ghoulish in the glow of the compass stone.

"Look who finally caught up. I was going to used one of the two Herrschaft idiots, but it will be much more satisfying to choke the life out of you." He grinned. "Look on the bright side. If it works, you'll be the first person in two thousand years to be resurrected. Maybe you can start your own religion." He gave her a shove to get her moving. "Then again, I might just kill you twice. Double your pleasure, double your fun." He threw back his head and laughed.

Jade stepped as close as she dared to the edge of the depression, and then stepped across without breaking her stride. She closed her eyes and prayed. *Please, please, please...*

Issachar's laughter cut off into a yelp of surprise as the limestone beneath his feet shattered.

Jade looked back, expecting to see a gaping hole in the floor, but instead she saw Issachar stuck up to his armpits in the hole. He was frantically trying to push himself up and out, but he was wedged in tight. He bellowed and thrashed about, but lapsed into silence when his movement caused him to slip a centimeter. He looked up at her, his eyes shining in bewilderment.

"Get me out of here."

Now it was Jade's turn to laugh. He had dropped the skull when he fell, and she scooped it up— an awkward task with her bound hands. She looked at the tunnel behind him. There was no way she could get past him, and even stuck as he was, he was strong enough to hurt her. She would have to find another way out.

"It's been fun, Issachar, but I've got go. Don't bother to write."

"You help me, Ihara!" he cried. "Help me!"

Still too unnerved to laugh, she hurried down the passageway, his cries ringing in her ears.

Chapter 16

"Looks like they were definitely here." Maddock kicked at the chunks of ice that had been cleared away from the tunnel entrance. "Somebody's hacked this up. You can tell by the marks."

"Maybe it was Krampus." Bones winked. "Relax, Maddock. We're going to get her back."

"I'm not tense; I'm focused." Maddock didn't look at Bones. His friend would see the lie in his eyes. "Let's move."

The passageways beneath the Sternspitze icefall were just as Adler has described— a confusing, twisting, turning mess that was sure to baffle even the most skilled spelunker.

"It's like walking through Swiss cheese," Bones said, running his hand along the pale limestone walls.

"Well, we are in the Alps, though not in Switzerland."

They each carried a skull and followed in the direction indicated. The stones had, so far, proved to be excellent compasses.

"Keep an eye out for holes," Maddock said. "This place doesn't seem very solid."

"Dude, I'm busy trying not to bash my head on the low ceiling. I can't win."

They picked their way through the eerie silence. Bones managed to avoid bashing his head, though he frequently complained about his sore back. Maddock suspected the complaints were his friend's way of keeping Maddock's mind off of Jade. It didn't work, but he appreciated the effort.

"Cover the stones. Quick!" Bones whispered.

The world was doused in black as Maddock and Bones put their hands over the glowing compass stones. Maddock looked all around, all his senses alive.

"What was it?"

"I saw a flash of light down that side passage. It's gone now." Bones exhaled slowly. "Think we should check it out?"

Maddock frowned. He was sure Issachar had the other skull, which meant he was probably following its compass stone. He felt their best bet was to follow wherever the stones led. That was where he hoped to find Jade and the truth behind this mystery. He explained his thinking to Bones, who grimaced.

"But what if they've already gotten there and are on their way back out."

"They'd run into us, wouldn't they?" Unless they made a wrong turn. "Fine, let's check it out."

They crept into the tunnel, each cupping a hand over their compass stone to permit only a minimum amount of light to come through. They moved forward like shadows, alert for any sound or sight that would alert them that someone– or something– approached.

And then Maddock heard it. It was a clicking sound, like a deer skittering across pavement. They froze, dousing their lights. Maddock's heart pounded and he stood, nerves tingling, ready to draw his weapon and start shooting. The noise grew louder and then ceased. He caught a faint whiff of a musky, animal scent, and then the sound faded into the distance.

"What the hell was that?" Bones muttered.

"Maybe Adler really did see something." Maddock set his jaw. Whatever it was hadn't tried to mess with them. That was a good sign.

"Go a little farther?" Bones asked.

"A little." Maddock glanced down at the compass stone on his skull, which was pointing back the way they had come. "Good thing this isn't a talking GPS."

"Make a U-turn now," Bones mimicked. He looked like he was about to continue, but his features froze.

Footsteps were coming their way and moving fast. They covered their lights and drew their pistols. Up ahead, the bend in the passageway began to glow with a faint light that grew brighter as the sound of someone moving grew louder. Now Maddock could hear heavy breathing like a marathon runner at the end of a race. He tensed.

"Make sure Jade's with him," he whispered to Bones. If it was Issachar, they'd have to try to overcome him without killing him– at least until they found out what happened to Jade.

But it was not Issachar.

"Jade!" Maddock cried when she turned the corner.

Jade screamed and dropped the skull she was carrying. The bronze crown clanked when it hit the floor. She recovered her wits instantly.

"Maddock?" she breathed.

"And his better-looking amigo." Bones uncovered his compass stone as Maddock rushed forward and clutched Jade in a tight embrace.

"Are you all right?"

"Fine. Just banged up and worn out." She pressed her cheek to his chest and he stroked her hair.

"Where's Issachar?"

"He fell into a hole in the floor and got stuck. I took the skull and ran." Her breath came in gasps. "Had to try and find a new way out. I've just been doing the opposite of what the stone told me to do."

"You're headed in the right direction, but it's a long way back," Bones said.

"I'm just glad you're all right." Maddock didn't want to let her go.

"Maddock, there's a branch of the Dominion in Germany."

"I know. You can fill me in on the way out. Let's go." He took her hand and turned to lead her back up the tunnel and was surprised when she held him back.

"Are you kidding me?" She looked from Maddock to Bones and back to Maddock, a disgusted look on her face. "I travel across Germany, get kidnaped, all to solve a stupid mystery and you don't want to see it through to the end?"

"Jade..."

"Don't 'Jade' me. You two are here now. I'm safe. Let's finish this."

Maddock hesitated. Of course, he didn't want to stop now.

"You do what you want," Jade said. "Bones and I are going. Come on, Bones." She brushed past Maddock and headed down the tunnel.

"You attract the stubbornest chicks, Maddock." Bones clapped him on the shoulder. "We might as well go with her."

Shaking his head, Maddock drew his gun and followed Jade.

As they went along, Jade recounted Issachar's belief that he would find the Magi's gift of myrrh and that it could resurrect the dead. Maddock remembered what Ulrich had told him about Heilig Herrschaft's plan, and was about to fill her in when Jade came to a sudden stop. Right in front of her a deep hole barred their way.

"Good catch." Maddock put a protective hand on her arm. "Wouldn't want to step into that."

"He was here." She knelt and shone her light into the hole. "This is where Issachar was stuck. I'm sure of it."

Maddock and Bones added their light to hers. All they could see was darkness.

"Nothing we can do about it now. We'll just have to keep an eye out." Maddock stood and hoisted Jade to her feet. Now he was even more alert, he took the lead as they moved deeper into the labyrinthine tunnels.

With each step, the compass stones seemed to shine brighter, and the tunnel filled with a bluish-white glow.

"I don't think it's the compass stones doing this," Maddock said. The glow was coming from the end of the passageway. They turned the corner and stopped dead in their tracks.

Maddock looked at his friends and then at the sight that lay before them.

"I don't believe it."

Chapter 17

They stood on a ledge overlooking a yawing cavern so wide they could scarcely see the other side. Floating in midair down below them was a glowing blue-white orb. Its surface pulsed and sparkled, bathing the jagged rocks of the cavern in a pale glow. The light had an odd quality to it– though Maddock sensed an intensity to it, he could look on it without so much as squinting. And though the cavern was a comfortable temperature, the thing was obviously not giving off heat.

"What's keeping it up in the air?" Bones asked.

Maddock shook his head. He had never seen anything like it. It seemed to be a self-contained ball of pure energy. "I want to know what fuels it. It can't just burn perpetually, can it?"

"Guys, look at this." Jade held up the skull she was carrying. The stone gleamed with light the exact color and quality of that which burned below. "It's the same."

"All along, these compass stones weren't pointing to a pole." Bones scrutinized his own Magi skull. "They were pointing to this place."

"Jade, what's the German word for light?" The pieces were falling together in Maddock's mind.

"Licht," she said, mesmerized by the pulsing ball of light.

"Remember what the dying priest said? '*Ewige l...*' He wasn't saying '*eternal life,*' he was saying '*eternal light.*' He meant this light."

"Whoa." Bones took a step back. "Like how we thought the stones were making their own light! If this is a source of perpetual light..." He looked at Maddock.

"A limitless supply of clean energy without the need for fuel. Unless we're way off base." He took a deep breath, trying to envision a nation harnessing such power. Even if it was not put to any sort of military use, it could give a country's economy such a boost that it could re-allocate massive resources to its military. It would be a treasure far beyond the rumored gifts of the Magi.

Jade suddenly tugged at Maddock's wrist. "Maddock, you remember the story Adler told about the star the Wise Men followed being hidden underground! Do you," she swallowed and her voice became very small, "do you think this is the Star of Bethlehem?"

"Maybe. Or at least, it's whatever is behind the story. It's obviously not an actual star." He chuckled. "Nothing like stating the obvious, huh?"

"I wonder..."

Jade did not get to complete her thought because they suddenly found themselves surrounded by men armed with spears and arrows tipped with blue stones that shone like the ball of light down below. They had crept up silently and taken up positions in a semicircle, leaving Maddock, Bones and Jade trapped between a pit with no visible bottom and a line of armed men.

Except they weren't men.

Horns protruded from their long, shaggy brown hair, and though they appeared human, if overly muscular and hairy, from forehead to waist, they were definitely animal-like from the waist down. At the waist, their body hair grew thick and glossy, and coated their thick thighs and lean calves. Their legs, which bent backward, ended in dark, cleft hooves, like a...

"A goat," Maddock whispered. "They're satyrs." His thoughts flashed to the pagan temple beneath the cathedral in Cologne. Satyrs were associated with Dionysus, or Bacchus, depending on your preferred mythology. A creature like this was the Krampus whom Adler had seen so many years ago.

One of the goat men cocked his head at the word 'satyr,' and nodded once. He pointed and Maddock realized he was indicating the pistol tucked inside his jacket pocket. Slowly, Maddock took it out and laid in on the ground; Bones did the same. The satyr gave another nod and came forward to collect them when a loud voice rang out in the cavern.

"Nobody move or the goat dies!" Issachar emerged from a nearby passageway. His left arm was wrapped around a satyr, holding it tight. In his right hand, he held a knife pressed to its throat.

They emerged into the light of the cavern and Issachar's eyes fell on the glowing ball of energy. Unlike the others, he did not seem mesmerized or even impressed. Instead, his face contorted in rage.

"Where's the myrrh?" he screamed.

The satyrs exchanged glances, their expressions so foreign to Maddock as to be unreadable.

"It's not here, Issachar. You had it all wrong."

"I wasn't wrong." There was a pleading tone to his voice. "The secret to eternal life..."

"Eternal light!" Maddock corrected. "Ewige licht, not ewige leben."

The satyrs looked at him as if the German words were familiar. Maddock could have sworn one of them looked at Issachar with a scornful grin.

"There is a miracle here, but not the one you thought you would find." Maddock took a step forward. "Let him go."

"I don't believe you. The Magi's treasures are here."

"The one treasure is here. The Star of Bethlehem, whatever it is, but you can't take it with you. Do yourself a favor, give it up and run. You might even get away." He took another step forward and the ring of satyrs parted to make room for him.

"But Lazarus... Jesus... how did they rise from the dead?"

"I don't know." Maddock shrugged. "Maybe it was a regular old miracle. Whatever it was, you won't find the answer here." He spoke the last slowly, as if to a dimwit. "Let him go."

"What do you care about a goat?" Issachar's eyes burned with hatred.

"I don't care. I care about kicking your ass." Maddock grinned. "Again."

"That's what I'm talking about," Bones said.

Maddock's grin split into a broad smile as rage boiled in Issachar's eyes.

"Come on," he goaded, "don't you want to get me back for what happened at Zion? Be a man."

Issachar roared like an enraged lion, but before he could make a move, the satyr he was holding raised a leg and kicked him in the shin with the force of a bucking bronco. Issachar's roar turned to a shriek of pain as his shin snapped. In a flash, six satyrs were on him. They bore him up and carried him away, still screaming, into the darkness.

The satyr who had first approached Maddock turned and stared at him. They stood there, listening to Issachar's cries fade away, and waited. There was an odd, almost expectant look in the satyr's eyes, like he was waiting for something. Maddock thought for a moment, and then realized he was still holding the Magi skull.

He held it out in front of him like an offering and then laid it carefully on the ground. Bones and Jade followed suit, and they all backed to the edge of the cliff.

The satyr folded his arms, looked down at the skulls, then took a long look at each of them, and nodded. He motioned three others forward. Each drew a knife and approached the three people standing on the cliff edge.

"What do we do?" Bones whispered from the side of his mouth.

"I think we're okay," Maddock said. "If not..." He let the words hang in the air. If not, they'd have to fight the best they could.

The satyrs stopped when they reached the skulls. Each one of them used his knife to pry a compass stone from one of the crowns. One by one, they hurled the stones into the cavern.

They looked like little meteorites, shining like little balls of pure light as the pulsing light drew them in. When the job was done, they handed the skulls back to Maddock, Bones, and Jade.

The satyr whom Maddock had come to regard as the leader now approached them. One by one, he placed his hand over each person's heart and made another of his little nods. When he was done, he pointed to the way out.

"I don't think we can find our way back," Maddock said.

The satyrs might not speak English, but they seemed to understand his doubtful tone. One of them moved to the mouth of the tunnel and beckoned for them to follow.

Their glowing spear heads showing the way, one satyr led and another followed them out through the maze of dark tunnels. The path they took was more direct than the way they had come, because it seemed in no time they were standing on a snow covered ridge looking down on the twinkling lights of Drekonhas. The sun had just bedded down for the night and, to the west, its last delicate glow coated the tips of the Alps in burnished gold.

They turned and waved to the Satyrs, who looked at them with grave expressions. Finally, one of them bobbed his head and, giving them what Maddock swore was a wistful look, drove his spear into the roof of the tunnel.

There was a flash of blue light, a sound like a grenade exploding, and the roof of the passage caved in. When the dust cleared, only a pile of rocks and rubble remained where the entrance had been.

"Is somebody there?" Angel's voice cut through the night air and, a moment later, a flashlight appeared in the distance. Angel appeared, picking her way along the ridgeline to where Maddock and the others waited.

She crushed Maddock and Bones in a tight embrace, crying and cursing them in turn. She wasn't so rough with Jade, about whom she was clearly worried.

"How did you get here?" Maddock asked.

"I told those douches in town," she pointed down toward the lights, "what happened, but they wouldn't even take a missing person's report at first. Finally, the lady at the inn threw a fit, so they wrote it up, but they insisted the only way under the mountain was through these caverns. The old lady lent me her car and I followed the cops up here. They poked around for a while and then went home." She breathed a deep sigh. "I'm just glad you're all right. You jerks scared the crap out of me running off like that."

"It's all good." Bones assured her. "We're safe and sound, and I've got one hell of a story to tell you when we get back to the pub."

"Well, you don't have to buy me a gift," she said. "You guys getting back safe is enough for me."

"Good thing," Bones said, "because I didn't buy you jack!"

"Ass!" she punched him on the shoulder. "You'd better have gotten me something." Laughing and arguing, they headed back across the ridge, with Maddock and Jade following behind.

Jade looked up at the starry night sky and smiled. "I don't suppose I'll ever think of the Christmas Star the same again."

"Me neither," Maddock agreed. He leaned down and kissed her gently on the lips. "Merry Christmas, Jade."

"Merry Christmas, Maddock."

~End~

BUCCANEER

A Dane Maddock Adventure

Prologue

January, 1698

It was a stormy day on the Arabian Sea. Dark clouds hung low on the horizon and an angry wind scoured the decks with salt spray. William Kidd stood on board the *Adventure Galley*, surveying his prize. The merchant vessel sailed under Armenian colors, but carried French passes guaranteeing its protection, and that made it fair game. They'd taken it with little resistance offered by its crew. If its cargo holds carried half the wealth he hoped, he would be a rich man.

"Captain, may I have a word?"

He turned to see an ashen-face Joseph Palmer standing behind him, shifting his weight from side to side and looking about as if fearful of being overheard.

"What is it, Palmer?"

"We have a problem." The sailor dropped his gaze, reluctant to continue.

"What is it? It can't be the cargo. The ship was riding too low in the water for her to be empty."

"No, Captain, it isn't that. It's the finest haul we've ever made. Gold and silver, silk and satin, and all sorts of fine things."

Kidd tried not to let relief show on his face. It would not do to reveal that he'd had even the slightest doubt. Loyalty among his crew was tenuous at best, and the dogs would bite at the first show of weakness on his part.

"So, what is this problem?"

Palmer cleared his throat and looked up at the gray sky.

"It is not a French vessel."

Cold fear trickled down Kidd's spine. The man had to be mistaken.

"It is an Indian ship," Palmer continued, "captained by an Englishman."

"That cannot be. It is under French protection. French!"

"It's the truth all the same." Palmer shrugged. "The captain of their vessel, he wants to see you."

"Then he may come and see me. I will show him all the proper courtesies." His thoughts raced. He was a privateer, not a pirate, but, after this incident, it might not be seen that way back in England. Perhaps he could reach an arrangement with this captain. "Bring him aboard."

"There's a problem with that. We tried to reason with him, but he wouldn't stop fighting. Finally, Bradinham stuck him in the gut. He's in a bad way, and I don't think he'll last much longer. He says it's important. He said he..." Palmer stopped and scratched at his chin whiskers. "What was the word? It was something like *ignore*."

"Implore."

"That's the one." Palmer's expression brightened. "Shall I take you there?"

Kidd saw no way other than to face the problem and work his way out of it.

"Very well, sailor. Let us go."

The wounded captain sat propped up on the bed in his cabin. His quarters were austere, not at all befitting a man of his rank, Kidd thought. Blood soaked through the heavy bandages wrapped around his abdomen, and loss of blood had drained him of any color he might have had. He forced a smile as Kidd came through the door.

"Be welcome, Captain." His voice was as thin as old parchment. "Please, close the door."

Puzzled by this courteous reception, Kidd complied.

"I understand you wish to see me."

The man's gray eyes, glassy with shock, locked on his.

"Are you a man of God, Captain Kidd?"

It was not a question he would have expected, considering the circumstances.

"Of course," Kidd replied.

"You are needed to do God's work." A series of painful coughs racked the captain's body, and red froth oozed from the corners of his mouth. "I need you to deliver something to England. It must not be lost or fall into the wrong hands." He handed Kidd a canvas bag. Inside was an ivory document case, very old and ornately carved. Bound to it was a sheet of parchment with instructions on where and to whom to deliver it.

Kidd frowned. The man's urgency indicated this was something of great value. Perhaps he could profit from this transaction.

"Captain Kidd, please listen to me." The man could scarcely manage a whisper now. His time was short. "Do not think to circumvent God's will. That way leads to ruin."

Kidd nodded. He was above such superstitious nonsense, but no harm in humoring a dying man.

"Believe me." He pulled down the neck of his shirt, revealing a brand on his left breast. He was a hairy man, and the brand was now a pale scar, but Kidd recognized the symbol immediately.

Surprised, he took an involuntary step backward, his head swimming, and clutched the wall for support.

"It can't be," he gasped. "They are all dead!"

The dying captain managed a weak smile.

"Not quite. Not yet."

Chapter 1

It was like walking on Swiss cheese. Avery chose her steps with care as she wound between sinkholes and abandoned shafts. Damn treasure hunters. They'd torn the island apart over the last two centuries and for what? A legend. Then again, she wouldn't be here if she wasn't a believer.

She paused, straining to listen for any sound that would tell her where work was going on. She didn't know exactly where the crew would be, probably somewhere near the reputed location of the famous Money Pit.

It had been a long hike from the causeway. Not so long ago, you could drive onto and around the island, but no longer. The local government had taken it over and shut it down, citing safety concerns. Now, no choice remained other than hoofing it. One hundred forty acres sounded small until you had to walk across it in the blistering sun, all the while worrying that your next step would send you plunging down into darkness and whatever lay beneath.

She brushed a stray lock of hair back from her face, feeling the damp sheen of sweat and humidity that clung there. *Good old Nova Scotia summer heat.* She knew she should have made an appointment, but when she'd heard the news about the new crew undertaking the search, she couldn't wait, knowing she might not get a chance like this again. Now, if she could only make him listen.

Passing through a dense stand of the oak trees that gave the island its name, she looked out across an open space where workmen had, over the years, stripped away the native forest. There! Far across the clearing, workers milled about, setting up equipment and surveying the area. Pleased that she'd been correct about their likely starting point, she picked up the pace. She thought she saw one of the workers, a tall, dark man with long hair, turn and look her way.

Avery felt the ground give way beneath her feet. She sprang back a moment too late. Her scream didn't quite drown out the muffled snap of rotten wood shattering. She reached out, her fingers digging furrows in the soft earth as she struggled in vain to hold on to the edge of the abandoned treasure pit. She caught hold of a thick tuft of grass and, for one blessed moment, hung motionless over the void.

And then, with a tortured, ripping sound, her lifeline tore free. She battered the inside of the shaft as she slid downward, grasping for a handhold. Sharp pain lanced through her as jagged rocks sliced her palms and pummeled her legs. Her ankle caught on a thick root, turning painfully beneath her, but the protrusion slowed her fall enough that she was able to grab hold and loop one arm around it.

Frozen with shock, she could only gasp for breath as she gazed up at the circle of light far above her. She could have sworn she'd fallen a hundred feet, but it was more like twenty. It might as well have been a mile for all the hope she had of climbing back out. She thought of the man who had looked her way. Might he have seen her fall? Maybe, but she couldn't count on it.

"Help!" Her scream was not one of panic, but more a matter of hedging her bets. She didn't know if anyone at the work site could hear her from so far away, but it couldn't hurt to try. She considered adding, "I've fallen and I can't get up," but even her morbid sense of humor wouldn't permit it. She shouted again, this time loud enough to send a sharp, stabbing pain through her vocal cords. "I fell in a shaft! I need help."

She tried to calculate how long it would take for someone to run from the work site to the place she'd fallen. Not long. If the guy didn't show soon, she had to figure he hadn't noticed her.

Her elbow burned and her shoulder felt like it was about to be wrenched from its socket as she struggled to hang on. She managed to take hold of the root with her other arm, giving her a measure of relief. The toes of her shoes slid across the rocky wall of the pit until she found purchase on a tiny protrusion. It wasn't much, but it eased the pain in her shoulder.

What to do now? Instinct told her no one was on the way to help her. Climbing up was out of the question. Could she climb deeper? It was a crazy idea, but maybe there was a place lower down where she could safely wait for help. Twisting her head around, she took a look down into the depths of the pit.

Big mistake.

"Oh God! Oh no!" Her head swam as she gazed down at the small circle of light reflected on the water far below her. There was nothing between her and the bottom that she could hope to stand on, and she'd never survive such a fall. She closed her eyes and took three deep, cleansing breaths. The whirlpool in her head slowed to an eddy and she opened her eyes again.

Cold, harsh reality slapped her back into focus. She'd set off for the island without letting anyone know where she was going or when she'd return, not to mention she hadn't obtained permission to even be on the island in the first place. No one knew she was here.

Then she remembered her cell phone. How had she forgotten her lifeline to the rest of the world? If she could manage to get a signal down here, and she wasn't that far below the surface, she could call for help.

She let go of the root with her right hand and her body slid downward for one sickening moment, but she kept her toehold and her grip with her other arm. Fishing into the pocket of her jeans, she worked her phone free and tried to position it so she could see the screen.

Damn! It was locked. Cursing her choice of phone, she balanced it on her palm and tapped in the numbers with her thumb. 1... 7... 0... 1... Unlocked! Still working one-handed, she began to tap in the number. 9... 1...

Her foothold suddenly gave way and she screamed as she fell, scarcely clinging to the root that was now the only link between her and survival. Her cries quickly melded into a stream of curses as her cell phone slipped from her grasp. She watched its luminescent screen as it tumbled through the air, landing with a pitiful splash in the water below.

Now, to quote her father, she was screwed like a Phillips head.

"Drop something?"

The voice caught her off guard and she almost lost her grip. Down below, a diver smiled up at her. He had short, blond hair, blue eyes, and an easy smile. She recognized him immediately. So this was the famous Dane Maddock. It certainly wasn't the way she'd planned on meeting up with him. Nothing like making a good first impression.

"What are you doing down there?" Despite her predicament, Avery couldn't keep a tone of annoyance from her voice. Couldn't he see she was holding on for dear life?

"My friend and I were exploring a channel under the island when this fell in front of me." He held up her phone.

At that moment, another diver surfaced. This man had a shaved head and skin the color of dark chocolate. He looked at Maddock, who pointed up at her.

"Hey girl, what's up?"

"Me, obviously," she snapped.

"Well, you ought to know the water is only about five feet deep here and the bottom is solid rock. You definitely don't want to let go."

"No, really?"

"Sorry," Maddock said. "Willis loves to state the obvious. How are you doing up there?"

"Hanging in there." Just then, the root gave a little, dropping her a few inches. Her cocky façade dissolved in a girly shriek that, as soon as she realized she wasn't plummeting to her death, at least not yet, turned her face scarlet.

"I'm coming up to help you," Maddock said. "Don't you let go."

Avery gave her head a tiny shake, fearful that greater movement would dislodge her for good.

"You can't climb that!" Willis protested.

"Sure I can. You just get back as quick as you can and bring Bones with some rope. I radioed as soon as I saw her, but I doubt they got the message." Maddock had removed his air tank and was already feeling the wall for handholds as he gave instructions.

Avery wondered if "bones" was some sort of climbing gear or rescue device. She couldn't think of any reason for Willis to bring actual bones, unless they were going to rescue her with some weird voodoo magic.

"Yeah, I heard it." Willis tapped his mask. "Sweetheart!" he called up to her. "You know how to do a cannonball?"

"Yes." Avery's voice was so small she doubted he could hear her.

"Cool. If you slip, and I ain't saying you're going to, do a cannonball. Whatever you do, don't straighten your body out. Got me?"

Avery nodded, not wanting to consider the possibility that she might fall, but grateful for the advice. She stole another glance down and saw that Maddock had already covered a good ten feet of the wall.

"What are you? Some kind of spider?"

"Nope, just a SEAL." Through his wetsuit, cords of muscle stood out on his shoulders and arms, showing the strain of the climb, but his expression and voice were relaxed. "So, how does a nice girl like you find herself hanging around in a place like this?"

"I just felt like dropping in," Avery grunted. It was crazy to be bandying words with this guy like they were clever college kids, but it kept the fear and discomfort at bay. Her muscles cramped and she was losing feeling in her hands. She couldn't hang on much longer.

"Did Crazy Charlie hire you?" Maddock asked as he hooked his fingers in a cleft in the stone so shallow Avery couldn't even see it.

"I don't know anyone by that name. I was actually coming to..." The root slipped again, this time accompanied by a cracking sound. Avery was too frightened to cry out. She just hung there, gasping for breath. Her foot found a tiny fissure and she pressed her toe into it, more for the comfort it afforded her than the weight it bore.

"I'm almost there." Maddock was maybe ten feet away now, but he looked like he was moving in slow motion. He was never going to get to her in time.

The sound of her rapidly beating heart pounded in Avery's ears. She was keenly aware of the sensation of abraded flesh against smooth wood, cold sweat running down the back of her neck, the smell of brine in the damp pit, and the crack of the root giving way.

And then Maddock was there. He drew a sinister looking knife and jammed it into a crevice just as the root finally snapped.

Avery felt only a momentary lurch and then a strong arm had her around the waist. She looked into Maddock's eyes, so like the sea, and her panic subsided.

"I've got you. But if you can get your fingers into that crack right there, it would help."

She looked up and realized his knife bore most of their weight, though he still had small footholds. She couldn't believe he'd made it up here, but time to marvel would come later.

She worked her left hand into a crevice, and draped her other arm around Maddock. She looked at him, uncertain what to say. She'd expected to dislike him, but now she wasn't so sure.

"How are you holding up?" Maddock asked, his thickly muscled arms trembling and his knuckles white.

"That depends on how much longer you can hang on." Avery struggled against the urge to look down.

"Are you kidding? I'm in this for the long haul."

Avery forced a smile and felt herself slip a little bit. "I'm sorry about this. It's not the way I intended for us to meet."

"So you don't spend your days hanging around pits with strange men?"

Her fingers slipped again and she wondered, for a moment, if she should just let go. This was all her fault and it wasn't fair for Maddock to go down with her. Literally.

"Did somebody say hanging?" Just then, a rope with a looped end dropped down alongside them. "Don't worry. It's not a noose."

"Bones!" Maddock exclaimed. "It's about time you got here."

"Talk about ungrateful. Now, how about you and your new friend take hold of this rope before you both fall?"

Avery reached out, slipped one arm through the loop, and grabbed hold of the rope. She started to rise and, next thing she knew, strong hands lifted her up and onto solid ground

Her rescuers were tough-looking men. One, a stocky man with short brown hair, introduced himself.

"I'm Matt," he said. "This is Bones."

Bones stood well over six feet tall, with striking Native American features, and a mischievous twinkle in his dark eyes. He wore his long, black hair pulled back in a ponytail, and his t-shirt displayed a giraffe with a speech bubble that read, "Moo! I'm a goat."

"Maddock's got to go back down for his air tank and other crap," Bones said. "He'll meet us back at headquarters, if you can call it that."

"Okay." Avery could barely find words. She was still freaked out about her near death experience and she was exhausted from the ordeal. "Are you part of Mister Maddock's crew?"

"He's my partner. Or I'm his. It gets a little confused at times. And don't bother with the 'Mister.' He just goes by Maddock." He raised an eyebrow. "You got a name?"

"Avery Halsey," she replied. "Sorry, I'm usually much friendlier."

"I hear you." Bones took her by the arm and guided her toward the work site. "What are you doing out here anyway?"

"If you're Maddock's partner, then I have a business proposition for the two of you."

Bones didn't break his stride or even look at her, but threw his head back and laughed.

"Did I say something funny?"

"No," he said. "It's just, we get that all the time."

A motley group awaited them at the work site. The two who stood out to her were both Native American. One was an attractive young woman with the body of an aerobics instructor. Avery wondered if she was Bones' girlfriend, and found the thought raised a pang of jealousy. Whatever. She'd known the guy for all of two minutes.

The other was a man of about sixty. Unlike Bones, he wore his long, silver-streaked hair down, with a black leather headband holding it back. His weathered face was handsome and, like Bones, mischief danced in his eyes. He wore a coat and tie, blue jeans, and cowboy boots.

Bones introduced the man as his uncle, "Crazy" Charlie Bonebrake, and the girl as his sister, Angelica, or Angel for short. Now that she saw them up close, the family resemblance was unmistakable.

"Glad to see you're okay," Angel said. Her handshake was firm, almost manly in its strength, but the air about her was distinctly feminine, though with a touch of tomboy.

"We had no idea anyone was coming out to the site," Crazy Charlie said, a touch of disapproval in his voice. "If we hadn't gotten Willis's call, we'd never have known."

"I still can't believe I fell. I've been coming to this island since I was a little girl. I know better than to let my mind wander."

"So, what brings you here?" Charlie crossed his arms and waited for an answer. The transformation was immediate, as his expression went from warm and inviting to cold and calculating in a flash. Two men moved in to flank Avery on either side. What was going on?

"You need to chill, Uncle." Bones stepped in between them. "She's here to see me and Maddock."

Charlie considered Bones' words before dismissing his men with a jerk of his head. He looked at Avery a moment longer.

"All right, then. Just be sure to let us know before you visit the work site again. For safety reasons."

Avery nodded. She doubted that safety was Charlie's primary concern, but she couldn't very well argue with him. After all, she'd just demonstrated the perils of wandering the island alone. Still, what was with the thugs? Just treasure hunter paranoia, she supposed.

"I understand. Sorry for coming unannounced."

"I'll leave you to the kids, then." Charlie winked at Bones, patted Angel on the shoulder, and left.

"Gotta love old folks," Bones said. "They never forget you were once five years old."

"Maybe if you didn't still act like you were five," Angel said in a scornful tone. She turned to Avery. "Let me look at your hands." She gave them a quick inspection before leading Avery to a nearby tent where she cleaned and bandaged them. Maddock arrived just as they were finishing up.

"So, you never told me what you were doing here," he said without preamble.

"I came here looking for you." Avery bit her lip. "It's about your father and his research."

The color drained from Maddock's face. He looked at her, nonplussed. It was an odd expression for a man who, minutes before, had bravely scaled a wall to rescue her.

"I'm sorry. I don't know much about his research, and he's been dead for years."

"Please." She felt a lump forming in her throat. "I wouldn't ask if it weren't important. Could we, maybe, meet somewhere and discuss it, at least? It's a long story and it might take a while to tell it."

Maddock and Bones looked at one another, as if each were reading the other's thoughts. Finally, Bones gave a shrug and nodded.

"All right," Maddock said. "No promises, but you name the time and place and we'll be there."

Chapter 2

"Oh, come on." Avery balled her fist and pounded the dashboard of her Ford Ranger. She found the loud thump satisfying. Not so satisfying was the hot air that continued to pour out of the vents. She supposed punching the dash wasn't air conditioning repair 101, but it was her only option at the moment. She'd just have to roll down the windows and deal with it.

Springtime in Kidd's Cross with no air. This would do wonders for her hair. Was she fated to look like a slob every time she and Maddock met?

Already imagining rivulets of sweat pouring down her back, she pulled into the parking lot of the Spinning Crab, narrowly missing a drunk college kid who reeled into her path. He shouted and gave her the finger, but froze when their eyes met.

Avery rolled down the window as she guided the little pickup into the nearest empty parking space.

"Let me guess," she called to the dumbstruck young man. "You're telling me I'm your number one professor."

The boy grinned sheepishly.

"Sorry Miss Halsey. I guess I had a couple too many."

"Don't forget you've got an exam coming up. I think it would be a good idea for you to impress me, if you get my meaning."

The young man nodded and hurried away amid the good-natured ribbing of his friends. Considering the quality of his academic performance so far this semester, Billy Dorne wasn't likely to impress her or anyone else with his brilliance, but maybe the dunce would at least crack a book.

She killed the engine and checked her hair and makeup in the rear-view mirror. Not as bad as she'd feared. She just needed to get inside before she started sweating like a pig.

"All right, Avery," she said to herself as she climbed out of her truck. "You know what's at stake. Time to sell this baby."

"Ave, what are you doing here?"

"Rodney, what a surprise." Avery turned to face her ex-boyfriend and his idiot friends. Now, as ever, she wondered why she'd ever consented to a single date with the man, much less four months of dating. Actually, she knew why. She was a lonely girl working in a college full of academics with sticks shoved so far up their... Anyway, Rodney had been a distraction. He was handsome and uncomplicated.

He was also a bully. She hadn't seen it at first but, once she spotted the signs, she put the brakes on the relationship. In her mind, it was over. Rodney, however, didn't see it that way.

"You really shouldn't be coming alone to a place like this," he said, folding his thick arms across his chest and smirking. "Drunk guys everywhere. You never know when you might run into someone with bad intentions." He grinned with pride, as if he'd made a brilliant joke. Behind him, his buddies, Carl, Doug, and

Reggie, guffawed.

Don't encourage the buffoon, she thought.

"I'm not alone. I'm actually meeting someone. Now, if you'll excuse me." She tried to move past him, but Rodney blocked her way.

"Meeting somebody?" Rodney's voice rose an octave as the idiot chorus behind him began to *ooh* like a bunch of twelve year-olds. "One of those Einsteins from your work? You'd be safer going in there alone."

"It's none of your business who I'm meeting. Now, get out of the way. I've got an appointment and you're going to make me late."

"Cancel it." Rodney's voice was suddenly cold. "Me and you should go somewhere and talk."

"We have nothing to talk about. Now get out of my way." She tried to keep her voice calm, but the frustration welled inside of her. She hated this feeling of helplessness. She couldn't make Rodney move and she wasn't about to leave. She couldn't. This meeting was too important.

"Watch out Rod. She'll call the cops on you, man," Reggie crowed.

Avery hoped she wasn't blushing. Rodney's father was the sheriff of Bridge County, and his son used that relationship as a shield. Rodney worked as a bouncer at a local club and had abused his position too many times to count. He took pleasure in humiliating, and sometimes seriously injuring, bar patrons. Any other employee would have been terminated, even prosecuted, several times over for such conduct, but everyone tiptoed around Rodney.

Sick of standing there, she tried to brush past him, but he grabbed her by the arm and held her tight.

"Sorry we're late." The strong voice cut across the chatter, and everyone turned to look at the speaker. It was Dane Maddock, followed by Bones and Angel. He clearly understood what was happening. "Are we interrupting something?"

"Yeah, you are," Rodney said, releasing his grip on Avery. He turned and looked down at Maddock, who stood a few inches shorter, and smirked. "Why don't you step off?"

"I never miss an appointment," Maddock said, stepping closer. "Give her your number. Maybe she'll call you, but I doubt it."

Avery tensed. She'd felt a momentary relief at Maddock and Bones' arrival, but Rodney and his friends outnumbered her would-be rescuers, and they all loved to brawl.

"I'm not gonna tell you again." Rodney thrust out his chest and took a step toward Maddock.

"Good. I'm getting tired of the sound of your voice." If Maddock was at all fazed by Rodney, it didn't show.

"Your breath is pretty stank, too," Bones interjected. "I can smell you from over here."

Tension crackled in the air. A few patrons had come out front to watch the inevitable fight. Avery's eyes flitted from one man to the next, wondering who would throw the first punch.

Surprisingly, it was Angel.

Bones' sister pushed her way past Reggie and held out her hand to Avery. "Let's go inside." She smiled and gave Avery a reassuring nod.

"Mind your business." Doug, the third of Rodney's cast of stooges, grabbed her roughly by the upper arm.

That was a mistake.

Faster than Avery would have thought possible, Angel lashed out, and Doug cried out in pain as she crushed the bridge of his nose with the back of her fist. His hands came up to protect his face, and she punched him in the gut, and followed with a knee to the groin. As he staggered a few steps, she kicked him in the side of the knee.

Everyone flew into action. Rodney reached for Maddock, who sidestepped and struck back with a barrage of crisp punches that sent the larger man reeling.

Reggie was slow to react, drawing back his fist just as Bones drove an overhand right into his temple. Reggie looked like a marionette whose strings had been cut as he flopped, rubber-legged, to the ground. Carl took one look at his fallen friend and ran.

Bones stepped over Reggie to help his sister, who had leaped onto Doug's back and was choking him. Red-faced, Doug wobbled toward Bones, who smiled and delivered another one-punch knockout.

Angel rolled free as Doug slumped to the ground, and came up cursing.

"Damn you, Bones! That one was mine." Her face, so beautiful only moments before, burned with a dark fury. "You've got to cut that out."

"You should have finished him sooner," Bones said, still smiling. Angel made an obscene gesture at him, and then they turned toward Maddock.

"Quit playing with him, Maddock!" Bones called. "I'm hungry."

Maddock was still peppering Rodney with punches and easily avoiding every attempt to take him down. Rodney's face was a mask of red; he was bleeding from his nose, mouth, and from cuts above both eyes. Maddock winked at Bones as he ducked a wild punch, then struck Rodney on the chin so hard that Avery swore Rodney's feet came off the ground.

His eyes rolling back in his head, Rodney fell into Bones' arms. Bones slung Rodney over his shoulder like a sack of potatoes and turned to Avery.

"Car or dumpster?"

It took her a minute to understand what he meant.

"That's his truck over there." She indicated a battered pickup truck on the other side of the lot.

Bones dumped the semi-conscious man into the bed of his own truck.

"Anyone else need a lift?" he called to Reggie and Doug, who had regained their feet but clearly wanted no part of him, Maddock, or even Angel. They cut a wide berth around the trio as they made their way to Rodney's truck. Reggie fished the keys from Rodney's pocket, and he and Doug climbed in and drove slowly away.

"Now that we got that out of the way," Bones said, offering her his arm, "let's eat. I worked up an appetite."

Avery suppressed a grin as she hooked her arm in his and allowed him to escort her toward the entrance. She froze halfway there.

"We might have a problem."

"What's that?" Bones asked as Maddock and Angel fell in on either side of them. "Don't tell me that anal probe is your boyfriend."

"He is... I mean, he was. But it's not that. His dad is the sheriff here."

Maddock and Bones exchanged knowing looks.

"It's cool," Bones said.

"But he might make trouble for you. He's the reason Rodney gets away with so much."

"We don't run from bullies," Maddock said, "even ones who wear a badge. Besides, if we leave, that makes us look guilty. If daddy shows up, we'll deal with it then."

Maddock held the door for her and Angel, then stepped in and closed it in Bones' face.

"They're like kindergarteners sometimes," Angel said, rolling her eyes.

"Well, they are men," Avery said, eliciting a knowing chuckle from Angel. "I have to ask. Where did you learn to fight like that?"

"It's sort of my profession," Angel said. She looked a little embarrassed as she explained that she was a professional mixed martial arts fighter, and was, in fact, in line to fight for the bantamweight title.

"That's awesome," Avery said. "How did you wind up working with these two?"

"Oh, it's just a little vacation for me." Her eyes flitted toward Maddock, who stood talking with someone at the bar, and her face fell. "Besides," she continued, her expression quickly back to normal, "I live to annoy my brother. He's such a loser."

"I heard that." Bones had caught up with them. Ignoring the sign that read "Please Wait to Be Seated," he sat down at a table with a view of the parking lot and flagged down the first waiter who passed by.

"Dos Equis for me and my friend, who'll be back in a minute," he nodded at Maddock's empty chair. "Nothing for this girl," he indicated Angel. "Indians can't hold their liquor, you know."

The young man looked thoroughly befuddled.

"Just kidding, bro. Get them whatever they like. Oh, and another thing." Bones took out his wallet and handed the young man a twenty. "Keep an eye out for me. If any cops or angry dudes who look like they just got slapped around show up, let me know."

Maddock came back, a grin on his face. Bones gave him a questioning look, but he shook his head. Avery wondered what he was up to, but that wasn't her biggest concern.

They lapsed into an uneasy silence while they waited for their drinks. Maddock clearly wasn't going to broach the subject, and Avery had been nervous enough without wondering when Rodney's dad would show up. When her rum and coke arrived, she took a healthy gulp, hoping to find some liquid courage there. Maddock seemed like a good man, after all he'd saved her twice, but when she'd mentioned his father, his blue eyes had turned to ice. There was something cold and hard inside him that made her distinctly uncomfortable. She sighed. There was no help for it. He was her best hope.

"I guess," she began, "we should get down to business."

Chapter 3

"I'm all ears," Maddock said. Truth was, he had a feeling he knew exactly what Avery wanted to discuss, and he wasn't eager to talk about it.

"Like I said, it's about your father's research."

Maddock kept his expression blank. "Right. You mentioned that earlier."

"Specifically, Captain Kidd." Avery must have seen something in his eyes because she hurried on. "Understand, I'm not some nut job or amateur treasure hunter. I'm an associate professor. I teach at the local community college. Captain Kidd is my area of professional interest."

"Seems like an odd thing to build your profession around."

"I have my reasons." A shadow passed across her face, but it was gone as quickly as it arrived.

"What's so weird about researching Captain Kidd?" Angel asked. "Isn't it his treasure we're searching for on the island?"

"We're investigating the so-called Money Pit, that's all." Bones said. "We're not necessarily looking for something Kidd left behind."

"Kidd's treasure is a legend," Maddock said, "and a far-fetched one at that. He buried a few chests on an island down south but, other than that, there's no reason to believe he had more to hide than that. If he had, he would have used it to bargain his way out of prison before they executed him."

"I think that's exactly what he did." Avery's gaze grew hard. "I've done extensive research on Kidd, much of it I've kept secret, and probably will continue to do so until I decide I can trust you. But believe me when I tell you I have evidence that he did, in fact, have a treasure of immense value, and he tried to use it to buy his freedom."

"Didn't work out for him, did it?" Bones took a swig of beer.

"No, but the important thing is, the treasure was real and quite valuable."

"How do you know?" Maddock couldn't keep the doubt from his voice.

"I told you, I've done extensive research, more than anyone who's studied Kidd or the island."

"That might be but, if you want my help, you've got to convince me."

"Your father believed it."

Maddock shifted in his chair. She was probably right, but that didn't make it true.

"Did you know his father?" Angel asked.

Avery's face reddened and she looked down at the table.

"He's familiar to me. He and I followed the same trails in our research."

"Dad enjoyed his pirate research, but it was a hobby, that's all. I doubt he took it seriously." Maddock took a long, cold drink of Dos Equis to cover the brief wave of sadness that washed over him. His parents, Hunter and Elizabeth Maddock, had died in an auto accident years before, and he still found it hard to talk about.

Avery sighed and brushed a stray lock of blonde hair out of her face. She looked down at her hands, eyes narrowed. When she looked up again, her expression was resolute.

"Captain Kidd hid clues, probably maps, in four sea chests. Your father owned one of these chests."

Maddock raised an eyebrow.

"That's true, or at least he believed it belonged to Kidd. We don't have it anymore, though. He donated it to..."

"The New England Pirate Museum." Avery completed the sentence. "I've already examined it." She saw the confusion in Maddock's eyes and hurried on. "I found a hidden compartment. Inside was a brass cylinder where a document could have been rolled up and hidden inside."

"But it was empty?" Maddock asked.

"Afraid so." Avery nodded. "I think your father found whatever was hidden inside before he donated the chest to the museum. In fact, I'm fairly certain of it."

"What makes you so sure?" Maddock wanted to dismiss her claim out of hand, but his instincts told him she was reliable.

"Around the time he donated the chest to the museum, he wrote seeking permission to explore the island." She paused, probably waiting for Maddock to object or question her, but he remained silent, so she went on. "He indicated that he had new evidence that could be authenticated if need be."

"I guess they turned him down?" Angel asked.

"Yes. Around here, you have to throw a lot of cash around to get anywhere." Bitterness cast a dark shadow across her face. Then, something seemed to click into place and she looked at Bones, eyes wide. "No offense intended toward your uncle."

"Get real." Bones waved the apology away. "We have no illusions about how Charlie does business."

"Anyway," Avery said, visibly relieved, "I don't know if your father didn't have the money or simply was unwilling to play the game."

"Maybe a little of both." Maddock shrugged. "I'm sorry to have to tell you this, but I looked through my dad's research shortly after he died, and there was nothing like what you're talking about."

Avery hesitated. "Could I examine his papers? Perhaps there's something you missed. I mean, you probably weren't searching for a clue to Captain Kidd's treasure when you were going through them."

Maddock considered that. Sorting through those books and papers would dredge up memories he'd buried long ago. Besides, while Avery was correct- he hadn't been looking for anything in particular when he went through his father's research, he was certain something like an authentic document from Kidd would have caught his eye.

"Captain Kidd's sea chests hold the key to unlocking the secret of Oak Island. I'm certain of it."

Maddock rested his chin on his fist, thinking it over.

"If need be, I'll take you to the museum and show you the secret..." She froze, staring over Maddock's shoulder.

Maddock turned around to see a stout police officer of late middle years standing behind him. He was blocky with gray eyes and hair to match. The calm detachment with which he eyed the people at Maddock's table said, *I own this town and everyone knows it.* Rodney's battered face peeked over the man's shoulder. He spotted Maddock and whispered something to the officer, who nodded and approached the table.

"Good evening." The man's gravelly voice held no emotion. He took a chair from a nearby table and sat down. "Miss Halsey." He nodded to Avery, whose face reddened as she whispered a soft hello.

"My name is Charles Meade," he said to Maddock and Bones, ignoring Angel. "I am the sheriff and, as such, it is my duty to keep the peace." The man's calm demeanor and articulate speech took Maddock by surprise. He'd been expecting an older version of Rodney.

"Everything's peaceful around here," Bones said, his tone easy.

"That is gratifying." Meade steepled his fingers and his gaze turned flinty. "But I understand that was not the case only a short while ago. I need to see your identification, please."

Maddock, Bones, and Angel all produced identification, but Meade declined Angel's proffered driver's license with a flick of his index finger.

"Only the gentlemen, please." He examined the licenses. "Dane Maddock and Uriah Bonebrake," he pronounced, like a principal calling unruly students into his office. Maddock saw Avery glance at Bones when Meade read his name. Bones hated his birth name. "You are a long way from home, gentlemen."

"That's not a crime, Sheriff," Maddock said. "As I'm sure you're aware."

"But aggravated assault is a crime, Mister Maddock. As I'm certain *you* are aware. I don't know what your relationship is with Miss Halsey, but I can assure you I do not condone beating up ex-boyfriends."

Avery started to argue, but Meade silenced her with a cold glance.

"You and your friend provoked a fight with my son. Were it not for the presence of his friends, his injuries might have been even worse."

Now it was Maddock's turn to quiet Avery. Meade thought the game was his, but Maddock held the trump card. He had to play it just right, though.

"I assume you've taken statements from witnesses?" Maddock said.

"Of course." Meade smiled, leaned back in his chair, and folded his arms across his chest.

"Witnesses other than your son's friends, I mean,"

Meade shifted uncomfortably in his seat.

"They all tell the same story. Rodney and Miss Halsey were talking out their differences. You interrupted, my son spoke rudely to you, and the two of you attacked him. His friends pulled you off, both of them sustaining injuries in the process."

"Well, allow me to retort," Bones said, quoting a line from his favorite movie, *Pulp Fiction.*

"Did your son and his friends tell you he was manhandling Avery?" Angel snapped, cutting across Bones' rebuttal with one of her own. "I tried to get her away from him, and was forced to defend myself when one of his friends grabbed me. Or do you condone violence against women in this county?"

"That is not the story as I heard it." Meade's voice remained calm but Maddock did not miss the annoyed glance he shot at Rodney, who, beneath his mask of bruises, wore a guilty expression. "Can you produce witnesses to support your version of events?"

"You've got four witnesses sitting right here," Bones said. "Two of them decorated veterans of the United States Navy."

"You're not in the States, Mister Bonebrake. In any case, your ribbons and medals hold no sway in my county." Meade looked around the table. "Do you have any unbiased witnesses who can support you?"

"You know everyone in this county is afraid to testify against Rodney," Avery said," because they're afraid of you."

"I'll take that as a no, then," Meade said. "I'm afraid I'll have to ask you gentlemen to come with me. Please know I have deputies waiting outside should you resist." His smile indicated he welcomed the thought.

"You're an elected official, aren't you, Sheriff?" Maddock asked. The question stopped Meade as he rose, his bottom hovering a few inches above the chair.

"Why do you ask?"

"I take it you have not yet reviewed the security video."

Meade eased back into his chair.

"The video confirms our story. The owner was kind enough to make a digital clip of the incident and email it to me. I'd rather not post it online and send links to the local news outlets." From the corner of his eye, Maddock saw Rodney shuffle away from his father, who had gone stock-still. "Let's be realistic," Maddock said. "We both have the power to make trouble for each other, but why bother." He hardened his voice. "I've been in all kinds of battles, Sheriff Meade, and one thing I've learned; it's better to avoid them whenever you can."

Meade was intelligent enough to see reason.

"Clearly I was misinformed. But next time you have a problem with someone, let the authorities deal with it. That is our job, not yours."

Angel looked like she was itching to make a sarcastic comment, but Maddock nudged her under the table.

"We will," Maddock said. "Thank you for hearing us out."

Meade nodded to the ladies and beat as fast a retreat as dignity would permit.

"I can't believe him!" Angel said. "Like it's so easy to stop and call the cops when some guy's got his hands all over you."

"We let him save face," Maddock explained. "That way, maybe he'll stay out of our hair."

Angel thought for a moment, then nodded. "You know, you're a lot smarter than Bones gives you credit for."

Maddock grinned and called the server over for another round of drinks. Their meals arrived, and they passed an easy hour of beer, seafood, and conversation. Angel, who had joined Crazy Charlie's island work crew at the last minute, steered the conversation away from Kidd's treasure, asking about the history of Oak Island and its fabled Money Pit.

"It all goes back to 1795," Avery began, "when a young man found an old block and tackle hanging above a depression in the earth. This area was thick with pirates back in the late seventeenth and early eighteenth centuries, and kids around here grew up hearing stories of buried treasure. So, the young man came back with some friends and they started digging. Within a few feet, they hit a layer of flagstones. Not a layer of natural rock, but actual, hewn stones. They kept digging, but kept hitting wooden platforms at regular intervals. That, plus the pick marks on the sides of the shaft, made it obvious to them they were dealing with something man-made."

"Now the story rings a bell," Angel said. "I hadn't put that particular legend together with our project. Bones was always more into legends than I was. If I recall, since that first discovery, treasure hunters have tried to excavate the shaft but, no matter how deep they go, they just hit more platforms."

"Correct. And the pit keeps flooding," Avery said. "The island is filled with underground channels."

"Which is where we come in," Bones said. "Charlie wants us to locate every channel we can find and see if any appear to be man-made."

"Which they don't," Maddock added.

Bones nodded. "He also wants to see if they can be sealed and the water drained out."

"No one's tried it before?" Angel asked.

"They have, but they've always failed." Avery shook her head.

"So why keep trying? It sounds like an impossible task. Has anyone found a single bit of treasure?" Angel's brow was knotted and she pursed her lips. "Have we signed up for a wild goose chase?"

"A few things have been found over the years." Avery stiffened and raised her voice. "Seafaring-related artifacts, bits of gold chain, parchment, and, of course, the stone."

"What stone?" Angel asked.

"A stone inscribed with strange symbols," Maddock said. "The message was translated as *'Forty feet below two million pounds are buried.'* Its authenticity is questionable, though."

"I have more evidence than that," Avery said. "Accounts no one else has seen. I know there's something down there." She turned to Maddock. "That's why I need to see your father's research." She held his gaze. "I'm not a quack treasure hunter. This has been a scholarly endeavor for me from the start. My colleagues haven't taken me seriously, but I'm right on the verge of proving them wrong. I've got everything I need to publish except..." She fell silent and looked down into her half-empty mug of beer.

"Except proof," Maddock said. Avery nodded and looked up at him again. Maddock saw the pleading in her eyes. "I don't want to get your hopes up," he sighed. "I've been through Dad's papers, and there's nothing there. But I'll take another, closer look. If there's anything at all that might help you, I'll give you a call."

"I suppose that's as much as I could have hoped for," Avery said glumly. "Thanks."

Maddock went out of his way to avoid looking at Bones. He knew what his friend was thinking, but Bones was wrong. This was not the beginning of another of their crazy adventures.

Chapter 4

The door to his parents' vacation cottage overlooking Mahone Bay felt heavier than usual as Maddock pushed it open. Sensing his mood, Bones and Angel slipped past him like shadows to their respective rooms. At Bones' suggestion, they'd seen Avery home safely before returning to the cottage for the night.

For a moment, he considered leaving his father's research where it lay and telling Avery he'd checked, but the coward's way out was not for him. This reminder of his parents' death was something he'd have to face.

In the kitchen, he slid the microwave oven from its cabinet and grinned. Leave it to his father to ignore the seascape painting in the bedroom, where any normal person would hide a safe, and put it behind a kitchen appliance instead.

He opened the safe and withdrew a fat envelope. He hadn't touched it since shortly after the accident. Leaving the safe open and the microwave on the counter, he moved mechanically to an armchair by the fireplace, and emptied the contents of the envelope onto the coffee table.

It was much as he remembered: printouts of articles, scans of documents, and a thick sheaf of notes written in his father's elegant, yet masculine hand. He let out a low chuckle as he recalled, as a teenager, trying to imitate his father's signature on a bad report card, only to be forced to own up to the bad grades and the failed forgery.

Along with the stack of research, a smaller manila envelope held brochures of museums and other pirate-related sites his father had visited, and loose bits of paper with notes jotted on them. Last was a small, leather-bound print of Edgar Allan Poe's story, *The Gold-Bug*. Fitting, he thought, as it told the story of a search for Captain Kidd's treasure. He turned it over, surprised to discover that the book looked brand new. This was not some old volume his father had taken notes in. He opened it to the middle and flipped through a couple of pages, then turned it over and gave it a shake in case anything was hidden inside, but no luck.

He set the book aside and started with the pile of research. The first several papers were various Kidd biographies, peppered with handwritten annotations. He read through them and found nothing new or unusual, certainly no references to Oak Island or the Money Pit.

He laid them on the table, rested his elbows on his knees, and buried his face in his hands. This was a waste of time. He was putting himself through this for nothing. In fact, he'd been foolish to stay here at all, where reminders of his father were everywhere and his presence seemed to hang in the very air. The weight of an unbearable burden of sadness pressed down on him. He should have stayed in the travel trailers Crazy Charlie had set up for the crew, and where Willis, Matt, and Corey were bunking.

He sensed movement behind him and a pair of gentle hands rested on his shoulders. He looked up to see Angel smiling sadly at him, sympathy shining in her eyes. She kept her silence and, for that, he was grateful. He gave her hand a squeeze and indicated that she should sit down.

She dropped into the other armchair and picked up the papers he had been examining. Understanding dawned on her face as she scanned them.

"This can't be easy for you. I remember when my grandmother died. Seeing to her affairs and taking care of her things wasn't so painful for me. That just felt like work. It was the personal things, you know. Letters she'd saved, pictures of me she'd written my name on. It was all too... real."

Maddock nodded.

"I can do this for you, Maddock. There's no reason you should have to dredge up painful memories."

"It's okay. I've been avoiding this place and these papers for years. Besides, I told Avery I'd do it."

"How about some help? Two of us can get through it faster than one."

"All right." He shrugged. "You know what we're looking for: clues to a treasure on Oak Island. I don't think a document old enough to be a clue from Kidd himself would have escaped my notice the first time I went through this stuff, so keep an eye out for anything that looks like a scan or copy of something older."

They set to the task, working in companionable silence. Occasionally, Angel would call his attention to a mention of treasure or the island, but they found nothing like what Avery was looking for.

The night wore on and he found that, the deeper he delved into his father's research, the more academic the endeavor became. His malaise melted away as he focused his thoughts on the subject. It was interesting, but shed no light specifically on the Oak Island mystery. By the time he finished reviewing his share of the material, he found himself eager to take a look at the rest. Angel, too, was eager to keep going.

When both sets of eyes had passed over every paper, he was forced to admit defeat. Whatever Avery was looking for, had it even existed, was not here.

"Sorry, Maddock." Angel gave him a quick hug.

"Thanks for getting me through it. Avery's going to be disappointed, but it was a pipe dream anyway." He gathered the papers and returned them to the safe, but held on to *The Gold-Bug*. Perhaps a bit of pleasure reading would help him relax.

Retiring to his room, he dropped down on the bed, opened the book, and froze. There, on the first page, was an inscription from his father. The date was December 25 of the year his parents died. This was to have been Maddock's Christmas gift. They had lost their lives only a few weeks before the holiday. His father must have written this shortly before his death.

Dane,
I know you think my search for a pirate's treasure is a fool's game. Perhaps, by the end of this book, you will wish to join me on this adventure.
Dad

He closed the book, dropped it on the floor, and turned out the light. He'd always, perhaps a bit childishly, believed his dad's pirate research to be something from which Maddock was excluded. But now... He rolled over and stared out the window, his mood as black as the night.

Rodney cursed and shifted in his chair, trying to find a comfortable sitting position. He was battered and bruised, and was pretty sure he had at least one fractured rib. He'd get his revenge on that Maddock guy, but that wasn't foremost in his mind at the moment.

He'd only caught snatches of the conversation Avery had with those jerks, but he'd heard enough. Captain Kidd had a treasure and he'd hidden the clues in old chests. Now, the treasure bug had bitten Rodney, and he was determined to be the one to find whatever it was Kidd had left behind.

Like many locals, he'd done his share of poking around on the island in his youth, but gave it up as hopeless. So many treasure hunters had excavated Oak Island that no one knew which pit was the original. Besides, he lacked the knowledge and equipment to carry out a proper search but, if he could find something definitive, a treasure map, maybe, he was sure he could get help in that area.

He looked at the monitor screen and his shoulders sagged a little. He'd never been much for research, or anything related to education, for that matter. Classes were just hoops to jump through so he could play football, wrestle, and meet girls. Tonight, he was wishing he'd paid a little more attention in school.

He'd tried the obvious research sites, searching for any mention of Captain Kidd's sea chests, with no success. He'd felt a momentary thrill when he found an account of Kidd burying a treasure on some place called Gardiner's Island, but read on only to find the treasure had been recovered shortly thereafter and used as evidence in Kidd's trial. The more he searched, the more discouraged he became.

Finally, he stumbled across a website that focused on the Oak Island mystery. Navigating to the forums, he was pleased to see an entire section dedicated to legends about Kidd's treasure. It took him a few minutes to figure out how to use the search function, but he got there in the end. He typed in "Kidd chest maps legend" and hit the enter key.

Nothing.

Finally, he overcame his revulsion at the thought of being a big enough loser to actually join an internet forum. He created a sufficiently masculine username, HotRod69, and made his first post.

does anyone know anything about a legend where captain kidd hid maps or clues inside sea chests

He stared at the screen, waiting for a reply, but to no avail. After ten minutes, he went to the kitchen for a beer and two pain relievers, but returned to more disappointment. What the hell? People were logged in to the forum. He could see the number of users online down at the bottom of the page.

And then he remembered the circular arrow at the top of the browser. He didn't remember what it was called, but Avery had shown him how to click it to update the page back when he'd been following a football game he'd bet on, and wondered why the score wasn't changing. Proud he'd figured this out on his own, he clicked the button and was happy to see he'd gotten a reply.

Do you mean the Gardiner Island treasure chest?

He gritted his teeth and banged out a harsh reply.

no idiot i dont

That shut the guy up. A few minutes later, he received a private message from a user named "Key."

Not familiar with a sea chest legend. Where did you hear of it?

Frustration at this idiot wasting his time dueled with pride at actually knowing something that, apparently, no one else did. This was a new, heady experience for him, and pride quickly won out. He typed a reply.

I know a researcher who found one of the chests

Key's reply was immediate.

Who?

Rodney didn't like the question. For one, it was none of the guy's business. What was more, it made Rodney seem less important if he was simply passing along information someone else had given him.

don't matter do you know about it or not??

He added the second question mark to show he meant business. He waited for Key's reply, but none came. Returning to the forum, he was puzzled to discover his post was gone. That was weird. He re-typed his initial message, posted it again, and watched the screen. Two gulps of beer later, the screen flickered and the website vanished, replaced with an error message.

"What the hell?" He banged his fist on the desk, spilling his beer all over his keyboard and lap. Upending the keyboard over the wastebasket, he drained the remainder of the foamy liquid, then rubbed it on his shirt. It didn't help. The keyboard was dead. Using the mouse, he refreshed his browser a few times, only to get the same error message. The website was down.

He shook his head. Just his luck. Maybe it would be up and running again in the morning. In any case, he wasn't beaten. If web searches didn't pan out, he'd simply have to try another tactic. As he settled into bed, he vowed he'd find a way to get to that treasure before Avery and her new friends did. And he didn't care what he had to do to get it.

Chapter 5

"One more quick dive and we knock off for lunch." Bones squinted up at the midday sun that hung high overhead. "Maybe for the day. I'm hungry and I'm bored. This whole thing is a wild goose chase."

Maddock nodded. He'd called Avery this morning and given her the news that there was no clue among his father's papers. The disappointment in her voice had been palpable, but she'd thanked him and asked him to contact her if he found anything. So far, nothing they'd seen today gave him any reason to believe he'd have any good news for her.

Every channel they'd explored had been natural. Not a hint of chisel marks or anything that would indicate human hands had altered it in any way. Each time they finished exploring a passage, Charlie set a crew to sealing it off. Maddock thought this was a waste of money and effort. The island sat on what was very much like a giant sponge. The hope of eventually sealing off all the waterways beneath its surface seemed futile to him. But, Charlie had the resources to make it happen, and remained undaunted by the lack of discovery. He bounced around the island, inspecting the work sites and keeping up a steady stream of encouragement.

"How long do you think Charlie will keep us at it?" Maddock sat down on *Sea Foam's* side rail next to Bones. "I know he can afford it, but I feel a little bit bad taking his money."

"Don't." Bones grinned. "If he doesn't give it to us, he'll just spend it on his latest bimbo girlfriend. Anyway, he'll keep us working until he can prove to the local authorities that the pit's a hoax, or a natural formation."

"What?" Matt stood nearby, making ready to dive. "You mean we're not here to find a treasure?" He looked affronted.

"I mean Charlie always has a backup plan. If we find the treasure, great. If we prove there never was a treasure, he's already laid the groundwork for building a pirate-themed casino on the island."

"And by laying the groundwork, you mean greasing the palms of local politicians," Maddock said.

A knowing grin was all the answer Bones gave.

"So, who's got tunnel seventeen and who's going to inspect the next stretch of shoreline?" Maddock asked.

"It's you and Matt in the creepy, dark tunnel this time," Bones said. "Me and Willis get the easy duty."

"Are you sure about that?" Matt asked.

"Yep. I checked the schedule and everything." Bones exchanged evil grins with Willis, who had joined them at the rail.

"Maddock, you never should have delegated that job to Bones," Matt said.

"Somehow, the Army guy keeps getting the crap duty."

"Seems fitting," Bones said, leaning away from Matt's playful jab.

"All right, y'all better get going," Willis called. "Don't be mad, now. Nothing but love for you."

Maddock rolled his eyes, pulled his mask on, and flipped backward into the water.

The cool depths enveloped him and he swam through shafts of green light, headed in toward the channel they'd labeled number seventeen. The entrance was well hidden in the midst of large, jagged rocks where the surf's ebb and flow surged with relentless force. He led the way, swimming confidently through the perilous passage.

A few feet inside the tunnel the light melted away. Maddock flipped on his dive light, setting the passageway aglow. Like all the others they had explored, the passage was wide enough for a man to swim through comfortably, the way irregular, and the rough edges worn smooth over time. This time, though, something immediately caught his eye.

A groove, two inches thick, had been carved up each side of the entrance and across the bottom. There was no way it was natural-the lines were too sharp and straight, the groove almost perfectly square. His first thought was someone had slid planks into this groove to form a cofferdam.

"Matt, do you see this?" he asked through the transmitter. The long-range communication devices were state-of-the-art, and came courtesy of Charlie's generosity.

"Yeah. Looks like someone tried to block this channel. Pirates?" He said the last in a comic, throaty growl.

"Or treasure hunters. Charlie isn't the first to try to dam up the channels under the island."

"You, my friend, are no fun."

Grinning behind his mask, Maddock led the way into the passageway, which ran back only about forty feet before it made a sharp bend to the left and came to a dead end.

"That was easy," Matt said. "We'll check this one off the list and be back on deck, drinking a cold one, before Bones and Willis drag their soggy carcasses back."

"Hold on." Maddock played his light slowly up and down the wall that blocked their way. He saw immediately that it wasn't like the sides of the passage. Instead of a smooth, regular surface, a pile of rubble blocked their way. A thorough inspection revealed an opening at the top, and darkness beyond.

"Think we can make it through?" Matt moved alongside him, reached out, and gave the topmost rock a shove. It gave an inch. "I think we can move it."

Maddock nodded and together they worked the stone, which was the size of a small microwave oven, free, and let it fall. Matt vanished from sight as a cloud of silt roiled in the water.

"There's no current carrying it away," Maddock observed. "I don't think this tunnel goes much farther."

"Then there's no point in wasting time waiting for things to clear up. Let's keep working."

Three large stones later, they had cleared a space large enough for one man to swim through. After securing one end of a strong cord to a length of branch that jutted up from the pile of rubble, Maddock went in first. He held on to the rope in case he lost his way and moved slowly due to the limited visibility, not wanting to injure himself or damage his equipment on an unseen snag. As he cleared the pile of debris, he felt a tug on the cord and knew Matt was behind him.

As he had predicted, the passage did not extend much farther, perhaps another forty feet, before it came to another dead end. This time, it wasn't a pile of stones blocking their way.

"Holy crap!" Matt's voice was dull with disbelief.

The twin beams of their dive lights shone against a wall of stone, and a carving of a Templar cross.

Chapter 6

Morgan plucked the phone from its receiver on the first blink. Her sisters never answered immediately, thinking it a subtle way of showing they had more important things to do than to take a telephone call. She brooked no such nonsense. She was a firm believer in immediate, positive action in all things, even the smallest.

"Yes?"

"Locke is here, Ma'am. He wishes to speak with you if you will consent."

"Of course." She hung up the phone, closed the file folder she had been reviewing, and stared expectantly at the door, which opened a moment later. Jacob knew her philosophy on wasting time, and made a point not to do so. He appeared in the doorway, his shaved, black head gleaming in the artificial light, and his broad shoulders filling the door frame. He gave her a respectful nod and stood aside for Locke.

The two could not have been more different. Where Jacob, formerly of the Elite Royal Marines, was built like a bull, the tawny-haired Locke was lean like a puma and moved with the deadly grace of one of the big cats. Formerly of MI-6, his whiskey-colored eyes shone with intelligence. Every member of her personal staff was an asset, mentally and physically, and he was her top man.

"Ma'am," he said without preamble, as was always her expectation, "we have a potential lead on the Kidd chests."

She felt her entire body tense. Locke often surprised her with information, but nothing of this magnitude.

"How strong a lead?"

"We can't be certain yet. Someone in Canada posted a query on a message board. He claims to have been tipped off by a researcher who gave him the location of one of the chests. An agent in the area is following up on it as we speak."

"A message board? I assume the post is gone?"

"We actually took down the entire site. We'll restore it, the post in question deleted, of course, after we've investigate the claim. Could be a crackpot." He sounded doubtful.

"For three centuries we have suppressed every mention we could find of these chests. It is not something one would accidentally stumble upon." She turned in her chair and gazed out the window. Truro lacked the size and bustle of London, and she liked it that way, but the modern world intruded here too. There was too little appreciation for the old ways, and old powers. "I want you there. Depart as soon as possible."

"As you wish. Should I wait until after your training session?"

"Jacob can train with me today." Morgan turned around just in time to see the ghost of a smile play across Locke's face. Jacob hated their training sessions. He was averse to striking a woman, which was a fatal weakness Morgan exploited to its full extent. Locke had no such compunction, but this task was more important. "Jacob, you may go. Meet me in the training room."

Jacob nodded and left quietly.

"There is something else." His hesitation was so brief that none but Morgan would have noticed. "A potential complication."

"What?" Her word cracked like a whip as suspicion sent hot prickles down her spine.

"Two others viewed the post before we eliminated it. I traced the ip addresses. One is an American from a small town in the south. A bit of a nutter who blogs about Bigfoot and aliens and the like."

"Erase him and his internet presence." Morgan would not accept even the tiniest risk of the legend of the chest spreading across the internet.

"Already done," Locke said. "It was a house fire. Truly, those so-called mobile homes are veritable death traps."

"Very good. And the second person to see the post?"

"That one is problematic. It took a great deal of doing, but I traced the source to Germany. Büren, to be precise."

Morgan froze. "Wewelsburg?"

"I cannot say for certain, but..." Locke shrugged.

"Herrschaft," Morgan whispered. "We must assume they have the same information we do." Her eyes met Locke's. "We *will* get there first."

"It will be as you say. Anything else before I go?"

"No, that will be all."

Morgan returned to her desk as Locke saw himself out. She performed a series of calming mental exercises to slow her racing heart, opening her eyes when she was, once again, her serene, rational self.

She gazed at the family portrait on the far wall. How unlike sisters they looked: Tamsin, a raven-haired beauty, Rhiannon, with her coppery tresses and emerald eyes, and Morgan, a blue-eyed blonde. They were not sisters by blood, only distant cousins, but they were bound by something deeper. How she longed to call the assembly and deliver the news that a chest had been found. Soon, perhaps, she would be able to do just that. But not until it was in her possession. To tip her hand too soon would be an unnecessary risk. Her position at the top of the order was strong, but she was not immune to the machinations of her Sisters.

She struggled to return to her work, but her duties as director of the British History Museum suddenly seemed mundane, even trivial, in light of what her people might soon uncover. Rock-hard discipline overrode any distractions, and she made quick work of her list of emails and telephone messages. She then took a half-hour to compose a carefully crafted opinion piece for *The Times* in which she questioned, but did not criticize, the Prime Minister's position on a key budget item.

Since being elevated to the leadership of the Sisterhood, she had used her connections to gradually raise her public profile, meticulously honing the image of one who took great pride in her nation's heritage and fought for its history without being perceived as backward. Though never presenting herself as having any interest in politics, her name was already being bandied about as a candidate for Parliament, even Prime Minister. Her aspirations, of course, were higher.

By the time she'd sent her submission to the editor, she could no longer curb the flow of energy that coursed through her. She buzzed Jacob.

"Close the offfice and meet me in the fitness room."

"Yes, Ma'am." He almost managed to cover his tone of resignation. The fitness room was never fun for him.

Smiling, she tapped in a code on her telephone keypad and watched as the painting on the far wall, "Le Morte D'Arthur" by James Archer, slid to the side, revealing her private collection of weapons. Morgan's eyes swept lovingly across the sharp, gleaming blades and angry spikes. She excelled at hand fighting and with firearms, but medieval weaponry was her true love. She selected a long sword and held it out in a two-handed grip, savoring its weight and balance. With a step and a twist, she sliced a whistling arc through the air. Yes, this was the one.

She caught sight of her distorted reflection in the blade. Like this image, the world did not yet see her for what she truly was, but they would. Oh yes, soon they would know.

Chapter 7

Maddock drifted in for a closer look at the cross. He shone his light across it and saw a thin circle carved around the image.

Matt ran his fingers across the surface of the carving, his fingers gently probing the recess.

"Careful," Maddock warned. There was something odd about it, but he could not put a finger on it.

"I think I can get a grip on it." Matt shoved his fingers into the groove and twisted.

"Matt! No!" But Maddock's warning was too late. The stone circle rotated a quarter turn and, with a whooshing sound like a drain opening, the stone vanished, pulling Matt's arm into a hole in the wall.

Matt shouted and struggled against the force of the water that was being sucked into the hole. Maddock grabbed hold of Matt's free arm but, before he could pull him free, he heard a hollow thud and Matt's cry of pain burst through the transmitter.

"My arm!" Matt yelled.

Maddock directed his light into the hole and saw, to his horror, that a section of wall had come down, crushing Matt's arm and trapping him. The smooth, regular edge of the stone told him in a single glance that it was not a natural rock fall.

"A booby trap," Maddock said. "Hold on." He called into the transmitter. "Bones, Willis, Corey, you guys copy?"

Nothing.

He made a second attempt and again got no reply.

"We're too deep under the rock." Matt's voice was thick with pain. "You've got to get closer to open water if they're going to hear you."

"I don't want to leave you here." Maddock knew Matt was right, but he hated to leave an injured man behind.

"What? You think I'm scared of the dark? I'm a Ranger, not some girly SEAL."

Maddock grimaced. "All right. How much air do you have?"

"It doesn't matter. Just go." There was just enough light that Maddock could see Matt glaring at him through his mask. "I'll watch my air supply. If you aren't back when it gets to ten minutes, I'll cut my arm off and swim the hell out of here. Now go." Matt closed his eyes and leaned his head against the rock wall.

Maddock swam with desperate fury, all the while calling for his team members. He squeezed over the pile of rubble and, with powerful kicks, zipped back up the passageway toward open water. He had just caught a glimpse of light when one of his calls finally got a response.

"Yo, Maddock, what's keeping you? We're done." Bones said.

"I need you guys here quick. The tunnel was booby-trapped. Matt's stuck and he's hurt. Bring pry bars.

"Roger." Bones and Willis spoke over the top of each other as they acknowledged Maddock's message.

"Corey, you call for help."

"Already on it," came the reply.

Maddock gave Bones and Willis a quick description of the underwater tunnel, then turned and headed back down the passage. When he reached Matt, he feared the worst. His friend sagged limply against the wall, his trapped arm supporting his weight.

"Matt, you still with me?"

"Yep," came the weak reply. "I'm *hanging* in there. Get it?"

The next few minutes seemed to stretch into hours as Maddock watched and waited for help to come. He worked at the stone that pinned Matt's arm down, first with his bare hands, then with his knife, but could not budge it. He knew it was futile, but Matt needed hope to strengthen his resolve. All the while, Maddock kept up a steady stream of encouragement until Matt told him to shut the hell up and go look for the others. Just then, a glimmer of light appeared, and two dark shapes swam into view.

"His arm is trapped under a stone block. You guys pry it up." Maddock instructed. "I don't know if he has the strength to pull himself free."

"That's what you think," Matt growled, rising up and placing his free hand against the wall. "You guys just get me loose."

Bones and Willis worked their pry bars into the open space beneath the rock and heaved. The rock moved, but no more than a centimeter. The two men tried again, groaning from the strain, and it budged a little more. Matt pulled back, roaring in anger and pain, but his arm scarcely budged.

"Again!" Maddock barked.

They continued to work at the stone. Maddock took Bones' knife in one hand, his own in the other, and used both to help lever the rock upward. The effort was tiring them rapidly and none of them had much air left.

"Cut it off." Matt gasped.

"Ain't no way," Willis said. He and Matt were tight, and he seemed to They be taking this accident as a personal affront.

"It's not going to work." Matt's voice was barely discernible. "We're all going to run out of air soon. Just do it."

"We'll give it one more try," Maddock said. "When we lift, you pull with all you've got."

"That's not much, but okay."

Maddock counted down from three and they all lifted one last time. Maddock's muscles burned and the strained grunts and groans of his team rang in his ears.

"Now, Matt!" he shouted.

Matt threw himself into the attempt and his arm gradually slid free of the trap. And then he collapsed, folding onto himself like an accordion.

Maddock dropped the knives and grabbed hold of his friend, yanking him free of the trap just as the stone crashed back into place. Together, they hauled their semi-conscious comrade up the tunnel and out to their waiting boat.

Maddock bandaged Matt's crushed arm while Corey piloted them to shore, the sound of approaching sirens telling them help was on the way. By the time they got him to shore and into the waiting ambulance, Matt was alert, though in tremendous pain.

"You guys don't worry about me," he said. "And don't let those asshole pirates beat us. Finish the job."

"We'll talk about it at the hospital," Maddock said as the ambulance doors closed. He turned to his crew. "We're done for the day. Does Charlie know what happened?"

Corey nodded.

"Good. We'll head to the hospital and we can talk about it more while we wait."

"I'm telling you right now," Bones said, "I want another crack at that tunnel."

Everyone gave him a quizzical look.

"I got a look inside just before the stone fell. I don't know what it is, but something is back there."

There it was again. A flicker of shadow, like someone moving past the back window. Rodney muted the television, rose slowly from his chair, and headed to the back window. Squinting against the afternoon sunlight, he scanned the back patio, but saw nothing. Weird. He was working later, so he'd had only one beer. Must be his imagination.

He returned to his chair, a cracked leather number he'd bought cheap at a garage sale, and reached for the remote.

"Do not move." The voice was cold and hard, but carried a hint of a pansy British accent.

Still pissed about being jumped by that Maddock guy and his friends, Rodney sprang to his feet, whirled about, and flung the remote in the direction he'd heard the voice. It flew through empty space and shattered against the wall.

He saw a blur at the corner of his eye and something struck him a hard blow in the temple, followed by a flurry of kicks and punches so lightning-fast he hardly knew what was happening. The next thing he knew, he was flat on the ground, knee buckled, head ringing, ribs screaming, and fighting for breath. Someone bound his wrists and ankles with cable ties. He twisted his head around and caught sight of his captor.

The guy was not what he expected. He looked like a banker, clean-shaven and dressed in a coat and tie. The only odd thing about his appearance was the pair of latex gloves he wore.

And the razor he drew from his breast pocket.

Rodney gasped, the relief of the sudden intake of breath failing to overcome his abject terror.

"What do you want?" He hated the way his voice squeaked and the hot, damp feeling in his crotch as his bladder released. "I'm broke, man, but take what you want."

"What I want," the man said in a voice like a schoolteacher in an old movie, "is information."

"I don't have any information. Ask anybody."

"On the contrary, you do indeed." The man knelt and pressed the flat edge of the razor against Rodney's cheek. "Tell me what you know about Captain Kidd's sea chests."

"What?" *How did the guy know about that?* "I don't know what you're talking about."

The man flicked his wrist and a line of hot fire blossomed on Rodney's cheek. He was too shocked to cry out.

"This will go much easier for both of us if we do not lie to one another. To encourage you to be truthful, I will cut something off each time you tell a lie or attempt to hide something from me: ears, fingers, toes, eyelids, lips."

Rodney whimpered and tried to squirm away, but the touch of cold metal on his eye socket froze him in his tracks.

"In the interest of fairness, I shall, of course, be truthful with you. You posted a query on a message board last night, asking about the legend of the Kidd chests. You also indicated that a researcher gave you this information. Now, tell me what you know."

"I heard that Captain Kidd hid treasure maps in his sea chests."

"Good. That wasn't so hard, was it? What else do you know?"

The man's friendly tone chilled him almost as much as the razor. It was like the guy did this every day. He racked his brain, trying to remember exactly what he'd overheard.

"There's one in a museum."

"Which one?" The man's voice was sharp as the crack of a whip.

"I don't know which one. Aren't they all the same?"

"Not which chest, which museum, you imbecile."

"The New England Pirate Museum, or something like that." He didn't mention Avery's connection to the chest. She might hate his guts, but he still felt like he ought to protect her. It was the closest thing to a brave act he could manage in what might be the rest of his very short life.

"Excellent. You're doing very well. Now, do you know the locations of any other chests?"

"No. Only the one."

"Anything at all? Rumors, legends?"

"No. I swear," he pleaded. He wanted desperately for the man to believe him. Maybe if he realized just how little Rodney knew, he'd let him live. "That's everything."

"Very well. Now, I need to know from whom you learned this information."

He couldn't give the man Avery's name. He just couldn't.

"I heard somebody talking in a bar."

The man sucked his teeth and gave his head a disapproving shake. With a deft movement, he sliced Rodney's ear and held the bloody gob of flesh, his earlobe, out for Rodney to see.

"I told you to hide nothing from me. You might have been given this information in a pub, or bar, as you put it, but you know the person who told it to you. What is he or she called?"

"Maddock!" Rodney blurted the first name that came to mind. "Dane Maddock. That's all I know about him."

"Very good. I appreciate your honesty."

Rodney relaxed. Whether the man killed him or let him live, at least it was over.

"I now have the unfortunate duty of confirming your honesty. That requires a more severe test of your veracity. We shall start with your thumb, I think."

The man stuffed something into Rodney's mouth, which made it very hard to scream.

Chapter 8

"All right! Let's dam this baby up!" Charlie rubbed his hands together and grinned, the lines on his face crinkling. He paced to and fro along the rocky bluff overlooking tunnel seventeen, his exuberance lending a youthful bounce to his step. The prospect of solving the mystery seemed to have taken twenty years off of him.

Maddock had to smile at the old man's excitement. Matt's arm was broken in several places but, given time, he'd heal. Once his recovery was assured, Matt had maintained his insistence that Maddock and the crew finish what they'd started. He further vowed to be back on the job the minute he was released from the hospital.

After spending much of the night at the hospital, Maddock, Bones, and Willis got back to work. They returned to the passageway and made a failed attempt at opening the trap, after which they used GPS to chart the twists and turns of the tunnel, though their signal crapped out before they got to the area behind the wall. Charlie's plan was to block up the passageway, pump the water out, if possible, and drill down directly into the chamber. It was far from the craziest thing the man had tried in his lifetime.

"I'm telling you, Charlie, I don't know what I saw back there," Bones said. "Not trying to shoot you down, or anything, but it might not be anything big."

"You're full of crap, boy." Charlie dismissed Bones' words with a gesture like shooing a fly. "Why would anyone put a booby trap in front of a chamber unless they had something they wanted to protect?"

"To be a douche?" Bones volunteered.

"Bah! All the evidence says that tunnel's important. They didn't carve a Templar cross at the chamber entrance for no reason. And, you said yourselves, it looks like someone dammed it up."

"How did searchers manage to miss it all these years?" Angel asked. "There have been, what, thousands of people looking for the treasure. You'd think someone would have found it by now."

"They've all been focusing on the Money Pit," Maddock said. "There probably haven't been too many skilled divers experienced in marine archaeology who've explored these channels." He looked out across Smith's Cove, where a single boat plied the waters, a white dot on the gray horizon. "Those who did could easily have missed this particular passage, or found it, but were fooled by the debris blocking the way. Matt and I almost missed it."

"Well, you boys found it and that's what matters." Charlie clapped his hand on Maddock's shoulder, his grip strong, despite his age. "We are going to be the ones to finally solve the riddle. I just know it."

"How long do you think it will take to dam up the tunnel?"

"Should be finished this afternoon. Then we'll start pumping the water out and see what happens." He looked like he was going to say more, but something out on the water caught his eye.

Maddock turned to see a police boat drift up to shore. Two uniformed deputies sat inside. The pilot gave a curt nod, but that was all. They gave neither an indication of landing the craft, nor leaving.

"Wonder what the hell they want." Charlie scratched his chin. "They'd best leave me alone. I've got work to do."

"Maybe they heard about Matt's accident and came to check things out?" Angel said.

"Then why don't they get out of the boat?" Charlie kicked at the ground with his booted foot. "Meddling government types is what they are. Can't let a simple businessman go about his work."

"Uncle, you are hardly a simple businessman," Bones said.

The sound of an approaching vehicle cut off Charlie's retort. They all looked toward the road in surprise. It had been closed long before their arrival and had fallen into a state of disrepair. The trucks that delivered Charlie's equipment were the only traffic they'd seen.

Maddock's instincts told him something was not right, and he keenly felt the absence of his Walther. He hadn't felt there was a reason to be armed on the island, so he'd left it back at the cottage. The impulse fled as quickly as it had come, and he suddenly understood the reason for the police boat.

"I think we're about to be paid a visit by the local authorities," he said.

"What for?" Bones frowned.

"I guess we'll find out."

A police cruiser appeared around a bend in the tree-lined road and coasted to a stop near where they stood. Two deputies climbed out, exchanged nervous looks, and approached Maddock and the others.

"They look scared." Bones grinned, his eyes alight with ill intentions. "Should I mess with them a little?"

"Hell no!" Charlie snapped. "This is my work site. Play your games somewhere else, young man."

"Yes, Uncle." Bones actually managed a respectful tone, so unlike his normal manner.

The deputies fanned out as they drew closer and stopped ten feet away. One, a short, attractive woman with fair skin and brown hair, rested her hand on her sidearm. Her partner, a tall man with wavy brown hair and a moustache, spoke first.

"We're looking for Dane Maddock and Uriah Bonebrake." He fidgeted and ran a hand through his hair.

"You found them." Maddock's mind raced. What did they want? He and Bones hadn't done anything wrong, but getting entangled with the police, especially outside one's home country, was not a good thing. "What can we do for you?" He and Bones took a few steps away from the rest of the group.

"I'm deputy White," the dark-haired man said. "This is Deputy Boudreau. The two of you are wanted for questioning."

"Okay, shoot." Bones smiled and managed not to make it look predatory.

"We'll need you to come with us."

"Are we under arrest?" Maddock kept his tone easy.

"Not yet," Boudreau snapped. She glanced at her partner and blushed as he gave a quick shake of the head.

"You don't have to come with us," White said. "I can tell you, though, if you don't, our orders," he nodded toward the boat, "are to make sure you don't leave the island until the sheriff obtains warrants for your arrest."

"All right," Maddock said. "Can I ask what you're going to question us about?"

White shrugged and forced a sympathetic smile. "It's not allowed. Sorry."

It was a short ride to the sheriff's department, but it felt longer thanks to Bones' need to fill every silence with annoying snatches of song or conversation. When he broke into "Achy Breaky Heart," Deputy Boudreau whirled around and promised to gag him and put him in the trunk if he didn't shut up. Bones winked at Maddock, clearly pleased he'd gotten under the deputy's skin, but Maddock was grateful for the peace and quiet.

They were taken to separate rooms, and left to simmer for a good twenty minutes before a man in slacks and a blazer, a single button straining to hold back his paunch, entered.

"I'm Detective Williams of the Kidd's Cross Police Department," he said, dropping heavily into a folding chair on the other side of the table where Maddock sat. He paused, perhaps waiting for Maddock to introduce himself in turn, but gave up after ten seconds of silence. "I understand you know a Rodney Meade."

"The name sounds familiar, but I can't place it."

Williams raised his eyebrows. "The two of you had a fight two days ago. Ring a bell?" He folded his arms, rested them on his belly, and leaned back in his chair.

"The sheriff's son. Sure, I remember."

"I understand the two of you were fighting over a girl."

"Are you telling me you haven't already reviewed the incident report and the security footage?" Maddock took pleasure at the sight of the man's obvious discomfort. "Or did the sheriff sweep it under the rug?"

"He declined to make a report due to a lack of evidence." Williams cleared his throat and sat up straight. "I'd like to hear your version of the events."

"What did you hear from the sheriff?"

"I already told you what I heard…" Williams bit off the sentence, his face now beet red. Clearly he'd just realized he was answering Maddock's questions instead of the other way around. "I'm investigating a crime and I'm asking you for an answer."

"I'll be happy to give you one, detective." Maddock folded his hands and rested them on the table. "But you'd do better to forget fallible eyewitness testimony and simply get a copy of the security tape from the owner of The Spinning Crab. I'll be happy to wait while you go get it."

"I want to hear your version of events."

"Detective, I'm sorely tempted to say nothing at all and make you do the detective work you should have done already, but I know how small towns operate and I'm sure you're doing the best you can, so I'll indulge you. Rodney assaulted a young woman, and one of his friends put his hands on another young lady who was part of my group."

"And you decided to beat him within an inch of his life for it?" Williams snapped.

"Actually, my friend fought back against the guy who was trying to manhandle her, and that's when Rodney and his other buddy started swinging. Like I said," he raised his voice and held up a hand to forestall the argument he could see Williams was about to make, "don't take my word for it. Check the video and decide for yourself."

"So he messed with your girlfriend..."

"Acquaintance," Maddock corrected.

"...and started a fight. I suppose you were pretty mad at him. Maybe wanted to get back at him?"

"For what?" Maddock couldn't stifle a laugh. "Detective, I'm sorry for how this sounds, but those guys got what was coming to them and they didn't leave a scratch on any of us. As far as any of us are concerned, it was over as soon as the fight ended."

"Fine. Let's suppose I believe you." Williams opened a file folder and made a show of inspecting the contents. "Where were you yesterday between the hours of two and eleven p.m.?"

That was an unexpected question, but Maddock had an easy answer.

"At the hospital. One of my crew was injured on the job. We stayed with him until well after midnight."

"Can anyone verify that?"

"My entire crew and maybe some of the hospital staff. There's a nurse there with frizzy gray hair and crazy eyes who wouldn't stop hitting on me. I'm sure she, at least, remembers."

Williams actually cracked a smile.

"I know her. Sorry to break it to you, but you're not her first." He took a deep breath and let it all out in a rush. "You realize I can check hospital security video to confirm your story?"

"I'm counting on it," Maddock said. "I'm guessing something bad happened to Rodney."

"You could say that." Williams closed his folder. "Give me a few minutes." He pushed himself up from his seat and lumbered to the door. "Can I get you anything to drink?"

"No thanks." Maddock hoped the abrupt ending to the interrogation, if it could be called that, and William's sudden bout of courtesy were good signs.

Williams returned twenty minutes later. He opened the door and leaned inside. "How long do you plan on being in town, Mister Maddock?"

"Until the job's finished. I don't know how long that will be."

"All right. You're free to go." Williams didn't seem angry or upset. Whatever follow-up he'd done seemed to have persuaded him that Maddock was not responsible for whatever had happened to Rodney.

"I'll need a lift back to the island. Are the deputies still here?"

Williams' expression darkened for a moment. "It would be better if I drove you. The deputies are..." He shrugged.

"Out for my blood?"

"Maybe not your blood, but they want a pound of flesh from somebody, and you two were the prime suspects."

Maddock took note of the past tense and nodded.

Williams guided Maddock and Bones out of the station. As they exited through the front doors, they heard shouting and turned around. Sheriff Meade, apoplectic, was struggling to escape the clutching arms of the three deputies who held him back.

"You killed my son!" he cried.

"My partner's going to talk to him," Williams said, ushering Maddock and Bones out the door.

"A horse tranquilizer might help," Bones said.

Williams smirked and shook his head.

"So, Rodney's dead." Bones made it a statement, not a question.

"Very." Williams' expression grew grave. "Until we find the killer, I suggest you two steer clear of the sheriff. He's a powerful man and he can be a dangerous enemy."

"That's fine," Maddock said. "So can we."

Williams stopped and looked at them each in turn. "I believe you."

Chapter 9

"They have one, Ma'am." Jacob's expression was studiously blank. He never said so, but he disapproved of this exercise.

"Very well. I'll be down there shortly."

Her phone rang as Jacob was closing the door. It was Locke. "Yes?"

"We found the chest and it was empty."

Though Locke had delivered the news exactly as she preferred- swiftly and succinctly, like a clean cut, she still felt a momentary thrill followed by a sagging disappointment. She'd been so certain.

"So it was another false trail." She hated the hollow sound of her voice.

"You misunderstand me. The secret compartment was there, but someone must have gotten to it first. I've secured the chest so our people can examine it, though I doubt they'll find anything. I took a few other items of no great value and ransacked an office as well. No need to call attention to the chest."

"Very good." Her head spun and her heart raced. So Kidd's story was true. She'd never doubted it, but this was the closest thing to definitive proof they'd found.

"I know it isn't the news you hoped for, but at least we have a path to follow."

"Who took it?" An overwhelming rage filled her, and she wanted nothing more in the world than to have the responsible party right there in front of her, where she could put her hands around his neck and choke the answer out of him.

"I don't know yet." How could Locke remain so calm? *"But the chest was donated by a man called Hunter Maddock. He told the museum he believed it belonged to Blackbeard."*

"A cover story," Morgan spat.

"Possibly. Or, he truly did not know what he had, and was ignorant of the compartment."

"In which case, whatever was hidden inside could have been removed by someone at the museum." The wheels of Morgan's mind were turning at a rapid clip.

"Or it was removed before the chest came into Maddock's possession." Locke completed her thought, as he often did.

"Pursue all angles." Morgan's flare of anger was settling into a cold fury. "Investigate the museum. Acquire it if you must. Our New York branch could stand to expand its reach."

"Yes, Ma'am. The budget for this acquisition?"

"At your discretion." She would not have given anyone other than Locke such a free rein. "Find this Hunter Maddock and wring the truth out of him. I don't care how you do it. If he doesn't have the clue, find out from whom he obtained the chest."

"He is deceased, with only one living relative. A son, a military type and a bit of an odd bird."

"How so?"

"He is a treasure hunter of sorts and his name is associated with some sensational rumors. It also seems that someone at a high level of the American government has worked very hard to hide information about him, though I can find no evidence that he has worked in any official capacity since he left their military. I know he is well-trained and keeps company with similar men. He would be difficult to kill or capture." He paused. Two eternal seconds of silence dragged past.

"What is it?" Morgan snapped. Locke knew better than to waste time.

"I can't be certain, but it appears he is on Herrschaft's list."

That was a surprise. What were the odds that an American civilian would have run afoul of the German sect of the Dominion? Morgan frowned, considering this new detail.

"In that case, perhaps an arrangement can be reached," she mused. "The enemy of my enemy, as they say."

"I will consider all angles."

"Is there anything else?"

"There is yet another treasure hunting expedition underway on Oak Island. Probably the same sort of misguided buffoons as always. Should we investigate?"

"Yes. As you say, it is not likely to amount to anything, but if it does, take control in any way you see fit." Morgan ended the call, pocketed her phone, and walked to the window.

Modron was her personal retreat. Built in the style of a medieval castle, it stood atop a lonely tor in Bodmin Moor. It was well off the beaten path, surrounded by a dense wood planted two centuries ago by her many-greats grandmother and cultivated by later generations, providing her the solitude she craved and the privacy she required.

She looked down onto the grounds, where a tidy formal garden gave way to acres of forest. The vast grounds were protected by a variety of security measures designed to keep intruders out... and other things in.

She espied movement among the trees, a brief glimpse of gold and green, and then it was gone. She smiled at the sight. She would have enjoyed a walk in the forest right now, but she should not keep Jacob waiting. The exercise would be a satisfying release after Locke's call.

From her private study, she descended a narrow, winding stone staircase. There was no light here, and each step carried her deeper into the darkness, a fitting twin for her mood.

The stairway emptied into a square room. To her left, a heavy oaken door barred the way. Suits of armor stood sentinel in each corner and, to her right, arched windows flanked a floor-to-ceiling tapestry depicting a scene from the Battle of Ager Sanguinis. She glided behind the tapestry and her hand went automatically to the trigger stone.

The door swung open on silent hinges, revealing a jarringly bright room. Built in an octagonal shape, it was thoroughly modern, from the soft, blue carpet, to the fluorescent lights, to the high-definition television set high on one wall. In contrast, a medieval-looking rack of weapons lined the wall to her left: swords, long knives, a mace, a morning star, and staffs of varying lengths and thicknesses.

Jacob stood watch over a handcuffed man in his late twenties, who scowled at her when she entered. Morgan looked him up and down. He was tall and solidly built, and the scarring on his knuckles indicated he'd done his share of fighting. Dark stubble dusted his shaved head and cheeks. He wore sagging blue jeans, jack boots, and a West Ham United football jersey.

"So who is she, then?" he growled. "Why'd you bring me here?"

"Why are you here?" Morgan echoed. "That is an excellent question, for which I shall give you an honest answer." She accepted a black leather portfolio from Jacob, opened it, and flipped through the contents.

"Richard MacKenzie, originally from Liverpool, late of Falmouth," she read. "You came to our attention because you beat your girlfriend two weeks ago."

"Them charges didn't stick, now, did they?" He grinned, his crooked, beige teeth gleaming like jagged fangs in the artificial light. "If you're one of them bizzies you can just bugger off and let me go on my way."

"You set a car on fire during the riots," she continued, "and you have an impressive list of criminal offenses."

"That's not all that's impressive about me, blondie." He moved his hips suggestively.

"I do not see here that you have a job, or have ever held one." She cocked her head and waited for a reply.

"See now, I've worked here and there." His smug grin flickered. "It's hard, you know. Not many jobs to be had."

"You have never held a job for which you earned a salary or paid income taxes."

"So what if I haven't? That's not a crime now, is it?"

"You are a parasite, Mister MacKenzie. Britain has provided you with support for your entire life, yet you repay her by preying on good and decent people."

"Most of them wasn't decent, Miss. No more than me, anyhow." His grin was back.

"Give me one reason I should let you leave here alive, Mister MacKenzie."

His face turned beet red and he trembled, not with fear, but rage. "Bollocks. You ain't going to do nothing to me." The man was either too arrogant or too lacking in imagination to understand he was in her power.

"Let us try again. If you ceased to exist at this very moment, give me one example of how Britain would be the worse for it."

"Piss off!" If his hands had not been cuffed, Morgan was sure he would have attacked her right then and there. Good!

"Nothing, then? Because I can think of several ways in which your death would improve our country immensely." She sniffed. "Not the least of which would be the absence of your foul stench."

"Let me go or I'll..." He glanced down at his handcuffs.

"What will you do? You'll hit me, like you did your girlfriend?" She nodded to Jacob who produced a key and removed MacKenzie's cuffs. "That is exactly what I want."

"What?" The confusion in his eyes was comical.

"I want to fight you, Mister MacKenzie. You may use any of the weapons you see here." She nodded to the rack. "I shall be unarmed. If you fight me and win, Jacob will drive you home and give you one hundred pounds for your trouble. Should you lose, you may still walk out of here."

"What if I don't want to?" He looked all around the room, searching for a way out. "There's some kind of trick here. Let me go."

"If you do not fight me, Jacob will shoot you and bury you in the moor."

"You're out of your mind." He took two steps toward her and froze, recognition dawning in his eyes. "I've seen you before. You've been on television and whatnot. Just wait until I tell my story. Somebody'll pay me nicely for it."

Jacob glanced at her and she smiled.

"Fight me, and you will be free to go and tell your story to anyone you like." In one swift movement she closed the gap between them and slapped him across the face. The loud crack and sharp sting felt good. "Hit me." She struck him again, this time with a closed fist.

Richard reeled backward, pressing a hand to his split lip. He raised his bloody hand, eyes filled with disbelief.

"You crazy bitch!"

He swung a wild right cross that Morgan easily ducked. She sidestepped and drove a fist into his side where his ribs ended. He grunted in pain but managed another swing, which she ducked. This time she drove a roundhouse kick to the inside of his knee then followed with a right cross to his nose. Her fist struck home with a satisfying crunch.

Richard flailed blindly, trying to grab hold of her, but she was too fast for him. Another kick to the knee and he stumbled to the floor.

"You fight like a Frenchman," she hissed. In an actual life and death situation she would have finished him, but this was something else entirely.

Richard found renewed strength and, with a roar, leapt at her. He almost managed to grab hold of her, but she sprang to the side and he crashed into the wall. Now, mad with rage, he went for the weapons. He grabbed a longsword and charged.

Morgan easily eluded his clumsy strokes and feeble thrusts. It was not long before he began to tire- he struggled to keep the sword aloft, and his breath came in ragged gasps. Summoning the last of his strength, he raised the sword and rushed in for a vicious downstroke. Morgan dodged and drove a roundhouse kick into his unprotected middle. The breath left him in a rush, and he dropped to one knee. Knowing he would offer no further meaningful resistance, she delivered an axe kick to the back of his skull.

It took Richard ten minutes to recover whatever wits he had at his disposal. Jacob wiped the blood from his face, congratulated him on a "bloody good fight" and offered him a glass of water. He sipped it, staring daggers at Morgan.

"I'll show you out if you're ready," Jacob said.

"Where's my hundred pounds?" Richard snapped.

"You didn't win." Morgan said. "But you do get to leave here alive."

Richard didn't bother to argue. He lurched to his feet and followed Jacob out.

Jacob returned a few minutes later. "I assume you want to watch." His voice was as dull as the look in his eyes.

"Of course," Morgan said. Her eyes turned to the television on the wall. Jacob turned it on, revealing a wide-angle shot of the formal garden. Jacob zoomed in on Richard, who was limping toward the wood. "Your disapproval saddens me, Jacob." Morgan kept her eyes on the screen as she spoke.

"I don't mind the fighting," he said. "These blokes all deserve an ass whipping, and you're more than fair about it. But this..." He gestured at the screen. "I just don't know."

"We are culling the flock. Can you honestly say our nation would be better off with him and the others alive?"

Jacob shook his head.

"Besides, the children need to hunt. It is their nature." She smiled as the feed switched over to a camera in the wood. Richard was already jumping at every sound. He sensed danger.

"I would respectfully argue it is their training, not their nature, Ma'am."

"Centuries of breeding and, yes, training have made them what they are today. Perhaps it was not in the nature of their ancestors, but it is their nature. It amounts to the same thing."

"True," Jacob said. "Let me know when you wish for me to press the button."

They lapsed into a tense silence as they watched Richard move into the depths of the wood. Things were about to get very interesting.

A branch rustled somewhere behind him. Richard spun around, sending a new burst of pain shooting up his injured leg. He hadn't taken a licking like that since school. The bitch must be some kind of soldier or spy or something. He'd be well shut of her and this damn forest.

He didn't like it out here. He couldn't properly say he knew anything about the outdoors, he was a city lad after all, but this place was all wrong. It felt unnatural. The trees weren't planted in rows or anything, but it had an orderly feel to it, as if everything were laid out according to a plan. And there were no bird sounds, only the occasional rustle of something heavy moving through the treetops or scuffling along the ground.

He quickened his pace, not entirely certain where he was headed. The black fellow had told him to keep going straight ahead and he would find a gate that opened onto a path leading into town. Richard had been too out of sorts to ask the name of the town or how, exactly, he was to get back home, but he didn't much care. He just wanted away from this place. And when he got home, he'd call one of those reporters who made their living exposing public figures, march right back to this place, and show the world what a nutter the woman was. He'd make her sorry she'd crossed him.

This time, the sound came from his left, and he saw a flash of movement. So there *was* something out there. Now he knew for certain he wasn't imagining things, but he'd have preferred his own paranoia to what he had just seen. It wasn't much- only a glimpse of a mottled hide of dark green and gold or orange, he couldn't be sure, covered in a lattice-work pattern of raised ridges. What the bloody hell was it?

He veered off to his right and quickened his pace, hoping he would not lose his way. There were more sounds now, coming from every direction, and moving closer. He scanned the ground for a stick, a rock, anything he could use as a weapon, but the forest floor was clean; another thing that lent to its unnatural feel.

A noise right beside him made him jump. With a scrabbling and scratching like sharp claws on a wooden surface, something climbed the tree where he stood. The thick trunk blocked the thing from view, but he caught a glimpse of a scaled tail vanishing into the leaves up above.

So complete was his panic, he was scarcely aware of the warm, wet feeling as he soaked his boxers. Clutching a belt loop to keep his pants from sliding down and tripping him, he ran blindly. Limbs slapping his face, he bounded like a pinball from tree to tree.

From somewhere close by, he heard a low moan that he realized was coming from his own mouth. He'd heard that sound many times in his life, always from someone he'd robbed or beaten up. It was the sound someone made when they finally realized they were powerless to stop what was about to happen to them. Now, it was finally his turn.

He broke through a thick tangle of brush and suddenly he was flying. He cried out in shock and flailed his arms as he hurtled through the air and, with an icy shock, plunged into darkness. Down and down he went, certain this was the descent into hell.

Then his feet touched something solid, and he realized he had fallen into water. He pushed up, but his booted feet held fast in the soft muck. Panic, which had momentarily faded, rose anew, and he struggled to break free. He worked his way out of one boot, then the other, only to have his baggy jeans tangle around his knees. He tried to cry out and got a mouthful of water for his trouble. Choking and thrashing about, he opened his eyes and saw a glimmer of light up above. He'd never get there. It was too far.

Somehow, all the fear and panic washed away in the face of his inevitable demise, and he was able to think again. He stopped his flailing about, slipped out of his jeans, and swam for the surface. Light and blessed air seemed to dangle tantalizingly out of reach as he kicked and paddled with every drop of his remaining energy. He clenched his jaw and fought the impulse to breathe. Just a little farther.

And then he broke the surface and pulled in a loud, rasping breath. Sweet air filled his lungs, and even the overcast England afternoon seemed bright and sunny after the depths of the pond and the darkness of the forest. He struck out for the shore, which was only a few meters away, hauled himself up onto the steep bank, and rolled over onto his back. He was dead tired, but he was alive.

It was only after he'd caught his breath that he remembered why he'd run pell-mell into the water in the first place. What had happened to the things that had been following him? Were they still there?

He rolled over again and looked up to where the sloping bank met the edge of the wood. He saw naught but trees and scrub, and relaxed.

And then a grayish-green snout poked out from the undergrowth. It was only there for a moment, but it was enough. Richard whimpered and scrambled crablike along the shore. He had to get away.

He had gone perhaps ten meters when a high-pitched tone, almost above hearing, rang out. It hung in the air for the span of two heartbeats, and then... nothing.

He looked all around. Had it been a signal of some sort?

And then he raised his head.

Something detached itself from a treetop and drifted down toward him. As it drew closer, he realized just how big the thing was, and were those... wings? He was frozen in place, stupefied by the sight. It couldn't be.

But it was.

And then the world exploded all around him, and he found his voice long enough for one bloodcurdling scream.

Chapter 10

"I'm afraid pumping the water out of the passageway isn't going to work." Charlie looked like he'd been sucking lemons. "We've been at it for hours and the water level hasn't gotten much lower."

"It's not unexpected," Maddock said. "This island is like a sieve."

"Somebody sealed that tunnel up once before, and all they had were primitive tools compared to what we've got. This is crap."

"That was a long time ago, Charlie. New cracks could easily develop over two centuries."

"You're probably right," Charlie agreed. "You know what? Screw the drilling! We're going straight for the chamber and, when we break through, you diver boys can do your stuff."

"We're not certain of the location," Maddock said. "You have our best guess, and that's it."

"I'll take your best guess every day of the week and twice on Sunday. Now, if it was Bones doing the guessing..." Charlie made a face.

Maddock laughed. There were some significant differences between Bones and Charlie, but they both had a long sarcastic streak that he appreciated.

The old man gave him a wink and headed over to give his crew their new instructions.

Maddock checked his watch. It was late afternoon, two days after the discovery of the underground chamber, and progress was stalled. He and the crew had continued surveying the shore, but they hadn't found any more underwater tunnels like this one. One more day and boredom would set in in earnest.

No sooner had the thought crossed his mind than his phone vibrated. It was Avery.

"Maddock, I've got some weird news."

"Okay." What news could she have that would be of interest to him?

"Your father's chest was stolen from the museum."

"Seriously? When?"

"Two nights ago. The same day Rodney was murdered."

Maddock pondered this new development.

"You don't think the two are related, do you? Unless you let Rodney in on what you knew about the chest."

"Of course I didn't tell him anything, but who knows how long he was lurking out of sight that night at the Spinning Crab? He might have heard me telling you about the chests." She lowered her voice to little more than a whisper. *"Rodney was an ass and, frankly, I'm not surprised someone killed him. But he was the kind of guy who gets knifed in a parking lot, not tortured."*

"Tortured?" Alarm bells were going off in Maddock's mind. "What do you mean?"

"I'm not supposed to know this, but one of the deputies is an old friend. They cut off his ears, his fingers, his eyelids. All kinds of crazy stuff you think only happens in horror movies."

"Somebody wanted information."

"Right, and believe me when I tell you, Rodney had no information in that head of his. None."

In spite of the grisly news, Maddock couldn't stifle a grin at Avery's dry sense of humor. Then a thought occurred to him that wiped the grin from his face.

"Do you think he gave them your name?"

"I've been wondering that very thing." Her voice was tight. *"I think they would have come after me by now if he had. At least, that's what I keep telling myself."*

"Is there any place you can go, anyone you can stay with, where you can hide out for a while?" He didn't know why he was bothering with the question. He already knew how this conversation was going to end.

"Maybe." Doubt tinged her voice. *"Classes ended today and I'm not teaching this summer, so I suppose I could leave town, but what if they found me? I'm not a helpless Barbie girl, but I don't think I could do much against professional killers."*

"You can stay with us. Gather what you'll need and I'll send Bones to get you." Maddock wanted to kick himself. Why must he always try to rescue the damsels in distress? He had to admit, he had no romantic interest in Avery, but he felt an odd affinity for her. In the few hours they'd spent together, she'd seemed to really get him, and understand his way of thinking. He liked her and didn't want to see her get hurt.

"I don't want to be any trouble. You guys have work to do and I'm sure Bones doesn't want to chauffeur me around."

"Trust me. The dive work is done for the moment and a bored Bones is an annoying Bones. He'll be happy to get off the island and I'll be glad to not listen to his grumbling."

"All right, then. Thank you."

He had just hung up the phone and was about to go find Bones when two sheriff's department cars pulled up to the work site. Deputies White and Boudreau climbed out of one, while Sheriff Meade, grinning ear to ear, and a tall man in an expensive suit exited the other.

"What the hell is this?" Charlie had noticed their new visitors and had come to stand beside Maddock.

"Charles Bonebrake?" Meade didn't wait for a reply to his question. "I have an order here for you to cease operations and leave the island." He held out a document which Charlie snatched.

"You mind telling me what this is all about?" He scanned the document, his countenance growing darker as he read.

"A man almost lost his life on your job site. The local authorities need to conduct a safety inspection, after which time the Bailyn Museum will be taking over the project."

"The hell they will! I've got a permit!"

"Which has been revoked, effective today." Meade's grin grew predatory, his straight, white teeth gleaming in the sunlight. "I'll need you and all of your equipment off the premises by five o'clock."

"That's impossible," Charlie snapped. "We're in the middle of a job here. It's not that easy just to pick up and walk away."

"It's a thousand dollar a day fine for trespassing."

"Pocket change." Charlie's grin matched that of the sheriff.

"And you'll be arrested for criminal trespass and your equipment impounded." Meade tucked his thumbs into his belt and rocked back on his heels, awaiting Charlie's next protest. Behind him, Boudreau looked pleased and White uncomfortable. The third man's expression was one of polite interest.

"Why is the museum taking over the project, Sheriff?" Maddock knew the truth, that the sheriff blamed him for Rodney's death and this was payback, but he was curious what the excuse would be.

"Indian artifacts have been found on the island. We need qualified researchers to do a complete archaeological survey before any other work can proceed. Since they're going to be doing the survey, it's more expedient for them to follow up on any leads you might have."

"Son, the only Indian artifact on this island is me." Charlie's voice and demeanor were serene, which meant he was already working on a plan. The old man never surrendered, but he knew when to make a strategic retreat.

"On the contrary," Boudreau said. "I found this arrowhead just lying on the ground when I got out of the car." She held up a leaf-shaped, fluted projectile point.

"That's a Folsom point." Maddock hadn't heard Bones approaching. "And it's obsidian, so it's from the American southwest. If you're going to pull a scam, at least try not to make yourself look like an idiot."

Boudreau's face reddened, but she was undeterred.

"In that case, I'm sure the museum will be interested in determining how it got here."

"Oh, I think we all know how it got here," Maddock said.

"We're wasting our time with these ignoramuses," Charlie said. "I'll give my men their marching orders. Bones, you and Maddock tell your fellows to clear out until I take care of things." He stalked away, muttering, "*When I buy somebody, he stays bought.* "

Maddock noticed the man in the suit do a double-take at the mention of his name. Now, the man approached Maddock and offered his hand.

"Dillon Locke. I'm with the Bailyn Museum in New York." The man had a strong grip and he looked Maddock square in the eye as if he were trying to read Maddock's thoughts.

"You're a long way from home, Mister Locke."

Locke laughed. "I'm a bit of a vagabond. New York is home for now, but I fear I'll never lose my accent." His smile faded into an earnest look. "I'm sorry about this, mate. This was all arranged between the local authorities and someone at the museum with a higher pay grade than mine." He shrugged.

"You're not buying this charade, are you?" Bones asked.

"I'm just here to do my job." Locke shrugged. "The arrowhead was absurd, I'll grant you that, but I promise I've no interest in local politics. We'll do our best to continue the good work you've done here." His eyes fell on the drilling apparatus Charlie's crew was already disassembling. "Looks like you're on to something over here."

"A dead end," Maddock lied. "We thought there might be something in this spot, but we were wrong."

"A shame. Sorry if this is an insensitive question, but is there anything at all you can tell me that might guide our search?"

"Give up and go home. There's nothing here but legends." Maddock hoped his words sounded sincere rather than spiteful. True, the museum wasn't at fault, but he wasn't going to give this Locke fellow a bit of help.

"Too bad. Hopefully the museum won't keep me on this wild goose chase for too long." He bade them good day and left.

"If that guy's an academic, I'm a ballerina." Bones glowered at Locke's receding form.

"I don't think you're in danger of having to wear a leotard any time soon," Maddock said. "He's got a military bearing about him, doesn't he?" There was definitely more to Locke than a simple museum employee. "Since we've got some free time on our hands, I think we should see what we can find out about the Bailyn Museum."

Chapter 11

Maddock stretched out on the sofa in the living area of his parents' cottage, feeling the bone-wearying fatigue that had plagued him since the sheriff had shut them down. He hated to think they'd wasted their time, but what did they have to show for their work? One injured crew member and a chamber they hadn't managed to penetrate. He despised failure.

He was tired, but sleep eluded him. There was too much on his mind.

He opened his eyes and rolled over onto his side, and his gaze fell on *The Gold-Bug*. He'd read a few pages, but not gotten very far. Might as well give it another go.

It was the story of a man who had to decipher a cryptogram in order to find a treasure buried by Captain Kidd. It wasn't the best book Maddock had read, but it held his interest to the final page. And what he found there made his heart lurch.

Beneath the words *"The End,"* his father had written another personal message.

"So, what do you say? Are you in?"

After the inscription, an arrow pointed to the edge of the page. The next page was blank, with another arrow, beneath the words

"Keep going!"

He flipped to the back page cover and was disappointed to find it blank. He was about to toss the book on the floor and try and get some sleep when he saw it. The dust jacket was taped to the cover, and peeking out from underneath it was a thin, wax paper envelope, with a yellowed sheet of paper inside.

"Bones!" he shouted, springing to his feet. "Get out here now!"

Seconds later, Bones burst through his bedroom door wearing only a pair of boxer briefs and holding his Glock. Moments later, a bleary-eyed Avery came stumbling out of the bedroom Maddock had given over to her, while Angel, not wearing much more than Bones, scrambled down the stairs that led to the loft where she was bunking.

"What's wrong?" Bones had needed only a glance at Maddock to realize they weren't in danger, and had lowered his pistol.

"What's wrong is, I'm an idiot. Look!" He held out the book for Bones to see what he'd found.

Bones whistled.

"What is it?" Angel was pressed up against him, one hand resting lightly on his shoulder. Maddock's eyes drifted to her taut stomach that her tank top didn't quite cover, and quickly tore his gaze away, cursing himself for ogling his best friend's sister. He glanced up to see if Bones had noticed, but Bones was checking Avery out, and making little effort to hide it.

"I think it's whatever was hidden inside the sea chest. My dad left a note in this book inviting me to help him search for a treasure." Under any other circumstance, he would have felt a lump in his throat and found it difficult to continue, but excitement and a measure of discomfort at Angel's closeness served to distract him. "It was supposed to be a Christmas gift, but he never got the chance to give it to me."

"He wanted *you* to help him find the treasure?" Avery's voice held an odd note he couldn't quite define.

"I'm his son, and treasure hunting is what I do." He shrugged. "Anyway, everybody grab a chair and let's check this thing out."

"I'm just glad you woke me for a good reason," Bones said. "I was dreaming about a Victoria's Secret model."

"Which one?" Avery asked.

"I don't know. They all look alike to me."

With the utmost care, Maddock worked the envelope free of the tape that bound it to the book cover, and removed its contents. There were two items inside: a sheet of stationery covered in symbols, and another sheet, folded, yellowed with age.

"Want me to do that?" Avery spoke in hushed, reverential tones. "I have experience with old documents."

"Sure. Have at it." Maddock slid it over to her.

"Give me a moment." She hurried into her room and returned with a pair of latex gloves. "I was going to color my hair," she explained. Maddock didn't miss the way her eyes flitted toward Bones and her cheeks reddened a touch. "This is more important."

A silence borne of anticipation fell as they watched Avery go about her delicate task. When the sheet was finally spread out before them, they all broke out in grins.

"It's the island," Bones said.

It was an aged map of Oak Island, rendered in exquisite detail. It alone would have been an exciting find, but there was more.

"X marks the spot." Angel gave Maddock's arm a squeeze. "That's the place you and Matt found, isn't it?"

"Looks like it," Maddock said. "We can't say for sure, since it's probably not to perfect scale, but I think it's the same place."

"And check this out! There's a way in." Bones indicated a dotted line leading from a different location on the island to the chamber.

"It starts on land, so it's unlikely to be an underwater channel," Maddock mused. "Unless it's become flooded over the years. That's a possibility."

"I know where this is!" Avery exclaimed. "I can lead you right to it. If the sheriff will let us back on the island, that is."

"That's not going to happen," Maddock said. "He said he's going to arrest anyone who wasn't gone by the end of the day. No way he lets us come back."

"What are we going to do?" Avery was on her feet, fists clenched. "We have to get to that secret passage before Locke drills into the chamber. That won't be long!"

"Chill," Angel said. "You forget who we've got on our side."

"She's right." Bones rocked back in his chair, hands folded behind his head. "Maddock and I are experts getting into places we're not invited."

"Only because you were never invited to any parties in high school," Angel jibed.

Bones' obscene gesture was half-hearted at best. He loved the adrenaline rush of anything dangerous, and was clearly focused on finding a way onto the island. "You've got to figure he'll have deputies guarding the road that leads to the island, and, maybe, a boat patrolling the coast, though I doubt it. He thinks he's beaten us, so he'll probably be lax."

"Don't count on it. His ego is huge, but he doesn't miss a detail. We'd better plan on two boats, and a patrol on the island as well." Avery cupped her chin and narrowed her eyes as she stared at the map. "We'll have to go in at night without lights or a motor. Kayaks?"

"You've got a good head for this sort of thing," Bones said. He gave Avery an admiring smile and she blushed.

"I love kayaking!" Angel exclaimed. "Let's rock this!"

"Hold on." Maddock held up his hands. "Avery's right about going in at night, but any kind of boat is too risky. Besides, I want to do this tonight. Bones and I will swim it."

"No!" Avery shouted and sprang to her feet. "You can't do that."

"We're pros," Bones said. "We've done the same thing hundreds of times, and trust me, the stakes were much higher. Worst that can happen here is we get arrested and Charlie bails us out."

"I need to go too." Avery clenched her fists until her knuckles were white. "I have to show you the way in."

"I'm sure you can tell us all we need to know ahead of time," Maddock said. "Show us on the satellite images."

"It's cool, Avery. We've got this." Bones reached out to take her hand but she snatched it away.

"This is my project. I'm the expert. Besides, I've done plenty of diving. I can handle it."

"You wouldn't be able to keep up if we ran into trouble," Maddock said. "Look, I've been on plenty of treasure hunts and I know how you're feeling." Avery shook her head and, too late, Maddock remembered that a man should never tell a woman that he knew how she felt. "If the circumstances were different, I'd have you right there with us, but this is just one of those times when it needs to be me and Bones. Only me and Bones." He said this last to Angel, who made a pouting face that sent a shiver down his spine. He looked back at Avery, trying to ignore how warm he suddenly felt. "I'm sorry, but this is the way it has to be."

"Besides," Angel said to Avery, "this is Maddock's treasure hunt. His father left it for him."

"You don't understand," Avery whispered as a solitary tear trickled down her face. "He was my father too."

Chapter 12

Maddock sat, dumbfounded, gazing up at Avery, who seemed almost as shocked by her words as he was.

"I'm sorry," she mumbled. "I've been trying to figure out a way to tell you. This wasn't how I wanted to do it."

Maddock looked from Angel, who was likewise speechless, to Bones, who frowned, and then his face split into a broad grin.

"I can totally see it!" He pounded his fist on the table, threw back his head, and laughed. "The hair, the eyes, the thing you both do when you're thinking hard. I should have figured it out."

"How is it possible?" Angel asked.

"Our father," Avery said, settling back into her chair and studiously avoiding Maddock's gaze, "spent a lot of time here. Sometimes he was with his wife, but other times he came alone. He and my mother had a fling; two ships passing in the night and all that. They didn't carry on any sort of long-term affair, but he sent money every month and made sure I had everything I needed. He even helped me with college." Her eyes grew moist. "Once every summer, he would spend a few days with me. We'd always do something related to his pirate research. I suppose that's why I chose the career path I did."

"So, this is more than an academic pursuit," Angel said. "This is personal."

Avery nodded.

"Say something, Maddock," Bones urged.

"Sorry, I'm just shocked. I never..." He trailed off, lost in dark thoughts. He'd never dreamed his father would lead a double life.

"Let's leave these two alone," Bones said to Angel. "I think they've got some talking to do." He rose from his seat and headed out the back door onto the deck. Angel gave Maddock an encouraging smile and followed her brother out the door.

"I'm not lying," Avery said after a lengthy silence. "I'll even take a DNA test if you want me to."

"I don't guess I want that," Maddock said. "Bones is right. It's kind of obvious once you know what to look for. How long have you known about me?"

"All my life. I don't mind telling you I've hated your guts for as long as I can remember. You got my dad fifty-one weeks out of the year. I got the leftovers. And now, after all the times he and I spent researching Kidd's treasure, I find out it was you he wanted to share it with." Her tears flowed freely now, but her eyes shone with resentment.

Maddock nodded, unable to summon any words of comfort. He couldn't blame her for feeling like she did.

"So, how do you feel about me now? Still hate me?"

"I haven't made up my mind yet." Avery managed a tiny laugh. "You're bossy as hell and you don't listen to anyone but Bones. That much I've already figured out."

"I'm not bossy, I'm decisive." He grinned. "And I do listen, it's just that everybody else is wrong most of the time."

"We really are an awful lot alike. Creepy." Avery wiped her eyes with the back of her hand. "So, what else do we have in common? Are you as unlucky with the ladies as I am with the guys?"

"Maybe." Before he realized what he was doing, he was telling her about his wife, Melissa, and her tragic death, a subject he studiously avoided even after all these years. Then it was on to his ex-girlfriend, Kaylin, and, finally, his current sometimes-girlfriend, Jade. "Things just aren't working out between us. Sometimes I think Jade and I are too much alike, you know?"

"I've got to hand it to you, Maddock. I never suspected you had that many words in your vocabulary, much less that you were the kind of guy who would talk relationships for ten minutes straight." She reached out, tentatively, and took his hand. It was a good feeling: companionable and comforting.

"That's the longest I've ever talked to anybody about relationship crap," he said, knowing he sounded a bit too much like Bones. "Is this typical sibling conversation?"

"Don't ask me. I'm new at this, too. Are we good?"

"Yeah," he said after a long pause. "I think we are. It's still weird, though."

"Totally," she agreed, slipping her hand from his grasp.

"How about we bring the two peeping Toms back inside and let's make a plan for getting to whatever Dad wanted us to find?"

Bones and Angel were making no effort to hide the fact that they were watching Maddock and Avery through the window. When Maddock motioned for them to come inside, they bounded through the door like children headed to recess.

"This is so cool!" Angel said. "Now I have somebody who can understand what I go through with this assclown." She glared at Bones, who feigned innocence and pressed his hands to his heart.

"Time's short. Let's get to work," Maddock said.

"Bossy," Avery said to Angel in a confiding tone. "I just told him about that."

"They don't listen," Angel said in a mock-whisper. "You have to learn how to push their buttons to get what you want. I'll show you." She smiled at Maddock, eyes sparkling, and winked.

Once again, he found himself feeling uncomfortably warm, and hurried on.

"It's going to be me and Bones going in. You get it, right?"

Avery gave a grudging nod.

"What can you tell us about this spot on the map?" Maddock asked.

"We'll have to compare it against contemporary maps and photos." She couldn't hide her guilty expression. "I lied. I have no idea what spot on the island this correlates to."

Maddock buried his face in his hands. "Why me?"

"Just kidding. I know exactly what this spot is."

Bones and Angel burst out laughing and Angel high-fived Avery.

"Fine," Maddock sighed. "Fill us in."

"The spot here is in the swamp." She pointed to the mark that denoted what they presumed was the entrance to the passage. The swamp was a triangular body of water that virtually cut the island in two.

"I thought the swamp had been investigated and dismissed as a possibility," Maddock said.

"Sort of. Back when portions of the island were privately owned, someone tried to drain it. As the water receded, he found what looked like a wooden shaft rising up out of the water, but when they investigated it further, it turned out to only be a few feet deep. He gave up his efforts to drain it any further. After that, there were disputes over the swamp between the different people and groups who owned parts of the island. Eventually, the government took control and, since then, the swamp has been ignored."

"Do you think this map is pointing to that shaft?" Bones asked. "If we have to dig, there's no way."

"It's not. Look here." She pointed in turn to six circles. "These indicate the locations of huge granite stones that form what we call the Oak Island Cross. The width of the cross," finger hovering millimeters above the aged map, she traced the line, "is 720 feet, with the center stone perfectly centered. The distance from the center stone to the bottom of the cross is also 720 feet, and 360 to the top. Everything is perfectly proportioned except for this one." She pointed to a circle between the middle and bottom stones.

"That's the entrance," Angel whispered.

"This stone ought to be halfway between the center and bottom stones, but it isn't. Researchers have always wondered why it alone is disproportionately spaced. Now we know." Avery looked around the table, her expression triumphant.

"Is it in the swamp?" Bones asked, leaning down for a closer look.

"It juts out into the water," Avery said. "I'll bet there's a hidden passage underneath it."

"What if the stone is covering the passage? They'll never be able to move it." Angel pursed her lips and tugged at her earlobe. It was one of her little habits that made Maddock smile.

"I guess we'll find out." Maddock's eyes drifted to the bottom right corner of the page. "What are these symbols?" A tiny block of glyphs, triangles, circles, squares, some incomplete or slashed through with diagonal lines, had escaped their notice.

"They look like the same glyphs that can be found on the stone that was discovered in the pit back in the 1800s." Avery gave the symbols a long, appraising look. "This uses some of the same symbols, but it's a different message entirely. No wonder no one has ever been able to make sense of it!" She sprang from her seat and hurried into her bedroom, returning shortly with a battered briefcase.

Maddock's eyes widened when he saw the case. "I remember that." It had belonged to his father. Maddock could recall being surprised when Hunter Maddock had returned from one of his research trips with a shiny, new briefcase instead of his beloved old one.

"Dad always had this with him whenever he visited," Avery explained. "When I was little I used to like to play with the clasps. As I got older, I guess I came to associate it with the good times we had together. He gave it to me on my sixteenth birthday. I hope it doesn't make you feel weird."

"It's cool. He told me the airline lost it. I'm glad it's still around."

"Anyway," Avery said, opening the case and extracting a folder, "here are some possible translations of the original stone. Maybe they can help us figure it out."

"What about this?" Angel held up the other paper that had been in the envelope. "It's got a bunch of those weird symbols plus a code." She flipped the paper around for the others to see.

"That looks like the cipher in *The Gold-Bug*," Maddock said, reaching for the book that lay forgotten on the table. He flipped to the pertinent page and turned it around for the others to see.

"No way!" Avery's eyes grew wide. "Do you think Dad translated the runes, and then encrypted them?"

"Definitely." Maddock was certain of it. "He would have thought it added to the fun and made it more secure in case the wrong person stumbled across it. Besides, to the average person, it looks like a long math problem."

"Do either of you know how to break this code?" Bones asked. "Because I hated Calculus."

"I'll bet there are plenty of *Gold-Bug* decryption sites online," Avery said. "Bones, want to grab my laptop?"

"Only if you sit on my lap top." Bones had scarcely gotten the words out when Angel hit him over the head with *The Gold-Bug*.

"Get the computer, you creep."

Ten minutes later, they had their translation. "Shaft south," Bones read. "Tunnel divides. Lower shaft. Third tunnel north. Upper shaft."

"What do you make of it?" Angel asked.

"I think there are a maze of tunnels in this part of the island," Maddock said, "and these are directions for navigating them." He looked up at Bones. "You up for a swim?"

Bones grinned. "Let's do it."

Chapter 13

"That doesn't look like a deputy to me." Bones kept his voice so low that

Maddock could scarcely hear him over the gentle ebb and flow of the surf. They were a scant twenty yards from shore, floating in the dark waters of the bay under a moonless sky.

"You're right," Maddock agreed. The causeway leading to the island had indeed been guarded by the sheriff's department- White and Boudreau to be exact, and they'd swum unseen past a patrol boat anchored offshore. He imagined another boat guarded the island's far side. But the man who stalked the shore of Oak Island was nothing like the deputies. He was tall, lean, and prowled the coastline like a predator on the hunt, his eyes taking in everything around him. Despite the quiet night and calm surroundings, he was clearly on alert.

"Let's slip right past him. You know, a little SEAL-style stealth for old time's sake," Bones said.

"Maybe, but we'll give him a minute and see if he moves on."

They watched as the man continued on his way, eventually disappearing around a bend. Maddock and Bones didn't wait, but swam for the shore, their powerful kicks driving them through the water like torpedoes locked onto their target. They hit the shallows, slipped their fins off and tucked them into dive bags- they'd need them again soon.

There was no need to speak. They'd done this so many times Maddock had lost count. His eyes took in everything to the east, while Bones scanned the island to the west. At first glance, all appeared clear, but then the smallest of glimmers caught his attention. The scant starlight flashed off a badge as Sheriff Meade himself strode out of the forest.

Maddock needed only to incline his head a fraction of an inch to indicate the man's presence. Bones scowled and nodded once. Moving as one, they submerged and worked their way along the coastline, moving in the opposite direction.

They emerged in a pool of darkness on the rocky beach a stone's throw from the swamp. Meade had positioned himself on the sea wall that separated the swamp from the beach. The sheriff stood with his thumbs in his belt, gazing out at his patrol boat.

Maddock led the way, creeping wraith-like through the deepest shadows and noiselessly moving through the undergrowth that surrounded the swamp. He paused when he reached the edge of the brackish water. Here they would have to cover ten feet of open ground before reaching the swamp. He glanced at Meade, who had not moved, and then back to Bones. It was unlikely the sheriff would spot them, but Meade just might be mad enough to take a shot at them.

Bones held up a fist, thrust his chin in Meade's direction, and gave Maddock a quizzical look. The question was clear- *Want me to knock him out?*

Maddock shook his head. He wanted to slip in and out with no one the wiser. If they harmed the sheriff, the finger would point either to them or to Charlie and his crew. They didn't need that. Besides, this way was more fun.

After slipping back into his fins, Maddock stretched out on the ground and slithered forward, keeping his eyes on Meade, who shifted his weight, but continued to gaze out at the bay. He aligned himself with the stone that marked their destination, and entered the swamp. The water, warm after the chill of the bay and the night air, enveloped him as he vanished into its dark depths. Visibility was almost zero, but he navigated the tangle and muck with ease. Finally, he arrived at the stone, Bones sliding up beside him.

Now would be the most precarious stage of the operation. They didn't know what they might find when they surfaced. For all Maddock knew, someone might be standing above them when they emerged from the water. Also, they'd need light to inspect the area around the stone.

Slowly, like a sodden log drifting upward, Maddock rose up until his mask broke the surface of the water. He immediately looked for Meade, and felt the shock of cold surprise to see the sheriff facing them. Reflexively, he reached for his Recon knife, not that it would do any good at this distance, but, as his fingers closed on the handle, Meade turned away again.

The sheriff unhooked his radio and spoke into it.

"You boys awake out there?" So the boat crew *was* on his mind. Maddock couldn't make out the garbled reply, but it must have been a question or a complaint, because Meade barked out a sharp retort. "It doesn't matter if you haven't seen anything. We're keeping this place sealed tight."

As the sheriff continued his tirade, Maddock seized the opportunity to turn on his waterproof flashlight and sink down beneath the water at the place where the stone vanished beneath the surface.

He saw nothing but mud.

Unwilling to give up, he scrubbed at the silt, stirring up a muddy cloud. He was about to give up when his fingertips scraped on coarse rock. He kept working until he had uncovered a stone, two feet square, with a cross carved in its surface. Remembering Matt's accident, he inspected it closely. Unlike the seal on the booby-trapped opening he and Matt had found, this cross was sunk deeper in the stone and was wider on the inside than at the surface. It was like it was made to grip.

He considered for a moment. He was convinced this stone had to be removed in order to gain access to the passage shown on the map. But what if it was another trap? Somehow, he didn't think so. This passage was marked on the map while the other was not, thus indicating that this one was the way in. The directions telling them which passages to take were likely the safeguard on this end. He'd have to take a chance.

Maddock had taken hold of the stone with both hands when Bones, who was keeping watch, grabbed him by the shoulder. He raised his head out of the water and looked around. Meade was still talking on his radio, but someone else was approaching. It looked like the same man they'd seen patrolling earlier.

They'd have to hurry. Meade might be useless as a guard but Maddock felt certain the other guy was of a higher caliber. Speaking in the lowest tone possible, he gave Bones a hasty set of instructions, and the two of them sank beneath the surface, took hold of the stone, and pulled.

It did not budge.

Maddock surfaced and stole a glance back toward shore. Meade had spotted the approaching figure and was walking in his direction. Neither had spotted the intruders in the swamp.

Submerging again, he made a corkscrewing gesture, indicating they should add a counterclockwise turn this time. They tried again, pouring all their strength into the effort. Maddock felt the burn from his hands all the way to the base of his neck as he strained against the rock. Finally, as if something had broken free, the stone rotated a smooth quarter turn and stopped with a hard knock of stone on stone. In the silence, it sounded like an explosion, and he dared another look above the surface.

"Fisher," Meade greeted the approaching man. "Quiet night?"

"So far," Fisher replied in an accent twin to Locke's. "Of course, anyone could have slipped past while you were waffling on with your mates out there and we'd never have heard."

Meade started to say something but, just then, a burst of sound that Maddock recognized as a drill filled the air. Locke and his crew were already trying to break through to the chamber. On the positive side of the ledger, the noise should cover any sound they might make removing the stone.

He and Bones set to the task, and worked the stone free of its socket just as the sounds of drilling ceased. This time there was no whooshing sound, as the passageway they had uncovered was already filled with water. They lay the stone aside and Bones forged ahead. Maddock was just about to follow when a glimmer of light up above caught his eye. Someone was playing a flashlight across the surface of the water directly above him! The mud and debris they'd stirred up made it impossible for anyone to see him, but it would be obvious, even to as dim a bulb as Meade, that something or someone was down here. And when they investigated, they'd find the underwater passageway.

The thought had just occurred to him when a bullet sliced through the water inches from his face. These guys weren't messing around. Adrenaline surging through him, he plunged into the passageway, wondering what they would find, and how they would get out again.

What the bloody hell is going on here?" Locke called as he trotted up to the shore of the swamp. Sheriff Meade leaned against one of the boulders that formed the so-called Oak Island Cross, staring down at Fisher, who was waist deep in the water, shining his light all around. "I heard a shot. Who fired?"

"It was your man here," Meade said. "I don't know how you do things at your *museum*, but we don't take pot shots at everything that moves."

In the reflected light of Fisher's torch, Locke could see the sheriff's scornful sneer.

"Remind me to put up a sign reading *Trespassers Will Be Shot On Sight*," Locke said. "Because that is precisely what will happen to anyone who invades my work site."

"I'm the law around here, not you people." Meade's back was ramrod straight and his voice trembled with anger. "I don't care who you've bribed. I will take you to jail."

"Of course you will." Locke gave the man a tight smile and turned to Fisher. "What concerns me is, in shooting at a muddy swirl and not a target, you might have alerted potential intruders that they have been spotted."

"Nobody came out of the water," Meade said. "It was probably a beaver."

"A beaver." Locke could not keep the sarcasm from his voice. "As a professional law enforcement officer, that is your assessment of this situation?"

Meade grimaced but had no reply. Just then, Fisher called out.

"I've found something. Hold my torch." He handed the light to Meade, who shone it where Fisher indicated. Fisher took a deep breath and vanished beneath the dark surface, emerging ten seconds later clutching something to his chest. He staggered to the bank and set the object on the ground and Meade turned the beam of the torch onto it.

The circle of light revealed a stone disc with a Templar cross adorning its surface.

"God in heaven," Locke whispered. "Someone has found it!" He produced his own torch and shone it on the boulder, where his sharp eyes immediately caught something Fisher and Meade had not noticed. "There's an outflow of clear water coming up from underneath the stone. See what's there."

Fisher swam for the stone, vanished from sight, and resurfaced moments later.

"There's an underwater tunnel down there," he sputtered, water streaming down his face.

"You're certain it's a tunnel, not a chamber?"

"I think so," Fisher gasped. "I couldn't see well, mind you, but it looked like a long, narrow tunnel."

"Good. I want divers down there immediately." He rested his hand on the grip of his Browning HP Mark III. Meade noticed and frowned. "Sheriff, please put your people on high alert and resume your patrol. I will see to things here."

Meade didn't bother to argue. He returned Fisher's torch, unhooked his radio from his belt, and walked away, barking orders as he went.

Locke gazed down at the Templar symbol. Finally, after centuries of searching, they were close, and no intruder was going to stand in the way...

...or live through this night.

Chapter 14

The darkness in the underwater passage was absolute, and Maddock moved forward cautiously, keeping one hand on either side of the tunnel. He wasn't worried about running into anything in front of him; Bones would encounter any obstacle before Maddock did.

He estimated he'd gone twenty feet when a light blinked on in front of him. Now that they were well away from the entrance, Bones had turned on his dive light. Maddock followed suit, revealing a tunnel identical to the others they'd surveyed.

He caught up with Bones and they swam side by side, following the passageway as it curved to the right and angled downward, gradually narrowing. Bones fell back, letting Maddock scout ahead. Just as the way was growing uncomfortably tight, they came to place where the main shaft continued forward, while a wide passageway branched off to the left and another, much narrower, broke off to the right. The first direction in the map had been "shaft south." Maddock checked the compass on his dive watch, and confirmed that the tunnel to the right would take them south.

This passageway, though narrower than he would have liked, was straight and its walls worn smooth, and they made good time as they penetrated its depths.

Maddock's confidence in the map's directions grew as they came to a divide. One shaft led up and to the left, the other almost straight down.

Tunnel divides. Lower shaft, he thought as he took the lower passage. This tunnel corkscrewed at a dizzying rate before angling back up again. Now thoroughly confused, he checked his compass and confirmed they were once again heading east.

The first tunnel they passed branched off to their right, leading south. The next clue was *"third tunnel north,"* so they kept moving. It was odd, as the chamber they sought lay somewhere to the south. Maddock was suddenly grateful they hadn't stumbled across the entrance to this chamber on their own. Without the directions, they'd be lost, and who knew if more booby traps could be found in some of the other shafts?

Soon they came upon three tunnels in a row on the north side of the passageway, and Maddock halted. Now they had a problem. Did the directions mean "take the third north-facing tunnel," or did they mean "at the third tunnel, go north?" He looked at Bones, who shrugged, then pantomimed a coin toss. Maddock grinned, motioned for Bones to stay back, turned, and moved to the third tunnel.

He inched forward, looking for anything that might indicate the presence of a trap. The walls here were irregular, and his light cast deep shadows on the pitted ceiling. He drifted forward, fingertips touching the bottom in case he had to arrest his forward motion on short notice.

He had gone no more than ten feet when he caught sight of a row of dark, jagged rocks looming up above like the teeth of a giant shark. The beam of his light flashed across them and he realized they were not stone at all, but rusted iron points like spear heads. He grabbed onto the nearest outcroppings and pushed, trying to shove himself out from under the spikes.

One of his handholds was solid, but the other gave way, rotating forward with an audible clack. He yanked his hands back and twisted as the iron spikes crashed down. One grazed his forearm, tearing his suit and slicing through flesh. He was scarcely aware of the pain. Instead, he was imagining what would have happened had he been even a moment slower in getting out of the way. Being pinned to the bottom of the tunnel for eternity was not his idea of fun.

He felt a hand on his ankle and looked back to see Bones behind him. He gave his friend a thumbs up and crooked his finger toward the second tunnel; the one he'd passed up. Bones nodded and retreated from the passageway.

Maddock was about to follow when he had an idea. He took hold of the lever he had first mistaken for a stone, and pulled back on it. With a hollow grinding sound, the spikes slowly retracted into the ceiling. No need to narrow the choices for anyone who might follow behind.

The other tunnel, the one he'd bypassed, looped around and led south. This, Maddock's instincts told him, was the direction in which the passage lay. Minutes later, they emerged in an underground cavern. As they shone their lights around, his heart lurched.

This was no simple underwater cave- it was a chamber of some sort. The walls on either side were carved with scenes of knights in action, and the vaulted ceiling was supported by ornate columns. Maddock had the feeling he'd seen carvings like this before, or, at least, carvings much like these.

Against the opposite wall, three steps led up to a small altar, behind which, six crosses in circles formed a larger cross on the wall itself.

Bones tapped him on the arm and directed his attention to the center of the floor. Bones' light illuminated a great seal, ten feet across, showing a temple and encircled by the words *"Cristi de Templo."* Now he understood.

The seal was one of the ancient symbols of the Knights Templar!

Bones shook his head, and Maddock knew what his friend was trying to say: *No freaking way!*

Maddock had to agree. He and Bones took out their digital underwater cameras and quickly took pictures of this strange room. As he worked, Maddock could not help but wonder what was the purpose of this place? It was reminiscent of a traditional Templar church. Had it been a center of worship which had to be abandoned when it flooded? But that didn't make sense. There was no evidence that the Templars had ever lived here. Why build a church on the other side of the Atlantic? And how did the Money Pit fit in?

And then it hit him. There was another direction they had yet to follow.

Upper shaft.

Amazing as it was, this chamber was not the end of the journey. But there were no shafts leading out, save for the one through which they'd entered. Where to go now? Beneath the seal? That wouldn't make sense.

He took another look around, searching for a clue. He looked at the walls, the columns, the altar, the cross...

The cross!

The circles that formed it were very much like the stone seal that blocked the entrance to the secret passageway. Furthermore, it was laid out in exactly the same proportions as the Oak Island Cross! He signaled for Bones to follow and swam to the uppermost circle.

Bones clearly understood what Maddock was thinking because he immediately set his fingers into the grooved edge of the cross and turned. The circle spun but, this time, did not come free. Instead, it rolled sideways into the wall, revealing a dark tunnel beyond.

Maddock and Bones exchanged glances. He imagined they were thinking the same thing. *What if it closes behind us... or on us?* Nothing they could do about it. He shrugged and entered the tunnel.

There was no sign of them. Fisher cursed the minutes they had wasted getting prepped for the dive. Worse was Locke's ire at Fisher letting someone slip past him and into the swamp. He knew it would do no good to point out that the sheriff had been guarding the swamp, with more of his own people anchored just offshore, so he held his tongue. The only thing that would make this right would be for him to find the intruder, or intruders, and take care of the situation.

He held his pneumatic speargun at the ready. Thirty centimeters long, it could be carried in a holster and fired double-barbed steel shafts with deadly power and accuracy at short range. It could not be purchased on the open market, for it was not made for fishing, but for killing. He swam with reckless abandon, eager to put his weapon to good use. Behind him, Baxter, Penn, and Hartley followed, all armed and ready.

They came to a place where the tunnel split into three. He made a quick signal and the divers fanned out. Hartley shot up the left passage. He was, perhaps, the most enthusiastic of their group. He was always spouting his theory that Francis Bacon was the true author of Shakespeare's plays, and the proof lay hidden beneath Oak Island. Baxter, a tall, lean fellow, took the narrow shaft in front of them, and Penn took the one on the right.

Hartley was the first to return, shaking his head and making a dismissive gesture.

Fisher grimaced. One dead end.

No sooner had the thought crossed his mind than a dull rumble sounded from the passage in front of them, and a cloud of debris spewed forth. Fisher didn't need to look in order to know what happened, but he had be sure.

Twenty meters down, the tunnel ended in a heap of rubble. Only Baxter's foot, swim fin dangling from it, jutted out. Fisher reached out and gave the foot a squeeze, but no response. Baxter was gone. His mood grew blacker at the loss of a good fighter, even if the man did crap on a bit too much about how much he loved Russell Crowe movies.

Retreating from the cave-in, he and Hartley took the tunnel Penn had scouted. They caught up with her at another split. Here, one tunnel went up, the other down. Hartley took the upper passageway, this time with a touch more caution after Baxter's accident. Penn took a similar approach to the lower tunnel.

Seconds stretched into eternity as Fisher fretted over their slow progress. And what if their quarry had gone down the passageway that was now caved in? What if they found a way out on the other side? He was just ruminating on this new, unhappy thought, when he heard a sound like a bowling ball rolling down the lane. The sound grew louder and, with a thud, a massive stone ball lodged in the entrance of the passage Hartley had taken. Fisher tried with all his might to dislodge it, but the rock held fast. He thought of Hartley trapped in the tunnel, and hoped there was a way out on the other side.

His heart beat like a snare drum and the blood coursing through his veins set up a roar like a hurricane in his ears. Now he knew the truth. What happened to Baxter had not been an accident. This place was a death trap, and he had no choice but to try and make it through.

Once again, he followed behind Penn. The woman was a zealot, perhaps a bit too blindly devoted to Morgan, though he'd never say that aloud, but she either had good instincts, or was very lucky. Perhaps her good fortune would help them carry the day.

This passageway took him round in a descending series of circles before ending at a juncture where a single tunnel broke to the right. He frowned. Penn should have stopped here and waited for him, but she was nowhere to be seen. He decided to continue along the main tunnel a little farther, eyes peeled for traps. A bit farther down, he came upon a series of shafts leading off from the main tunnel. No sign of Penn. He was about to go back and investigate the first tunnel he'd passed when something caught his eye- a trickle of something dark drifting out of the last shaft. Heart sinking, he went to investigate. Two meters down the shaft, he found Penn.

She lay pinned on the floor by thick iron spikes. Her arms and legs were contorted in a grotesque tableau. She had lost her mask, and her eyes stared blankly upward, her face frozen in a mask of agony.

A black rage descended on Fisher. He no longer cared for booby traps, treasure, or Locke's wrath. He wanted revenge.

This tunnel opened into a smaller chamber, circular, like a turret. A double line of repeated symbols spiraled down from the peak of the domed ceiling, where an odd, wedge-shaped pattern was carved, running all the way down to the floor. The seal at the center of this room showed two knights riding a single horse- another Templar seal. To their left was the trap that had injured Matt's arm. To their right stood another stone altar, but this one was not empty.

A wooden casket, two feet long, sat atop the altar. As Maddock swam closer, he could see it was coated with some sort of resin that gave it a glossy sheen and had protected it from who knew how many years of immersion. Like many ancient caskets, it was shaped like a split log: wide and flat at the bottom, rounded on the top half. Its hinged lid appeared to be sealed with lead.

Maddock reached out and gently took hold of it, fearing all the while that the wood would crumble at his touch. It did not. Emboldened, he lifted it. It was deceptively heavy. Either the casket was lined with lead, its contents were extremely heavy, or both.

Despite the dim light and the dive mask, he could see excitement shining in Bones' eyes. They were about to solve the riddle of Oak Island. He put the casket in a mesh bag and hooked it to his belt as an added precaution, though he'd have to carry it. Now, to get out of here unseen and unscathed.

He turned to make for the exit tunnel, hoping it had not closed behind them, when a beam of light sliced through the water. Someone had caught up with them.

Chapter 15

Maddock and Bones drew their Recon knives, extinguished their dive lights, and moved to either side of the passageway that led back to the underground church. Any small ember of hope that the unseen person did not know they were there was doused when something silver flashed through the water and embedded in the limestone wall. Whoever was out there had a spear gun.

Their only hope was to take their pursuer unaware as he entered the chamber. Of course, they'd need to be quick and luck would have to be on their side. The intruder's dive light cast a faint glow- just enough that Maddock could see Bones swim to a spot above the passageway and cling to the wall Spider-Man style. Good thinking. Their adversary was likely to look to the sides and down before looking up; an instinct honed by life outside the water.

They waited in near-darkness and absolute silence. Energy coursed through Maddock, every nerve on edge. It was amazing how alive he felt when possible death was near. Danger brought everything into focus.

Seconds passed, then minutes. Nothing. The guy was waiting for them to make a move, and who could blame him? He had the projectile weapon and the full length of the tunnel to take shots at them. It would be like a carnival game to him- Maddock and Bones were sitting ducks.

Maddock glanced up at Bones who shook his head and tapped his pressure gauge. Their supply of air was limited. Right now they had sufficient reserves, but it wouldn't last forever, and only a fool let his tank get close to empty. They were screwed.

He racked his brain for a possible solution. Going down the tunnel was out of the question unless they had something they could use as a shield, which they did not. He wondered if the top of the altar would work, but dismissed the thought immediately. He couldn't get anywhere close to it without placing himself in the line of fire. Besides, it wasn't wide enough to provide suitable cover. What they needed was a way out.

And then he remembered the booby-trapped shaft he and Matt had discovered. If they could get through, they could make their way out to the shore, and to open water. He swam to the blocked shaft, turned on his light, and inspected the space closely.

The shaft was three feet square and sealed off by a solid stone block. He already knew it couldn't be pried up, but he remembered the iron spike trap they'd encountered and the lever that sprang and released it. Besides, he had to believe that whoever constructed this chamber would have left themselves a secondary exit in the event that the tunnel leading to the temple collapsed.

The ornate bands carved in the wall angled past on either side of the shaft. Maddock gave them a close look, all the while wondering when their stalker would show up and start shooting. He pressed on anything that resembled a button, but to no avail. And then his hand passed over a carving of a chalice. This particular image was raised farther than those surrounding it, and the top of the cup was scooped out. Maddock hooked his fingers inside and pulled.

The chalice tilted forward and, with a scraping sound made to seem all the louder by the silence in the chamber, the stone block rose.

He signaled to Bones, who swam over. Maddock released the chalice and the stone remained in place. But would they trigger the trap again by swimming through? He inspected the shaft, searching for anything that would spring the trap, but he saw nothing.

Without warning, the block fell again with a resounding crash. Bones held up ten fingers and shrugged. *Ten seconds?* Keeping one eye out for the man with the speargun, Maddock pulled the lever again and watched the stone rise. He counted down and, twelve seconds later, the trap sprang.

So that was the trick. You could open the trap from the inside, but you had twelve seconds to make it through. The shaft was only a couple of feet. They could do it.

Just then, the light in the tunnel winked out, followed an instant later by the plink of another spear against the wall. Their pursuer's patience was at an end. He was coming for them.

Bones brandished his knife and made to swim for the tunnel to meet the attack, but Maddock grabbed him by the arm. Bones understood the reason a moment later when another projectile sliced through the water. The man wasn't taking any chances.

Maddock pointed to Bones, then to the tunnel as he yanked down on the lever. Bones knew him well enough not to argue, but dove through before the stone came crashing down.

Time was almost up. Maddock turned out his light, plunging the chamber into inky darkness. He pulled the lever and, relying on instinct and sense of direction, shoved the casket through the shaft as the stone was still rising.

A light blinked on behind him and another spear whizzed inches past his face. He knew it would take the man a few seconds to reload, but he was already on his way through. He felt Bones take hold of his arm and yank him through as the trap fell again. Something yanked at his foot as he tried to swim down the tunnel. For a moment, he thought his foot was trapped, but then he realized his fin was caught. He wasted no time working his foot free and swimming down the passage with the speed and grace of a one-legged frog. Bones, carrying the casket, was well ahead of him.

Maddock figured it was only a matter of time before the lever that released the trap was discovered, but their enemies would be waiting for them to emerge in the swamp, not on the shore. He hoped.

A small circle of light swam into view overhead. This was the spot where Charlie's crew had tried to pump the water out of the tunnel. Charlie's crew! They had sealed up the end of the tunnel before beginning the pumping. He and Bones had almost found themselves in a dead end.

He flicked his light on and off to get Bones' attention, and pointed to the opening. It was their only option. Bones stared for a moment, then seemed to catch up with Maddock's train of thought.

Maddock went first, wondering what he'd find waiting when he stuck his head out of the hole. He treaded water, listening for any sound that would warn of danger, but he heard nothing, not even the rattle of the drill. Locke's crew must have stopped working when they became aware of his and Bones' presence. Figuring there was no time like the present, he hauled himself out onto solid ground.

No one was about. Breathing a sigh of relief, he helped Bones out of the hole and, breathing the sweet, night air, they crept into the trees, moving away from the work site and the swamp.

On the north side of the island, they hid in the shadows beneath an ancient oak tree and assessed the situation before hitting the water. By the time they came ashore more than a mile away from the island, they were both spent.

"It's been a long time since our training days," Bones panted as they made their way to the place, far from shore, where they'd arranged to meet Angel and Avery.

"I can't say I miss the six mile swims," Maddock said. They emerged on a hill overlooking a dirt road. Down below sat Avery's car.

It was empty.

Chapter 16

It took every ounce of Locke's self-control to keep from pacing. He waited at the edge of the swamp, impatience battling with eagerness. More than once he considered putting on dive gear and going in himself, but that would not do. He was in charge and needed to act like it.

He consulted his watch for at least the tenth time. What was keeping Fisher and his team? Having only begun operations the previous evening, they'd not yet had the opportunity to investigate the warren of tunnels beneath the island. For all he knew, his people were navigating a veritable maze. And then there were the intruders. Who were they? Were they armed? There was too much he didn't know.

He was about to check his watch again when Fisher appeared. To Locke's surprise, he didn't emerge from the swamp, but from the direction of the drilling operation. The look on his face told him the news was not good.

"Report," Locke snapped, his harsh tone a concession to his mood.

"It's a death trap down there. The tunnels are like a honeycomb and whoever built this place added a few nasty surprises. I lost everyone." He took a deep breath and looked away.

"Tell me the rest." The back of Locke's neck warmed with his rising anger.

"There is a church down there, clearly built by the Templars. Behind it, I found a hidden chamber." He paused, stiffened, and swallowed hard. "The intruders got there first. Whatever was in that chamber, they took it."

"How did they get away?" Locke bit off every word. Calm on the outside, his insides quaked with rage.

"I thought I had them trapped, but the Templars built in an exit. The lever that opened it was hidden and I had to search for it. By the time I made it through..." He shrugged.

"Where are they now?"

"They made it to the surface. I tried to track them, but they left little sign. I finally found a few tracks on the north side of the island. I think they swam for it."

Locke grabbed his radio, ordered his men to scour the island, and instructed the sheriff to send both of his boats to the island's north side. It was clear from Meade's tone that he did not appreciate taking orders from a civilian, but Locke couldn't care less. Even as he put his forces in motion, he knew it was too late. He would have to admit his failure to Morgan.

Who could have done this? Who had the skill to infiltrate the island, move like shadows through armed and alert guards, navigate the underground tunnels, and swim to freedom? Almost as soon as the question crossed his mind, he had the answer.

Maddock!

A commotion coming from the direction of the causeway drew him from his thoughts and he looked up to see two of his men escorting a handcuffed woman toward him. Two of Meade's people, White and Boudreau, followed closely behind.

"This is our prisoner!" Boudreau shouted. "You can't just take her. We want to see the sheriff about this."

"Who is she?" Locke asked as he looked the prisoner over. She was an athletic-looking woman, dark of skin, eyes, hair, her lovely face at odds with the stream of vulgarity she spewed as she yanked at her bonds. She managed to land a kick to the knee of the man who held her, almost sending him to the ground.

"Our people picked her up along the coast road. We were told to be on the lookout for anything suspicious," White explained. "She was looking out over the water like she was waiting for someone. She had a car parked nearby."

"I wasn't waiting for anything," the girl snapped.

"You were just sitting on the shore, in the middle of the night, doing nothing at all?" Locke took a step closer. "Or were you waiting for someone? Dane Maddock, perhaps?"

"Who the hell is that?" She looked like she wanted to bite his face off.

Now he could see she was Native American, and something clicked into place.

"You are with that fellow who was running the operation here before we took over."

"I don't know what you're talking about you poncey..."

Fisher stepped forward and drove a fist into her gut. Surprisingly, she absorbed the blow and grinned.

"Is that all you got?"

Fisher tensed, but Locke put a stop to his foolishness with a wave of his hand.

"Enough." Everyone fell silent, even the Indian girl. He turned to the deputies. "Something of value was stolen from the island tonight, and I suspect this woman is an accomplice."

"We'll take her to the jail." Boudreau took a step toward the prisoner but Fisher blocked her. "Step away from me." Her hand went her weapon but, just then, Sheriff Meade returned.

"What's this now? We have a prisoner?"

"You do not have a prisoner, Sheriff. I do." Several of his men had gathered round. All were well-armed and obeyed orders without question. As the Sheriff and his deputies became aware of their presence, Locke could see the fire in their bellies flicker and die. "Get my helicopter ready. We're leaving."

"To the museum?" Fisher asked.

The idiot! Locke tried to silence him with a glare but to no avail. "I can question her first, if you like."

"No." Would he have to choke Fisher to get him to shut his mouth? Clearly, the ordeal beneath the island had rattled him, but that was no excuse.

"Wait a minute, Mister Locke." Sheriff Meade swallowed hard, took a deep breath, and went on. "I understand you have the support of some important people, but the law is the law. I cannot allow you to take this woman away. She..."

Locke stared him into silence, then stepped so close he could see the one silver hair in the man's left eyebrow. The sheriff stood his ground, but he worked his jaw nervously.

"Sheriff, you have two choices." He raised his index finger. "You can set your people back to guarding this island so my museum staff can continue its work here undisturbed, and we shall remain friends. Or," he raised a second finger, "you and your two deputies can take out your sidearms and attempt to stop us. I would prefer we remain friends, and I would consider it a great personal favor if you permitted me some time alone with this woman before I return her to your custody."

For an instant, he thought Meade would go for his weapon, but the sheriff thrust his hands in his pockets instead and stalked away.

"Have her back to me by morning," he said to no one in particular. The deputies sent twin withering looks in Locke's direction before following Meade.

"Are you sure you don't want me to question her?" Fisher asked when they were out of earshot.

Locke turned and punched Fisher in the jaw. The man crumpled to the ground.

"What was that for?" he mumbled.

"Stupidity," Locke said. "You speak of interrogation in front of the man whose son you tortured and killed only a few days ago?"

"He's too dumb to put it together," Fisher said, still holding his jaw.

"You don't know that. In any case, your special brand of questioning gained us no new information and added a complication. Between that and tonight's fiasco, I no longer trust your judgment."

"I'm sorry. I always give everything I have to the cause."

"Morgan will decide whether or not to accept your apology. For now, I want everyone out of here except the museum staff. They may continue their research just as we planned. You will remain here as security until your fate is determined."

"I'll see to it immediately." Fisher wobbled to his feet and staggered away.

Locke shook his head. Fisher's failure notwithstanding, Morgan would consider this Locke's responsibility, and it was. Morgan could temporarily be assuaged by the news of the temple beneath the island, but he would have to produce results soon or she would grow impatient. Perhaps this girl could help him bring things back into balance.

Chapter 17

Where could they have gone? Maddock looked around, but there was no one in sight.

"Maddock?" A voice called from the woods. "Bones? Thank God." Avery appeared from the shadows and hurled herself into Bones' arms.

Maddock raised an eyebrow and Bones shrugged.

"What happened?" Maddock asked.

"Angel's been arrested. I went over to the shore to look for you and, when I came back, they were putting her in their patrol car. I feel like I should have tried to stop them, but what could I do?"

"Nothing," Bones reassured her. "They would have taken you in too." He looked over the top of Avery's head and scowled. "Let's go get her. Meade and his crew have pushed this too far. They can't just take my sister in on some bogus charge."

"I know," Maddock said. "First, we need to get out of here in case they come back. Then we'll figure out the best way to handle this."

Avery handed him her spare set of keys and, only then, did she notice the casket they'd recovered from the island. She looked at him in surprise and excitement.

"It's sealed shut. We'll take a look at it when we're somewhere safe. Bones, you ride in the back and keep the casket with you. If we get stopped, you might have to slip away."

"No problem," he said.

Maddock took them on a route that led up the coast, away from town and, he hoped, the sheriff's patrols. As he drove, he fought to suppress the rage that boiled inside of him. Right now, all was forgotten except the thought of Angel locked in a jail cell. He wanted to go in, guns blazing, and rescue her. He had a vague picture in his head of carrying her out through the front doors, action hero style, and laughed inside at the image. Where had this sudden hero complex come from?

As rational thought took hold, he considered their options. He and Bones were on the sheriff's radar, and likely wouldn't get anywhere if they showed up at the jail. Besides, they were in a foreign country. What she needed right now was bail money, a good attorney, or both.

"We need to call Charlie," he finally said. "He's got money and connections we don't have. If we show up there, we might get arrested too."

Bones considered that for several seconds before acquiescing. "Yeah, Charlie's the man for the job. He can take care of getting her out while we follow up on this." He tapped the casket.

"The mystery's solved," Maddock said. "That casket was the only thing on the island. Once it's opened, that's it."

"Hardly," Avery said. "There were three chests. Three treasures. I don't think Dad planned on quitting after only one. He'd follow it all the way to the end."

"You know how it goes with us, Maddock." Bones leaned forward and rested his chin on the back of Avery's seat. "The first thing we find is never it. There's always more."

"Yeah, I know." Maddock chuckled. "You can't blame a guy for wishing for a quiet life."

"I'm not even going to comment." Bones sat quietly for a minute, then suddenly burst out laughing.

"What's so funny?" Avery asked.

"Angel's going to be pissed when she finds out we started without her. She's been dying to go on another of our little adventures."

"Do you do this sort of thing often?" Avery looked from Bones to Maddock, who grinned ruefully.

"You have no idea."

They contacted Charlie, who assured them he would take care of Angel, as well as send a couple of his men to the cottage to collect everyone's remaining belongings. They didn't provide him with any details of what they had discovered beneath Oak Island, but assured him the search was over and encouraged him to pack up his crew and return to the States as soon as possible. By the time they rendezvoused with Corey and Willis, who met them aboard *Sea Foam*, they had filled Avery in on all the details of the hidden Templar church. She was fascinated and couldn't wait to see the pictures they'd taken, but was even more eager to see what was hidden in the casket.

While Willis piloted the boat toward international waters, Maddock, Bones, Corey, and Avery gathered belowdecks. Using small chisels, Maddock worked at the seal until he freed the lid. He paused and took a long look at the others. This was the moment he relished- the edge of revelation.

"Stop titillating us and open it already," Corey said.

"Dude, you said *tit*." Bones elbowed Corey, who winced and rubbed his arm.

"Are they always like this?" Avery cast an annoyed glance at Bones and Corey.

"What did I do?" Corey complained.

"Never mind," Maddock said. "Masks on and we'll do this." When they had all donned surgical masks, Maddock took hold of the lid and lifted it free.

The inside was stuffed with a tangle of stringy brown material.

"Coconut fiber," Avery said. "It was used for packing material. They even found some in the Money Pit."

Maddock reached a gloved hand inside and pushed the fiber aside to reveal a dagger with a dark, mottled blade and a gleaming white handle. He looked up to see Avery holding the casket lid in trembling hands, and Bones and Corey looking over her shoulder.

"Carnwennan." She turned the lid so Maddock could see the Latin word carved on the inside. The word was unfamiliar, but the look in her eyes told him it was significant.

"And what is that?" he asked.

"King Arthur's dagger." She leaned in for a closer look. "He had three legendary weapons: Caliburn, which we know as Excalibur, Rhongomnyiad, his spear, and Carnwennan, his dagger."

"Wait, so we've just found proof that..." Bones began.

"King Arthur was an actual, historical figure?" Maddock finished. His mind was numb with shock. He'd expected to find treasure beneath Oak Island, but not this.

"It was one of the legends associated with Oak Island, but probably the most far-fetched one of them all." Avery's voice trembled.

"But why would somebody try to kill us for it?" Bones asked. "I mean, it's a huge discovery, but there's got to be more."

Maddock withdrew the dagger and held it up to the light. The blade was made of a substance unfamiliar to him. It was mottled gray, its surface covered in a hexagonal grid of alternating light and dark metals. The blade was honed to razor sharpness, and the butt was translucent, almost black, like obsidian.

As he gazed at it, the handle began to pulse with a dull, bluish-white glow that gained strength with every beat.

"What is it doing?" Avery took a step back as if it were a venomous snake.

Maddock didn't reply, but removed his hand from the hilt and, carefully holding the knife by the blade, held it up to the light. The pulses came faster, the light more intense until it shone so bright that Maddock had to avert his eyes, and a low hum filled the room.

And then it stopped.

The hilt no longer shone, but it glowed a brighter white than before. Pinpoints of light like tiny galaxies sparkled deep in the handle and butt, and threads of blue flickered around the hexagonal patterns on the blade.

"It's like it absorbed energy from the light," Avery said. "I've never seen anything like it."

"We have." Bones grimaced.

Maddock examined the dagger closely, carefully running his finger along its length. There was something odd about the way the butt was made. It was concave on the bottom and flattened out so that it did not quite conform to the dimensions of the hilt. Frowning, he pressed his thumb into the recess. Nothing. Then he gave it a twist.

The dagger vibrated and his vision swam for a split second.

"What the hell?" Bones said.

"Maddock! Where did you go?" Avery sounded panicked.

"I'm standing right here."

"No way." Bones reached out awkwardly, as if he were playing Blind Man's Bluff, and grabbed Maddock by the forearm. "He really is here," he marveled.

"But... how?" She gaped at a spot a few inches to Maddock's left.

"What are you two talking about?" Maddock looked back and forth between the two of them. If it were only Bones, he'd figure it was a lame joke, but Avery appeared rattled.

"Dude, you're invisible." Bones' matter of fact tone was void of humor. "One second you were there and then you were gone."

"It must be the dagger." He explained what he had done, and what he had seen and felt.

"The stories are true," Avery whispered. "Legend says Carnwennan had the power to cloak its owner in shadow. It really does make you invisible."

Maddock turned the butt back and, once again, the room swam for an instant.

"He's back!" Bones said. "Here, let me see that."

Maddock handed him the dagger and, a moment later, Bones vanished.

"I don't feel anything," Bones' voice said from nowhere. "Am I really invisible?"

"Yes, but we still recognize your foul stench," Maddock deadpanned.

"*Star Wars* quotes are my job," Bones said.

Maddock stared at the spot where he heard Bones' voice. He thought about what Avery had said. Carnwennan *cloaked* its bearer in shadow. He wondered...

"Bones, do me a favor and move side to side a little."

"You mean like line dancing? You know I hate anything redneckish."

"Just do it."

"Fine, I'll do the Casper Slide. Ready? To the left!" Bones began chanting lyrics and, presumably, dancing.

Maddock followed the sound and, sure enough, he saw movement.

"Avery, Corey, can you see it?" He drew them to his side and pointed. "If you really focus, you can tell a difference between the space where Bones is and the wall behind it."

Avery narrowed her eyes and, a few seconds later, smiled.

"It's like an imperfect piece of glass. You can see through it, but something's just a little bit off."

Bones stopped chanting and, an instant later, reappeared.

"I don't think a woman's ever called me imperfect and a little bit off in one breath."

"No one's ever made the mistake of thinking you were only a *little bit* off." Maddock relieved his friend of the dagger and held it out so everyone could see it. "Look at the pattern on the blade and think about what this dagger does."

"It's a cloaking device!" Bones said, following Maddock's line of thought almost immediately. "This isn't some magic weapon. It's seriously advanced technology."

"Scientist are in the early stages of developing technology that bends light rays, making a particular spot invisible," Maddock said, noticing Avery's confused expression. "Nobody's achieved anything like this, though."

"But this has clearly been down there for centuries. And if it's really Carnwennan, how did they get their hands on such technology?"

"I don't know," Maddock said, though he was turning over a myriad of ideas in his mind. "But now we know why someone would kill in order to get their hands on it."

Chapter 18

Angel sat stock-still, her eyes on the widening band of gray light where someone was opening the door to her small room. She was locked in what looked like a basement storage room, but she didn't know where. A dark figure loomed in shadow, and then a light clicked on. In the instant before she closed her eyes against the sudden glare, she caught a glimpse of a blocky man with red hair.

"Glad to see you're awake." He smiled. "We need to talk."

Angel's only reply was to suggest he use an orifice other than his mouth when speaking. She usually liked a guy with a British accent, but not under these circumstances.

"That won't do." Still smiling, he shook his head, his eyes roving up and down her body. "I'll explain." He pulled up a stool and sat down next to her. "We want information, and we will have it. If you talk to me, things will go easier for you. If you talk to Locke..." He let the words hang there, and gave her a look that told her Locke was the last person she wanted to deal with.

"Where am I?"

"We're in the museum. Now, tell us what we need to know and we can have you back with your friends in a thrice."

"Right." She didn't believe a word of it. "Explain to me why I should believe anything a kidnapper tells me."

"I didn't kidnap you, love. I'm merely gathering information." He winked, making her stomach twist. Even if he wasn't her captor he'd be creepy. That big, moon face and massive body reminded her of the inbred killers that hacked their way through so many horror flicks. "I'm not one of the bad ones."

"So, you'll take these off of me," she indicated her handcuffed wrists, "and let me go."

"Sure."

The reply surprised Angel. She searched his eyes for signs of deception.

"I'll take the cuffs off right now to show you I'm a reasonable man and, after you answer my questions, you can walk. Hell, I'll even give you a lift to the airport."

No way in hell was she getting in a car with this creep, not that she believed for a second that he intended to release her, but she played along. If he was willing to uncuff her, that meant he didn't expect a girl of her size to pose any kind of threat. At a good two hundred-fifty pounds, she imagined few women, or men for that matter, were a threat. She'd have to be fast and would need a bit of luck on her side, but what did she have to lose? They were going to kill her anyway.

"Fair enough." She held up her hands, and watched as he fished a key out of his pocket and unlocked one side of the cuffs. The moment he turned his attention to the other cuff, she struck.

She drove her fist into his Adam's apple, and he reeled back, gasping and clutching at his throat. Angel sprang to her feet and whipped her left hand around. Still locked onto her left wrist, the handcuffs cracked across the bridge of his nose, sending up a spray of blood that spattered across the wall. She attacked with fury, knowing the blows she had struck were far from incapacitating. She poured all her strength into an overhand right that caught the taller man squarely on the chin, followed it up with a knee to the groin, and pounded away with a rapid flurry of punches to the chin, face, and temple. It was like chopping down a tree. He was too stunned by surprise and the force of her blows to do more than throw up his beefy hands in a weak attempt to fend off her attack.

It did no good. Angel was a well-conditioned professional athlete and this was nothing more than a training exercise to her. She threw in a few hard kicks to the side of the knee and, slowly, the man slid down to the floor, Angel delivering kicks and elbow strikes as he went down. When he finally fell into a sitting position, his eyes were glassy and his face a mask of blood. She drove her knee into his forehead for good measure, smashing the back of his head against the wall. His eyes rolled back in his head and he was out.

She made a hasty search of the floor, found the handcuff key, and freed her wrist, then searched his pockets for a weapon or anything else that might be of use, but all she found was a key ring. She took it just in case and crept to the door, tried the handle, and found it unlocked. Holding her breath, she opened it an inch and peered out.

She was looking at a narrow corridor lit by a row of bare bulbs. At the far end, a staircase led up into the darkness. Her pounding heart was the only sound she heard, so she slipped through the door and closed it behind her. She tried three keys on the ring before finding the proper one, and locked the thug in.

Smiling, she trotted down the corridor, almost wishing someone would try to stop her. She was ready to take somebody else down. She wasn't *that* stupid, though, so she proceeded up the stairs with caution.

At the top, she found herself in the middle of a long hallway lined with doors on one side. None were marked.

"How the hell am I supposed to choose?" she whispered. Figuring one was as good as the other, she tried the closest door. It wasn't locked. She peeked through and found herself staring at a dark figure holding an upraised sword. She gasped and almost slammed the door shut, but just as quickly had to suppress a laugh.

It was a wax figure, a pirate armed with a realistic-looking sword. He loomed over another wax figure posed as a cowering woman. She had discovered the access door to one of the museum's exhibits. She inferred from the dim lights and empty museum that it was early morning and the place was not yet open. Good!

Only a low rail separated the exhibit from the museum's viewing area and, across the way, a window beckoned to her. She crept into the exhibit area and closed the door behind her when heavy footsteps sounded in the quiet room only feet from her. She lay down behind the woman on the floor and tried to cram herself into the tiny space behind it. She watched, heart in her throat, as an armed man walked past. He wasn't a uniformed security guard, and that frightened her even more. She'd take a rent-a-cop over a dude who looked like he could handle himself any day of the week.

He was a tall, muscular man with a shaved head. He wore a pistol on one hip and a knife on the other. He moved with detached ease, as if nothing could harm him, but his eyes were alert. As a fighter, she was always the aggressor, taking the battle to her opponent without fear. That same drive urged her to jump the guy, but common sense prevailed. This guy wasn't a careless idiot like the dolt she'd taken out downstairs. She'd need more than her bare hands to deal with this fellow.

She held her breath, convinced he could hear the pounding of her heart, and prayed for him to pass her by without seeing her.

After three eternal seconds he did just that, continuing on through the museum. She didn't permit herself to breathe until his footsteps faded in the distance. When she was certain he was gone, she counted to three before rising and peering around the side of the exhibit. He was gone. What was more, the lobby was only fifty feet or so to her right. As she watched, a woman in a cleaning uniform appeared from somewhere near the lobby, unlocked the front door, and left. She did not lock it behind her.

Angel didn't hesitate. She sprang to her feet, knocking the pirate to the floor, vaulted the rail, and made a dash for the door. Outside, the cleaning lady was climbing into a van. Maybe Angel could catch a ride.

She hit the lobby at full steam and was just reaching out to push the door open when her world dissolved into ice and pain. She slammed face-down on the tile floor, her arms and legs suddenly useless. The wind was knocked out of her and she tasted warm, salty blood in her mouth.

"Was my little dove trying to fly the coop?" Locke loomed over her, holding a taser and smiling. "I must say, I do enjoy shattering dreams at the very moment they are to be realized."

"She almost made it." The big guy she'd seen patrolling moments before stood behind Locke, looking equally pleased. "I wonder what she did to Charles?"

"Yes, I wonder that as well." Locke dropped to a knee and leaned in close. "Charles was a test. He's a great fool, and I'd have been disappointed had you not escaped him. Just know that you can't escape me." He reached into his pocket and withdrew a syringe. "By the time we get you back to your cell, you should be most tractable."

Angel watched in horror as the needle descended toward her limp arm. She heard someone screaming, then realized it was her.

Tamsin gazed across her desk at the surprise guest who had just interrupted her day. He was a pale man, his blond hair nearly white. She'd have mistaken him for an albino, but his eyes were alarmingly blue. He grinned, his perfect white teeth blending in with his pale face. Ordinarily, she'd never have granted an audience to a perfect stranger, but his cryptic explanation of his business had been enough to get her attention. He knew something about Kidd, or so he claimed.

He smiled at her, his manner easy as if this were his office and she the visitor. Was he ever going to speak?

"Who are you and what do you want?" She immediately chastised herself for speaking first. Patience had never been her strong suit. "Tell me now or I'll have you tossed out." It was a feeble attempt at regaining the upper hand, but it was all she could think of. For a moment it seemed as if she would be forced to make good on her threat, because the man continued to smile. But, just as she was reaching for her intercom, he spoke one word.

"Herrschaft."

She held on to her calm exterior with the greatest of effort. Inside, she was a mess. Why would anyone from Heilig Herrschaft, that vile branch of the Dominion dedicated to restoring the Nazis to power in Germany, using the church, of all things, as its vehicle, dare come anywhere near her or any Sister? Was he an assassin? Surely not.

"Please, Fraulein." He spoke with only the mildest German accent. "Be at ease. I know who you are."

"Then you are a fool for coming here today." She ought to have him taken into custody immediately, but something stayed her hand.

"Perhaps, but a brave fool, no?" Each time he smiled, he seemed ever more wolflike. "There is enmity between our organizations, that is true, but I believe we can find common ground."

"Morgan would never hear of it."

"Not with Morgan and not with the Sisterhood. With you."

"What could we possibly have in common?"

"A common enemy. Your sister." He held up a finger, silencing her protest. "How much has Morgan told you about Oak Island?"

Tamsin's stomach lurched. The honest answer was 'nothing,' but she didn't care to admit it.

"Yes, I see," he said, correctly interpreting her hesitation. He leaned forward and adopted a conspiratorial tone. "Morgan has found something on Oak Island."

"Impossible. The island has been searched countless times, and nothing has ever been found. The Money Pit is well named, for too much money has been wasted looking for treasure that is not there."

"You know it is not treasure we seek." He paused. "A Kidd chest has been found."

This time she could not keep the surprise from her face. "How do you know?"

"Of course I cannot tell you that. It is enough that we know, and now, you know."

Tamsin stared at the man without seeing him. It was no surprise that Morgan was keeping secrets, but it galled her nonetheless. And this was one secret that belonged to all three sisters. It was what they had been working for.

"How do I know you are telling the truth?"

"You do not, but you can find out. Put the question to your sister. Look into her eyes and see the lie. Or, perhaps, she will tell you the truth." He shrugged, as if the whole issue was of no import to him.

"Assuming you *are* telling the truth, and Morgan has found... something." She could not bring herself to say what, exactly. "What is it you want from me?"

"We want you to take control away from Morgan, with our help if you like. In turn, when you find what you seek, we ask only to be permitted to make use of it one time. Nothing more."

"You believe the stories?" she scoffed. "They are symbols, and only to Britons at that. To the rest of the world, they are mere curiosities." Her words rang false, and she knew it. She'd had enough glimpses in her lifetime of powers not understood by the modern world to know better.

"We believe," he said simply. "If you think they are, as you say, curiosities, then surely there is no harm in permitting us to try."

"Suppose it will do what legend says. How will you use it?"

"That is our affair." He sat up straight. "You should not so easily cede control to Morgan. What power does she truly wield, save the court of public opinion and the allegiance of a few politicians? You have authority."

"I am Chief Constable of the transport police. That is a far cry from powerful."

"You underestimate yourself, and we both know you have forged many alliances behind Morgan's back. Let us help one another. In fact, I have some information that might be of interest to you. Someone in America is making quite an effort to find Kidd's chests. I can provide you with specifics, should you choose to work with us."

"What benefit is there to helping Heilig Herrschaft? The last time your people controlled Germany, our nations tried to destroy each other."

"Yes, and now America has come to dominate the world. What if we had formed an alliance, instead? Where might both our nations be?"

She shook her head. Dealing with the Dominion? The very idea was mad. Then again, perhaps this was the opportunity she had long sought. She rose from her chair, turned, and gazed down at the slow-flowing waters of the Thames. On the opposite side, the London Eye stuck out like a festering boil on the landscape of her beloved city. Too few held on to the things that truly mattered any more. The ancient things rooted in history and tradition; things that held power to make modern inventions seem trite by comparison. If the Dominion could help her obtain them... Perhaps it was time to take a risk.

"Tell me more."

Chapter 19

"Jimmy has something for us!" Maddock proclaimed, scrolling through the email he'd just received from Jimmy Letson, an old friend and accomplished hacker. "I gave him a list of everything in Dad's research to see if he could come up with any leads on Kidd's chests."

"And what did he find?" Bones lounged on the deck of *Sea Foam* with a steaming mug of coffee in his hands. "I'm already bored."

They'd met up with Charlie in a coastal town in Maine. He'd returned their belongings and informed them that Sheriff Meade wouldn't let him post bail for, or even visit, with Angel until Monday morning. The sheriff also declined to say what she was charged with. Incensed, Charlie vowed to bring all his resources to bear on the situation. He'd been disappointed to learn that his Oak Island project was at an end, but had been downright giddy to hear of what Maddock and Bones had discovered and to see the pictures they'd taken.

Now they were cruising south somewhere off the coast of Massachusetts. Matt, who had come along with Charlie, had rejoined the crew and was piloting the ship.

"He's got a few possibilities," Maddock said. "There's a museum on Gardiner's Island..."

"Already checked it," Avery said. She was seated next to Bones, drinking a cup of chai tea. "No joy."

"Okay. How about the Maritime Museum in Port Royal?" The thought of a trip to Jamaica definitely appealed to him.

"Been there. Done that." Avery frowned. "No offense, but I don't think your friend has much chance of finding the Kidd chests. It's not like I'm the first who's tried."

"Don't underestimate Jimmy," Maddock said. "He's talented and has access to some really obscure stuff."

"Not necessarily legally," Bones added.

Maddock ran through Jimmy's list, growing more discouraged as Avery eliminated each possibility. Finally, he was down to the final two items.

"Trinity Church, on Wall Street," he began.

"Nope. Nothing belonging to Kidd in their archives. I've been there several times, and so had Dad."

"But they just added the journal of a William Vesey."

Avery sat up straight, her eyes boring into Maddock with raptor-like intensity.

"I take it that's somebody important?" Bones asked over his coffee mug.

"He was the first rector of Trinity Church," Avery said. "He served there while Kidd was a member."

"Jimmy read an email from the donor to an archivist at the church which says it includes an account of Kidd's confession to Vesey and," he paused for dramatic effect, "Vesey alludes to a treasure map."

"How did he get access to their... oh, never mind." Avery took a sip of her tea and pondered this new information. "No mention of a chest?"

"Not in the email. Jimmy would have mentioned it. But maybe in the journal?"

"It's possible," she mused. "I've researched Vesey and there's no indication that he ever possessed a sea chest, but maybe Kidd told him where one or more could be found. It's worth following up on. Anything else on the list?"

"It's not specifically a sea chest, but there's a chest connected with the Poe Museum. It once belonged to Edgar Allan Poe."

"No connection to Kidd?" Bones asked.

"No. I guess he made the connection because I included *The Gold-Bug* in the list of Dad's research items."

"Poe was a Kidd aficionado," Avery said. "But I've been to the Poe Museum and there were no chests there that fit the bill."

"So, cross Baltimore off the list," Maddock said.

"You mean Richmond," Avery corrected.

"No, the Poe House and Museum in Baltimore."

"What? That place is tiny. There's almost nothing there, and definitely no sea chest." Avery stood and began pacing.

"She's definitely got that Maddock intensity," Bones observed before breaking into laughter as Maddock and Avery shot dirty looks his way.

"He's added a link here, let me check it out." Maddock tapped on the hyperlink Jimmy provided and it opened to an article from the Baltimore Sun, in which a director at the Baltimore Maritime Museum bemoaned the city's refusal to continue funding the Poe House. Maddock read it over twice and saw no mention of a sea chest. "I don't see anything here."

Avery snatched his phone away and read the article. Frown lines appeared in her brow and disappeared almost immediately.

"It's in the picture!" She tapped on the image that accompanied the article. "You missed it because it's so tiny on the screen, but check it." She held up the phone for both to see and, sure enough, a wooden chest sat on a shelf in the background over the director's shoulder. "You've never seen it, but this is an exact match for the Kidd chest that Dad discovered!"

"Do you think this director guy found this chest at the Poe House and helped himself to it?"

"Could be. Even if this is a Kidd chest, unless you know what's inside, it doesn't have much value. I can see how someone who admires Poe and also loves maritime history could give in to temptation."

"That would explain why it's never been identified as a Kidd chest. As far as anyone knew, it was just another wooden chest that Poe stored his crap in," Bones interjected. "Who knows, it might have been gathering dust in an attic somewhere until this guy found it."

"I think they're both worth checking out. Which one do we follow up on first?" Avery asked.

"New York's on the way to Baltimore," Bones said.

Maddock nodded. "Wall Street here we come."

"Questioning her will not get us anywhere." Locke shook his head and closed the door behind him. He had hoped Bonebrake's sister would be a reliable source of information, but it was not to be.

"Are you certain? I could use some more... intense techniques." Shears ran his hand over his shaved scalp. He wasn't prone to the excesses that made Fisher so erratic, but such efforts were not needed.

"No. She told me everything she knew, which is not much."

"With all due respect, where's the harm in making certain?" Shears didn't quite meet his eye as he spoke. Clearly, he had more on his mind than gathering information.

"Torture only motivates the victim to tell you whatever they think you want to hear." Locke kept his tone patient, though frustration was wearing on him. He dreaded his next call to Morgan. He needed a breakthrough. "Besides, if we keep her largely intact, we might possibly make use of her."

"How do you mean?" Shears asked.

"Never mind. Just keep an eye on her and let me know when she's fully awake. She and I are going to make a telephone call." He left Shears to guard the cell. Dane Maddock had stolen the prize out from under his nose, but now Locke had a bargaining chip.

Returning to his office, he logged onto his computer and performed a search on Angelica Bonebrake. He had not expected to find much, perhaps a social networking page from which he could glean a few bits of useful information, but the pages of hits that filled his screen took him aback. The girl was a professional fighter and a minor celebrity.

He stroked his chin and smiled. He did not yet have a treasure to give to Morgan, but this girl's unique set of skills would make her a perfect plaything for Morgan's little games.

Chapter 20

"This is most unexpected, Sisters." Morgan ushered Tamsin and Rhiannon into her private study. "Our next meeting is not for two days."

"We felt it was necessary for us to come early," Tamsin said. "We are certain you were eager to share your news with us."

"Of course."

Three chairs formed a triangle in the center of the room. They met in the middle, joined hands, and spoke the ritual words. As the ancient speech rolled across her tongue, Morgan felt a strong kinship to their forebears. She could almost feel the power coursing through her veins. How satisfying it would be when the three were made one again, and she wielded a power long forgotten by the world.

When the ritual ended, they took their seats and Morgan began her explanation.

"It's nothing really," Morgan said. "I have received yet another request to run for Parliament along with a hint that I would make for a fine Prime Minister."

"That is not what I'm talking about." Tamsin glowered at her. "What have you found at the island?"

It was the question Morgan had anticipated the moment they had appeared at her doorstep, and she was prepared.

"I have news, though it is not all I had hoped it would be." She described in great detail the Templar church that had been discovered beneath Oak Island, omitting the smaller chamber where the lost item, whichever one it was, had been kept. She showed them the photographs researchers had taken, apologizing that she had not assembled them into a proper presentation.

"So you see," she finished, "the discovery confirms that the Templars did, in fact, reach Oak Island, but we have not recovered any of the items we seek." She gave a false sigh. "If the news had been better, I would have summoned you immediately but, considering the limited success of our search, I was not eager to give you my report." There. That should settle them.

"Do we have any leads on the artifact that was stolen from the church, or on the man who took it?"

Morgan froze in the act of shutting off her computer. How had Tamsin come by this information? She knew all of her sister's key operatives and their activities and whereabouts. None of them could have possibly known. And Rhiannon's base of power lay in the church, so she could not be the source. It was a conundrum that would require her attention, but not right now. Now was the time to stand firm.

"Locke is working on it," she said simply. Maintaining her calm exterior, she returned to her seat, sat with her hands folded in her lap, and smiled at Tamsin. Ordinarily, Morgan would not waste time sitting in silence, but she knew Tamsin put great store in such trifles as not being the first to speak, thinking it somehow gave her power. Let her believe that. Right now, Morgan could use it to her own advantage. She watched as Tamsin's cheeks reddened and she began to chew on her lip and fidget slightly until finally she could take no more.

"What is this plan?" Her voice was hot with anger.

"We have taken into custody a young woman who is close to the culprit. When he has finished questioning her, Locke will arrange an exchange. The girl for what was taken."

"Details, please." These were the first words Rhiannon had spoken, and her velvety voice betrayed no emotion. Of the two, she posed the greater potential threat to Morgan. Tamsin had no guile, while Rhiannon was cool and calculating. Tamsin had authority, but lacked the ability to capture the hearts and minds of the people. Rhiannon was beloved as a spiritual leader, though if the world knew her true religion, she would be cast down. Fortunately, Rhiannon had never given any indication that her position, a step below Morgan, chafed at all.

Morgan could see no use in prevaricating. She outlined Locke's plan, assuring them that the long sought-after treasure would be in their hands in a matter of days.

"Do we know which of the three it is?" Rhiannon maintained her calm, courteous manner.

"No." Morgan had her suspicions, based on accounts of the thieves' escape, but she would not share them.

"Very well," Tamsin sighed. "I need not remind you that the plan..."

"I know, Sister."

"Then you understand our concern," Rhiannon said smoothly. "The window of opportunity is a small one. If our quest confounds us again, we will be forced to wait."

"Need I remind you that, a few days ago, we were utterly without hope?" Morgan met their stares each in turn. "Now that hope is rekindled, and I am doing everything in my power to see to it that we do not miss this opportunity. But do not forget, Sisters, the mere possession of any of these artifacts is no small thing. We can use them to cement our power and entrench ourselves in the imaginations of the people. We will be queens!"

"*You* will be Queen," Rhiannon corrected. "Your bloodline is more direct than ours."

Morgan smiled at the thought. Prime Minister was well within her reach, but her aim was higher. She longed for the day they could finally set the plan in motion. A wave of change was about to sweep the world, and she would ride its crest.

"Sister, do we know the thief's name?" Tamsin seemed, if not cowed, at least placated.

"Maddock," Morgan said. "Dane Maddock."

Chapter 21

Trinity Church sat at the corner of Wall Street and Broadway. Its ornate spire, nearly three hundred feet high, stood in stark contrast to the modern buildings all around. A wrought iron fence ringed the property, as if to stave off the intrusion of city life. Maddock found it disorienting to look upon the centuries-old brown stone church, the gothic architecture, and the historical cemetery, with its weathered gravestones, crypts, and monuments, then turn his head to see congested streets choked with taxi cabs and sidewalks where pedestrians navigated an obstacle course of vendors' carts and gawking sightseers. He, Bones, and Avery paused in front of it, taking a moment to admire the famed landmark.

"So this was Kidd's church, huh?" Bones asked.

"It was." Avery quickly donned the mantle of lecturing professor. "Not this building, of course. This is actually the third Trinity Church. The original structure was built in 1698. During its construction, Kidd even lent the runner and tackle from his ship to help them move the stones."

"That's pretty old, for white Americans, that is." Bones gave her an evil grin and Maddock chuckled. "The cemetery looks pretty cool. Maybe we'll have time to check it out."

"There are a lot of famous people buried here and in Trinity's other two cemeteries. Alexander Hamilton, Horacio Gates, Robert Fulton, John Jacob Astor..."

"Wait, the Jingleheimer Schmidt guy is buried here?" Before Avery could reply, Bones laughed and gave her arm a squeeze.

"Good thing Angel isn't here. She'd have punched you for that one." Maddock felt a pang of regret and realized how quickly he'd grown accustomed to Angel's presence. He missed her easy laugh, her self-confidence, and the way she rode herd on Bones.

"Yeah. Don't you know she's climbing the walls in that rinky dink jail?"

"You don't seem too concerned that your sister is sitting in a jail cell," Avery said. "Are you two not close?"

"She's fine." Bones waved her concern away like a wisp of smoke. "This isn't Angel's first rodeo. She wasn't as bad as me when we were kids, but she had her moments. I just feel sorry for her jailer. You think I can get under someone's skin, you ought to see her in action."

Maddock smiled at the thought, but couldn't escape a feeling of guilt that they hadn't found a way to get her out of her predicament.

They spent a moment longer admiring the church and the grounds, soaking in the history.

"Doesn't it seem like we go to a lot of these places?" Bones asked.

"Yeah, but no complaints here." Maddock examined the architecture, its blend of sturdy lines and artistic trappings. He loved these pockets of history that stood against the disposable construction of recent generations "At least, not too many complaints."

"You guys keep dropping these little comments about places you've gone and things you've done," Avery said, "but you won't dish. It's starting to tick me off." She gave them each the evil eye and stalked into the church.

Maddock grimaced and looked at Bones, who chuckled.

"She's a spitfire." He started to say something, then hesitated. It was a strange thing for Maddock to witness. Bones was never uncertain about anything. At least, he never let it show. "Say, Maddock, I've been meaning to ask you something."

"All right. Shoot." As eager as he was to go inside and begin the search, he was, at the moment, even more curious about what Bones wanted to talk about.

"It's kind of weird for a guy to have a thing for his best friend's sister, don't you think?"

Maddock felt his face grow hot. All his conflicted feelings about Angel rose anew. Had he been that obvious? How long had Bones known?

"Bones, I don't know what to say."

"Look, if you want me to stay away from her, I will. She's your sister and I don't want to mess up our friendship, but I wouldn't mind hanging out with her. She's cool." He looked at Maddock then looked away.

It took Maddock a moment to realize what Bones was talking about, and then he laughed.

"Oh! You mean Avery." Relief flooded through him.

"Yeah. Wait, who did you think I meant?" Bones cocked his head and looked quizzically at him.

"Nobody." He quickened his pace and didn't meet Bones' eye. "Yeah, that's cool. I could tell you have a thing for her, and she's only been my sister for a couple of days."

"Dude, you suck at math. She's been your sister all her life."

"You know what I mean. It might be different if we'd grown up together."

"Yeah, that might be a little different." Bones sounded thoughtful.

"We'd better get going." He strode through the gate, headed toward the entrance, relieved Bones didn't press the issue.

By the time they caught up with Avery, she had used her credentials and charm to gain a look at the journal. She sat at at table under the close scrutiny of an archivist, a stocky man with light brown hair, blue eyes, and a youthful face. He gave Bones a funny look before returning his attention to Avery, who was carefully turning the pages with gloved fingers. Maddock and Bones sat down on either side of her and watched her work.

The journal was thin, its pages yellow, and the script faded. Avery worked her way through the book at a steady pace, her blue eyes moving back and forth across the page as she devoured the text, putting Maddock to mind of a typewriter carriage. When she finally reached the end, she frowned.

"What is it?" Maddock asked.

Avery held up her hand, cutting off further questions, and slowly leafed back through the journal. After a few pages, she paused and leaned closer.

"Careful," the archivist cautioned. "No sneezing or drooling allowed." He smiled, but his comment was not entirely meant to be humorous.

"Pages have been torn out." Avery slid the book across the table so the archivist could take a closer look. The ragged edges were just visible.

"Are you sure?" The man took a closer look. "Holy crap." He dragged it out into a good four syllables, and Maddock thought he detected a trace of a southern accent, so out of place in the heart of New York City. "I'm sorry. I'm going to have to take this back." He donned a pair of gloves and gingerly reclaimed the journal from Avery.

"Do you know if the page was there when it came into your collection?" Maddock asked.

"I assume so, but I haven't read the entire thing. The donor is meticulous and I think she would have mentioned if it was incomplete."

"Who else has looked at the journal since it came into your collection?" Avery sounded like a prosecuting attorney interrogating a witness, and her manner seemed to take the man aback.

"Only the..." He reddened and shook his head. "Only the donor." He averted his eyes, but Maddock could see the lie there.

The guy was obviously protecting someone, but who, and for what reason? Instinct told Maddock that the archivist was not a bad sort. Maddock decided to take a chance.

"The part of the journal you read, was there any mention of Captain Kidd?"

"There was." The man's face brightened. "It was interesting and a little weird. Kidd was in trouble with the crown and he knew it, so he came to Vesey because he said he had a secret he wanted to confess. Vesey doesn't go into detail, but Kidd says a secret was entrusted to him that he didn't want to let die. He gave Vesey what he called a 'treasured possession,' but Vesey inspected it later and couldn't see that it had any value."

"Did he say what it was?" Avery had stripped off her gloves and now clutched the edge of the table.

The man shook his head.

"We're interested in Vesey," Maddock began. "Are any of his personal effects on display at the church, or anywhere else? Maybe a wooden chest?"

"There is an old chest that's bounced around the church since Vesey's time, though I don't know if it belonged to him. It's nothing fancy, and has been ill used, I'm afraid. It was passed around and used for storage until someone finally realized its age and thought it was worth preserving. At the moment it's in St. Paul's Chapel."

Avery smiled and nodded at Maddock. The pieces were falling into place. They thanked the man and left the chapel in a hurry. When they reached the street, Avery didn't pause, but turned left and took off down the sidewalk at a fast walk that bordered on a jog.

"So where is St. Paul's?" Bones asked, his long legs allowing him to easily keep stride with her.

"Just a few blocks down the street," she said. "It's a part of Trinity Church. I know where it is, but I've never been there. It's even at the corner of Broadway and Vesey Street. I'm so stupid."

"You're just like Maddock. Don't be so hard on yourself," Bones began, but clammed up at one look from Avery.

St. Paul's was a Georgian-style church, boxy and surmounted by an octagonal tower on a square base. From the Broadway side, a portico sheltered a statue of Saint Paul, which was flanked by double doors on either side. To the left of the entrance, in a fenced, grassy area, stood an obelisk, on which was carved an eagle and a man's profile. Maddock wondered if this Masonic symbol could have any connection to the Templars who built the church beneath Oak Island.

The interior of the chapel was elegant, but was not awe-inspiring like Trinity Church. Cut glass chandeliers cast slivers of light across the ceiling and the rows of white pews. All around them, banners memorializing the tragic events of the terrorist attack on the World Trade Center a decade before hung as stark reminders of the disaster that St. Paul's had, according to Avery, miraculously avoided.

They fell in with the other tourists and made their way around the church. The history of the place was interesting. It had withstood not only the 2001 attack, but also the Great New York City Fire of 1776. Both George Washington and Lord Cornwallis had worshiped here at different times, as well as other figures of historical significance. Though he found it all interesting, Maddock was growing impatient. Where was the chest?

And then he saw it.

A simple, wooden chest sat atop a plain table in the back corner. It was afforded no special place. In fact, it was being used to hold brochures. Maddock took that as a good sign. No one who knew anything about the Kidd legend or the potential connection between this chest and the legendary pirate would ever put it to such a pedestrian use. If this was the chest they sought, there was a good chance its secret remained undiscovered.

He nudged Avery and inclined his head toward the chest. Her eyes lit up.

"That's it. It's identical to the one Dad found." She took a hasty step in toward the back corner, but Bones grabbed her by the arm.

"Slowly," he said. "Don't draw undue attention to yourself."

They moved casually in the direction of the chest, still looking around as if no single thing held their interest. When they reached the corner, Maddock turned to Bones.

"Turn around and look scary."

"Can do, boss." Bones pretended to answer his phone, twisted his face into an agitated scowl, and began speaking in a harsh whisper. Maddock had to admit Bones was a pretty good actor when he put his mind to it.

"Let's see if it opens the same way as the other chest." Avery pressed her finger against a raised wooden square and moved it side to side, then up and down in the shape of a cross. The square came free, revealing a hidden compartment.

Smiling, Avery reached in and removed a brass cylinder, uncapped the end, and plucked out a roll of aged paper, much like the Oak Island map. She handed the cylinder to Maddock and was about to unroll the paper when someone called out.

"What's this now? Give me that."

A big man with a shaved head approached them from near the doorway. If his British accent didn't set off warning bells, his hand resting on the pistol at his hip did. The man took a step closer and held out his free hand.

"That's right, hand it over now."

Maddock tossed the cylinder at the man's face and, as the fellow reached up to grab it, drove his fist into the man's chin. The big man's knees turned to rubber and he went down in a heap, his eyes glassy. Maddock grabbed Avery by the arm and steered her toward the door. All around them, people were talking and pointing. A few had taken out cell phones and were probably calling the police.

"He was a Red Sox fan," Bones explained before following Maddock and Avery out the door.

Beneath the portico, Maddock looked out at the street and saw a dark-haired man leaning against the fence that ran along the sidewalk. Their eyes met and the man stood ramrod straight and reached behind his back.

"Gun!" Maddock shouted. Still holding Avery by the arm, he made a hard right and ran around the corner of the church and onto the churchyard. They sprinted past the obelisk just as a bullet deflected off its surface.

"Looks like it's time to call in the cavalry!" Bones shouted, punching up a number on his phone while running at full speed. "Church Street at Fulton," he barked, then tucked the phone back inside his leather jacket.

They dashed through the cemetery, navigating the tombs, hurdling low gravestones, and ducking in and out of the trees that shaded the yard. They reached the end of the church and veered to the right just as another muffled pop sounded and a bullet buzzed past Maddock's ear. The streets were busy, but the guy didn't seem to care who he might hit.

"Get Avery to the street."

Bones nodded and pulled her along, ignoring her protests.

Maddock leaned against the wall and waited. He heard the sound of footfalls and someone breathing hard. As their pursuer came around the corner, eyes on the receding figures of Bones and Angel, and his pistol leveled, Maddock lashed out with a vicious roundhouse kick, catching the man across the shins and sweeping his legs out from under him. He landed face down on the stone path with a sickening thud, his breath leaving him in a rush.

Maddock hastily relieved him of his weapon, as well as a radio and cell phone. He rolled the man over. His nose was broken, his forehead split, and his face thick with blood and mucous. He gasped for breath, staring up at Maddock with hate-filled eyes.

"I know you're Locke's man," Maddock snarled. "You tell him to back off. I might not be so nice to the next man who takes a shot at me. Got it?"

"You..." the man panted... "don't give orders... to Locke. He has... something you want."

"What do you mean?" Had Locke found the other chest?

The man clammed up.

"Maddock! Get over here!" Bones called from the street.

Maddock left the man lying there and ran toward the sound of his friend's voice, dashing through the gate and arriving on the sidewalk by the entrance to the

Church Street Subway station just as a motorcycle screeched to a halt in front of them, scattering pedestrians who shouted and cursed. Willis raised the face shield and smiled broadly at them. He loved bikes.

"Matt and Corey are on the way." He said.

"Get Avery out of here," Maddock told him.

This time, Avery didn't argue, but leapt onto the back of the bike, pulled on the spare helmet, and wrapped her arms around Willis as he rocketed out into traffic.

"Look out!" Bones shouted, pushing Maddock to the ground as a bullet whistled over their heads and the few people who hadn't been driven away by Willis's bike ran for the subway or the churchyard. The big man from inside the church had recovered his wits, circled around the outside of the churchyard, and was now coming at them head-on.

Maddock reached for his Walther but, before he could draw it, a beat-up van flashed past them, and bounded up onto the sidewalk. As it drew even with the approaching man, the passenger stuck out his arm, encased in a hard cast, and clotheslined their attacker under the chin, linebacker style. The surprised man flew backward and tumbled down the stairs to the subway.

"Holy crap, that hurt!" Matt groaned as Maddock and Bones clambered into the van and Corey hit the gas. Sirens sounded in the distance but Maddock wasn't worried. They'd be long gone before the police arrived. Besides, it had been the other guys shooting at them, and in front of witnesses at that, and neither was in any condition to get up and run.

"Why did you hit him with your cast?" Maddock asked as Corey wove the van through traffic.

"I don't know, it seemed like something Bones would do," Matt groaned, holding his arm to his chest.

"Amen to that, my brother." Bones high-fived Matt's good hand. "Nice rescue, by the way."

"Did you find it?" Corey asked, eyes locked on the street. "Because if I get points on my license, I want it to be for a good cause."

"We did, and as soon as we catch up with Willis and Avery, we'll see where it leads."

Chapter 22

"Let's see what we've got here." Avery took out the paper they'd recovered from the chest and laid it on the table in their hotel room. She carefully unrolled it, revealing another map. Unlike the Oak Island map, however, there was no code to break. Instead, someone had added on to the original map. The older, more faded ink, showed a river and a stretch of shoreline. A dotted line led inland to a spot marked with a cross. Distances were lined out to specific landmarks: a tree, a boulder, and a bend in a stream. In the bottom right corner, the creator of the map had drawn three of the cross-in-circle symbols they'd seen on Oak Island arranged in a triangle around another familiar symbol- two Knights on a horse. Over the top of this map, someone had inked in a street, a building, and an "x."

"That's the cross symbol we saw at Oak Island," Maddock said, pointing to the corner of the map.

"I don't believe it," Avery said. "This is Trinity Church."

Maddock hadn't even noticed the labels. Sure enough, the street was labeled "Wall" and the building "Trinity."

"Kidd, or one of his contemporaries, must have added these details," he said. "The land had probably changed so much that the landmarks on the original map were useless."

"So, once more into the breach?" Bones asked, drawing an amused look from Avery. Maddock had long ago grown accustomed to Bones' occasional lapses in which he let his intelligence show, but people who didn't know him well were sometimes taken unaware.

"We'd have to be crazy to go back," Corey said. "They know we're here and they know what three of us look like. Surely they'll be watching for us."

"Maybe not," Maddock mused. "They know we found the map, but they have no idea where it leads. They probably figure we're already on the way out of town, headed for wherever this map leads."

Just then, Bones' phone rang. He answered it, listened for a minute, then uttered a stream of curses. The conversation didn't last much longer, and when he hung up, he cursed again and slammed his fist into the wall.

"Locke's got Angel."

Maddock felt like he'd been dropped into freezing water. He sat there, unable to speak, or even move.

"Charlie went back to see Meade. I don't know what he said, but the sheriff broke down and admitted they don't have her. The deputies tried to bring her to Meade on the island, and Locke's people basically intimidated them into turning her over."

The icy shock was melting quickly, warmed by Maddock's kindled fury. He pictured Angel in Locke's power and suddenly felt a blood rage he'd only experienced in the heat of battle in the service.

"Locke said he'd give her back." Bones' tone of voice made it clear what he thought of that promise.

"Oh my God." Avery looked like she was about to faint. "This is crazy."

"We're going back to the island," Maddock said. "Screw the treasure hunt. I'll kill every one of those..."

"They're gone." Bones cut him off. "He left some researchers behind, and that's it."

"Damn!" Maddock stood and began to pace the room. "Does Meade have any idea where they've taken her?"

"He gave us two clues: the museum, and somebody named Morgan."

"The Bailyn Museum?" Avery asked. "That's where Locke supposedly works, and it's right here in New York."

"Let's go." Maddock headed to the door, his thoughts bent on mayhem.

"Hold on there, bro. We need a plan." Bones motioned to the chair Maddock had vacated. "Sit down and let's think this through."

Bones acting the calm, rational part was such a departure that it brought Maddock up short. He turned back to face the others, but didn't sit down.

"I want to hurt somebody too," Bones said, "but if we just go storming in there, we could get Angel killed, assuming she's even there. We need to do this right, and we need you at your best."

"You're right." Maddock squeezed his eyes shut and turned the problem over in his mind. "They know me, you, and Avery by sight, but they don't know the rest of the crew. Corey, if we get you close enough, could you hack into their network?"

"Jimmy would be the better choice, but it's possible," Corey said. "It depends on what kind of security measures they have in place."

"It's worth a try. We don't need access to everything, just their security camera footage."

"I'll call Jimmy right now. Maybe he can give me some pointers." He excused himself and stepped out onto the balcony to make his call.

Maddock turned to Willis.

"Would you be willing to go inside, take a look around?"

"Hell yes. Let me put on my nerd clothes and I'll be ready to roll." His smile, normally so open and friendly, was hungry and dangerous. "Nobody messes with our girl."

"What about me?" Matt raised his broken arm. "I'm ready to bash some more bad guys with my cast."

"I have a job for you too. We," he indicated Bones, Matt, and Avery, "are going wherever this map leads."

Chapter 23

Corey parked the van in the parking lot of the Bailyn Museum as close to the building as possible, cut the engine, and moved to the back, out of sight of passers by. He quickly located the Bailyn's wireless network, clicked to access it, and activated a program Jimmy had given him. He nervously drummed out the beat to "Apache" as the program began trying security codes at a dizzying rate. He worried that the Bailyn would have systems in place to detect intruders, but Jimmy had assured him this program was as good as invisible.

In a matter of minutes, he was in. Jimmy had programmed an Elvis icon that gave a thumbs-up and said, "Thank you very much," upon a successful hack. Corey chuckled at the image and moved on.

A few keystrokes and a list of directories scrolled down the screen. He selected /security and Jimmy's program began its work. Two minutes later he was looking at a list of sub-folders containing video from various parts of the building. Where to begin? Angel had been taken less than twenty-four hours earlier, so he chose a likely time frame and began his search.

He sighed, wondering how long this was going to take. He hoped Willis was having better luck.

Willis, clad in khaki pants, a baggy polo shirt, and glasses, and wearing a camera around his neck, made his way through the museum. It wasn't the greatest disguise in the world. He was more than six feet tall, so he stood out in any crowd, but at least he was dressed appropriately for the setting.

He regularly consulted the map in his brochure, but it wasn't the exhibits he was interested in. He was marking off the rooms he had inspected, searching for access to offices, storage, or mechanical rooms. So far he'd met with no success. The few doors he had seen were locked and required electronic clearance to enter.

The only room he had not yet checked stood adjacent to the entryway. If he struck out here, he wasn't sure what he'd try next. Maybe go outside and look for a service entrance. The exhibits here were devoted to pirates. He took that as a good sign. A replica of a seventeenth century pirate ship hung suspended from the ceiling, with a second-floor viewing area up above. Tall windows lined the wall to his left and a series of exhibits filled the wall to his right.

He passed wax figures of Blackbeard, Captain Kidd, and Black Caesar. A heavy tarp was draped across the next exhibit and a sign taped to the rail indicated it was "closed for repair." That didn't necessarily mean anything, but he had a feeling about it, and his instincts had kept him alive through a youth spent in one of the worst neighborhoods in Detroit, and then through service in the Navy.

He checked to make sure no one was looking, then peered behind the plastic. A wax figure lay on the floor, one arm broken. Nothing too weird about that. And then he spotted something very out of place- the tip of a sneaker print. Even that might not have seemed unusual if it weren't for the fact that he'd seen enough bloody prints in his life to know one when he saw it. Whoever had come through here had stepped in blood. He leaned farther in and spotted a doorknob on the back wall.

"Can I help you?" A big man with a shaved head and battered face stood behind him. The man wore a museum ID badge that named him A. Shears, a radio on one hip, and a pistol on the other.

Willis immediately recognized him by the description Maddock had given. This was the man who had accosted Maddock and Bones in the chapel earlier in the day and whom Matt had taken out. He suppressed a grin, wishing he'd seen what Bones had described as an "epic takedown." He had to hand it to Shears, though. The guy bounced back quickly.

"Just wondering what this display was. First time I've been here, you know."

Shears looked him up and down before answering.

"Nothing special, just a diorama of a pirate raid. The bloke got himself a broken arm."

"All right. Cool." He continued down the line of exhibits, feeling Shears' gaze boring into him. He checked his watch. Forty minutes until closing time. If Shears didn't move along soon, he'd have to find a place to hide.

Thirty minutes later, he stood alone on the second floor balcony that afforded visitors a view of the pirate ship. Shears still stalked the ground floor, ushering the last visitors out of the museum. As the last group of people left, Shears mounted the steps, heading up to the second floor.

Willis was cornered. The stairs were the only way down and, with Shears already suspicious of him, he had no way to explain his presence here. He looked for a way out. He had less than ten seconds before Shears reached the top of the stairs, turned, and spotted him. He looked around, seeking a way out, and his eyes fell on the pirate ship.

It would be a bit of a leap, but he could do it. His mind made up, he clambered up onto the rail, not looking down at the floor below. Hoping this wasn't the day his impulsiveness finally came back to bite him, he jumped.

His stomach fluttered on the edge of nausea as he flew through open space. Next thing he knew, his arms and legs were wrapped around the stout cable that supported one corner of the stern. He slid down its length, his hands burning as the rough steel scoured his palms, and dropped with scarcely a sound into the ship.

He hit the deck and reached for the Beretta M9 he wore concealed underneath his shirt. If Shears spotted the gentle rocking of the ship, he might investigate, and Willis was through playing around. He waited, wondering if he'd be spotted and, if not, how he was going to get down.

"It's somewhere around here, I think." Avery let out an exasperated sigh and stamped her foot. "This is so frustrating. We need more to go on."

They stood in the Trinity Churchyard, looking at the rows of gravestones, many of which had eroded over the centuries until the engraving on them was nearly illegible.

"If we're looking for another Templar church, we have to assume it was built long before Trinity Church or this graveyard were here," Maddock said.

"Thanks for that ray of sunshine," Bones replied. "If we don't find something soon, I'm going to get all weepy and emo like that Keep America Beautiful Indian."

"Iron Eyes Cody?" Avery said. "Did you know he wasn't even an Indian? He was Italian."

"Shut it! No freaking way."

"Yes, way." Avery laughed.

"Focus." Maddock knew Bones was trying not to think about Angel. Maddock too was having a hard time keeping his mind on the task at hand. "The map has three of the cross-in-circle symbols set in a triangle. Why don't we see if we can find that same pattern on any of the gravestones?"

They spread out, moving quickly because evening was rapidly approaching and the light growing dim. Maddock soon found what he was looking for on the gravestone of William Bradford. The three crosses formed a triangle around a cherub face. Hope rose, but fell as he realized it was only a simple headstone and could not be the entrance to anything.

"Got one!" Bones called. "Three crosses around an angel dude. Just a headstone, though."

"Same here." Avery sounded disheartened.

"Well, that was a big, freaking fail," Bones said. "What now?"

Maddock considered the situation. Like the crosses, the headstones formed an equilateral triangle, and at the center of that triangle stood...

"Alexander Hamilton's tomb," Maddock whispered.

The tomb of Alexander Hamilton was perhaps the most impressive of all the structures in the churchyard. Square at the bottom, with columns at each corner surmounted by urns, the tomb was topped by a weathered obelisk.

Maddock knelt down behind Bradford's headstone and followed the cherub's line of sight. Sure enough, it pointed directly at the obelisk. He instructed Bones and Avery to do the same with the headstones they had found and, moments later, they confirmed his theory.

Maddock made his way over to the tomb and circled it, searching for any indication that this was what they were looking for. An epitaph to the famed patriot was engraved on one side, but he saw no Templar symbols. He let his eyes drift upward to the top of the obelisk where he thought he saw the faint outline of a circle engraved on the weathered top.

"You two, keep a lookout," he said to Bones and Avery, and climbed onto the tomb. The obelisk was short enough that he could easily see the four sides of the capstone.

"They're here!" he exclaimed. "A templar cross on three sides of the point. This is it."

"But Hamilton wasn't a Freemason. Why would that symbol be carved onto his tomb?" Avery looked puzzled.

"It *shouldn't* be here. Someone put that mark here for a reason." Maddock had no doubt he was on the right track.

"What do we do now? Say *open sesame?*" Bones asked.

Maddock looked down at the symbols and two details immediately caught his attention: a groove ran around the capstone, as if it were a separate piece; and on the fourth side, instead of a cross, a small arrow was carved. It was so tiny he almost missed it, but it was there.

"What's that thing you're always saying, Bones? Righty tightie, lefty loosie?" With that, he took hold of the capstone and gave it a deft twist. It didn't budge.

"Impressive." Avery smirked, then turned and gave Bones a wink.

"Thanks for the support." Maddock got a better grip this time and poured all of his strength into the effort. Slowly, inch by inch, the capstone began to rotate, and rose as it turned. After a quarter turn, Maddock heard a loud thunk and the capstone froze. "Anything?"

"Nothing," Avery said.

"There are three crosses," Bones said. "How about three turns?"

"Or maybe three quarter-turns," Avery added.

"You're already correcting me, woman?" Bones asked. "We hardly know each other."

Maddock tuned them out and gave the capstone another twist. He felt the strain in every muscle of his shoulders, arms, and back as he turned the stone another quarter-turn, and then another. When he'd completed the third turn, the tomb vibrated beneath his feet and a hollow, grating sound rose up from down below.

"Yahtzee!" Bones exclaimed.

"You did it, Maddock," Avery whispered.

Maddock leapt down and looked down at the base of the tomb on the side facing away from the street. The entire side of the tomb had sunk into the ground, revealing an empty space below. They had found it!

Chapter 24

Corey sighed and opened the last sub-folder. His search had been utterly fruitless, and now it was closing time. He wondered if Willis had fared any better. Considering how long he'd spent in the museum, he'd better have found something. If Willis had been browsing museum displays while Corey worked his butt off, they would have a talk later.

This folder contained footage from the security camera in the delivery area. He quickly scrolled through the clips, as the museum apparently didn't get many deliveries. One clip after another, all showing an empty loading bay, rolled by. He was ready to give up, but figured he might as well keep going, at least until Willis showed up, which ought to be any minute now.

The most recent clip was from this afternoon, and ended shortly before they'd arrived. For no particular reason, he skipped down to it and double-clicked. This clip began the same as the others, footage of an empty room, but it soon grew interesting.

On the screen, a heavy-set man with a pistol on his hip opened the bay door and a black sedan with tinted windows rolled in. Another man, short and dark, also armed, stepped out. The two spoke for a minute, then moved off screen. Two minutes later, they returned, supporting a figure in jeans and a t-shirt.

It was Angel.

She could barely stand, as if she was under the influence of some sort of drug. She also might have been injured, and unable to walk on her own, but he didn't want to consider that. Her hands were cuffed in front of her and ankles shackled. They weren't taking any chances with her.

They put her into the back seat and the big guy got in after her, while the dark-skinned man took the wheel. A minute later, a lean, tawny-haired man climbed into the passenger seat and they drove away. Corey scrolled through the rest of the clip, but the car did not return.

Angel was gone. They had missed her by a matter of minutes.

Corey reached for his cell phone, then thought the better of it. They had agreed Corey would not call Willis, in case his phone should ring at an inopportune time, but Willis would call Corey if he needed help.

When they weren't certain anything was amiss at the museum, he hadn't been too concerned about Willis, but now things had changed. What if the guys he'd seen leaving in the car weren't the only armed, dangerous men on the premises? Willis should know that Angel was gone and there was nothing more he could do in there, but how could Corey let him know? He supposed he could go in after him, but the very thought made his stomach threaten to heave up. He was a computer guy, not a soldier. Besides, what if he walked into a trap and they both wound up...

He dismissed the line of thought with a shake of his head. Willis had been in worse situations than this plenty of times. He'd be okay.

Willis checked his watch. Thirty minutes since he'd heard so much as a footstep down below. Hoping Shears and the rest of the museum staff had gone, he crawled to the bow of the pirate ship and peered over the edge.

Down below him, the museum was empty. He watched for another five minutes before deciding it was safe to come out. But how to get down? He scanned the deck and his eyes fell on a coil of rope in the stern. Unlike most of the ship, which was constructed from new materials, this appeared to be an authentic rope from an old sailing ship. It looked dry and brittle, but he had no choice.

He lashed the rope to the stern and tossed it over the edge. It was too short, ending about ten feet above the floor, but it would have to do. Not willing to waste time fretting over something beyond his control, he took hold of the rope, climbed over the rail, and shimmied down.

The coarse rope scoured his already scraped hands, but he worked his way down in a controlled slide.

Halfway to the floor, he heard a snap and the rope gave an inch.

"Oh hell." He dared a look down. Twenty feet was too far to fall.

Another snap as strands of the aged rope began to break under the strain of his weight. And another.

He slid a little faster, bracing himself for the fall that now seemed inevitable as, far above him, the rope frayed and, fiber by fiber, fell apart. He was twelve feet up when it finally gave way.

He hit the ground hard, landing skydiver style, but the impact on the hard floor jolted him all the way up his spine. He grimaced as pain lanced through his knees, and he wondered if he'd torn something. It didn't matter, though. He had a job to do.

One positive was that he didn't have to leave a length of rope dangling from the stern of the ship where it could draw unwanted attention. He coiled up the fallen rope and carried it with him to the closed exhibit where he hid it beneath the fallen pirate figure. He paused to listen in case anyone was still here and had heard his fall, but the museum was silent as a tomb. Figuring it was time to move on, he took a deep breath and stepped through the door at the back of the exhibit.

He found himself in a spartan hallway that ran along the back of the exhibit hall. Doors on either side provided access to the various exhibits. In front of him, a stairwell led down to a lower level, and he spotted another smudged, bloody footprint a few steps down. Hand resting on his Beretta, he made his way down into the darkness.

He found himself in a poorly-lit basement area. He spotted more footprints and followed them past doors labeled according to what was stored inside them, to a small room, perhaps a large janitor's closet. Inside, he found a folding chair and a stainless steel table.

And a great deal of blood.

A dark spatter slashed across the wall to his right, and more spots trailed down to the floor, where more dark, dry patches spotted the gray surface. Trembling with rage, he gave the room a once-over, in case he'd missed an important detail. A small wastebasket was shoved into the corner on his left. At first, he thought it was empty, but then he spied a glint of silver. He knelt and fished it out. It was a broken necklace with a turquoise and silver Kokopelli pendant. He recognized it as Angel's. This was definitive proof she had been here.

"I'm gonna kill somebody," he muttered, pocketing the necklace.

"Not today, my friend," someone said from behind him. Damn! He'd let his anger distract him, and someone had crept up behind him. "Very slowly take that gun out of the holster."

"Hey man, I was just looking for the john. Is it anywhere around here?"

"If you don't want a hole in your head, do what I say, and do it now."

He did as instructed, slipping his Beretta out of the holster with two fingers, making it clear he was not reaching for the trigger, and setting it on the ground.

"Good. Now turn around slowly."

Still squatting down, Willis turned to see Shears pointing a gun at him. The man smiled, clearly pleased with himself.

"Slide the gun over to me."

Willis did as he was told. He gave the Beretta a shove, sliding it toward Shears' gun hand with enough force that it slid past him.

Shears took his eyes off of Willis for only a split second, but that was all Willis needed. He whipped his Recon knife from his belt, hurled it at Shears, and dove into a forward roll as a bullet pinged off the ceiling. He came to his feet ready to wrestle the gun from Shears, but there was no need. Willis' aim had been true, and the hilt of his knife protruded from Shears' chest. He'd gotten him in the heart.

Willis retrieved his knife and his Beretta, and dragged Shears' lifeless body into the room where Angel had been held. He regretted taking the man's life, not because he placed any particular value on it, but because he would have liked to question him. As it was, he had no clue as to Angel's whereabouts. He only knew she had been here. He guessed that would have to be enough.

The space beneath Hamilton's tomb was a tight box, but deep enough that even Bones could stand up straight. A round seal was carved in the center of each wall: the Templar cross, an Eagle clutching a spear in its talons, and the familiar temple seal and two knights seal.

Maddock moved immediately to the two knights on horseback, as it was the one drawn in the corner of the map. He ran the beam of his flashlight back and forth across the carving. It didn't take long to realize what made this seal different from the traditional rendering. In most versions of the seal, each knight carried a lance. In this carving, the two lances were carved as one thick lance with a prominent point. Closer scrutiny revealed a fine seam running around the top half of the lance. Maddock blew the dust away from the edges.

"This looks like a button," Avery said. "May I?"

"Sure." Maddock stepped back and watched as she gingerly pressed on the top half of the lance. It sank into the stone with a hushed click, and the seal slowly rolled to the side, vanishing into the wall and revealing a dark shaft with handholds in the side leading deeper into the ground.

"Maybe you should stay here." Maddock looked at Avery. "I don't know how far down we'll have to climb. It could be dangerous."

"Are you stupid?" Avery looked scandalized. "This is Dad's quest and we're going to finish it together. Besides, despite what our first meeting might have indicated, I can climb a little." With that, she clambered through the hole, ignoring Maddock's urges for her to exercise caution, and began her descent.

"Sisters," Bones said. "You gotta' love 'em." He grinned. "I'll make sure she doesn't get into trouble." He followed Avery into the shaft, and Maddock went last.

At the bottom of the shaft, a doorway opened onto a dark chamber, with steps leading down into the bottom. Maddock and Bones played their lights around the room. It was another Templar church. Like the church beneath Oak Island, the walls were adorned with ornate carvings but, instead of scenes showing knights in combat, the images told the story of the crucifixion. Directly in front of them, behind a simple stone altar, the image of the centurion piercing Jesus' side looked down upon them. The agony on Jesus' face was almost palpable.

"This is amazing!" Avery took out a camera and began snapping pictures. "A Templar church beneath New York City. Hard to believe." She paused, lowering the camera. "Wait a minute. This had to be here long before the Hamilton tomb was constructed. So that means..."

"Someone was in on the secret and built the tomb specifically as a cover-up," Bones finished.

"The Freemasons?" Avery asked.

"I think it was Elvis and The Colonel, but that's just me."

"You're useless." Avery looked around, and her eyes suddenly widened. "But if someone or some group knew about this place, what if they took whatever was hidden here? I don't see anything."

"If it's like the church under Oak Island, and I think it is, this place hasn't revealed all its secrets." Maddock pointed to a spot high on the wall and the symbol of six crosses in a circle, identical to that in the Oak Island church. "If my guess is right, the map to this temple didn't include everything someone would need to know. Bones, a boost?"

Bones chuckled and hunched down against the wall below the crosses and served as a ladder for Maddock to climb. Bones stood up straight, then took Maddock by his feet and lifted him up until Maddock reached a ledge beneath the crosses.

"Maddock, you have got to lay off the bacon cheeseburgers," Bones grunted. "You're too fat for me to keep doing this."

"Quit whining." Maddock hoisted himself up onto the ledge and cautiously climbed to his feet. The ledge was narrow and the drop was far enough that he didn't want to risk a fall.

"Careful," Avery warned.

He smiled down at her, then reached up to the topmost cross, took hold, and turned it in the same way Bones had turned its counterpart in the Oak Island church. It didn't budge at first, but then, slowly, it moved. Gradually, he rolled the circle back into the wall, and climbed through.

The space here was much like the one beneath Oak Island- a domed, turret-like chamber with the same double-line of symbols spiraling from ceiling to floor and the same wedge-shaped pattern in the ceiling's center, and a stone altar off to one side. In this chamber, however, there was no wooden casket atop the altar, but a long wooden cylinder. He took a minute to make a photographic record of the chamber before moving to the altar.

He was tempted to crack open the cylinder right then and there and see what was inside, but common sense won out. He hefted the cylinder and carried it back to the entrance.

"Hey Bones, can you catch this?" he called.

"Only if you don't throw like a girl."

Maddock chuckled and tossed it down to Bones, who managed to snag it in both arms before it hit the ground.

"What's inside?" He turned it over, giving it a close look.

"Don't know. We'll see when we open it."

Chapter 25

"What do you think it is?" Matt asked. "It's really long."

"That's what she said," Bones jibed. He elbowed Avery, who gave an exasperated sigh and shook her head.

They were back on board *Sea Foam*, docked, and waiting for Corey and Willis to return. There was no word from them, and he didn't know how to interpret that, though he kept his hopes up.

"Let's find out." The cylinder was a good five feet long, and capped on each end. The caps were held in place by resin. Maddock needed only a few minutes to work one end free. He twisted the cap off and pulled out a handful of coconut fibers.

"I see it," Avery whispered.

A brass circle gleamed beneath the stark light. Maddock took hold of it and drew forth a spear. The shaft featured the same spiral band he had seen on the walls of the two chambers. The oversized spearhead was made of the same mottled metal as Carnwennan and, like the dagger, a deep channel ran down one side of the blade. The head was held in place by a band of the now familiar white stone. As he held the spear out for the others to inspect, lights began to swirl deep in the stone.

"It's Rhongomnyiad. King Arthur's spear. It's got to be," Avery said. "It's clearly a mate to the dagger."

"Is it a cloaking device too?" Bones asked.

"There's no legend of invisibility surrounding the spear. In fact, there aren't many legends about it at all." Avery looked thoughtful. "The only one I can think of says it could take a life with a single touch. But the same story claimed that it carries life within it."

"So, who wants to be the one to touch the big, scary spear?" Bones asked. No one volunteered. "Let me see that thing." Bones took the spear from Maddock and looked it up and down. "Do you think the butt turns it on, sort of like the dagger?" Before anyone cold object, he pressed on the bronze butt and the spearhead flickered. "Sweet. I wonder..."

"Bones, don't..."

Before Maddock could finish the sentence, Bones prodded a metal folding chair with the spear. Avery screamed and everyone covered their faces as, with a loud crack, the spear sent up a shower of blue sparks and the chair flew across the cabin and clattered to the floor. Bones hurried over and picked it up so everyone could see the smoking hole the spear had burned through it.

"Well, now we know what it does." He grinned. "Who's next?"

"Bones, give me the spear before you sink us." Maddock took the spear back and held it loosely by his side. He turned to share a pained smile with Avery, and was surprised to see her gaping at him.

"Maddock," Bones said, "your butt is glowing."

Maddock looked down and saw that the dagger, which he had tucked into his belt, and the stone band around the spear, had begun to shine. The closer together he held them the brighter they shone.

"This is crazy." Avery said. "How can you guys be so calm about this?"

"Like we said before, we've seen this phenomenon a couple of times." Maddock drew Carnwennan and held it next to Rhongomnyiad. The white stones glowed like small suns, though they produced no heat. Strangely, he felt a tingling down his arms, and decided he shouldn't toy with forces he did not understand.

"Stones like this are unheard of." Avery took the spear from Maddock for a closer look. "So, what are they? Did you study them?"

"We've never actually been able to do that. We sort of keep losing them."

Just then, Maddock's phone vibrated, sparing him further questions. The number was unfamiliar.

"Hello?"

"We each have something the other wants."

He'd only heard the voice once before, but he recognized it instantly. It could only be one person.

"Locke." He couldn't keep the growl from his voice. Silence fell in the cabin as everyone stared.

"*One and the same. Now, time is short, so I shall keep this simple. I want what you found on the island...*"

"I don't know what you're talking about."

"*Mister Maddock, I assure you I have no attachment to this girl. In fact, I find her crass and tiresome. The only value she has to me is as an object for trade. If you do not have what I want, rather, if you insist on pretending so, she will no longer be of use to me, and I shall dispose of her. Now, shall we begin again?*" He took Maddock's silence as assent, and continued. "*I want what you found on the island, and I want the map you recovered from Saint Paul's.*"

Maddock's mind worked furiously. As he'd predicted, Locke knew about the map, but assumed it led to somewhere else entirely. That was good.

"What do you want with the map? It was right here in New York all this time, right under your nose. Why didn't you take it?"

"*Yes, disappointing, that. You beat my men there, literally and figuratively, by minutes.*"

"We have a bad habit of doing both those things."

Locke ignored him.

"*For your convenience, we will make the exchange in Baltimore. I believe you are already headed in that direction. Don't bother with the Poe House. My people will be there before you.*"

Maddock's heart pounded and thoughts hummed through his mind at a lightning pace. Locke had caught him off guard with that detail.

"I'm not making any kind of deal with you until I talk to Angel." Just saying her name felt like a vice clamping down on his chest. He could hardly breathe, so powerful was his rage.

"*How cliche,*" Locke sighed. "*Very well, if it will make you feel you have some semblance of control, you may speak to her. But first, I want something in return.*"

"What?"

"*Tell me which one you have. My man got a good enough look that I know it is not the spear.*"

"The dagger." Maddock saw no point in lying.

"*Excellent. Very well, here's your bird.*"

Two seconds of agonizing silence hung in the air, and then he heard Angel's voice.

"*Maddock?*" For a moment, she sounded fearful, almost childlike, and then her resolve hardened. "*Are you there?*"

"Yeah, are you all right?" He wondered if the look on his face or the tone of his voice revealed anything to the others in the cabin, who still looked on in rapt silence.

"*Doesn't matter. Don't you give this poncey asshat anything.*" Now she sounded like her old self. "*I'll kick your ass if you do. You hear me?*"

"Sorry, Angel. You know I don't follow orders very well. You just hang tight, okay?" He almost smiled at the stream of profanity she hurled at him.

"*Very well.*" Locke was back on the line. "*Tomorrow at one o'clock in the afternoon. You will receive specific instructions at noon. If I, or any of my people, have so much as a hint you've notified the authorities, she dies, and then I will hunt you down and kill you too. Do we understand each other?*"

"Yes to the first part. As to the second, you're welcome to try your luck any time." At that moment, Maddock would have liked nothing more than a shot at Locke, but he had Angel to think about.

"How I do love bravado." Locke chuckled. *"By the way, don't believe her when she says she doesn't want you to come for her. She made some very interesting admissions under sedation."*

Maddock was about to tell Locke exactly where he could stick his advice, but heavy footsteps on deck distracted him momentarily, and he looked around to see Willis and Corey hurry in.

"Maddock," Willis began, "Angel was at the museum, but she's gone."

Maddock nodded and turned away.

"Just make sure you've got her there tomorrow."

"It's a date, then," Locke said. *"Be sure to dress smart."*

The call ended and Maddock stared at his phone for a moment before tucking it in his pocket.

"They'll trade Angel for the map and the dagger. They don't know we've already found the spear."

"A trade's not good enough." Bones took a deep breath, holding in his anger. "I want to hurt somebody, and I really don't want to give them the dagger."

"We might not have to," Maddock said. "I've got a plan."

Chapter 26

Avery looked out at Baltimore's Inner Harbor, drinking in the sunshine and watching the boats zip across the gray waters of the harbor. She looked to the southeast to see if she could catch a glimpse of Fort McHenry, but the distance was too great. All around her, tourists swarmed like insects, visiting the various attractions, including historic ships and the National Aquarium. Despite the pungent air that carried a hint of rotting fish beneath the damp salt smell, it was a pleasant enough place. She looked across the harbor to the west, where she could just make out the shape of the *U.S.S. Constellation,* and wondered how Maddock fared.

"Miss Halsey? I'm Director Sweeney." A brown-haired man with a thick circle beard approached, smiling, and shook Avery's hand.

"Thank you so much for meeting me on short notice." Avery put on her most coquettish smile. "I know how busy you must be, and here you are giving us a private tour."

"Not a problem. We don't get many college professors here, and none from Canada that I can remember. Certainly none as attractive as you." He leaned in just a little too close. Oh well, flirting was part of her strategy, so she couldn't blame the guy for responding.

"Aren't you sweet?" She reached out and gave his arm the gentlest touch. "I'd like you to meet Corey, he's my graduate assistant."

Sweeney's smile, which had faltered when he saw Corey, returned immediately.

"Good to meet you." He shook Corey's hand and turned back to Avery. "I thought for a minute he might be your husband. I was afraid I was going to have to get jealous."

"Nope. Single as they come." Avery wriggled the fingers on her left hand, calling attention to her bare ring finger. She hated this girly-girl crap, and the guy probably deserved better than to be manipulated, but this was too important to let feelings get in the way.

"Well, if you're ready to see the lighthouse, we'll go on in."

Seven Foot Knoll was like no lighthouse she'd ever seen. The squat, round metal building, painted barn red, was supported by a stilt-like metal framework and topped by a short beacon.

"It looks like some Wisconsin dairy farmers tried to build a UFO," Corey observed.

Sweeney flashed him an annoyed look, but quickly forced a smile.

"It's called a screw pile lighthouse. The supports, or piles, are screwed into the sea bottom or river bottom and the lighthouse is built atop them. It's not the design most people think of, but it's not uncommon. This is the oldest screw pile in Maryland."

Avery could tell by the look in Corey's eyes that he was about to make a really bad pun, and shook her head. She had no doubt this was Bones' influence.

"I guess these have the advantage of not needing to be waterproofed against the rising tides?" Avery asked, feigning interest.

"Very astute," Sweeney said, leading them up a staircase to the deck that encircled the lighthouse. "Of course, the primary advantages were their relative cheapness and ease of construction. Here we are." He opened the door and ushered them inside.

The interior was well-lit by the sunlight streaming through windows all around. Avery gushed over the various displays, asking detailed questions about the model ships and other exhibits, while Corey wandered around pretending to take notes.

Their plan was simple. Avery would keep Sweeney distracted while Corey found the chest and removed the map. She'd told him how to open the compartment, and hoped he wouldn't be too clumsy about it.

"Is that the Mayflower?" She pointed to a model high on a shelf.

"Good eye. She doesn't really belong in a Maryland museum, but she's a personal favorite of mine." He shrugged and gave her an embarrassed smile.

"I thought I detected a touch of Massachusetts in your accent."

"Wow. Nothing gets past you. You ought to be a federal agent." Sweeney winked.

Out of the corner of her eye, she saw that Corey had found the chest, and her pulse quickened. Now was the moment. Cursing herself for what she was about to do, she pulled Sweeney's head down and kissed him, at the same time turning him around so his back was to Corey. He tensed, then relaxed and put his arms around her and kissed her back. It wasn't the worst kiss in the world, but she'd never been one to use her sexuality to manipulate a guy, which made this all the more uncomfortable. That, and she sort of had a thing for Bones, and hoped Corey wouldn't say anything to him about this.

Hurry up Corey.

The kiss stretched beyond all natural and comfortable limits, and Sweeney started to pull away. Avery tangled her fingers in his hair and held on.

"Ahem!"

Avery broke the kiss and saw Corey standing beside them, an amused smile on his face.

"Sorry to interrupt, but we have a plane to catch." He tapped his watch. "We need to head out."

"Oh." Sweeney was clearly disappointed. "Do you need a ride to the airport?"

"That's good of you, but we're flying out of Dulles, and we're in a rental car." She gave his arm a squeeze. "Thank you so much for showing us the museum. I'll text you next time I'm in town."

"Sounds good." He still seemed a bit dazed. "I'll email you. You know, so we can keep in touch."

They left as quickly as they could without rousing suspicion. It wasn't until they were crossing the Harbor Bridge Walk that she felt comfortable asking the question that was foremost on her mind.

"Did you get it?"

"Yep." He unzipped his jacket, pulled out a brass cylinder, and handed it to her.

The smooth metal was cool to the touch and she held it in trembling fingers, excited by the thrill of discovery. She couldn't wait to take a look. She removed the end cap and withdrew the paper inside. Passing the cylinder back to Corey, she unrolled the paper, revealing another map. She wanted to take time to examine it, but suddenly felt a keen sense of vulnerability. She was standing in a very public place, and Locke's men could be anywhere.

"Hold this, and don't you dare drop it!" She handed Corey the map, took out her phone, snapped a few pictures of it, then uploaded them to a private album. "Better safe than sorry," she explained. Before she could return it to the cylinder, Corey frowned and looked over her shoulder.

"That guy keeps staring at us."

Avery glanced over her shoulder and gasped. It was one of the men who had chased them at St. Paul's church. She looked away, but not before their eyes met. She saw recognition in his face, and he began walking toward them.

"Get out of here!" Corey gave her a push in the back to get her moving, and then followed along behind her.

"What do we do?"

"He sees I've got the cylinder. When we get to the next bridge, I'll lead him away. You blend in with the crowd and make your way back to the street and meet up with Matt. You and the map need to stay out of their hands."

"But, you..."

"There's the bridge. Go!"

Before she could protest, Corey took off in the opposite direction. Avery hated to leave him to the mercy of Locke's men, but what could she do? Cursing him under her breath, she weaved through a crowd of college kids who were poking along, taking in the sights. When she reached the end of the second bridge, she stole a glance behind her.

Corey's ruse had not worked. The man was after her.

Maddock stood on the deck of the U.S.S. *Constellation,* a nineteenth-century sloop-of-war. The last remaining intact Civil War ship and one of the last sailing warships built by the United States Navy, she had also seen action in both World Wars prior to her final decommissioning in 1955. She was now a National Historical Landmark and served as a floating museum and attraction.

"Right on time, I see." Locke seemed to materialize out of the crowd. The man was good. He stopped a few feet from Maddock. "Do you have them?" His tone was relaxed, as if they were two friends engaged in a casual conversation.

"Where's Angel?" Maddock hated feeling he was at Locke's mercy. Hopefully, their plan would turn the tables.

By way of answer, Locke pointed toward the harbor, where a speedboat floated fifty feet from *Constellation's* stern. A man stood guard over the hunched figure of a dark-skinned young woman. She was gagged, her hands were bound, and her face was a mask of bruises. Anger surged through him.

"You bastard. I'll kill you for that."

"Not today, unless you want your girl to meet the same fate. Now, give it here and don't try anything foolish." He held out his hand.

It was only by supreme force of will that Maddock did not knock the man's teeth down his throat. He looked again at the speedboat, and spotted an odd disturbance in the water by its stern. Good!

"Fine. But I want Angel released now." He slid off the backpack he'd been wearing over one shoulder, and handed it to Locke.

"Of course." The lie was evident in his eyes. Locke opened the backpack just enough to expose the dagger's white hilt. He fished deeper into the backpack and withdrew a clear plastic bag that held the map. "Very good. Now..."

He cut off in mid-sentence as two men, so pale they looked almost like albinos, converged on him. Somewhere in the crowd of tourists, someone yelled, "Stop right there!"

And then it all went to hell.

Bones hauled himself over the speedboat's stern, careful not to make a sound. At his hip, the dagger gently vibrated, concealing him from sight. He wondered absently if someone who looked in his direction would see water dripping from... nothing. He wasn't about to waste time finding out.

There were two men in the boat: one at the helm and the other standing behind Angel. He wore a pistol at his hip, but his arms hung loosely at his side. Both were staring up at *Constellation*, where Maddock and Locke should be making the exchange right about now.

Bones crept up behind the guard and, fast as lightning, slipped the gun from its holster, clamped his free hand over the man's mouth and nose, and pressed the gun to his temple.

"Don't move and don't make a sound," he whispered, quiet enough not to be heard by the man in the helm over the sound of the idling engine. The man froze. If the barrel of a gun against his temple wasn't enough to guarantee his cooperation, the shock of being held by an invisible enemy did it. "Down on your knees."

The man complied instantly. Bones clubbed him across the back of the head with the pistol and he crumpled to the ground.

Angel still sat slumped forward, and hadn't seen him. Even though she was gagged, if he frightened her, she might cry out and alert the man at the helm, so he reached down and pressed the dagger, turning off the cloak.

"Angel, it's me." He kept his voice soft. "I'm getting you out of here."

Angel sat up fast and jerked her head around.

It wasn't Angel.

"Who are you?" Bones whispered, forgetting for a moment the danger and that the girl couldn't speak. "Never mind. Let's go." He helped her to her feet, removed her gag, and led her to the stern.

"What's happening?" she whispered, her voice trembling.

Just then, chaos erupted on the *Constellation*. An instant later, the boat lurched forward as the man at the helm made a beeline for the sailing ship's stern.

The woman was thrown off balance and tumbled into the water. For a split second, Bones considered letting her swim for it. If he waited on the boat, maybe he could ambush Locke, but the woman had sunk out of sight and showed no sign of surfacing.

His decision was made for him when a bullet zipped past his head. Someone on shore had spotted him. Cursing his luck, he dove into the dark water.

Avery hurried on, looking back on occasion, only to see the guy gaining on her. Every time she thought she'd lost him in a crowd, he turned up again- sometimes ahead of her, sometimes behind her, but always closer. She looked around for a police officer, security guard, anyone who might offer some help, but there was no one.

As desperate panic welled inside her, her eyes fell on an oblong, modern building of gray metal and glass. The National Aquarium. Surely they'd have a security staff there. She made a beeline for the front door. Let them bust her for gate crashing. She'd be safer in custody than out here pursued by Locke's man. She circled around an arguing young couple and there he was again. He stood twenty feet away barring her way to the entrance, smiling.

"No more of this foolish chase. Give it to me and you can be on your way."

She didn't even think. She just ran. Behind her, she heard him call out, more in annoyance than surprise, and then she heard his feet pounding the concrete, hot on her tail.

She rounded the building and saw a man in a work uniform unlocking a side door.

"Hold on!" she cried, adding a burst of speed she hadn't thought she had at her disposal. The man gaped as she sprinted past him, crashed through a set of double doors, and clambered up a staircase to her left.

She had only a moment to consider where she might be. It definitely wasn't any sort of public area. At the top of the stairs, she brushed past a girl in a polo shirt and khaki shorts, causing the girl to spill her bucket of chum or something equally stinky.

"Hey! You can't go that way! That's..."

Whatever it was, Avery didn't know because her pursuer chose that moment to take a shot at her. Avery and the girl both screamed as the roar of the gunshot filled the stairwell and the bullet tore through the ceiling. The door in front of her was propped open and Avery dashed through.

Big mistake.

She had only a split second to realize her mistake and then she was flying through the air. She flailed her arms and legs as if she could take wing, and then she splashed down into deep water. As momentum and the weight of her sodden clothes dragged her down, she kicked and paddled, trying to arrest her descent. When she finally got herself headed back up to the surface, she opened her eyes. Another mistake.

The cold salt water stung but that wasn't the worst part. A dark gray shape swam into view, bearing down on her. A shark! She had run right into one of the tanks. She opened her mouth to scream as the creature came closer, and choked on a mouthful of salt water. If the shark didn't get her, she'd likely drown.

She watched in horror as distance between her and the fierce aquatic predator shrank. Ten feet. Five feet.

And then the shark veered to the side at the last instant, its rough hide brushing her bare arm. And then it was gone. For a moment she hung there, shocked into immobility by her close call. Looking down, she saw the ghostlike shapes of aquarium visitors watching her through the glass. She wondered if they thought they were seeing a performance, or if they realized what was really happening.

And then she looked directly beneath her. There wasn't one shark in the tank, there were a half dozen, and they were circling. All thoughts fell away except the need to get the hell out of that tank and fast. The map, the man with the gun, Maddock and Bones' attempt to save Angel, all forgotten. She fought for the surface with everything she had, but no matter how hard she swam, it seemed to come no closer. She felt as if an invisible hand were holding her underwater, inches from precious air and a chance at safety.

Suddenly, she broke the surface, gasping for air. Half blinded by the salt water, she swam for the edge, wondering when the feeding frenzy would begin. Her vision cleared as she reached the side and found herself staring at a pair of shiny, black shoes. She looked up into the barrel of a gun.

"Dead end," the man said. "Now, give me the map."

The map! What had she done with it? She remembered tucking it into her bra when Corey first hurried her away from their pursuer.

"It's right here." She reached her numb fingers into her shirt and pulled out a sodden wad of brown paper. "It got a little wet." She held it up to the man, wondering if she might be able to pull him down into the water when he reached for the map, but he stood stock-still.

"You carried it into the water?" He trembled, either from shock or rage, and his finger twitched on the trigger.

"I didn't exactly plan to jump into a shark tank. It might not be ruined. Take it."

"You've bloody well ruined it, I'm sure." He chewed on his lip, thinking for a moment, and then his eyes lit up. "But you got a look at it."

"No," Avery said immediately. "I didn't have a chance before you came after us."

"We'll soon find out. We have people who are very good at getting answers. Now come on."

She heard a sick thud, and the man's eyes rolled back in his head. His knees buckled and he tumbled into the tank. Jimmy stood there, smiling, holding the lid of a toilet tank.

"I passed a bathroom on the way up. It was the only heavy thing I could grab."

"I'm glad you did. Here, pull me up." She was surprised at the strength with which he hoisted her up. He'd never seemed very physical. "Thank you." She gave him a quick hug. "Now, let's get out of here."

"I'm afraid you *will* be leaving," said a voice behind Jimmy. Two police officers stood, weapons drawn. "But it's going to be with us."

Chapter 27

As the two men converged on him, Locke whirled about and made a dash for the stern rail. Surprised by the sudden chaos, Maddock was an instant late with his attempt at tackling the fleeing man. Three strides and Locke vanished over the edge. Maddock regained his feet in time to see Locke swimming for the speedboat, which was on its way to pick him up. Angel was no longer aboard, and he soon spotted Bones helping her swim to shore.

Relieved, he turned around just as shots rang out. One of the attackers was firing wildly into the crowd, which broke apart as everyone fled for safety. His partner had gone over the rail after Locke, but he wasn't a strong swimmer and was losing ground with every stroke.

Maddock didn't know who these guys were, and what he really wanted was to get the hell out of there, but he couldn't let this madman kill an innocent person. He sprang onto the gunman, pinning the man's arm to his side as he wrestled him to the ground. He wound up on top of the man, one hand pinning his gun hand to the ground, the other at his throat.

"Who are you?"

The man's blue eyes, so pale as to almost be white, shone with icy contempt. He worked his lips and then spat on Maddock. Maddock raised his fist, intending to turn the guy's nose into a waffle, but a sharp voice rang out.

"Hold it right there! CIA!"

Maddock froze as three men, weapons trained on him, came running up.

"Put your hands in the air," one of them barked.

"I will as soon as you relieve this guy of his weapon." He wasn't about to give the albino a chance to take a shot at him or anyone else.

In an instant, the government agents, all clad in plain clothes, had him and the other man cuffed. They were patting him down when a familiar voice rang out.

"Oh no! Oh *hell* no!"

As he turned his head to face the music, he couldn't help but smile.

Tam Broderick was an attractive woman, with a solid, athletic build, dark skin, and big eyes. At least, she was pretty enough when she didn't look like she was about to waterboard someone. They'd met under unusual circumstances and forged a temporary alliance. Since then, they'd spoken a couple of times, but only to discuss a situation he and Bones had stepped into the previous winter. She marched up to Maddock, her hand resting on the Makarov he knew she carried, and stopped, her face inches from his.

"Dane Maddock." She spoke his name like a curse. "Every time I get a lead on the Dominion, you stick your big, ugly nose in and jack it all up."

"My nose is not big," he said. "I know for a fact that you like my nose."

"Save the wise comments or I will cut you." She was still angry, livid in fact, but there was now a flicker of amusement behind her glower. "Now tell me, why does the Dominion keep following you around?"

Her words hadn't registered the first time, but now they brought him up short.

"Wait. Locke is with the Dominion?" The Dominion was a shadowy organization about which little was known, yet Maddock and Bones had a knack for running afoul of them. Had it happened again?

"Who is Locke?" She threw her hands up in the air.

"The guy who went over the side. The first guy, that is. He kidnapped Bones' sister and we were getting her back." He looked around, wondering where Bones had gone.

"And you didn't think to notify the authorities? Never mind, don't bother." Tam sighed. "Let him go, but take mister pale and pasty into custody, and see if you can fish his partner out of the harbor." She turned and looked down into the water. "Don't hurry. Looks like he's a floater." Tam put her hands on her hips and fixed Maddock with a disapproving stare while her man uncuffed him. "Give him his weapon back," she said. The agent gave her a quizzical look, but followed orders.

"Where are the rest of your boys?"

"Matt's waiting in the getaway vehicle. Willis is down below, incognito, as it were, and Bones and Angel ought to be climbing out of the water by now."

"Let me get this straight." Tam pressed her fingertips to her temples. "You boys tried to stage your own rescue operation in the middle of the Inner Harbor, where who knows how many innocent people could have gotten killed?"

"We didn't choose the location," Maddock said. "And yes, we rescued Angel."

"No we didn't." Bones and Willis, both in handcuffs, were being ushered to Tam by a pair of agents.

"What do you mean?" Maddock felt cold all over. "I saw you with her."

Bones shook his head.

"It wasn't her. They found a girl her size and coloring, then beat her beyond recognition." Bones glared out at the water, as if he could take flight and chase down Locke and his men.

"Where do you think she is?" Maddock couldn't remember feeling more helpless.

"Enough!" Tam shouted. "I want to know who the hell this Locke is and why you almost got a whole mess of civilians killed out here."

"Calm down, girl," Willis said. He and Tam had fought side-by-side in the Amazon, and were on friendly terms. "Nobody likes an angry black woman."

"I am not an angry woman, I just have a low tolerance for stupidity." She glared at Willis until the smug grin melted from his face. "I suppose you can take the cuffs off of these two dummies too, and give them their weapons back. You boys won't try to run, will you?"

Bones and Willis shook their heads, both looking like chastened schoolboys.

"Even the dagger?" the agent standing behind Bones asked, holding up Carnwennan.

Tam's eyes narrowed as she looked at the odd weapon.

"What kind of knife is that?" She took it from the agent and held it up for a closer look. "You boys have a whole mess of explaining to do."

"I know," Maddock said. "But not until we go somewhere private, and the sooner the better. We've got to find out what Locke's done with Angel."

"Fine," Tam sighed. "I commandeered an office downstairs. We'll go there."

"Do you want us to go with you, Ma'am?" The agent who had handed her the dagger looked at Maddock and the others like they were about to sprout fangs.

"No. Just take the lead here. You know what to do." When the agent looked uncertain, she raised her voice. "Agent Paul, as hard as it might be to believe, I owe my life to these three stooges. I'll take one man to guard the door, but that's it. I'll be safe with them. Besides, they just might be able to help us." She turned back to Maddock. "Come on. This sounds like it's going to be a long story."

On the way downstairs, Maddock remembered something.

"So, when did you become CIA? Last I knew, you were FBI."

"Oh, right about the time somebody stirred up a branch of the Dominion in Germany." Her glare left no doubt whom she meant. "All of a sudden our little domestic problem became international."

"Hey, I filled you in on that right away," Maddock protested.

"Yes, you did." She sounded neither pleased nor upset. "Funny how you keep butting heads with the Dominion, but you don't want to join in the fight against them."

Maddock didn't bother to argue. They'd had this conversation before. The previous summer, Tam had asked him and his crew to join her in her work rooting out the Dominion.

When they settled into the small office in the museum section of the *Constellation*, he wasted no time bringing her up to speed.

"So, we've got the dagger and the spear, but Locke still has Angel," he finished.

Tam looked down at the dagger lying across her lap.

"You're telling me this thing is..."

"Carnwennan. King Arthur's dagger. We also have his spear."

"Oh, holy Lord Jesus." She rested her head in her hands. "Would it kill you to have an ordinary life?" She sighed for what felt like the twentieth time, and handed him the dagger. "You really expect me to believe not only was King Arthur real, but that thing belonged to him? It doesn't exactly look ancient."

"Think about what we found in the Amazon," Bones said. "Then ask yourself if this seems any more unlikely."

"I don't suppose it does, at that, but it's hard to get used to." She stood and moved to the window that looked out on the harbor. "You've got the spear and the dagger. Aren't you missing something important?"

Maddock, Bones, and Willis exchanged glances. They'd discussed this very subject. The way they saw it, the final map could only lead to one thing.

"We have a lead on one more map," Maddock said. "My sister is looking into it."

"Avery Halsey?" Tam turned around and grinned at him. "You finally found her?"

"Yeah, she's... Wait a minute! You knew about her?" Maddock trusted Tam, but to find out she'd been keeping a secret like this hidden from him? It was hard to swallow.

"Not until recently. I've done my homework on you and your whole posse. By the way," she turned to Willis, "there's a stripper in Detroit who said to tell you the baby is yours."

"What?" Willis gaped at her.

"Don't worry about it. I checked. The boy's daddy is a five foot nothing Latino." She smirked.

Willis sagged, visibly relieved.

"How do you know all this stuff?" Bones asked.

"I'm with the government, sweetie. We've got resources you've never dreamed of."

"Any other long lost relatives I should know about?" Maddock asked, only half-jokingly.

"Oh no. You don't get access to privileged information." She paused. "Unless you're ready to take me up on my offer."

Maddock grimaced. Arguing with Tam was pointless. She was one of the most focused people he'd ever met.

"You never told us how you wound up here," Bones said. "What's the Dominion's connection to all this?"

"I don't know how they're connected. For months I've mostly combed through the phone and financial records of suspected leaders in the Dominion, but I haven't gotten anything solid. Just suspects from every walk of Christendom. And then, after not hearing a peep from them since your Christmas vacation..."

"Shitter was full!" Bones said in his best Cousin Eddie voice.

Tam went on as if he hadn't spoken.

"...we finally got a hit on Heilig Herrschaft. You know, your German Dominion buddies. Two suspected members, twin brothers, were instructed to be here at one o'clock today and to intercept something the Dominion wanted. We were waiting for them to make their move, so we could get them and whatever it was they were after."

"And then Maddock screwed it up," Bones finished.

Maddock ignored the jibe. His thoughts drifted back to something Tam had said moments before. She had tremendous resources at her disposal. But would she agree to help them?

"Tam, look, I'm sorry we interfered. You do know we had no way of knowing the Dominion was involved?"

She sat down in an antique wooden chair and drummed her red lacquered fingernails on the armrest.

"I'm sensing you've got more to say and, whatever it is, it's going to make me cuss. I don't even have my swear jar here."

"We need help finding Angel. The only clues we have are Locke and the museum. For all we know, they've taken her to England. We don't have a prayer of tracking her down, but you can." He took a deep breath. "Please?"

Despite her prediction, Tam didn't cuss. She stared at him for a full ten seconds. Bones and Willis looked on, afraid to break the silence. Finally, her features softened.

"You've got a thing for this girl, don't you?"

Maddock couldn't stop his face from reddening, nor could he keep himself from looking at Bones. To his surprise, both Bones and Willis looked to be on the verge of laughter.

"The lady asked you a question, Maddock." Bones crossed his arms and smiled expectantly.

Maddock couldn't find his voice.

"Wait a minute!" Willis laughed and slapped his thighs. "You'd take on a whole army with nothing but your bare hands and never flinch, but can't admit you like a girl?"

"He doesn't like her," Bones said. "He loves her. He can't hide something like that from me."

"I want to hear it from him," Tam said, clearly enjoying the moment. "Well?"

"Maybe," Maddock said, watching as the others exchanged frustrated looks. How could he make them understand? After the way his wife had died, he felt... cursed. Like he'd bring misfortune onto the next woman he truly loved. He knew that wouldn't fly with any of them, though.

"Dane Maddock," Tam took on the lecturing tone of a middle school teacher scolding an underachieving student, "it's no wonder you won't join up with me. Willis is right. You're not afraid of dying. You're afraid of real commitment."

"No I'm not. I'm a decorated veteran in case you've forgotten."

"I know that. I also know when and why you quit the service." She looked like she wanted to say more, but a knock at the door interrupted her. A moment later, the agent standing guard ushered Matt into the room. He greeted Tam and then turned to Maddock.

"When I saw the Feds had taken over here, and you guys hadn't shown, I figured my getaway driver services were no longer needed. Anyway, I just got a call from Corey. He and Avery have been arrested."

"You've got to be kidding me. Is it at least a real arrest? Locke doesn't have them too?"

"No. One of Locke's men chased them into the National Aquarium and Avery wound up jumping into the shark tank, or falling in, or something. Corey bashed the guy's skull pretty good. It's a mess."

Maddock groaned and closed his eyes. When he opened them, he saw Tam grinning at him like a cat who had cornered a mouse.

"I guess I might need two favors."

"Join my team and I will. We can wait til all this is over to work out all the details. I've got a place for all four of you, plus the little nerd boy."

"Dude, are you seriously blackmailing us?" Bones anger was returning.

"Excuse me? You forget, I know *all* about you. If I wanted to blackmail you, I could have done it long ago. Defacing national historical sites?"

"That was Maddock." Bones pointed at Maddock.

"The Fremont ruins?" she asked.

"Okay, that was sort of me," Bones said.

"Desecrating graves?"

"It was only one grave," Maddock said, "and I didn't exactly..."

"Kidnapping a patient from a hospital in Utah."

"Me again." Bones raised his hand.

"Missing Italian nationals who, rumor has it, were sent after you."

"Good. I was feeling left out," Willis said to Bones.

"Bringing down half a mountain in Jordan. Lord only knows what you did in Utah. Breaking and entering all across Germany. And," she paused for effect, "we found the bodies in that well."

There was nothing Maddock could say. Everything she mentioned had an explanation, a greater purpose, or was a case of self-defense, but they'd never be able to defend themselves in court. The cumulative weight of the charges against them was too great.

"But, as I said, if I wanted to blackmail you, I would have already done it. I've been in the field with you. I know what you can do. I trust you." She stood and offered her hand to Maddock. "I'll get your friend and your sister out, and I'll help you get your girl. But you've got to help me."

Maddock looked at Bones, Willis, and Matt. They exchanged glances, then all nodded solemnly.

"All right." Maddock clasped Tam's hand. "You've got a deal."

Chapter 28

Maddock sat aboard the jet Tam had secured for a flight to England, waiting for takeoff and for her to tell him what she had learned. He passed the time by scrolling through the pictures they'd taken of the two underground Templar churches they'd discovered. It wasn't long before something caught his attention.

"Hey guys, check this out," he said to Bones and Avery who were seated behind him. "You see how, right at the top of the ceiling in both of these places, there's this pie-shaped carving?" He clicked between the images to illustrate his point. "They aren't exactly the same, but don't they look like pieces of a map?"

"You might be on to something," Bones agreed.

"Each one is about one third of a circle. I'll bet, when we find the last chamber, we'll find the missing piece."

"And that will lead us where?" Bones mused.

"I don't know. I'm going to message Jimmy and ask him to see if he can match it up to any known locations." Just then, Tam arrived.

"All right. Here's what I've got." She took the seat next to Maddock. Bones and Avery listened in, as did the others, who were seated all around.. "Locke is former MI6. He was a rising star with an exemplary record, but he left unexpectedly to go to work for this woman." She held out a photograph of a blue-eyed blonde woman of early middle years.

"Smoking hot!" Bones said.

"Oh, is that what you like?" Avery snapped.

"I just like women." Bones smiled at Avery who made a face at him.

"Morgan Fain. She is the director of the British History Museum in Truro. The same museum that owns the Bailyn."

"Wait a minute." Avery cupped her chin, thinking. "One of the biggest treasure hunts on Oak Island was conducted by the Truro Syndicate back in the mid-1800's. Could there be a connection?"

"Hers is an old and powerful family, so maybe."

"Truro. That's kind of off the beaten path, isn't it?" Maddock asked. He'd imagined any powerful players in England would be based out of London.

"It works for her," Tam said, returning the photograph to the folder and pulling out a sheet of paper. "She has political aspirations, and she's set herself up as an outsider. She's never held public office, but she writes editorials for the biggest newspapers in Britain, and makes guest appearances on news shows. Ninety percent of the time, she's talking politics, not history. When she does talk history, it's about England's past greatness."

"That doesn't sound so bad," Avery said.

"Her underlying message, and I'm paraphrasing here, is that the lowlifes and scum are dragging all of the United Kingdom down, and they've got to go. She wants all the resources that go to supporting the bottom feeders to go toward re-establishing their military strength and political influence. She even thinks Ireland should bend the knee and join the United Kingdom. I won't go so far as to say she sounds like Hitler, she's too smart to talk like that, but I don't think she'd be too disappointed if the people she thinks are not 'true Britons' vanished off the face of the earth."

"Plenty of American politicians talk that way," Maddock observed.

"True, but there's more here than meets the eye. I don't know for sure how the pieces fit together, but here's what I've got. People have been begging her to run for Parliament for years, even talk about her being a shoo-in for Prime Minister, but she won't do it, even though it's obvious that's her long-term goal."

"It's like she's waiting for something," Maddock said. "What else do we know about her?"

"She's also got people working hard to strengthen her royal bloodline. There's no question she has royal blood but, rumor has it, she thinks she has a better claim to the throne than the current monarch or her heirs."

"Who is she tracing her roots back to that she could make such a claim?" Avery looked puzzled.

"Arthur," Maddock said, half to himself. "Think about it. If she can produce Arthur's weapons as proof that he was an actual, historical figure, and as evidence that she's his heir, wouldn't that capture the minds and hearts of the British people?"

"It's not enough," Avery said. "Even if she could convince people the weapons aren't fakes, that won't prove she's descended from Arthur."

"But if she finds his body, DNA testing certainly could," Bones said. "Hey, if he really lived, and it looks like he did, that means his body's got to be somewhere, doesn't it?"

"Even then, the Queen's not going to abdicate," Avery argued.

"Not voluntarily." Tam's tone was dark. "If half of the rumors we've gathered are true, Morgan's reach is broad, and she's got people in all segments of society who are devoted to her. The Dominion agent we captured mentioned something called "The Sisterhood," but clammed up when I mentioned her name. He seemed scared. Anyway, she lives in a castle, a compound, really, outside of Truro, and her private staff is all ex-military or ex-intelligence. Guys like Locke. When I put this all together, it paints a grim picture."

"You think, once she's got her connection to Arthur established, she'll move into the political arena," Maddock began, thinking it through as he spoke, "become Prime Minister, and then..."

"She uses her connections to make sure something terrible and permanent happens to the Queen," Bones continued.

"Not long afterward, it's revealed that the beloved Prime Minister is descended from the legendary King Arthur," Maddock finished.

"I'm not convinced she's going to wait that long," Tam said. "She's hosting an event this weekend at her estate, and the Queen will be there."

"Only the Queen?" Maddock asked. "What about the rest of the Royal Family?"

"Morgan might act now and step into the gap later. She might figure if she cuts off the head, the monarchy will fall. Who can tell?" Tam shrugged.

"Have you notified the British authorities?" Maddock asked.

"I've told our people what I suspect, but I did not tell them anything about King Arthur, which makes my suspicions pretty flimsy. What do I really have but a bunch of theories about a politically connected woman who doesn't seem very ambitious? On paper, she looks like an upstanding citizen, if maybe a bit too conservative for some people. She gives a lot of money to charity. She supports genetic research to fight all sorts of diseases. They even named the reptile house at the London Zoo for her because of all the money she gave them. She ain't bulletproof, but she's close."

"Queen and Prime Minister," Avery said. "And if she can find a way to harness the power of Arthur's weapons, replicate it, even, there's no telling what she could do."

Tam nodded thoughtfully.

"An army that can become truly invisible. Objects that can amplify rays of light into powerful energy weapons."

"You'd never have to reload," Willis said.

"And we haven't even found the final piece of the puzzle," Matt added.

"Okay, you've convinced us she's up to no good. But what have you found out about Angel?"

"We've got her arriving in England, alive, with Locke." Tam handed him a grainy printout of a frame of security footage. "We've got her being put in a van." She handed him another printout. "And a van like this one showed up at Morgan's headquarters an hour ago." She took a deep breath. "I can get you in and out of the country, and I can give you what you need to pull off this rescue, but I can't be directly involved and neither can my people. It's on you."

"I understand," Maddock said. "Now, tell me all you know about this compound."

Chapter 29

"Who the hell are you?" Angel said to the man who opened the door. He was a solidly built black man with a shaved head. As he stepped into the room, she revised her opinion. He wasn't just solid, he was built like a rhinoceros.

"Jacob." His soft voice stood at stark odds with his build. He stopped in the center of the room and stared at her. There was no kindness in his eyes, nor was there cruelty. He was a blank slate.

"You don't look like a Jacob. You look more like a Rufus." Perhaps she shouldn't cop an attitude with these people, but she was resigned to the fact that they were going to kill her, so she really didn't care what they thought of her. If her needling made them kill her sooner, fine. She was tired of being held captive.

Jacob didn't answer. He hoisted her to her feet and walked her toward the door.

"You don't say much. Are you stupid or something?"

"No," he replied, just as softly as before. He steered her along a featureless hallway of gray stone that ended at a suit of armor.

"How the hell do you get lost in a freaking hallway? Remind me not to let you navigate next time. You probably don't even stop to ask directions, do you?"

This time she didn't even get a one-word answer out of him. He pushed up the face guard on the helmet, revealing a number pad, punched in a code, and stepped back as the suit of armor swung forward, revealing an elevator.

"Where am I, some kind of Scooby Doo haunted castle?" She realized her chatter was covering for a rising fear she thought she'd worked past early in her captivity. Truth was, she wasn't eager to die, no matter what she told herself.

"You're at Modron, on Bodmin Moor near Truro," Jacob said as the elevator door closed and they began to descend.

"Okay, now I wish I'd paid attention in Geography class." She'd hoped that might have elicited a smile or a chuckle from Jacob. Any sign of emotion would be welcome at this point. "So, where are you taking me?"

"Morgan wants to see you."

"Captain Morgan? I could go for a drink right now." Still no emotion.

The elevator came to a stop and the door opened onto an octagonal room with blue carpet, a television, and a rack of nasty looking weapons. Angel stepped out onto the soft carpet and looked around.

"Cool dungeon, bro."

"It's merely my exercise room." She hadn't noticed the woman standing off to the side. She was about Angel's height, but fair and blonde. "This is where I hone myself to a fine edge."

"I take it you're Morgan."

"I am. And you are no longer of use to us." Morgan stared at her as if expecting a reply.

"Yeah, I don't play well with others, especially when they kidnap me."

"Fortunately for you, that time is at an end."

Angel's stomach lurched and she looked at the weapons rack. Was this where she was to die? She swallowed hard.

"Cool. So I can go, right?"

"Yes. After you fight me." This time Morgan did smile, but there was neither laughter nor guile in her eyes. She was serious.

"That's stupid. If you're going to let me leave, just point me to the door and I'll be gone. No need for anybody to get hurt."

"That is my condition, the same one I give everyone who is of no use. Fight me. If you win, you leave by the front door. If I win, you leave by the back door. It's all very simple."

"Right. I win and your lackey shoots me in the back, I suppose."

"No. I meant what I said. Leave with honor or leave in disgrace, but you will not leave until you fight me. Locke thinks you might afford me a challenge."

"You're crazy. I guess you want to fight with those swords and spears and crap?" Angel hoped the answer was "no." Knife fighting she could handle. Maybe a spear, if it was anything like a bo staff. But a sword? No way. And she didn't even recognize some of the weapons, which looked medieval and more than a little sinister.

"If you wish. I prefer hand to hand fighting," Morgan said.

"Mano a mano, huh?" Angel stared into Morgan's eyes for a full five seconds, waiting for any indication that this was all a big joke. No dice. As she stared, she reminded herself that this woman was apparently the boss, which meant she was the one responsible for Angel's kidnapping. Now she stood there, the arrogant cow, wanting to fight her. Fine. If there was one thing Angel knew how to do, it was throw down. "All right. Take these cuffs off of me and let's do this."

Jacob removed her bonds and Angel took a moment to rub her wrists and work the kinks out of her shoulders. This wasn't an ideal situation. She'd been captive for a few days now, and her body wasn't at its best. There was nothing for it now. She took a deep breath, turned, and faced Morgan.

"Say when."

Morgan raised her fists and flowed gracefully into a fighting stance. Despite her beauty queen appearance, she looked like she knew what she was doing. They circled one another, eyes locked.

Angel snapped a quick jab which Morgan evaded with ease. She'd obviously done this before. Angel had better take her seriously.

Morgan whipped a roundhouse kick that Angel checked and answered with a kick of her own that just missed. If she was fit and warmed up, she'd have landed it. Morgan grabbed Angel's leg and tried to take her down, but Angel kept her balance and fought free. They traded kicks, to little effect, and Angel missed with a jab.

Now Morgan drove forward with a flurry of punches. Angel blocked them, landed an elbow that split Morgan's cheek, and followed with a back fist that Morgan sprang away from. Angel pursued her backpedaling opponent, knocking her into the wall with a front kick, but Morgan danced away before Angel could close the gap.

It became a chess match. Morgan kept Angel at bay with kicks and jabs, always circling. She had correctly assessed that Angel was a brawler who hated this kind of fight, and thus refused to get in close. Angel's lip was bleeding, her eye was puffy from taking several solid punches, and she was wearing down. Her arms felt like they were made of lead.

Morgan feinted a jab and, when Angel raised her hand to block, drove a side kick into Angel's ribs, sending her sprawling to the carpet.

Knowing she was in serious trouble, Angel rolled to her feet before Morgan could pounce. *Okay, time to get to work.*

She stalked Morgan, watching the woman's footwork, the way she held her hands, the movements that indicated she was about to strike, looking for a pattern. Morgan pivoted her back foot, a sign that a roundhouse kick was on the way.

As Morgan's weight shifted to her front leg, Angel lashed out with a kick of her own that smacked into Morgan's kneecap. Morgan grunted in pain and tried to circle, but her leg betrayed her and she staggered.

Angel sprang into the air and drove a knee into Morgan's gut. Morgan absorbed the blow and caught Angel on the chin with a left hook, but there was no power behind it. Angel barely felt it as she grabbed Morgan by the back of the neck, held her head down, and punished her with a flurry of knees to the face and body.

Desperate, Morgan struck blindly, clawing at Angel's face, but scratches weren't going to stop her. And, if Morgan could fight like a girl, so could she. She grabbed a handful of blonde hair, slammed Morgan's hair into the wall, and followed with three hard punches to the side of the head that wobbled Morgan, followed by an uppercut that put her on the ground.

Morgan struggled to rise, made it to her knees, and fell again. She raised her battered and bloodied face, glared at Angel, and whispered two words.

"Kill her."

Chapter 30

"Here comes one." Bones stepped into the roadway and raised his hands. The delivery van slowed to a halt and the driver rolled down the window. Willis approached the vehicle, holding a clipboard.

"Is there a problem?" The driver sounded annoyed. "I'm already behind schedule."

"Modron security," he said in a lame British accent. "We need to inspect your vehicle."

"But Modron's another kilometer down the road. Why are you stopping us out here?"

"Only following orders." Willis shrugged as if to say, What are you going to do? "We'll need to inspect the cab as well as the cargo bay. If you'll step out, we won't waste any more of your time than necessary."

The driver frowned, and Bones wondered if the man had picked up on Willis' fake accent. He looked Willis up and down, taking in his plain, black clothing and the radio clipped to his belt. Finally satisfied, he nodded, and he and his passenger climbed out of the cab.

Before the men knew what was happening, Bones and Willis had them stunned, bound, and hidden near the side of the road. Later, they'd make sure the authorities got an anonymous tip on the men's whereabouts, and they'd be sure to implicate Morgan's security staff. Matt and Corey, who had been hiding nearby, joined them.

Matt took the wheel, and Willis joined him in the cab, while Bones and Corey climbed inside the cargo area, which was packed almost to the ceiling with tents and folding chairs for the upcoming event, and rolled the door down behind them. As the truck lurched into motion, Corey fired up his laptop and prepared for his part of the job.

"This had better work," Bones muttered.

"Think positive." Corey's words rang hollow. He hated these types of situations, and much preferred to remain somewhere safe and make his contributions from a distance. Bones had to hand it to his crew mate. Corey had really stepped up the past couple of days. Perhaps his confidence would grow. "They don't have any reason to turn us away, or even inspect the truck closely. Matt and Willis have the driver's paperwork. That should be enough."

"But if they do turn us back, we're going to have to find a way past motion detectors, over an electrified fence, and past whatever other security measures they've put in place." Bones gripped his pistol and imagined how he might put it into use. Ever since Angel's abduction, he'd tried very hard to remain optimistic. Things always seemed to work out for him and Maddock, and he figured it would be the same for her. He'd even managed to block the worries from his mind, until now. He was angry and a little afraid- not for himself, but for his sister.

"Getting past those things is Maddock's job. Besides, when did you turn into a rain cloud?" Corey asked. "Usually he's the one talking about everything that could go wrong."

The truck made a sharp right, then came to a stop. They waited in tense silence, straining to hear the conversation outside, but all Bones could make out was the muffled sound of voices. His fingers itched, and he felt the sudden urge to jump out of the truck and start fighting. He stilled his rising ire and waited.

Finally, he heard the doors of the truck close and they began to move again. He and Corey exchanged relieved smiles that were quickly wiped off their faces when Willis' voice sounded in their earpieces.

"Bad news, boys. They bought the ruse, but they want their people to do the unloading. Left us standing outside the gate. Looks like you two are on your own for now. The guy at the gate is watching us close. If you need us to take him out, just call."

"Great." Bones turned to Corey. "Get as far back into the truck as you can. Make yourself a space behind the boxes. That'll buy you some time."

Even in the dim light that filtered in, he could see Corey swallow hard, color draining from his face, before clambering out of sight. Bones squeezed into a gap to one side, where he wouldn't be readily visible when the back doors opened. He waited, Glock in one hand and Recon knife in the other, but the doors did not open. A minute passed. Then another. Nothing.

"How are you coming on that hack, Corey?"

"The signal's weak, probably because we're inside a metal box, but it looks like the same system that was in place at the museum, at least the security part of it. I'll see what I can do with it." A minute later, Bones heard Corey's triumphant whisper. "I'm in. Are you ready?"

"Always." Bones sheathed his knife, but kept his Glock handy. Tension and exhilaration surged through him in equal measure as he raised the back door a few inches, peered outside to make certain the coast was clear, and climbed out. Now, to find Angel.

"This is a stupid idea, Maddock." Tam grimaced as she looked him up and down. "Have you ever even used one of these things?"

"Sure. Bones talked me into it." It was the truth. He'd used a wingsuit exactly one time, though he'd found the experience exhilarating.

"From a helicopter?" Avery looked at him nervously. It was odd to once again have a family member worry about him, but it wasn't bad.

"No, but I can handle it. Trust me."

"Are you sure you don't want to use a regular parachute?" Avery asked.

"No. The wingsuit is the better choice because I can be cloaked all the way in. By the time I have to deploy my chute, I'll be well beyond their perimeter and into the forest."

"Be careful." Tam's expression was grave. "Remember, I can't come in after you. Once you jump, you're on your own until you find the girl and get off the property."

"I understand. Thanks for everything." They clasped hands briefly. "See you when I get back."

"Maddock?" Avery said, her voice tremulous.

"Yeah?"

The next thing Maddock knew, she was crushing him in a tight embrace. He hugged her back, a little awkwardly. When she let go, tears glistened in her eyes.

"Don't get yourself killed. We haven't finished Dad's quest yet."

Not trusting himself to answer, Maddock gave her a wink before fixing his goggles in place, taking out the dagger, and depressing the butt.

"That's seriously messed up," Tam said as he vanished.

Maddock chuckled, turned, and dove out into open air.

The speed at which he descended was breathtaking. He soared over the desolate moor, his eyes locked on the thick forest that covered several acres behind Modron and, not for the first time in his life, he envied the eagles and other great birds of prey. The sea was his first love, but flying was pretty sweet.

As he approached Modron, he could clearly see the high brick wall, topped with an electrified fence, that ringed the property. Outside the wall, a dry moat afforded another layer of security, and he knew from Tam's intelligence that the entire property was guarded by security cameras and motion detectors. He flew on, passing high above the perimeter wall and looked for his chosen landing place.

There it was! In the very center of the forest lay a small clearing and a pond, its waters glimmering in the sunlight. He angled toward it, waiting until the very last moment to release his parachute. This was the most dangerous part. The dagger would not cloak an area much larger than his body, so if someone looked his way at the wrong time, they might spot the parachute. Oh well, what was life without a little risk? He released it, and felt a hard jolt as it arrested his momentum. He held his breath, waiting for bullets to fly, until he floated down below the level of the treetops.

When he hit the ground, he hastily stripped off his wingsuit, stowed it in the trees, and then took a moment to get his bearings. The forest was unnervingly quiet, yet he sensed a presence there. Someone, or something, was watching him. Well, not for long. He moved into the shadow of an ancient oak tree, and activated the dagger.

Time to storm the castle.

Chapter 31

"Kill her." Morgan's eyes glazed over and she lapsed into unconsciousness.

Angel looked at Jacob. He was too far away for her to close the distance between them before he could draw his gun. Besides, she didn't know if she had enough left in the tank to take him on. Her eyes flitted to the weapons rack. If she had a knife, maybe she could... no. It was too far. She was at his mercy.

Jacob looked from her to Morgan's supine form, then back to Angel. For the first time, emotion registered on his face. Uncertainty.

"I won. That means you show me the front door, right?" She tried to sound confident, but fatigue gave her voice a breathless tenor that made her sound weak.

"I can't let you go." Jacob looked down at Morgan again, as if she would rise and tell him what to do.

"This is bullshit." She tried to keep the rising panic from her voice. "A deal is a deal."

Morgan groaned and began to stir, which spurred Jacob into action. He hurried over to Angel and grabbed her by the arm.

"You can leave by the back door, but we have to be quick about it."

She stumbled along beside him as he guided her through a dark corridor, stopping in front of another suit of armor.

"More secret doors?"

"Yes." He opened this door in the same manner as the last. Behind the suit of armor, a narrow corridor led to a wrought iron gate. Jacob hit another button and the gate began to rise. "Go straight ahead. Follow the path through the forest. You'll find a gate at the far end. Go!"

Angel didn't wait for him to change his mind. She ran and didn't look back.

Locke found Morgan lying on the floor in her workout room. He helped her to her feet and escorted her back to her study, reluctant to comment on her injuries.

"You were correct," she said. "The girl was a worthy opponent." She sat down behind her desk and looked up at him, her eyes their usual icy calm. "Report."

"The map that Maddock gave us was accurate. We located the Templar church beneath the graveyard at Trinity Church." He did not want to tell her the rest, but knew better than to make her ask. "There was nothing there. Maddock, or someone else, got there first."

For one of the few times since he'd begun working for her, Morgan looked weary. She closed her eyes and went through a series of calming exercises, breathing deeply and exhaling slowly. When she finally opened her eyes again, her face was a mask of serenity, though anger lurked beneath the surface.

"I had the dagger examined by experts at the museum. It is a fake."

Locke did not react to this bit of news. Dane Maddock had outwitted him, but the game was not over.

"Where is the girl?" he asked. "You did not let her go, did you?"

"Of course not. I told Jacob to kill her." She logged on to her computer and called up the security cameras that overlooked the grounds. "He should be burying her about now." She pursed her lips. "It looks as if he put her out the back door. I intended for him to kill her himself, not feed her to the children." Scowling, she turned the monitor around so Locke could see the young woman running through the forest.

"He must not have sent the signal yet. One of them is just watching her, see there?" He pointed to the upper branches of a leafy tree, where a scaly green and gold figure perched. "I'll go get her."

"No need," Morgan said. "I can send the signal from here." He tried to stop her, to tell her he had further use for the girl, but it was too late.

A high-pitched tone sounded all around her. It was there only for a moment and, when it faded, something rustled in the trees high above her. Angel kept running, looking up to see what was there, but she saw nothing. Her feet kept pounding the soft earth and she wished she knew if she was close to her goal, but the forest up ahead seemed to go on forever. Her body ached and her lungs burned, but she kept going.

It's just like training, she told herself. *Feel the burn. Embrace the pain. Fight through it. Keep chopping wood.* Every bullshit phrase a trainer had ever spoken ran through her mind, each more absurd than the one before. *I just want to get out of here.*

Up ahead, something moved among the trees. She quickened her pace and, as she hurdled a fallen log, something leapt out and snapped at her feet. She cried out in alarm as razor sharp teeth closed on empty air where her foot had been an instant before, hit the ground, and kept running.

Her eyes must be playing tricks on her, because what she'd seen wasn't possible. Behind her, the thing was in pursuit and it was gaining on her. Up ahead, a low hanging limb dangled over the path. She leapt up, grabbed hold, and swung herself up into the lower branches of the tree. Down below, she heard an angry hiss and the scraping of claws on the tree trunk. She began to climb, and didn't stop until she was a good fifteen feet off the ground.

She sagged against the tree trunk, gasping for breath. What the hell was that thing? She could still hear it down on the ground. Apparently, it couldn't climb, and that was fine with her. She didn't want to look, but she had to know what was after her. Clutching the tree so she didn't fall, she leaned over to peer through the foliage.

A vision from her darkest nightmares peered back at her. It was reptilian, and at least ten feet long from its snout to the tip of its powerful tail that lashed back and forth. Its body was dark green in color, its throat copper. Its toes ended in sharp, black claws that dug furrows in the ground and shredded the tree trunk as it struggled to get at her. Her first thought was of a komodo dragon that forgot to take its Ritalin. It had the size, general shape, and forked tongue of the giant lizard, but there were some significant differences. Aside from the coloring, the creature's hide was sleeker, and its movements more agile. The biggest difference, however, was the bright orange and gold frill that flared out behind its head.

"What the hell are you?" she muttered. Of course, the real question was, how was she going to get away from it? Climbing from tree-to-tree was out of the question. The limb she sat on would not support her weight should she move more than a few feet out from the trunk. Outrunning it wouldn't work either. The thing would be on her as soon as she hit the ground. How could she have been so stupid as to let herself get treed?

As she contemplated her next move, panic welling inside her, she heard another hiss. She looked up to see another of the lizard-looking creatures high in a tree farther down the path. It had spotted her, and it flared its flame-colored frill and hissed angrily. And then it leaped out of the tree. She watched, mesmerized, as it spread bright red wings and glided toward her.

"Holy crap," she whispered. "It can fly."

The man, a powerful-looking black man with a shaved head, stood staring at a suit of armor. That was weird. He was the first person Bones had seen since entering the castle, so Bones decided not to kill him... yet. Maybe the guy would lead him to Angel.

All of a sudden, the man shook his head, turned, and headed off down the corridor. His Glock at the ready, Bones crept after him. The man came to a door with an electronic keypad lock, entered in a code, and the door swung open. Bones moved in behind him, ready to shoot should the man go for his weapon, but he seemed unaware of his surroundings as he walked slowly across the blue carpeted room, picked up a remote, and turned on a flat screen monitor, which displayed what looked like security footage of the grounds. He pressed a few buttons, and four images appeared on the screen, each displaying a section of forest.

Bones was disappointed to see that no one else was in the room. He guessed it had been too much to hope that Angel would be in the first room he entered. So much for that. Time to see if he could squeeze any information out of this guy.

Three silent steps, and he held the barrel of his Glock to the base of the man's skull. The man froze.

"I'm in a really bad mood, so I suggest you don't make any sudden moves." Bones poured every ounce of his hate and anger into his voice. "Put your hands out in front of you. Slowly." The man complied, and Bones relieved him of his weapon. "What's your name?"

"Jacob." His voice was dull, not so much unafraid as uncaring.

"All right, Jacob, where's my sister?" He figured he'd have to do some persuading, maybe with his knife, but Jacob answered right away.

"She's gone. I let her go."

Bones wanted to feel relieved, but he wasn't buying it.

"The hell you did. Tell me the truth, or I'll cut your eyes out and feed them to you for lunch."

Now Jacob didn't seem so uncaring.

"I swear. She's not here anymore. Morgan will probably kill me for it, but I let her go."

Bones didn't know why, but he sensed the man was telling the truth.

"Is she all right?" He bit his lip as he waited for the answer. If something had happened to Angel, he'd burn this place to the ground, that is, if Maddock didn't do it first.

"She was when she left here. A little banged up, but not by me."

Bones finally took a moment to look around the room. There was little to see, except a rack of weapons.

"What are the swords and crap for?" He had a few ideas the uses someone could find for such a sinister array of weapons, but he forced those thoughts from his mind.

"Morgan trains with them."

As he continued to look around, his eyes fell on a dark spot on the carpet. Blood. He turned to ask Jacob whose blood it was when he glanced at the monitor on the wall, and what he saw erased all other thoughts from his mind.

"What the hell is that?" The image of a winged creature with a long, scaly tail and a fiery frill filled the screen.

"A dragon," Jacob said.

"Don't mess with me." Bones dug the barrel of his pistol into Jacob's neck. "What is it, really?"

"That's what Morgan calls them. They're lizards, really. Her family began importing different varieties from around the world centuries ago: komodos, frilled dragons, flying dragons. They bred them and culled out the smallest and weakest. But when Morgan took over, she started messing with their DNA."

Bones remembered what Tam had told them about Morgan's philanthropic efforts. *She gives a lot of money to charity. She supports genetic research to fight all sorts of diseases. They even named the reptile house at the London Zoo for her because of all the money she gave them.*

"Is she crazy?"

"Maybe. But she's fascinated with dragons, it's sort of a legacy, and if she couldn't have the real thing, she was determined to create the next best thing."

"Don't tell me they breathe fire." Bones didn't bother to keep the scorn from his voice.

"No, but they're deadly all the same. The one on the top left has the power and ferocity of the komodo, and the agility of the frilled lizard. The one on the bottom right is almost as big, just as vicious, and it can fly."

Bones' mouth was suddenly dry, and a sick feeling hung in his gut. Maddock was out there with these so-called dragons.

"Morgan has them trained to hunt at a signal," Jacob continued. "And the smartest one will even obey her commands." Just then, a high-pitched note, almost like a whistle, rang out, and the dragons on the screen suddenly became alert.

"Oh no." Jacob wobbled and almost lost his balance. "Morgan must have seen her and sounded the call. I thought she could get away."

"You thought who could get away?" Bones asked, though he already knew the answer.

Jacob hesitated, and when he finally replied, his voice was cold.

"Your sister."

Chapter 32

Angel wanted to scream, but her voice was frozen in her throat. The beast glided toward her, growing ever closer and ever more frightening. She had nowhere to go, but she'd be damned if she would sit there. If she was going to die, she'd die trying to escape. She looked down, searching for a soft place to land. She was up on the balls of her feet, ready to make the leap, when a shot rang out and the creature in the air shrieked.

Two more shots rang out, one tearing a gash in one of the creature's winglike membranes and causing it to veer off into the woods. The second shot caught it in its belly, and it tumbled to the ground and thrashed about in pain.

The creature at the bottom of the tree cocked its head, sniffed the air, then tore off down the path toward the sound of the gunshots. As Angel watched, another shot came seemingly out of nowhere, pinging off its skull and tearing a ragged hole in its frill. It hissed and kept moving. The thing was tough.

Another shot rang out, the bullet striking the beast in the foreleg, and she thought she saw a muzzle flash in the middle of the pathway, but that couldn't be. There was nothing there, but somehow she knew who had come to her rescue.

"Maddock!" she shouted. Suddenly, all the fear and uncertainty of the past few days overwhelmed her, and she burst into tears. Crap! She didn't want Maddock to see her acting girly, but right now, she couldn't help herself.

The creature continued to charge, ignoring its wounded leg. Angel wanted to help, but what could she do without a weapon? As the tears welled in her eyes, the world became a kaleidoscope, where a myriad of crystallized lizard beasts attacked an invisible assailant.

Two more shots rang out. She didn't see where the first one struck, but the second one did the job, catching the beast in the eye and dropping it in its tracks. Ten feet down the path, the air rippled and Maddock appeared, holding a pistol in one hand and a weird-looking knife in the other.

Sobbing and laughing, Angel shimmied down the trunk of the tree and, by the time she hit the ground, he was there. She wanted to save face by saying something sarcastic but, before she could open her mouth, Maddock swept her up in his arms and kissed her. She kissed him back, the way she'd wanted to for years. He broke the kiss all too soon, and she was suddenly aware of the sounds of more of the lizard things approaching from all directions.

"I love you," she blurted.

"Yes you do." He winked and smiled, and she punched him in the chest.

"Ass." She kissed him again. "You were, like, invisible. How..."

"Not now. We need to get out of here." He took her hand and turned to lead her back in the direction from which he'd come, and froze. Two beasts barred the way. "The other way, I guess. Hop on my back."

"I can run," she protested.

"Just do it. I'll explain later."

She saw no point in arguing. She hopped up on his back and, as they headed along the path back toward the castle, something strange happened. The air shimmered around them and the world got weird for a second.

"What did you do?"

"The knife is a cloaking device." If he was feeling any strain from the added burden of her weight, he didn't let it show. He kept up a steady pace, though she could hear the beasts on their tail coming closer.

She was about to steal a look behind them when she saw one of the beasts leap from a tree up ahead and come soaring at them. She called out a warning, but Maddock had already leveled his pistol and fired two shots. Both of them caught it in the wing and sent it spinning into the trees. Now she looked back.

"Maddock, I think they can smell us, and probably hear us. They've almost caught up!"

He quickened his pace.

Angel held her breath as the castle appeared in the distance. Would they make it?

"Come on, come on," Corey urged as he waited for Jimmy's program to worm its way into the cracks of Modron's security system. It hadn't taken this much time at the museum. Surely it wouldn't be much longer. He wondered how Bones and Maddock were faring. If he couldn't break into the system, they might not be able to get out again. No, he couldn't think that way.

He looked down at the spinning icon that indicated the program was still at work and tried to hurry it along by tapping the screen. Waste of time, he knew, but he hated this impotent feeling.

Just then, he heard voices close by, and the cargo area was suddenly bathed in sound and light as someone rolled up the back door. They were finally getting around to unloading the truck. Corey performed a few mental calculations. If it was only a couple of guys and they worked slowly, he might have ten minutes before they found him.

He was keenly aware of the weight of the pistol on his hip. He wasn't much of a shot. Heck, he didn't even know what kind of gun Tam had given him, but he would have surprise on his side. No way they'd be expecting an armed geek to be hiding here. Maybe he could get them first. He'd have to try.

Heart racing and palms sweating, he sat back and waited, hoping the computer, or Maddock and Bones, or both, would hurry up.

"You sent my sister out there with those things?" Bones snapped. "You're dead."

"No! I was trying to help her escape," Jacob protested. "I couldn't take her out the front door, so her only chance was the security gate in the back. The dragons don't attack unless the signal is sounded. I thought she could make it."

"What security gate? This whole place is walled and fenced in."

"There's a hidden gate in the wall at the far end of the property. Morgan thought it would give people a sporting chance against her children, as she calls the dragons. The path leads directly to it. You can't see it from the outside."

"How many people have made it out?"

"The next one will be the first." Hands still outstretched, Jacob slowly turned to face Bones, who kept his Glock trained on the man's head. "I don't expect you to trust me, but you'll need me to get you past the security system if you want to go after her."

Bones knew Jacob was right.

"Fine, but consider this an audition for the rest of your life. You do anything else to piss me off, I'll kill you, and I just might shoot you in the gut first. You know, to make sure it hurts."

Jacob nodded and, hands on his head, led Bones back the way they had come.

"The suit of armor hides a passageway leading out," he explained, "and there's a security gate at the end. I have to put in a code to open them."

They turned a corner and Jacob stopped short, his hands falling limply to his sides. The suit of armor was swinging open of its own accord. Behind it, Bones saw a gate slowly rising, and daylight glimmered beyond. Jimmy had done it!

He clubbed Jacob in the temple with the butt of his Glock and dashed past him before the man hit the ground. Maybe he'd just been knocked unconscious, maybe Bones had scrambled the guy's brains. He didn't care about anything but finding Angel.

He dashed out of the tunnel onto a manicured lawn. The overcast afternoon gave everything a dull, gray overtone, matching his mood. He ran toward the distant forest and the path Angel had taken. He was a hundred yards away when three dragons burst forth from the forest, making a beeline for him. He dropped to one knee and took aim.

"Bones! Hold your fire! Hold your fire!" Maddock's voice came from somewhere in front of him, but where was he?

Then it clicked in Bones' mind. The dagger! Maddock was cloaked. Bones concentrated on the space between him and the charging dragons and, in an instant, he spotted it. A rippling outline, like heat rising in the desert, coming right at him. Now that he knew where Maddock was, he took aim again at the dragons, who were gaining ground fast.

"He said don't shoot, you assclown!" It was Angel. Maddock had found her.

"Relax. I got this," he shouted as relief spread through him.

"Go for the legs!" Maddock shouted.

Bones took careful aim and fired two shots at the closest dragon. One bullet found its mark and the dragon shrieked and stumbled, but got right back up again and continued its pursuit. The other two dragons quickly overtook their wounded counterpart, and Bones stepped up his rate of fire. Most of his shots deflected off their solid skulls or grazed their tough hides, but a few were on target, and soon all three were hobbling along, slowed, but still relentless in the pursuit of their prey.

Suddenly, Maddock appeared, carrying Angel on his back.

"Let's move!" he shouted. He slowed long enough for Angel to hop down, and the three of them headed for the open gate.

"Corey took control of the security system," Bones said, "but who knows how long he can keep it?"

"Just lead the way." Maddock was clearly winded from the run, but he kept pace with Bones, as did Angel.

"Take the dagger," Maddock said to Angel. "Press the butt to activate the cloaking mechanism. Don't argue. Just stay close and, if it comes to a fight, don't get in our line of fire."

To Bones' surprise, Angel did as Maddock said without a word of complaint. Moments later, she vanished. Bones thought he'd never get used to that. It was too creepy.

As he ran, he ejected his Glock's magazine, which was nearly spent, and replaced it with a fresh one. He had a feeling he was going to need it.

"The cameras just shut off," Morgan said. She clicked the mouse a few times, but nothing happened.

Locke circled around behind her desk, grateful for the distraction. They had discussed his failures at length, and he had grown weary of the conversation. He knew he was still useful to Morgan, but she was very unhappy with him right now.

"It's probably your computer," he said. "Try shutting it down and restarting it."

The computer was in the process of rebooting when he realized they had greater problems than a frozen computer. A loud popping sound came from somewhere in the distance.

"Are those gunshots?" Morgan rose from her chair, a little slower than normal, and tapped a button on her phone. "Jacob, where are you?"

No reply.

"Jacob, can you hear me?"

Still no answer.

Locke heard another rapid burst of gunfire, and then all was eerily quiet. He hurried to the window and looked out. The forest was alive with dragons. They charged out of the woods or launched from the trees, all headed for the castle. What the hell was going on?

Then he spotted three dragons hobbling across the lawn. They had clearly been injured. But by whom? He knew immediately.

"We've been infiltrated by Dane Maddock."

Bones led them through a series of twists and turns, moving deeper into the heart of the castle. They made their way without encountering resistance but, when they reached the underground garage where Bones had left the truck, Morgan's men were ready.

A torrent of bullets zipped through the space where Maddock's head had been only a moment before. He hit the ground, rolled, and came up firing. One man went down, but the other retreated into the truck's cargo bay, took up a defensive position, and continued firing. Maddock cursed. It would take time to dig this guy out- time they didn't have.

He was about to tell Angel to give him the dagger when a single shot rang out.

Seconds later, a stunned-looking Corey appeared at the back of the truck. He dangled a pistol loosely at his side. He looked at them in shocked amazement.

"I got him."

"Hell yeah!" Bones shouted as they dashed for the truck. "I'm driving." He ran to the left side of the cab and cursed when he remembered he wasn't in America.

Maddock took the wheel and fired up the engine while Angel joined Corey in the back. Tires squealed as he stepped on the gas and the truck peeled out of the garage. In the rear-view mirror, he saw a body go tumbling out- the man Corey had shot. As they barreled down the long drive, Maddock was pleased to see the security gate standing open. Corey's hack had done the trick.

He was not pleased, however, to see armed men barring the way, and others dashing across the moor in hot pursuit. Modron's grounds suddenly resembled an upset anthill. Shots rang out, and bullets pinged off the sides of the truck. Bones returned fire, sending the attackers diving for cover. Up ahead, the gate guards leveled their weapons at the oncoming vehicle...

...and went down in a heap.

Matt and Willis had entered the fight. They now turned their fire on the rest of Morgan's security force. Surprised by this new development, many of them retreated, while others went down, never to rise again. At the gate, Maddock slowed down so Willis and Matt could climb inside.

They continued firing at the remaining security guards, keeping them at bay. For a moment, Maddock thought they were home free, but then a new threat reared its head. A group of riders on motorcycles shot down the drive and fell in behind the truck. As they gained on the vehicle, they drew weapons and began to fire.

Maddock yanked the wheel hard to the left, then back to the right, zigzagging across the road.

"You're making it kind of hard for us to shoot back!" Bones shouted. He leaned out the window and fired off a shot at the pursuing motorcycles.

Maddock glanced back and had to laugh as folding tables came flying out of the back of the truck and tumbled across the road. Angel and Corey must be unloading the remainder of the cargo. The motorcycles scattered, one rider losing control and skidding off the road.

One biker managed to skirt the flying furniture and accelerate past Matt and Willis' line of fire and, as he drew even with Maddock, he raised his weapon. Before he could pull the trigger, Maddock kicked the driver's side door open, sending him tumbling off the road. Behind them, the tables kept flying, followed by chairs. Two more bikers crashed and another fell to gunfire. After that the pursuit melted away. Maddock turned to Bones and managed a grin.

"We did it. Now, call Tam and tell her we're ready for a pickup."

Locke stopped his bike on the side of the road, dismounted, and went to check on his men. It galled him that Maddock had gotten away, but a squad of men on motorcycles stood little chance against men who could aim and fire from the back of a truck. He also had to admit that pitching the tables and chairs onto the roadway had been resourceful, and it had been the girl who had done it.

For a moment, he considered following them on his own, but the appearance of a helicopter landing atop a tor farther up the road told him he'd missed his chance.

He smiled, in spite of the grim circumstances. He hadn't lost them entirely. As long as the girl remained alive, he could track their every move.

Chapter 33

"Nice boat." Maddock admired the sleek lines of the cabin cruiser Tam had secured for them. The helicopter pilot had dropped them at the coast, not far from Bodmin, where one of Tam's agents, a tall, dark-haired man who introduced himself as Greg, had been waiting for them. They were now headed north along the coastline.

"Glad you like it. Your boy, Jimmy, came through for us about two minutes after you jumped. He's got a location for the map Avery found, and he's working on something else that I'll tell you about after you finish the next job." She tilted her head and looked thoughtfully up at the cloudy sky. "He's pretty good. You think he'd come to work with us?"

The word "us" gave Maddock pause. He still wasn't accustomed to the idea that he and his crew would soon be working for Tam.

"Doubt it. He's not the type, but I think we could count on him for some freelance work here and there."

"You don't give classified information to a hired hand, Maddock," Tam sighed. "Lord have mercy, I've got so much to teach you."

Maddock smiled, leaned against the bow rail, and gazed at the dark water up ahead, feeling the cool salt spray on his face and breathing deep of the sea air. He thought of Angel, down below, nursing her wounds, and Avery, who had narrowly avoided capture just the day before. Was it worth risking their safety just to track down a treasure?

"Do you think we should hand things over to the authorities?"

"You don't really mean that," Tam chided. "This is your family's quest. Your daddy passed it down to you and your sister. Besides, I know enough about you to know you never leave a job unfinished."

"But what about Angel and Avery?"

"Don't worry about them. I already offered to fly them both back home but they wouldn't hear of it."

"I figured as much. I just don't want them to pay the price for my hubris." He took a deep breath and let it out in a rush. "I lost my wife and my parents in a very short time..."

"And now you're in love, and you've got a family again, and you're afraid of losing them," Bones said, dropping to the deck alongside him.

"I didn't know you were there."

"No one expects the Cherokee Inquisition." Bones made a face, and then grew serious. "Listen to me, Maddock. Until this mystery is solved, none of our group are safe. They'd kidnap us like they did Angel in order to get information, or they'd kill us to shut us up. You know that. We've been in situations like this before."

Maddock nodded. He'd had the same thoughts.

"Another thing. When I was growing up, my grandfather didn't spend a lot of time telling me what I should and shouldn't do. He taught me what it meant to be a Bonebrake. He said every family has something they stand for, and a set of values they live by. That's what holds them together. And that doesn't just go for blood relatives."

Maddock thought he knew what Bones was getting at. Their crew was a family, and their dedication, their courage, and their commitment to one another was what gave them their identity.

"And don't forget the Dominion," Tam said. "Even if Morgan was out of the picture, they're still out there. And if they want to get their hands on whatever we're going to find, it's important enough for us to get there first."

"Understood. So, are you going to tell us where we're headed next?"

"Tintagel Castle."

Maddock frowned. The ruins of Tintagel Castle stood atop high cliffs on the peninsula of Tintagel Island in Cornwall. Legend held it to be the birthplace of King Arthur, and a nearby coastal cave was known as Merlin's Cave.

"That can't be right. It's a popular tourist destination and it's been thoroughly excavated. Plus, it's in Morgan's backyard. She has to have already searched it."

"Oh, it's not in the castle, it's under it. Way under it. Now, you boys go down below and get your speedos on. We'll be there in a few minutes and you've got work to do."

Twenty minutes later, he and Bones were suited up in full diving gear, and standing on deck in the shadow of Tintagel Island. They were anchored in a sheltered area between the island and another peninsula to the east. He had to hand it to Tam. She worked fast.

"All right," Tam said. "The entrance should be underwater between those two rocks." She pointed to two huge rock formations poking out of the water. "It's got to be well below the low tide mark, or else someone would have found it by now."

Maddock and Bones exchanged glances, both thinking the same thing. What if someone *had* already found it?

"Don't you make that face," Tam scolded. "The map shows a channel that runs straight west. The only clue we have is, *Walk in the Way of Sorrows.*"

"Great," Bones said. "We're looking for an emo treasure."

Tam checked her watch.

"We've got plenty of daylight, but don't dally. Once you're in the water, we're going to head up the coast. We don't want to draw undue attention. Call us when you're out, and be careful."

Angel and Avery hugged Maddock and Bones in turn, and Willis complained about the lack of a third set of diving gear. Matt, who had taken over the helm, guided them as close as he dared to the stones shown on the map, and Maddock and Bones dived in.

"Report," Morgan snapped as Locke entered the room. She seemed to have recovered her faculties and energy, though the cuts and bruises on her face bore testimony to the damage she'd taken.

Jacob had not bounced back so quickly. He'd sustained a severe blow to the head when Maddock, or one of his men, had crept up on him from behind just as he was about to set the dragons on the Bonebrake girl. He still attended Morgan, as always, but he seemed detached. Probably a mild concussion.

"I planted a tracking device on the girl while she was sedated. I sent two men to follow them."

"Only two?" Neither her tone nor her expression betrayed her feelings, but he knew she disapproved.

"We've been decimated here. Worse than decimated, in fact. They only killed a few of our men, but too many have sustained serious injuries." He stopped there. Morgan knew what she had to do, and she wouldn't thank him for telling her how to respond to present circumstances.

"Of the losses we've sustained, how many are essential to our plans for the Queen's *visit?*" She raised her eyebrows as she said the last word.

"Only a few. SO14 is the critical piece, and our people have been in place there for years." SO14 was the branch of Special Operations that provided protection for the Royal Family, and several of its members were loyal to Morgan and the Sisters.

"Very well. Are you tracking Maddock right now?"

"Of course. They appear to be headed to Tintagel Castle."

Morgan threw back her head and laughed. It was a rare display of amusement from the stolid woman.

"Tintagel? They must not have the third map, or else they would not be wasting their time. The castle has been thoroughly excavated."

Locke nodded, though he lacked Morgan's confidence. Maddock had already surprised him too many times for Locke to underestimate him.

"In any case, our men will keep us apprised of the situation."

Locke nodded again. With so many of his men out of commission, he'd been forced to send two of his younger, more enthusiastic charges. He'd given them clear instructions, but worried they'd overextend themselves by trying to be heroes.

"Most of our remaining men will need to remain here to clean up the damage and prepare for the event. How large is Maddock's party?"

"Seven, that we know of, including the women. At least, as far as we know. Four of them ex-military."

"Seven. A number of power, but fitting somehow. Even better, it is a number we can easily overcome, with help." Morgan struck the desk once with her open palms and rose to her feet. She turned toward the wall where "Le Morte D'Arthur" hung, and gazed almost lovingly at the image. "The time has come. Summon the Sisters, and tell them each to bring their seven best men. We will follow Maddock, and be prepared to strike at any moment."

"Seven of our own men as well?"

"In addition to you and Jacob, I want four reliable men." She turned to face him, the ghost of a smile on her face. "And bring Mordred."

The water was cool and the dull sunlight shone gray-green beams into the depths. As Maddock swam deeper, the two stones converged, leaving a space between them not much wider than a chimney. He followed it to the bottom, which was not as deep as he'd expected, and found nothing. Undeterred, he began digging in the loose sand, and soon exposed a portion of the rock face that was unnaturally smooth and even.

Bones lent a hand and, within minutes, they found what they were looking for--a stone circle carved with a Templar cross. Working together, they turned it until it gave way. The stone rolled out of sight, exposing a dark tunnel. Maddock turned on his dive light and swam inside.

The passageway dropped straight down for twenty feet, then made a sharp right angle and, as Tam had said, led west, back toward Tintagel Island. They swam through the featureless tunnel until it took a sharp bend upward and then, thirty feet up, they broke the surface and emerged in an underground cave, facing two stone doors.

Each had a circle and cross stone where a doorknob should be, and each depicted a scene from Jesus' life. The door on the left showed a nativity scene. The door on the right showed Jesus struggling to carry the cross to his crucifixion.

"I know which one looks like sorrow," Bones said.

Maddock contemplated the doors. What was it about the Way of Sorrows that rang a bell? He had it!

"*The Way of Sorrows* is another name for the stations of the cross. We're looking for scenes of Jesus on his way to the crucifixion. It's the one on the right."

He spun the Templar cross and the door opened on a passage that led up and curved to the left. He shone his light inside, looking for signs of danger, but finding none. Holding his breath, he moved into the passageway and followed it up into the heart of the island.

They continued on until they'd passed through six sets of doors, each juxtaposing a triumphant event of Jesus' life with one of his road to Calvary, and every subsequent passage winding higher and higher. He wondered what lay behind the other doors, but didn't really want to find out.

At the seventh set of doors, they faced their first real conundrum. The doors were identical. Each showed the entombment of Jesus, with seven people, four male and three female, carrying him toward the tomb, which lay in the background on the left. In the background, on the right side of the picture, stood Calvary, with its empty crosses looking down on the scene.

"Any ideas?" Bones was looking at the doors like they'd insulted his mom.

"Take a closer look," Maddock said. "See if anything's different."

"Man, that's too much like those stupid puzzles in the newspaper. I vote for the door on the right."

"Fine. You can go first." Maddock grinned and pushed his friend aside as he moved in for a closer look. They spent five frustrating minutes gazing at the two doors. The images seemed to meld together until he couldn't separate them in his mind. Finally, he rubbed his eyes in frustration and backed up to look at it from a distance.

And then he saw it.

"Bones, come back here and take a look." When Bones joined him, he pointed to the crosses atop Calvary. "What do you see?"

Bones stared blankly at the doors, and then his eyes widened. "The crosses on the right are Templar crosses. How did we miss it?" He moved forward a few steps. "You have to be in just the right place to see the subtle differences. I wonder..." He walked up to stand between the doors and rubbed an identical spot on each with the tips of his index and middle fingers.

"Bones, those aren't boobs."

"Check out the stone that blocks the tomb. It's too small to see, but I can feel a cross carved in the one on the right."

"Just like the stones that have gotten us into the treasure chambers." Maddock nodded approvingly. "You want to do the honors?"

Bones grinned and opened the door on the right. It slid back to reveal another chamber. In its center stood a three foot tall block of stone, and protruding from its center…

"Holy crap!" Bones exclaimed.

Even though it had been what he'd expected to find, the sight of a sword embedded in a stone took Maddock's breath away. He entered the room, feeling like he was in a dream, and stopped in front of the sword.

"Excalibur." He spoke the word reverentially. From the moment Avery told them they'd found Arthur's dagger, he'd known they were on a path that would lead to the legendary sword, but the reality was still more than he could comprehend. Arthur had lived, had borne this sword, and, apparently, had drawn it from a stone.

Much of the sword was buried in a three foot-high block of stone, but he could see enough of the blade to know it was made of the same metal as the spear and dagger, while the hilt was made of the same white stone that gave them their power.

"Well, who's worthy to draw the sword?" Bones asked with a sly smile.

"You first."

Bones reached out, took hold of the handle, and pulled. It didn't give an inch.

"Fine," Bones sighed. "Your turn."

Maddock gave him a knowing look and aimed the beam of his flashlight onto the white stone hilt. Lights immediately began to swirl in its depths, reminding Maddock of a line from Tennyson's "Morte d'Arthur."

"And sparkled keen with frost against the hilt, for all the haft twinkled with diamond sparks." The stone pulsed faster and faster until it finally shone with a steady light.

"Here goes nothing." Maddock pressed the stone, and flickers of light began to dance along the flat of the blade and run up and down the fuller. The edge shone a bright blue, and the light seemed to run up one side and down the other.

He took Excalibur in his hand and pulled. The blade slid free easily. He knew he should shut it down right then and head back to the boat, but the little boy inside of him, the one that, in his youth, had daydreamed of being a Knight of the Round Table, wouldn't let him.

"Stand back," he told Bones. "I want to try something." He took aim, raised the sword, and brought it down at an angle. Excalibur sheared the corner off of the stone like the proverbial hot knife through melted butter.

"Sweet! My turn." Bones looked like a kid on Christmas morning as he sliced two more corners off the stone. Then his expression grew sober and he pressed the pommel. As the lights in the blade faded and died, he handed the sword back to Maddock. "This is serious stuff, you know."

"I know." Maddock had pondered the implications of their discoveries many times. The weapons might be ancient, but they represented an advanced, maybe even unearthly, technology.

"A cloaking device. A weapon that turns a little bit of light into a powerful electrical weapon. Now a sword that can cut through stone." Bones shook his head.

"And none of them require a power supply," Maddock added. "Just solar energy, or even a little bit of artificial light. If scientist can unlock the technology, they could do incredible things."

"Or incredibly terrible things." Bones rubbed his chin and stared down at the ground. "Tam's going to want to turn them over to the government, you know."

Maddock nodded. "Better that than the Dominion getting its hands on them."

"I guess. Let's take some pictures and get out of here."

While Bones made a photographic record of the chamber, Maddock finally took the time to look around. It did not differ in any significant way from those chambers on the other side of the Atlantic: circular with Templar symbols carved in the walls, the double band of code winding down the walls, and a wedge-shaped image up above.

Maddock took a last look at the stone where Excalibur had been embedded minutes before, still amazed and intrigued by what they'd found. He stowed the sword in a bag Tam had provided, slung it over his shoulder, and began the trek back to the outside world. Back on the surface, he radioed Tam to pick them up.

"Three down," Bones said. "I wonder what Jimmy has come up with. This kind of feels like it should be the end of the line, you know? Arthur only had three legendary weapons."

Before Maddock could answer, their cruiser appeared around the tip of the peninsula, and shots rang out from up above. He turned and saw that two men had taken up positions on the cliffs below Tintagel and were firing on their cruiser. Nearby, a sleek-looking boat bobbed in the surface. He and Bones had been so dizzy with success that they'd ignored what was right in front of their faces.

"Tam, get out of there now!" he barked into the radio.

"We're coming to get you!" came her reply.

"I've got a plan. Just get out of range and fast!" He breathed a sigh of relief as, moments later, the cruiser turned and headed back around the peninsula.

"Are we swimming for it?" Bones asked.

"We'd never outrun them. Give me a minute." Before Bones could ask what he had planned, he submerged and swam to the boat. He surfaced on the side opposite the gunmen, who were clambering down from the rocks. He didn't have long.

He drew Excalibur from his pack, gave it a few seconds to absorb the sunlight, then activated the blade. He could almost feel the energy coursing through him as the edges shone with blue light. He checked to make sure the men still had their backs to him before he took his first swing. The sword sliced through the hull with ease and, moments later, he'd cut a gaping hole near the stern, just above the waterline. He covered the hole with a life jacket, knowing the ruse wouldn't last for long, but maybe it would be enough.

He met up with Bones just as the men got into their boat and fired up their engine. The boat shot past them and, moments later, it slowed and began to sink. The men cursed in surprise and anger, the chase abandoned as they tried to plug the leak with whatever they had on hand. Maddock smiled as he and Bones hit the water, keeping well below the surface and passing unseen beneath the foundering boat. Now, to finish the job.

Chapter 34

"That place is crazy-looking," Bones said, looking out the porthole.

"Inishtooskert," Tam said. "They call it the Sleeping Giant, or The Dead Man."

"How many skirts was that?" Bones asked.

Tam shook her head and Angel punched him.

Maddock had been correct about the wedge-shaped images on the ceilings of the three chambers. When put together, they formed a map to this, the northernmost of the Blasket Islands off Ireland's southwest coast. The lonely island had been uninhabited for years, and was home to many ancient ruins. And, as its nickname suggested, when seen from the east, the island did, indeed, look like a man lying on his back. Blanketed by silver moonlight, it put Maddock to mind of a corpse lying on a funeral bier.

"What do you think we're going to find there?" Maddock asked no one in particular.

Everyone exchanged glances, unwilling or unable to hazard a guess. Finally, Avery spoke up.

"Avalon. Legend holds it was somewhere across the water. They could have crossed the Irish sea and rounded the coast until they found the perfect place. What better place to lay a king to rest than an island that looks like a giant crypt?"

No one disagreed.

"You think King Arthur is somewhere inside that island?" Willis asked.

"Why not? If our theory is correct, Morgan believes she's his descendant and would need his remains in order to conduct a DNA test. She's a museum director, so the public wouldn't look at the find with the same suspicion they would if some random person claimed he'd found Arthur's final resting place."

"I guess we'll find out soon enough," Maddock said, "So, who's going and who's staying?"

Everyone spoke at once. None of them wanted to remain behind. Not even Corey.

"We can't all go. Somebody's got to stay with the boat." He looked pointedly at Matt's broken arm. "And we need a lookout and someone to be our communications man."

"That's me, as always," Corey grumbled.

It was agreed that Greg, Tam's agent, would go ashore and find high ground from which he could serve as lookout. As the rest of the group made their preparations, Maddock pulled Angel aside.

"I really think you should stay behind. You've dealt with too much already."

"Forget it. After what I've been through, I deserve to see this to the end as much as anyone, if not more. Besides, you can't tell me what to do." She grinned, gave him a quick kiss, and left him standing alone belowdecks.

She was right. He couldn't tell her what to do, though he wished he could. He vowed to keep her close and not let anything happen to her.

"There you are." Avery poked her head in the door. "You *are* coming aren't you? I mean, we can handle it without you, if you'd rather stay here." She reached out, took his hand, and pretended to haul him up the stairs. He played along, feigning reluctance. When they reached the deck, she laughed and gave him a hug.

"We're going to do it, Maddock! After all these years, Dad's quest is at an end."

"Do you think he had any idea where it would lead us? This is a far cry from a pirate's treasure."

"I doubt it, but I think he'd have loved every minute of it." She stopped, blinked a few times, and cleared her throat. "I wish he was here."

Maddock looked out across the moonlit water, and fought down a sudden wave of sadness. He put his arm around Avery's shoulders and gave her a squeeze.

"Me too."

It was a steep climb up the side of the Dead Man, and they were all exhausted from the ordeal of the past few days but, buoyed by enthusiasm, they made the climb in good time. Reaching the top, they paused to look out across the water at the chain of islands to the south. It was a beautiful sight, and he found himself wishing he and Angel were here alone, with no thoughts of Morgan or the Dominion to distract them. He looked down at her and could tell by the look in her eyes she was thinking the same thing.

"All right, Maddock," Tam said, "take charge of your troops or I'm going to do it for you." She handed him a flashlight and a sheet of paper.

Jimmy had made a major breakthrough. He'd broken the bands of code carved on the chamber walls. The resulting message, they hoped, marked out the path they were to follow.

"Okay, the first line reads, *Beneath the eye of the giant lies the door to eternity.*"

"I hate poetry," Bones mumbled.

"The head is that way." Avery pointed to the east.

They picked their way across the rough terrain, navigating the old ruins, then faced an even more challenging climb up to the jagged rocks that formed the giant's head. Avery shone her light across the rocks and cried out in triumph. Where the right eye should be, a round boulder four feet across sat in the center of a circular depression.

"The eyes have it," Bones proclaimed. He, Maddock, and Willis rolled the boulder out of the way, revealing a shaft carved into the rock. Handholds ran down to the floor twenty feet below. Maddock insisted on going first, in case there was a trap. The ladies exchanged wearied looks, but didn't argue. He reached the bottom without incident, and looked around.

He stood in a cave. Evidence of occasional human presence in the distant past lay all about in the form of fire rings, the charred bones of small animals, smoke-stained walls, and carvings. What he did not see was any sort of door, trapdoor, or portal, and certainly no Templar cross. The others reached the bottom and joined him in examining the cave.

"What's the next line?" Bones asked.

"The three come together and show the way to the Dead Man's heart."

"The three what? Wise men? Amigos? Blind mice?"

"The three weapons, genius." Angel said, pointing to Rhongomnyiad, which Bones wore strapped across his back.

"Definitely," Maddock said, pretending he'd known all along. He suspected he wasn't fooling anyone, but that was all right. "Everybody spread out and look for carvings that resemble the sword, spear, or dagger.

It wasn't long before Willis found what they were looking for. A triangular shape formed by carvings that exactly matched the three weapons.

"So what do we do now?" Avery asked.

"I think the weapons are the key." Maddock drew Excalibur and pressed it into the carved outline. As if some magnetic force were pulling it, it clicked into place and light danced in the stone haft. Next, he set Carnwennan, then Rhongomnyiad. For a moment, the three blades burned like a blue sun and, when the light winked out, the men found themselves staring at an open doorway. The weapons no longer glowed, but hung in the stone doorway. Gingerly, Maddock touched Excalibur. When it didn't zap him into oblivion, he removed it and the other weapons, and they moved on.

The passageway opened onto a sheer cliff. Maddock shone his light down into the yawing abyss, to the rock-strewn bottom a hundred feet down.

"Did I mention I don't like heights?" Avery asked, moving back from the edge.

"It's not the height that scares me," Angel said. "It's falling from heights."

"Hey, I'm the one who's supposed to make the bad jokes," Bones protested.

Maddock shone his light up ahead. Two stone bridges spanned the gap, each only wide enough for one person to cross at a time. He consulted their list of clues. *"The hand of God will carry you across.* That's got to be the bridge on the right. In Biblical times, the left hand was unclean."

"You'd better be sure," Tam said. "That's a long way to fall."

"One way to find out." Bones turned and strode out onto the bridge. He reached the center, stopped, and turned back. "Seems pretty solid, and I'm heavier than any of you, so I think we're good." He hopped up and down to illustrate his point and, with a crack, a chunk of the bridge rail broke off and fell down into the abyss. "Sorry."

"Holy crap, Bones." Maddock shook his head. "I still think this is the only way to cross. Anyone who wants to hang back, that's fine." They all shook their heads in unison. "All right. One at a time. Heaviest first." Tam, Angel, and Avery all exchanged appraising looks. "Fine. Willis first, then the ladies in any order you like." He watched with bated breath as, one by one, his companions crossed over, and then he followed. On the other side, they followed a steep passageway and disappeared down into the darkness.

"I've lost the signal." Locke pocketed his tracking device. "They must have gone underground."

Tamsin looked at her sisters. Rhiannon, flanked by her men, was her usual, calm, detached self. The ocean breeze whipped her red hair about like a fiery halo. She didn't meet Tamsin's eye, but stared at Morgan, waiting.

Morgan's implacable stare had been replaced by a manic gleam once they arrived at their destination. She didn't bat an eye at Locke's news.

"It is of no matter. Mordred will track her."

Mordred was Morgan's prized pet. Bottle green with a bronze chest and red streaked frill and wings, he was the the most successful product of her genetics experiments. At sixteen feet long and standing nearly four feet at the shoulder, he was the largest of Morgan's children, as she called them. He was also vicious, but that was not what bothered Tamsin about the beast. Mordred was intelligent... too intelligent. He was well-trained, responding to Morgan's every command, much like a loyal dog, but one look in his eyes suggested there was a limit to his restraint. She only hoped she was not there when he finally broke free of his mistress's control.

Morgan took a scrap of bloody blue carpet from her pocket and held it out in front of Mordred. The dragon flicked his forked tongue several times, even licking it once, then looked up at her, indicating his readiness.

Tamsin shivered at the sight.

"Hunt."

At Morgan's single word, the dragon dropped his head close to the ground and began flicking his tongue in earnest. Back and forth he went until he hit on something. He stopped, turned his head to look at Morgan, and hissed.

"He has the trail," Morgan said. "Come." She moved to walk alongside her pet, while her men kept a safe distance behind. Rhiannon and her men followed.

Tamsin hesitated, stealing a glance at the horizon before following. She had kept her word to the Dominion, secretly apprising them of the Sisters' departure and notifying them as soon as she knew their destination. Now she waited for them to fulfill their end of the bargain. They had assured her they had resources embedded in England, ready to move at her call. If they did not arrive soon, all would be lost.

Mordred led them to a passageway at the eastern end of the island amongst the rocky crags. He paused only long enough to make sure the others were coming, then disappeared into the hole. Only one person could climb down at a time, so Tamsin again held back, hoping for some sign of her new allies. Finally, as she was about to descend, she caught sight of a light in the distance, growing larger as it approached. A helicopter! They had not abandoned her after all. Smiling, she began the descent toward her destiny.

"Maddock, can you hear me? Tam! Come in!" Corey cursed and pounded the console. All of his attempts to reach Maddock had been unsuccessful. Wherever Maddock and the others had gone, they were well out of radio contact.

"I didn't get a good look," Matt said, dropping a pair of binoculars in a chair, "but I think it was Morgan and her men. I caught sight of them at the top of a ridge."

"How many?" Corey asked. They were anchored in a sheltered cove, well out of sight, but still he worried about being discovered before Maddock and the others returned.

"A lot. Close to twenty." Matt drummed his fingers on his pistol grip and worked his jaw. "I thought about following them, but it would take me forever to climb up there. They'd be gone."

Just then, they heard the drone of an engine. Matt hurried out of the cabin, returning minutes later, his face ashen.

"That was an AS532 Cougar."

"One more time, in English," Corey said.

"A German transport helicopter. It just dropped a dozen armed men up on the slope."

Shots rang out in the distance.

"I hope that wasn't Greg."

"I'm going to find out. You keep trying to reach Maddock, and be ready to get the hell out of here at the drop of a hat."

"Matt! You can't do that! You'll be killed!"

But Matt was gone. Corey punched the console again and returned to the radio. It was all he could do.

Chapter 35

They entered a cavern honeycombed with side passages, large and small. The floor was cracked and wisps of steam rose all around.

"I don't like this." Tam looked down at the ground, as if expecting it to give way at any moment.

They shone their lights all around, the beams slicing through the mist and revealing carvings of mythical creatures above the various passageways. The room was a veritable menagerie: a griffin to the left, a manticore to right, and various others all around. All of them looked fierce... and hungry.

"How about we move along?" Bones asked, looking nervously around.

"The directions say we're supposed to feed ourselves to the dragon," Maddock said. "Look around for it, and watch your step."

They scattered and, moments later, gunfire and shouting erupted from the passageway by which they'd entered. Everyone looked around in alarm, those who were armed drawing their weapons.

"Find the dragon and let's move!" Maddock shouted, moving as quickly as he dared across the precarious ground and shining his light above every passage.

No sooner had he spoken than a group of armed men burst into the cavern. Though the mist limited visibility, the ambient glow of a dozen flashlights playing off damp stone was sufficient to see the gleam of weapons in their hands. The newcomers froze for an instant at the sight of a cavern full of people, then opened fire.

The chamber thundered with the sound of gunfire. Maddock hit the ground, turned off his flashlight, and returned fire, as did the others in his party. The mist, moving lights, and confusion made him feel as if he were in a madhouse. Bullets ricocheted all around, adding to the danger. More men poured into the chamber, and Maddock knew his side was outgunned.

"Maddock! The dragon's over here!" Angel shouted from behind him.

"This way!" he called, keeping low as he ran toward her voice. "Let's get out of here."

Avery was nearby, and vanished into the tunnel along with Angel. Maddock looked around for the rest of his group, but they had all killed their lights. He could tell by the occasional gunshot from the cavern's perimeter, however, they were scattered all around and cut off from him.

"Just go!" Tam shouted. "We'll catch up with you."

"No way." Maddock dropped to the ground as someone fired off a shot in his direction.

"Maddock, you get out of here or I'll shoot you myself!" Bones' voice came through the fog. "Finish it!"

Indecision kept Maddock frozen in place long enough to realize the sounds of gunfire on the perimeter were growing fainter. His friends were retreating into the side passages, drawing the attackers away from him. Cursing and blessing them in the same breath, he turned and dashed down the passageway.

Tamsin stumbled through the darkness. Her face was bloody and her body bruised from tripping over unseen obstacles and banging into walls. Her men had abandoned her the moment the fighting started and the Dominion operatives didn't seem to care who they killed. They had surprised the Sisterhood's forces and started shooting. They were supposed to have made contact with her and joined forces. How had it gone so wrong?

She grimaced at the question. It had gone wrong because she had placed her trust in Heilig Herrschaft, the most sinister sect of the Dominion and had been betrayed. Now she and her Sisters were paying the price. Morgan had lost all her men except Locke and Jacob. Rhiannon's force had fared better, taking up defensive positions and holding the attacking force at bay, though who knew how long they could keep it up? If Tamsin's own men had stood their ground, they might have turned the tide, but the cowards had shown their true colors and now she was alone.

As she reeled forward, she sensed that the space around her had opened up. She had lost her flashlight when the fighting started, and was now, for all practical purposes, blind. She slowed her pace and felt all around her. She was definitely in a large chamber of some kind. She felt around for a wall to guide her and stepped out into open space.

She fell, screaming and grabbing for a handhold. Her fingernails tore as she clutched at rough stone, still falling. And then she hit the ground hard. For one irrational moment, she thought she had fallen to her death. Then she laughed. Feeling around, she realized she'd landed on a ledge. Of course, she didn't know how she was going to get out of this predicament, but at least she was alive. If only she could call for help, but there was no way her phone would get a signal so far underground. *Her phone!* She cursed herself in three languages as she dug her phone from her pocket and turned it on, using its faint glow to light the space around her. She saw immediately that she had not fallen far, and the rocky face above her was ripe for climbing. Relief flooded through her, renewing her energy.

After climbing up, she had just raised her head and shoulders over the top of the ledge when she heard a faint sound coming toward her. It wasn't exactly footsteps, but more of a scraping sound. She froze, hoping it would pass her by, but it came right toward her and, as it approached, she knew what it was.

Mordred.

She knew she should climb back down and wait for the dragon to go away, but fear kept her frozen in place, and she was trembling so hard she was afraid she would lose her grip and, this time, miss the ledge. Mordred had always terrified her, but this was far beyond any fear she had ever felt.

Far down the passageway behind Mordred, she saw a flicker of light. Someone was coming. She tried to cry out, but managed only a whimper. As the light grew stronger, she could finally see the dragon. Its snout was inches from her face.

She shook her head, furtively praying that the beast would go away, but it hissed, and opened its mouth wide.

She found her voice in time to manage a shrill scream that cut off when razor sharp teeth closed around her throat.

Chapter 36

"Oh my God," Angel whispered as they emerged into a vast cavern. Like the one from which they'd just come, tunnels branched out from it on all sides, but that was where the similarities ended. Its walls were sprinkled with crystals that twinkled like tiny stars, the source of their light not readily apparent. In the center of the room, a pit, twenty feet across, plunged down into the earth. Deep in its depths, a vortex swirled, sending up wisps of steam.

All around them, carvings depicted events from King Arthur's life, but they weren't exactly what Maddock had expected. One showed Arthur climbing out of a deep pool, clutching his three weapons- no lady in a lake to be seen. Another image showed him standing before a glowing man. At least, Maddock thought it was a man, but there was something different about him. He looked... alien.

"Bones would love that one," Angel said.

"Do you see what's written below it?" Avery's voice was filled with wonder. "Merlin."

Not for the first time in the past few days, Maddock felt overwhelmed by the magnitude of their discoveries. His mind was abuzz, wondering if what they saw here connected with other, similar finds he and Bones had made in the past.

"Do you want to see him?" Avery's voice drew him from his thoughts. "Arthur," she whispered, as if they were attending a viewing in a funeral home. "Come on."

Two stone footpaths formed a cross above the chasm, supporting a central platform. Upon it, a casket of blue-tinted crystal lay on a bier in the center. As they drew closer, Avery gasped.

"He looks like he just died yesterday."

Indeed, Arthur's had to be the most remarkably well-preserved corpse he had ever seen. He was a handsome man of early middle years. His wavy brown hair and thick beard were streaked with silver. He wasn't as tall or broad of shoulder as Maddock had imagined, but had probably been a big man for his day. He had been put to rest in simple garments- no armor or chain mail like Maddock had always imagined. His expression in death was serene, as if he were enjoying a pleasant dream.

"What is he holding?" Angel asked, pointing to a simple, stone bowl Arthur held upon his chest. It was carved of chalky white stone, but sparkled throughout with the same substance found on his weapons. It was deeper than an ordinary bowl, and three holes, evenly spaced, were bored just below the rim.

"I think it's the Holy Grail." Avery's face was as pale as the stone from which the bowl was carved.

"Doesn't look like a chalice to me," Angel said.

Maddock considered what he knew about Grail lore.

"There are a lot of different ideas about the Grail. Some said it was a chalice, a bowl, even a dish. One legend said it was a stone that fell from the heavens, and later fell into the hands of the Templars."

"Lapis Exillis," Avery whispered. "Though some people call it Lapis Elixir."

"The Philosopher's Stone," Maddock finished. "I see how it could be both. It's a bowl that could be used to catch blood, but it also looks like a chalky stone someone could scrape a bit off of and use it for an elixir."

"Yeah," Angel said. "It's sort of got that Alka Seltzer look to it."

"It's not quite that simple."

They whirled about to see Morgan enter the chamber, flanked by Locke and another man on one side, and a huge dragon on the other. She and her men aimed their pistols at Maddock.

"Hello, Jacob," Angel said to the man standing between Morgan and Locke. "Thanks for letting me go, but you forgot to tell me about your boss's reptile fetish."

Jacob looked uncomfortable, but Morgan ignored Angel.

"I must commend you on your resourcefulness," she began. "I did not anticipate the challenge you and your people would pose, but we beat you in the end. Now, I want the three of you to lay down your weapons. You should know, Mister Maddock, that if you try anything, we will shoot the ladies first."

Maddock gritted his teeth. He didn't see a way out of this one. He wasn't fast enough to kill all three before they could take a shot, and even if he could take hold of Carnwennan, which he had sheathed on his hip, its cloaking power would not help Angel or Avery. Slowly, he drew his Walther and laid it on the ground. On either side of him, the ladies did the same.

"Very good. Now, back away from them."

They did as they were told, moving to either side of Arthur's casket.

"Arthur," Morgan breathed, her expression enraptured. "After all this time, I shall finally fulfill my destiny." She looked up at the glowing walls. "And tonight is a full moon. How fitting. It only remains to be decided who will provide the sacrifice."

An icy certainty crept over Maddock. If Morgan was going to sacrifice someone, it wouldn't be him. Morgan would delight in his agony as he watched the woman he loved, or his sister, die. He couldn't let that happen.

Morgan took two steps closer, then froze. "Where is it?" She hissed. "Mordred will drink your blood for this."

Maddock just stared at her. What was she talking about?

"Where?" she shrieked. "Where is Rhongomnyiad?"

"It's right here, you crazy witch." Bones stepped out of a side passage and hurled Rhongomnyiad at Morgan. She dived out of the way and the spear embedded in the far wall in a flash of blue light. The crystals all around the cavern shone white hot and showered the chamber with sparks.

Maddock made a move for his Walther, but Mordred was almost upon him. He sprang back, unsheathing Excalibur. He hit the pommel and its blade burned.

"Get out here!" He called over his shoulder to Angel and Avery, who turned and ran. He only had a moment to register that people were pouring like angry bees from a hive out of the warren of passageways and into the chamber. He heard someone bark orders in German, and he caught a glimpse of Tam and Willis entering the room, guns blazing, and then Mordred was on him.

He thrust the glowing sword at the oncoming dragon, but it sprang back with incredible agility. Maddock drew back, and the creature stalked him. The chaos all around him seemed to fall away, like turning down a television set. It was him and the dragon. And then it struck him that, as a child, he'd often pretended he was a knight doing battle with a dragon. He almost laughed.

Mordred sprang forward again and he thrust. The blade opened a smoking gash in the dragon's hide, but it kept coming. Maddock continued to backpedal around the crystal casket, keeping the dragon at bay, but not dealing it enough damage to incapacitate it.

The dragon charged again, and he took a mighty swing, hoping to split the beast's head in two, but Mordred sprang to the side and Excalibur sheared off a chunk of its frill. The creature hissed and slashed at Maddock's leg with its razor sharp claws. Maddock wasn't quick enough, and the dragon opened a gash in his leg. Maddock stumbled, and Mordred lashed out with his powerful tail. Maddock leaped just high enough to avoid a broken leg, but the strike knocked him off his feet.

Mordred tensed to strike, but a torrent of bullets stopped him in his tracks. Avery had circled around and retrieved both her pistol and Maddock's. Most of her shots missed, but enough struck home to put the dragon on the defensive.

As she emptied the magazines and her weapons fell silent, Maddock regained his feet, raised Excalibur, and brought it down with all his might, cleaving the dragon's head from its body. Still snapping, the head rolled off the platform and down into the pit.

Maddock leapt back from the dragon's tail that, even in death, lashed about with deadly force, and ran back across the footbridge onto solid ground.

"Avery, you've got to get away," he ordered, and pushed her toward the nearest tunnel. He looked up just in time to see Locke standing before him, clutching Rhongomnyiad.

"Say good night, Maddock." Locke thrust the spear at him and Maddock parried, sending up a shower of sparks, and struck back. Locke blocked his stroke, and the blades flashed as they met.

They circled one another, locked in a dance of death. Maddock's injured leg slowed his movement, and he found himself increasingly on the defensive. Each of Locke's slashes and thrusts came ever closer to striking home. Step by step, he drove Maddock out onto the foot bridge, forcing Maddock to give way until Locke had him backed up to Arthur's casket.

Maddock glanced behind him and saw his chance. As he fended off another vicious slash, he pretended that his injured leg had given way, and reeled backward. As a gleeful Locke leapt in for the kill, Maddock threw himself over Mordred's still-thrashing body.

Locke, whose attention had been focused entirely on Maddock, sprang right into the path of the dragon's powerful tail, which struck him square in the side of the knee. Locke went down, screaming agony. The tail caught him again, this time in the side of the head, and Rhongomnyiad fell from his limp fingers and rolled to the edge of the platform.

Maddock dashed around the far side of the casket and scooped it up before it could go over the edge. He stood over Locke, who looked up at him with bleary, hate-filled eyes.

"I know how you think, Maddock. You won't kill an unarmed man. You're too noble for that."

"Maybe." Maddock reversed Rhongomnyiad and held the tip just above Locke's heart. "But I'll kill any man who lays a hand on my girlfriend." Fear flashed through Locke's eyes in the moment before Maddock drove the spear home. Blue light danced across Locke's body and smoke poured from his mouth, nose and ears. Maddock grimaced as the sickly sweet odor of burnt flesh filled his nostrils. He watched as Locke's body burned down to a blackened husk and crumbled to dust.

And then a voice sounded above the din, cold and clear. "Drop the spear or the girl dies!"

Chapter 37

Maddock heard Morgan clearly over the waning sounds of the battle. It sounded to him as if a lot of people had run out of ammunition, been killed, or both. He wanted to look around for Angel and his friends, but he could not tear his gaze away from Morgan who held a pistol trained on Avery. Maddock's sister stood with her hands upraised, quaking with terror. Why hadn't she run?

The room fell silent. All around them, the fighting stopped. Willis and Tam were on their knees, hands behind their heads, guarded by three white-clad men, as was another man he didn't recognize. Bones, knife in hand, faced off with another man in white, who aimed a pistol at him, but seemed reluctant to use it. Behind Morgan, Jacob had Angel in a headlock, though she was still fighting to free herself.

"I will not be denied." Morgan spoke the words like an oath. "Especially not by you."

"That is enough, Sister. It is over."

A beautiful woman with red hair and green eyes entered the chamber.

"What are you talking about, Rhiannon? Have you forgotten who I am?" Morgan quaked with rage, but she held her gun steady.

"I know exactly who you are, and it is time I put a stop to your plan." She snapped her fingers and the men who guarded Willis and Bones now trained their weapons on Morgan. "Jacob, stop choking that girl," she ordered. "And you," she said to Bones, "may stand down. We mean your people no harm."

Maddock nodded at at Bones, who reluctantly lowered his knife.

Morgan's beautiful face was cold with fury. For a moment, it looked as if she would turn her weapon on Rhiannon, but instead she lowered it a few inches.

"A wise choice," Rhiannon said, walking toward Morgan.

"You mean to take my place."

"I mean to stop your foul plan, and to prevent this," her gesture took in the entire chamber, "from ever being revealed to the world."

"Why?"

"Show him, Adam." One of Rhiannon's men pulled down the neck of his shirt, revealing a brand on his chest. A Templar cross!

"No," Morgan whispered. "The Templars are dead."

"We are very much alive, Sister, and we find your pagan rites foul in the sight of God."

"God." Morgan laughed. "After what we know about these weapons, you still believe in your God?"

"Perhaps His creation is greater than our imaginations, but He is still the author of it all."

Morgan began to laugh. It was a crazed, mad sound that chilled Maddock to the bone. But her laughter cut off when her eyes fell on Mordred's body. The dragon's death throes had nearly subsided, and he now twitched weakly.

"You killed him!" she cried in a voice that was beyond pain, beyond sanity. "Very well." Her entire body quaked. "You kill my family, I kill yours."

"No!" Jacob dove at Morgan, wrapping her in his bearlike arms and bearing her to the ground just as she pulled the trigger. Morgan cursed and fought him with all her might, struggling to free her gun hand, but Jacob held her down. "Don't do this," he pleaded. "I believed in you. Believed in your vision for Britain, but I don't believe in this."

Morgan spat in his face and fought to break free. In the midst of her struggles, Maddock heard a loud pop. Morgan gasped, her eyes wide with shock. Jacob took the gun from her limp fingers and rolled off of her, revealing a gaping wound in her side. She raised her trembling, bloody fingers in front of her face.

"Damn you all," she gasped.

Maddock barely heard her. He rushed to where Avery lay on the ground, blood seeping between her fingers as she held them pressed to her stomach.

"We've got to get you out of here," he said. "Somebody give me something I can bandage this with." His voice rang hollow. She wasn't going to make it. It was Melissa and Mom and Dad and too many good friends all over again.

"Shut up, Maddock." Avery managed a smile. "I hate it when you treat me like a child. Big brothers are all alike."

"I don't want you to die," he choked.

Tears spilled down Avery's cheeks as she reached out and took his hand. Suddenly, Maddock was aware of someone shaking him hard. It was Rhiannon.

"I said, it's not too late to save her. Give me the dagger."

Dumbly, Maddock handed Carnwennan to her.

"Bring me the Grail," she snapped as she collected Excalibur and Rhongomnyiad.

Bones and Willis hurried to the casket and raised the crystal lid while Maddock reached inside and withdrew the Grail.

Up close, it looked even more ordinary than it had before. The outside still sparkled in the light, but he noticed the inside was stained a dark reddish brown. He sat the Grail down next to Rhiannon and returned to Avery's side. She lay with her head in Angel's lap, looking up at the ceiling.

"It's beautiful here," she whispered. "I think Dad would have liked it."

"He would," Maddock said. "Now just hang on a little longer."

Rhiannon knelt down beside Morgan, who stared balefully at her.

"We need a sacrifice, Sister. Will you give it?"

"No," Morgan hissed. "Sacrifice her and save me instead."

"I will not. I am giving you this chance to make your final act in this world one of redemption. Perhaps you can atone for the evil you have done."

"I'll do it." Jacob said, dropping to a knee beside Morgan. "For all the wrong I've done in her service."

Morgan looked at him in bewilderment, and then, to Maddock's utter amazement, began to cry. She took Jacob's hand and kissed it.

"No, Jacob," she whispered, "I will do it if you will hold me up. I want to face death on my feet."

Jacob lifted Morgan like a baby and stood her up, wrapping his arms around her to keep her from falling.

Rhiannon lay the three weapons in a triangular pattern as they had seen on the doorway to this place. They all watched as the weapons shone brighter and brighter, each seeming to draw energy from the other. When they shone so brightly that Maddock could not stand to look at them, she reached down and picked up the dagger. The glow subsided, but each weapon pulsed with palpable energy.

"Hold the Grail for me," she said to Maddock. "This should be done by family." Maddock picked up the stone bowl and, together, they turned to face Morgan.

"Are you ready?" Rhiannon asked.

Morgan nodded.

Rhiannon sliced open the front of Morgan's shirt, turned the knife flat side up, held it above her heart, and slowly pushed it into her Sister's body. Morgan gasped as the blade entered her, but she maintained her mask of serenity.

Rhiannon did not push the knife in deeply, only far enough to draw blood. She waited until the fuller, the groove in the center of the blade, filled with blood, and then she turned and poured it into the Grail. She repeated the process with the spear, and then she hefted Excalibur.

As she pressed the sword to Morgan's chest, their eyes met.

"Goodbye, Sister," she whispered.

"May the gods forgive me," Morgan replied, closing her eyes.

With a powerful thrust, Rhiannon drove the sword deep into Morgan's heart. Morgan made not a sound as her lifesblood flowed onto the blade. When Rhiannon withdrew the sword, Jacob laid her gently on the floor.

When Rhiannon poured this last measure of blood into the Grail, it began to glow. Flecks of light swirled, and the blood inside bubbled and steamed.

"She must drink it now."

Maddock knelt in front of Avery and tipped the cup into her mouth. She choked and gagged, but was too weak to resist. In a few moments, she had gulped down the contents of the cup and, with a sigh, fell back onto Angel's lap.

She lay there for only a few seconds before her eyes jerked open. Her breath came in gulps and her legs twitched. She clutched her wounded stomach and cried out in pain.

And then, she was calm.

She looked up at Maddock in disbelief. Rhiannon knelt and raised Avery's shirt high enough to reveal that the wound was healed.

"It worked." Maddock shook his head. Another thing he couldn't believe.

"Is she, like, immortal?" Bones asked, looking at Avery in wonder.

"No. All Morgan's remaining years now belong to her. Morgan was a healthy woman, so she should have a long life ahead of her."

Now that he knew Avery was going to be all right, Maddock had questions.

"So, you're a Templar?"

"We are what remains of them," she said.

"Did you know about this place?"

"We knew of its existence, but its location was lost over three hundred years ago, along with the hiding places of the three weapons." She sighed. "The knowledge was believed to be lost forever, until 1701, when William Kidd, imprisoned in Newgate for piracy, offered three lost Templar maps in exchange for his freedom."

"But how did he get the maps in the first place?" Maddock asked.

"Through one of his acts of piracy. The captain of the ship he took was a Templar. He had recovered the maps and was taking them to England when he was mortally wounded in Kidd's attack. Kidd promised to deliver them, but he betrayed the captain. He tried to recover what he assumed was a treasure from Oak Island. When he failed, he left a false trail in the form of a stone inscribed with runes. By this time, accusations of piracy were catching up to him, so he tried a new tactic. He hid each map in a sea chest and secured them in various locations for safe keeping until he could see his way free."

"But it didn't happen," Bones said.

"No. He attempted to negotiate his release, but no one in authority believed he had anything real to offer, and Kidd refused to provide proof until he was set free. Finally, on the eve of his execution, he made his confession to a priest, though he refused to tell to whom he had entrusted the chests. We began our search immediately, but failed to locate them, and the secret faded into legend."

She picked up Excalibur in one hand and Carnwennan in the other.

"Now we can finally complete our task." With a look of regret, she stepped to the edge of the pit and tossed them in.

"Wait! What the hell?" Bones, Avery, and Angel shouted over one another.

"Why did you do that? Those are irreplaceable treasures. The technology..." By the look on Tam's face, it was a good thing she no longer had a loaded gun.

"They're too powerful," Maddock said. "Imagine if one nation harnessed that technology, or a terrorist group got hold of it."

"It is more than that," Rhiannon said, picking up the spear and the Grail. "People need faith, and these," she held them up for emphasis, "have the power to destroy that faith."

"Why, because they might be alien artifacts, or leftovers from an undiscovered, advanced civilization?" Bones asked. "Hell, I've believed in that stuff for years."

"No. It is because of what they are. What they were used for."

Understanding began to trickle through Maddock.

"That's the Holy Lance!" he exclaimed.

"Precisely. But it never pierced Jesus' side. And the Grail did not catch his blood. Quite the opposite, actually."

"Wait a minute." Avery, who was now back on her feet, held up her hands as if trying to slow Rhiannon down. "What are you saying?"

"Just as Morgan's blood saved you, the blood of another restored Jesus to life after his ordeal on the cross."

"Whose?" Avery looked stunned.

"Who among those closest to him died shortly after the crucifixion?"

"Judas," Maddock said. "Are you saying he wasn't a traitor? He didn't kill himself out of remorse?"

"The betrayal was planned, as was his sacrifice for his lord."

"I don't buy it," Willis said in a scornful tone. "That might be the story you all have passed down, but that don't mean that's the way it happened."

"Perhaps not," Rhiannon mused, "but, in any case, we cannot risk that story getting out. You can see the damage it could do."

One by one, they all nodded, except for Tam, who was doubtless thinking of the uses to which the government could put these items.

With a sad smile, Rhiannon dropped the Holy Grail and the Holy Lance into the pit. Maddock watched them fall, wondering if they'd made a mistake, but knowing deep down they had not.

"So, what happens now?"

Rhiannon's sad expression melted into a look of determination.

"I am the last remaining Sister, so I shall assume leadership. Morgan's body will be found on the grounds of Modron, a victim of her misguided attempt to tamper with nature. I shall also put a stop to her plot against the Royal Family."

"What about this place?" Avery asked.

"We will move Arthur's remains to a secret location, and then this chamber, and the passageways leading to it, must be destroyed. I suggest you leave as soon as possible."

"If you're leaving, we scored a sweet helicopter." Matt entered the chamber, followed by Greg. "It belonged to the Dominion, so we figured it was okay."

"How did you find us?" Willis asked.

"Just followed the dead bodies. You guys really make a mess."

"That's another thing," Maddock said to Rhiannon. "How did the Dominion get involved in all this?"

"I suspect my Sister, Tamsin, betrayed us, but I cannot be sure. We will know more after we question our prisoner." She reached out and shook Maddock's hand. "You should go now. Good luck."

"I don't know how to thank you for saving my sister's life."

"Keep our confidence, and continue the fight against the Dominion."

The moon hung low on the horizon when they returned to the surface. Maddock put his arms around Angel, holding her close and feeling more alive than he had in he didn't know how long. There was no need to talk. He could tell she felt it too.

"You two going to stand there all night?" Bones asked.

"I guess we'd better get going," Maddock agreed. "We've got a long trip home."

"So, who's riding in my awesome helicopter?" Matt asked.

"I could go for a ride," Tam said. "Who else is coming?" Willis and Greg volunteered. "How about you, Maddock?"

Maddock looked from Angel to Avery to Bones.

"I don't think so," he said. "I think we'll go for the relaxing cruise. You know, have a little family time."

Tam smiled.

"Enjoy your night, then. Because, tomorrow, you start working for me."

~End~

ATLANTIS

A Dane Maddock Adventure

Prologue

"We have emptied the city, Eminence." Albator shifted his weight and stole a glance at the temple door. "It is only the two of us and a few acolytes who wait to block the door as you instructed."

"You have done well, my son. Now it is time for you to go." Paisden pointed a long finger at the exit. "You don't want to be here when they arrive."

Instinct battled obligation in Albator's gray eyes. Clearly, he wanted to get away, but as Paisden's highest-ranking acolyte, his place was here in the temple. His lips formed soundless words and his feet continued their dance of indecision.

"Perhaps it won't come to war," he finally managed. "Why would the lords do this to us? We are of their line."

"We are their greatest mistake, or so they believe." Paisden's outward calm reflected the serenity that came with accepting one's fate. "They feel they never should have let us leave the mother city. We did not hold to the old ways. We interfered."

"We helped!" Albator swept a shock of stringy hair off of his high forehead. His voice took on a strident tone. "The people knew nothing. We taught them so much. We bettered their lives."

"The lords do not see it that way. To their minds, the knowledge was not ours to give. And then there were those of us who did not rein in our baser instincts."

Albator's red cheeks confirmed something Paisden had long suspected.

"Who is she?" Paisden now regretted the long hours he spent in the temple. Perhaps if he'd ventured outside more often, he'd have known more about Albator's life.

Albator's eyes fell. "Her name is Malaya, and she is kind and beautiful. If the lords could only see how much we care for one another, perhaps they could understand that a union such as ours…"

"Will always be an abomination to them. On this, and many other things, they are intractable." Paisden hated to bring the young man up short, but the sooner this conversation came to an end, the sooner Albator could make his way to safety. "Now, go to your woman. It is not too late for the two of you to build a life together. I hereby discharge you from your obligations to the temple."

"I don't want that." Albator held up his hands and took a step backward.

"What you want no longer matters." Paisden delivered the words like a slap to the face. "By this time tomorrow there will be no temple."

"We should fight them." Albator looked around as if searching for a weapon. "There are more of us than there are of them."

"Impossible. You know we have nothing with which to fight. For years, under the guise of needing resources in other parts of the empire, the lords have gradually stripped us of our weapons and energy sources. By the time we realized what was happening, we had but one machine and nothing with which to power it."

Paisden winced. The memory of his own naiveté stung. He remembered the pleas for help from their sister cities—pleas to which he was helpless to respond. Disasters, none of them natural, befell the cities, until only Paisden and his followers remained. He sent envoys to the lords, but none returned.

And then, yesterday, a single messenger, so weak from hunger and exhaustion that he could scarcely walk, staggered into the temple and uttered three words.

"They are coming."

Paisden sprang into action, ordering everyone to flee inland, taking only what they could carry on their backs, for he knew the weapon the lords would use against them, and he was powerless to stop it. When the messenger recovered sufficient strength, he told Paisden that the lords were, perhaps, a day behind him. And thus, did Paisden finally know the number of his days.

"There is nothing more you can do. Our people will need leadership, and you are their strongest remaining link to the temple. You and the other acolytes must close the door and then go, before it is too late."

"I'm not a stronger link than you." The flash of puzzlement in Albator's eyes dissolved in understanding. "You mean to remain here."

"I do. I am sworn to this temple. If fate wishes me to live, it will be so."

"You can't." A tear trickled down Albator's cheek. "Is there anything I can say to change your mind?"

"No." Paisden embraced the young man who was the closest thing to a son he would ever have. He kissed Albator once on each cheek, tasted the salty tears and perspiration, and then, gently, pushed him toward the door.

Albator stole a single glance over his shoulder as he stepped out into the sunlight. Moments later, he and the others began piling up stones at the temple door. Soon, it would be dark and Paisden would be alone.

Paisden took one last look around the place he had called home since his youth. Though wrought by human hands, the temple was perfect. Every stone fitted together seamlessly, every line was perfectly straight, just as Paisden's people had taught them. He took one last look at the sun, breathed deeply of the tangy salt air, and then went about his business.

He spared not a glance at the statue that dominated the room, but trailed his hand across the cool, smooth surface of the altar rail as he headed deeper into the temple. In the adyton, he clambered up into the steep shaft that led to his hidden quarters. Despite his years, he still had little trouble making the climb. With his demise looming, he savored every breath, every sensation. The rock shaft seemed alive beneath his hands, each trickle of sweat a living thing dancing along his flesh.

At long last, he crawled into his cell. It was a tiny, dark room, but he found comfort in the close quarters. He wanted to sleep, but he had set himself a task worthy of his final years, and he would see it completed. He lit a taper, plugged the tiny doorway with a stone block, and gathered the tools he would need.

He forsook the hammer, chisel, and stone tablets. There was too little time. Instead, he filled several wooden frames with dry clay, added water, stirred, and then smoothed them. His tablets ready, he found a sharp wooden stylus, settled onto his pallet, and began to write the story of his people.

Chapter 1

Sofia Perez mopped her brow and looked out across the sunbaked flats of the Marisma de Hinojos. Heat rose in waves from the parched earth, shimmering in the summer sun. Sunburned workers chipped away at the baked mud, excavating the canals that ringed the site. The scrape of digging tools on hard earth, and snatches of conversation, drifted across the arid landscape. It was hard to believe the transformation this drought-ridden salt marsh outside of Cadiz, Spain had undergone since early spring. Considering the level of funding their primary donor provided, progress was not just expected, but demanded.

"It's hot as Satan's butt crack out here." Patrick fanned himself with his straw pith helmet. His fair skin was not holding up well under the Spanish sun. In fact, his entire body glowed almost as red as his hair beneath a thick layer of sunscreen. "I don't know how you handle it."

"I'm from Miami. This is nothing." That wasn't entirely true. She kept going to her backpack for the can of spray-on sunblock to protect her olive skin. She hated sunburns—the itching, the way her clothing rubbed raw in all the wrong places. It was something she avoided at all costs. She noticed the way the corners of Patrick's mouth twitched and raised an eyebrow. "So, are you going to stand there trying not to smile, or are you going to tell me what's up?"

"You're needed in my section." He stopped fanning. "We think we've found the entrance to the temple."

Now it was her turn to keep her emotions in check.

"No vendas la piel del oso antes de cazarlo," she said under her breath.

"What's that?"

"Something my abuela used to say. It means, D*on't sell the bearskin before you hunt it.*" She permitted herself a sad smile at the memory. Her grandmother had been so proud when she'd graduated from college, but wasn't impressed by her choice of Archaeology as a vocation. She'd been hoping for an attorney in the family.

"It's more colorful than, D*on't count your chickens before they hatch*, I'll grant you that. Now, are you coming?"

They navigated the busy work site, waving to workers who called out greetings to them. Spirits were high. This had been a controversial undertaking from the start, and everyone feared it might end up a black mark on their résumés. Sofia had more hope than confidence, but the money was too good to pass up. Since then, her results continued to vindicate her. The circles originally spotted in satellite imagery and scoffed at by almost everyone had proven, upon excavation, to be ringed canals. And at the center…

"The Temple of Poseidon." Patrick's beatific smile made him look ten years younger. "I can't believe we've really found it. It's almost like a dream."

Sofia tried to ignore the flutter in her chest at his words. "You're a scientist, Patrick. Be professional."

"Even if it's not what we think, it's still a spectacular find. The architecture is classic, the golden ratio is everywhere. We uncovered a shaft that runs down into the temple at precisely the same angle as one of the shafts in the Queen's Chamber of the Great Pyramid, except it's much bigger. A few inches wider and I'd have climbed down there myself. It's a great find, Sofia. We're going to be in the history books."

"We can't draw any conclusions until we get inside and see what, exactly, we're dealing with. It would be pretty embarrassing if we told the world we've found the legendary temple at the heart of Atlantis and it turns out to be a grain storage building."

"I'll bet you a romantic, candlelight dinner that it's not a grain storage building."

Sofia laughed. "Even if I win that bet, I still lose. I'm only saying we need to be sure before we tell anyone outside the dig about this. It's just common sense."

Patrick's eyes fell and he turned away.

Sofia stopped in her tracks, grabbed him by the shoulder, and yanked him around to face her. "Tell me you didn't." The look in his eyes was all the answer she needed.

"I only sent one text. I was supposed to report in if we found anything promising. You've got to admit, *this*," he pointed to the peak of the temple roof where it rose out of the earth, "is interesting."

She couldn't argue with him. The temple, for despite her professed reservations, it was clear that's what it was, was remarkably well preserved. The carving on the pediment, the triangular upper portion of the temple facade, showed an angry Poseidon slamming his trident into the sea, sending ferocious waves in either direction. The supporting columns were massive pillars fluted with parallel, concave grooves. At their peaks, the capitals, the head pieces that flared out to support the horizontal beam beneath the pediment, were carved to resemble the scaled talons of a sea creature, giving the impression that the roof was in the clutches of a primordial beast. The sight of it sent chills down her spine.

"Who did you tell?"

"Mister Bishop. I mean, I told his assistant. That's the only number I had. They're staying somewhere nearby, so we can expect a visit." His voice took on a pleading tone. "Come on, Sofia. They're practically footing the entire bill for this dig. They've given us everything we could want. You think we could have written grants to find Atlantis in southern Spain and gotten anything but ridicule for our trouble?"

"I know." She hated to admit it, but he was right. "It's just weird that the Kingdom Church is paying us to find Atlantis. Noah's Ark, I could see, but this? It's weird."

"I don't care as long as the checks keep coming in. Now, how about you quit worrying and let's get down there so they can open this door? You said not to open anything without you, and we took you at your word."

"Good. I'm glad to know you can use common sense when you have to."

Patrick mimed thrusting a dagger into his heart and then stepped aside so she could be first down to the dig site. A forty foot ladder descended into the pit where the excavation was ongoing. She climbed down, almost losing her footing once as she daydreamed about what they might find inside.

Several people stood around the entrance to the temple. They had cleared the entire front of the temple and back through the pronaos, the covered area that led back to the naos, the temple's enclosed central structure, and now waited for her to give the word. She could almost feel their excitement as she mounted the steps and approached the doorway. This was the moment!

"The door is weird." Patrick removed his helmet and scratched his head. "It's not really a door at all. It's more like a patch."

She didn't need to ask him to explain. The exposed portion of the naos was solid marble. The entryway, by contrast, was sealed with loose stones and mortar.

"Looks like they wanted to keep something out." She ran her fingers over the rough stones. "Maybe they knew the flood was coming?"

"Or they wanted to keep something in." Patrick made a frightened face, eliciting a giggle from a plump, female grad student.

Sofia brushed her hands on her shorts and stepped back. "Clear it out carefully. Try to keep it in one piece, if you can."

The crew didn't need to be told twice. Clearly, this was what they'd been eager to do since uncovering the entryway. They worked with an efficiency that made her proud. Sooner than she would have thought possible, they worked the plug free.

"Ladies first." Patrick made a mocking bow and motioned for her to enter the temple.

Sofia paused on the ambulatory, crinkled her nose at the stale air wafting through the doorway, and tried to calm her pounding heart. Was she about to make one of the greatest archaeological finds of all time? Heart racing, she fumbled with her flashlight, turned it on, and directed the shaky beam inside.

The cella, the interior chamber, hadn't gone unscathed in the disaster that befell the city. The floor was covered in a foot-deep layer of silt and all around were signs of leakage, but it could be worse. Much worse. This place had been closed up tight and must have been quickly covered by dirt and sand, at least, quick by geological standards, to have kept it in such pristine condition. Mother Earth had wrapped it in her protective blanket, protecting it against the ravages of time.

She played her light around the room, and what she saw took her breath away. Twin colonnades, the columns shaped like the twisting tentacles of a sea serpent, ran the length of the room, framing a magnificent sight.

"What do you see?" Patrick had hung back, like he knew he was supposed to, but his anxious tone indicated he wouldn't wait much longer.

"Poseidon!" A twenty-foot tall statue of the Greek god stood atop a dais in the middle of the temple. Like the image on the pediment outside, this was an angry god, driving furious waves before him. Unlike so many modern interpretations, he was not a wise, grandfatherly figure, gray of hair and beard, but young and virile, with brown hair and long, sinewy muscles. Wait! Brown hair?

"You can still see some of the paint!" Through the use of ultraviolet light, researchers had determined that the Greeks had painted over their sculptures, sometimes in bright primary colors, other times in more subdued, natural tones. Thus, the classic marble statues seen in contemporary museums did not accurately reflect their appearance in ancient times. This sculpture appeared to have been done in the latter style. Besides the traces of brown in the hair, she could see hints of creamy skin, as well as flecks of silver on his trident. The waves beneath his feet were speckled with aqua and the crests streaked with white. Had leaks in the roof eroded the paint, or had the pigments faded over time? One of the many questions they would doubtless try to answer as they studied this fabulous place.

Her crew could wait no longer, and crowded in behind her, adding their own flashlight beams to the scant light hers provided.

"Whoa." Patrick, focused on the Poseidon statue, stumbled on the soft, uneven dirt. "It's just…" Words failed him, so he shook his head, continuing to gaze at the sculpture of the god of the sea.

"What's the Stonehenge thing?" The grad student who had been so amused by Patrick indicated a circle of stone that ringed the statue. Though the stones were marble, and their lines sharp, the thick bases and circular arrangement did suggest Stonehenge in miniature.

"I guess it's an altar." Overwhelmed by the temple, Sofia found thinking a challenge.

"And there's an obelisk where the heel stone should be." Patrick rounded the statue, kicking up a cloud of dust as he went. "Hey, wait a minute." He froze. "Sofia?"

"What is it?" She joined him on the far side of the statue and followed his line of sight. The back wall that divided the cella from the adyton, the area to which only priests were admitted, sloped away from them, and each layer of stone grew progressively smaller, giving the illusion of…

"A pyramid," Patrick whispered.

"Why not? We've got an obelisk here. Perhaps Atlantis was, in some way, a cultural forerunner to both the Greeks and the Egyptians." She wanted to kick herself for uttering such an unexamined theory. Such speculation was unscientific and unprofessional. She turned the beam of her flashlight into the adyton and almost dropped it.

The light gleamed on a contraption of silver metal supported on four stone pillars. It was a pyramid-shaped frame made of a metal that looked like titanium. Suspended beneath it was a metal bowl shaped like a satellite dish. The pyramid was capped by a grasping silver hand. Only the hieroglyphs running around the cap just below the hand looked like something from the ancient world. Otherwise, its appearance was thoroughly modern…

…and thoroughly alien.

Chapter 2

"What the hell is that thing?" Patrick's words, whispered in a reverential tone, gave voice to Sofia's own thoughts.

"Everybody stay out until I call for you." She wanted to make a complete photographic record before anyone else entered the chamber. But more than that, she wanted to experience it by herself, to get the feel of the space and let her intuition speak to her. It was something she'd always done—her way of communing with the past.

She circled the odd contraption wondering just what in the world it was. She'd never seen its like in an ancient world site, but here it was, inside a temple that had spent the last few millennia buried under twenty feet of silt. She took a few minutes to photograph the chamber before turning to a tiny doorway in the back wall. She ducked through and found herself in a small room that was, surprisingly, faintly lit by sunlight. She identified its source as a shaft high in the opposite wall above a stone shelf that might have been a priest's bed. Moving closer, she looked up and saw a square of sky at the far end. This was the shaft her crew had uncovered. Patrick was right. It looked like a larger version of a pyramid's air shaft.

"Sofia." Patrick called, soft but urgent, from the cella. "Mister Bishop's here and he's brought armed men with him."

"What?" She whirled around. "That doesn't make sense. Why would they need to be armed?"

"I don't know. A few of them are Guardia Civil, and others look like Americans."

Just then, gunfire erupted somewhere outside, reverberating through the stone chamber like thunderclaps. A final scream pierced the air, cut off in an instant by a single shot.

"You've got to get out of here!" Patrick hurried up to her. "The shaft. I'll give you a boost."

Before she could argue, Patrick scooped her up and lifted her toward the opening. She struggled to find handholds in the smooth stone, but Patrick kept pushing. He was stronger than she'd imagined. A few more shots rang out just as Patrick got his hands under her feet and shoved her the rest of the way in.

"What about you?" She felt like a coward, fleeing this way.

"I'll be fine. He likes me." His words rang hollow. "You just climb as fast as you can. I'll stall him."

Fighting back tears, she scrabbled up the shaft, her feet finding purchase on the sides and forcing her upward. Why had Mister Bishop done this? Behind her, she heard Patrick's voice.

"Mister Bishop, what happened out there?" His voice quaked with every word.

"Nothing you need concern yourself with." Bishop's deep voice echoed in the shaft. "Where is Doctor Perez?"

His words chilled Sofia to the bone. She had no doubt he planned on killing her and Patrick once he'd extracted whatever information he sought. She didn't know why he wanted to find Atlantis, but now that she'd discovered it, she, and her people, were expendable.

"She's out on the dig site. Inspecting one of the outer canals on the south side, I think."

"There are two sets of footprints." His voice was cold.

"One of the assistants took some pictures and then I sent her back out."

If she hadn't been deathly afraid for her life, Sofia would have admired Patrick's ability to invent on the fly. The fear was gone from his voice. She wished he could have escaped along with her but, should the worst happen, she was determined not to let his sacrifice be in vain. She continued her climb, now almost halfway to the top.

An unfamiliar voice, rough like sandpaper, spoke up. "What's that opening behind you?"

"We think it's an air shaft like the ones in the Great Pyramids." Patrick reply came out fast and unnatural. Sofia could hear it, and she was sure Bishop and his cronies could too. "We got lucky. It was capped up at the top. Otherwise, it and this whole chamber would have filled with silt. We'd have had a heck of a time uncovering this thing, not that we know what it is." He was clearly trying to divert their attention to the strange contraption.

"Oh, we know exactly what it is." Bishop cleared his throat. "To be more precise, we know what it does."

Don't say anything else, Patrick. The more you know, the worse it is for you. Just run away.

Perhaps if Sofia were a telepath, Patrick would have heard her plea and clammed up. Instead, he rambled on. "Really? What does it do? It looks like…"

A gunshot rang out and Sofia muffled a cry of grief and fear. She looked up at the square of light at the end of the shaft. It was no more than ten meters away, but at the rate she was going it might as well be a thousand. If Mister Bishop, or one of his men, looked into the shaft, she was dead. She tried to quicken her pace, reaching out as far as she could, and her hand closed on cold metal.

"Pack up the machine." Bishop was all business. His voice carried no hint that he had just witnessed the slaughter of innocent people. "Carefully, now, and be certain to crate it up before you take it out."

"Yes, Bishop," the man with the rough voice replied.

"I wonder." Mister Bishop now sounded thoughtful. "Could a person fit inside that shaft?"

Sofia's pulse roared in her ears, and panic dulled her senses. She realized she was gripping a metal handle of some sort. She scooted closer and saw two brass handles embedded in a block of stone. It was a plug like the one archaeologists found in the Great Pyramid! She grabbed hold of the handles and yanked with all her might.

It didn't budge.

"I'll check it out, Bishop."

With renewed strength born of abject terror, she heaved at the plug, and it came free in a cloud of dust and stale air. There was a chamber there! It was pitch black, but instincts honed from years of experience told her there was a large, open space inside. She slithered through the opening and took the plug along with her. Moments later, she heard the rattle of gunfire. Bullets pinged up the shaft, inches from where she squatted.

"Did you see someone?" Mister Bishop asked.

"Just being thorough. It's not like there's anyone left out there for me to hit." The man's guttural laugh echoed through the chamber.

"Doctor Perez is still unaccounted for. Find and dispatch her with all due haste. I'll meet you back on the ship."

"Yes, Bishop. We'll have the machine out of here in ten."

Sofia bit her lip, thinking hard. If they were looking for her, it would be too dangerous to try and climb out right now. She'd have to wait them out. She hefted the plug and pushed it back in the hole, handles facing inward, and then took out her small LED flashlight and flicked it on. Through a curtain of dust that tickled her nose and made her eyes burn, she followed its beam.

The space was no more than three meters square, its walls smooth and unadorned. She directed her light down onto the floor and her heart skipped a beat as it fell on a skeleton. It lay on its side in a pool of dust that might have once been clothing or a blanket. Near its hand lay a thin wooden rod with a pointed end—a stylus, and a jumble of rectangular tablets not much bigger than index cards. She knelt down for a closer look and saw they were all covered in tiny hieroglyphs. Many she recognized as identical to their Egyptian counterparts, but most were either slight variations on the Egyptian writing, or were unfamiliar.

"A codex." Depending on what was written here, this could be the single most important find of the dig. After first checking to make sure the opening to the chamber was sealed, she photographed each one, moving them about as if handling a newborn baby. They were made of clay, and she feared they would crumble at her touch, but they held together. When she'd made a photographic record, she took another set of pictures with her phone, vowing to text them to… she didn't know… someone she could trust, the moment she got out of this temple and into cell phone range. If she and the tablets should fall into Bishop's hands, she didn't want the secret to die with her.

The absurdity of her thoughts struck her in a flash. Here she was, hiding from men who had apparently just murdered her crew, and now were after her, and her paramount concern was preserving a codex. She would have laughed, had the situation not been so dire. This was her life's work, and she wasn't going to let a crazy man stop her. With great caution, she stacked the tablets and wrapped and bound them in a bandanna. It was the best she could do for now.

She checked her watch. Nearly twenty minutes had passed since she first entered the adyton. Were the men gone? As carefully and quietly as she could, she shifted the plug aside and strained to listen.

"We can't find Doctor Perez, Bishop. If we'd kept Patrick alive we might have extracted her whereabouts from him."

"The Guardia Civil will put her on our list." The speaker's voice was deep with a Spanish accent.

"Thank you," Mister Bishop said. "Are we certain she is not among the dead?"

"I can't be sure. My men like to aim for the head. It's good for target practice but bad for identification purposes."

Bishop let out a long, slow breath. "In that case, she is most likely dead. If not, it won't matter for long. We will cleanse the site, as planned."

She froze. What did he mean by that? She knew what it meant for her—she had better find a way out of here sooner rather than later. She listened for more sounds, but Bishop and the others seemed to have gone. She performed some quick mental calculations, and decided she should wait ten minutes to make certain the men were well clear of the temple before she climbed out. She watched the minutes pass by with agonizing slowness until, finally, it was time.

She tucked the codex into her shirt, listened again for a few seconds, and heard nothing. Heart pounding and dizzy from fear, she took a deep breath and clambered out into the shaft. The ascent seemed to take hours. Every second she expected to hear the gunshot that would end her life. Her breath came in ragged gasps and cold sweat soaked her clothes, but she labored on until she reached the top.

She peeked her head out and scanned up and down the trench her workers had dug in order to reach this part of the temple. The trench was empty and all was quiet, save the rush of distant waves. Of course, she had no idea who might be waiting up above. It didn't matter. Her gut told her she needed to get as far away from here as possible, and fast. She hurried to a nearby ladder, ascended in silence, and paused at the top to peer over the edge.

A small whimper escaped her lips as her eyes fell on the bodies of two crew members. Bullets to the head rendered them unrecognizable, but she grieved for them all the same. She wondered again at the reason for this senseless slaughter. Furthermore, how had Bishop gotten the local authorities on his side? Money, she supposed. There would be time enough to figure that out once she'd gotten clear of the dig.

She heard the faint roar of an engine in the distance and looked to the south to see a van driving across the flats, escorted by two pickup trucks, their beds packed with men. She couldn't quite make them out, but the light glinted off of what she presumed to be firearms. Bishop was leaving, which meant it was a good time for her to go, too.

Not wasting time, she scrambled out onto level ground and sprinted in the opposite direction. It was not until she'd run for an hour, the stabbing pain in her lungs and leaden feeling in her legs reminding her how long it had been since her last 10K road race, that she felt safe enough to stop in the shelter of the tall grass in one of the few remaining marshlands.

She took out her phone and first used it to pinpoint her location. She would need it when she made her next call. But would he want to hear from her? It didn't matter. She didn't have many connections in Spain, and certainly no one else who would be okay taking in a fugitive from the Guardia Civil, perhaps Spain's most corrupt branch of law enforcement. And then there was the matter of the codex, her taking of which violated all kinds of laws. Of course, he couldn't possibly take the moral high ground on that score. Besides, he owed her after the way he'd left her in Peru. She punched up the number and held her breath. He picked up on the first ring.

"Sofia, is that you?"

So he hadn't deleted her number from his phone. That made her smile.

"Hey, Arnau. Long time, no speak."

"Oh my God, it is you! Are you all right?" The genuine concern in his voice moved her, but then a different thought chased the good feeling away.

"Why wouldn't I be?" Had word of the killings already leaked out?

"You don't know?" He sounded befuddled. *"Where have you been? There was a tidal wave or something down on the salt flats. Your whole dig is gone."*

Chapter 3

"Yeah! I freaking love this thing." Bones tapped on the transparent ceiling of the small submarine. "It's sturdier than I expected. I know! Let me try the torpedoes."

"No way." Dane Maddock stifled a grin as he took the craft into a steep dive. "Tam just gave us this new toy. We're not getting it taken away after our first test run."

Down below, the barnacle-encrusted hulk of a sunken ship grew ever larger as they approached. Maddock slowed the craft and drifted toward the gaping tear in its hull. The two former Navy SEALs turned treasure hunters, along with their crew, had recently agreed to work for a clandestine branch of the CIA that sought to root out the Dominion, a powerful group of religious extremists that had given Maddock and his partner, Bones Bonebrake, more trouble than they cared to count. This submarine, which Bones christened *Remora* after the suckerfish that attached itself to a larger host for transportation, protection, and food, was just one of the benefits.

"I don't think we can make it through that gap," Bones said from his seat behind Maddock. "How about I make that hole bigger?"

"Fine, but no torpedoes. What do we have in our arsenal?"

"How about this?"

Maddock watched as a mechanical arm extended from the sub and, with a flash of white light, began slicing through the hull. A cloud of silt and debris engulfed the sub. When it cleared, Bones had carved out a semicircular section of hull large enough to pass through.

"Laser cutter, baby!" Bones sounded like a kid on Christmas morning. "Hey, you know that riverboat casino my Uncle Charlie's all worked up about? With this, we could send that thing to the bottom of the river in no time."

"You know something? I was kind of hoping you wouldn't be able to fit inside here. Being at close quarters with you gets old fast." It seemed something of a miracle that the hulking Cherokee had managed to squeeze his broad-shouldered, six foot-five frame into the tiny sub.

"Always hating. I can't help it if you need a gallon of hair gel to get to six feet tall."

Maddock shook his head. It wasn't only the contrast between the blue-eyed, blond-haired Maddock and the dark-skinned, long-haired Cherokee that made them an odd pair. Bones was brash and aggressive, while Maddock was prone to think twice before taking action. They hadn't cared for one another in the early stages of SEAL training but, over time, found that their strengths complemented each other. Now, though they still managed to annoy one another, they were closer than brothers.

Maddock poked *Remora's* nose into the ship's open cargo hold. The hull had collapsed in places, leaving insufficient room for the craft to make it all the way in. He shone the light around, revealing indistinguishable piles of silt and rubble. Nothing to see here. "Why don't you try out the retrieval arms and then we'll head back?"

Two more mechanical arms extended from the bottom of the sub. Maddock followed their progress on a video display. Bones used them to lift and move items of various sizes. Finally, one of the arms came up with a thin chain hooked on its grip. Bones raised the arm so they could examine the object through the transparent bubble that topped the pilot's area.

"A necklace. That'll clean up nice," Bones said. "Hard to believe it didn't break. I am good."

"What are you going to do with it? Give it to Avery?" Avery Halsey was Maddock's sister whom his father had kept a secret from him. They'd met a few months before and now she was dating Bones.

"Yeah, Maddock, I need to talk to you about that." Bones stowed the necklace in the sub's tiny hold and retracted the arms while Maddock reversed the craft and turned back toward shore. "She says she's found a job and is moving down here so she can be closer to us."

"From Nova Scotia to the Keys? That's quite a change, but that's cool. Wonder why she didn't tell me." Maddock paused. "Hold on. Are you two moving in together? If so, you're moving out of my guest room."

"Hell no! I broke up with her. That's what I wanted to tell you." Bones hurried on. "I just hope it doesn't make it weird between us."

"Why would that be weird?" Maddock rolled his eyes. He wasn't entirely surprised that the relationship hadn't lasted. A few months was actually a long time for Bones, who sometimes referred to himself as "Pollinator in Chief," considering it his duty to expose as many women to his charms as humanly possible.

"You know what *was* weird?" Bones ignored the sarcasm. "Each of us dating the other's sister. That was messed up."

Bones' sister Angel, a model and professional mixed martial arts fighter, was Maddock's girlfriend. Unlike Bones and Avery, they were still together. She had joined them on a couple of their adventures, but was currently in North Carolina training for a championship fight. The very thought of her made him smile. After years of forcing himself to think of her as a friend, she'd finally broken through the wall he'd constructed between them.

"What is this, a pajama party? Cut the relationship talk and take over." Maddock chuckled at Bones' triumphant shout as he took control of the craft and they surged forward, climbing up toward the light.

"Let's see if we can find a military ship and try out the cloaking on this baby."

Maddock's good-natured groan died in his throat as the power in their sub flickered. When it returned, all the displays went crazy for a split second before returning to normal.

"Looks like we've found our first bug," Maddock said. "What did you do? Turn on the cloaking?"

"No, I was kidding about that." Bones sounded puzzled. "I was taking us in, holding steady, when everything went on the fritz for a second, if that long."

"Everything looks normal now. Let's take it back to shore and give Tam our report."

"Aye aye. Let's hope this thing doesn't crap out on us before we get there."

"I hope they're enjoying themselves." Willis Sanders cast an angry look at the dancing blue waters of the Gulf of Mexico. "Me and Matt are getting that sub tomorrow. I don't care what Maddock says."

"I'm the boss, not Maddock," Tam reminded him for what felt like the hundredth time. "I said you two can take it out tomorrow and that's final. Now shut up before I change my mind."

She'd recently brought Maddock and his crew onto her team, and Willis, in particular, found adjusting to the new power structure difficult.

"Girl, you're grouchy. Is the Key West humidity getting to you?" He grinned down at her. He was a handsome man, tall, and well-sculpted, with skin just dark enough to lend him a hint of mystery, but even if he wasn't her subordinate, he got under her skin way too often for her to take an interest in him.

"What have I told you about calling me girl? I used to think you were too arrogant to stop, but now I think you're just a slow learner." She would never admit it, but there was some truth in his words. She felt as if she was in a steam room most of the time, and the humidity played hell with her hair. More and more, she found herself in a foul mood, and she was putting far too many dollar bills into her cussing jar. She mopped the sweat from her damp brow and attempted to maintain her stern expression.

Willis hung his head and attempted to look chastened, but failed badly. His mischievous grin seemed permanently fixed in place.

For a moment, Tam considered shoving him off the pier, but he'd probably find that funny, too.

"It's your fault for hiring a bunch of SEALs." Matt Barnaby, a sturdily built man with brown hair and a fresh beard that he couldn't stop scratching, gazed out at the water. "The Army actually teaches discipline." He was a former Army ranger, which led to plenty of good natured ribbing amongst the crew members.

"Crazy talk." Willis shook his head.

"One word: Bones."

"All right, you got me there." Willis threw his head back and laughed. "I'll bet he's down there testing out the torpedoes right now."

"All right, ladies, break time's over. Let's finish our run." Tam raised an admonishing finger. "And I don't want to hear any more complaints about cardio. I don't care how well you boys swim…" The words died on her lips. Along the shoreline, the water receded across a wide swathe, and the gentle roar of the waves dissolved into an ominous, sucking sound.

"You were saying?" Willis folded his arms across his chest and cocked his head.

"It's a drawback!" she shouted. "Tsunami!"

Chapter 4

Tam dashed down the pier, the sunbaked planks trembling beneath her feet as she pounded along its length. All around, people looked at her in confusion.

"Tsunami!" she shouted. "Everybody get to high ground as fast as you can!"

Everyone looked at her like she was crazy, and well they should. The idea that a tsunami could hit with zero warning, and from the inland side of the island, was absurd. That, and there was no "high ground" to be found here.

She slowed her pace and turned on her most commanding voice. "Move it! Get to the upper floors of a building! Now!"

The authority and urgency in her voice seemed to convince a few people, who began trotting along in her wake, but others just stared.

"Come on, y'all. Look at the water!" Willis pointed to the receding waterline. "I'm a Navy SEAL and that's a warning sign of a tsunami. Now move your asses!"

Whether it was the bizarre sight of the water drawing back, or the force of Willis' words, the people on the dock were finally convinced. That was both good and bad, as some turned and ran, while others froze in fear, and some even began to scream.

"Sure." Tam put her hands on her hips and frowned. "The woman yelling *tsunami* is hysterical, but if a *man* says it, they jump. Forgive me, Lord Jesus, but stupid people do vex me."

Matt and Willis brought up the rear urging the stragglers along, while Tam ran ahead, continuing to call out her warning to those who might not have heard.

She knew they didn't have much time. The wave period for a tsunami averaged twelve minutes, but there was nothing average about this situation. She stole a glance over her shoulder to check on Matt and Willis. They were falling farther behind as they tried to get everyone moving off the pier. She knew enough about them to know they wouldn't want to leave anyone behind. A tsunami in Key West! Why had she let Maddock talk her into setting up shop here?

By the time she hit the end of the pier, the warning had spread and people all along the shore were streaming away from the beach, but it wouldn't do any good if they couldn't get above the waterline. She scanned the area, looking for anywhere safe. Most of the buildings in this area were small waterfront bars, restaurants, and shops, but beyond them, she spotted a four-story hotel building.

"Everybody to the hotel! Get to the second floor or higher!" She ground her teeth in frustration. These people were slower than boyfriends to a bridal shower. She grabbed a dazed-looking, heavyset woman who seemed to be clogging the flow of traffic, took her by the chin, and looked her square in the eye. "You see that hotel right there?" The confused woman nodded. "Good! You're in charge of getting everybody to the top floor. Can you do that?"

The woman nodded again, shook like a dog fresh from its bath, and turned around to face the oncoming throng. "We're going to the hotel!" she bellowed in a voice suited for a football coach. "Follow me!" With that, she lumbered away, the rest following in her wake.

Tam could almost hear her grandmother chiding her for lack of tact, but she'd gotten the job done, hadn't she? Matt and Willis trotted up as the last of the stragglers cleared the deck of the pier.

"Where to now, boss?" Matt didn't look the least bit concerned about the impending disaster.

Down the shore, a crowd milled about, some staring at those fleeing the beach, but not making a move to escape the wall of water that would soon sweep them all away if they couldn't manage to outpace it. Willis and Matt followed her line of sight and they took off running. All three were in good shape but Willis outpaced his shorter colleagues, reaching the crowd well ahead of them and ushering them away from the beach. It didn't take long for panic to take over as people realized what the receding water meant, and they fled in every direction.

"If that's all the stragglers, we need to get ourselves to some place safe." Tam pressed her hand to the stitch in her side, hoping she wouldn't have to run any farther.

Matt turned toward the water and his expression grew stony. "I think we're too late."

Sure enough, a wave rolled toward them. It was difficult to tell at this distance, but Tam estimated it to be least four meters high, which meant the swell behind it would be powerful. They'd never outrun it.

"Time for some body surfing." All signs of fear were absent from Willis' face, but a hint of resignation lay beneath his words. "I always did like riding the waves."

Tam looked around for anywhere close by they could go to escape the water. "We ain't done yet. Come on!"

A nearby sign read "Glass Bottom Boat Rides" and two of the crafts sat on damp sand where the drawback had left them high and dry. Willis untied one from the dock while Matt kicked in the office door and retrieved a key ring. He tossed them to Willis and joined them in the boat.

"You think we'll make it?" Tam tried to sound braver than she felt. The wall of water was now a hundred yards away and closing fast.

"The boat's pointed the right way." Matt couldn't keep his eyes off the wave. "We've got a chance."

"Y'all put on your life jackets," Willis said found the proper key and put in the ignition. No sense cranking up the engine until they were actually afloat. If they managed to ride the wave, that was.

Tam strapped on her life jacket and braced herself as the wave broke fifty yards from where they waited and an avalanche of foamy white water came roaring toward them. When it struck, the boat shot straight up, its bow pointed to the sky. For one, heart-stopping instant, she was sure they were going to flip over backward, but then, as if in slow motion, the craft fell forward and hit the water with a loud crack. She felt the impact from head to toe, and icy water soaked her, but the boat didn't capsize. She spat out a mouthful of salty water and blew more from her burning sinuses. This was crazy, but they were alive. For the moment.

The boat rocked and spun as Willis fired up the engine and struggled to gain control, but the water carried them inland at a breathtaking pace. They rode a swell and teetered perilously as they crested it and came down, sending up another curtain of cold salt spray. "Can't you drive any better than this?"

"It's just like a ride at Disney World!" Willis laughed. He was enjoying himself. Gradually, he turned the craft, but not out into open water, as Tam expected. Instead, he pointed it back toward shore.

"What the hell are you doing?" The roof of a submerged beachfront bar stuck up like an iceberg in their path, and they bore down on it with alarming speed.

"We can't fight the water." All traces of humor had vanished from Willis' face. "Engine can't handle it."

"Well, you better make a right turn quick."

With agonizing slowness, the boat turned, but not fast enough. The stern struck the roof of the bar, sending them spinning. Tam tried to see where they were headed, but couldn't focus. She felt, more than heard, another crash. The next thing she knew, she found herself lying face down on the glass bottom, staring through drops of blood and churning water at a paved road beneath the swirling water. She touched her forehead and her hand came away red and sticky. That was going to be attractive.

Matt hauled her to her feet and leaned in to inspect her wound, but she shoved him away. Grasping the side rail for balance, she blinked to clear the cobwebs from her mind and looked around. The boat still turned, but slower now, and the surge carried them along a thoroughfare through the middle of town. Buildings, half submerged, spun past, making her dizzy. She tried looking down, but the transparent bottom was little better.

"Hang on!" Willis shouted and, moments later, they careened off the top of a lamppost and crashed into a brick building. The impact jolted them, but the craft took no serious damage. "Man, this thing is tough."

The current slowed as it swept them inland, and Willis gained control of the boat. Tam looked around, surveying the damage. She didn't know what the rest of the key looked like, but this section was devastated. Only buildings two-stories or higher were visible. The tops of palm trees rose like shrubbery just above the surface of the water. Debris clogged the surface, and she spotted the occasional body carried along by the current. She was no stranger to death, but the sight made her wince. How could such a tragedy occur with no warning whatsoever?

"It doesn't make sense." Matt seemed to read her mind. "This is the twenty-first century. We detect these things ahead of time and issue warnings, but not this time. If you hadn't noticed the drawback, no telling how many people would have been caught off guard."

"That ain't the strangest part." They turned to look at Willis. "Didn't y'all see? That wave, it wasn't natural."

"What do you mean?" Tam felt her insides turn cold.

"It was, I don't know, concentrated. I could see where it ended on both sides. It was like somebody aimed a surge of water right at this spot."

"Are you sure?"

"Definitely."

"What could cause a phenomenon like that?" Tam mused. "Setting off a nuclear bomb underwater?"

"No." Matt shook his head. "That would send out waves in an ever-widening circle, which isn't what Willis saw."

"I'm dead serious. It seemed like the devil scooped up some water and pushed it right at us."

"I hope Bones and Maddock are okay." Matt turned and looked back in the direction from which they'd come.

A shrill scream rang out. Tam turned and saw a woman clutching a child in one arm and hanging on to a treetop with the other. The current battered her as she struggled to maintain her grip. Instinct kicked in.

"Somebody needs help," she barked. "Step on it."

Chapter 5

"Muchas gracias! Dios le bendiga!" The sodden woman lay in the bottom of the boat, her body limp, but her eyes were alive with gratitude. She clutched her son, probably no more than five years old, to her chest. The boy stared up with glassy eyes, but he had no visible injuries.

"It's fine. We just need to get you somewhere safe." Tam didn't know if the woman understood her, so she made sure to keep her voice calm and her expression friendly. Not her strong suit under duress, but such was life.

"I see somebody over there." Matt pointed to a woman clinging to a boogie board. "You get these two to safety while I get her." He didn't wait for a reply, but kicked off his shoes and dove in.

"You boys expect me to believe you were ever in the military when not a one of you knows how to take orders?" Tam glanced at Willis. "You see anywhere we can take these two?"

"How about that church over there?" Willis indicated a high-steeple white church backed by a two-story brick building. A few faces peered out of second floor windows, gaping at the devastation. Willis guided the boat to the church and pulled up next to one of the open windows. A blocky, middle-aged man stared at them with unfriendly eyes.

The man didn't give Tam a chance to speak. "We're full up. No room here."

"These people need help." She couldn't believe what she was hearing.

"Get it somewhere else. I told you, we've got no more room." He set his jaw and fixed her with a flinty gaze. Those eyes held no compassion.

"I don't know how full the rest of your church is, but I can tell from here that the room you're standing in is empty, save for you." Tam pointed to the space behind him. Soft music and the aroma of fresh coffee and cinnamon rolls wafted out into the air. The people inside were having a social while the world outside lay in chaos. "You can take them in."

"Come on man," Willis said. "This is a church, and you're supposed to help strangers in need. Do I need to start quoting scripture to you?"

"I don't need a Sunday school lesson from an uppity…" The man bit off his retort and swallowed hard. He didn't need to complete the sentence for everyone to know what he'd been about to say. "Just move along. There's a Methodist church around the corner. They'll take *anybody*." He screwed up his face to show what he thought of the Methodists.

"I want to talk to the pastor." Tam had to stop herself from slapping the fool look off the man's face.

"I am the pastor." More than anything else he'd said, this news stunned Tam. "And I will go to any length to defend my flock." He opened his jacket to reveal a holstered revolver.

Tam's fingers twitched and she felt the lack of her Makarov, which she'd left back at headquarters. She vowed she'd never go jogging unarmed again.

"Let's go before I take that toy away from him and give him an enema." Hot fury burned in Willis' words.

Tam nodded. "This is no house of God. We'll shake the dust off our feet and move along."

The pastor's face turned beet red at the insult, but he didn't reach for his weapon. Apparently, he believed Willis could, and would, follow through on his threat.

"Do you keep office hours, Pastor?" Willis asked.

"Why?"

"Because, when this is over, I just might drop by and teach you some manners. Keep your appointment book open." Willis gunned the engine, drowning out the man's sputtered retort.

Tam kept her eye on the pastor as they drifted away. If he wanted to shoot them, there was nothing they could do but duck, and she wanted to be ready. Thankfully, the man settled for staring daggers at them until they were out of sight.

They collected Matt and the woman he'd rescued, a Hooters girl who declared him her hero and offered to give him her number. While Matt searched in vain for pen and paper, they continued on until they came upon a group of survivors gathered on the roof of a local bar.

"Oh man, not Sloppy Joe's." Matt raised his hands in dismay. "Best joint in town underwater."

The survivors atop the building welcomed the newcomers, particularly the Hooters girl, who was already eying one of the men on the roof. Their charges now safe, Tam decided they should continue to look for others who might need help, at least until they ran low on fuel.

They continued their search, finding victims, but few survivors. They passed two more churches, both packed with refugees. They were considering trying to make their way to safety when they caught sight of two men clinging to a child's inflatable raft and struggling to keep their heads above water. Here, floating debris choked the streets. They had scarcely closed the gap between them and the struggling swimmers when a diver surfaced near the two men.

"Thank God!" one of them cried. "Can you help my partner? He can't hold on much longer."

Something glinted in the sunlight and the man fell back, clutching his throat as a curtain of scarlet poured from the gaping wound below his chin. He treaded water for a moment, the disbelief in his eyes evident even at a distance, and then he sank. Still clutching the inflatable raft, his partner managed only a startled cry before the diver's knife flashed again and the second man disappeared beneath the water.

"What the hell are you doing?" Tam shouted. The diver jerked his head in her direction, and then disappeared beneath the water. Tam gaped at the empty space where, moments before, two cold-blooded murders had been committed before her eyes. The world had gone mad. "Get after him!" she shouted to Willis.

"He could be anywhere," Matt said.

"Just go that way." She pointed to the spot where she'd last seen the diver. After a few minutes of searching, though, they had to give it up as a bad job. The man was nowhere to be found. "Dammit." She pounded her fist into her palm.

"Sorry," Matt said. "There are just too many places he could have gone."

"It's not just that. He made me cuss, and I had a three day streak going." She sighed. "Well, another dollar in the jar."

"You might want to add a few more dollars." Willis pointed down the submerged street to a boat speeding toward them. A man stood in the bow. At first, Tam thought he was pointing in their direction. Then a bullet smacked the water a foot from their boat, and she heard the report of a rifle.

They were being attacked.

"Something strange is happening up on the surface." Maddock checked the readouts on the display in front of him.

"How so?" Still distracted by the bells and whistles of this new craft, Bones sounded disinterested.

"I'll skip the details and just say I think Key West has just been hit by a tsunami."

That got Bones' attention. "No freaking way! Corey would have let us know about any warnings." Corey, their crew's resident techie, was minding the shop back at their temporary headquarters.

"I'll bet you a bottle of Dos Equis." Maddock wouldn't mind losing that bet, but he knew better. His heart sank at the thought of his home being struck by such a disaster. And then he thought of Matt, Willis, and Tam. "Say, do you know what Tam and the guys had planned for today?"

"Besides bitching about us getting first crack at the sub? They were going to… Holy crap! They were going for a run somewhere around the pier. She's been ragging Willis about his conditioning."

"I'm taking over. See if you can raise Corey on the radio."

Bones made several attempts to reach their friend, but failed. "He's got to be okay. He's minding the radio, so he wouldn't be down on a bottom floor."

"He probably lost power," Maddock said as the sub sliced through the water, headed for the dock. As they approached, he gradually brought the sub to the surface.

"Up periscope." Bones tapped a button and an image of Key West appeared on their monitors.

Maddock groaned. The island, or at least this part of it, lay under a good eight feet of water. The topmost portions of buildings rose above the churning surface, and all around, people sat perched on roofs or leaned out of second-story windows to witness the disaster.

"What do we do?" Bones asked.

"Let's see if we can get closer. Maybe we'll run into the others." Maddock felt the conspicuous absence of conviction in his voice, and he tried to force down the rising doubt. "They've been in worse situations than this. I figure they're partying on a rooftop somewhere."

He grew concerned as they made their way into the city and began to navigate the flooded streets. He wasn't sure how far he dared take *Remora*. The sub was small and maneuverable, but the streets were choked with debris and submerged vehicles. If they found themselves stranded, at least they'd have a chance to try out some of the special features.

"Hey, check this out. An external mic!" Bones exclaimed. A moment later, a cacophony of noises filled the cabin: rushing water, people shouting… and gunshots. "What the hell? Surely nobody's looting when the water's this deep."

"I don't know," Maddock said. "Let's find out."

Chapter 6

"Listen up!" Willis shouted over the whine of the engine and the crackle of gunfire. "When we round the corner up ahead, there's an office building with a broken window. I remember passing it. I'm going to swing in close and you two are going to jump in there. I'll draw them off."

"You can't outrun them." Matt stole a glance back at the boat that followed in their wake. "They'll catch you in no time."

"I don't need to outrun them. I just need to draw them off of you and then I'll swim for it."

"Without diving gear? You're crazy. I won't allow it." Tam grabbed for the wheel. "Let me."

Willis gave her a level look and held on to the wheel. "I know you're the boss, but this time, neither one of you needs to argue with me. I'm the only one of the three of us who can pull this off."

"I hate it when he's right, but of the three of us, he's by far the best swimmer." Matt turned to Willis and gripped his friend's shoulder. "If you don't make it back in one piece, I'm going to kick your ass."

"You just fire up the barbecue and have me some ribs and a cold one waiting. Now, you two better be quick about it. Don't let them see you."

They approached the corner at a rapid clip. At least, rapid for the glass-bottom boat. As they turned and swung toward the gaping window, Tam and Matt moved to the edge of the boat and tensed to spring.

"You first, and be quick about it," Matt said. "One… two… three!"

Tam flung herself through the window, tucked her shoulder, and rolled out of the way as Matt followed on her heels. He landed at an awkward angle and hit the floor with a thud.

"That sucked." He rolled over and drew in a deep breath.

"Get up. We need to help Willis." Tam didn't wait for him, but dashed through the empty room and out into a hallway. To her right, she spotted the door that led to the stairs. With Matt hot on her heels, she dashed to the top floor, the fourth, and hurried along the hallway until she found the room closest to the corner of the building. Inside, she spotted what she'd hoped to find: a heavy wooden desk. "Help me turn this over."

Matt bared his teeth in a predatory grin. Clearly, he understood what she had in mind. Together, they flipped the massive desk over onto its smooth top.

"You ready?"

"Just like football practice." Matt put his shoulder to the desk and they pushed, gaining momentum until the desk slammed into the floor-to ceiling window. The sturdy glass cracked but did not shatter.

"Again," Tam huffed. They repeated the maneuver two more times. The first time sent a spiderweb of cracks splaying across the glass. The second time, the glass shattered, leaving a gaping hole four feet high. "That's what I'm talking about."

Matt peered around the edge of the window frame. "Here they come. "Let's do it."

The boat rounded the corner, traveling as fast as the tight quarters would permit. Its momentum forced the craft to swing wide, bringing it right up to the side of the building where Tam and Matt waited. She caught a glimpse of the armed man in the bow. His eyes were locked on Willis. Slowly, he raised his rifle.

"Now!" Tam said. They threw their weight against the desk. It slid forward, teetered on the edge, and then plummeted down onto the unsuspecting men. It struck the boat near the stern with a resounding crash, taking a chunk out of the boat's side and eliciting cries of alarm as the boat tipped hard to port, taking in water over the damaged section. It didn't, however, sink, and a hail of bullets answered their improvised bomb. Broken glass scoured their exposed flesh as they dove away and scrambled out into the hall.

"What do we do if they send men in after us?" Matt said as they dashed for the stairwell.

"I don't know. Hide and pray, I guess." It galled Tam to admit it, but she could think of no better plan.

"Is that Willis?" Maddock looked at the boat that filled his screen as it churned through the debris-filled water, coming right at them. Sure enough, their friend stood at the wheel, jaw clenched. As he piloted the boat, he stole the occasional glance back over his shoulder. He appeared to be running from something. And he was alone. "Where are the others?"

"Maybe they're in that other boat down the way?" Bones said.

In the distance, a second boat appeared. And then an odd thing happened. A desk came tumbling down from an upper story of a nearby building, and smashed into the corner of the boat. After a moment of shock, the passengers raised weapons and sent a barrage of bullets up at the building from which the desk had been dropped.

"I think we've got our answer," Maddock said. Up ahead, the gunfire ceased and the second boat roared off in pursuit of Willis. Two men took potshots at him as they pursued the glass-bottom boat. At their rate of speed, they'd catch up with Willis quickly.

Just then, Willis spotted their sub and slowed down.

Maddock flipped on the two-way audio. "Need a lift?"

"I'm trying to draw them off of Tam and Matt!"

"You won't last long. Here's what we're going to do." Maddock hastily outlined his plan, then took the sub down as far as he dared.

"Think it will work?" Bones asked.

"We'll know soon enough."

"You two, into the building and find whoever dropped that desk!" Karl shouted. The men obeyed immediately, and Karl gunned the engine as soon as they were clear of the craft. Though the debris in the water slowed their progress, he felt confident he'd catch the glass-bottom boat quickly. Three of them, armed, against one man made for fine odds. One fewer witness, and an undesirable for good measure. He smiled as the gap closed between him and his quarry. It was a fine day on the sea. Beside him, Abel and Henry fired off a few shots.

"Looks like he's slowing down, sir." Abel pointed at the boat ahead of them.

Sure enough, the glass bottom boat drifted to a stop. The pilot, a tall, black man, had apparently lost control, and the craft slowly rotated until it faced them broadside. The pilot spared them one panicked glance, then dropped down into the bottom of the boat.

"Broken down or out of fuel, I gather. It doesn't matter. He is ours." As they approached the foundering craft, Karl slowed their own boat and ordered his men to exercise caution. He assumed the man they pursued was unarmed, but there was no need to make a mistake.

"Where is he?" Abel leaned over the starboard rail and narrowed his eyes.

"Hiding, no doubt. You and Henry will board his boat and root him out. I'll cover you."

With a loud thump, their boat shuddered and a high-pitched grinding sound filled the air. "What the hell?" A whirring blade sliced through their hull. They gaped as it tore a ragged line across the bottom of the boat. What could do such a thing?

Panicked, Henry fired off two shots at the protruding blade, adding two holes to their already damaged craft.

"Stop it, you idiot!" Karl began working the controls, trying to break free of the blade before they sank. When they began to take on water, Abel and Henry grabbed buckets and bailed. Above the sound of the cutting blade, the engine roared and, with a jerk, they started moving in reverse. The blade disappeared, but the damage was done. They'd be lucky to get away before they sank. They needed to get to the church, and get there unseen at that.

As Karl turned the boat about, an alien-looking metal claw appeared over the port bow, clamped down on Abel's head, and plucked him out of the boat. Abel screamed in terror and fired his AK-47 with wild abandon. Henry went down, clutching his stomach as a seeping flow of crimson spread across his midriff.

Karl let loose a stream of curses and gunned the engine, hoping extra speed would help keep the craft afloat until he could get away. He spared no more than a single glance at the building where he'd left his other two men, but didn't slow down. There was no time. If he stopped for them, the boat might sink, or, worse, whoever... whatever had attacked them might catch up. Right now, the only thing he wanted was to get as far away from this disaster as possible.

"This had better work," Matt grunted, the strain evident in his voice. "I don't think I can hold myself in place up here much longer."

"Shut up. I hear them coming." Tam had little confidence in her plan, but, as improvised attack plans went, it wasn't the worst. She stood just outside the door that led into the darkened stairwell and listened as the footsteps drew closer. Thinking they had nothing to fear, the men who pursued them weren't making any effort to keep quiet. Tam didn't care if they were arrogant or just plain stupid, either was a point in her favor.

The sounds grew louder until she was sure they were almost upon them. This was it. Whispering a quick prayer, she dropped to one knee as she heard a loud thud and a shout of surprise as Matt dropped down onto the man in the lead. By pressing his hands and feet against the stairwell walls, he'd managed to climb up to ceiling level and wait until he could take their pursuers by surprise.

Before either man could react, Tam squeezed the lever on the fire extinguisher she'd taken off the wall nearby. She heard another surprised shout as gas filled the stairwell. She emptied the canister and then flung it into the cloud, then rolled aside as bullets flew through the open doorway.

"Come after me," she whispered to herself. "I dare you." She clenched her fists, ready to spring. She'd have to get the drop on the gunman, and that was an iffy proposition since she and Matt had just sprung an ambush on them, but it was her only hope. Every nerve alive, every muscle tensed, she readied herself to spring.

Another burst of gunfire rang out.

And then silence.

She waited, not daring to breathe. Her heart pounded out a steady beat.

"I'm okay."

She sagged with relief at the sound of Matt's voice. "What took you so long?"

"You try wrestling a gun away from a guy and knocking him out before his buddy shoots you. Of course, I knocked him out after I shot the other guy. Now, help me haul this dude out of here."

"Not bad," Tam said as they dragged the unconscious man out of the stairwell and into the nearest room. "I don't think your crew mates give you enough credit."

"Please. I'm a Ranger. I eat SEALs with barbecue sauce."

"If you say so." Tam smirked. "I'm going to grab the other guy's rifle and make sure he's dead."

"Oh, he's done, but check if you like." The semi-conscious man was already beginning to stir, and Matt took a step back and trained the procured rifle on him. By the time Tam returned, their captive was awake, if not fully alert. He gazed up at them with hate-filled eyes, but he didn't move.

"Who are you?" she asked. No reply. "How hard did you hit him?" she asked Matt, who shrugged. "Okay, dummy. You don't know your own name, so how about telling me why you're out there shooting at people instead of saving them?"

"You can't talk to me like that."

"I believe I just did. What's the problem? Mister murderer don't like taking orders from a woman?"

"It's not murder. It's a cleansing." As soon as the words left his mouth, the man blanched. Faster than Tam would have thought possible, he sprang to his feet and ran, not at her and Matt, but for the closest window.

"Stop!" she called, but the man flung himself against the glass, which shattered on impact. He flew out into open air and disappeared from sight. She ran to the window and looked down, where their prisoner of seconds before now floated in the water, his head caved in on one side. He had struck the top of a lamppost just before hitting the water.

"So much for questioning him," Matt said. "What do you think he meant by a cleansing?"

"I don't know for sure." Tam felt cold inside. "But I think we'd better figure it out."

I think I squeezed his head too hard. He looks pretty out of it to me." The man

Bones had snatched out of the boat using one of the sub's remote appendages lay atop an awning just above water level, held fast by the remote arm. He'd lost his weapon, and now stared up in disbelief at the sub's high-density cutting blade, which hovered inches above his chest.

"We'll see how he handles questioning." Maddock once again engaged the external audio and spoke into his mic. "Nod your head if you can hear me." The man nodded. "Good. What's your name?" The man frowned and pressed his lips together. "Let's try this again," Maddock said. He spun the cutting blade and lowered it an inch for emphasis. "Give me your name or this is about to get painful for you." He wasn't about to slice this fellow apart, but hopefully, his bluff was convincing.

The man's face twisted in anger then sagged. "Abel." He looked like he was going to be sick.

"See how easy that was? Now, tell my why you were shooting at my friends."

Abel took a deep breath and narrowed his eyes. For a moment, he looked as if he might refuse to answer. "The cleansing."

"What the hell is that supposed to mean?" Bones asked.

Abel's eyes bugged out and he gaped, but it wasn't the sound of Bones' voice that elicited the reaction. A diver rose from the water, inches from him. With a single, swift movement, he sliced Abel's throat, and sank back into the water.

Maddock released Abel's body and tried to snatch the diver using the mechanical hand, but the man moved too fast. Maddock took *Remora* down while Bones engaged the sonar and began pinging the area all around them, but the diver was gone.

"We're not going to find him," Maddock said. "Too much silt and debris in the water for visual or sonar, and he's not a large target. Besides, he could swim through any of these submerged buildings and get away."

"What just happened?"

"Not a clue," Maddock said. It was the truth. Try as he might, he could not construct a scenario in which the murder they'd just witnessed made any kind of sense. "Let's pick Willis up and then find Matt and Tam. Maybe they can help us figure it out."

Chapter 7

Sofia rolled the mechanical pencil back and forth between her teeth, her index finger tracing an invisible line under the row of symbols. She cursed, dropped the stack of papers onto her lap, and fell back onto the pillow. She needed sleep, but she couldn't turn her brain off. Since her arrival in Huertas, a barrio of Madrid, she and Arnau had made progress deciphering the codex. As she had suspected, the codex bore a strong similarity to Egyptian hieroglyphs, but too many of the symbols still eluded them.

She moved to the window and gazed down at the street below. Streetlights shone on a young couple enjoying the night life, and a few stray singles who cast envious glances at the two lovers. Under different circumstances, she'd be down there among them, drinking in the local culture and perhaps enjoying tapas and cerveza at Magister or Viva Madrid. Right now, though, she couldn't bring herself to put the codex aside.

"Five more minutes, and then lights out," she told herself. She sank down on the lumpy bed in Arnau's guest room and returned to her stack of papers. Wanting to protect the ancient codex, she and Arnau were working from blown-up images of the artifact. She had abandoned her plan to send copies to colleagues skilled in ancient languages because she could think of no one whom she could completely trust. Some would turn her in to the authorities for stealing the codex. Others would seek to discredit her find, while still others would try to translate it on their own and steal the credit for themselves.

And then there was Arnau. She was not entirely comfortable working with him either. His dealings with her, as far as she knew, had always been honest, but the fact he'd been caught trading in stolen antiquities strained his credibility. Then again, considering her present circumstances, who was she to judge?

She decided to begin by re-reading what she'd translated so far. It was not a literal translation. The symbols conveyed meaning, but could not be directly transcribed into complete sentences, so she and Arnau had fleshed things out, using a combination of educated guesses, wild speculation, and trial and error. In the places where they were least confident about the translation, they'd inserted their best guess in brackets.

The words of Paisden, priest of [Atlantis?] We are betrayed by our [Fatherland? Motherland?] Our crystals have been taken and our [machines?] [fail?] My [servant?] leads our people to [safety?] but I remain [steadfast? Dedicated?] The deluge shall soon [unknown] I believe we are the last [remnant]...

The rest remained untranslated, save for a few words, including an intriguing reference to temples. She gained no new insights, and put the papers down even before her allotted five minutes was up. Weariness weighed heavy on her and her eyelids drooped. Tomorrow, she'd look at the codex through fresh eyes.

"Let's see if the Marlins have made any more stupid trades." She took out her phone, opened the web browser, and punched in the Miami Herald's website. She gasped when she saw the headline.

Killer Tsunami Strikes Key West

She read on, concern turning to disbelief as she read the report. A freak wave had struck Key West without warning, causing death and devastation to a small section of the island. The tsunami was odd, not only because it seemed to come out of nowhere, but because its size and behavior were so far out of the norm. It had come from the direction of the mainland and was reported to be a concentrated wall of water rather than a typical, broad wave. Strangest of all, scientists could determine no cause for it. Seismic detectors all around the Gulf of Mexico and in the Atlantic detected no activity whatsoever. The sole clue was a brief burst of energy, emitted by an unknown source, minutes before the wave struck.

Sofia leaned back and considered this terrible news. It wasn't just the tragedy that impacted her, but the similarity to the wave that had swamped her dig site. In both cases, a wall of water appeared out of nowhere, with no obvious cause, and behaved in a way no known tsunami ever had. The articles she'd read hadn't mentioned a surge of energy preceding the event in Spain, but that didn't mean it didn't happen.

Something in the back of her mind nudged at her thoughts. What was it? The codex mentioned machines, and a deluge to come. The machine in the temple! What if... No, the very idea was absurd. Of course, belief in Atlantis seemed absurd until she'd unearthed the city.

"Oh my God. I have to tell somebody." But who? Could she really go to the American embassy with this story? They'd think her a lunatic. But she couldn't just let this drop. She was certain she was onto something.

A loud knock startled her. Someone was at the apartment door. She heard Arnau moving through the front room. He opened the door and whispered something unintelligible.

"Why the need to be so quiet?" a deep voice said. "We are alone, no?"

"I don't want the neighbors to hear us."

"Always overcautious," said a second voice. "Perhaps it is for the best. There is no harm in taking a few precautions. Now, where is it?"

"Just a minute. It's in my safe."

Sofia's heart lurched. Damn Arnau! He thought to sell the codex. She gripped the doorknob, ready to storm in and confront him, but then she paused. Some of the people who bought stolen artifacts were little more than wealthy eccentrics or gluttons who wanted to own a piece of history. Others, however, were dangerous. What sort were the men outside? Indecision rooted her to the spot.

"Here. Give me the money and go." Arnau's voice trembled. "I want this out of my house."

"Let us see what we have here. Ah, very nice. You say this came from Atlantis?" The man's tone expressed his obvious skepticism.

"That's what I was told. I've studied it enough to be satisfied that it's a genuine artifact. "

"You've studied it." The voice sounded flat.

"Yes, but only to authenticate it. Nothing thorough." Arnau spoke quickly. "I don't know what it says."

"From whom did you acquire this piece?"

"You know I can't reveal my sources."

A dull pop made Sofia jump. On the other side of the door, she heard a thump and Arnau's cry of pain.

"It is not a fatal wound, but the next one will be unless you tell me the truth. I ask again, from whom did you acquire the codex?"

Sofia's stomach heaved. She had a feeling the fatal wound was inevitable, regardless of what Arnau told the men.

"I only know his first name," Arnau groaned. "It's Abed. He lives in Cairo."

Another muffled pop and another cry of pain. That must have been what a silenced weapon sounded liked.

"I've given you a measure of grace, Arnau. You'll lose your leg, but you might live if you receive medical attention soon." The speaker lowered his voice to a husky whisper. "You got this from Sofia Perez, didn't you?" Arnau's silence was all the answer the man needed. "Very well."

Sofia didn't need to hear any more. She was halfway out the window, her few belongings stuffed inside her shirt, when the next gunshot sounded. She clambered down the fire escape, dropped the last ten feet and rolled her ankle when she landed hard on the pavement. Fear gave her strength and she hobbled down the street at a half-run. The hour was late, but the hotel district wasn't far, and there were always taxis about.

By the time she flagged down a cab, she was soaked with sweat and her white tank top wasn't quite opaque any more. If the driver thought it odd to pick up a young woman in her nightclothes, he gave no indication, though he didn't bother to hide the way he undressed her with his eyes. He sat up straight, though, when she told him her destination.

"United States Embassy. I'll double your fare if you get me there fast."

Tires screeched and horns blared as the cabbie stepped on the gas and pulled the cab out into traffic. Sofia watched the lights and the people flash past and wondered if anyone would believe her story.

Chapter 8

"I expected something fancier from a government agency." Bones scowled at the faded carpet and plain, white walls as they moved along a narrow hallway at the back of the Truman Little White House. The famed building had suffered a great deal of water damage, but this section must have been waterproofed. The carpet was dry and the sheetrock walls unblemished.

"After all those years in the military, you still think the government splurges on people like us?" Maddock shook his head and chuckled. "Come on."

"We're, like, agents now. James Bond gets all those fancy toys. Why not us?" Bones scratched his chin. "Must be a British thing. You think I could fake a British accent?"

"I've heard your accent. Hate to tell you, but it's not the best." He ignored Bones' expression of feigned insult. "Besides, this building was underwater only a few days ago, or have you already forgotten?"

"Sloppy Joe's and Captain Tony's got washed out. Trust me; I'll remember this for a long time."

"They'll be back." Already they'd seen many of the island's residents pulling together in the wake of the tragedy that had taken so many lives and caused such devastation. It was both sad and heartening to witness.

"Misters Maddock and Bonebrake?" A husky man dressed like a banker barred their way. Maddock didn't need to see the holster inside his coat to know he was a professional, probably military. His rigid posture and clipped manner of speaking spoke volumes.

"That's us," Maddock said.

"Very good. Follow me, please." He led them to a bookcase.

"Thanks, but I've switched to e-books." Bones ran a finger down the spine of a very old copy of Tom Sawyer. The shelves held complete works of Alexandre Dumas and Mark Twain. "Besides, I don't read anything published before nineteen hundred. Not enough sizzle, if you take my meaning."

The man grinned and withdrew a battered copy of The Count of Monte Cristo, revealing a small keypad. He entered a code and re-shelved the book as the bookcase swung forward, exposing a blank wall of gleaming metal and a small black screen. "Left thumbs on the scanner, please."

Bones held his thumb up. "Mine's been up my butt half the day. Is that going to be a problem?"

The corners of the man's mouth twitched. "Not for me. I never touch that scanner."

Maddock and Bones pressed their thumbs to the scanner and, with a hiss, a previously invisible door slid to the side, opening onto an elevator. Inside stood Tam Broderick. She checked her watch and gave them an impatient look.

"Late for the first team meeting. Not the way to impress me."

Bones yawned and stretched. "Whatever gave you the idea that I care about impressing anybody? Besides, we're five minutes early."

"Five minutes early is ten minutes late to me. Now get in here and let's get to work."

"All I see is a down button," Maddock said as he stepped inside and the elevator began its descent. "Should I have brought my dive gear?"

"Sweetie, this place has been here longer than you've been alive, and we know how to waterproof when we want to."

"I can't believe there's been a secret installation here all this time," Bones said. "Seems like a conspicuous place to hide spook central."

"Sure has. The government built it during World War II and kept it going all through the Cold War. It got shut down for a few years, but reopened again right after the start of the War on Terror. They were about to close it again when I requested we be headquartered here. Now it's all ours."

The elevator stopped and the door slid back, revealing a welcome area with plush, blue carpet, leather sofas, and an attractive receptionist with shoulder length, black hair and blue eyes, seated behind a mahogany desk. Five doors were evenly spaced along the wall behind her, with no signage to indicate where they led. Fine works of art lined the walls to their left and right.

"Everyone's in the conference room, ma'am."

"Everyone except for these two." Tam rolled her eyes in Maddock and Bones' direction. "Joey, meet Dane Maddock and Uriah Bonebrake." Tam smiled sweetly as Bones' smile flickered. He hated his given name.

"Call me Bones," he said, taking Joey's hand in a familiar way. "How about you and I get to know each other while Tam and Maddock go to their meeting?"

"Bones?" Joey frowned, and then realization dawned in her eyes. She stole a quick glance at Tam and then smiled at Bones with what Maddock could have sworn was a touch of sympathy. "It's very nice to meet you and I look forward to working with you."

"You ain't getting out of the meeting that easy, Bonebrake. Let's go." Tam led them through the door on the far right and down another hallway.

"Did you tell Joey not to talk to me or something?" Bones asked.

"No, I just warned her that, ever since your injury, you try to overcompensate by hitting on every woman you meet, and she should be patient with you but not encourage you."

"What injury?"

"You got shot in the pelvis and now you can't do your manly duty. That's why we call you 'Bones.' It's one of those ironic nicknames."

Maddock smothered a laugh in a rasping cough while Bones' cheeks turned crimson.

"That *was* you, wasn't it?" Tam asked with a straight face. "Or did I confuse you with somebody else? I'm sorry."

"Not bad," Bones admitted. "You do realize the next move is mine?"

"I'm counting on it, sweetie. Just don't forget I'm the boss."

The door at the end of the hallway opened into a well-lit conference room painted in bright colors and furnished with tropical plants. A giant, high definition screen on the far wall showed rolling surf and palm trees swaying in a gentle breeze. Just above the edge of hearing, the sound of waves crashing onto shore whispered from invisible speakers.

A long, oval table sat in the middle of the room. All the seats were occupied but three. Some of the faces were unfamiliar, but Matt, Willis, and Corey, the rest of Maddock's crew, were there, smirking at Maddock and Bones like the two were school kids who'd just come from the principal's office. A blonde sat with her back to them, but Maddock didn't need to see her face to recognize her.

"Avery?"

At the sound of her name, his sister turned around. He'd expected her to look contrite, if not downright guilty, but instead, she set her jaw and raised her eyebrows.

"Yes?"

"What are you doing here?"

"I work here. You have a problem with that?" The look in her eyes told him it would be a bad idea to answer in the affirmative.

"Man, I love it when she gets all Maddock Junior on him." Willis laughed and slapped his thigh. "That's exactly what you look like when you act stubborn," he said to Maddock.

"Come on, now. Maddock isn't stubborn." Bones put a protective arm around Maddock's shoulders. "When he knows he's right, he sticks to his guns. And he's right *all the time*."

Everyone joined in the laughter, even the unfamiliar faces. Maddock shrugged Bones' arm away and turned to his friend. "You knew about this, didn't you?"

"I told you she was moving down here because she got a new job."

"You left out one important detail."

"Not that long ago, you didn't even know I existed," Avery said. "This way, we get to spend even more time catching up on all those lost years."

He couldn't argue. It had only been a few months since he learned that his father, Hunter Maddock, had a daughter a few years younger than Maddock. Avery was the sole blood relative he had left in the world, and the idea of her being a part of their new team worried, even frightened him a little. Except for Angel, all the people he cared about were now part of this team, and that meant their lives were in peril. He knew they were adults and the responsibility was not his, but he couldn't like it.

"It doesn't matter," Tam said. "I needed to add to our research staff. I like her and, more important, I trust her. She's one of the few people in the world I can be one hundred percent sure isn't connected to the Dominion. Are we clear?"

Maddock nodded. As he took his seat, the others greeted him. He shook hands with Greg Johns, a tall, lean man with close-cropped, dark hair. They'd worked together once before, and Greg was a solid agent. The other two agents were Joel Berg, a sandy-haired man of about forty, and Kasey Kim, an attractive woman of Korean descent, who looked to be in her late twenties.

"You forgot to save me a seat." Bones smiled at Kasey, who made a wry face and shook her head. "It's cool. I'll grow on you."

"Like a fungus," Corey chimed in.

"You two can paint each other's toenails after the meeting. Let's get to work."

Tam picked up a remote, clicked a button, and the image on the HD screen changed to a satellite image of Key West. Red circles dotted the map. "The circles are places where someone witnessed a murder during the tsunami, or a body was found with a gunshot or knife wound."

"I don't see a pattern, but that's a lot of people," Maddock said.

"Twenty three. And those are just the ones we know about. The waters receded quickly. No telling how many might have been washed out to sea."

"But the island was under water for, what, an hour?" Bones cupped his chin and stared thoughtfully at the map.

"Exactly. Think about that. What are the odds that the killers saw the tsunami hit, spontaneously cooked up a scheme to ride around in a boat murdering people, and pulled it off in such a short period of time?" Tam looked up and down the table.

"Or that a guy would run home, strap on his diving gear, and start cutting throats," Matt added.

"You're saying they knew the tsunami was coming and they were ready." Maddock shook his head. "But how?"

"We'll get to that in a minute. You said you didn't see a pattern in the circles, and that's true, but Corey's found something." The screen now filled with head shots. "These are the victims. See a pattern there?" No one answered. "Corey?"

"They're all minorities."

"Most of them are, but there are a couple of white dudes up there too." Bones gestured at the screen.

"I did some checking and they're gay." Corey ran a hand through his short, red hair. "Willis told me about the killing they witnessed. He said one man referred to the other as his partner. That was my first clue."

"That church we went to turned away the Latina woman and her little boy." Willis scowled. "Bet you they'd have taken her in if she was white."

"It could be a coincidence," Tam said, "but I've got a feeling we're on the right track. There's more. We've been checking on our dead men—the one who came after me and Matt, and the one Bones snatched with his new toy. Both were members of the same church. The one who turned us away." She paused, letting that sink in. "As far as we can tell, no other members lost their lives. Seems like every one of them just happened to be in the church at the time the tsunami hit. Every one."

"On a weekday during business hours." Maddock didn't bother to hide his disbelief.

"You catch on quick."

"What is this church like? Conservative?" It was the first time Joel had spoken, and Maddock noted the man's rich voice and the way he enunciated each word.

"Not conservative—crazy. Separatist, racist, misogynist, every bad stereotype you can think of."

"That guy we caught, the one who was killed, said something about a cleansing," Bones said. "That definitely sounds like something this church would approve of. What's a church like that doing in Key West? This place is chill."

"Good question. The building has been around for a long time, but this pastor and congregation are new. He moved here from Utah less than a year ago, bought the church and grounds, though we don't know for sure where the money came from, and managed to run off all the old members with his hate mongering."

The back of Maddock's neck began to itch. He was beginning to understand why this was an issue for their team. Tam suspected the Kingdom Church in Utah was the driving force behind the Dominion in the United States, though she hadn't yet managed to prove it. "You think this is a front for the Dominion."

"I think it's a possibility, even a probability."

"I've been running background checks on the church members," Corey said. "So far, I haven't found one who's from around here. It's like this whole group was planted here."

"Let's assume that's the case." Maddock chewed his lip, turning the details over in his mind. "We've got a group associated with the Dominion hiding out on the upper floor of their church, waiting for a tsunami to hit. While their own people are safe from the disaster, they send out killers to take out any undesirables who might have lived through the flood."

"We're still left with the question of how they knew the tsunami was coming when no one had any warning," Avery cut in.

"We think we know how it happened." Tam grimaced and looked away for a moment.

"Spit it out. We've seen all kinds of craziness in our lives. Can't be any worse." Maddock propped his feet on the table, folded his arms, and waited.

Tam took a deep breath and let it out in a rush. "We think the Dominion has found Atlantis."

Chapter 9

"You have got to be kidding." Kasey stared at Tam in disbelief.

"It's not as crazy as it sounds," Bones said. "Stick with us and you'll see all kinds of things you never thought were possible."

"So what's the story?" Maddock knew Tam would not share this with the team unless she was reasonably certain that the information was correct.

"As to that, I have someone I'd like you all to meet." She opened the side door and escorted a young woman inside. "This is Doctor Sofia Perez. She has a story I think you all need to hear."

Sofia Perez was an attractive Latina woman in her early thirties. Her soft brown hair hung just below shoulder length, and her brown eyes were big and round. Her skin was bronzed by the sun and she had about her an air of youthful vigor. She settled into the last empty seat, while Tam remained standing, and looked around, giving everyone a tight-lipped smile.

"Doctor Perez," Tam began, "why don't you begin by telling everyone about your most recent project?"

"Please, call me Sofia." She shifted in her seat, took a deep breath, and began. "I'm an archaeologist and one of my areas of interest is Atlantis. It's something I've mostly kept private for obvious reasons."

Maddock nodded. Professional archaeologists frowned upon colleagues who treated seriously what they considered far-fetched legends. Publicly declaring belief in something like Atlantis could derail a career, and someone like Sofia would be especially vulnerable, being both young and female.

"I spent a number of years researching Atlantis and made what I believed was a major breakthrough—a site in southern Spain that, I believed, fit Plato's description. But I lacked the resources and connections to excavate. About a year ago, a man, known to me as Mister Bishop, contacted me. He had somehow found out about my work and wanted to fund my research. I was suspicious at first, but when the first check didn't bounce, I stopped worrying about it."

Joel cleared his throat. "I have to confess my ignorance of the Atlantis story. Forgive me, but I always considered it nothing more than a myth, and an absurd one at that."

"Believe me, I understand." Sofia smiled at him.

"Why don't you give us a quick summary of the Atlantis story?" Tam asked. "Other than Bones, I suspect even those of us familiar with the story are fuzzy on the details."

"All right." Sofia rose from her chair and smiled. Clearly, she loved her subject.

"The story is told in Plato's dialogues: the "Timaeus" and the "Critias." He claimed to have learned the story from the writings of Solon, a Greek legislator and poet who heard the story from Egyptian priests during his travels in Egypt around 500 B.C.E—about one hundred fifty years before Plato.

"According to Plato, Atlantis was a utopian civilization and a great power. They worshiped Poseidon, and their residents were half-human, half-god. Their great navy permitted them to travel the world, and they mined precious metals and kept exotic animals. The city was located somewhere in the vicinity of, or beyond, the Straits of Gibraltar. The story is vague in that respect. Their home city was made up of a series of concentric islands separated by canals, with a great temple in the center. Atlas ruled as their high king, though sources name multiple kings of Atlantis and indicate there were as many as ten Atlantean cities, with Plato's being the motherland.

"I could go on all day, but for brevity's sake, I'll fast-forward to the end. Plato said the Atlanteans fell into moral decay and were eventually destroyed by a great deluge as their city sank into the sea in a single night. Virtually every scholar considers it a cautionary tale, but I believed that, even if Plato's story wasn't accurate in every detail, there was a true story there somewhere. So, I dedicated years to digging into the myths, legends, and theories. Finally, my work led me to Spain."

"So, did you find it?" Bones grinned at Sofia. Here were two of his favorite things: a crackpot theory and a beautiful woman. Avery shot a dark glance in his direction but kept silent.

"Yes." Sofia beamed and her smile seemed to brighten the room. "Near Cadiz, we found the remains of an ancient city. Its architecture bore resemblance to that of ancient Greece with elements of Egyptian architecture as well, as did its writings. The city itself was laid out in accordance with the Atlantean legend. We found a series of circular canals and, at the center, the temple of Poseidon." She glanced at Tam. "Do you want to show them the pictures?"

Tam clicked the remote and a snapshot of an ancient temple, half-buried, appeared on the screen. The architecture was striking, the details fascinating. The room fell silent as image after image flashed before them: an ancient temple, a statue of Poseidon, an altar reminiscent of Stonehenge, a pyramid-shaped structure. It was overwhelming. When Tam stopped on an overhead shot of the dig site, showing the concentric circles that surrounded the temple, no one spoke.

Sofia looked up and down the table, her eyes narrowed as if she feared they would scoff.

"Why haven't we heard anything about this?" Kasey asked. "If you discovered Atlantis, your find would be one for the history books."

Sofia took a deep breath. "Shortly after we opened up the temple, Mister Bishop showed up. He brought armed men with him and they killed everyone. Well, almost everyone. I escaped, obviously."

"I'm not seeing the connection to our situation," Maddock said.

"What if I told you that, after this Mister Bishop slaughtered Sofia's team, a freak tsunami flooded the dig site, destroying everything?" Tam raised an eyebrow. "But it was no ordinary tsunami. It struck the area of the dig site and left the areas on either side unaffected."

"Sounds familiar to me," Willis said.

"But our business is the Dominion," Bones said. "Where's the missing link?"

"Mister Bishop…" Maddock said. "Do you mean Bishop Hadel?" Bishop Frederick Hadel was the leader of the Kingdom Church in Utah, and purported to be the leader of the American branch of the Dominion.

"I don't know anything about this Dominion, or about Bishop Hadel," Sofia said, "but when I saw what happened to Key West, I immediately recognized the similarities to what happened at my dig."

"Sofia told her story to the people at the US Embassy. That's when I became aware of her," Tam explained. "I get pinged when certain words or phrases come up in government communication. We know the Dominion is interested in archaeology as it relates to ancient mysteries. That combination, along with the name Bishop, was enough to bring her to my attention. Her description of him matches Hadel to a T."

"Odd, isn't it? The Dominion usually takes an interest in items of religious significance. How does Atlantis fit in?" Maddock asked.

"I think they wanted the machine." Sofia bit her lip. "We found something strange in the center of the temple."

Tam clicked the remote again, and a bizarre, silver contraption appeared on screen.

"You think they used this machine to cause the tsunami?" Maddock ran a hand through his hair. This was a great deal to take in.

"Yes. I also found a codex. The translation is incomplete, but what I found indicates the Atlanteans possessed machines that were capable of such things. I believe the Dominion used it to destroy both my dig site and much of Key West. I also believe a machine like this was used to destroy Atlantis, or at least the city I excavated."

"Hold on a second." Maddock raised a hand. "If you found Atlantis, and this machine was still in the city, then who was responsible for the attack?"

"As I said, my translation of the codex is incomplete, but it seems that Atlantis was, in fact, made up of more than one city. A conflict arose, maybe a civil war. According to the codex, the city I excavated was unable to defend itself due to a lack of crystals, whatever that means."

Out of the corner of his eye, Maddock saw Bones sit up straighter.

"If you're correct, the Dominion can use this machine to attack any coastal city it chooses, with no one the wiser." Greg's brown eyes bored into the image on the screen.

"While Bones and I were trying out the submarine, we experienced a brief power outage just before the tsunami hit," Maddock said. "It didn't last more than a moment. Perhaps this machine creates a wave of energy of some sort."

"So they could strike anywhere," Greg said.

"I don't think so." Bones rocked back in his chair and propped his feet on the table.

"What makes you say that?" Tam asked sharply.

"I don't think they have any more crystals. You guys probably wouldn't know anything about this, since most people don't exactly share my taste in reading material, but there's been a rash of crystal skull thefts in museums around the world." Bones' love of legends, conspiracy theories, and cryptids was well known to his friends.

"Crystal skulls?" Avery didn't bother to hide her skepticism.

"Seriously? You can say that to me after what we've been through? After what *you've* been through?"

"Be professional, you two," Tam snapped. "Go ahead, Bones."

"There are four well-known crystal skulls: the Mitchell-Hedges skull, the Paris skull, the British Museum skull, and the Smithsonian skull. Over the course of the last few months, three of the four have been stolen, plus a bunch of other skulls that everyone knows are fake. The Paris skull is the only one that hasn't been taken." He looked at Sofia. "Does that more or less coincide with the timeline of your dig?" Sofia nodded. "Sounds to me like, once Bishop knew Sofia was on to something, he gave the order to acquire the skulls."

"But how would he know he needed the crystal skulls unless he had a copy of the codex?" Greg asked.

"Who can say for sure? Maybe he has information we don't. Or it might be a hunch. The crystal skulls have been associated with Atlantis myths for a long time; maybe he was hedging his bets." Bones shrugged.

"It's too big a coincidence to ignore." Tam turned to Greg. "I want you and Kasey in Paris tonight. Take Bones along." She ignored Kasey's exasperated sigh. "Keep an eye out for anybody trying to take that skull. Hell, steal it if you can." Greg nodded. "Anything else for us, Sofia?"

"I've got copies of the codex for everyone, along with what I've translated so far." She took out a plain manila folder and passed it around. Inside were several sets of stapled sheets, each with an enlarged photograph of a clay tablet etched with glyphs. Sofia had jotted her translation in the margins.

"Where are the originals?" Joel asked.

Sofia's face fell. "I was betrayed by the man who was helping me translate it. We went back a long way and I thought I could trust him, but he tried to sell it to black-market antiquities dealers. They killed him."

"Any chance these dealers were connected to the Dominion?" Maddock asked.

Tam nodded. "Let's assume so, just to be on the safe side."

"There's something I really don't get," Matt said. "Why Key West? We're not important in the big picture. Washington, New York City, those I could see, but Key West? It doesn't make sense."

"I bet we were a practice run." Willis scowled down at the translation of the codex in his hands. "Just to make sure they have their act together when the real fun starts."

"So they chose some place vulnerable," Kasey said, "a tourist town where they weren't likely to be caught."

"I'm sure they didn't mind that we're an inclusive town with a significant gay population here," Willis added. "They made sure their people were safe, and then they went around killing off anybody they could find who didn't fit their mold. Imagine if they can plot something like this on a large scale."

"The Coast Guard needs to be on alert. Have you notified anyone?" Greg asked Tam.

"I've shared my suspicions as much as I can, but we're still talking about the government here. If I go to the wrong person with a story about Christian terrorists using Atlantean weapons to run their own little genocide, we'll find ourselves pushing pencils on the bottom rung of the CIA. We need proof." She clapped her hands once. "We need to think like the Dominion. What are they up to?"

"If Sofia is right," Maddock began, "there are more Atlantean cities to be discovered, and more weapons. If I were them, I would assemble an entire arsenal so I could hit all the major coastal cities at once. A freak tsunami here and there would cause problems, but would also raise suspicions and put the country on alert. But if I could knock out all the big cities, the major ports, offshore mining operations all at once, I don't think America could cope with the disaster. Considering the shape our economy's in and the tendency of so many people to believe any wacko conspiracy about the government, no offense, Bones, the government could collapse."

"Especially if the disaster is accompanied by genocide." Kasey grimaced. "They could destroy the economy and the social order."

"So, we need to find these other Atlantean cities first." Bones rubbed his hands together. "Screw the crystal skulls. Who's with me?"

"Hold your horses," Tam said.

"Is that supposed to be some slur against Native Americans?"

"No, I would've said, 'Hold your fire water.' Corey, whenever Maddock doesn't need you, you're going to work on translating the rest of the codex. Sofia will get you started." Corey nodded. "You too, Avery. And you can dig into possible Atlantean locations. Sofia will point you in the right direction. Bones, if you have any suggestions, pass them along. Sofia, do you have any ideas on where we should look first?"

"The author of the codex, a man named Paisden, gives what I think are clues to the locations of Atlantean cities. I think he hoped someone might gather the weapons stored there and fight back. Combining what I've translated so far with what I know of potential Atlantean settlements, there is one place in particular that I think is worth investigating right away."

"Fine. Give Maddock and Willis a full report." She turned to Maddock. "This should be right up you dummies' alley. Tell me what you need and get a move on."

"Avengers assemble!" Bones raised a fist.

"What about us?" Joel inclined his head toward Matt.

"You two just found religion." Tam smiled at their puzzled expressions. "I want you to infiltrate our favorite local church."

"I'm an atheist," Joel objected.

"You're also an actor. Make it happen. Do it however you see fit, but I have a feeling Matt can pull off the role of a disgruntled ex-soldier with a grudge against the government. You'll have to be more creative." Joel smiled and nodded.

"What if I'm recognized?" Matt asked.

"I don't think there's much chance of that. The only men who got a look at you are dead, but shave that crap off your face, and put on some nice clothes, just to be safe. If somebody does recognize you and tries anything, take him down and bring him to me for interrogation."

"Shave my beard?" Matt raised a hand to his cheek. "But it's just now filling out."

"Shave it," Bones said. "It looks redneckish."

"I like it," Kasey said. "It makes you look tough." She shot a defiant glance in Bones' direction.

"All right people," Tam said, "let's do this. And don't forget, we might not have much time."

Chapter 10

Key West Church of the Kingdom was a rectangular brick building with white columns at the entrance and a tall steeple that loomed high above the other buildings in the area. The morning sun shone on the stained glass windows and the golden cross atop the steeple. Matt thought it was an oddly happy image for a place suspected of such dark deeds.

Since the water had damaged the sanctuary, the worship service took place in a large, crowded room on the second floor. Organ music wafted through the stairwell, guiding Matt and Joel upward. They entered just before the service began and settled into folding chairs in the back row. Joel, who seemed to know a lot about church for an atheist, explained that church visitors usually liked to remain inconspicuous on their first visit. That way, if the church wasn't a good fit for them, they wouldn't have to deal with awkward visits from the pastor or church members. Matt was happy to remain inconspicuous. He ran a hand across his smooth cheeks. He had gotten used to his facial hair, and now he felt naked without it.

Everything about the service was ordinary: hymns, prayers, and a sermon about repentance, followed by an altar call. By the closing hymn, he wondered if they were in the right place. He glanced at Joel, who nodded. Apparently he wasn't concerned. After the benediction, they took their time leaving. A few people sitting nearby greeted them and shook hands, but most stared at them with varying degrees of suspicion.

After a few minutes, they joined the crowd making its slow way downstairs and out onto the street. When they reach the front steps, a sandy-haired, middle-aged man in a three-piece suit greeted them.

"Welcome." He shook hands first with Joel, and then with Matt. He had a firm grip and a tight smile. "Is this your first visit?"

"Sure is. Me and my brother here just moved to the area." Joel inclined his head toward Matt. "We are opening a business, and thought it would be a good idea to start getting to know some of the people in the community." Matt had to hand it to Joel. With just a few subtle changes in his posture, facial expressions, and vocal inflection, he had adopted an entirely new persona.

The man's features relaxed when Matt was introduced as Joel's brother. "I forgot to introduce myself. I am Davis Franks. So, what sort of business are you all in?"

"We'd like to open a pistol range. Maybe sell handguns and ammo. Matt here is ex-military and a pretty fair instructor. Of course, with the way the winds are blowing, it might not be the best business to get into."

"Gotta love the government." Matt rolled his eyes, playing the role of disgruntled soldier. "It's like they've never heard of Constitutional rights."

"Amen to that, brother." Franks nodded sympathetically. "What branch of the service were you in?"

"Army." Matt didn't say anything else, letting Franks guide the course of the conversation.

"I take it you didn't like it very much?"

"I liked the Army fine. It's the federal government I don't love." Matt looked around, then lowered his voice. "I guess that's not a popular opinion around here, is it?"

"No, not in Key West, but you'll find sympathetic ears in this church. If you don't mind my asking, why did you decide to settle here? Most of the locals aren't exactly firearms enthusiasts."

Joel gave an embarrassed smile. "The worst reason in the world. I love Jimmy Buffett. I've wanted to live down here for twenty years. We just hope we can get the required permits and find enough like-minded people to keep our business afloat. If not, we'll figure out something else." He shrugged as if to say, "*What are you going to do?*"

"Well, you've already found one," Franks said. "I love to shoot, and so do a lot of the fellows here. We've got to keep in practice. You never know when you'll be called to stand up against tyranny." He paused, thinking. "Listen, we have a men's group meeting tonight at six o'clock. If you two would like to visit, I'll give you directions. I think you'd enjoy it. Lots of potential customers in that group."

After they accepted his invitation, he introduced them around. The church members were much friendlier now that Matt and Joel had been accepted by one of their own, and by the time they left, they'd already fielded and politely declined three invitations to lunch, explaining they needed to start scouting around for possible places to open their business.

"Good work today," Joel said as they headed back to their car. "We'll make you an undercover agent yet."

"Do you think we're on the right track?"

"Can't say for sure, but I bet we'll find out tonight."

Chapter 11

"This place is freakish." Bones couldn't help but stare at the frontage of the Quai Branly Museum. Set in the shadow of the Eiffel Tower and a stone's throw from the Seine, the building was, in itself, a work of art, with its tall, glass panes and protruding blocks of varying size and color. "It looks like a living cubist painting."

"I don't think you understand cubism." Kasey made a face and looked to Greg, who ignored her, apparently having decided to tune out the bickering.

"Tell me that doesn't remind you of *Factory, Horta de Ebbo*." Bones pretended not to notice Kasey's surprise. "Obviously, there's no glass in that painting, but the way Picasso represents the sky…" He gestured toward the building and then watched out of the corner of his eye as she gave a reluctant nod.

"I see your point." Kasey tugged at her ear, something she did, Bones noticed, whenever she felt annoyed.

Bones nodded. Truth was, he didn't know much about art, but he'd picked up a few things here and there, mostly back when Maddock was dating Kaylin Maxwell, who worked as a professor of fine arts and was a painter herself. As with many other subjects, he knew just enough to carry on a conversation, or even take someone by surprise with his knowledge.

"You should see the green wall," Kasey said.

"At Fenway Park? Been there, done that."

"No, it's a section of the museum's exterior." This time, she even sounded amused. "Imagine an office building with big, modern windows, but the rest of the building looks like it's made of jungle. They call it a vertical garden. I've seen it in pictures, but never in person."

"Sounds pretty cool, actually. How big is it?"

"Two hundred meters long, twelve meters high."

"I could climb that easy. How about we grab a bottle of wine and race to the top?" Bones winked.

Kasey lowered her eyebrows and pursed her lips.

"Or we could do the Eiffel Tower. Your choice."

"Okay, time to get to work." Greg remained on his usual, even keel. "We'll split up. You two go in first, I'll follow in a few minutes. Keep in touch." He tapped his ear, indicating the communication devices with which they'd all been outfitted.

"Why do I have to go in with *him*?" Kasey stressed the last word.

"Because you two argue like a couple that's been together forever. Nobody will look at you twice."

"Chicks always look at me twice, sometimes more," Bones said.

"I don't know why karma has it in for me." Kasey sighed and took his hand. "Come on, you big ape. If we're going to do this, let's do it right."

"You know something? You and my sister would get along."

"You have a sister?" Kasey winced. "Give me her address. I want to send her a sympathy card."

The interior of the museum provided an odd juxtaposition of modern architecture and displays of artifacts from primitive cultures. Sinuous, shoulder-high partition walls snaked across the floor, and many of the exhibits were encased in glass on all sides, giving visitors an oddly distorted view of people and objects in the distance.

"Pretty creepy." Bones looked around at the primitive displays. "I didn't expect such funky stuff in a snooty place like Paris."

"Their subject matter is interesting. That's for sure." Kasey paused to inspect a sculpture of a Maya warrior. "This guy is imposing."

"Looks a lot like my grandmother, except she had a beard."

"Let's just find the crystal skull." Kasey sighed and resumed walking. They wandered through the exhibits, feigning interest in the items on display. They moved a little slower than Bones would have liked, but they didn't want to draw attention to themselves.

They reach the crystal skull display and stopped short.

"Lovely. Can't say I'm surprised." Kasey shook her head.

The pedestal where the skull normally stood was now bare, save for a sign reading, in French and in English, THIS EXHIBIT IS TEMPORARILY OFF DISPLAY. Kasey pressed a finger to her ear and spoke softly. "Greg, are you there?"

"I'm here. What have you got?" Greg sounded as if he were standing right next to them. Kasey told him about the skull. *"Okay. I'm working on getting into their server right now. You two wander around and keep your eyes open. Be ready to move when I give the word."*

"I don't know about all this cloak and dagger stuff," Bones said. "Normally, I'd just look around for a sign that reads *Do Not Enter*, and walk on through."

"It might come to that, but let's see what Greg can learn before you go blundering into a bad situation."

"We're in a museum, and one full of Frenchmen at that. How bad a situation could we possibly get into? I guess they could throw wine and cheese at us."

"You know, the more time I spend with you, the better I understand why Tam calls you a dummy." Though she stood a foot shorter than he, Kasey somehow managed to look down her nose at him. "Have you forgotten who else wants the skull?"

"Oh yeah." Bones scratched his head. "I actually *had* kind of forgotten. The company of a beautiful woman does that to me."

Just then, Greg's voice sounded in his ear. *"Could you two turn off your mics when you start in on each other? You're giving me a headache."* Kasey shot a dirty glance his way and Bones shrugged. *"You guys need to make your way to the southwest corner of the museum. When you get there, look for a door with a sign that reads* Do Not Enter.*"*

"See? Told you."

Kasey pointedly ignored his gloating smile. Despite his longer legs, he was forced to quicken his pace in order to keep up with her as she strode through the museum, not slowing down until they reached the corner of the museum. She paused in front of a display of primitive musical instruments, turned, and jabbed a finger against his chest.

"I want you to follow my lead when we get in there. You understand?"

"Yeah, but I have to warn you, I'm only good at following orders up to a point. Sometimes instinct kicks in and then…" He made a wry face.

She exhaled, long and slow. "Well, do the best you can." As she walked away, he heard her mutter something about Tam and choosing her own partners from now on.

Bones grinned and followed along behind her. Keeping an eye on the few visitors wandering the exhibit, they slipped around a display and out of sight. Kasey took one last look to make sure no one was watching, gave him a warning frown, opened the door, and stepped through. Give her time, he thought. Sooner or later, she'd come to appreciate him.

Chapter 12

The waters of Guanahacabibes off of the western tip of Cuba sparkled in the morning sun. Maddock sucked in a deep breath of the damp, salty sea air and smiled. Being out on the water felt like a reunion with an old friend. He never tired of it.

"So, this is supposed to be a sunken Atlantean city? I've never heard of it."

Sofia leaned against the rail and looked out over the water, her brown eyes glassy. She perked up at the sound of his voice.

"No one has really taken the theory seriously. About ten years ago, a research crew made sonar scans of the area, revealing what looked like roads, walls, buildings, even pyramids. Another researcher used remotely-operated video equipment to collect footage of the site, but all she got were some poor quality images of stone blocks and some formations that might be man-made structures. When she couldn't produce more definitive proof, skeptics concluded there was nothing to get excited about. The mild interest the discovery stirred quickly died down, and now the place is all but forgotten.

"The so-called experts don't like theories and discoveries that run contrary to their beliefs. Most of them have a lot more in common with religious fundamentalists than they'd like to admit."

Sofia raised her eyebrows and cocked her head. "You surprise me. You don't find many people who think that way. Except, of course, on the internet forums where the loonies congregate."

"Bones' second home." Maddock grinned. "I've seen some things over the past few years that have opened my eyes. I'm still a skeptic at heart, but I no longer dismiss theories out of hand just because they seem unlikely. There's more to this world than the average person would ever suspect."

Sofia nodded. "That's one of the reasons I haven't shared my findings from the dig site. All I have are photos and the codex, and the scientific community would point out that either could be fakes. When it's safe, and if the Spanish government will let me, I'll go back some day and re-excavate. Hell, I might live-stream the dig so everyone will know it's real." She spoke the last sentence with bitterness in her voice.

"You don't think the government would let you come back?"

"Who knows? I tried for months to get a dig permit and they stonewalled me. It took Bishop Hadel, or Mister Bishop as I knew him, getting involved to make it happen. When he killed my crew, he had a police officer with him. Somebody he bought off, I expect. Clearly, he's got connections at more than one level of government." She looked down at the blue-green water rushing by, and her eyes fell. "Governments can be weird, in any case. Look at how much trouble people have researching Noah's Ark."

"That's one I have trouble buying into. I have enough trouble spending a few days cooped up on a boat with Bones. Add a wife, kids, daughters in-law, and a ton of animals to the mix? No way."

"Don't be so sure." She nudged him with her elbow and smiled. "What did you just tell me about dismissing the improbable?"

"I'm not dismissing it. I'm just skeptical."

"Fair enough." Sofia's voice took on a tone of forced casualness. "Speaking of improbable, how is a handsome guy like you still single? No wedding band, no tan line where a ring should be. What's your deal?"

"I was married a long time ago, but she died." He left it at that. Melissa's death no longer haunted him, but he'd never feel comfortable talking about it.

"Sorry. I tend to say whatever comes to mind. When you work in a male-dominated field, you can't be passive."

"No problem. Bones is the same way and he and I are like brothers." Sofia smiled and the warmth in her eyes made him uncomfortable. "In fact, I'm dating his sister." He took out his phone and showed her a photo of himself and Angel.

"She's beautiful." Sofia laughed. "When you mentioned his sister, I imagined Bones in a dress."

Tam's voice rang out above the hum of the engine and rush of the sea breeze. "Bones in a dress? I'd pay to see that."

"You and no one else." Maddock returned his attention to Sofia. "So, what makes you think this place is worth our time?"

"I've had my eye on it since its discovery. A passage in the codex describes a sister city 'across the waves to the west,' with details that match photos of the sunken city. It was supposedly ruled by Azaes, a king of Atlantis who is associated with this part of the world."

"I don't know that name." Maddock had done his share of reading about the legendary lost city, but Sofia was miles ahead of him in that department.

"He's better known in this part of the world as Itzamna."

"Ah! The man who brought the arts and sciences of a destroyed civilization to the people of the Yucatan." Maddock had heard this story before.

"The old, bearded, white man who escaped a flood that destroyed his civilization," Sofia added. "Sound familiar?"

"Yeah, sounds like Noah."

"You're funny. Seriously, though, the Gulf of Mexico used to be much smaller and shallower. In fact, Cuba and the Yucatan Peninsula were once connected by a land bridge which included this area. A few years ago, archaeologists found three well-preserved skeletons in deep, underwater caves off the coast of the Yucatan. The remains dated back 11,000 years. It fits." Sofia sounded like an attorney making her closing argument.

"You think this was Azeas' home and, when it flooded, he fled to the Yucatan and started over?" Maddock couldn't deny the potential connection.

"I think it's a strong possibility."

"Corey says we're almost there," Tam called from the doorway leading into the cabin of Maddock's boat, *Sea Foam*. She wore shorts, a tight-fitting tank top, and an eager smile. "I've got to tell you, Maddock, this discovery stuff is fun. I spend too much time these days sitting at a computer going through files."

"You're sure you and Corey can handle things up here?"

A roll of her eyes was Tam's only reply.

"Corey says we're right over the spot." Willis appeared on deck. "I finally get to try out the sub. Let's do this!"

Maddock, Willis, and Sofia took their places inside *Remora*. They didn't bother with wetsuits, as they'd not be exiting the sub. When everyone was secure and Willis reported all systems were go, Maddock took *Remora* into a steep dive.

The waters turned from a bright aquamarine to a deep sapphire as they descended below the sunlight zone and into darkness where the sun's rays seldom penetrated. Maddock switched on the front lights and let the nav computer guide them to their destination.

"It's so dark down here." Sofia spoke in a reverent whisper. "It's creepy."

"This ain't nothing," Willis said. "Get down below 3,000 feet, that's the midnight zone. It's like diving in ink. You don't know which way is up."

"I've done some diving, but I've never been so far down."

"You won't dive this deep, girl. You've got to be in a sub if you don't want to get squished."

"Approaching one thousand feet." Maddock kept his voice level in spite of his excitement. The images Sofia had shown him of this city were remarkable, and he couldn't wait to see them for himself.

"Will the sub be all right this far down?" Sofia's casual tone didn't quite mask the concern in her voice. "Isn't the water pressure substantial at this depth?"

"It's rated for two thousand feet, so we'll be fine." Maddock hoped the rating was accurate.

Just then, a shape appeared in the distance. He slowed *Remora* and approached with caution. In a matter of seconds, they found themselves gazing at a massive structure of stacked, square blocks.

"It's a pyramid. Looks kind of like the ones the Mayans built," Willis said. "Except for the top. It looks more Egyptian. See how it's pointed?"

"Maya, not Mayan," Sofia corrected.

"Whatever. Hey Maddock, let's circle this bad boy and let me take sonar readings."

"Roger that. Corey, are you picking up on our feed?"

"Loud and clear. Audio and video. Tam says she wants you to scout the city before you zero in on any single structure."

"Sorry, you dropped out. I'll ping you again after we scout the pyramid." Maddock smiled when he heard Tam curse in the background.

"That girl is going to have serious cash in her cussing jar if she keeps working with us."

"You have got to stop calling her 'girl.' It's a dangerous habit." Maddock piloted the sub around the pyramid's base. Thousands of years of undersea currents had worn the sharp corners smooth, but it was still a remarkable structure, with well-proportioned levels and the remnants of steps still visible on the lower half of one side. As Willis noted, it looked like an amalgam of Maya and Egyptian architecture, with the stepped lower portions giving way to a classic pyramid structure at the top.

"This is amazing! Seeing this firsthand, I can totally believe the stories of an outside influence on Yucatan culture. I wish I could touch it, walk on it." Sofia sounded as if she were ready to climb out of the sub for a closer look.

"Scan's complete," Willis said. "Let's move along."

Not wanting to try Tam's patience, Maddock followed the route he and Sofia had plotted out earlier. They passed the remains of buildings, some largely intact, and three more pyramids. Streets paved with flat, square stones ran throughout the city. No vegetation grew here, so far from the sun, and strong currents kept the streets clear of silt. It felt like a sunken ghost town which, Maddock supposed, it was, after a fashion. By the time they completed their circuit and found themselves once again in front of the first pyramid they'd discovered, Maddock had no doubt that these structures were wrought by human hands.

"What now? Want to run a grid over the whole area?" Willis asked.

"We need to go to the center of the city. There's something we need to find." Sofia's excited voice rose as she spoke.

"Works for me. Time permitting, we can scout the rest of the complex afterward." Maddock redirected the sub, ignoring the navigation program and instead following the street that ran ramrod-straight through the city. Minutes later, a high hill, ringed by several canals, appeared up ahead.

"Rings of canals," Sofia said. "You can't deny the connection to Atlantis."

"It's impressive." Maddock was forced to admit he was captivated by this lost city that, all these years, had lain so close to his home.

"Looks like we're coming up on the target area," Willis said. "What's that dark shape up there?"

"We'll check it out." Maddock accelerated and they swept over the canals like a bird in flight. As they drew closer, the shadowy figure swam into focus. It looked like some sort of monster out of legend.

"What is that?" Willis whispered.

"Corey, are you guys getting this?" Maddock's heart pounded.

"We've got it." Maddock was surprised when Tam's voice sounded in his ear. *"I got tired of using nerd boy as a go-between. Approach with caution."*

"I always do."

"Right, I keep forgetting Bones isn't with you."

Maddock smiled, but keenly felt his best friend's absence. He found he actually missed Bones' constant chatter. Doubtless, if he were here, Bones would be spouting theories about aliens until he was blue in the face.

"What do you think Bones would make of this thing?" Maddock asked, but no one replied. All of them had fallen silent at the sight that lay before them.

The fine details had worn away over the years, but there was no mistaking the giant sphinx that sat atop the hill overlooking the city. Unlike its Egyptian counterpart, which lay in silent contemplation, this sphinx sat up on its haunches, its mouth open wide as if eager to devour anyone or anything that might intrude upon its watery domain. Maddock marveled at the size of the sculpture.

"This thing could eat us for lunch." Maddock found himself transfixed by the stone beast.

"We should call him Jared." Willis waited a few seconds. "Aw, come on. Eating a sub? Jared? If Bones had said it, you'd all be cracking up."

"We *want* it to swallow us," Sofia said. "Maddock, can you take us inside?"

"Are you serious? That seems… dangerous."

"Do it," Tam said in his ear. *"She and I have already discussed the plan."*

"Didn't bother to clue us in, did you?"

"I'm the boss of you, and don't you forget it. Take it slow, and don't get yourself into trouble."

"If you say so." Maddock shifted in his seat, sat up straighter, and steered *Remora* into the sphinx's gaping maw.

Inside, a wide pit ringed with stone steps plunged straight down. Cold sweat rising on the back of his neck, Maddock took them down into the inky blackness.

"Okay, so maybe this wasn't such a great idea." Sofia's breathy words were barely audible.

Indeed, it felt like they were descending into Tartarus. The pit seemed to go on forever, with only the steps hewn in the wall breaking the monotony. It felt like they'd never reach the bottom, but, at long last, their instruments indicated they were drawing near to solid ground.

When they reached the bottom, Maddock halted their descent and slowly turned the sub about. The walls of the pit were blank.

"Dead end. Guess we need to head back up." Willis sounded relieved.

"Run a few scans and see what you can find." Maddock searched the stones in front of him. There had to be something here. "Maybe we're missing something."

He heard Willis' fingers tapping buttons on his console. A minute later, his friend cried out in triumph.

"That's what I'm talking about! At ten o'clock, there's a break in the wall that's partially blocked."

Sure enough, they had overlooked an opening. It was almost large enough for *Remora* to pass through, but a pile of rubble and silt barred the way.

"I supposed we could use the arms to clear an opening, but it could take a while." Maddock scanned his monitors. They had an hour before they'd have to draw on their reserves of power and oxygen. He didn't want to cut it that close, especially since they and the sub were still getting to know each other, as it were.

"No need," Willis said.

Before Maddock could ask what his friend meant, a bright flash blinded him, debris pelted the plexiglass bubble, and a dull explosion reverberated through the pit. Sofia screamed as the sub pitched to the side.

"What the hell?" Maddock shouted, trying to blink the spots out of his eyes and struggling to right the craft.

"Sorry, y'all." Willis sounded sheepish. "It was one of the little torpedoes. I didn't go for one of the big ones."

"You have got to be kidding me. Even Bones wouldn't have done that." Maddock knew it was a lie, but didn't care. "What if you'd brought the whole place down on us?"

"My bad. I'll ask next time. But, check it out! I got the tunnel open."

Sure enough, the rubble was gone—blasted away by the torpedo. Through a curtain of silt, the sub's lights revealed a short tunnel and a large open space beyond. Hoping the blast hadn't destabilized the rock, Maddock plunged *Remora* through the passageway.

The space beyond proved to be almost a match for the temple Sofia had discovered in Spain: a column-lined chamber a good thirty meters long. A statue stood in the center, encircled by an altar resembling a tiny Stonehenge monument.

"I remember that old dude." Willis said as Maddock directed the lights upward.

"Poseidon," Sofia whispered. "It's just like the temple I excavated in Spain. This is proof that the Atlantean civilization spread across the ocean."

"I want to make a record of this place." Maddock tapped the console and a camera began snapping still pictures of the chamber. "Where to next?"

"Check around behind the statue. That's where the adyton should be."

Maddock stole another glance at the sub's readings. They still had time, but the window was closing. "You think there's a weapon down here?" He asked, navigating *Remora* to the back of the chamber, careful not to hit Poseidon or the altar.

"There it is! Straight ahead. See it?"

Inside an alcove beneath a pyramidal facade, something silver reflected the sub's light.

"It's a machine like the one Bishop Hadel took from the temple in Spain."

Maddock moved the sub in to get a closer look at the gleaming contraption. It was identical to the pictures they'd seen of the weapon Sofia had found: a metallic dish suspended beneath a pyramid-shaped frame, topped by a grasping hand.

"All right. Let's see if we can get this thing out of here in one piece." Maddock considered the instruments he had at his disposal and formed a strategy in his head.

"Man, you got to be kidding! This little sub can't handle that thing."

"It only took a few men to carry the one in Spain," Sofia said. "It must be deceptively light."

"We've got to give it a shot," Maddock said. If the Dominion had one of these things, it could only help them to study it and hopefully learn how it worked and what it could do. It also would be a good idea to keep it out of the Dominion's hands. If this machine truly could create a tsunami, the enemy could double the devastation should they obtain it.

He brought the sub as close as he dared, extended the robotic arms, and took hold of the device. "Watch out for old ladies crossing the street behind us."

"Beep! Beep!" Willis chimed in as Maddock reversed the sub.

Slowly, he dragged the Atlantean machine from the chamber and out into the temple. As Sofia had predicted, it was light and moved easily.

"Now for the tricky part." He released the machine and used the robotic arm to hook a cable around their prize. It took three tries and a rain of taunts from Willis before he got the job done, but finally, towing the machine behind the sub, he was able to lift it and carry it toward the exit.

"Be careful not to hit the…" Willis began, but before he could finish his sentence, the sub jerked to a stop.

"What was that?" Maddock glanced at the screen displaying the feed from the rear camera. The cable was snagged on Poseidon's trident, and the statue now lay atop the device, which appeared undamaged, but was pinned to the temple floor. What was worse, there was no way he could reach it with the robotic arms.

They were stuck.

Chapter 13

Silence fell as Bishop Frederick Hadel entered the boardroom. His eyes passed over the men assembled there, taking in their expensive suits and gaudy watches, the trappings of a materialistic society. One of the many things he would change when their plans came to fruition. Wealth was a means to an end, but not an end unto itself. Until that day, he would play their game, operating his headquarters from this opulent retreat center in the Wasatch mountain range, and deliver his weekly sermons from a gilded pulpit in a lavishly-decorated church. What was it about common people that obscene displays of wealth inspired them, even when the religion they purported to follow taught against the accumulation of material possessions?

He smoothed his flyaway gray hair and slid into an oversized chair at the head of a table of dark wood polished to a high sheen, and forced a smile. Everyone beamed at him, puppies eager to be scratched behind their ears. Those assembled weren't entirely worthless. All had some degree of power and influence in the secular world, but the men of true worth in the Dominion would not be found here, save one or two. Those men understood his vision and didn't mind getting their hands dirty to achieve their purpose.

"My friends," he began after a sufficient pause, "I am pleased to report that our first attempt was successful, and we are making plans for the next stage."

The men exchanged nervous glances before Utah Senator Nathan Roman cleared his throat.

"Bishop," he began, "we are all wondering about this next stage. Will it be similar to the last one?"

Hadel stared at the senator until the man broke eye contact. "If you are asking if we are targeting another city, the answer is yes."

"Do you think that is wise?" Roman stared at a spot just above Hadel's head. The others wouldn't notice, but the bishop could tell. "Another unnatural disaster and the feds might take notice."

"Do you think me a fool?" Hadel's voice was like ice, though the senator's question did not bother him in the least.

"Of course not." Mitchell Sanders, president of one of Utah's largest banks, spoke up.

"Then, by definition, my decisions are wise, are they not?" Hadel waited for a challenge he knew would not come. "Let them take notice. In fact, when the time is right, I intend to let the world know who we are and what we can do. I want the people frightened, with no confidence in their government's ability to protect them." A few heads nodded. "Look at what happened after the terrorist attacks of 2001. Yes, the United States changed the regime in Iraq, but to what end, and at what cost to the people? Americans rushed to surrender their liberties in exchange for the promise of security, surrendering freedoms the terrorists could never have taken from them. The terrorists might lose the battles, but in one sense, they are winning the war. We will capitalize on that fear, and that eagerness to be cared for at any cost."

"What happens then?" Roman shifted uncomfortably in his seat and adjusted his tie.

"I am not ready to reveal the subsequent stages, but we have solid plans and ample resources."

"What I would like to know is how we caused the destruction in Key West." Steven Ellis was a dean at Southern Utah University, and had a sharp mind, though it was slanted a bit too heavily toward the world of academia. "I assumed it was a bomb, but descriptions of the phenomena contradict that."

"I fear I am not qualified to explain the science behind it, but our researchers are preparing a report for the board, which I hope to have available at our next meeting. Suffice it to say, we have at our disposal a weapon unlike any in the world. Indeed, it is so remarkable that I can credit only the grace of God that we discovered it." The frowns around the table indicated a degree of dissatisfaction, but no one pressed him.

"Why are we spending so much money on archaeological expeditions?"

Sanders jumped back into the conversation with a question from his domain. "I can only describe these expenditures as exorbitant, with little to be gained."

Hadel smiled. If they only knew the real number, which was much higher than the one reported to the board. "As I have explained to you before, there are a number of reasons. First, the search for Biblical relics, the discovery of which would strengthen the devotion of our flock, draw new followers to our ranks, raise our profile in the Christian world, and prove to the skeptics the truth of Scripture.

"Second, we are a church, and it is important that we act like one, or else we risk unwelcome scrutiny from the outside. Supporting missionaries and, yes, Biblical archaeologists, and even the archaeology departments of Christian universities, are some of the things that churches like ours do. I also have other, more personal reasons, that I do not wish to share at this time." He steepled his fingers and stared at Sanders. "Repeating myself is not a good use of my time. I trust I will not be expected to answer the same questions at every meeting?"

Duly cowed, Sanders shook his head and lowered his eyes.

"We apologize for making you repeat yourself, Bishop. Understand, our motives are sincere." The speaker was a square-jawed man with intense, green eyes. He seemed uncomfortable in his finely-cut suit, but perhaps it was merely the juxtaposition with his powerful build and GI haircut. Jeremiah Robinson was the only board member whom he had considered bringing into his inner circle. To the outside world, he was a National Guard recruiter, but he was also one of the highest-ranking members of the Dominion's paramilitary branch. The other members of the board underestimated him, which made him a perfect mole. "Would you mind telling us which city is the next target?"

Hadel pretended to consider this. He and Robinson had, of course, planned this ahead of time. "San Francisco," he said. "We considered New Orleans, but we want to send the message that our power extends beyond the gulf." He made a show of checking his watch. "I thank you for your time, gentlemen. Members of my staff will meet with you individually to give you your instructions. I bid you a good day."

They all rose as he stood and left the meeting room. Some of the instructions the board members would receive were important, but most were inconsequential, serving only to convince the board members of their value to the Dominion.

He retreated to his private office. It was not the "secret" office known only to board members, which was, in fact, a red herring, but a conference room hidden in plain sight, where picture windows offered mountain views that calmed his nerves and reminded him of God's majesty.

Thirty minutes later, Robinson let himself in and locked the door behind him.

"Were you successful?" the bishop asked.

"I was able to speak with each of them individually, giving every one of them a different city as the "real" target. If one of them is leaking information, we'll know it soon enough." He declined the bishop's offer of a chair, instead standing with his hands clasped behind his back.

"How are we progressing on the skulls?"

"As expected, the Smithsonian skull is a forgery, and thus, is completely useless."

"And the Paris Skull?"

"Our man on the inside failed, and the skull has been taken off display. A team is on its way as we speak to acquire it."

Hadel rubbed his chin and watched a golden eagle ride an updraft. An omen of the Dominion's rising, perhaps? It was superstitious nonsense, of course, but pleasant to contemplate.

"So we will have but a single bullet in our gun, should the Paris skull be genuine."

"We have analyzed the skulls but, so far, have failed to synthesize them. We think we might have found an alternate source for crystals. A research team discovered a cave…"

Hadel held up his hand. "I don't need every detail. Put it in a written report. Now, what about the rest of the operation?"

"Sofia Perez has gone to ground in Spain. We've had her passport suspended, so she can't leave the country. We'll find her. Until then, we have people working on translating the codex."

"And the Revelation Machine?" Despite his best efforts at remaining calm, the bishop's heart raced.

"No more clues than what we've had for a year now, but we hope the answer lies in the codex."

"Very well." The bishop sighed. "Move forward with stage two, and keep me abreast of developments."

Robinson's right arm twitched as if he were about to salute. He settled for a sharp, "Yes, Bishop," turned, and strode from the room.

The bishop returned to watching the eagle and contemplating the future—a future in which he controlled the fate of the United States and, perhaps, the world.

"Lord, haste the day," he whispered. "Lord, haste the day."

Chapter 14

"**Upstairs or downstairs?**" Bones whispered. They stood on a landing behind the door through which Greg had sent them.

"Downstairs," came Greg's reply. *"When you hit the ground floor, turn left. You want the fifth door on your right. You'll pass some private offices. I haven't gotten access to their security system yet, so I'm blind. Be wary and try not to let yourself be spotted."*

"Don't worry about me," Kasey said. "I just wish you hadn't made me bring a bull into this china shop."

"Tell you what. If I give us away, you can make me a steer."

Kasey gave Bones a withering look before descending the steps on silent feet, Bones creeping along behind. The hallway was silent and empty.

"Remember," Kasey whispered, "I take the lead."

Bones winked and she sighed. *"Until you screw up,"* he mouthed at the back of her head. Kasey glided along like a shadow, peering through each office window as she went. The girl moved well, and looked good doing it.

They reached their destination without incident, and found the door locked.

"Need me to pick it?" Bones offered.

"It's electronic, genius." Kasey drummed her fingers on the door frame. "What's the holdup, Greg?"

"Something odd's going on. I'm being blocked, but it appears to be from the outside. Someone

else is hacking into the system." Bones heard the sound of furious tapping on a keyboard. "*You might want to duck out of sight until I get it.*"

Bones looked around, for what, he was not sure. The office closest to them was empty, but the door was ajar and the lights were on. He figured the occupant was likely to return soon. Shelves lined the walls, and a modest desk and chair, with a jacket draped across the back, faced the door. "Hold on," he said. "I got this."

He stepped inside, unclipped a security badge from the jacket, and brought it to Kasey. "I swiped it so you can swipe it."

"Oh my God, do you ever stop?" Kasey sighed. "But it *was* a good idea." She held the badge up to the sensor. A green light flashed and, with a click, the door unlocked. "We're in," she said for Greg's benefit, and they stepped inside and flicked on their Maglites.

Bones had expected a vault, or something equally imposing, but instead found himself in a simple storage closet. Bundles and boxes, all labeled, filled the metal shelves on his left and right, and a few more items lay on a trestle table.

He kept watch while Kasey searched the room. The hall remained empty, but his senses were on high alert, and Greg's next communication only stoked his nervous energy.

"*I think we're almost out of time. Have you found the skull?*"

"Not yet," Kasey said. "Why?"

"*The outside hacker just called up the skull's location in the museum's database. Two guesses who's behind it.*"

Bones gritted his teeth. "Is there another way out if they come down the stairs?"

"*Checking.*"

"I've got it." Kasey appeared at his side, clutching a fist-sized bundle. "Let's get out of here."

They hadn't taken more than a few steps when footsteps echoed down the hall.

"That's got to be them. In here, quick!" Bones shoved Kasey inside the open office, turned out the light, and closed the door.

"We'll be trapped in here."

"Trust me. I've got a plan." He turned on his Maglite and played it across the desk. The beam fell on a coffee mug. Bones dumped the contents on the floor and stuffed it into his jacket pocket.

"Not that there's ever a good time for stealing, but now? A coffee mug?" Kasey asked.

Bones ignored the comment. "Greg, you got an escape route for me?"

"*Far end of the hall, opposite the direction you came. Turn right. There will be a stairwell on your left.*"

"Roger." Bones turned to Kasey. "I'll lead them away. When they're gone, you get out of here. I'll connect with you when I can." Before she could argue, he kissed her hard on the lips, turned out his Maglite, and ducked out the door.

Three men, casually dressed, strode down the hallway. All were tall, fit, and moved with single-minded determination.

"Pardonnez-moi," one of them called. His accent was atrocious, but his attempt at French indicated he had taken Bones for one of the museum staff.

"Oui?" Bones called over his shoulder.

"You're an American." The man looked hard at Bones. "What've you got in your jacket?"

"Naked pictures of your old lady."

"He's got the skull!" The man shouted. "Come on!"

Bones turned and dashed down the hallway, keeping one hand clutched to his jacket pocket to maintain the ruse that he carried the skull inside. He turned the corner and slowed his pace a bit. If he lost them too soon, one or more of them might double-back and then Kasey would be in trouble. He stole a glance back to make sure all three were still behind him, and then sped up again.

He found the stairwell and took the steps three at a time. His footfalls thundered in the empty space.

"Bones, what's happening?" Greg asked.

"I'm heading up the stairs and I've got all three guys after me. Kasey, get out of there!"

"Way ahead of you," came her breathless reply.

Bones hit the first floor landing, shouldered through the door, and emerged in the middle of a display of primitive dress from around the world. All around him, faceless figures encased in glass stood sentinel. Before he could get his bearings, the glass pane before him exploded and he caught the faint pop of a silenced pistol.

"I thought they had gun control in France," he muttered as he took off through the maze of glass cases.

"Stay alive, Bones." Greg's voice remained implacably calm. *"I'm on my way."*

The shots continued, and screams filled the air as museum patrons made a beeline for the exit. All around him, glass shattered and bullets tore through the silent figures. He didn't know where, exactly, the shooter was, but the man was between Bones and the front door. He'd have to find another way out.

The three men who had been chasing him added their voices and bullets to the cacophony. Bones dove behind a marble pedestal and assessed the situation. The walls of glass, and their scant protection, were literally crumbling all around him. He was almost out of time.

"Spread out! One of us is bound to find him."

The voice was only meters away and coming closer. Bones tensed, ready to spring, and waited. He could now see the man's blurred form through one of the few standing displays. The man held his pistol at the ready, and moved at a steady walk. Knowing he needed as much of the element of surprise on his side as possible, Bones took the coffee mug out of his jacket and tossed it over his shoulder.

The man heard the clatter and crash, fired a shot in the direction from which the sound had come, and took off running. Bones stuck out a leg as the man sprinted past, tripping him up and sending him falling hard to the floor. His breath left him in a rush, and his consciousness followed a few seconds later when Bones hammered two vicious elbow strikes to the temple. Helping himself to the man's weapon, a nickel-plated Beretta 92FS, he grinned. The odds were not yet in his favor, but he'd shortened them considerably.

"Stevens! Did you get him?" someone cried out.

"He's headed back toward the stairs," Bones called in a nasal voice. He had no idea what Stevens sounded like, but if silence had greeted the question, the men might have jumped to the correct conclusion. This way, there was a slight chance he could throw them off the trail. He counted to ten, and then moved quietly in the direction of the front door.

No joy. A figure stepped out in front of him and opened fire. Bones dove to one side, came up in a crouch, and fired off a single shot that just missed. His target dropped to the floor and flattened out behind a pedestal covered in broken glass and the shredded remains of a display. Cursing the unfamiliar feel of the Beretta, Bones rolled behind a still-standing display, wondering when the others would arrive.

The man behind the pedestal opened fire. As broken glass rained down on Bones, the shots ceased.

He's reloading, Bones thought. *Time to move in.*

He rose up, Beretta at the ready, just in time to see a tall, lean figure move like a shadow across his field of vision. The man on the floor managed a cry of surprise that melted into a gurgle as Greg struck him in the throat, then put him to sleep with a chokehold.

Footsteps, more gunshots, and Greg melted into the shadows.

Two men appeared, looking around wildly. Bones recognized one as the man who had spoken to him downstairs. They spotted him at almost the exact moment he saw them. They raised their pistols, but Bones was quicker. He squeezed the trigger.

And nothing.

The Beretta was empty.

"Of course," he muttered. "Now what?" His eyes fell on the figure above him—a Maori warrior, clutching a tao, a traditional short spear. "Any port in a storm." He snatched the spear, gave the dummy a shove, and ran.

The ruse only fooled his pursuers for a moment. Bullets shredded the dummy, and then the men were on the move again.

Bones zig-zagged around the few displays that remained standing, bullets whistling all around him. They had to run out of bullets sooner or later... he hoped.

Up ahead, a broad staircase led up to the second floor gallery. Mounting the steps, he ducked his head as he climbed, regretting his height and broad shoulders. Shots pinged off the marble banister, one ricocheting inches from his head.

"If one of these bullets rips my jacket, I'm going to be pissed."

At the top of the stairs, he turned left and ran along the balcony overlooking the first floor. The men weren't shooting now. Though he hoped their magazines were empty, it was more likely they were merely conserving their bullets until one of them got a clear shot at him.

"Greg, where are you?"

"I'm following along behind you guys, but I don't have a weapon. The guy I took out had fired his magazine dry."

"Any idea where I'm headed?" Bones dashed along the balcony, wondering when the next hail of lead would fly. "All I see up here is a set of double-doors."

"Conference rooms, I think. No idea if there's a way down."

"Lovely." A bullet whizzed past his ear and struck one of the doors with a thud. Acting on instinct, Bones dodged to the side, whirled, and flung the spear at the man in the lead. It flew true, taking the surprised man in the thigh and sending him tumbling to the ground. His partner stopped short, gaping at the fallen man.

Seeing his chance, Bones dashed through the double doors as bullets flew again.

A short hallway led to a conference room, where windows framed in the thick vines of the so-called green wall overlooked the street below. There were no other exits. He was finally cornered. The last pursuer was closing in. Time was almost up.

A wooden podium stood at the far end of the room. Bones ran to it, picked it up, rushed toward the nearest window, and struck it, battering ram-style.

The glass cracked, but did not shatter.

"Seriously?" Bones dropped the podium and lashed out with a series of side kicks. Glass flew, falling to the sidewalk below. He finally cleared a hole large enough for him to fit through, and clambered out the window just as the conference room door flew open.

Down on the street, people cried out, and sirens wailed in the distance. Bones gripped the thick vines, his feet finding holds in the green wall's tangled foliage. Moving with the agility of a monkey, he clambered not down, but up and to the side. He'd just come level with the top of the window when his pursuer leaned out, looking down at where he expected Bones to be.

Bones was ready. He lashed out with a powerful kick, catching the man square on the chin. Stunned, he wobbled, and Bones caught him with an up-kick across the bridge of the nose, and then drove his heel into the base of the man's skull. The man flopped unconscious, half in and half out of the window, like a wet blanket draped over a clothesline, his gun falling to the ground two stories below.

Bones slipped back through the window to find Greg entering the conference room.

"That's the last of them."

"Good," Greg said. "Kasey's got the car and will pick us up. Let's get out of here before the police arrive."

Bones laughed. "If only I had a dollar for every time I've said that very same thing."

They circled the museum at a fast walk, and hurried down Avenue de la Bourdonnais to Rue de l'Universite, where they joined a crowd of tourists headed for the Eiffel Tower.

"That thing is huge." Bones gazed up at the famed landmark. He knew the iron lattice structure rose more than a thousand feet in the air, but he was unprepared for just how impressive it was, its bronze surface gleaming against the cornflower sky. "Dude, I would love to climb that thing."

"You could take the elevator," Greg said.

"The hell with that. I'm a climber."

"Let's hope it doesn't come to that. You'd be treed like a cat."

They strolled beneath the tower and wandered along the manicured green, reminiscent of the National Mall in Washington D.C., until they reached the Champ de Mars.

"Kasey should be along any minute." Greg glanced at his watch, then checked his phone. "No messages. I guess she's okay."

Bones looked up and down the street. "Either that, or she can't text while she's being chased."

"Why would you say that?"

Bones grimaced. "Wait a few seconds and see for yourself."

Chapter 15

"Why aren't we moving?" A note of panic resonated in Sofia's voice.

"We just hit a little snag, that's all," Willis reassured her. "Maddock, how you want to handle this? Release the cable?"

"I'd hate to have come all the way down here and leave without the device." Maddock carefully brought the sub about. "With all the gadgets we've got on board *Remora*, surely one of them will do the trick."

"Whatever you're gonna try, you'd better make it quick. Oxygen's starting to run low."

Maddock glanced at the panels in front of him. Willis was right; time was growing short. He tried pulling the device free. It was not so much a serious attempt, but a matter of eliminating the simplest solution first. No luck.

He brought the sub about, unable to maneuver well with the cable still attached, and moved closer to the fallen statue. Poseidon gazed up at them through dead eyes of stone, a faint echo of the life that once teemed in this sunken ghost city.

"Should we call to the surface for help?" Sofia asked.

"We lost contact with them a while ago," Willis said. "Too far below the surface and too much rock in between."

"There's nothing they could do anyway. We've got the only sub." Maddock extended the sub's mechanical arms, grabbed hold of the statue, and lifted, but the statue didn't budge. The point of the device was stuck between Poseidon's left arm, held down by his side, and his hip. Maddock tried again, but to no avail.

"New plan. Let's see if we can cut it free."

"You're not going to cut the statue!" Sofia protested. "It's thousands of years old."

"You'd prefer to leave the device down here?" Maddock asked. When silence met his question, he extended the sub's cutting blade and set to work on the statue. The stone was solid and the blade's first stroke scarcely made a scratch. Gritting his teeth, Maddock set to cutting again. Silt and bits of stone clouded his view, and he used a water jet to clear his view. Soon, he'd managed to cut more than halfway through.

"Will you get it before our air runs out?" Sofia's forced casualness lent a stiff tone to her voice.

"No problem." Maddock didn't know if that was necessarily true, but he saw no reason to worry her. "Not much more to go." He set to cutting again, the blade now chewing up the rock. Just a few seconds more…

"Maddock! Stop for a minute." Willis, usually unflappable, sounded concerned.

"What is it?"

"I'm picking up some odd vibrations. Hold on." Willis activated the sub's external microphones and turned them up. "You hear that? It sounds like…"

"Falling rock." Maddock's mouth went dry. "We've got to get out of here." He turned the sub about and gunned the engines. It strained against the cable. Maddock's finger hovered over the release switch that would free the sub from its tether. He didn't want to lose the strange, Atlantean device, but his desire to live was stronger.

Just as his finger touched the switch, they broke free, and the sub lurched forward, dragging the device behind it. Willis and Sofia cheered as *Remora* zipped toward the exit tunnel.

Up ahead, chunks of stone fell like giant snowflakes from the ceiling of the passageway. Maddock had no choice but to try to make it through, or else they'd be trapped in the pyramidal chamber.

"Guess those torpedoes were a bad idea," Willis said.

"We're about to find out." Maddock gritted his teeth as the mini sub entered the tunnel. Falling rock pelted the sub's exterior, but the little craft surged ahead. "Hang on!" Maddock barked, steering the sub hard to the right as a huge chunk of stone broke free and fell right in front of them.

They almost managed to avoid it.

The falling rock struck *Remora* on its port side, causing it to pitch to the starboard side, where it banged into the tunnel wall.

"Oh God!" Sofia cried.

Maddock struggled to regain control of the sub. The craft rolled, righted itself, and plowed forward again. The shower of rock continued unabated, debris now collecting on the tunnel floor, narrowing their window of escape.

"We're never going to get out," Sofia groaned.

Another huge chunk of rock fell in their path. Maddock took the sub hard to port...

...and then they were free.

He angled the sub upward, climbing the shaft as fast as they dared. A quick glance told him they had fifteen minutes of air remaining, and a long way to go before they reached the surface. As they emerged from the mouth of the Sphinx and began their ascent, they regained contact with *Sea Foam*.

"Maddock! Do you copy?" Tam sounded as agitated as Maddock had ever heard her.

"I copy. We've got the device and we're on our way back right now."

"We've got company up here," Tam said. *"The Cubans have located us. We're bugging out."*

"Wait! We've only got a few minutes of air left."

Five seconds of silence greeted this proclamation. Finally, Tam replied in her trademark, patronizing tone.

"Why don't you turn on the carbon dioxide scrubber, sweetie?"

Maddock felt his cheeks warm, Tam's words rendering him mute and more than a little bit embarrassed. During their training exercise in *Remora*, he'd focused on piloting and working with the various mechanical appendages, leaving most of the other details to Bones.

"Aw, hell," Willis finally muttered. "Okay, I got it."

"You think you boys can get Doctor Perez back safely? I mean, now that you can breathe again?"

"We'll be fine," Maddock said, "but what about you and Corey?"

"We've got a good lead on them, but it's going to be close. I don't know if we can make it back to international waters before they catch us. If we make it back in one piece, I'm arming this boat."

Maddock considered the situation. "I've got a better idea. We're going to ping you. Corey, bring her about and head for our location."

"Got it," Corey said.

"Just what are you planning, Maddock?" Tam sounded suspicious.

"I'm planning on atoning for my stupidity."

He brought *Remora* to the surface, and hovered just below water level. "Corey, have you got a reading on us?"

"Affirmative. We're closing on you fast. What's the plan?"

"I want you to pass right over me and keep going in a straight line. Make sure you're followed."

"That's not a problem."

The seconds crawled by, stretching into an eternal minute.

"What are you gonna do, Maddock?" Willis whispered.

Maddock didn't reply. As *Sea Foam* closed in, Maddock took *Remora* deep enough for the craft to safely pass above them. When the ship had jetted past, he swung the sub a few meters to port and brought it up to surface level.

"Cuban ship's closing fast," Willis said.

"I've got it." As the craft shot toward them, Maddock activated the targeting system and made ready to fire. "Now it's my turn to try out the torpedoes."

The Cubans were almost on top of them when Maddock fired. The torpedoes cut through the water and struck the ship on its starboard bow. Willis whooped at the sound of the explosion.

Maddock took them deep and made a beeline toward Miami. The ship wouldn't sink, but it wouldn't be following *Sea Foam.*

"Nice one, Maddock," Tam said. *"But you know you've got to write up an expense report when we get back. Torpedoes are pricey."*

Maddock couldn't help but laugh.

"Will do, and you're welcome."

Chapter 16

A sleek, silver BMW 4 Series wove in and out of traffic and screeched to a halt in front of Bones and Greg. The passenger side window lowered a few inches and Kasey called out to them. "Hop in fast, boys, and don't you," she said to Bones, "make any cracks about women drivers."

"Wouldn't dream of it." Bones stuffed his bulk into the back seat. "Some of the hottest drivers I know are women."

"Whatever." Kasey floored it, and the BMW screeched out into the sparse traffic. "In case you haven't noticed, I think someone's following us."

Bones stole a glance through the rear window where a white sedan bore down on them.

"They've been behind me for several blocks. They tried to play it off casual-like, but they just happened to make too many of the same turns as I did. I blew a few lights and got a lead on them, but it didn't last." She yanked the wheel hard to the right, sending Bones crashing into the driver's side door. Blaring horns and screeching tires drowned out Bones' protest. Moments later, they rocketed across a bridge spanning the Seine.

"Nice view." Bones gazed out over the water. "Kasey, once we shake these jokers, how about you and I go out for a romantic dinner?"

"No, I hate French food."

Bones chuckles and looked back again. The sedan closed in on them again.

They came down off the bridge and took a hard right, the BMW fishtailing as they rounded the curve, and soon they were flying along the banks of the Seine. Bones took in the serenity of the scene, where couples walked hand-in-hand by the slow-moving water, unaware that a deadly chase played out meters away from them.

A shot rang out, a bullet clanged off the wheel well closest to Bones. Kasey cursed and yanked the wheel hard to the left, and their car bounced over the low median and hurtled into the oncoming lane. A pair of smart cars parted like the Red Sea as the BMW shot between them. A horn blared and Bones looked up to see the grill of an oncoming box truck filling their windshield. Kasey cut the car back to the right, narrowly missing the truck. They bounced back over the median and onto the right side of the road.

"Holy crap, chick!" Bones shouted. "Nice maneuvering." He looked back to confirm they'd gained ground on the sedan, but for how long?

"We've got to make it out of town if we're going to catch our flight out of here." Greg remained as calm as ever.

"Do you seriously think I don't know that?" Kasey glanced at the rear view mirror and frowned when Bones caught her eye and winked. "I'm just trying to keep us alive."

"And you're doing a fine job. Keep it up."

Another bullet struck the car, this one shattering the corner of the rear window.

Bones' hand went to his hip, reaching for his Glock, which, of course, wasn't there.

"Greg, remind me why we didn't bring guns."

"Because we were supposed to be burglars, not armed robbers. Also, getting them into the museum would have added another layer of difficulty."

"Next time, I vote we take our chances with museum security. They don't worry me nearly as much as the Dominion does." Bones' eyes remained glued on the pursuing car. Kasey was doing a good job keeping traffic between them, but she couldn't manage to shake them.

"You're forgetting the most important reason of all," Greg said, his tone still serene.

"What's that?"

"Tam said no."

"Everybody grab what you've got!" Kasey cried.

Bones turned to see a massive stone arch barring their way. He had only seconds to take in the sheer size and spectacular artistry of the Arc de Triomphe before Kasey took them into the midst of the congested traffic circle that rounded the famed monument. He cursed as they barely missed sideswiping a Renault. Then, mostly to feel like he was doing something, he flipped off the driver of the car behind them, who blared his horn.

Kasey whipped the wheel back and forth until it was all Bones could do not to close his eyes as Kasey navigated the dense traffic. Greg even gripped the dashboard and pressed his brake foot against the floorboard. All around them, alarmed and angry drivers cursed and blew their horns as they tried to get out of the way of the BMW. Bones found himself holding his breath until, as quickly as they had entered the circle, they were out again, shooting south down the Champs Elysees.

The white sedan wasn't so fortunate. Bones watched as the driver, stuck in the inside lane, tried to force his way out. His vehicle struck another car, fishtailed, and smashed headlong into one of the concrete pilings supporting the chain that ringed the Arc de Triomphe, coming to an abrupt halt amidst a cloud of steam and smoke.

"Sweet!" Bones gave Kasey's shoulder a squeeze. "The Dominion might as well give up. We're too much for them."

Kasey managed a smile which melted away in a flash. "Nice going, Bones."

"What did I do?"

"I think you just jinxed us." Kasey didn't need to elaborate. Up ahead, a two-man helicopter hovered ten meters above street level. It turned broadside to the BMW and the man in the passenger side of the helicopter leveled a rifle at them and fired.

A bullet pinged off the BMW's hood and Kasey veered to the right, crossing back over the Seine and into the southern part of the city. She gunned the engine and the BMW leapt forward. Bones found himself fearing a crash almost as much as the Dominion helicopter, which followed behind them.

The chase went on for what seemed an eternity, Kasey barreling through Paris at a breakneck speed, weaving in and out of traffic, screeching around curves and even taking out a mailbox—an obnoxiously bright, yellow number that, in Bones estimation, had gotten exactly what it deserved. Meanwhile, the helicopter kept pace, sometimes deviating its course to avoid buildings, but always taking up the chase again. Periodically, the shooter sent a bullet their way. When the rear window exploded in a shower of glass, Kasey cried out in alarm and changed directions again, and the chopper temporarily disappeared from sight.

"If either of you has an idea about how to get out of here," she said "now would be a good time to mention it."

Brushing glass out of his hair, Bones looked around. They flashed past a familiar-looking sight: a statue of a lion. Where had he seen it before?

And then he remembered.

"If you can find a safe place nearby to stop, do it."

Kasey steered the car onto a narrow street and stopped halfway along the block. The helicopter would never make it through, but, without cover, they remained sitting ducks for the shooter.

"What now?" Greg asked, craning an ear toward the sound of the approaching chopper.

"Hop out and follow me." Bones sprang out and took off down the narrow street, eyes peeled, hoping his memory of a particular episode of one of his favorite paranormal shows was accurate. If he was wrong, they were dead.

"Are we looking for something in particular?" Kasey called from behind him.

"A manhole cover. Here!" He dropped to one knee next to the heavy steel plate, worked his fingers into the slot in the center, and wrestled the cover free.

"You're stronger than I thought," Kasey said.

"Thanks. I'll do some muscle poses for you later. Now get down there!"

The drone of the helicopter nearly drowned out his words. The Dominion had caught up with them again. As if announcing their presence, a bullet clipped the sidewalk inches from where Bones knelt.

Kasey blanched, but kept her composure as she disappeared down into the tunnel.

"You next." Bones held the manhole cover like a shield while Greg climbed into the hole. A bullet deflected off the solid steel plate, vibrating Bones' arms all the way up to the elbows. Out of time, Bones clambered into the tunnel and dropped the cover back into place as a third bullet missed his hand by a hair's breadth.

Daylight vanished, and they descended in total darkness. Time lost all meaning, and he was surprised when his feet hit solid ground. Finding his balance, he dug the Maglite out of his pocket and clicked it on, partially covering the beam with his fingers so as not to blind himself or his companions.

The thin slivers of light shone down a long stone corridor. The air was cool and heavy with the scent of stale water.

"This doesn't look like a sewer," Kasey whispered.

"It isn't," Bones said. "We're in the catacombs."

Chapter 17

"They call this place an island?" Joel scanned the shore of Bottlenose Island, a tiny patch of sand and palm trees off of Key West's northwest coast.

"I've seen smaller. But if this place is privately owned, somebody greased a lot of palms to get hold of it." Matt guided their boat toward the gleaming white sand beach where three empty boats sat beached.

"Sounds like the Dominion to me. They're never short on resources." Joel looked around and stiffened. "There's Franks. Time to get into character."

David Franks had traded his three piece suit for cargo shorts, flip flops, and a Ted Nugent concert tee shirt one size too small for his thick middle. He raised his hand in greeting and waited for Matt and Joel to drag their craft onto shore.

"Glad you found the place." Franks shook hands with each man.

"It's not hard to find. That is, if you know what you're doing," Matt added, remembering his adopted persona. "Anybody ever get lost trying to make their way here?"

"Once or twice. Anyone who can't make it here doesn't have what it takes to be a part of our group." Franks indicated they should follow him, and led them toward the edge of the wooded area.

"Is this some kind of sailing club?" Joel flashed a wicked grin. "Maybe orienteering?"

Franks' expression went stony. "It's a *men's* club, and we expect our members to live up to the name."

"Amen to that." Matt made a show of checking out his surroundings. "Lucky the tsunami didn't hit here."

"God is good," Franks said.

"Does this place belong to one of the group members?" Matt tried to make the question sound casual.

"It belongs to the church. We use it for small group meetings. It's not much, but it gets us away from the noise of the city... and prying eyes."

"There are a lot of things in the city I don't mind getting away from," Joel added.

"Definitely." Franks pointed up ahead. "It's just through those trees."

A faint scent of wood smoke hung in the humid air, and soon Matt heard low voices and a crackling fire. Nine men sat on benches around a campfire. They all fell silent when Franks, Matt, and Joel emerged into the clearing. Franks introduced them, first names only, and invited them to take a seat.

Franks waited for silence and then opened the meeting. "Brothers, we gather once again to reflect on the Lord's wisdom, and His perfect plan for this sinful world. Brother Bill, I believe you have the devotion."

Bill, a stocky man with thinning ginger hair, stood, opened his Bible, and cleared his throat.

"Hear the words of the Lord from the book of Ezra.

"When these things had been done, the Jewish leaders came to me and said, Many of the people of Israel, and even some of the priests and Levites, have not kept themselves separate from the other peoples living in the land. They have taken up the detestable practices of the Canaanites, Hittites, Perizzites, Jebusites, Ammonites, Moabites, Egyptians, and Amorites.

"For the men of Israel have married women from these people and have taken them as wives for their sons. So the holy race has become polluted by these mixed marriages. Worse yet, the leaders and officials have led the way in this outrage."

He closed the Bible, looked around at those assembled, and proclaimed, "The word of God for the sons of God."

"Thanks be to God," the group intoned.

The meeting began with a perfunctory discussion of the tsunami recovery efforts. It seemed the church was taking up a collection to assist members whose homes had suffered damage in the flood, while the men's group, which didn't seem to have a name, had helped clean up Key West Cemetery.

The discussion then turned to the topic of illegal immigration. Every man assembled stood opposed to anything short of removing non-citizens from American lands and beefing up border security, but their comments were much less incendiary than Matt would have expected. Some alleged a correlation between rising unemployment and an influx of foreign workers, while others discussed the impact on prisons, schools, and public services. Matt couldn't help but think the men were all tempering their comments until they had the measure of him and Joel.

Finally, Franks chimed in. "Such worldly issues are important, no doubt, but God is the ultimate authority."

"There's Deuteronomy, chapter 32," Brother Bill offered. *"He separated the sons of man. He set the boundaries of the peoples according to the number of the sons of Israel."* Everyone, even Matt and Joel, nodded.

Joel surprised Matt by chiming in. "What about Deuteronomy 28? *"The foreign resident among you will rise higher and higher above you, while you sink lower and lower. He will lend to you, but you won't lend to him. He will be the head, and you will be the tail."*

"Amen!" several men chimed.

Franks turned to Matt. "You've been quiet so far. What are your thoughts?"

"I admit I don't know the Bible as well as my brother." Matt spoke slowly, racking his brain for a believable answer. "But I seem to remember we're taught to stay in our places." He held his breath, hoping he'd remembered that detail correctly. Everyone stared at him, the silence so complete that he thought they must be able to hear his heart beat over the crackling campfire.

Finally, Franks nodded. "The Apostle Paul, in particular, taught that one should remain in his condition upon entering the church."

"And Proverbs tells us not to move land markers. The borders should not change and the people should not mix," another man added.

Matt's tension melted away. First hurdle cleared.

Franks checked his watch, then clapped his hands once.

"Brothers, our time is almost at an end. We need to set this week's fishing schedule."

Matt and Joel exchanged frowns. Matt enjoyed fishing, but this sounded like an awfully strong dedication to the sport.

Brother Bill went around the circle, assigning a pair of men to each night of the week. "I'll take tomorrow night." He looked at Matt and Joel. "Are the two of you up for some fishing?"

"Absolutely," Joel said. "But we don't have any tackle."

Everyone laughed and exchanged knowing looks.

"No need to worry on that account." Franks smiled broadly. "The Lord will provide."

Chapter 18

The Catacombs of Paris were comprised of 1,500 miles of caverns, sewers, and crypts that lay beneath the storied city. Formed from centuries-old limestone quarries, the caverns housed pockets of French resistance and German bunkers during World War II. A section of these passages had been converted to an ossuary containing the bones of six million Parisians, making it the world's largest necropolis. The ossuary was now a popular tourist destination, while the lesser-explored tunnels were the domain of cataphiles—people who illegally roamed the passageways.

Bones breathed in the faint scent of mold on the chill, damp air, and shone his light around. His breath rose in clouds to the ceiling, where moisture clung to the old stone. Droplets of water formed on the ceiling. This was one of the mining tunnels and not part of the actual ossuary, yet it was quiet as a tomb here, with only the occasional drip of water onto the floor to break the silence.

"Do you think they'll follow us down?" Kasey whispered.

"The pilot won't, but I'll bet the guy with the rifle will." Bones looked up, wondering how soon they could expect pursuit.

"Unless they call in reinforcements," Greg said. "No telling what kind of manpower they can call upon here. The helicopter was unexpected, so we'd better assume they've got more nasty surprises coming our way."

Kasey took out her own flashlight, a tiny keychain number with a high intensity beam, and shone it along the wall. "How did you know we could get down here through the manhole?" she asked Bones.

"*Casebook: Paranormal* did a show down here not too long ago. They contacted the spirit of a German soldier who died in a secret bunker."

"Really? What did he say?"

"I don't know. He spoke German."

Kasey sighed. "You don't buy into that stuff, do you? Ghosts, I mean."

"Let's just say I don't dismiss things out of hand just because they don't seem likely."

"Down here, I can almost believe it." Kasey shivered and rubbed her arms. "It seems like the kind of place a ghost would hang out."

"The Empire of the Dead," Greg said. "At least, that's what the sign above the front entrance reads. Saw it in *National Geographic.*"

They all turned and looked up when the scrape of metal on stone pierced the veil of silence.

"Here they come," Bones said. "Let's move."

They hurried along the tunnel, moving as quietly as possible and keeping an ear out for the sounds of pursuit. They passed a pillar of stacked boulders that appeared to be supporting the ceiling.

"It's best if you don't touch anything," Bones whispered. "Sections of these tunnels have collapsed in the past, sometimes taking entire houses with them."

"So glad you brought us down here." Kasey looked up at the ceiling as if might fall on them at any moment.

They went right at the first fork in the tunnel and followed it around a series of curves. Along the way they passed occasional holes big enough for a man to wriggle through, had he sufficient determination. Maybe as a last resort, Bones thought. He didn't want to find himself trapped down here, so finding an exit topped his list. They rounded a sharp curve and Bones stopped short, throwing out his arms to hold Greg and Kasey back. Before them, a pit barred their way.

"That's a long way down," Greg remarked as Bones shone his light into its depths.

"Yeah, I forgot. Lot of wells and pits in the floors."

"Any other potentially fatal details you forgot to tell us about?" Kasey thumped him on the chest.

Bones scratched his head. "Nothing fatal, but if we're unlucky, the tunnels might flood with sewage."

Kasey bit off a retort. The sound of running feet echoed through the chamber. The Dominion was closing in on them.

"We can't cross here." Greg turned around. His eyes scanned the dark passageway behind them.

"I saw a side passage back there," Bones said. "Come on."

A few paces back around the corner, they found a dark hole in the wall just below waist height. Bones shone his MagLite inside, revealing another, smaller tunnel. Kasey wriggled in first and Greg squeezed through behind her.

"Get in here," Greg whispered.

Bones considered the narrow opening. "I'll never fit."

"We'll pull you through." Kasey held out her hand.

"And get me stuck like Winnie the Pooh in the honey tree? No thanks." The footsteps came louder now and he saw the faint flicker of a flashlight beam. "I'll be okay. You two stay hidden. If we get separated, go on without me."

Before they could argue, he turned out his light and felt his way back around the corner to the edge of the pit, where he pressed against the wall and listened to the sound of the Dominion's approach.

Footfalls. Heavy breathing. Closer and closer.

This had better work, Bones thought.

A beam of light slashed through the darkness and then someone cried out in surprise. The man stopped at the edge of the precipice, just as Bones had. In that instant, Bones struck.

It wasn't the stuff of action movies or heroic epics. Instead, he kicked the man in the backside with all his might. That was all it took to send the Dominion's agent plummeting down into the darkness, his cries ending with the wet splat of flesh hitting stone at terminal velocity.

Bones paused, listening for more pursuers, but heard none.

"You guys can come out now." He spoke in a conversational tone, but it sounded like a shout in the stillness.

Kasey wormed her way out of the passageway and tried, in vain, to brush the grime from her clothing. "What happened?"

"I kicked his ass."

"Whatever. So, do we head back to the car, or do you think the chopper's still hovering around?"

"I doubt it, but I'll bet they've disabled our car and maybe even set someone to watch it." Greg knuckled the small of his back. "I'm too old for spelunking."

"Walking is good for that," Bones said. "Let's find a way out."

They retraced their steps, making it back to the first fork in the tunnel they'd encountered, before trouble found them again. Someone called out to them in French and shone a light in their direction.

"The police patrol this place regularly," Greg whispered.

Just then, a shot rang out, the bullet zinging off the tunnel wall.

"That's not the police!" Kasey took off running, with Bones and Greg bringing up the rear.

"You didn't manage to relieve that last guy of his weapon, did you?" Greg huffed.

Bones held out his empty hands in reply.

"Whoa!" Kasey froze and shone her light all around the room they had just entered.

The walls were lined with bones. Layers upon layers of skeletal remains were stacked to the ceiling, broken every meter or so with a ring of skulls, their eyeless sockets casting dark gazes on all who entered.

Bones ran a hand over one of the skulls and it came away covered in a fine coating of bone dust. He rubbed his fingers together, feeling the fine powder. "I wish we had time to look around, but I don't think that's a good idea. Sounds like our friend's getting closer."

They took off again. Chamber upon chamber of dry bones and leering skulls flashed by in a blur. Here and there, the floor fell away in a yawning chasm or dark pool. They hurdled the smaller ones and rounded the larger, all the while hoping the man chasing them would stumble, but he kept coming.

By the time they came to the intersection of two passageways, Bones found himself thoroughly disoriented.

"We should split up," Greg said. "Kasey, give Bones the crystal skull."

Kasey handed it over without a word of protest, and Bones tucked it into his jacket.

"It's our turn to play decoy. You just get the skull out of here, and don't even think about trying to rescue us if we get into trouble."

"No way, dude."

"It's our job. Now go." Greg gave Bones a gentle shove to set him in motion.

Bones took the tunnel to the left, cursing Greg under his breath. There were times when running away from danger was the right thing to do, but not when friends were in peril. He had to admit, though, Greg was right. It was imperative that they keep the skull away from the Dominion.

He kept his eyes peeled for the iron rungs that would indicate a way back up to the surface. So far, he hadn't seen a single one. He soon left the ossuary behind, and found himself back in old quarry tunnels. The darkness seemed to sharpen his other senses, and he caught a whiff of the rank smell of sewage. Nice.

The tunnel began to narrow and occasionally he was forced to duck to avoid a low section of ceiling. Beneath his feet, the tunnel floor grew rough and uneven. This must be one of the older sections, which meant the probability of finding a shaft leading up to the surface was small. He'd have to double back.

The thought evaporated at the sound of someone approaching. Apparently, Greg and Kasey hadn't managed to draw the Dominion's agent off his trail. That made him feel better. Now, the entire burden was on his shoulders—just the way he liked it.

He stole a glance back over his shoulder and, thankfully, did not see the flashlight glow that would tell him the Dominion agent was almost upon him.

A flash of red burst across his vision, hot pain shot through him, and, an instant later, he found himself on the ground, gazing up at a pile of rubble. The ceiling had collapsed here.

"You've got to be freaking kidding me." He looked around, his heart now racing, and his eyes fell on a tiny side passage. It would be a tight squeeze, but it was better than running headlong at an armed man. Holding his MagLite in his teeth, he forced his bulk through, and found himself in a small rubble-strewn antechamber, staring at an iron door.

"Now, where do you lead?" He tried the handle and was surprised when it turned. He slipped through and closed the door behind him. "Dude! What is this?"

Rodent droppings covered the moldering remains of burlap bags at the base of the wall to his left, while the rotted remains of wooden crates lay on the right. Rifle barrels and heaps of ammunition jutted up from the debris like islands in a sea of ruin. But it was what lay right in front of him that held his gaze.

Before another iron door, a skeleton lay curled in the fetal position atop a pile of dust and dirt that had perhaps been a blanket. Nothing remained of his clothing, but his dagger identified this as a Nazi bunker.

Bones picked up the dagger, feeling thrilled and repelled in equal measure. The history buff in him was amazed to have stumbled across a previously-undiscovered bunker, but the image on the dagger—an eagle, its spread wings forming the quillon, clutching a swastika in its claws, turned his stomach. Nonetheless, he needed a weapon. He tucked the knife into his belt, and then moved to inspect the old rifles. As he'd feared, the dampness had been unkind to them. Even if the seventy year-old ammunition was still good, the rifles were too fouled and rusted to fire.

"Too much to hope for," he muttered.

He would have liked to inspect the bunker further, but just then, he heard movement outside. His pursuer had found the antechamber, which meant he'd be coming through the door at any second. Bones' thoughts raced. Fight or flight?

He decided to take his chances with door number two. He forced it open, and found himself in a rough, dank tunnel. He looked around for an alcove, or any potential hiding place from which he could ambush the agent, but the passageway ran straight ahead, gently sloping upward into the darkness. Cursing his luck, he took off at a sprint.

He heard the door behind him open. Instinctively, he dodged to the side just as gunfire erupted and bullets deflected off the stone walls. Something needed to give, and fast.

The tunnel curved and sloped downward, and the sewage smell dissipated, replaced by the moist smell of clean water. The beam of his light glinted on a pool of water and he skidded to a halt on the slick stone floor. His breath caught in his chest as he stared out at a sight that many believed to be a myth.

Fed by an underground river and made famous by *The Phantom of the Opera*, the subterranean lake beneath Palais Garnier was, in fact, a cistern built by construction workers when they found themselves unable to remove the water from the ground where the foundation of the famed opera house was to be built. Now, the space was almost forgotten, though it was occasionally used by firefighters to practice swimming in the dark.

Bones shone his light up at the grate in the ceiling, his sole path to freedom, and knew he didn't have a chance of getting there before the Dominion's agent caught up with him. He had one hope.

The tunnel sloped downward at a steep angle and the way grew slick with moisture. Eric slowed his pace. It wouldn't do to fall and crack his skull or lose his weapon. He no longer heard the big Indian's running footsteps, which meant that the man had given up on running, and decided to turn and fight. Or, more likely, he was hiding in the shadows, waiting to spring.

Eric had gotten a good enough look at the man to know hand-to-hand combat was unlikely to favor him. He needed to locate the Indian before he attacked, and put a bullet through his heart. He shone his light all around, but saw nowhere the man could hide.

Up ahead, the tunnel opened onto a larger space. One filled with water! What was this?

"Where am I?" Eric whispered. He stood on a ledge looking out at a body of dark water of indeterminate depth, inside a concrete vault. He played his light around, inspecting the walls and ceiling. Aside from this tunnel, a single grate appeared to be the lone means of egress.

The Indian was nowhere to be seen. He must have gone into the water.

The thought had scarcely passed through his mind when a strong hand seized him by the ankle and yanked him into the water.

Eric lost his grip on his flashlight, and it clattered to the ground and bounced into the water. He managed to squeeze off a single, wild shot as he fell, but it went wild. In the muzzle flash, he caught a strobe-like glimpse of dark eyes and bared teeth, and then icy black water enveloped him.

He kicked and flailed, trying to get back to the surface, but wasn't a strong swimmer. His sodden clothing weighed him down, and he didn't know which way was up in the black water. His assailant seized him by the hair and, for an irrational instant, he thought the Indian would pull him free of the water. But then the truth hit him like a dagger to the heart—the man was holding him beneath the water.

Panic overrode rational thought, and he clawed at the hand that held him down, but the man's grip was like iron. His lungs burned and lights swirled before his eyes. His time was almost up. Desperation welled up inside him and he fought harder to dislodge the death grip. His lungs began to cramp, and he thrashed about like a fish on the line. He opened his mouth to scream and icy water filled his lungs. He jerked once and then relaxed in the face of his inevitable demise.

At least I gave all to the service of the Lord.

Something thin and sharp pressed against his throat, and he relaxed as death made him its own.

Chapter 19

"What do we think?" Maddock ran his hand along the smooth, silver surface of the thing they'd taken to calling, simply, the Device. They'd brought it back to headquarters, where it now sat on supports beneath a bank of fluorescent lights, looking like an inscrutable piece of modern art.

"I think it's dangerous," Tam said.

"Shouldn't we send it to a lab somewhere to be analyzed?" Willis eyed the Device like it was a rattlesnake coiled to strike.

"What lab and where?" Tam's face tightened and then relaxed. "Remember, we don't know who we can trust, and our little group doesn't carry any weight, or even credibility. Yet." Her features hardened and she raised her chin.

"Our group needs a name," Bones said. He, Greg, and Kasey had returned from Paris in the middle of the night, having managed to keep the skull out of the Dominion's grasp. "Something that doesn't sound like a coffee klatch."

Tam ignored him. "I've got someone coming in to look at it. He's an engineer from NASA. I've known him for a while and I'm sure he's not connected to the Dominion."

"How sure?" Maddock asked.

Tam's shoulders sagged. "As sure as I can be."

"I don't see what there is to figure out. You put this," Bones hefted the crystal skull, "in the hand, point, and shoot. Boom! Instant tsunami!" He strode over to the device and stepped up onto the framework that held it off the floor.

"Don't you dare!" Tam sprang forward and snatched the skull out of Bones' hand.

"Chill. I just wanted a closer look. Does it have a trigger?"

"You see that faint outline that looks like a handprint?" Corey pointed to a spot below the silver hand. "I think that's it."

"Sweet. I can't wait to fire this thing." Bones held his hand above the trigger point. "Those Atlanteans had small hands. Sucks for them."

"Your paws are just freakishly large." Maddock turned to Tam. "We should fire it. Hear me out." He took the skull from Tam and turned it over in his hands, feeling its cool, smooth surface. "Not here, and not alone. You say our group doesn't have any buy-in from the powers that be. Fly some movers and shakers down here for a demonstration. They'll have to believe us then."

"And snatch it away from us while the military squabbles over who gets to study it first? Not yet. Not until I'm ready."

"I get it." Maddock chose his words carefully. "Bones and I have trusted the wrong people before, and paid for it. But this is a national security threat. I don't think we should keep it to ourselves."

"I've already notified my superiors, plus a few contacts in other agencies. They know what we suspect—the Dominion has a weapon that can cause a tsunami."

"They aren't taking the threat seriously," Maddock argued.

"I don't know how they're taking it, and neither do you," Tam said.

"But…"

"Don't push me on this, Maddock. It's my decision, and I say no. At least, not right now."

Maddock, Bones, and Willis exchanged dark glances. Maddock knew Tam was on the right side, and she'd given him some much-needed help a few months before, but he still didn't trust her. Technically, he and his crew were working for her voluntarily, but she'd gone to a great deal of trouble to investigate their pasts, and now she held their misdeeds over their heads like a guillotine blade.

"If any of you have further objections, now would be a good time to keep them to yourselves."

"You know better than that," Bones said. "You buy the muscle, the mouth comes along with it. It's a package deal."

"I can live with that, so long as you remember who is the chief and who are the Indians."

Bones covered his mouth and pretended to sneeze. "Racist," he huffed.

The corners of Tam's mouth twitched. "Fine. I'm Achilles and you're my Myrmidons."

"I like that." Willis stroked his chin thoughtfully. "The Myrmidon Squad."

"I'll have some t-shirts printed up." Tam smirked. "Maddock, you and Bones come with me. You've got a new assignment."

They followed her to the conference room, where Sofia and Avery waited. Sofia smiled at them, while Avery drummed her fingers on the table and tapped her foot.

"About time. You're getting slow in your old age." Avery winked at Maddock before shooting Bones a dirty look. The three new arrivals took seats at the table and Avery began. "We think we've found another Atlantean site." She handed Maddock a manila folder, then offered one to Bones, but when he reached for it, she tossed it onto the floor with a flick of her wrist.

"Professionalism," Tam chided. "But I understand."

"Don't let them fool you," Bones said to Sofia. "Women really do love me."

"I'm sure." Sofia opened her own folder and got down to business. "Translating the codex has involved a great deal of guesswork. In some cases, it's pure trial and error. Last night, Avery matched one of my possible translations to an actual site—one I hadn't given serious consideration due to its location."

"Yonaguni." Maddock read the heading on the first page of Avery's report.

"I've heard of that place," Bones said. "It's in Japan. Sunken pyramids and stuff. But people dive there all the time. If there was anything there, wouldn't someone have found it by now?"

"Not if they don't have the codex." Sofia tapped her folder.

"Yonaguni features some very distinctive rock formations," Avery added. "We've matched what initially seemed to be a string of nonsense lines in the codex to these formations. We think they will lead to the temple."

"The codex mentions a temple?" Maddock asked, turning pages filled with underwater photographs of strange formations.

"No, but it stands to reason. The two devices that have been uncovered so far were each found in a temple, which appears to have been the center of Atlantean life." Sofia turned to Tam. "I'd like to go along. I'm an experienced diver, and no one knows Atlantis better than me."

"I need you here working on the codex," Tam said. "Losing a few hours on the Cuban site is one thing. Going to Japan is another. I've got an experienced archaeologist lined up on the other end. With her help, I trust Maddock not to screw this up."

Maddock wondered if she'd intentionally omitted Bones' name.

"You two pack your bags. You leave in," she checked her watch, "four hours."

"Who do you have lined up on the other end?" Bones asked. "Not some crusty old bone picker, I hope."

"Hardly. You know her quite well, in fact."

Maddock noted a hint of forced nonchalance to Tam's demeanor. His mind ran through what she had just said. Archaeologist. Japan. You know her quite well. The pieces fell into place and he sprang to his feet, upending his chair.

"You can't be serious." He clenched his fists, trying to control his anger.

"I'm dead serious." Tam met his scowl with an impassive gaze.

"No way. Play your mind games with someone else, Tam. I'm not joining in."

Tam's expression remained serene as Maddock's rage broke over her. "As I have told you before, the people I can say with one hundred percent certainty are not connected to the Dominion are few and far between. She's one of those people. Trust me, she wasn't any happier about it than you are. You know what they say about a woman scorned."

"Then send someone else. Willis, Matt, Greg…"

"I want you. Don't forget, you agreed to work for me."

Their eyes locked, and Maddock wondered if Tam referred to the implied threats she'd made months ago on board a ship in Baltimore's Inner Harbor.

"Oh, this is going to be all kinds of fun." Bones closed his eyes and rubbed his forehead.

"Wait. Are you talking about Jade Ihara?" Avery asked. "Maddock's ex-girlfriend?"

"The one I broke up with not too long ago."

"Good old, reliable Maddock." Bones chuckled. "You can count on him for two things: courage under fire, and cowardice in the face of an angry woman."

Sofia failed to cover her grin and Avery laughed out loud.

"I'm not afraid of women." Maddock's face burned as he spoke. "I just prefer to avoid conflict if I can help it." Seeing no one else was buying his explanation, he excused himself and left the meeting room.

It was a short walk from headquarters to his condo, and Maddock had only been home a few minutes when his phone vibrated. It was Angel.

"Hey." His voice sounded falsely cheerful to his ears, and Angel picked up on it immediately.

"What's the matter?"

"I'm good. Just a little stressed out." Grabbing a Dos Equis from the refrigerator, he headed out onto the deck overlooking the Gulf of Mexico, settled into his favorite chair, and began to fill her in on the events of the past few days. He told her as much as he was permitted to about his escape from the sunken city,

Bones' run-in with the Dominion in Paris, and their pending trip to Japan.

"Japan sounds fun. I wish I was going with you."

"Me too. You don't know how much I wish you were coming along."

"Aw, that's so romantic," Angel said. *"Which is how I know it's a load of crap. What's really going on?"*

"No, it's true. If you weren't in the middle of training, I'd take you in a heartbeat."

"Of course you would, but that's not the point. You're not telling me everything."

"You know I can't do that now that I work for the government."

"We both know I'll get it out of you sooner or later. I'm very good at that." Angel's gentle voice sent a wave of tingling heat coursing through him, and he wanted nothing more than to be lying on a beach with her somewhere far away. *"Spill it. I'll thank you properly the next time I see you."*

"You might want to wait until you hear what it is before you make that offer." Before he could reconsider, he told her about Jade.

The line went silent for so long he thought they'd lost the connection.

"Are you there?"

"Are you freaking kidding me? Tell Tam you won't go."

"It's not that simple."

"Only because you make everything complicated. Most things in life are simple: I love you and you love me, but how long did it take you to figure that out? You always have to look at every little angle so you can make the decision that you think will piss off the fewest people."

"If you'd let me explain. Tam has…"

"You're not hearing me, Maddock. This isn't one of those things that requires an explanation. It's the wrong thing to do, so you shouldn't do it."

Maddock flung his bottle of beer, still full, against the wall, where it shattered with a satisfying crash. The shower of beer that now soaked the front of his shirt, however, was not so satisfying. "Why don't you trust me? I'd never cheat on you, and you know it."

"That's not it at all, and the fact that you don't get that is a real problem." Angel sighed. *"Loving you is tiring, you know that?"*

Maddock managed a grin. "Just trying to make things interesting. I'm always hearing that women love a challenge."

"You know what they say—don't believe everything you hear, especially if my brother says it." She paused. *"I've got to go. Call me when you can."*

As if on cue, Bones stuck his head through the sliding glass door as Maddock hung up.

"I heard the crash and figured you needed another beer." His eyes fell to Maddock's sodden shirt. "And a poncho."

"I didn't hear you come in."

"You think Indians are only quiet in the forest?" He handed a beer to Maddock. They clinked bottles and drank deeply, Bones punctuating his swig with a loud belch.

"Nice." Maddock finished his drink in silence, savoring the smooth, malty flavor. "I guess we should get packing." He glanced down at his shirt. "After I shower."

"After you, bro."

Maddock had decorated his condo to reflect his love of the sea. The walls were painted a rich, Mediterranean blue, and trimmed in white. Paintings of old sailing ships hung in the living area, while his first-floor study was adorned with anchors, a ship's wheel, an antique compass, and an old cutlass. Nets hung from the ceiling, giving the room a comfortable, yet cocoon-like feeling. The upstairs was done in the same fashion.

"You probably ought to get your own place now that we're headquartered here," Maddock said over his shoulder as they mounted the stairs.

"You need me here," Bones said. "You're too reclusive when I'm not around. It's unhealthy."

"True, but it's going to be awkward when Angel comes to visit."

"Not awkward at all. You two can get a room somewhere." Bones hesitated. "Was that Angel on the phone?"

"Yep." Maddock really wasn't in the mood to talk about it.

"And you told her about Jade?"

"Yep."

"Maddock," Bones groaned. "You really don't know anything about women."

Chapter 20

"Permission to come aboard?" Matt asked Brother Bill, who waited aboard a sleek Wellcraft Sportsman fishing boat. The craft, a roomy twenty-footer with the most powerful engine one could get with that model, looked brand new. He hoped Bill would give him some time at the wheel.

Bill pursed his lips and his forehead crinkled. "I thought you were an Army man."

"I am, or was. Why?"

"The way you talk. That, and you're looking at my boat like you want to marry her." His face split into a gap-toothed grin.

"Can you blame me? She's a fine craft."

"That she is. Can't properly call her mine, though. The men's club bought her for our fishing trips and the like." He scratched his belly and his unfocused gaze ran from bow to stern. He seemed to remember himself, jerked back to full wakefulness, and invited the two men on board.

"Does she have a name?" Matt asked.

"We call her *Domino.*"

"Somebody must love pizza," Joel said.

Bill grinned. "It was a compromise. Some of us wanted to call her *Dominion*, you know, for the dominion of the Lord, but others thought that wasn't a fitting name for anything short of an aircraft carrier."

A chill ran down Matt's spine. It wasn't confirmation of the connection between the church and the shadow organization, but it was close.

"I'll say this much," Joel began as Bill steered *Domino* toward deep water, "so far, this seems like my kind of men's group. Most church groups are nothing but coffee and conversation. No offense."

Bill waved the apology away with one beefy hand. "I've been in my share of those."

To the west, the last rays of the setting sun colored the sky a blood red that faded to purple overhead and indigo to the east. Matt breathed the cool salt air and thought this would be a perfect night to wet a line and relax under the stars. If only they weren't on duty.

When the scattered lights on shore were but a memory, Bill cut the engine and let *Domino* drift. "Time to fish." He rubbed his hands together. "Should be a good night for it. Clear skies and calm water." Three fishing rods sat in holders at the stern, and he picked one up, freed the hook, and cast the line into the water.

"Don't you need bait?" Joel asked.

Bill paused. "That would look better, wouldn't it?" He opened a cooler, shifted the cans of beer aside, and pulled out a container of frozen jumbo shrimp. "You two want to bait your hooks, or do you need daddy to do it for you?"

Matt forced a laugh, and he and Joel each picked up a rod, baited the hook, and cast it into the water.

"That'll do for appearances in case the Coast Guard shows up." Bill returned the bait to the cooler and handed each of them a beer. "Drink slow, fellows. We need to stay sharp."

"What are we fishing for?" att asked.

"I'll give you two guesses." Bill took out a key, unlocked a large locker, and raised the lid. Inside lay three Colt AR-15 semi-automatic rifles.

"Sharks?" Joel guessed.

"Nope. Something much nastier. At least, some of them are."

Matt felt another chill as Bill passed him a rifle. It felt like dead weight in his hands as he contemplated the implications.

"Now, you fellows know anything about marine radar?" He tapped a screen next to the wheel.

Matt nodded.

"Good. We're going to cruise nice and slow-like. You keep an eye on the radar, especially for small targets. And I do mean targets."

Joel glanced at the radar. "I expected something that would find schools of fish."

"That's what this does," Bill said. "Only, the fish we want swim on the surface." With that cryptic comment, he returned to the wheel and took the craft into deeper water.

"Tell me about your time in the Army," Bill said after they'd cruised for an hour without catching a single fish or spotting a single boat.

"Not much to tell. I fought in Desert Storm, came home, got no help from the government when I got back. Been trying to make it ever since."

"Government," Bill spat. "At least you got a chance to put them Islamics in their places."

Matt shrugged.

"How about you, Joel?"

"No military service for me. I don't follow directions too well. I've mostly worked for private security firms. We're really hoping our new business venture will pan out. I mean, who doesn't like to shoot?"

"Too many people in Key West." Bill grimaced and shifted in his seat. "If you do open a shooting range, though, I can promise you'll get plenty of business from the men's group."

"I've noticed we don't fit in with many of the locals," Joel said. "But the men's group seems different. You all seem to be the out-of-doors type, like us."

"You two do much climbing? Caving?" Bill asked.

"Hell, yes," Matt said truthfully. "Been doing it since I was a kid."

"We've got a retreat coming up that the two of you just might like. Nothing's firm, yet. We just got word from the home church a few hours ago. If you're interested, I'll talk to Franks, put in a good word for you."

Just then, a blip appeared on the radar. Bill noticed it at the same time as Matt.

"We just might have a fish."

He zeroed in on the blip on their radar and, minutes later, they came upon three dark-skinned men floating on an inner tube raft. They paddled with old planks, but stopped when they spotted *Domino*. The two groups of men gazed at one another in silence until Matt spoke up.

"What's the plan? Turn them in to the Coast Guard?"

"Hell, no. You know what happens when we do that? They get processed and then turned over to their families in Miami or wherever. They never get sent back where they came from."

"And they stay here either living off the government dole or stealing jobs from Americans." Joel had managed to remain in character, while Matt fought to keep his dinner down. He'd killed men in his day, but never a cold-blooded execution.

"I'll give you the first shot." Bill said it as if he were bestowing upon Matt a great honor.

Matt thought fast. If he hesitated, he, at best, lost any chance of having his ticket punched to the men's group's inner circle. Worst case, he might rouse suspicion, thus putting the mission, and perhaps himself and Joel, into danger. But he couldn't kill the men on the raft, who had noticed the rifles and were frantically, and uselessly, struggling to paddle their raft away.

"Take us a bit farther away. I like a challenge, and this isn't it."

Bill considered this. "How far?"

"Fifty yards is good considering the limited light. Daylight, I'd make it farther." He made a show of examining his rifle while Bill took them farther away from the terrified refugees. He'd only delayed the inevitable for a few moments. He looked at Joel, who appeared completely at ease. "You aren't going to try to talk me into giving you the first shot?"

"Not at this distance. You're the marksman in the family."

Matt shrugged. "It's your call." He didn't dare emphasize the last word, lest Bill notice, but he raised his eyebrows as he spoke.

Joel winked. Message received.

"This far enough?" Bill asked, cutting *Domino's* engine.

"It'll do." Heart racing, stomach churning, Matt took aim. He had to make this shot perfect. Gently, he squeezed the trigger and felt the rifle buck against his shoulder. The shot boomed like thunder in the quiet night, the muzzle flash like lightning, and the men on the raft cried out in fear.

"You missed." Bill sounded disappointed.

"Look again. I hit what I was aiming at.""

Bill leaned across the rail and squinted. "You were trying to hit the inner tube? What for?"

"Just watch." Matt took aim again, taking as much time as he dared, and fired again. Another inner tube exploded. By the time he'd taken out three of the inner tubes, both Bill and the refugees understood his plan. The men were now desperately trying to paddle their raft away.

Bill, for his part, laughed and cheered Matt on. "Listen to them squeal!"

The sounds, both the laughter and the cries, sickened Matt. He bit down on the inside of his cheek, letting the pain distract him. A few more shots and the refugees would be in the water, either to drown or be finished off by Bill or Matt.

Another shot, and now the men clung to the few inner tubes that remained inflated. Matt understood enough Spanish to understand they were now begging for their lives.

"That's what you get!" Bill shouted. "This ain't your country!"

Matt considered turning the rifle on Bill, knowing that doing so would ruin everything, but he would not kill these helpless men.

"Someone's coming!" Joel barked, tapping on the radar screen. Sure enough, a boat was approaching. Joel's call had gotten through.

"Damn! Could be the Coast Guard." Bill took the wheel and turned *Domino* toward shore. "Sorry you didn't get to finish the job," he said to Matt. "But it was a good time."

"How'd you do it?" Matt whispered.

"Texted Tam and Corey. One of them must have pulled the right strings."

"Good work." Matt replaced his rifle in the locker, grabbed another beer, and took a seat. He took a drink and tried to relax, but couldn't. They'd avoided the close call with the refugees, but what might they encounter on the so-called retreat? Right then, he keenly felt Maddock's absence. Matt hadn't realized just how much he relied on his friend's leadership and calming presence. Now he was on his own. He supposed he'd better be prepared for anything.

Chapter 21

"Maddock and Bones! Long time, no see!" The tall, lean man stepped out of the crowd at baggage claim in the Yonaguni Airport and approached Maddock and Bones.

"Professor?" Maddock couldn't believe it. Pete "Professor" Chapman was an old Navy buddy with whom he and Bones had shared a few adventures during their days in the SEALs. "What are you doing here?"

"I've been sent to pick you up." Professor glanced down at the ground. "I work with Jade Ihara. Well, I work for her."

"Now that's one heck of a coincidence." Bones shook hands with Professor.

"I don't know about that. She looked me up a few months ago and made me an offer I couldn't refuse. She said the two of you spoke highly of me. And I needed the money." Professor shrugged.

"Okay, so not a coincidence, but I'm glad to see you all the same." Maddock slung his duffel bag over his shoulder and he and Bones followed Professor to their waiting car.

They spent the drive catching up with their old friend, though they avoided the subject of Jade. Professor had lived up to his nickname, earning his PhD after leaving the SEALs and working at the university level. "I never managed to secure tenure. They always blamed it on budget constraints, but I suspect it's my demeanor."

"What? You were the mellowest guy in our platoon," Maddock said.

"I was mellow by SEAL standards. The average college kid doesn't respond well to my... need for structure." Professor grimaced. "You should have read my end-of-course evaluations. *Intimidates students. We don't feel free to express ourselves.* What a bunch of crap. Every one of my students was free to express him or herself, provided the opinions expressed weren't stupid."

"There's the Professor we know and love," Bones said from the back seat.

They made small talk for the remainder of the drive, lapsing into silence when Professor parked the car in front of a small cottage.

"Home, sweet home." Professor cut the engine. "There are just the two bedrooms, so I'm afraid you two will be bunking on the floor."

Maddock's reply froze on his lips. Jade stood in the doorway, hands on hips, her expression hard.

She was as beautiful as ever. She wore her lustrous black hair in a thick braid slung over one shoulder, and her shorts and tank top accentuated her trim, athletic figure. She was half Japanese, but in this setting, she looked like a native.

Jade maintained her blank stare a few seconds longer, then smiled and hurried forward, arms extended. Maddock stepped forward to meet her, but she brushed past him as if he weren't there.

"Bones!" she cried. "It's so good to see you again." She caught the big Cherokee in a tight embrace which Bones, surprised but clearly pleased, returned. "Come on inside. I need to bring you up to speed so we can get started. You aren't too tired from your flight to do a little diving, are you?"

"Never," Bones assured her.

She led the way inside, once again pretending Maddock wasn't there.

"Brrr!" Bones shivered and rubbed his arms. "Good thing I brought my jacket."

Professor whistled between his teeth. "Not fun when she gets like this. She'll warm up. Just give her a few minutes to get used to seeing Maddock again."

"A few minutes?" Maddock smirked. "You don't know Jade like I do." For all her good qualities, and there were many, Jade had always been short-tempered and could hold a grudge like few people Maddock had ever known.

Inside, Jade had hooked her laptop to an HD television set. The screen now displayed a three-dimensional rendering of what looked like a series of staircases, terraces, and block-shaped structures atop a rectangular mound. When everyone was seated, she launched into a description of the Yonaguni site.

"The Yonaguni Monument was discovered in 1986. It lies about five meters below the surface. As you can see, it has several distinctive features, including steps, terraces, roads, and odd-shaped stones. Theories abound in regard to its nature. Some connect it with Lemuria, others say it's a civilization destroyed by Noah's flood. There's never been a serious scientific study, but it's a fascinating place."

"I did a bit of reading about it on the way here. Some say it's nothing more than fractured sandstone, sections of which just happen to look man-made," Maddock said.

Jade didn't even look at him, but instead glanced at Professor.

"That's certainly at play here, but we believe human hands have worked many spots here. Check out this staircase." He tapped the touch pad and an image of a narrow staircase, with walls on either side, filled the screen. "What are the odds that this happened due to fracturing?"

"It's too perfect." Bones rested his chin on his fist and stared thoughtfully at the screen. "I've seen fracture patterns that sort of looked like steps, but for a staircase-shaped section to pop out of the middle of a huge block of stone, with the sides still intact? That's a heck of a coincidence."

"We think so too." Jade took up the discussion again. "There are also engravings that seem to be wrought by human hands. These glyphs, for example." She clicked over to a close-up picture of a wall covered in what looked like writing. "The photos available online leave much to be desired, so we'll want to try and get some high-resolution images while we're down. Professor will take care of that."

Maddock tried again to engage her in conversation. "Do you think there's a connection between these glyphs and the Atlantean writing Sofia Perez is working on translating?"

Again, Jade ignored him. After an uncomfortable pause, Professor jumped in.

"Possibly. Some of the images are similar to Kaida script, an old writing system found only in this part of the world, but others resemble Atlantean."

"If Yonaguni were an Atlantean city, the writing could have evolved over time," Bones said.

"That's what we're thinking." Pete glanced at Jade.

"This place looks like it's made of solid rock," Bones said, "but we're searching for something that could hide a weapon—an underground chamber or something. Has anyone ever found something like that?"

"No one's ever looked for it. Very few people take Yonaguni seriously as a site of historical interest. We're hoping the clues from the codex will lead us to just such a place."

Maddock struggled to keep his annoyance in check. Jade couldn't ignore him forever. They had to work together. "Even if the Dominion hasn't deciphered this section of the codex, we have to assume they're keeping an eye on any site that's reportedly Atlantis-related."

Jade turned to Professor. "You finish up with Bones. I need to get some things ready. We leave in an hour." Still refusing to meet Maddock's eye, she stalked out of the room.

Maddock rose from his seat and made to follow her.

"Are you sure you want to do that?" Bones asked.

"Definitely." He strode out into the warm sun to find Jade standing alone, staring out toward the sea.

"You're going to have to talk to me sooner or later. You know that, don't you?"

"I *don't* have to do anything." Jade's cheeks turned a delicate shade of pink, clearly annoyed that Maddock had gotten her to break her silence.

"So you do know how to talk. I mean, to someone other than Bones."

Jade turned her back on him, fists clenched.

"You knew when you agreed to this job that you'd be working with me. Why don't you stop being a child and..."

Jade's full-armed slap cut him off in mid-sentence. She'd caught him right across the ear, the loud pop setting off a clanging in his head that nearly drowned out all other sound.

Jade's eyes widened and she covered her mouth. "Sorry."

"No, you're not."

"You're right. Of course, it didn't feel as good as I'd hoped it would."

"I'm just glad you went with the open hand."

"I'd planned on a roundhouse, but I was afraid I'd fracture a toe on your thick skull." Amusement flickered in her eyes, but died again just as quickly. "I never wanted to see you again, Maddock."

"Then why did you take the job?"

"Because I hate the Dominion even more than I hate you."

That stung. He knew she was angry with him, even furious, but what had he done to earn her hate?

"Jade, I never cheated on you. You and I weren't even seeing each other when Angel and I got together." Jade didn't say anything, so he went on. "Let's face it. It seemed like you and I could never keep things going for more than a few months at a time. You started working in China, and then Japan, and we never saw each other."

"Why do you think I went to China in the first place?" Her eyes glistened with unshed tears. "I wanted you to come and get me."

"What?" This was the last thing he'd expected her to say. If there had been one thing in their relationship he thought he could count on, it was that Jade didn't play games. Yes, she was jealous and short-tempered, but she also told him exactly what was on her mind.

"I thought if I was on the other side of the world, you'd realize you needed me and would ask me to come back." Jade forced a laugh. "The first and last time I played a head game like that."

"I didn't know," Maddock said. "I didn't want to be one of those boyfriends who tried to hold you back. After a while, I just figured I wasn't that important to you."

Now Jade looked him in the eye for the first time since he'd arrived. "Listen to us talking like a couple of lovesick teenagers. This is stupid. I'm not going to waste my time with someone who didn't feel for me what I felt for him." She glanced at her watch. "Let's go. We've got work to do."

Maddock watched her as she returned to the cottage. All the anger had melted from her stride, and she moved with her usual, catlike grace, her braid swinging and her hips…

Maddock closed his eyes and gave his head a shake. "Get a grip," he muttered to himself. "You already have enough problems with women. Don't go creating another one." Cursing inwardly, he followed Jade inside, wondering how he could avoid screwing things up.

Chapter 22

"Who's first?" Bones sat perched on the rail, ready to take the plunge into the sparkling, blue water.

"You two lead the way. I'll bring up the rear." Maddock knew his friend was eager to dive, having missed out on the Cuban excursion.

"Excuse me. My boat, my expedition." Jade threw a challenging look in his direction. At least she was finally speaking to him. "Bones first. Me second. Maddock third." Spotting Maddock's perplexed smile, she added, "I know sense when I hear it. Now, let's go."

"Wish I was coming with you." Professor had a wistful look in his eyes.

"Do you usually dive alone?" Maddock asked Jade.

"We haven't dived since I brought Professor in." She adjusted her SCUBA tank. "I have grad students who could have held down the fort, but I didn't want to bring more people into the circle than necessary."

Maddock nodded. He doubted any of the students was a Dominion plant, but word of this mission didn't need to get out.

"Speaking of Professor, how'd you come to hire him?"

"He had the qualifications I was looking for and his name rang a bell. You two always spoke well of him."

"I'm surprised my recommendation carries any weight with you," Maddock said.

"It does in some areas. I wouldn't take relationship advice from you." Jade paused, cocked her head to the side, and smiled. "Are you jealous, Maddock? Or maybe you thought I hired him to get back at you in some twisted way?"

"The thought never occurred to me," he lied. "Just wondered. I haven't kept in touch with him, so I was surprised to see him, that's all."

"You have a habit of discarding the people you used to care about." Jade turned her back on him and clapped her hands twice. "Let's do this."

"As you wish." Bones checked his mask one last time, winked, and flipped backward into the water, Jade a few moments behind.

A feeling of comfort enveloped Maddock the moment he plunged into the water. He'd loved diving for as long as he could remember, and the prospect of adventure was icing on the cake.

Maddock knew the monument lay just below the surface, but he was unprepared for it to fill his vision the moment he hit the water. He gazed at a pair of columns that almost reached the surface and marveled that so remarkable a place had lain forgotten until modern times. The staircases, passages, and multiple levels put him in mind of a step pyramid.

"Dude, this place is wicked." Bones' voice sounded in Maddock's ear. "Too bad we can't stay all day."

"Maybe we'll come back some day and bring the crew," Maddock said.

"I'll bring the beer."

"If you two can focus, we need to look for the first clue." Jade's voice cracked like a whip.

"Remind me what it is again?" Bones asked.

"*Behind the watcher's starry eye.* There's a sphinx-like sculpture, called the totem, somewhere in the complex, but I couldn't find anything online that pinpoints its location."

"Do we want to spread out?" Bones asked.

"We'll stay together for now. Let's start at the bottom and work our way up." Jade pointed to the base of a steep staircase.

They circled the base of the monument, inspecting its smooth walls and sharp angles. They made three circuits, rising as they went. The stairs and terraces were bare, and they reached the top without spotting anything that could be called a watcher. At the top, they swam through narrow passageways, past walls constructed at perfect right angles, and around octagonal stone pillars, but still no watcher.

"No way this place is a natural formation," Bones said. "It reminds me of ruins I've seen in South America. Saksaywaman?"

"It definitely reminds me of the sunken city in Cuba, but there's one big difference. There aren't any ruins here. It looks like it was all carved out of one solid block."

"It's assumed that what we see here is the foundation upon which temples and the like were constructed. Look there." Jade indicated a row of perfectly round holes bored in the stone.

"Postholes," Bones said.

"That's the assumption. Whatever was here must have been washed away in whatever deluge submerged this place."

Something moved in the corner of Maddock's vision and his hand went to the small spear gun he wore at his hip. "What's that?"

The three divers stared as a half-dozen shadows approached. Maddock tensed, on the verge of sending Jade back to the boat while he and Bones attacked. The shapes grew larger and more alien as they drew closer. Long, thick bodies, wide flat heads with bulbous eyes on the sides, emerged from the distance.

"Hammerheads," Maddock breathed.

"I forgot to tell you," Jade said, "this place is teeming with them."

Maddock relaxed. Like most creatures, the hammerhead was more than happy to leave you alone provided you extended it the same courtesy. In fact, they were his favorite sharks. While some people found their appearance frightening, he considered them ugly ducklings, and always looked upon them with a degree of affection and something like sympathy.

"They are awesome," Bones said, reaching out to almost touch one as it passed him by. "Weird that people are so afraid of them."

"That could work to our advantage," Maddock said. "If the Dominion sends divers in, maybe the sharks will put a scare into them."

"We can hope. Let's keep looking." Jade didn't wait for them, but kicked hard and swam over the edge of the monument and down toward the smaller structures.

Maddock couldn't help but fondly remember all the dives he and Jade had made together. She'd always taken the lead, trusting he'd always be right behind her. For the briefest moment, he fought down the urge to chase her down and catch her up in a rough embrace, just like the old days.

"Did you find something?"

Bone's voice yanked him back to reality.

"No, just taking a last look around," Maddock lied. "Let's catch up with her before she does something reckless."

"Wouldn't want that to happen," Bones said. "Reckless is my domain."

When they caught up with Jade, she was hovering over an odd-shaped rock formation.

"The turtle." Jade indicated the five-pointed, humpbacked formation atop a stone platform. "It's one of the features mentioned in the codex." She took out an underwater camera and snapped a few pictures before continuing on.

They searched for nearly an hour, working in a grid pattern around the monument. They passed through more channels beneath archways and around blocks of stone that might have been remnants of old structures, and discovered hieroglyph-like carvings of which Jade made a thorough photographic record, but no totem. It was a shallow dive, and the three of them were experienced divers, so none of them had expended much more than half her or his supply of air, but they decided to surface for fresh cylinders, not knowing what they'd encounter once they located the totem. After fending off Professor's attempt to switch places with Bones, even trying to bribe him with beer, they returned to the water.

Their search of the final quadrant bore fruit almost immediately. They passed through a deep stone channel and exited to find a stone face staring back at them, and they swam in for a closer inspection. The currents had eroded its sharper features, but the long face, sunken eyes, and protruding forehead were easy to make out.

"You know what this thing looks like?" Bones asked.

"Moai."

Maddock's first thought upon seeing the totem was its resemblance to the moai, the statues made famous by Easter Island. He ran a hand across the huge, stone brow, wondering what it could mean. Was there a connection between Yonaguni and the island on the far side of the Pacific? Considering what they and Sofia had found so far, the possibility did not seem far-fetched.

"What now?" Bones asked.

Maddock recited the clue from the codex.

"Behind the watcher's starry eye, at the center of the trident, the crone points the way to Poseidon."

"Open up and try not to blink," Bones said to the statue as he shone his light inside the eye socket. "Lots of gunk in here. Let's see if it's covering anything." He took out his dive knife and began scraping. Maddock did the same to the right eye.

It wasn't long before he uncovered a rectangular stone bar set in a grooved track.

"I found what looks like a lever."

"Me too," Bones said. "Should we pull them both and see what happens?"

"No!" Jade said. "Think about the clue. The watcher's starry eye, not eyes. I think we're just supposed to pull one of these handles."

"How do we know Sofia translated it correctly?" Bones asked. "Do hieroglyphs have plurals?"

"I don't know about that," Maddock said, "but why make specific mention of the 'starry' eye unless the word is important?"

Bones flitted his light back and forth between the eyes. "No stars here. If the clue refers to a constellation the figure faced back when this place stood above water, we're screwed."

Maddock had a different idea. "Jade, where is the turtle formation from here?"

"Just over there." She pointed to their left. "Why?"

"Except for the rounded back, I didn't think it looked much like a turtle, did you?"

"You're right. Some people call that formation 'the star.' Let me check it out." Again, Jade swam away without waiting for a partner, returning in less than a minute. "It points directly at the totem. The right eye, to be exact."

"You're sure?" Maddock asked.

"Only one way to know for sure." Bones thrust a hand into the eye socket.

"Hold on," Maddock said. "Remember what happened to Matt?" On a dive at Oak Island, their crewmate had tried something similar and almost lost his arm.

"There's one big difference," Bones said.

"What's that?"

"I always come out on top." Before anyone could stop him, Bones pulled the lever. Everyone swam back as a rumbling sound broke the silence and the totem sank out of sight. "Score!" Bones shone his light down into the hole the totem had revealed. Not only the statue, but a square ten feet across had sunk into the earth, and an angled passageway of the same shape and size lay before them. "A word of advice. Never play me in Russian roulette."

The passageway sloped downward for about fifteen feet, then leveled out, heading straight for the main monument. Whatever lay at the end would likely be found beneath the mountain of stone.

The passageway through which they traveled was perfectly square. The block walls and slab ceiling were made of the same rock as the monument, while the floor was lined with huge paving stones.

"Reminds me of the Bimini Road," Bones said.

"Is there anything that doesn't remind you of a conspiracy theory or far-fetched legend?" Jade asked.

Maddock didn't disagree with Jade, but he came to his friend's defense nonetheless. "You can say that to him after all the things we've seen?" In fact, Jade had been by their sides during some of their most remarkable discoveries.

"Don't be so touchy, Maddock. You're like a soccer mom or something."

Maddock bit back a retort and kept his eyes straight ahead.

"Looks like we've reached the proverbial fork in the road." Bones slowed down and shone his light around. Here, the tunnel split into three seemingly identical passages. "Three roads diverged in a creepy tunnel."

"When you make it to the afterlife, I'll bet Robert Frost will be waiting for you with a shank and a baseball bat," Jade said.

"And miles to go before I'm appreciated," Bones sighed. "So, which tunnel?"

"I think this tunnel is the trident the clue mentions," Maddock said. "A straight shaft, splitting into three at the end."

"Sounds good to me, dude. The center, then?"

A short way in, Maddock noticed a change in the passageway. "No more bricks and slabs," he noted. "Just a smooth tunnel carved in stone."

"We must be under the monument," Jade said.

"And it's about to get weirder. Look up ahead." Their lights glinted on the surface of the water up ahead. "There's a pocket of air down here. Maybe a big one."

They broke the surface together and looked around. They were in a pool in the center of a thirty foot-high chamber. Maddock climbed out of the pool and offered Jade a hand up, which she ignored, and hauled herself up to the stone floor.

"Wonder what the air-quality is like in here?" Bones said.

"No telling." They were wearing full masks so their communication devices would work. "I don't care to find out, though."

Maddock turned his attention to the far end of the room where three statues of Greek goddesses, each at least three meters tall, stood on a ledge above three tunnels. Each figure pointed downward at the tunnel beneath her feet, which was partially obscured by a curtain of water pouring from her mouth.

The goddess on the left exuded strength and vigor. She was posed in midstride, looking to the side and reaching back for the bow slung over one shoulder. The figure in the center wore a cylindrical crown, held a piece of fruit in her right hand; a mature beauty seemed to emanate from her solemn face. The figure to the right held a torch aloft, and spikes radiated from her crown.

"I guess this is where the crone points the way, "Jade said. "But which one is she?"

Maddock looked the statues up-and-down. Each was a woman from Greek mythology, but he thought he knew the answer right away.

"It's Hecate, the one on the right."

"Are you sure?" Bones asked.

"Definitely. The one on the left is Artemis. You probably know her as the hunter, but she was also known as the maiden. Hera, in the center, is the mother, and Hecate, on the right, was the crone. What's more, she's associated with crossroads and entryways."

"Sounds like a winner to me." Bones moved in for a closer look. "You're right about the center passage. Check it out."

Maddock and Jade stepped around the water falling from Hera's mouth and shone their lights down the passageway. In the distance, at the very edge of their dive lights' glow, a skeleton lay impaled by a broken spike.

"I'll bet it was designed to go back into the floor so it could catch the next person," Maddock said. "It must have broken when it caught this poor fellow."

"Or lady," Jade added.

Maddock ignored her comment. "Hecate was my suggestion, so how about I lead the way?"

Jade made a show of mulling this over before agreeing.

Maddock led the way up the corridor. He felt certain he had chosen the right path, but the knowledge there were booby-traps in this place made him cautious. The gently sloping passageway soon opened up into a temple much like the others they had discovered. The now-familiar Poseidon stood watch over his domain.

"Whoa!" Bones exclaimed, staring at Poseidon. "Awesome."

While Bones marveled at the sights and Jade snapped pictures, Maddock moved to the chamber at the back of the temple. His heart fell when he shone his light inside and found it empty.

"What do you see?" Bones asked.

"Nothing. If there was anything here before, it's gone now." Maddock's stomach twisted into knots. They had come all this way and worked so hard for nothing.

Hearing his words, Jade hurried over. When she saw the empty chamber, she seemed to deflate, disappointment marring her beautiful face.

"What do you think happened?"

"I don't know." Maddock shrugged. He shone his light on the floor and spotted a line of scrapes and gouges in the flagstone. "It looks like something heavy was dragged through here."

"The Dominion?" Jade asked.

Maddock considered this, remembering the entrance to the passage that had led them here. "I don't think so. We had to clear away a lot of silt and growth on the levers. Unless there is a back door, and I don't see one, whoever got here first beat us by several years."

"Great," Bones said. "Now we just have to figure out who it was."

Maddock nodded. "Another mystery."

Chapter 23

"That's it." Sofia pushed away from the desk and gazed at the computer screen. She had finally completed her translation of the codex.

"Let me take a look." Avery rolled her chair next to Sofia's and read aloud.

"Our only hope lies in our collective strength. Few of us remain, but we must continue to resist, lest we leave this world on its own to face the great city and its deadly power."

Avery rested her elbow on the desktop, cupped her chin, and gazed at the screen. "Not a very cheerful message, is it?"

Sofia shook her head. As she read these words she could not help but wish she had never sought Atlantis.

"It sounds like the tsunami machine is nothing compared to whatever the so-called great city had at its disposal."

"And by great city you think they mean…"

"Atlantis. The true Atlantis. The capital or mother city, if you will, of the Atlantean civilization." She sighed. "It's funny. A few weeks ago, I would have given anything for definitive proof that Atlantis was more than a myth. Now I wish I could somehow undiscover it. This is all my fault." The back of her throat pinched but she forced herself not to cry.

"If it hadn't been you, it would have been someone else. If I've learned anything from my brother and his cohorts, it's that the Dominion is relentless. They'd have kept on until they achieved their goal." Avery gave her a tight smile. "I'm glad it was you. Another scientist might have given up, or worse, joined their cause."

"They didn't give me a chance to join. They tried to kill me as soon as I found the temple." Sofia winced at the memory.

"Because they knew you'd have refused. Evil is not in your character. Believe me; I've known some very bad people in my lifetime." Avery gave Sofia's shoulder a squeeze. "Okay, enough feeling sorry for yourself. We've got work to do."

Sofia sat dumbstruck for a moment, but then she broke into laughter. "Some bedside manner you've got there."

"It's the Maddock in me coming out. But I'm right." She winked, and Sofia laughed again.

"This is so frustrating." Sofia ran her fingers through her hair. "The author of the codex seems to think the location of the mother city was common knowledge, but directions to the other cities were needed."

"His breadth of knowledge is impressive. So much specific detail. It makes you wonder if they had some sort of advanced communication device." Avery forced a smile, uncertain how Sofia would react to that comment.

"They had a machine that could create a tsunami, so I don't think that would be so far-fetched an idea."

Avery took a deep breath. The idea was a test balloon to see how Sofia would react. She'd been hesitant to make any suggestion that might seem too "out there." She already felt like an imposter amongst this group of accomplished agents and experienced soldiers. Even Corey, who might not have a resume to match that of

Maddock or Bones, had played an important role in their adventures. And Sofia was as smart as she was beautiful, which would have rankled if she weren't also annoyingly kind and congenial. Though Avery didn't doubt her own skills and knowledge, she feared that the others viewed her as little more than Maddock's little sister.

"Speaking of far-fetched ideas, I have one." She paused, trying to read the expression on Sofia's face, but the archaeologist merely looked at her with polite interest. "We can surf websites filled with crackpot theories about Atlantis all day long."

"And we have," Sofia added with a grin.

"Touché. Anyway, everyone has his or her own theory about the location of Atlantis: Mediterranean, Antarctica, the middle of the Atlantic, you name it. The one point of agreement, however, is that once upon a time, a record of Atlantis' true location did exist."

Sofia's jaw went slack. "You're talking about the lost library of Alexandria."

"Exactly." Avery felt her cheeks warming and she hurried on. "Hear me out. No one questions that the library existed, and though it was destroyed, scholars generally agree that most of its knowledge was dispersed long before its final destruction. Considering what we now know about the power Atlantis wielded, I can't help but believe that information about it would be considered highly important. Surely, someone, somewhere preserved some part of it." She swallowed hard and waited for Sofia's response.

Sofia sat in silence for several seconds. "It's an angle I considered. In fact, I had just begun researching it when I was diverted by the dig in Spain." Her eyes fell. "Anyway, I agree with you. I think the knowledge is out there somewhere, but I doubt we're going to find it in any of the traditional sources of information."

"So what do we do?" Avery was grateful to be taken seriously.

"In my research, I kept turning up one name: Kirk Krueger. He's an author and researcher who has devoted his life to tracking down the knowledge from the Great Library."

"Are you sure he's not a crackpot?" Avery asked.

Sofia grinned. "I can't say for sure, but he doesn't act like one. For one, he doesn't seek the spotlight. He's a recluse who never makes public appearances and doesn't make guest appearances on those wild theory-based television shows. He hasn't even written any books, for that matter."

"He's definitely not trying to profit off his research, then," Avery said.

"Exactly. Which is why I suspect he might be reliable. He publishes an essay here and there, or makes a post on the discussion board. On even rarer occasions, he'll speak with a fellow researcher, but never on the record."

"Great! Where does this guy live?"

"That's the problem," Sofia said. "I tried to track him down, but he seems to have disappeared."

"You think the Dominion had something to do with it?"

"Considering he disappeared right about the time they hired me, yes."

Avery probably should have found this news discouraging, but instead it only made her more determined. "In that case, I think we need to start a manhunt, and I know a great person to help us."

Chapter 24

"**Another round?**" **Bones** didn't wait for an answer, but headed to the bar and returned with four bottles of Asahi Black.

"Cheers, Bones!" Professor clinked bottles with Bones, Jade, and Maddock, and they all filled their mugs with the dark liquid.

Maddock watched the foamy head dissolve, then took a gulp. The beer wasn't as cold as Maddock would have liked, and was a touch on the heavy side, but it had a strong flavor that reminded him of coffee beans with a hint of dark chocolate. They were lucky to have found any sort of bar on this tiny island.

"I didn't think we'd find a bar on this island, much less a dive like this," Bones said, echoing Maddock's thoughts. "My kind of place." There was nothing about the place, save the clientele, to remind them they were in Japan. This bar, with its musty air seasoned with the sour aroma of spilled beer, uneven wood floor, chipped Formica-top bar, and cheap neon beer signs, would have fit in any number of places back in the States.

"It's for the tourists, as few as they are." Jade picked at the wrapper on her bottle. Her attitude toward Maddock had warmed, but the air between them crackled with unease.

They sat in discouraged silence, watching the beams of afternoon sunlight journey across the mats that lined the floor.

"What do we do now?" Jade finally asked. "Go door-to-door asking if anyone has seen an alien-looking machine that might have belonged to the Atlanteans?"

"It's a small island," Professor mused. "Maybe we start with the recreational divers. Surely somebody knows something." He took a sip of beer and glanced at Jade.

"I don't know. I'm still too stunned to think straight. Who would have thought we'd find an Atlantean temple only to find someone's beaten us to it?" She sighed and ran a finger down the side of her untouched mug.

"I don't suppose there's a library or local newspaper we could check out?" Maddock doubted it, but he had no better idea. He glanced at Bones, who sat with his chair rocked back on two legs, grinning broadly. "What are you smiling about?"

"You guys are thinking about this all wrong." Bones took a long, slow drink, dragging out the moment.

"So, enlighten us." Jade put a foot on the front stretcher of Bones' chair and slammed it down to the floor.

"Careful, chick. You almost made me spill my drink." Seeing her angry look, he hurried on. "A tiny place like this where pretty much everyone has lived in the same place for generations, what you want is a storyteller." He frowned at their blank looks. "You know, the revered old dude who knows everyone and all their secrets. Every small community has at least one. That's where we should start." He took another drink, a self-satisfied expression on his face.

Jade considered this. "It's not the worst idea. I'll see what I can learn." She rose from the table and approached the only other occupied table. The three men, all middle-aged Japanese men with weathered faces, watched her approach with unconcealed eagerness.

Maddock felt his fists clench, wondering if he'd have to intervene, but Jade remained unfazed, pulling up a chair without waiting for an invitation, and chatting away.

"I thought Japanese men didn't appreciate assertive women," Bones said.

"See the way they're looking at her?" Professor smiled. "She can do anything she wants. Clever and beautiful. It's a dangerous combination."

Maddock shifted in his seat and took a sudden interest in the world outside the dirty window by the front door.

After a brief conversation, Jade returned to the table, smiling. "I've got a name and directions. Let's go."

Daisuke Tanaka lived in a shack overlooking the sea. Wrinkled and graying, he sat on the ground, a bottle of beer in one hand, and watched their approach with suspicious eyes.

Jade stopped a few paces away and bowed low. Maddock and the others awkwardly followed suit. Finally, the man inclined his head, and they straightened. At the advice of the men in the bar, Jade had brought along a half-dozen bottles of beer, and Daisuke's eyes immediately wandered to them.

"Daisuke-San," Jade began, but the old man waved her into silence.

"Please, just Daisuke. I'm too disreputable for *San.*"

Jade smiled. "Daisuke, we're archaeologists, and would like to learn more about Yonaguni, specifically the monument, and we were told you are the man to ask."

"I see you brought payment." He pointed to the ground in front of him and Jade laid the beer down. "Sit."

There was nowhere to sit but the ground, so they settled down in a circle.

"Your English is excellent," Bones said.

"So is yours." Daisuke drained his beer, opened another, and took a long drink. "Almost as good as this beer."

Maddock waited to see if he would offer his guests a drink, but no luck. Daisuke made short work of the second beer and opened a third. Maddock was just beginning to wonder if they'd have to wait for him to finish the entire six-pack when Daisuke finally spoke again.

"It begins with the dragons."

"Dragons?" Jade asked.

"Many call this," he gestured toward the water, "The Dragon Sea." It is haunted by the spirits of the dragons that protected Japan in ages past."

Maddock and Bones exchanged surreptitious glances. This could get weird.

For the next hour, Daisuke regaled them with stories of sudden storms, lost ships, and spectral apparitions. By the time full dark was upon them, Maddock was convinced they were in the midst of another Bermuda Triangle.

"What can you tell us of the monument?" Maddock asked when it seemed Daisuke had run out of steam.

The old man thought for a moment. "I dove there many times when the place was first discovered. I probably know them better than anyone." He took a drink. "It was once the home of an ancient people who are now gone."

"Who were they?" Bones asked.

"No one knows, but they left behind the curse of the dragons to protect their city. That is why the storms claim so many ships. To keep them from uncovering what they should not."

"Not good for tourism," Jade said. "I understand Yonaguni hopes to become a popular destination for divers."

"Tourists." Daisuke virtually spat the word. "Fouling the island and the waters. I think the dragons hate them too. Lots of their little boats find our sea inhospitable." His laugh was coarse like sandpaper.

"Have many divers explored the location?" Maddock asked.

"Not too many. The dragons chase them away." Daisuke laughed again.

Jade bit her lip and glanced at Professor before asking the question that lay foremost in their minds. "Have you heard tell of anyone bringing back any artifacts from the monument?"

"Artifacts?" Daisuke asked sharply.

"I mean… relics of whatever civilization lived there." Jade continued. "Any rumors at all? It might have been years ago."

"No." He returned to his beer, turned his gaze back to the sea, and his eyes went cloudy.

After a few minutes of silence, they made a few more attempts at conversation, but the old man had clammed up. They might as well have been invisible for all the acknowledgment they received from him. Finally, discouraged, they returned to the house where Jade and Professor were staying.

Maddock sat staring at the moon and turning his cell phone over in his hands. He had tried calling Angel, but she was still letting his calls go to voicemail. Since they'd last spoken, his only communication from her had been a couple of curt text messages saying she was busy and they would talk later. He sighed deeply and gazed down at the blank screen, wondering if he should give it one more try. A gust of cool air, moist with the damp of the sea, made him shiver, but he didn't go inside. Right now, he needed the quiet.

"Somebody's being antisocial."

He looked up to see Jade standing behind his chair.

"I figure it's more comfortable for both of us if I give you space," he said.

"Don't be like that, Maddock." She laid her hands on his shoulders and began kneading the taut muscles as she had done so many times in the past. "I know I gave you a hard time when you got here, but can you blame me? You know what they say about a woman scorned."

Maddock closed his eyes and felt the tension drain away. Jade had the perfect touch—just enough pressure to work out the knots but soft enough to turn a man to butter. It was one of the things he'd always loved about her. His eyes popped open and he stiffened again. "You know it was never going to work between us, don't you?"

Before she could reply, Bones called out from the doorway.

"Hey you two, Professor thinks he's on to something."

Jade jerked her hands away as if she'd been burned, and Maddock sprang to his feet.

"Great," he said. "Let's see it."

He followed Jade back to the house. When she disappeared through the front door, Bones grabbed Maddock's arm.

"What the hell is going on out here?"

"Nothing." Maddock yanked his arm free. His first instinct was to tell Bones to mind his own business, but his friend deserved an explanation. "I was trying to call Angel, and Jade came out and started talking to me."

"She was doing a little more than that." Bones raised an eyebrow.

"She just started rubbing my shoulders and, before I could say anything, you stuck your big head out the door and interrupted us. You've always had bad timing."

Bones folded his arms and looked down at Maddock with the air of a disapproving schoolteacher. "You have any witnesses to back up your story?" And then he grinned. "Maddock, if I didn't know you were one of the good guys, I'd probably kick your ass right now, but I guess you've at least earned a little bit of trust over the years."

Maddock relaxed a little. "There's nothing going on. You've got my word on it."

"But will it stay that way if Angel keeps ignoring your calls? If it takes us a while to find whatever was taken from the temple, you and Jade are going to be working at close quarters. Can you handle it?"

For all his clowning and buffoonery, Bones could be insightful when he made the effort.

Maddock met his friend's eye and gave a single nod.

"Good enough for me. Let's see what Professor has for us."

Inside, Professor paced back and forth, almost bouncing with scarcely contained excitement. He held a roll of papers and slapped them into his open palm.

"I think," he began, grinning at Maddock and Bones, "that our friend Daisuke knows more than he is letting on."

Chapter 25

"**What do you** mean?" Maddock asked, now interested.

"I did some checking on Daisuke. He was in the papers all the time, back when the monument was first discovered. Basically, there were two camps: one sought to use the discovery as a way to bring in more divers and tourists, and draw attention to Yonaguni; the other wanted exactly the opposite."

"No need to hazard a guess as to which one Daisuke belonged," Maddock said.

"Definitely not. In fact, he was the most extreme of his group. He wasn't only opposed to tourism; he didn't even want researchers to visit the site. He wanted it completely closed off."

"I can't totally blame him," Bones said. "Even the best of the academics can disrespect sites that others hold sacred. Just ask my people."

"That's an interesting angle considering some of the things you and Maddock have done." The corner of Jade's mouth twitched.

"I'm a complex man, my dear." Bones winked. "And, as I recall, you were along for a few of our hijinks."

Jade fixed him with a disapproving look and then turned back to Professor. "But what makes you think he knows something about the missing device?"

"I've been researching the Dragon Sea and I've learned that most of the problems he talked about— the storms, shipwrecks, lost sailors, happened in the past twenty-five years."

The others absorbed the information for a moment.

"So?" Bones asked. "What does that mean for us?"

"By itself, nothing." Professor unrolled the papers he was holding. "This is a map of the Dragon Sea. I've plotted the locations of the various incidents. What do you see?"

"They're pretty much all in a single place. Or at least, very close together." Jade rested her chin on her hand and nodded.

"So you think the missing Atlantean device is causing all these problems?" Maddock asked.

"I've heard crazier." Bones tugged absently at his ponytail. "I mean, the device the Dominion found, and presumably the one you recovered, causes tsunamis, so why not another device that affects the seas?"

Maddock glanced at Professor and saw he was grinning. "There's something you haven't told us yet."

"What if," Professor began, "I told you that this spot right here," he uncapped a ballpoint pen and made a dot on the coastline, "is Daisuke's house?"

Bones and Jade looked puzzled, but Maddock immediately saw where Professor was headed. "You think he's got the device?"

Professor nodded sagely.

"Wait. What?" Bones looked from one man to the other.

"You might be right," Jade whispered. "He said he was one of the first to discover the monument, and he…"

"… hates tourists with a bitter passion," Bones finished. "Let's kick his ass."

"Maybe we should leave you here," Maddock said to Bones. "Professor's idea makes sense, but it's still pretty far-fetched. We need to investigate, not come down on the guy like an avalanche."

"Show of hands. Who votes avalanche?" Bones raised his hand and looked at the others. "You guys suck."

"Don't worry about it. This way, you get to use some of that famous Native American stealth you're always bragging about." Maddock turned to Jade and Professor. "All right, folks, it's time to devise a plan of attack."

Two hours later they anchored off the coast a short distance from Daisuke's home. This time, Jade had drawn the short straw, and would wait with the boat while the others made the dive. To Maddock's surprise, she had acquiesced with only the slightest protest when he pointed out that, of the four of them, the three former Navy SEALs were most likely to be able to complete their task without being seen.

After a brief, invigorating swim, they found themselves at the cliff below the house. As they had planned, Bones stripped off his fins and quickly scaled the rock wall. He would keep a lookout while Maddock and Professor searched. Maddock had reasoned that the device would not be inside the old man's home, but hidden somewhere nearby, in a place with a good view of the sea. Using his map, Professor had determined what he considered to be the likely starting point: a central point from which the old man, or an accomplice, could have used the device on unsuspecting ships.

Maglite in his teeth, Maddock ascended the cliff. He was an experienced climber, so he would take the high ground while Professor would cover the area just above the shore. His fingers dug deep into the cracks and crevices and his feet searched for toeholds as he made his way up. He tried to bear the weight mostly on his legs, but in a few places, he had to swing from one spot to another with only his arms holding him up. He soon felt the burn in his neck, shoulders, and lower back, but it was a good feeling. In the early days of their friendship, when they still had not learned to trust one another fully, he and Bones had bonded over their mutual interest in climbing. The first time he had met Angel was when Bones took him back to North Carolina on a climbing trip. She had just finished high school then, and a relationship with her had been the furthest thing from his mind. In fact, he found her abrasive and annoying. A lot had changed over time. The memory made him smile.

"Find anything yet?" Bones' whispered question startled him.

"Did I say I found something?"

"Touchy. The house is dark, so I'm going to scout along the cliff. I figure, if he comes down here regularly, he might have worn a path, and he definitely would need a way to climb down."

"Definitely," Maddock agreed. "Of course, it's hard to imagine Daisuke scaling a cliff."

"Don't be so sure. My grandfather kept climbing well into his sixties, until my grandmother put her foot down."

"I imagine you'll be a lot like your grandfather. Now, shut up and let me work."

Maddock turned his attention back to his climb, ignoring the obscene gesture that he knew Bones was directing his way. Down below, over the gentle rush of the surf, he heard Professor picking his way through the rocks.

"Somebody's forgotten how to be quiet," Maddock said, just loud enough to be heard.

"I figured if you two Marys could have coffee and conversation, there wasn't much need for stealth," Professor replied. "You do remember we have communication devices, don't you?" He tapped his ear.

Maddock shook his head, though he doubted his friend could see him in the dim light. Was everyone going to bust his chops?

He continued to work his way along the cliff face. Although he wanted to find Daisuke's hiding place, if it existed, he was enjoying himself nonetheless. What if he gave up treasure hunting altogether? He could move to North Carolina with Angel and they could spend their free time up in the mountains doing what they loved. For a moment, he imagined them sitting on the porch of a mountain cabin watching the sun set.

So distracted was he by the daydream that he almost fell when his right foot came down in empty space. He cursed and dug in his fingertips. Idiot! He'd been climbing instinctively, and lost his focus.

He turned his light downward and saw that he had stumbled across a recessed area over a rock ledge. Inspecting the area above, he could just make out what looked like handholds carved in the rock. His heart skipped a beat. Could this be it? Cautiously, he dropped down onto the ledge and looked around. It was a narrow space, not much wider than his shoulders. He could see how it could easily be overlooked by passersby. But, when he shone his light back, he was disappointed.

There was nothing here but a rock wall.

His shoulders sagged, and he let his hands fall to his sides. He'd been so sure. And then something on the ground caught his attention. A glint of metal. He dropped to a knee and brushed aside loose gravel and sand, revealing an iron ring. Smiling, he took hold of cold metal, and pulled.

A hinged trapdoor, one meter square, swung up and to the side until it rested against the rock wall. He shone his light inside, revealing a padlocked door. Smiling, he called for Bones and Professor, this time remembering to turn on his mic and speak in a low voice. His companions joined him a few minutes later.

"Bones, do you think you can pick that lock?" Maddock knew that Bones had some skills in that area, developed during his teenage years.

"Easy as picking my nose," Bones assured him. Flashing a roguish grin, he slid down through the trapdoor and went to work on the lock.

"He really hasn't grown up at all over the years, has he?" Professor asked.

"Would we really want him any other way?" Maddock chuckled and considered his own question. The truth was, he wasn't always sure of the answer.

"We are in," Bones called a minute later.

Maddock and Professor followed him through the door and froze. They were inside a small cave. The walls and ceiling showed signs of past habitation. Soot stained the ceiling, storage niches were carved in the walls, and an array of broken tools and household items lay scattered across the floor. But it was the thing in the center of the room that rendered them speechless.

Their triple beams of light shone on what could only be an Atlantean device.

"What the hell is it?" Bones finally asked.

"It definitely looks like a weapon of some sort," Professor said.

Maddock had to agree. Standing on a makeshift bamboo tripod, the device looked to him like an oversized titanium telescope. On one end, he saw a trigger and what looked like an eyepiece, perhaps for sighting in a target. On the other end, four crystals came together in a point. He reached out and ran his hand along its perfect surface. Even after seeing the other device, it amazed him that the Atlanteans could have done such precise metalwork so many millennia ago.

"What kind of metal is this?" Professor ran the beam of his Maglite up and down its length. "Titanium?"

"They're still running tests on the device we recovered," Maddock said, "but my money is on something previously unknown."

"A previously unknown metal? What are the odds?"

Maddock and Bones exchanged looks. Once before, they had encountered such a metal. What if there was a connection? It was too much to consider at the moment.

"What are these things?" Bones pointed to a row of depressions running along the top of the cylinder near the eyepiece. They were of varying shapes and sizes. Clearly they served a purpose.

"Maybe it's where they put the crystals that powered it."

"But if this thing runs on crystal power, how did Daisuke use it?" Bones mused.

Maddock looked around and found the answer almost immediately. Nearby lay an old dive bag, and when he opened it and shone his light inside, he found what he was looking for.

"This is how." He reached inside and scooped out a handful of crystals. The shapes, sizes, and colors were varied, as were the quality. Some were finely shaped gems, while others were raw stones in smoky hues of blue and green.

Bones took one and held it up, shining his Maglite so that the beam refracted in tiny slivers of red all over the cave. "This one looks like it was made to go into this first slot. Should I try it?"

"No!" Maddock and Professor exclaimed in unison.

"Just kidding." Bones tossed the crystal back into the bag. "Where do you think he got all these?"

"I'll bet he found them in the temple. He was probably the first person to discover it, so I imagine he cleaned the place out."

"And then he used it as his own high-tech, *Keep Out* sign." Bones shook his head. "I'd love to see his face when he comes down here and finds it gone."

Maddock put his arms underneath the device and checked its weight. It was astonishingly light. They would have no problem getting it out of here. He replaced it on the tripod.

"Let's call Jade and let her know we found it. Then, we need to touch base with Tam and have her make arrangements to get this thing home. I don't think we can put it in our checked luggage, and I'm not sure it will fit in the overhead bin."

"Wait a minute." Professor frowned. "Shouldn't we notify the authorities? If he's been using this thing to cause ship wrecks, and who knows what else, he should be made to pay."

"Good idea," Bones said. "As soon as we get back to the house, you can call the police and let them know that a local drunk found a weapon from Atlantis, and used it to turn the Dragon Sea into the Bermuda Triangle."

Professor's jaw went slack as he considered Bones' words. Finally he laughed. "Okay. I'll defer to your judgment. I don't have as much experience as you with this sort of thing."

"Stick with us." Maddock clapped his friend on the shoulder. "You'll have all you can stand."

Chapter 26

Are you sure we're in the right place?" Sofia looked doubtfully at the bookstore facade. Perched in front of a four-lane highway, the big, square building with large glass panes across the front looked like an old grocery store.

"Jimmy says his debit card is swiped in the coffee shop here every weekday around this time," Avery said. Jimmy Letson was an accomplished hacker and an old friend of Maddock's. He'd done a little searching on their behalf, and discovered that Kirk Krueger was living in Rachel, Nevada under the name James Ronald. Tam had sent Avery, Sofia, and Willis to search for him.

"So this road is seriously called the Extraterrestrial Highway?" Willis asked.

"It's the town closest to Area 51," Avery said. "It's small, but it draws a fair number of tourists."

"Kind of weird, a conspiracy theory nut living this close to Area 51, of all places, don't you think?" Willis ran a hand across his shaved scalp.

"Perhaps he's hiding in plain sight?" Sofia offered. "I guess we can ask him when we find him."

"How about we get going?" Avery said. "We'll go in separately and do some browsing. If one of us spots him, text the others."

"Look at the little girl taking charge." Willis smiled indulgently.

"You have a problem with that?"

"No, girl. It's just the Maddock in you coming out."

"Whatever. Remember, I don't want you approaching him," she said to Willis. "Sofia and I are a bit less intimidating. You just hang back in case we need you."

Willis nodded.

"Okay, let's do it." Avery waited until first Willis, then Sofia, entered the store, then followed a minute later. The bookstore was packed with rows of overstuffed shelves teeming with books, DVDs and CDs. New and used items were shelved together. She inhaled the aroma of slightly scorched coffee beans and smiled. This was her kind of place.

She spotted Willis' head bobbing along above the shelves in the movie section. Sofia was nowhere to be seen. Avery thought for a moment. Where might an expert on the lost library browse? She approached the register and asked the sleepy-looking cashier to direct her to the section on ancient mysteries. He waved her toward the back corner of the store and slumped back onto his stool, a defeated look on his face.

The ancient mysteries aisle was empty of customers, so she selected a book at random and wandered toward the coffee shop. Krueger wasn't there. She bought a cup of house blend, one sugar, no cream, in a to-go cup, and resumed her wanderings. She hadn't gone ten steps when her cell phone vibrated. It was a text from Sofia.

Seating area beside the magazines.

Avery rounded the magazine display and found a circle of sofas, chairs, ottomans, and side tables. Sofia was curled up in an overstuffed armchair reading a magazine. Avery couldn't help but notice, and envy, the way Sofia did everything, even sit in a chair, with such natural grace. She wondered, with a touch of resentment, how long it would be before Bones got his hooks into the beautiful archaeologist. Pushing the juvenile thoughts aside, she refocused.

You're here to find someone, she thought. *Where is he?*

And then she spotted him. Directly across from Sofia sat a slender, fair-skinned man with blue eyes. He wore his shockingly blond hair in a flat top cut, and he was clad in jeans and an Oxford cloth shirt. He was flipping through the sports section of the Roswell Daily Register, his coffee untouched on the table beside him.

His eyes barely flitted in her direction as she sat down in the chair next to his. She smiled and he made the faintest of nods before returning to his paper. She took a sip of coffee, opened her book, and pretended to read. She'd inadvertently grabbed a book titled Mysteries of the Ancient World, and now wondered if Krueger would notice and fear something was amiss. Way to be heavy-handed, Avery.

Out of the corner of her eye, she spotted Willis loitering in front of the magazines—the Playboys, to be exact. The guy had spent too much time with Bones. She glanced at Sofia, who looked meaningfully at Krueger and nodded once. Avery took a deep breath.

"Excuse me, could I borrow the front page?"

Krueger looked up at her, surprised, and then held out the front page section. As Avery accepted it, she leaned in close and whispered, "We need to speak to you, Mister Krueger."

Krueger sat up straight. "I'm sorry," he mumbled. "You have the wrong person."

"Please," Sofia said, unfolding her legs and leaning toward him, urgency in her eyes. "We need your help."

"There's nothing I can help you with." He folded his paper and made to rise, but Avery stood and blocked his way.

"Too many people have already died. We need your help to stop it."

"People you've killed," Krueger retorted. "I don't know how you found me, but I promise you, I won't go down without a fight." He reached down and grabbed the cuff of his jeans.

Avery's stomach lurched as she caught a glimpse of a small revolver, and then Willis was there. He seized Krueger's wrists from behind and held him still.

"No need for that. Whoever you're running from, we ain't them."

Alarmed, Krueger looked back at Willis and then, strangely, relaxed.

"You're right. You aren't."

Willis released Krueger and sat down on the arm of the chair on the side of Krueger opposite Avery. From there, he could be on the man in an instant should he make another try for his weapon.

"I'm glad you can see that," she said. "Do you know who's after you?"

"I don't know who, exactly, they are, but I know what they want and why. Best I can tell, they're no better than Nazis. They probably saw my surname, saw a picture of me, and figured I'd be a sympathizer." He smirked at Avery. "I could believe you were one of them, but a Latina and a black man? Not a chance. Tell your friend to relax." He tilted his head toward Willis. "I'm not going to run, and I definitely won't try for my gun again."

"Glad to hear it." Avery waved at Willis, and he slid down into his chair, though he still appeared as tense as a runner waiting for the starting pistol.

"So, who are you and what do you want?" Krueger asked.

"We're part of a team dedicated to rooting out the people who are after you," Sofia said.

"Who are they, exactly?"

"We're not supposed to talk about that." Avery bit her lip, wondering how he would respond.

"If you want my help, you're going to have to trust me, at least a little bit." Krueger's gaze was rock hard.

"Fine. They're called the Dominion. They claim to be a Christian group, and they have roots in many churches, but they've also infiltrated branches of government. We're new to the team and aren't privy to all the information our director has, but their leanings definitely tend toward Nazi beliefs." Avery paused while Krueger mulled this over.

"What are their aims? Overthrow the government?"

"More like take it over organically," Avery said. "For some time now, they've been building their power in the shadows, both in the religious and secular spheres. But something they did very recently leads us to believe they're either changing their strategy or, more likely, expanding it."

Krueger frowned at her.

"Did you hear about the tsunami that struck Key West?" Kruger said he had, and Avery filled him in on what they knew, and what they thought they knew, about the disaster.

Krueger stared at her for a full ten seconds, and then he laughed.

"Atlantis? Right. Tell you what, I'll let you get back to your book," he tapped the book on ancient mysteries, "and your whacked-out ideas. I need to find a new town and create a new identity."

"Would you like to see some pictures of the weapon?" Sofia asked softly.

Krueger froze, half in, half out of his chair.

Sofia took out her iPad and flipped through a series of images, all showing the Atlantean device they had recovered off the coast of Cuba. Next, she showed him several images of the temple, all screenshots taken from the submarine's video feed. Finally, she showed him the pictures she had taken of the temple in Spain before its destruction.

"Mister Krueger," she began, "I'm not a crackpot conspiracy theorist. I don't believe in Bigfoot or Nessie."

"Don't let Bones hear you say that," Willis interjected.

Sofia rolled her eyes and continued. "I've already found two cities that we believe were part of the Atlantean civilization. We've seen the devastation wrought by a single Atlantean weapon, and the codex hints that the mother city holds an even deadlier weapon. We must get there before the Dominion."

"Why do you need me?" Krueger asked weakly.

"You know why." Avery looked him hard in the eye and he seemed to melt under her gaze.

"I suppose I do. If Atlantis was real, and it seems that it is," he glanced at Sofia's iPad, "that means it's likely that the Great Library contained information about it."

"Can you help us find it?" Avery held her breath while Kruger looked at the three of them in turn, a lingering look of disbelief in his eyes. Finally, the last remnants of skepticism appeared to fall away.

"I think I can."

Chapter 27

"Mexico." Matt looked down at the fresh stamp on the fake passport Tam had provided for him. "This wasn't what I expected when they invited us on a camping trip."

"Not much to see out here." Despite the situation, Joel managed to sound bored.

Matt gazed out the window of the van in which they rode. The dull brown of the hilly landscape was speckled with a touch of green here and there, but there was no forest to be seen. Since they'd left the Villalobos Airport in Chihuahua, they'd seen little more than dust and dirt.

"I'm told the camping isn't the best." Bill glanced at them in the rear-view mirror. "But the caving is supposed to be out of this world."

"Caving, huh? Sounds like fun." Joel's eyes widened and his voice held a tone of forced bravado.

"Claustrophobic?" Matt whispered, but his friend didn't answer.

"I don't care for it myself. I don't fit too well into small places." Bill barked a laugh and Matt and Joel joined in. "I'll be staying back at the campground, running things."

"What's there to run?" Matt asked. He didn't miss the glance Bill stole at Greer, another member of the men's group, who was seated in the passenger seat. It was just the four of them, and a ton of equipment. The remaining seven members of their party rode in a second van.

"Just camping stuff," Bill said. "Planning the meals and the Bible study and stuff."

"Has your group done much caving?" Matt asked, more to alleviate boredom than out of any interest.

"This is the first time. The mother church is sending a man down from Utah to be our guide. He'll have special equipment for us."

Matt perked up at the mention of Utah. "What's the name of the mother church?"

"The Kingdom Church." Bill looked like he was about to say more, but Greer silenced him with a tiny shake of his head.

Matt considered this new information. According to Tam, the Kingdom Church, led by Bishop Hadel, was believed to be, if not the headquarters of the Dominion in America, one of its strongest outposts. She had been trying for some time to gain evidence of Hadel's connection to the organization, and hinted that she was coming closer by the day.

They rode in silence through a small town called Naica, and stopped in the foothills to the west of the city. They climbed out and looked around. There was nothing to distinguish this flat patch of brown dirt from the rest of the landscape, but Bill called it a "campground," and began unloading the van. By the time a forest green jeep bounced up the dirt road and parked alongside the van, they had set up camp. Matt and Joel, as the new guys, had been tasked to dig the latrine, and both were coated in dust and sweat by the time they finished.

The newcomer, who introduced himself as Robinson, had them pile back into their vans and follow him to a mining operation. While everyone milled around the vans, Robinson went to speak with someone. Pretending to look at the mountains, Matt wandered out of sight of the group and fired off a quick text to Tam.

Caving in Naica, Mexico. Man from Kingdom Church is here.

As soon as he'd sent the text, he deleted it from his Sent Messages folder, pocketed the phone, and returned to the group. Robinson emerged from a dilapidated-looking office building a few minutes later and led them into the worksite.

A man in a hardhat with a light on the front, who introduced himself as Rivera, led them down through the mine until they finally stopped in a hollowed-out chamber of gray stone. Conduit ran along the walls and down the middle of the ceiling above, where lights hung every twenty feet or so. When Bill had said they were going caving, Matt had expected cool, even chilly caverns, but it was hot in here. Uncomfortably hot.

Rivera stopped in front of a metal door and turned to face them. He was a tall, thin Latino man with a wispy mustache and a thin beard that didn't quite cover his pockmarked face.

"On the other side of this door is the Crystal Cave of Giants," he began in lightly accented English. "It was discovered by accident during mining operations in the year 2000. Inside, more than three hundred meters below the surface, you will find the largest crystals known to mankind. The largest are more than ten meters long and weigh up to fifty five tons." He paused to let that sink in.

He went on to describe the makeup and formation of the crystals, and give them a brief description of the caverns, including the dangers.

"Footing can be treacherous inside, and many of the crystals are razor sharp. If you slip, you can find yourself impaled on a selenium spike. In fact, one of the chambers is called the Cave of Swords because the walls are coated with dagger-like crystals. But that is not the greatest danger the cavern poses."

The group members exchanged glances. A cave brimming with crystal swords ready to slice them apart seemed dangerous enough to them.

"Because the cave rests above a magma chamber, the air temperature is more than fifty degrees Celsius, or more than one hundred-twenty degrees Fahrenheit. The relative humidity of ninety percent makes the air feel more than double those temperatures. Without proper protection, you will quickly lose your higher brain functions, which increases the chance of a fatal fall." He smiled, as if pleased by the thought. "In as few as fifteen minutes, your body will begin to shut down, and death follows soon after. No one lasts more than thirty minutes."

The words scarcely registered with Matt. As soon as Rivera said the word "crystal," he knew why they were here. Somewhere in these caverns, the Dominion believed they would find crystals that could power the Atlantean machines, and they'd sent the more than expendable members of the men's group into this deadly environment. He looked at Robinson, who wore a revolver on his hip and an expression of calm determination. He wondered if the man had any intention of letting the men leave here alive. He thought about messaging Tam, but he knew he'd get no signal so far below the earth's surface.

They were on their own.

Chapter 28

"We need to know what this thing does." Bones looked like a kid on Christmas morning as he looked over the Atlantean weapon. "Let me and Maddock take it out into the middle of the Gulf and give it a shot. Pun intended."

"I don't like it. What if it you set off some sort of natural disaster?" Tam gritted her teeth. She hated not knowing what this device could do, but was averse to the risks inherent in testing it.

"Why didn't you interrogate the old man and learn from him how it worked?"

"You didn't meet him," Maddock said. "I can read men, and this one was as stubborn as they come. We would have had to torture the information out of him, and he didn't deserve that."

"Tell that to the families of the men who lost their lives in those storms he cooked up," Tam snapped.

"It doesn't matter now. We didn't extract the information from him, and we need to know how this thing works." Maddock softened his voice. "Obviously, Daisuke experimented with the weapon before he used it against anyone, and he didn't set off any natural disasters—only small, localized events. I give you my word we'll exercise caution."

Tam sighed. What Maddock said made sense, and a good leader didn't ignore reason just because it came from an underling. Like her grandfather used to say, "Sooner or later, a stiff neck breaks."

"All right. I'm relying on you to keep the big dummy," she pointed at Bones, "under control."

"Great. We'll need Corey."

"I can't spare him. You can break in our two new team members. Don't argue with me!" she added sharply. "I've heard all I'm going to hear about Ihara and Professor. I have my damn good reasons for wanting them on board, and I didn't tell you before because I don't want to listen to your hissy fits. You're on the team; she's on the team. Deal with it."

"How long until my debt to you is paid in full?" Maddock's tone was perfectly polite and nothing more.

"When the Dominion is finished. Now you two get this contraption out of here before I change my mind."

Maddock hefted the device and carried it out of the room, Bones following with the bag of crystals.

"Lord, don't let them sink Havana," she muttered. Behind her, Kasey leaned against the wall, gazing thoughtfully at Tam. "Do you have a question?"

"What's the story with Maddock and Ihara?"

"Why do you need to know?"

"Because we're a team, and if there's an issue between them that could affect the way we work together, I want to know about it." Kasey grimaced. "I'm not questioning your choice. I just want to know."

"They used to be an item, but Maddock dumped her in favor of Bones' sister."

"Awkward," Kasey said.

"Very. But Ihara is an asset. I've profiled her thoroughly, and she's smart, tough, and resourceful. She's got a lot of what Maddock has, and I know for a fact she's not hooked up with the Dominion. In fact, she wants to see them done in as much as I do."

Kasey frowned.

"Don't ask why. That's her story to tell."

"Fair enough. Any word from Avery?"

"They found their target and are proceeding as planned." Tam's cell phone vibrated. "It's a text from Matt." She read the message twice. "Do you know anything about caves in Naica, Mexico?"

"No. Hold on." Kasey moved to a nearby computer and performed a quick search.

"It's a small city in Chihuahua, about a hundred and fifty miles south of the border. Not much there except for mining operations." Kasey paused as she scrolled down the page. "The only cave I see mentioned is one that houses the biggest crystals in the world."

"Crystals?" Tam's blood turned to ice. Her eyes snapped to the crystal skull resting on a table, and then to the machine they'd recovered from the Cuban temple. "Lord Jesus, if they've found a way to power their tsunami machine…"

"Every city on the coast is in danger." Kasey's eyes went wide.

"I need boots on the ground in Naica as soon as possible. Call Maddock back, and tell Greg to scare up weapons and transportation. I want you three there as soon as humanly possible."

"You realize what this means?" Kasey said as she headed for the door. "Bones is going to try out that weapon without adult supervision."

"One battle at a time, sweetie. One battle at a time."

Chapter 29

"We're going to go inside the caves without protective gear. We will only stay for fifteen minutes. The purpose is to impress upon you just how dangerous the heat and humidity are." The guide turned, unlocked the door, and opened it.

Matt didn't need any convincing. It seemed like common sense. But, he followed the others inside.

The heat assailed him immediately. His knees trembled the moment he hit the wall of hot, damp air. His discomfort, though, was immediately forgotten when his eyes took in his surroundings.

The cave was magnificent. The giant crystals, gleaming in the dim light, were so huge as to give the experience a dreamlike quality. They were everywhere, jutting up at angles like countless, miniature Washington Monuments. He glanced at Joel, who appeared immune to the magic of the caves. His eyes flitted from one member of the group to the next, his face set in a look of concentration.

"What's up?" Matt kept his voice low.

"Just keeping an eye on things. I don't trust any of these men."

His words reminded Matt that they weren't here for sightseeing. He searched out Robinson, who stood off to the side, his expression bored and detached.

There was nothing memorable about Robinson; nothing to make him stand out in a crowd. To an ex-military man like Matt, however, subtle clues named the newcomer a fellow veteran: his posture, the way he walked, his general bearing. Of course, a military background wasn't a crime, but knowing he was associated with the Kingdom Church made him someone upon whom Matt and Joel would want to keep a close eye. Matt and the rest of Maddock's crew had run afoul of the Dominion's paramilitary elements too many times not to be on his guard around someone like Robinson.

"This place gets to you, doesn't it?" Bill came staggering up to Matt. "I'm feeling a little…" His legs gave out and Matt grabbed him before he collapsed.

"I think he needs to get out of here." Matt, aware of how weak he, too, felt, looked at Robinson, whose face remained impassive.

"All right." Robinson motioned to Rivera, who ushered the group back out through the door.

The temperature in the tunnel outside the crystal cave was probably more than ninety degrees, but stepping through the doorway felt like being immersed in a cool bath. Rivera opened a cooler and passed around bottles of water.

Robinson moved to the center of the circle of men, his presence commanding their immediate attention. "We'll take a ten minute breather," he began, "after which, we'll suit up and get to work."

"We're starting right now?" Bill sat with his back against the wall, clutching his water bottle like a lifeline.

"We have work to do, and it needs to be done quickly."

No one in the group seemed surprised at this. Apparently, only Joel and Matt had been led to believe this was a recreational trip.

"Do the rest of us need to be armed?" Matt asked.

"What?" The question had caught Robinson off guard.

"I notice you're carrying, though I can't imagine what we might encounter in there. Some kind of underground dwellers?" He forced a grin and the others chuckled.

Robinson's face turned to stone, but softened in an instant. The smile he directed at Matt didn't quite reach his eyes.

"Just a habit. I won't be carrying inside."

Matt doubted that very much, but he didn't say so.

"Are you trying to put him on the alert?" It was amazing how well Joel could enunciate without moving his lips. "We're already the new guys. Why call attention to us?"

"I don't know," Matt admitted. "I guess I don't want him thinking he can bully us. Besides, isn't it the new guy's job to ask stupid questions?"

"Only if the new guy is stupid. You might want to let me take the lead until things get physical."

Matt set his jaw. He knew he was clueless as a spy, but he always trusted his instincts, and right now, his gut told him that Robinson needed to know that not all the men in this group were sheep.

"Time to suit up!" Robinson announced.

The suits they donned had two layers—an outer layer fitted with refrigeration tubes connected to a backpack filled with a cooling agent, and an insulating interior layer to protect the skin from the icy tubes. Each man was also outfitted with a breathing apparatus and a futuristic-looking helmet with a light on the forehead.

"I feel like a space marine," one of the group, a man named Davis, said. The others chuckled, except for Robinson and Greer.

Robinson explained that these suits would keep their body temperatures in the normal range for over an hour, and were an improvement over older models that were good for no more than forty-five minutes. "You might milk an hour and a half out of it if you're lucky, but I don't recommend it. You'll be exerting yourselves, which will raise your body heat and exhaust the cooling agent faster than if you were at rest. Exercise caution and good sense."

"Gentlemen, let us take a moment to reflect on our work today." Brother Bill had recovered from his bout of fatigue, and seemed ready to launch into a sermon. A stern look from Robinson nipped that in the bud, and he settled for a reminder that they were about the work of the church, which meant they were doing God's work, and that they numbered twelve, which assured His blessing upon them. When he had finished, they headed back into the cave.

That neither Bill nor Robinson had told them what, exactly, their work would entail, was not lost on Matt. Nor was the lump inside Robinson's suit. Evidently, he'd lied about leaving his weapon behind.

The journey into the caves quickly turned from fascinating to laborious and, finally, to perilous. Several men slipped on the slick surface and just missed impaling themselves. They navigated several passageways, the way tight due to the forest of giant crystals in their path.

At one point, they climbed a sheer face seventy five feet high and crawled through a tiny passageway into a new set of caverns, an effort that left Bill gasping for breath and whispering prayers to Jesus.

No telephone pole-sized crystals filled this next system of caves. Instead, the floor, walls, and ceilings bristled with tiny crystal daggers, with the occasional head-high pyramidal-shaped selenite blocks. They navigated the treacherous caves slowly, knowing what would happen if one were to fall on the carpet of sharp crystal.

"How long do you think we've been in here?" Joel finally asked as they exited a winding chamber of white and blue crystal and entered a narrow crevasse.

Matt consulted his mental clock and conservatively estimated they'd been moving for at least thirty minutes.

"Long enough that we'll have to turn back soon if we want to make it back alive. Which means, wherever we're going, we must be almost there."

He was half-right. In the next chamber, they found a large tent into which several air conditioners pumped a steady stream of cool air. Here, the tired men rested and replenished lost fluids while Robinson outlined the next stage of the excursion.

"This is what we are looking for." He held up a tiny spike of transparent crystal. "As you saw on the way here, the crystals so far have all been opaque and white in color. Somewhere beyond this point is a single, tiny cavern filled with crystals of a different sort. I won't go into detail about what makes this special." He brandished the crystal, which, Matt noticed, flickered blue in the glow of the bare bulbs hanging over Robinson's head. "In fact, I don't understand it myself, but that isn't our concern."

He turned to a dry erase board where the cave system had been sketched out. "We've had time to explore and completely eliminate this passageway." He marked a red X over a tunnel that branched out like the limbs of a tree. "These others," he tapped two more lines, "remain unexplored. That's why the map is open-ended in these places. We will divide into two groups and scout them out."

Matt raised his hand. "What if the cave we're looking for is farther than we can go with our cooling suits?"

"Fair question. A caver using the old-style suits managed to reach the cavern, recover this crystal and another, larger one, and make it back safely. That means it should be well within our reach."

"He couldn't tell you where the cave was?" Bill asked.

"Obviously not." A shadow passed over Robinson's face, but he quickly donned another of his phony smiles. "His cooling suit, which relied on ice and chilled water, lost its cooling capacity long before he made it out. He was disoriented and suffering from heat exhaustion by the time he reached the surface. He remembers the way to this cavern, but gets foggy after that." Robinson paused. "Any more questions?" Robinson's tone indicated that questions would be tolerated, but nothing more than that.

A rangy, sandy-haired man named Perkins raised his hand. "Why does the church need crystals? Aren't they part of the new-age heresy?"

"Imagine the rarest, most valuable mineral in the world." Robinson smoothed his gruff voice. "Now imagine the church owned it all. How much would it be worth, and how much good could we do with the proceeds?"

"And imagine how far down the road toward our aims we would be," Greer added. The others nodded, their expressions ranging from solemn to beatific. Once again, Matt realized that he and Joel, as newcomers, were out of the loop on something important.

They donned fresh cooling suits and Robinson divided them into groups of six, putting himself in charge of one of them, and placing Greer at the head of the other. He also handed out small backpacks containing rock hammers, in case they found the cavern quickly and had time to get to work. Matt and Joel found themselves in Robinson's group, along with Perkins, Brother Bill, and a red-haired man named Logan. Before they entered the tunnels, Robinson pulled Matt aside.

His senses on high alert, Matt tensed to fight should Robinson reach for his weapon. Instead, Robinson laid a hand on Matt's shoulder and whispered in a conspiratorial tone.

"Keep an eye on Bill. He's not in good shape, and I can tell you know how to handle yourself."

Matt nodded once but remained silent.

"You served," Robinson said. "I can tell. Army?"

Matt nodded again.

"Rangers?"

"Kicked out," Matt lied. No need to reveal too much.

"It happens." Robinson thanked him in advance for keeping an eye on Bill, and led the way into the passageways.

The final pieces were falling into place in Matt's mind. The Dominion believed these crystals would power the Atlantean machines. But what did they plan to do with them when they got their hands on them? And, more immediately, what would Robinson do once they found the cavern?

He spied a dagger-sized spike of crystal. Slowing, he let the others get ahead of him, hastily used his rock hammer to break it free, and then tucked it into his bag. It might serve as a weapon later.

He caught up with Bill, who was already flagging.

"Are you going to be okay?" Matt asked.

Bill nodded.

"I'm curious. What are these 'aims' Greer mentioned? I realize I'm new to the group, but I'd like to know what I'm working toward."

"It's more than I can tell you right now," Bill huffed. "For the short term, let's just say I wouldn't be buying any real-estate in Savannah if I were you."

Matt's heart lurched. So the Dominion planned to continue destroying cities. The loss in human life and damage to infrastructure aside, should a tsunami strike the Savannah River nuclear plant, it could be an unmitigated disaster.

"But that's small potatoes. Wait until we find the Revelation Machine."

Matt swallowed hard. "What's that?" He tried to keep his tone casual.

"Can't say, exactly. I'm not even supposed to know about it, but I heard talk. When we get ahold of it, we'll make sure the world is a whole lot better than it is today."

Matt forced a smile. Whatever this Revelation Machine was, it didn't sound like something the Dominion ought to get its hands on. Somehow, he had to get word to Tam.

Chapter 30

"The Great Library of Alexandria was like nothing in the world at its time. It held the world's largest collection of books—legend places the catalog at well over half a million scrolls." Krueger handed Avery a coffee table book with a painting of the fabled library on the cover.

He'd taken up residence in Rachel's only apartment complex. From the looks of it, he'd quickly made himself right at home. He'd set up a computer station along with four cheap shelf units stuffed with books and papers.

"How did they get all the books?" Avery thumbed through the pages as she spoke. Unlike Sofia, her own knowledge of the library was limited.

"Any way they could. They borrowed and copied manuscripts or traded them. When a ship came into port, any books on board had to be lent to the library for copying. Sometimes they were even returned." Krueger winked. "Travelers passing through had their books confiscated, though they were reimbursed for them. Basically, anything in the world that was written down, the library tried to make copies."

Krueger filled four cups of coffee and set them on the battered coffee table along with milk and sugar. Avery and Sofia had taken the only chairs, so he and Willis sat on the floor.

"It was burned down, right?" Avery asked.

"It's not that simple. The library gradually declined over several centuries. Fires played a part, but so did war, politics, and religion. There are legends of Christian and Muslim leaders, at different times, ordering documents burned that did not agree with their respective holy books. There's no firm evidence that the more sensational stories are true, but there's no doubt that some of that occurred."

"What about war and politics?" Willis asked.

"If you know the history of Alexandria, it was a Greek city founded in Egypt, eventually taken over by Rome, and torn apart by Roman civil war. We don't know exactly how much of the library was destroyed, but we do know that much of the contents of the library was taken back to Rome."

"I understand that you've managed to trace much of the lost contents," Sofia said. "Can you tell us how?"

Krueger took a drink of coffee and sat in silence for a few seconds, as if weighing his answer.

"First of all, we need to remember that most of the books in the Great Library were copies of books that came from somewhere else. It's not like many of the books were actually written in Alexandria. Virtually all of them existed in other parts of the known world. Also, part of the library's mission was to disseminate information. Sharing knowledge through copying and distributing books was a major part of the daily work. So, it's not completely accurate to call the library "lost." The building was lost—we don't even know where it stood, but the knowledge is still out there."

"All of it?" Avery asked.

Krueger smiled. "Good question. Let me show you my work."

He moved to the computer desk, turned on his laptop, and called up a map of the world. Circles in varying sizes and colors were dotted all across it.

"I'll give you the short version of what I do. I created a master list of all the 'hot' topics, if you will, of the first few centuries of the library's existence: science, philosophy, you name it. To that, I added the names of the great thinkers and teachers of the day, and any scholars who were known to have been associated with the library.

"Next, I searched out the places where knowledge from this period seems to have been preserved."

"You mean, like, in museum collections?" Willis asked.

"Sometimes," Krueger said. "But it goes deeper than that. I looked for cultures or regions where the ancient wisdom appeared to have the greatest impact. I looked for literature that referenced the great teachers and contained unique insights. As you can see, there's plenty." He tapped the touch pad, and only the smallest dots, all pale green, appeared.

"The greatest concentrations are in expected places, like Rome, but there are others." He tapped the pad again, and larger circles, all blue, appeared. "I also considered the historical events, like the Roman civil war, that could affect the dispersal of knowledge."

He fell silent for no apparent reason.

"Are you all right?" Avery asked.

"Sorry. I have a flair for the dramatic." Krueger winked at her. "Finally, I assessed all the legends and theories—even the wacky ones. I evaluated them for frequency, consistency, and whether or not they made sense. Adding them in, you see the end result here."

A final tap and now only a few circles appeared on the map.

"The bright green circles are your repositories of basic knowledge: science, philosophy, and history."

"Cairo, Rome, Paris, London, Washington, no surprises there." Sofia sounded disappointed.

"What about the blue circles?" Avery tapped a fingernail on a blue dot in Washington D.C.

"Those represent arcane knowledge. The special documents that would have been hidden away, either from religious leaders, or by them. Or hidden by governments."

"You think our government is hiding secrets from the ancient world?" Avery asked.

"Come on," Willis chided. "Do you really think there's anything our government won't hide from us?"

"I'm not saying the knowledge is definitely there," Krueger explained. "I'm saying all the signs point to these places. If such knowledge exists, that's likely where it will be found."

"Do you know where, exactly, in Washington?" Sofia rested her hands on Krueger's chair and leaned forward eagerly.

"I have a theory, but that's all that it is."

"What about the other places?" Willis asked.

"Jerusalem. Possibly beneath the Temple Mount, though I suspect whatever was hidden there is long gone. Wewelsburg Castle in Germany—a Nazi stronghold."

"And the other?" Avery asked.

"The Vatican's secret archives."

"You've got to be kidding." Sofia stood and pressed her hands to her temples. "I've tried so many times to get in there. There's no way."

"Well, I do have some good news." Krueger spun about in his chair. "Based on what you've shown me, there's little doubt that Atlantis, or a society that inspired the legend, existed, which means there almost definitely would have been a record in the library. Our best bet, though, is not the library."

Avery wondered if the expression on her face was as dumbstruck as those of Sofia and Willis.

"What is it then?" Sofia asked.

"We want the Egyptian Hall of Records."

"The what?" Avery and Sofia said in unison.

"It's a mythical library supposedly buried under the Great Sphinx of Giza. It's said to have housed the history of the lost continent of Atlantis, plus ancient Egyptian history. Sort of an Egyptian counterpart to the Great Library."

"That don't make sense," Willis argued. "Why wouldn't that knowledge be part of the library at Alexandria?"

"Because Alexandria was, essentially, a Greek city that just happened to be located in Egypt. Alexander the Great founded it. Ptolemy ruled after his death, and was responsible for founding the library. The Egyptians wouldn't have handed their knowledge over to foreigners."

Avery didn't know what to make of this new information. She turned to Sofia, who frowned at Krueger.

"I've never heard of such a place. Like you said, it's mythical."

"So was Atlantis until you found it," Krueger retorted.

"I love how people keep throwing that in my face." Sofia brushed a stray lock of hair out of her face. "All right. Suppose this place is real. How do we go about looking for it?"

"I can help you with that." Krueger smiled. "I know where the doorway is."

Chapter 31

"What do we know about this crystal cave?" Maddock scanned a map of the area where the cave was located. He, Greg and Kasey were winging their way across the Gulf of Mexico in an S-6, a modified version of the Saker S-1, a jet capable of cruising at more than 1,100 kilometers per hour. While unable to reach such speeds, the S-6 could exceed 800 kilometers an hour, and carried six passengers. It was also equipped with an ejection mechanism so passengers could parachute from the plane. He had to hand it to Tam—she had some useful connections.

"The main access is through a mining operation," Kasey said. "It was discovered by accident, and it's only the turbines that pump underground water from the mine that prevent it from flooding. If the mine ever shuts down, the Mexican government will either have to foot the bill for keeping the pumps going, or let the caverns flood." She consulted her notes. "The place is dangerously hot and humid. You have to wear a special suit or you won't last long. We'll have suits waiting for us."

"How do we find Matt once we're there?" Maddock took out a second map, this of the caverns. "There are so many channels to choose from. He could be down any of them."

"Matt *and Joel*," Kasey frowned at Maddock's omission of their team member, "will probably be down one of the passages that hasn't yet been completely mapped. If there's a source of Atlantean crystal, it stands to reason that's where it will be found."

"I just got something from Tam." Greg tapped his iPad and read the message aloud. "Kevin Bray, geologist, was found dead in his apartment in Los Angeles."

"I hope there's more." Kasey didn't look up from her notes.

"There is. His laptop, journal, and all his research were gone. Cash and other valuables were still there. And the kicker? He had recently returned from an excursion to the Cave of the Crystals. According to his colleagues, he got lost, and when he finally made it out, barely alive, he had with him a crystal that he claimed was unlike anything known to science."

"That's promising." Maddock leaned over and read Tam's message for himself. "Friends thought the heat exhaustion had messed with his head."

"I can see how a scientist who, all of a sudden, begins talking about crystal power could seem hippy-dippy to his colleagues," Kasey said. "So, the Dominion got to him first."

"If not, it's one heck of a coincidence." Greg closed the message and consulted his watch. "We're almost there. Get ready to jump."

Chapter 32

"What do you mean, you found the door?" Avery searched Krueger's eyes for signs of deceit, or even humor, but his gaze held firm.

"You've heard of Herodotus?" he asked.

"The Greek historian," Sofia supplied.

"Also known as the Father of History." Avery felt pleased by the others' surprised faces. "I was a history professor. Give me a little credit."

"Herodotus traveled in Egypt sometime after 464 BC," Krueger continued, "and wrote extensively about the nation and its history. In the course of my research, I came across a single piece of his writing that I've never seen anywhere else. It was part of someone's private collection. I don't think the man even knew what he had. To him, it was just another piece in his collection."

"I assume we're talking about a black market collector?" Sofia asked.

"Is that really important right now?" Krueger replied. "Anyway, in this scroll, Herodotus wrote an account of a massive temple complex he called the labyrinth. He said it contained 1,500 rooms and many underground chambers he wasn't permitted to enter."

"I've heard of a labyrinth being uncovered at the Hawara pyramid near the Fayyum oasis," Sofia said.

"One and the same." Krueger drained his coffee and headed to the kitchen for a refill. "Anyone need a warm-up?" he asked, sticking his head through the doorway and holding up the coffee pot.

Avery suspected he was stalling for some reason. Willis apparently had the same feeling, because he stood and began pacing back and forth in front of the windows overlooking the dusty street.

Krueger noticed their discomfort immediately.

"I know I'm dragging this out. The truth is, I'm not a people person, but I do enjoy company every once in a while, and this is the first chance I've had to talk shop with anyone since I went into hiding. I'm having fun."

"We understand," Sofia said. "Can you tell us how Hawara connects to Giza?"

"Funny you should ask. It connects in a literal sense." Kruger pulled a battered notebook down from a shelf and turned a few pages. "Here's what Herodotus writes:

"*There I saw twelve palaces regularly disposed, which had communication with each other, interspersed with terraces and arranged around twelve halls. It is hard to believe they are the work of man. The walls are covered with carved figures, and each court is exquisitely built of white marble and surrounded by a colonnade. Near the corner where the labyrinth ends, there is a pyramid, two hundred and forty feet in height, with great carved figures of animals on it and an underground passage by which it can be entered. I was told very credibly that underground chambers and passages connected this pyramid with the pyramids at Memphis.*"

"Memphis?" Willis asked.

"The ancient capital of Lower Egypt," Sofia said. "As Alexandria rose, it declined. The Giza Plateau, where the Sphinx and Great Pyramids are situated, was a part of Memphis." A tone of skepticism colored her words. "That sounds pretty far-fetched. After all, Herodotus was also called the Father of Lies."

"That name wasn't entirely deserved," Krueger said. "Yes, he had a habit of occasionally presenting his findings through the accounts of fictional eyewitnesses, but he collected folk tales and legends as much as historical fact. Also, many of his claims, even the ones that seemed most doubtful, have proved true. Take Gelonus, for example. No one believed Herodotus when he spoke of a city a thousand times larger than Troy, until it was rediscovered in 1975."

"We can debate Herodotus later," Avery interrupted. "Tell us how this relates to the Hall of Records."

"At first, I was as skeptical as Doctor Perez, so I continued my research and found even more accounts. The historian Crantor spoke of underground pillars that contained a written record of pre-history, and said they 'lined access ways connecting the pyramids.'" Krueger turned a page in his notebook and went on. "I found account after account: Pliny, Marcellinus, Altelemsani, and more. But these are the most powerful." He turned another page. "It's by a Syrian scholar named Iamblichus.

"*This entrance, obstructed in our day by sands and rubbish, may still be found beneath the forelegs of the crouched colossus. It was formerly closed by a bronze gate whose secret spring could be operated only by the Magi. It was guarded by public respect, and a sort of religious fear maintained its inviolability better than armed protection would have done. Beneath the belly of the Sphinx were cut out galleries leading to the subterranean part of the Great Pyramid. These galleries were so artfully crisscrossed along their course to the Pyramid that, in setting forth into the passage without a guide throughout this network, one ceaselessly and inevitably returned to the starting point.*"

He paused, glancing up from his reading, as if to see if they were impressed.

"And this I found on an ancient Sumerian cylinder seal:

"*The knowledge of the Annunaki is hidden in an underground place, entered through a tunnel, its entrance called Hawara, hidden by sand and guarded by a beast called Huwana, his teeth as the teeth of a dragon, his face the face of a lion, is unable to move forward, nor is he able to move back.*"

He closed his notebook with the solemnity of a liturgist.

"What's the Annunaki?" Engrossed by Krueger's tale, Willis had left his post by the window and now stood behind Avery. "I never heard of them."

"Mesopotamian deities," Sofia said. "Their name means, 'royal blood,' or 'princely offspring.' In the Epic of Gilgamesh, they are the seven judges who punish the world before the storm."

"Wait a minute." Avery sat up straighter. The connections were rapidly coming together. "The Epic of Gilgamesh is a flood story. And your translation of the codes indicates that the Atlanteans, for some reason, decided to flood their subordinate cities."

"Precisely!" Kruger said. "It all connects. And when I saw the inscription on Herodotus' tomb, I was convinced he'd had a life-changing experience at, or perhaps somewhere far below, the Sphinx."

"What was the inscription?" Willis asked.

"Herodotus, the son of Sphinx."

They lapsed into silence, with only the low hum of an engine somewhere in the distance to disturb the quiet.

"So, you think there's a door at Hawara that leads to the Hall of Records?"

"I know there is," Krueger said. "In fact, I found the entrance to the hall." His smile vanished in a blink, alarm spreading across his face. "Oh my God," he rasped. "They found us."

Chapter 33

"We'll have to turn back soon." Matt took a gulp of fresh air from his supplementary supply. "Maybe the cavern's not here."

"Is that a bad thing?" Joel asked. "We'd prefer the Dominion not find it."

"If our group discovers it, maybe there's something we can do to stop them in their tracks. If the other group finds it..." He left the rest unspoken.

"I think I've found something!" Up ahead, Logan stood at the edge of a five meter wide fissure. A single, meter-wide crystal spanned the yawing chasm, ending at the entrance to a cavern.

The others moved to join him, all training their lights on the cave.

"But the crystals in there are white, like the others." Bill gestured with his flashlight.

"Not the ones on top. See how that one cluster in the ceiling is transparent with a touch of blue?" Logan pointed. "They look like the crystals Robinson showed us."

"I think you're right. Truly, the Lord blessed you this day. You have found what He needs in order to continue His work." Robinson looked at the gathered group. "Who wants the honor of being the first to enter the chamber?"

"I found it," Logan said, and Matt could see zeal gleaming in his eyes. Or was it a touch of madness brought on by the heat? "I'm going in. It's God's will."

"We need a safety rope. The surface of that crystal has got to be..." Matt's words were cut off by a scream as Logan took two steps, lost his footing, and tumbled into the gorge."

"...slick."

They shone their lights down into the fissure. Logan lay impaled on a crystal spike, the blood pouring from his mouth redder than his hair. Perkins turned away at the sight, and Bill retched.

"A sacrifice for the Lord is the noblest sacrifice of all. We must soldier on." Robinson dug into his pack and pulled out a rope. "I wish Brother Logan hadn't been so hasty. Your idea," he leveled his gaze at Matt, "was a good one." He secured the rope to a stout crystal and handed the other end to Matt. "Lead on."

Matt's first instinct was to attack. Perhaps take Robinson by surprise and drop him into the cavern alongside Logan. But then he realized the man had already drawn his weapon.

"What's that for?"

"Times like these are when men tend to lose faith. Our task is too important for fear to take hold. Now, show us the way."

Grimacing, Matt secured the rope around his waist and moved out onto the crystal. The surface was slick as ice, and he had to choose each step with care. Once, his foot slipped and he teetered above the ten meter drop, arms flapping like a bird in flight, before recovering his balance. Finally, he made it to the cave and climbed inside.

The cave was about five meters deep, and the same across. The floor and walls bristled with tiny, white spikes. A few lay broken, presumably by the man who had originally discovered this place. Choosing his steps carefully, he moved to the center of the cavern where the transparent crystals hung from the ceiling. Somehow, perhaps through minerals leaching down through the bedrock, a distinctive type of crystal had formed here. It was a small cluster, enough to fill his backpack and no more.

"I've got this," he called. "It shouldn't take me long." He heard a rustling noise, and turned to see Bill, his face pale despite the heat, entering the cave, with Perkins right behind him.

"What's going on?" Matt asked.

"It's Robinson," Perkins whispered. "He's got your brother."

Matt peered through the cave opening to see Joel on his knees, hands behind his head. Robinson held his pistol at the base of Joel's neck.

"Insurance!" Robinson shouted. "Bag up the crystals and toss them to me and I'll let him go."

"I won't do it until you let him go." Matt knew the threat was empty, and Robinson did too.

"Fine. If you prefer, I'll shoot all of you and retrieve the crystals myself."

Matt glowered at him, vowing to kill Robinson the first chance he got. Why had he come without a weapon of his own? Foolishness. Rage burning inside him, he set about chipping away at the crystals. In a matter of minutes, he had filled his backpack.

"Walk out onto the bridge," Robinson said when Matt poked his head out of the cave. "Just a few paces."

Matt did as instructed.

"Toss the bag over there." He indicated a place off to the side. "If you attempt to distract me by tossing the bag directly at me, or if you do anything other than follow my instructions to the letter, your brother dies. And you'll be next."

Matt could see no way around the situation. Robinson was armed, and Matt had only a rock hammer and a crystal spike. Reluctantly, he tossed the bag of crystals onto the ledge near where Robinson stood.

"See how easy that was? Now, back into the cave with you."

"Let him go."

"When you're in the cave." As Matt backed into the cave, Robinson sidled away from Joel, keeping his pistol trained on the kneeling man. It was clear from the way his eyes kept flitting about that Joel was looking for an opening to attack, but saw nothing more than Matt did. Robinson was being careful, and he held his pistol like he knew how to use it.

True to his word, Robinson did not shoot Joel, but sent him across the crystal bridge and into the cave. He had just clambered inside when Robinson snatched something from his backpack, hurled it toward the cave, and ran. Matt saw the object over Joel's shoulder as it flew toward them.

"Grenade!" Matt shouted.

It seemed to happen in slow motion. Joel leapt out of the cave, catching the grenade in midair. His eyes met Matt's as he fell into open space. Matt hit the floor as the world turned to fire and ice.

Bill and Perkins barely had time to scream before razor-sharp shards of crystal shredded them like tissue. Pain like a thousand needles stung Matt's back, but, shielded by the low wall beneath the cave's opening, the worst of the blast passed over him.

Ears ringing, pain lancing through him, and heat creeping up his back through his damaged cooling suit, he pulled himself to his feet and looked out.

Joel was gone.

And so was the bridge.

Chapter 34

"Everybody get down!" Willis shouted.

Avery felt him shove her hard in the back and she hit the floor, her breath leaving her in a rush. The windows exploded in a shower of glass and the sound of gunshots boomed all around. She struggled to her feet, brushing glass from her hair. Willis had shoved the sofa against the front door and now peered out of one of the shattered windows.

"There's at least four of them. They'll probably come at us from both sides, and have another man guarding the door."

Krueger shoved a stack of notebooks into Avery's arms.

"As soon as I moved in, I cut a bolt hole in the floor of the bedroom closet. Move the shoes aside and pull up the carpet. It'll take you down into the basement, which runs the length of the building. You should be able to get out that way."

"We'll all get out that way." Willis flinched as the kitchen window shattered. "Come on."

"Somebody has to stay here, or else they'll know we've gotten away." He reached behind a bookshelf and drew out an assault rifle. Avery was no expert, but she knew an AK-47 when she saw it. "Those notes can't fall into the Dominion's hands, and you're more capable of getting the ladies out of here than I am."

A burst of gunfire shredded the front door, and Krueger fired back.

"Go!" he shouted. "Or else this is all for nothing!"

Willis hesitated for a split-second before ushering Avery and Sofia toward the back room.

Avery found the bolt hole, yanked it open, and dropped down into the cool, dark basement. Above her, the gunfire continued. She heard another window shatter, Willis return fire, and a man cry out in pain. Good!

Sofia dropped down next to her and Willis followed a moment later.

"I'll get you away from here, and then I'm going back for Krueger." They dashed down the length of the basement, passing storage cubes made from two-by-fours and cheap chicken wire, each labeled with an apartment number, and ending in a laundry room.

Willis held up a finger for silence and then slipped out the door. He returned moments later.

"We can't get to the car. There are too many of them."

"I saw a couple of motorcycles in one of the storage cubes," Sofia said. "Too bad we don't have the keys."

A wicked smile split Willis' dark face. "I don't need keys."

"Can you not squeeze so tight?" Avery grunted. They were roaring south along the Extraterrestrial Highway atop a freshly-hotwired Honda Shadow. Willis had wanted them to take both bikes, but not only had Sofia never ridden one, she was deathly afraid of them.

"I'm not letting go." Sofia's voice quaked. "We don't even have helmets. What if we crash?"

"We'll definitely crash if you suffocate me." Avery felt Sofia's python clutch ease a little. "I don't get it. You're an outdoorsy girl. You SCUBA, you climb, what's so bad about a motorcycle?"

"What's bad is flying down the street with nothing between me and death but the clothes on my back."

"Fair enough. Just hang in there. Willis should catch up with us soon."

Ten minutes later, a man on a motorcycle appeared in her rear-view mirror. She recognized him immediately and pulled to the side of the road. Willis stopped alongside them and cut the engine.

"I called Tam. She says it's too dangerous to try to make it all the way to Vegas. She's hooking us up with a flight out of a little airfield about a half an hour from here." He grimaced.

"We wouldn't have had time to hit the casinos," Avery chided.

"Naw, it's not that. It's Krueger."

"What happened?" Avery had noticed Willis was alone, but didn't want to broach the subject.

Willis shook his head. "Right after you left, Krueger's gun went silent. Must have run out of ammo. They were hauling his stuff out of the apartment. I would have gone in, but there were more of them than I thought, and they were better armed than me. Besides, I needed to get the two of you out of here."

"Going in there would have been a suicide mission. You're not Bones; you're smarter than that."

"If you say so," Willis sighed. "Anyway, Krueger's either dead or their prisoner."

"Which means," Avery said, "the Dominion might soon know about the Hall of Records."

Chapter 35

"Two guards," Maddock whispered into his mic.

"I see them." Kasey's voice didn't lose the serene quality it always held.

"Which one do you want me to take out?" Maddock held his Walther ready to fire.

"We've got this one," Greg said. "Cover us in case we get into trouble."

Maddock watched as two dark figures appeared seemingly out of nowhere. Greg took one guard out with a sharp strike to the temple and a knee to the forehead. Kasey eliminated her target with a strike to the chin and a roundhouse kick to the head as he fell. They dragged the men away from the entrance, bound them with zip ties, and motioned for Maddock to join them.

Keeping to the shadows, they passed through the gate and headed toward the mining company's main building.

They dispatched two more guards at the entrance. No need, Greg noted, to kill the men if they could help it. As far as they knew, these were locals and had no affiliation with the Dominion.

It wasn't until they located the security office that they ran into trouble. Two men burst forth, spraying the hallway with automatic pistol fire. Greg and Kasey hit the floor and, before they could return fire, Maddock took both men down with head shots.

"Wow!" Kasey said as he helped her to her feet. "I guess the SEALs' reputations are deserved."

"Sometimes."

"Can Bones shoot like that?"

"Yep. Almost as good as me." Maddock winked. "At least, that's what he claims."

"I figured he was full of crap." Kasey fell in alongside Maddock as they followed Greg into the office.

"Oh, he's definitely full of crap, but he's also very good at what he does. The two aren't mutually exclusive."

"Do you think you two could manage to guard the door while you gossip?" Greg was already working on hacking into the computer system.

Maddock and Kasey took up positions just inside the door where they could watch the hall in both directions.

"I have to admit, he handled himself pretty well in Paris."

Maddock looked at Kasey. "Don't tell me you've got a thing for him. His ego doesn't need the boost."

"No. He's just… interesting." Kasey looked away, but Maddock didn't miss the way her cheeks turned a delicate shade of pink. Bones was going to eat this up.

"I've accessed the security cameras," Greg called. "The good news is I don't see anyone between us and the entrance to the crystal caverns."

"Going by the tone of your voice, it sounds like you've got some bad news to deliver," Kasey said. "Spill it."

"Interesting choice of words. Come see for yourselves."

The heat assailed Robinson the moment he stripped off his useless cooling suit. The sudden wave of heat staggered him, but he smiled despite his weariness.

Twenty minutes from now, he would be free of this hell and on his way back to Utah with the crystals that the bishop so fervently desired. His triumph was certain to earn him a spot in the inner circle, one which he believed he richly deserved.

A harness hung at the end of a stout cable and he strapped himself in before pressing the button on the wall. Ten seconds later, a mechanical hum filled the shaft and he began to rise.

Two thousand feet deep, the Robin Hole was a ventilation shaft originally drilled by miners to ventilate lower chambers. When they broke through into this remote section, they widened the hole just enough to lower, or lift, a man through the hole.

The ascent seemed to go on forever as he scraped and banged against the stone walls. Sweat dripped from every pore of his body, and his breath came in gasps. It shouldn't be taking this long, should it?

Finally, he felt cool air on his face and he rose from the shaft to see Rivera's smiling face.

"You did as instructed?" Robinson asked as he removed the harness.

"I called the number you gave me and said what you told me to say. I also set off the charges I placed on the turbines." Rivera frowned. "What about the rest of your men?"

"They won't be joining us. Now, where's the way out?"

"That tunnel over there." Rivera pointed off to his left. "May I ask when I can expect the rest of my money?"

"Your money." Robinson smacked himself in the side of the head. "I almost forgot. Thank you for reminding me." He reached into his bag and took out his 9 millimeter.

The expression on Rivera's face turned from pleased to confused to panicked in the instant it took Robinson to pull the trigger.

"Pleasure doing business with you. Sorry to run, but I have a ride to catch."

"What is it?" Maddock's eyes went to the bank of monitors on the wall and his throat clenched.

Water was pouring into the caves.

"The pumps are no longer working. The caverns will be flooded in no time." Greg kept his voice calm, but strain was evident in his eyes as he pounded the keyboard.

"Can you turn them back on?" Kasey asked.

"I thought I might be able to, but check this out." He pointed to a screen showing what looked like a cavern filled with scrap metal.

"What is that?" Maddock asked.

"Those are the turbines. Somebody didn't just shut them down; they blew them up."

"Joel and Matt?" Kasey's voice trembled.

Greg turned away from her, his posture rigid. He gazed at the bank of monitors for a second before finally giving his head a single shake.

"There's no hope."

The jagged outcropping sliced into Matt's hand as he hauled his weight ever upward. He didn't know if this crevasse would lead him out of the cavern, but it was his last hope. When Robinson blew the crystal bridge, damaging Matt's cooling suit in the process, the way back had been eliminated as a possibility. The gap was too wide and the sides too sheer to climb. Any thoughts of playing Superman were dashed with a single glance down at Logan's remains, now shredded by the grenade blast, still impaled on the crystal spike.

For a moment, he'd considered giving up, but then he thought about the man who'd found this cavern. Somehow, he'd made it to this cavern and out again. It was possible he could have made it to the cavern before his cooling suit gave out entirely, but there was no way he could have survived the return trip.

Unless he'd found another way out.

Matt had searched the cavern and found this narrow crevasse which, promisingly, climbed upward at a steep angle. His damaged suit would hinder his progress, so he'd removed it, chipped away a few remnants of what he now thought of as Atlantean crystal, and pocketed it, before beginning the climb.

Twenty minutes later, his strength flagging, he found himself flat on his stomach, feet pressed against the sides of the shaft, inching his way upward. His body, slick with sweat and blood, burned with the effort, and the heat, though intense, had abated somewhat. He felt like he was back in the midst of a firefight in some unknown patch of jungle, which was an improvement over crawling through the Fifth Circle of Hell.

He pressed his fingers into a crack in the rock and tried to pull himself up, but the stone crumbled in his grasp and he slid back. He tried again, and again his handhold crumbled. He lay there, gasping for breath, feeling the last of his strength melt away. He couldn't go on any more. He'd just lie here and gaze at the stars.

The stars! Up ahead, in the midst of unrelenting darkness, Orion's belt shone in a sliver of gray light. The way out!

Calling upon reserves he hadn't realized he possessed, he resumed climbing. Inch by painful inch, he moved toward the twinkling lights. They seemed to inch ever closer until he thought he could almost reach out and take hold of them. As if in a dream, he extended his hand.

A cool breeze raised goose bumps on his exposed flesh. He dragged himself out into the night air and rolled over on his back, relishing the shivers that racked his body. He was free.

He lay there, eyes closed, listening to the wind... and the roar of an approaching engine. He opened his eyes and spotted the approaching craft: a Russian Kamov Ka-52 Alligator attack helicopter. He staggered to his feet and watched as the chopper landed atop a nearby hill. A man carrying a backpack came running out of the darkness. Robinson!

Matt's hand went to his hip, reaching for a weapon that wasn't there. Cursing in impotent rage, he started running toward the chopper. There was nothing he could do, but he couldn't bear just standing there and watching the murderous Dominion operative escape.

It seemed someone else had the same idea. As the Ka-52 rose into the air, gunfire erupted from the direction of the mine. Who could be firing on the chopper? He strained his eyes, but could not make out the figures, only the muzzle flashes, always in different places, as the shooters remained on the move.

Undeterred, the chopper rose into the air, fired off a single burst in the direction of the shooters, turned, and zoomed off into the night.

Matt's knees went weak and he crumpled to the ground. Joel was dead, Robinson escaped, and the Dominion now possessed the crystals it needed to unleash their weapon.

Over the sound of his own ragged breathing, he heard shouts and the cries of someone in pain. At least one of the attackers was down. He could just make out some of the words.

"Hang on, Kasey! Help's on the way."

He knew that voice.

It was Maddock. And that meant they were another man down. Forcing himself to move, he headed toward his friends. How, he wondered, had this mission gone so wrong?

Chapter 36

"Kasey's out of commission for the foreseeable future." Tam looked around the table at her "Myrmidons," as they had taken to calling themselves. Everyone appeared shell-shocked. With Joel dead, and Kasey seriously injured, spirits were low. It was up to her to keep them going.

"I won't pretend to know exactly what each of you is feeling, but I can tell you I'm hurting. I knew Joel longer and better than most of you, and I've known Kasey almost as long. I also feel bad about Krueger. Just remember this. We are the last line of defense against the Dominion. Hell, we're the only line of defense."

"I take it our tip about an attack on Savannah wasn't taken very seriously." Greg sat rigid as a statue. He was taking the failure harder than anyone.

Tam laughed. The only response she'd gotten was, *"We'll give it due consideration and take all precautions we deem necessary."* Translation, *"We'll put it in the file with all the other crackpot tips."* She'd also shared the information with a few trusted contacts, but none of them had the power or the inclination to do anything about it.

"Not a chance. So it's all on us." She paused, and began pacing to and fro. Her uncle was a preacher, and he'd taught her a few oratorical tricks to captivate an audience, and the judicious use of silence was one of them. Too little, and you got no effect. Too much and you lost their attention. She watched for the little signs: narrowed eyes, a slight cock of the head, subtle demonstrations of interest. When the time was perfect, she continued. "We've got to find this Revelation Machine before the Dominion gets its hands on it. I think it's pretty clear that they believe it, whatever it might be, will bring about the end of days." She let that sink in for a long moment.

"I don't care how much pain we've suffered. I don't care if you don't approve of the people I've brought onto our team. And I really don't care about your relationships or family issues or your histories together. This is bigger than any of that."

Out of the corner of her eye, she saw Avery cast an embarrassed glance at Bones, who grinned and winked at her. Jade lowered her head a notch. Only Maddock didn't react to her words. The man could be hard when he wanted to be, but that wasn't all bad.

"I need to know right now. Is everyone here still committed to the cause? Because if you're not, I swear to Jesus I'll find somebody else who is, and you can put on a skirt and work as my secretary until this is over."

"Hell yes!" Bones pounded his fist on the table. "I mean, yes we're committed, not yes to the skirt thing."

The tension broke. Each person reiterated her or his commitment to bringing down the Dominion and paying them back for Joel and Kasey.

"So, what's the plan?" Greg asked.

"First of all, I don't know if there's anything we can do about Savannah, but we need to try."

"I think the biggest problem we face is the fact that the Dominion won't come in a destroyer or any other sort of military vessel," Maddock said. "They'll have attached the weapon to an ordinary ship so as not to draw attention."

"I agree, and that's both good and bad. Bad because it's difficult to spot; good because it's easier to sink." She looked Maddock in the eye. "Can we use your boat?"

"I won't be with it?" he asked.

"I need you somewhere else. Besides, it's Matt and Corey who make her go, right?" When Maddock didn't argue, Tam turned to Greg. "Take Matt and Corey and Willis. And take *Remora*. That way, you can patrol above and below the waterline. Maybe we'll get lucky."

She dismissed the four men with a jerk of her head.

"I want my archaeologists in Egypt. Maddock, Bones, Jade, and Sofia—I want you to take the information Krueger provided and find this Hall of Records, if it exists."

"I'm going too," Avery protested. "Sofia and I are the ones who've been working on…"

"You're not an archaeologist. I want you here. He gave you more information than just the Hall of Records research. Follow up on it. Besides, I need at least a couple of people to watch my back in case something comes up. If I send all of you across the Atlantic, I've got no one."

A touch of the Maddock obstinance flashed in her eyes, but she didn't argue.

Relieved, Tam dismissed the rest of the team, but grabbed Maddock by the arm as he walked by. He stopped and waited until the others left.

"I want to tell you," Tam began, "that no matter how much the things I do piss you off, I need you and I'm glad you're on my team."

"Same here." Maddock's eyes softened. "Like you said, I don't always love the way you operate, but you're on the right side."

Tam gave his shoulders a squeeze.

"Good luck," she whispered. "And try to bring them all back alive."

Chapter 37

Standing at the entrance to the Fayyum Oasis, the pyramid of Amenemhet III looked more like an Indian mound than an Egyptian monument. Constructed of mudbrick over a series of chambers and corridors, the pyramid once boasted a limestone facade. Over the years, the exterior stone had been stripped away for use in construction, leaving the mudbrick core exposed to the elements. Now, its original pyramidal shape was barely evident. The last rays of the setting sun lent a reddish-brown cast to the once-magnificent monument. All in all, it made for an unimpressive sight.

"It looks like a pile of dirt," Bones observed.

"That's a good thing," Jade replied. "It's not an impressive sight, which means it doesn't draw tourists like the Giza complex does."

"Where's this awesome temple and labyrinth?" Bones sounded affronted.

"All that's left are stones from the original foundation." Sofia gazed at the scattered remnants of Egypt's past glory, a sad smile on her face.

"We don't care about that. We need the entrance to the underground chambers, which, according to Krueger's notes, can be accessed through the main pyramid entrance." Maddock had spent the entirety of the flight studying the notes. Sofia was already familiar with the details, but Jade and Bones hadn't had the chance to study them. Or, more accurately, Bones chose to sleep his way across the Atlantic, while Jade was either too proud, or felt too guilty about the way she'd treated Maddock in Japan to ask for a turn. That, of course, did not prevent her from stealing glances over his shoulder whenever she got the chance.

Sand crunched beneath Maddock's feet and a dry breeze ruffled his hair as he approached the pyramid. A hand-lettered sign identified the pyramid as Middle Kingdom, gave its height as fifty-two meters, its base width one hundred, and directed them toward the entrance which lay at the pyramid's south face.

A narrow walkway led to the spot where three monolithic slabs of limestone formed the entryway. Here, portions of the interior corridors peeked out from the eroded mound of bricks. Taking one last look around for unwelcome visitors, be they local authorities or Dominion agents, Maddock led the way into the darkness.

They descended a stone staircase that ended in a small, rectangular chamber. Maddock shone his Maglite on the ceiling, revealing an opening.

"Bones, will you do the honors?"

"Sure. I love being your personal stepladder." One by one, Bones boosted his three companions up to the chamber above them, and then, with a helping hand from Maddock, climbed up himself.

This chamber ran at a ninety degree angle to the one below, ending in an alcove, where Anubis, the Egyptian protector of the dead, stood watch. The paint was faded, but the god was easily recognizable. Moving as if in sync, Jade and Sofia took out digital cameras.

"No time for that," Maddock said. "Besides, I'm sure you can find pictures of this chamber online. It's not exactly a secret."

"But there is a secret passageway somewhere?" Bones asked.

"There is. This chamber was a decoy. Once upon a time, stout doors guarded that alcove. Grave robbers would waste time breaking them down, only to find themselves cursed by Anubis." He shone his light on hieroglyphs carved above the god's jackal head. "The true path lies above." He pointed to another trapdoor in the ceiling. "You have to pass through three of these dead-end chambers in order to get to the burial chamber. But we don't need to go quite that far."

"What do you mean?" Bones asked.

"You'll see in a minute."

Like the chamber they'd just exited, this one was also rotated at a ninety degree angle to the one below and ended in an alcove guarded by Horus.

"Do we go up again?" Bones glanced up at the ceiling.

"We would if the burial chamber was our goal. But what Krueger discovered is that this particular chamber isn't quite the dead end it appears to be." He made his way to the alcove, stepped up onto the ledge, and ran his fingers across the hieroglyphs, the ancient stone cool and smooth to the touch. A shiver passed through him as he reflected on the fact that someone had stood in this very spot, nearly four thousand years ago, and carved these symbols. For a moment, he felt a brief kinship with that workman. What was life like for him? Could he have imagined how long his work would endure?

"Are you awake?" Sofia asked.

"Don't mind him," Jade said. "He's a history buff and he sometimes gets weird around very old things."

"You should have seen him scamming on my grandmother last Christmas." Bones chuckled.

Maddock ignored them. His fingers stopped on a flat hieroglyph that resembled a rowboat.

"This is the symbol for a door or gateway." He pressed his fingers against the glyph and felt it give way. It slid back, creating a handhold which he gripped and rotated a quarter-turn, then released as the entire wall slid to the side.

"Awesome," Jade marveled, while Bones hummed the theme to Indiana Jones.

The passageway behind the trapdoor was so steep that they were forced to descend with the aid of handholds on the wall. By the time they reached the bottom, Sofia dripped with sweat and gasped for breath. Jade was in better condition, though she leaned against the wall to catch her breath.

"It's good thing we've got Krueger's notes, or else we'd be screwed." Bones shone his light down the corridor. It ran straight ahead, well beyond the Maglite's glow, and intersected a cross-hall every ten meters. An engraved column stood at each intersection. "There's something we need to decide right now."

"What's that?" Maddock consulted Kruger's notes.

"Which one of us has to fight the Minotaur?"

"Wrong culture." Sofia laughed and squeezed Bones' arm.

Jade and Maddock exchanged knowing glances.

"Straight ahead, seventh passageway on the left." Maddock headed off down the corridor at a brisk walk, forcing the others to hurry to keep up.

"How did Krueger find his way through here?" Jade tried to walk and take in the scene all at once. She stumbled, and Maddock caught her around the waist.

They froze for an instant, gazing into one another's eyes, the sudden closeness foreign, yet so familiar.

"Get a room," Bones jibed.

Jade pulled away from Maddock and brushed invisible dirt from her knees. "Such tact." She shot a dirty look Bones' way. "It's truly a wonder some woman hasn't snapped you up."

"I'm a roller coaster," Bones replied. "I'm a short ride, but it's always fun while it lasts."

"You should try thinking about baseball," Maddock suggested.

"I didn't mean…" Bones sputtered while the ladies laughed. "Forget it."

"Krueger found the chamber by looking for places where Anubis and the gateway hieroglyph appeared together. Like this." They had reached the seventh cross-hall. Here, Anubis faced left, the gateway symbol hovering between the tips of his long ears.

Aided by Krueger's notes, they followed where the jackal god led, winding through the labyrinth in a dizzying set of twists and turns, until Maddock was certain the whole thing was an elaborate ruse and they would spend the rest of their short lives wandering through this dark maze of sand and stone.

"Does Krueger say how long it should take to get there?" Jade's tone held a hint of nervousness.

"It probably took him quite a while since he didn't have directions to follow. He would have been forced to inspect every column and make notes along the way." Maddock flipped to the next page in Krueger's notebook. "If we haven't made a wrong turn somewhere along the way, it should be around the next corner."

"Don't jinx us, Maddock," Jade said. "I don't have the energy to go back and start over."

There was no need to start over. The next turn led them to a dead end, just as Krueger said it would. And to what he claimed was the doorway to the Hall of Records.

"It looks just like the photographs." Sofia beamed. Krueger's journal included several snapshots of this wall, where, beneath the now-familiar gateway hieroglyph, an Egyptian carver had rendered the constellation Orion.

"Orion? Here?" Bones gave Maddock a knowing look. This wasn't the first time Orion had figured into one of their mysteries.

"This definitely seems out of place." Jade reached out and ran her fingers along the curved line of stars that formed the hunter's shield. "But if this is a door, where's the handle?"

"And what makes you think we can get in when Krueger couldn't?" Bones added.

"Take a close look at his belt." Maddock winked at Sofia while Bones and Jade shone their lights on the carving.

Bones saw it first. "The stars are shaped like the indentations on top of the Atlantean weapon we took from Daisuke."

"Avery and I both recognized the shapes the moment we saw the photographs." Sofia's voice trembled with excitement.

"Did anyone bring the crystals?" Jade asked.

Maddock drew a small pouch from his pocket. "What? Did you think we were going to scout it out and then fly back for the crystals?"

"Don't be an ass," Jade snapped. "I was just asking."

"Quiet, you two." Bones hissed.

"He has no call to talk to me like that."

"I hear it too," Maddock said. "Listen."

The corridor went dead quiet as they all strained to listen. Maddock heard it again—whispered voices somewhere in the labyrinth.

They looked at one another. Jade and Sofia appeared stunned, Bones determined. There was only one logical conclusion.

The Dominion had taken Krueger alive, and they were about to catch up.

Chapter 38

It was a dark day on the Atlantic. A gray blanket of storm clouds cloaked the sky, and a chill wind stirred up waves that battered *Sea Foam*, sending icy salt spray over her gunwales. Soaked to the bone, Matt stood on the foredeck holding a pair of binoculars. He knew he should get out of the weather, but he felt as though he were doing a penance for his failure in Naica. He wanted his revenge on the Dominion for what they had done to Joel, and right now, this was all he could do to help. He felt impervious to the cold, maybe because he found it a pleasant change from the deadly heat of the crystal caves, or perhaps his anger kept him warm. Either way, he stood fast.

The foul weather kept all but the largest ships ashore, and Willis and Professor took *Remora* in for a closer look at every craft that plied the waters off the coast of Savannah, but they'd met with no success. He wiped the lenses for what felt like the thousandth time and traced the dark line of the horizon—an inky divide between dark sky and darker water. Nothing.

And then he spotted a white dot. He wiped the lenses again and tightened the focus on the binoculars. Something was there! Feeling a touch of hope for the first time in hours, he turned and waved to get Corey's attention. A moment later, Corey's voice sounded in his ear.

"Did you forget we can talk to each other?"

"I did. Still not accustomed to this high tech gear. Take us north-northwest. I think I see a boat."

"Must be a small one. Radar doesn't show… wait. There it is!"

Sea Foam rolled in the choppy sea as Corey turned her about. A moment later, Greg joined Matt on deck.

"Can I take a look?" The tall, lanky agent, always so unflappable, still seethed with scarcely-contained rage. Matt knew no one blamed him for what happened to Joel, but he couldn't help but feel a pang of guilt around one of Joel's longtime colleagues. He handed the binoculars to Greg, who took a long look before handing them back. "Keep looking. Let us know when you have a visual." He turned and stalked back into the cabin.

Matt locked his gaze on the target and watched it grow larger in his field of vision. As they drew closer, the boat came into clear view. His heart leapt when he got his first good look at the boat.

"I think this is it!" he called into his mic.

"Dude, no need to shout," Corey said.

"What makes you think so?" Greg asked in clipped tones.

"That boat is identical to the one Bill took us out on for the so-called fishing expedition. Who, in their right mind, would be out fishing on a day like today?"

He felt the vibration beneath his feet as Corey opened up the engine and *Sea Foam* crashed through the waves, making a beeline for the fishing boat.

"Willis, Professor, did you hear that?" Greg asked.

"Roger," Professor replied.

"We're on the mother!" Willis cried.

Nervous energy boiling up inside him, Matt hurried into the cabin and grabbed an M-16. Please let me get a chance to use it. For a moment, he wished he had the Atlantean gun Maddock had found in Japan, but Bones had only managed to generate a few waves with it. For now, its secrets remained hidden.

Returning to the deck, he watched as they bore down on the fishing boat. He could make out two figures in rain gear looking in his direction. He dropped to one knee, rested his M-16 on the gunwale, and waited.

One of the men in the boat spotted Matt. He shouted something to his comrade, who sprang to the wheel and gunned the engine.

"They're running!" Matt called.

"Not for long," Willis said.

Ten meters in front of the fleeing fishing boat, mechanical arms extended like a creature from the depths, *Remora* surfaced. The pilot yanked the wheel to the right just as a wave crashed into the boat, nearly capsizing it. As he struggled to recover, Corey cut *Sea Foam* across their bow.

Matt stood and trained his rifle on the pilot.

"Hands in the air! Now!"

Both men raised their hands and stared up at Matt in horror. Up close, he saw that both had the weathered features of men who spent most of their time on the water. He had a sinking feeling they'd chased down the wrong craft. Willis seemed to confirm that a moment later when he reported no weapon attached to the craft's underside.

"Whatever you want, just take it." The pilot's voice trembled. "But we don't have much."

Greg appeared at Matt's side and flashed his identification.

"We're with the D.E.A. We need to inspect your boat." It was a lie they'd agreed on at the outset of the mission.

The men's frozen faces melted with relief.

"You two move to the stern and put your hands behind your heads," Matt ordered. No harm in maintaining the ruse.

Greg inspected the boat, proclaimed it "clean," and apologized for the inconvenience. The relieved men assured him there was nothing to apologize for, and headed back to port without complaint.

"Sorry," Matt said. "I really wanted it to be them."

"Me too." Greg gazed out at the sea. "But we're searching for a needle in a haystack here." His phone rang. "It's Tam." He answered, listened for a few seconds, grimaced, and then hung up. "We're aborting the mission."

"Why?" Matt protested. "There's no way those guys could have already complained about us. Besides, they think we're D.E.A."

"It's not that." Greg pocketed his phone and pounded his fist on the gunwale. "Bill gave you a bad tip. The Dominion just hit Norfolk."

Chapter 39

The sound of voices drew closer. Bones drew his Glock and took up a position at the corner where he could see the Dominion operatives' approach.

"Give me some light," Maddock whispered. Jade and Sofia trained their Maglites on Orion's belt. Quickly, Maddock placed the crystals in their proper spots. As he pressed each into its slot, some invisible force, almost like magnetism, snatched the crystal from his fingers and held it fast.

"I can see their lights," Bones whispered. "We're almost out of time."

"Got it." Maddock set the last crystal into place and the door swung inward. He shone his beam inside, making a cursory inspection for booby traps, and then ushered the others inside. After they all entered the chamber, he pried the crystals free and pushed the door closed. With a hollow click, it locked into place. "Now, let's see if Krueger was right."

Turning around, he swept his light around the room.

"Oh my God," Jade whispered. Her free hand found his and squeezed. "This is it!"

Statues of Egyptian gods lined the Hall of Records. Between each statue, the walls were honeycombed with alcoves for storing scrolls. A band of hieroglyphs ringed the chamber just above the alcoves. It was laid out like the Atlantean temples, but with a large stone table at the center where the altar to Poseidon would have been.

Jade and Sofia immediately began snapping pictures.

"We don't have much time," Maddock said.

"Why not?" Sofia asked, still clicking away. "We're in here, they're out there, and they don't have the crystals."

"I don't think that will slow them down for long. The best we can hope for is they try the door for a few minutes. Once they realize they can't get in, I believe we can count on them to resort to other means."

"Like what?" Sofia asked.

"Like blowing the door," Jade said. "Maddock's right. We need to hurry. I just hope we can find the information we need in time."

"What happens when they do blow the door?" Sofia's voice dropped to a scant whisper.

"You two will hide while Bones and I deal with them." Maddock wished he felt half as much confidence as he feigned. He had a feeling the Dominion would have sent enough trained men to make sure a job this important came off without a hitch.

"Guys, there's something weird in here." Bones pointed to the nearest statue—Osiris. "Notice how every statue has been defaced?"

"Every one?" Jade asked, moving deeper into the hall. "That can't be right."

"He's right," Sofia said. "Every face is smashed. That can't be an accident. Someone's been in here."

"That's not the worst part. Check out the alcoves." Bones shone his light along the wall.

Every alcove was empty.

"No!" Sofia wailed. She balled her fists and pressed them to her forehead. "All this work, and grave robbers beat us to it."

"Not grave robbers," Maddock said.

"How do you know?" Jade cocked her head to the side and fixed him with a questioning look.

"The thieves left a calling card." He shone his light on the wall above the door, where someone had carved a few squiggly lines and a familiar symbol.

"The Templars? No freaking way." Bones looked like he was about to say something else, but just then, they heard voices on the other side of the door.

Maddock couldn't make out the words, but it was clear by their excited tone that they knew they'd found the entrance to the Hall of Records. He looked at Bones.

"There are a bunch of guys out there, Maddock." He said it with the clinical detachment of an engineer sizing up a challenging task.

"We'll have surprise on our side, and they'll have to come in two at a time."

Maddock thought fast. "We'll lay our Maglites in alcoves, with the beams directed at the door. They'll aim for the lights at first. That will buy us a little more time."

"Maybe we won't have to fight." Sofia grabbed him by the arm and pulled him deeper into the hall.

"We can't hide from them," Maddock said. "When they find the chamber empty, they'll give it a thorough search."

"That's not what I mean." Sofia continued to pull him through the hall. Bones and Jade followed behind them, bemused expressions on their faces. "This place is laid out exactly like the Atlantean temples."

"So?"

"So, that means there should be an air shaft leading out. That's how I got away in Spain." She released Maddock's arm and hurried ahead.

Maddock glanced at Bones. "It's worth a try."

"It's here!" Sofia called. "Come on!"

"Okay, everybody into the shaft," Maddock ordered. "Bones take the lead; I'll bring up the rear."

"No way. Why do you get the good view?" Bones winked. "Besides, I'm the biggest. If I get stuck along the way, everyone behind me is stuck too."

"Fine." Maddock stuck his Maglite in his teeth and began to climb. He'd made it about ten meters when an explosion rocked the passageway. "I guess they blew the door." He wondered if the others could even hear him. If their ears were ringing half as loudly as his, he doubted it. He looked back to make sure everyone still followed, and continued the climb.

The climb through the shaft went on with agonizing slowness. The stones were fitted together with such precision that he found it difficult to find handholds. Every muscle ached from crawling in a hunched position. It felt like boot camp all over again.

As the ringing in his ears abated, the voices of the Dominion's men rose. Angry shouts and arguing reverberated through the shaft. *I know how you feel,* he thought. *You came all this way for nothing.* Listening to the men in the hall below, a sudden thought struck him.

"Everybody turn out your lights," he said around his own Maglite, which he still held between his teeth.

"Why?" Sofia asked.

"In case they look into the shaft." He paused enough to douse his light. "I don't think Bones' butt is big enough to block the light."

"Hey, my butt is perfect. Just ask your old lady."

"Your sister is my old lady," Maddock retorted.

"Oh, yeah."

Even Jade laughed at this, though they quickly fell silent.

"Do you see anything yet?" Jade whispered. "Any light at the end of the tunnel?"

"Not yet, but we entered the labyrinth just before sunset. It will be dark outside."

He couldn't deny he was worried that the shaft wasn't a true air shaft that would lead outside. If a shaft this size were open at the other end, wouldn't it have been discovered by now? Nothing to be done about it, he supposed. At worst, they'd hide in the shaft until they were certain the hall was empty, then try to sneak out the way they'd come in.

His fears were confirmed minutes later when his skull met a stone wall. He halted, and Jade crashed into him a moment later. He heard twin grunts as Sofia and Bones joined the pileup.

"Why have we stopped?" Jade whispered.

"End of the line."

"There's got to be a way out," Sofia protested.

"I don't know." Maddock ran his hand across the wall in front of him. It was smooth, just like the sides of the shaft. He felt for a seam, but the stone was seated tightly in the end of the shaft. "I think we're out of luck."

"Let me see." Light blossomed in the darkness and Jade squeezed in beside him.

"Warn me when you're going to do that." Maddock tried to blink away the spots in his eyes.

"Somebody had to find the doorknob. Look."

He squinted against the too-bright light, and looked at the spot where she'd trained her beam.

"It's a slot for a crystal. I must have missed it in the dark."

"Duh. Now hurry up. I want a bath and a beer, and not in that order."

"Can I join you?" Bones asked.

"Only for the beer."

"Just like old times." Maddock pulled out the bag of crystals, found the one that fit, and set it in place. Silently, the shaft swung open. Cool breeze and the glow of artificial light bathed his face. He looked around at his surroundings and laughed.

"What's funny?" Jade asked.

"You'll see. Just be very careful climbing out. Bones, be sure to take the crystal and close the door behind you." Carefully, he climbed out of the hole. When they all reached the ground, they stood, looking up, and laughing.

"I can't believe that we just climbed out of the eye of the Sphinx." Bones couldn't tear his eyes away from the battered stone face of the ancient monument.

"Believe it," Maddock said. "Let's get out of here. If we hurry, we should be able to get back to the car long before the Dominion gets out of the labyrinth."

They took off at a slow trot. Maddock and Bones could have stood a faster pace, and probably Jade, who always kept fit, but he didn't know if Sofia would be able to handle it.

As he ran, he punched up Tam's number. She wasn't going to like his report.

Chapter 40

"With us live from his church in Utah is Bishop Hadel of the Kingdom Church." Patricia Blount, the news anchor, was an attractive blonde of middle years, but her pleasant smile belied her reputation as a hard-nosed interviewer. She didn't quite manage to disguise her frown as she introduced Hadel. Though the Dominion was an organization unknown to most, Hadel was well-known, both for his altruism and his controversial opinions. *"Bishop, it is my understanding that representatives from your church are already on the scene in Norfolk, providing aid to displaced families."*

"We call them missionaries," Hadel corrected. *"And, yes, they are on the scene. When*

tragedy strikes, we reach out in loving compassion to our brothers and sisters in need."

Hadel's easy smile turned Tam's stomach. She knew what a monster the man was, even if the world didn't, and the fact that she couldn't yet prove it made it all the worse.

"*With thousands already confirmed dead, tens of thousands more having lost everything to the second freak tsunami to hit the United States in less than two weeks, how do you comfort people who might think to give up hope in your God?*" Blount winced at her own brief lapse in professionalism.

"*He's everyone's God, Patricia, whether they know it or not.*" Hadel smiled like an indulgent grandfather. "*And we provide reassurance through acts of mercy like those we are performing in Norfolk.*"

"*How did your missionaries happen to be on the scene so quickly?*"

"*We have sister and satellite churches throughout the nation who assist us in our work.*" Hadel said with a touch of pride.

"*What do you say to those who claim a merciful, loving God would not allow a tragedy like this to strike innocents?*"

"*I would say there are few innocents in this world. Norfolk, I am sad to say, is not immune to the infection that is rotting our nation from the inside out. Norfolk is rated as one of the hundred most dangerous cities in the United States, with crime rates well above the national average.*"

"*May I ask why, in the face of this tragedy, you took the time to study up on Norfolk's crime statistics?*" Blount bore down. "*It seems like you'd have other priorities.*"

Hadel remained unflappable. "*I sought to understand the reason for this seemingly-senseless tragedy, and came to the inescapable conclusion that God's judgment and righteous wrath are at play here. This is a city peopled with some of the lowest of the low…*"

"*Who do you consider the lowest of the low?*" Blount snapped, but Hadel rode over her.

"*Not to mention the strong presence of the United States military, which aids and abets our corrupt government.*"

Blount redirected the conversation. "*Bishop, we're going to play a cell phone video captured by one of the victims of the tsunami and we'd like your comments on it.*"

"*Of course.*"

"*The video shows your missionaries rescuing a white family from the flood waters, and then, almost immediately, fighting off a drowning African-American man…*"

Tam's phone vibrated just as an indignant Hadel shouted something about 'ambush journalism' and the tendencies of overcrowded boats to capsize. It was a text from Maddock. She fired off a reply and sagged against the wall, eyes closed. Why had she ever wanted to be in charge? What she wouldn't give right now to be out in the field, matching wits with her quarry. Maybe she'd even get to shoot somebody. That would relieve her stress.

"What's wrong?" Avery looked up from Krueger's notebook. She was still upset with Tam for keeping her at headquarters, but she'd been working diligently since the others left on their respective missions.

"First the Dominion attacks the wrong city, making me look like a fool, and now Maddock finds the Hall of Records."

"Really?" Avery sprang to her feet, upending her chair. "Where was it? What did he find?"

"It was under the Sphinx, just like Krueger said. And it was empty."

The gleam in Avery's eyes flickered and died. "What?"

"The Templars got there first. He's sending me a picture of…" Her phone vibrated again. "Here it is. The Templars left a calling card." She handed the phone to Avery.

"The cross looks authentic. Lord knows we've seen enough of these lately." The Templars had been at the heart of a mystery Tam aided Maddock and his crew in solving. "But these squiggly lines are odd." Avery's gaze went cloudy and she bit her lip.

"What?" Tam could tell the young woman was deep in thought, but she dared not get her hopes up.

"I think I know where this is!" She snatched up the notebook and flipped through to a hand-drawn map. "See how the lines on this carving match up?"

Tam looked at the map. It showed a stretch of river and an island. "It's not an exact match. The Templar carving doesn't show this island." She tapped a chili-pepper shaped stretch of land that ran parallel to the shore, joined to the mainland by bridges at its north and northwest tips.

"That's because this island wasn't built until the 1800s but, according to Krueger, it's one of the Templars' most notorious 'hide in plain sight' constructions. He believes it's the place where the Freemasons, the modern descendants of the Templars, hid their most sacred knowledge." She paused. "And it has Atlantean connections."

"Where is this place?" Tam held her breath. Hope stirred inside her again, though she was reluctant to believe it.

"It's in Washington D.C. I know it must seem like a stretch, but Krueger was right about the Hall of Records. Isn't it at least worth having Maddock and the others check it out?"

For the first time in she couldn't remember how long, Tam permitted herself a genuine smile. Now she recognized the location.

"Girl, forget Maddock. There's no time to waste. Besides, I'm the one who can get us inside. Grab your toothbrush. You and I are going on a trip."

Chapter 41

"You realize I know what you're up to?" Bones lay stretched out on the hotel bed, tossing his Recon knife in the air and snatching the falling, spinning blade just before it hit him in the face. He'd been at it for the past ten minutes, complaining all the while about boredom and insomnia.

"What are you talking about?" Maddock groaned. Sleep eluded him as well, but he'd at least tried harder than Bones to catch some shut eye.

"Only getting two rooms. You're hoping I'll keep you from hooking up with Jade."

"I'm not going to hook up with her. You're the hookup guy in this partnership."

"You're not planning to hook up with her, but I know how things go when you meet up with an ex. It starts out friendly, and then it gets nostalgic. Next thing you know, you're wondering why you ever dumped her in the first place. It's psychology and hormones." Bones caught the knife again and flung it across the room where it stuck in the back of the desk chair.

"You're paying for that." Maddock sat up and rubbed his eyes. "You've been through this before?"

"Are you kidding? I hook up with my exes whenever I get a chance. It's a lot like makeup sex. The difference is, I don't get into long, committed relationships like you do. I've tried a few times, but it doesn't last." He got up, retrieved his knife, and sheathed it. "It's bad enough you want me to run interference for you, but you're messing up my game. Sofia looks like a mountain I'd like to climb."

Maddock ignored the labored metaphor. "Wait a minute. You think it's bad I want you to keep Jade away from me? I'm being faithful to your sister."

"It's not faithfulness if somebody has to make you do it. If you're going to go back to Jade sooner or later, I'd rather Angel find out now, instead of down the road. It'll hurt her less."

"It gives me a headache when you say something that makes sense."

"Screw you, Maddock." Bones smiled to show he had not taken offense. "I'm going to get some fresh air before I go stir crazy."

There came a soft knock at their door. Bones gave him a look that said, *What did I tell you?* He opened the door to find Jade standing there, looking abashed.

"I… needed to talk to Maddock about something."

"Go ahead. I'm going out for a few minutes." Bones left without looking back.

Jade sat down on the bed, facing him, and gazed at him, her brown eyes shining with deep emotion.

"What did you want to talk about?"

"I'm not sure." She looked down at her hands. "It was fun today. You know, solving the puzzle, proving a legend was true, almost getting killed." She laughed. "God, I've missed it. I know that sounds crazy, but I never feel more alive than when I'm with you."

"Nostalgia's a funny thing. It makes you forget the bad times."

Now, Jade met his eye. Her gaze was hard, but her words soft. "You're trying to sound callous, but I know you better than that. Tell me you don't feel it too."

"Of course I do. And yes, our highs are pretty high, but you can't deny that our lows were sometimes about as low as you can get." He poured all his effort into ignoring her eyes, which always mesmerized him, and her other features that he found just as enticing, and concentrated on the bad times: the fights, the jealousy, the months apart.

"It's called a roller coaster, and people love them. How boring is life if there aren't any ups and downs?"

Maddock had no reply.

"You don't have to give me an answer. Just promise me you'll think about it. About us." Jade's smile faltered and faded into a tiny frown. She stood and headed for the door.

"Leaving already?" Maddock didn't know why he'd said that. From the time they'd checked into the hotel, he'd wanted nothing more than for the two of them to keep their distance from one another.

"I want to get back to the room before Bones tries something with Sofia."

"He won't be happy."

"He will when I remind him about the punishment for adultery in a Muslim country." She looked back over her shoulder, a wicked gleam in her eye. "I don't actually know what the law is in Egypt, but I'll make up something suitably horrible."

"Nice one." Maddock winked at her. "Sleep well."

Jade looked at him for another long moment before opening the door. "Goodnight, Maddock." She stepped outside and closed the door.

Maddock stared at the door, fighting an irrational urge to go after her. What was his problem? He was in a good relationship with a girl he'd known forever. Why would he even consider throwing that away?

He turned out the light, yanked the covers over his head, and, when Bones returned a few minutes later, pretended to be asleep. It was going to be a long night.

Chapter 42

"**According to Krueger,** Pierre-Charles L'Enfant, who designed the master site plan for Washington, D.C., also known as the 'L'Enfant Plan,' was a French architect and Freemason handpicked for the job by George Washington, who was also a Freemason. L'Enfant's original design incorporated Freemason, Egyptian, and even Atlantean symbolism." Avery had spent the flight from Miami to Washington devouring all of Krueger's research on the Templars' connection to the capital city, and supplementing it with her own research. The more she learned ,the more fascinated she became. A scholar could devote her entire career to studying the connections between the ancient world, secret societies, and Washington D.C. Now, as their driver, a government agent driving a boring, gray sedan, drove them to their destination, she shared her findings with Tam.

"Skip to the part we care about." Tam was checking email on her phone, but seemed to be listening intently.

"Just like the labyrinth Maddock and the others found at Giza, a network of passageways runs beneath the national mall and all the major structures in the vicinity. Somewhere amid this warren lies a vault containing the accumulated treasures of the Templars in America. Beginning in the late 1930s, the Freemasons constructed a new passageway to the vault, and hid the entryway beneath a memorial that incorporated both Templar and Atlantean symbology; the symbols to serve as a sign to the initiated."

"Tell me about the symbology." Tam pocketed her phone and gave Avery her undivided attention.

"Look at this aerial photograph." Avery laid Krueger's notebook between them. "See how the entablature is a perfect circle?"

"I've been there before, and I can see how it's reminiscent of a Templar church. But I don't see Atlantis here anywhere."

"Look outward from the memorial. What do you see?"

Tam stared for a moment, and then her eyes lit up. "Rings of concentric circles on a piece of land surrounded by water."

"Is that Atlantean enough for you?" Avery could have gone on, but she could tell Tam was convinced.

"We're here, Ma'am." The driver stopped the car and opened the door for them. "Shall I come with you?"

"Remain here with the car. I'll call if I need you."

Bathed in moonlight, its interior lights glowing, the Jefferson Memorial stood enshrouded in the ethereal curtain of fog that rolled in off the Potomac. In the silence of the midnight hour, the place had a ghostly quality to it.

Tam made a beeline for the monument, and Avery hurried to keep up. As they drew closer, she noticed yellow tape encircling the monument and signs reading, *Temporarily Closed.*

"Uh oh. I wonder why it's closed."

"Are you kidding?" Tam gave her a quizzical look. "I closed it. Rather, a friend closed it for me. And there he is. Hey, Tyson!"

Daniel Tyson was a tall, dark-skinned man who appeared to be about the same age as Tam. Light from the memorial reflected off his shaved head, and he greeted Tam and Avery with an easy smile and bone-crushing hugs. His tailored suit was cut to accentuate his athletic figure.

"Tyson is a friend and former colleague," Tam explained. "He used to be FBI, now he's with the NPS and calls it a 'step up.' He's also a Lakers fan, which tells you he knows nothing about basketball."

"Please." Tyson's speech was flavored with a light touch of the Caribbean, adding to his aura of congeniality. "You've never balled in your life, Broderick."

"Not on the court, anyway." Tam gave him a wink.

"My court is always open if you ever feel so inclined to brush up on your...skills!"

Tam gave his arm a squeeze. "Thank you for doing this for us. We'll try to make it quick."

"Not a problem. Do you need anything else from me?"

"Just keep prying eyes away." Tam thanked him again, gave him another hug, and led them into the memorial.

"I found pairs of numbers, get this, written in the margins in invisible ink. I think they correspond to words in the various inscriptions on the walls."

"Invisible ink? How'd you know to check for that?"

"My father was obsessed with pirate treasure, legends, and secrets. I picked up a few things here and there."

"Good job. Let's get to checking the panels."

"No need. I looked up the various inscriptions online and worked on it during our flight. I think I've come up with something that makes sense." She opened the notebook and read aloud.

"Progress of the human mind. Enlightened discoveries. Truths remain ever in the hand of the master."

"The master? You mean Jefferson over there?" Tam assessed the bronze statue. "He's big, but I don't think there's a tunnel in his hand."

"I've got an idea about that." Moving to the statue, Avery climbed up onto the pedestal. There was little room to stand and the surface was slick, but she clung to the president's cloak for balance.

Ever in the hand of the master.

In Jefferson's left hand, he clutched a scroll. Avery wasn't tall enough to get a good look, but, if she stretched, she could just reach it. She ran her fingers across the top and found what she was looking for. A pyramid-shaped indentation.

"It's here! Give me the crystals."

Tam, looking bemused, handed her an envelope in which she'd put one each of the crystals Maddock and Bones had recovered in Japan. The first crystal was not a fit, nor was the second, but the moment the third crystal slid into place, the empty rotunda echoed with the thrum of cogs turning somewhere below ground. The statue lurched and Avery leapt off the pedestal, not quite pulling off a clean landing. She sprang to her feet, but Tam hadn't noticed. She watched as the statue slid to the side, revealing a stone staircase.

Tam looked at Avery and smiled.

"Who needs them boys? You did it!"

Avery couldn't help but blush a little at Tam's praise. She had to admit she was more than a little proud to have done all of it: tracking down Krueger, finding the connection to the memorial, and deciphering the clues, without her brother's help. Okay, a lot of the credit went to Krueger, but she was still going to enjoy the moment.

"You coming?" Tam was already ten steps down the staircase, flashlight in one hand, Makarov in the other.

"Yeah, sorry." Avery took out her Maglite but left her 9 millimeter in her coat pocket. She couldn't imagine encountering anything down here that would require a weapon. Head buzzing with the thrill of discovery, she followed Tam down into the darkness.

The air grew damp and musty as they made their way deeper. After a long descent, they reached a level passageway. At first, Avery was taken aback at the relative modernity, but reminded herself that this tunnel had not been built by the Templars, but was a twentieth century link to the Templar vault. Cobwebs hung from the ceiling and a thin sheen of dust coated everything. No one had passed this way in years, maybe decades.

Minutes later, they found themselves facing a dead end.

"Okay. What now?" Tam shone her Maglite all around. "Did we miss a door somewhere along the way?"

"I don't think so." Avery moved closer and ran her hand down the wall. Her fingers passed over a soft spot and she paused. "I think I might have something." Pulling the neckline of her shirt up to cover her nose and mouth, she brushed away the accumulated dust and mold, revealing another indentation like the one on the statue. She quickly found the proper crystal and fitted it into the slot. Some unseen force tugged it into place and the door swung back.

They shone their lights through the doorway and Avery sucked in her breath. "This is really it!"

Chapter 43

The Templar vault looked like an oversize version of the interior of the Jefferson Memorial—round with a low, vaulted ceiling and columns interspersed around the sides. Shelves were carved into the walls between each set of columns, with piles of scrolls, books, and artifacts heaped onto them. The room itself was filled with statuary from all over the world and various historical epochs. She recognized Greek, Egyptian, and Chinese sculpture, as well as Roman busts on pedestals.

"This is…" Tam couldn't finish her sentence. "To think this has been down here all this time and no one knew."

"Someone knew," Avery said. "I can't imagine the Freemasons let the knowledge die."

"I wonder," Tam mused, "if they kept the knowledge within an inner circle, and something happened to those in the know before they could pass the information along. It would explain why nobody's been down here in forever." She shook her head. "That's a question for another day. We need to get to searching. Where should we start?"

"Um." Avery bit her lip. She hadn't considered how they would go about sorting through the accumulated treasures of the Templars. "This could take a while."

"Time we might not have. Unless the men they sent to Egypt were idiots, the Dominion knows the Templars cleared out the Hall of Records. They'll try to extract the information from Krueger. He's unlikely to hold out any longer than he did before he revealed the secret of the labyrinth."

"In that case, we'd better hurry. You go left, I'll go right?" Avery skirted the perimeter of the vault, examining the contents of the various shelves. She saw that there was at least some organizational system here. The first section contained Hebrew texts, a golden menorah, and a few artifacts she didn't immediately recognize. In addition to the ancient texts, the section also contained more recent copies of various writings, some in Latin, others in Greek, and still more in English. So the material was organized by topic as well as origin. Perhaps they should search out, not the Egyptian collection, but one devoted to Atlantis.

The next section contained Christian writings and a few small chests that likely contained relics. She took a few steps back to get a different perspective on the layout. As she ran her light up and down the wall, she noticed the symbols carved above each set of shelves—a menorah above the Hebrew section and a cross over the Christian section.

As her eyes followed the beam of her light as it swept in a circle around the vault, she saw more symbols: the eagle of Rome, the Eye of Horus, and…

"The trident! It's over here." She hurried over to where a statue of Poseidon guarded the shelves. Tam joined her a few seconds later.

"Some of this is really old. It might crumble if we touch it." Tam passed her fingers over a scroll, as if she could capture its contents through proximity. She hesitated. "How do we know which of these contains the information we need?" She swept her light up and down the shelves. "There's too much to carry."

"We need Sofia," Avery agreed. "I've picked up on the meanings of a few of the symbols but not enough of them to translate." Her eyes roved over the collection and fell upon an object so different from the others she almost wondered if it were mislaid.

Laying her Maglite on the shelf, she picked up a leatherbound journal and opened it to the first page.

"That's anachronistic," Tam said.

"It's more than that." Avery's hands trembled. "This journal is an eighteenth century scholar's attempt to tell the true story of Atlantis based on a lifelong study of this archive." She turned the page and almost dropped the book.

"Are you all right?"

"Look." Avery could scarcely manage to believe her eyes. A hand-drawn map of the world showed the locations of Atlantean cities: in Spain, Cuba, Japan, and the middle of the Atlantic. Dotted lines connected them all to one mother city. With trembling hands, she passed the book to Tam, whose jaw dropped.

"That can't be right," she whispered.

"Yes it can. You see, it wasn't always…" She paused as a beam of light coming from the direction of the doorway sliced through the darkness.

"Oh, my God. What have you two found?" It was Tyson.

"What are you doing down here? I asked you to keep people away." Tam's eyes narrowed at the sight of her friend.

"I'm sorry. I looked in to make sure you were all right and I saw the Jefferson statue moved to the side. Then I noticed the staircase and I just couldn't believe it. I called down to you and, when you didn't answer, I thought you might be in trouble." He shone his light around the vault, taking in the treasures of human history. "What is this place?"

"Sort of an old library," Tam said.

"Right." He glanced at the book in Tam's hand, and the map. Avery didn't miss the way his eyes widened. Without warning, he drew a Glock and leveled it at Tam's face. "Give me the book."

Tam didn't flinch. "How can you possibly be one of them?" She bit off each word, fire blazing in her eyes.

"Who? The Dominion?" Tyson laughed. "Not a chance. I'm too, shall we say, tainted by the blood of Cain for their liking."

"Then why are you helping them?"

"Let's just say that, on occasion, we have mutual interests."

"Who is we?"

"The Trident." As if by reflex, Tyson's free hand moved to a spot below his throat.

"You're a traitor to the country you devoted your life to serving."

"America." Tyson laughed again. "I never served this infant nation. I serve the oldest people of them all. Any job I took in this foul government served to put me into a position to help prepare for the return."

Tam held Tyson's full attention, and Avery took advantage of that fact, sidling away. What could she do to help? The man was too big to fight and, even if she could take him on, she couldn't do anything before he pulled the trigger.

"You're crazy," Tam whispered.

"And you're dead."

Before Tyson could pull the trigger, Tam struck, smashing the journal book into his gun hand.

As Tyson's shot went wild, Avery threw all her weight against the Poseidon statue. It toppled over with agonizing slowness, striking Tyson in the shoulder and knocking him to the side.

Tam lashed out with a roundhouse kick, knocking Tyson's Glock free. He reached for his weapon, and Avery remembered her own pistol.

She drew it, took aim, and shouted out with more confidence than she actually felt. "Hands up or I'll shoot!"

At the sound of her voice, Tyson flung his flashlight at her head and rolled to the side. Avery's shot went wild as the big man fled. She spun around, following the sound of crashing statues as he fled the vault, and fired a desperate shot.

"Let's go!" Tam had regained her feet, her Makarov, and the book. Avery snatched her Maglite off the shelf and followed. At the door, she paused to retrieve the crystal, then sprinted to try and keep up with Tam, whose light bobbed up and down ten meters ahead. Tyson stood well over six feet tall and looked like an athlete. It was unlikely they'd catch him, but Tam appeared determined to try.

They took the steps two at a time, their footfalls reverberating through the stairwell. And then, all sounds were drowned out by a low rumble. Avery felt the vibration in the soles of her feet.

"He must have taken the crystal! He's trying to lock us in down here!"

Up above, the statue slowly moved back into place. The square of bright light inexorably shrinking. Tam hurtled through the opening, which seemed to be shrinking even faster. Did Avery dare try it? But what if Tyson had taken the crystal? She might be stuck here?

She had an instant to make up her mind. What would Maddock do? With a cry something like terror, she flung herself upward.

She stumbled.

And fell, her legs half in and half out of the stairwell. She scrambled to crawl, but she slipped on the slick, stone surface. Almost there. She felt the statue's massive pedestal close on her foot.

Suddenly, Tam grabbed her wrists and yanked. For an interminable instant, she felt frozen in place, and then she slid forward. Something grabbed her toe and she jerked her leg. Her foot slid free, leaving her shoe behind.

"Could be worse," she mumbled as she scrambled to her feet. When Avery reached the portico, she saw Tam standing on the bottom step, Makarov at her side. The thickening fog rendered visibility almost nil.

"We lost him."

"It's my fault. If I hadn't fallen, you might have caught him."

Tam shook her head. "He had too big a lead, and the dude is fast. You saw them long legs. Besides, he'd have killed me if it weren't for you."

Avery doubted that, but appreciated the words of reassurance.

Through the fog, they heard the sound of running feet. They both aimed their weapons at the sound, but lowered them again when they recognized their driver.

"I've been trying to reach you," he said, skidding to a halt in front of Tam. "A terrorist group just claimed responsibility for the tsunamis. They've got a list of demands, and if they aren't met, they say a major city will be the next to fall."

"Does this group have a name?" Tam's tone of voice was razor sharp.

"The Dominion."

Chapter 44

Bishop Frederick Hadel read through a report from his agent inside the CIA. The contact was a low-level operative, and seldom had much of use to report but, on occasion, he delivered valuable information. Today, he'd picked up a useful tidbit. Someone within the agency had tried to warn the government about an attack on Savannah. Specifically, a man-made disaster.

"Our first leak," he said aloud. His mind ran through the list of false trails he'd laid. The Savannah rumor had been planted with the leader of the church in Key West. He'd have to address that situation immediately. A shame, really. Some of his most ardent supporters were members of that particular congregation, and they'd served him well during the tsunami and in Mexico.

Now, he opened a browser window on his desktop computer and navigated to the major news sites. As he expected, the internet was abuzz over the proclamation the Dominion had just released, in which they claimed responsibility for the tsunamis and demanded the President's resignation, along with that of the Vice President, a few select Supreme Court justices, and most of congress.

His demands would not be met, of course, but the implicit message would not be missed. One look at the list of representatives and justices whom the Dominion considered acceptable would deliver the message. The nation needed to change, and he would make it over by any means necessary. The next attack would prove the Dominion's power, and when they obtained the Revelation Machine…

His phone buzzed, interrupting his musings. He tapped the speakerphone button.

"Yes?"

"Mister Robinson to see you, Bishop. He says it's urgent."

"Send him in."

As always, Robinson knocked exactly two times before pushing the door open. It was an idiosyncrasy, or perhaps a compulsive behavior, that Hadel was happy to ignore, given Robinson's reliability.

"I just received a report from a contact within a friendly organization. A CIA agent named Tamara Broderick sought his help in accessing a vault beneath the Jefferson Memorial—one that, she claimed, contained a Templar archive."

Hadel sat up straight. "And?"

"It was there. Inside, she found information that pinpoints the location of the capital, if you will, of Atlantis. He failed to obtain the document in question, which he said appeared to be a journal of some sort, but he saw the map and knew exactly where it pointed."

Hadel laid his hands on his lap to prevent Robinson from seeing them tremble. He couldn't remember ever being so excited. But, when Robinson told him the location, he found himself puzzled.

"I've never heard of such a place. Just a moment." He returned to his computer and called up the location. When the first images appeared on his screen, he relaxed. "Atlantis," he whispered, "has been hiding in plain sight all this time."

"I'm assembling a team as we speak," Robinson said. "We await your instructions."

"Activate the failsafe plan."

"Bishop?" A furrow creased Robinson's brow. "But the failsafe is…"

"I know what it is, and now is the perfect time to activate it, because I'm going with you."

Chapter 45

The Range Rover bounced across the barren landscape, jostling its passengers. Maddock slowed the vehicle to a halt atop a rise. The sun beat down on the dry, rocky landscape below. It was hard to believe this was their destination.

They all climbed out, stretching tired limbs and knuckling sore backs.

"The Eye of the Sahara," Sofia whispered. "I never would have thought it possible."

Located in Mauritania, the Richat Structure, or the Eye of the Sahara, was a thirty kilometer-wide, collapsed volcanic dome. Visible from space, when seen from far overhead, its circular shape and symmetrical rings bore an eerie similarity to elements of Plato's description of Atlantis. Indeed, when Sofia had shown him satellite photos of the location, he'd been shocked no one had considered it before.

"It looks different from here," Bones said. "Not like Atlantis at all."

"That's because we aren't looking at it from overhead." Jade rolled her eyes.

"But how could Atlantis have been here? We're so far away from the ocean. I don't see how it could ever have flooded."

"Researchers have found evidence of salt water fishing in the area ten to twelve thousand years ago," Jade said. "So it's possible that the ocean extended further inland than it does now."

"Another possibility is that Plato's flood story referred to the site in Spain, which flooded and was buried beneath mud, just like the story says," Sofia said. "If the mother city stood here, it might have been so isolated that it could have been lost to memory."

"Seems like an awfully big place to just get lost," Bones said.

"Up until a little over ten thousand years ago, settlements in northern Africa were largely restricted to the Nile Valley. By the time the Sahara went through its monsoon period, the Atlanteans were gone. At least, that's our best guess." Sofia looked out across the landscape and smiled in disbelief. "I've worked at this for so long, and now we're right on the verge of finding it. I just can't believe it."

"Where do we start?" Maddock asked.

"There are no explicit directions, but it seems there's a system of caves somewhere near the center."

"According to my research, there's a small hotel there," Jade said. "That could make for a good base of operations while we search."

"As long as we can see the Dominion coming." Maddock hopped back into the Range Rover and cranked it up while the others piled in. Deep inside him, the thrill at the prospect of finding Atlantis battled with apprehension over the Revelation Machine. What if the Dominion got there first? Or, and he hated to entertain the thought, what happened if he found it first? Did any government deserve the power to destroy the world? But that was a problem for later. First, they had to find it.

"Were we supposed to make a reservation?" Bones asked as they pulled up in front of the tiny hotel that rested right in the center of the Eye. "Looks like they didn't leave the light on for us."

The small hotel appeared deserted. Maddock cut the engine. All was quiet. "I imagine this place doesn't get much business, but I have a bad feeling about this." Drawing his Walther, he climbed out of the Range Rover. Bones was at his side a moment later.

"Do you want us to stay here?" Sofia asked.

"I don't want you two to be alone, just in case."

"Maddock, you see these tracks?" Bones swept his hand in a half-circle. "At least two different vehicles were all over this place, and not too long ago or else the wind would have blown the tracks away." He narrowed his eyes. "Looks like Hummers to me."

Maddock didn't reply. He hoped that, if two Hummers had come this way, they weren't packed with Dominion agents. He led the way to the hotel.

The coppery scent of blood filled his nostrils as soon as he opened the door. He didn't need to look far to find the source.

A man lay bound to an upended chair. His eyes gazed blankly up at the ceiling. Congealed blood pooled on the floor around his head. Maddock grimaced at the ragged cut in the man's throat.

"Cause of death is pretty obvious." Bones pursed his lips as he looked at the grisly scene. "Looks like he was tortured."

The man's hands were smashed, his fingertips sliced and his fingernails torn out.

"I guess the Dominion got here first." Maddock hoped he caught up with the men who did this. He was eager to repay the favor.

"I can't imagine they got any useful information from a desk clerk," Bones said.

"We can hope," Jade said. "Say, what if it's not the Dominion? What if it's this Trident group Tam told us about?"

"All we can do is be prepared. Let's check the building and get out of here."

It didn't take long to determine no one else was about. Thankfully, they found no other bodies. When they'd completed the search, they gathered outside the door.

"What's our next move?" Bones asked. "This place is too big to just go wandering."

"I don't see that we have a choice." Jade turned to Sofia. "Unless you think there's something you missed in what Tam sent you."

Sofia shook her head. "I'll look again, but I don't think so."

"I have an idea," Maddock said. "I think it's safe to say the man inside didn't know the way to Atlantis. But, if he was local, he probably would have been familiar with any caves in the area."

"Which would mean the Dominion now knows the way," Bones grumbled.

"How would they know about the caves without the book?" Sofia asked. "Tam said her so-called friend only saw the map."

"It stands to reason that Atlantis, if it's here, is beneath the volcanic dome," Jade said. "They'd have wanted to know about any tunnels or caverns that might lead underground."

"So we do what?" Bones asked. "Drive around until we find some locals?"

"We could do that," Maddock said. "Or we could follow their tire tracks."

Chapter 46

The moment he spotted the Hummers parked at the base of a steep rise, Maddock pulled the Range Rover behind a rise, blocking it from view. Urging Jade and Avery to wait with the vehicle, and failing spectacularly to convince them, he and the others moved closer to scout the area.

"I'll bet it's somewhere on that ridge up there." Maddock pointed to a steeply-sloped wall of volcanic rock. "It stands to reason the entrance would be somewhere difficult to get to, and that doesn't look like an easy climb."

"Not for some people." Bones winked. He and Maddock had always been competitive when it came to climbing. "So, do we wait until Tam gets here with backup?"

"I don't think we can. If the Dominion, or anyone, for that matter, is ahead of us, we'd better catch up to them before they find the machine."

"Ladies, you should wait with the Range Rover." Bones held up a hand.

"Not a chance." Jade glared at the two men. "We've got as much right as you to see this through. Heck, Sofia has more right than any of us. This all started with the Dominion killing her team. Besides, you're probably outgunned, so you'll need all the help you can get."

"Someone needs to be here in case Tam tries to make contact."

"Have you checked your phone lately?" Sofia held up her phone. "We haven't had a signal for hours. Might as well be a tin can and string."

Maddock had had this same argument too many times to count, and not only with Jade, and he'd never won.

"No point in arguing. Let's move."

They found precious little cover as they moved toward the spot where the Hummers were parked, but they arrived without incident. Whoever had gotten here first hadn't left a lookout. Maddock made a cursory inspection of the vehicles. Both were empty, save a Bible lying on the passenger seat of the second vehicle. It wasn't confirmation that it was the Dominion they tracked, but it increased the likelihood. Meanwhile, Bones began tracking their quarry, complaining all the while about stereotypes and racial insensitivity. He identified eight sets of bootprints, probably belonging to men based on their size. As they expected, the tracks led up the rocky slope, part of one of the raised rings that gave the Eye its distinctive appearance.

The way up was easier than Maddock had anticipated, with plenty of natural hand and footholds. Jade was a skilled climber in her own right, and Sofia held her own. They experienced a bit of good fortune when, approximately two-thirds of the way up, they came upon a climbing rope affixed to pitons hammered into the rocky face.

"Nice of them to help us up the steepest part." Bones grunted as he heaved his bulk up the rock.

"Putting these in would have slowed them down, at least a few minutes," Maddock added. "We'll take any break we can get at this point, no matter how small."

Reaching the top, they fanned out and began searching for the caves that would, they hoped, lead down into the earth and to the fabled lost city. Minutes later, Maddock spotted a ledge a few meters below the place where he stood. From this vantage point, only a fraction of it was visible, but his sharp eyes espied it, as well as a scuff mark that might have been made by a boot. He waved the others over and then climbed down for a better look.

Rubble lay scattered across the ledge where someone appeared to have cleared away a rockfall, exposing a dark passageway.

"I think this is it," Maddock said.

"How will Tam and the others find us?" Jade looked doubtfully into the dark cave.

Maddock considered the question, then took his cell phone out of his pocket and stuck it in a crack in the rock.

"Maybe they can trace it." He made a noncommittal shrug before entering the cave.

A few meters in, the cave floor dropped down at a steep angle before leveling off in a small chamber where three round tunnels converged. Seeing no signs left by the Dominion's agents, they decided to take them one at a time, beginning with the one on the left.

"This is a lava tube." Jade shone her light around the rock-encrusted tube. "And maybe not the most stable one. There are cracks everywhere."

Maddock looked up at the fragmented crust coating the tunnel and winced.

"Maybe Bones should walk a little more softly," Sofia said.

"The day a white person teaches me how to walk softly…" Bones began.

"Hello? Latina here."

"Oh. You shut it too."

"I've got an idea," Maddock said. "How about we hold it down in case there's a Dominion agent or two waiting around the corner?"

"He's such a killjoy, but I suppose he's right." Bones squeezed the grip of his Glock.

The lava tube ended in a wall of rubble, and they were forced to retrace their steps. The second passageway was similarly collapsed a short way in.

"That leaves door number three," Bones said.

They entered the third passageway moving cautiously, not knowing when they might happen upon the Dominion. This lava tube was in a condition similar to the others, with cracks running through the rocks and shattered stones all over the floor, remnants of minor ceiling collapses. More than once, Maddock froze when he thought he heard the sound of cracking rock.

"It's held for more than ten thousand years," Jade whispered. "Surely it can last a little longer." She snaked her arm around Maddock's waist and gave him a quick squeeze.

"It'll be all right. Just keep moving."

Several anxious minutes later they came to a spot where two tunnels crossed.

"Holy crap." Bones glared at the tunnels as if they'd given offense. "This is going to take forever."

"Now I see how Atlantis could have gone undiscovered for all this time," Sofia said. "It's in an unlikely location, the cave was hard to find, and even if a local were to stumble upon it, they could wander around down here forever without ever finding anything of interest."

"And I'll bet you need a crystal to get inside." Maddock thought of the door to the Hall of Records and what Tam had told him about the entrance to the vault beneath the Jefferson Memorial.

"You figure the Dominion will blast their way in?" Bones asked.

Before anyone could reply, a deafening explosion rocked the ground beneath their feet. Maddock covered his head as chunks of ceiling began to fall.

"Which tunnel did it come from?" Bones cried, dodging a chunk of rock.

Maddock looked around and saw dust drifting out of the nearest tunnel. "That one. Come on!" He grabbed Jade by the arm and ran, Bones and Sofia hot on their heels.

As they ducked into the lava tube, the ceiling continued to crash down. They kept running along the curving passageway, the sound of falling rock loud in their ears. Finally, when they heard no sound except that of their own feet pounding the floor, they stopped to catch their breath.

"What's your plan, Maddock?" Bones shone his light back the way they had come. The tunnel behind them had completely collapsed. They were trapped.

"We do the only thing we can. Keep going."

Chapter 47

"I don't understand." Robinson nudged a silver box with his foot. "In most ways this place is primitive, but some of the things we're finding seem advanced—alien, even."

"Do not make assumptions. I am sure all will be made clear in time." Hadel kept his voice calm, though his mind was in turmoil.

In searching for Atlantis, he'd expected to find the remains of an ancient, human civilization, one that had perhaps stumbled across a previously unknown, yet terrestrial, power, and the discovery of the crystal-powered weapon seemed to confirm that, but now, he was not so certain.

It was true that there was an ancient world feeling about this place—every passageway or chamber they passed through thus far had been a natural formation or a room carved from stone. No one else seemed to notice that those rooms were carved with more precision than even the most advanced of the ancient stone masons. And their shapes were... off—the angles not quite square, the ceilings undulating, rather than flat. The deeper they'd penetrated into Atlantis, the more uneasy he felt. This place felt... wrong.

They entered another of these disorientingly-skewed rooms and Hadel felt his insides twist into knots as his mind sought to resolve what he saw into a normal picture. Here, the walls were hive-like, with oval pockets carved everywhere. It appeared to be a storage room of some kind, with clay pots and jars in some, and more alien-looking objects of various size and shape in others.

"I don't like this place," Robinson muttered under his breath.

Hadel turned an angry glare on Robinson, who did not wither under the bishop's stare as so many of his underlings might have. It wasn't that he disagreed with the statement. It was the way Robinson gave voice to Hadel's own fears that annoyed him.

"The artifacts, the crystals on the wall that absorb light and pass it along. What if they're dangerous?" Robinson asked.

"Some of them are likely to be dangerous," Hadel said. "That is why we are here, is it not? To find the Revelation Machine so that we may complete our work."

"Yes, but with so many things down here we don't understand, maybe we should take you somewhere safe, and then the men and I can come back here and complete the search."

"Is this a coup? Do you want to control the Revelation Machine?" Hadel snapped. He'd never have believed Robinson capable of such machinations.

The blood drained from Robinson's face. "Of course not. I only meant that we're expendable. You're essential."

"Very well." Hadel forced a smile and struggled to calm his nerves. Where had that flash of paranoia come from? Robinson had always been one of his most loyal lieutenants.

Somewhere in the distance, a shot rang out. Robinson froze, listening. After a few seconds, he turned to Hadel. "That must be Thomas. He wouldn't fire unless he had reason."

"Whatever is happening at the door, these men can see to it." Hadel inclined his head toward the five operatives who trailed behind them. "You and I will find the Revelation Machine."

It took one shot to eliminate the guard posted in front of the door to Atlantis. Maddock kept his Walther at the ready as he crept forward, keeping his eyes peeled for more enemies.

"Nice shot," Bones whispered. "Next one is mine."

Maddock relieved the guard of his AK-47 and paused to examine the remains of the door to Atlantis. The Dominion had blasted a hole in it large enough for a person to crawl through, but most of it still remained—a stone block half a meter thick, twice his height and nearly as wide. Like the door to the Hall of Records, someone had carved Orion into the stone.

"I could be wrong, but I'm beginning to think Orion is important," Bones said.

Maddock ignored him. He climbed through the hole, and waited for the others to join him. They were still in a lava tube, but here, the floor was perfectly level. Up ahead, the passageway shone with opalescent light.

"That looks familiar." Maddock shone his light on an opaque, diamond-shaped crystal. As soon as the beam struck the crystal, the surface swirled, and the light became brighter and more iridescent, gaining in strength until the passageway shone as bright as day. It set off a chain reaction as crystals further down the hall absorbed and amplified the light.

"I've never seen anything like this," Sofia marveled.

"We have," Maddock and Bones said in unison.

Maddock thought back on all places he and Bones had been and the things they had seen in the past few years: so many devices, and even weapons, powered by crystals, the powers of some of which were nothing short of miraculous. Was Atlantis the source of it all?

"Looks like there's a room up ahead." Bones raised the AK-47 to his shoulder and took the lead as they moved along the silent corridor.

A low wall barred entry to the first chamber, which was empty.

"Maybe it's a guard room?" Jade offered.

"Makes sense. All I know is, it's weird." The room was almost square, the walls almost perpendicular, but off just enough to give Maddock a feeling of discomfort. The arched, ribbed ceiling bulged in places, and the center line was not quite straight.

"It's like we were swallowed by a snake," Bones said.

"All I know is, looking at it makes me dizzy." Jade rubbed her eyes. "Let's get out of here."

Up ahead, the lava tube ended with a passageway running off to either side. They chose the one on the right, and found it to be cut at the same, not quite square, angles.

"Don't look at the walls," Maddock said. "Keep your focus straight ahead and you won't feel so dizzy." Taking his own advice, he locked his gaze on the way ahead, and they soon found themselves in a much larger, if no less disorienting, room than the previous one. What they found stopped them all in their tracks.

The walls were covered in maps and star charts, cut with such precision that they could not have been made with primitive tools. Running all around the base of the walls, like a giant honeycomb, a waist-high band of meter-wide, hexagonal cubes held stacks of stone tablets. Stone benches ringed a table in the center, where more tablets lay, as well as a few crystals and an object that looked like a titanium pencil.

"This is their archive!" Sofia picked up one of the stone tablets at random and examined it. "The writing is the same as in the codex I found in Spain. I'll bet," she looked around, eyes as big as saucers, "the whole story of Atlantis is here. What might we learn about human history once we translate them?"

"I think we'll find that the Atlanteans, at least the original ones, came from somewhere out there." Bones pointed to a star chart. "Probably from a planet orbiting one of the stars in Orion."

"Five years ago, I would have laughed at you," Maddock said. "But it makes sense. Remember Goliath's sword?"

"How could I forget?"

"If you guys are going to reminisce about things we weren't there for, you really ought to give us a bit more information." Sofia sounded affronted.

"It's a long story. Actually, it's several long stories." Maddock wondered how long it would take to recount their exploits of the past few years.

"I've heard bits and pieces of them from Avery. Just hit the highlights."

Maddock paused, considering how to sum it all up. "We've found things made of metal that didn't come from earth. We've found things powered by crystals that could do things that were so advanced that they seemed like magic... or very advanced technology."

"Like the tsunami machine and the gun," Sofia said.

Bones nodded. "That and more. An almost perfect cloaking device, a blade that could cut through stone, spears that fired bolts of energy, and all of them were powered by ambient light. And that's not even all of the things we've seen."

"And we found them in different places: Jordan, Germany, England, Ireland, even America." Maddock looked around as he spoke. "Looking at these maps, and taking into account the book Tam and Avery found, I think it's a reasonable assumption that this is where it all started."

"They had knowledge of the entire world," Jade said. "Every continent is mapped accurately."

"Some people believe that the great accomplishments of the ancient world were made possible by contact with aliens," Bones said. "But that's definitely a story for another day."

"I know you'd like to stay here and begin your studies," Maddock said, "but we should keep moving. I want to catch up with the Dominion before they get their hands on the Revelation Machine."

They left the library and entered a crypt. Skeletal remains filled alcoves in the walls. They were tall and slim, their arms too long for their bodies and their fingers too long for their hands. Their heads were overlarge, the skulls elongated, and their eye sockets large and round.

"These look like... aliens," Sofia breathed.

"Another thing we've seen before," Maddock said. "We..."

A thunder of gunfire cut him off in mid-sentence. Sofia's body jerked as a torrent of bullets ripped through her. Maddock knew in an instant there was no hope.

Jade dove behind one of the stone benches while Maddock and Bones took shelter behind the table and returned fire. Maddock saw a Dominion operative fall, clutching his throat, and felt a wave of satisfaction.

"You two duck out the back!" Bones shouted. "I'll cover you." Not waiting for a reply, he opened up with the AK-47.

Maddock grabbed Jade by the back of her belt, hauled her to her feet, and shoved her toward the exit beneath the world map. Bullets spattered the ground at their feet as they fled.

"Keep going!" Maddock shouted. "We'll catch up."

Jade looked up at him, tears streaming down her face and grabbed his collar. "You kill them, Maddock," she rasped, her voice husky. "Kill them all."

"I'll try."

Jade yanked down on his collar and kissed him, hard and fast, and then turned and ran.

Maddock heard Bones' AK-47 fall silent and hurried back to the doorway.

"Your turn, Bones!" Maddock emptied his Walther while Bones, ducking down as low as his frame would allow, ran for it.

More shots rang out as Bones dove for the tunnel, hit the ground and rolled, and came up in a kneeling position. He squeezed off two shots with his Glock.

"I've got one reload left. How about you?"

"Same here." Maddock ejected the magazine and reached into his pocket for a reload.

"Don't bother," said a cold voice. "Now, turn around slowly or the girl dies."

Chapter 48

Jade stood, hands on her head, her lips pressed tightly together. She trembled slightly, but the fire in her eyes told Maddock she wasn't frightened, but enraged. A tall, weedy blond man stood behind her with his rifle pressed against the back of her neck. A second man, dark-haired and broad shouldered, trained his weapon on Maddock and Bones.

"You two drop your weapons, put your hands on your heads, and stand up slowly." The dark-haired man gestured with his rifle.

Maddock assessed the situation in an instant and knew there was nothing he or Bones could do without Jade paying the price. Charging the men or throwing their knives was out of the question—the distance between them was too great and retreating to the archive room wouldn't work. The men would kill Jade and probably get to Maddock and Bones before they could reload their weapons. And then there were the men coming up behind them. He dropped his Walther and stood, Bones following suit an instant later.

"Don't hurt her. We'll cooperate." His only hope was to stay alive long enough to rescue Jade and, hopefully, sabotage the Revelation Machine.

"I'm sorry, Maddock. I didn't see them until I ran right up to them," Jade said through gritted teeth.

"It's all right."

He heard footsteps behind him, and felt the cold metal of a gun barrel pressed against his neck.

"Wilson, they got Douglas," a voice behind him said to the dark-haired man. "I think we should waste them right here."

"I don't know. I think the bishop should make the call. Frisk them. And if you two," Wilson's eyes moved back and forth between Maddock and Bones, "do anything stupid, I'll kill you in a second. The girl, I'll kill slowly."

The agent patted them down one at a time, relieving them of their recon knives and spare magazines. When he got to Maddock's front pocket, he paused.

"I'm not your type," Maddock said.

Ignoring him, the agent reached into Maddock's pocket and drew out the pouch that held the Atlantean crystals. He tossed the bag to Wilson, who upended the contents into his hand. He held the crystals out, letting the light dance off their surface.

"What do these do?"

"I found them on the floor and thought I'd add them to my rock collection." Pain blossomed through Maddock's skull as the man behind him struck him at the base of his skull with the butt of his rifle. Maddock grimaced but didn't fall or even cry out.

Smiling, Wilson pocketed the crystals.

"We'll take you to the bishop. If, by the time we get there, you haven't decided to come clean, we'll cut pieces off of your girl until you tell us what we want to know."

Maddock and Bones exchanged glances. Bishop Hadel was here? Maddock made up his mind then. If he decided escape was impossible, he'd find a way to kill Hadel.

The Dominion's operatives escorted them, at gunpoint, through the Atlantean complex. They passed through empty rooms and others where alien-looking artifacts lay on shelves or in the strange, hexagonal alcoves. This place would be a treasure trove of information if they could ever get away, but Maddock scarcely considered the thought. Rage burned hot inside him. His failure to protect Jade and Sofia was almost more than he could bear.

Bishop Hadel stood in the midst of a massive chamber—the largest they'd seen since entering the underground city. Maddock took in his surroundings. This room was clearly the model for the Atlantean temples they'd discovered. It had the same exact layout as the others, down to the pyramid-shaped facade at the back. But it was what stood at the center that separated it from the other sites they'd uncovered.

A circle of crystal spikes, each twice a man's height and breadth and tilted inward so that their points almost touched, stood behind a ring of gleaming silver metal reminiscent of the Stonehenge-like altars in the temples. A silver hand, its palm open, rose from the altar.

The bishop paced back and forth, staring at the crystals.

Another man, large and powerfully-built, stood nearby. He turned his gaze on Maddock and Bones as they entered the room. His green eyes bored into Maddock.

"Who are these people?" he snapped.

Before anyone could reply, Bishop Hadel turned on his heel and stalked toward the captives. His hands trembled and there was a gleam in his eyes that bordered on manic. Maddock had seen Hadel on television and in pictures, but the man always seemed so calm and self-assured. What he'd seen down here had unhinged him.

"I know who they are." Hadel's voice shook. "The Indian is Uriah Bonebrake, which makes this one," he pointed a trembling finger at Maddock, "Dane Maddock." He lowered his voice. "You two have a knack for stepping on my toes. I ordered you killed months ago, but we couldn't locate you. And now, here you are." He laughed, a cold cackle that echoed in the stone chamber. "Did you imagine you would stop us from setting off the Revelation Machine?"

Maddock glowered at him, but remained silent. If Hadel planned to set off the machine, the situation was worse than he had feared. Of course, now that he saw the device, if that's what this crystal circle was, he realized it wasn't something that could be carried away. If Hadel wanted to use it, he'd have to do it here.

"Bishop," Wilson began, "he had these with him."

The bishop took the pouch containing the Atlantean stones, looked inside, and smiled. "I think we now have what we need." He leaned in close to Maddock until their faces were inches apart. "Are you ready to die?"

Maddock didn't speak, didn't think. Instead, he head-butted Hadel across the bridge of the nose.

Hadel cried out in pain and reeled away, his hands unable to hold back the crimson flow that streamed down his chin and dripped onto the stone floor.

Behind him, the Dominion operative clubbed Maddock across the back of his head with the butt of his rifle. Maddock dropped to one knee, his head swimming. Hadel was about to use the machine. What could he do?

The big, green-eyed man hurried to Hadel's side, but the bishop shook him off.

"I'm fine, Robinson. Just keep an eye on these three in case they try anything else." His broken nose still dripping blood, he turned and headed for the machine.

"Shall I kill them?" Robinson asked.

"No. Let them see it happen. I want them to feel their failure deep in their bones before they die."

"With all due respect," Robinson said, "I don't think we should try the machine until we're certain of what it does."

Hadel turned a beatific smile in Robinson's direction. "I know what it does. It will bring about the end of times, as promised in the Book of Revelation."

Robinson swallowed hard. "I understand, but we should learn to control it before we use it."

"Control? You do not presume to control the power of God."

Maddock's vision cleared and he noticed the guards behind Jade and Bones shift uncomfortably. The time was drawing near and the only possible action would be desperate and likely fatal. Of course, if Hadel discharged the machine, the result would be the same. As Maddock planned his last, desperate attack, Hadel continued to rant.

"You saw what lies in this place. Abominations! The earth must be cleansed of this filth."

Robinson tried to argue but Hadel went on.

"This world has become an abomination. Our faith is persecuted daily as people bow to the altars of science and government. Imagine what the idolaters would make of what we've found here. They would use it as *evidence*," he spat the word, "against the truth of our Lord." His voice fell to a hoarse grunt. "Better they die in the Lord than live in confusion."

The bishop turned again and, as he approached the machine, the crystals in his hand began to flicker. He knelt before the machine and began to recite the Lord's Prayer.

"Robinson?" one of the guards said.

"Stand firm." Robinson ordered. "He is about the Lord's work."

Hadel laid a gleaming crystal in the silver hand rising from the altar. It snapped into place and began to glow. Behind the rail, the giant crystals that formed the machine also began to glow.

High above, unnoticed by anyone except Maddock, crystals set in the stone began to glimmer as Hadel laid more crystals into place. With each one, the machine shone brighter and the crystals in the ceiling sparkled.

Soon, Maddock recognized their shape. He took another glance in the direction of the machine, and then back up at the crystals in the ceiling. He now understood the machine's purpose.

As the bishop made to place the last stone, Maddock stole a glance at Bones and Jade. Their eyes met and he mouthed instructions. He didn't know for certain if they understood, because, just then, the last crystal clicked into place and the world exploded in blue light.

Chapter 49

"Where the hell are you, Maddock?" Tam stood, hands on hips, staring at the small hotel that stood in the middle of the Richat Structure. They'd found plenty of footprints and tire tracks, but no sign of Maddock or the others. Until they'd arrived, she hadn't appreciated how vast this place was. "I shouldn't have sent him in ahead of us."

She looked up as Greg and Professor emerged from the hotel.

"There's a body inside," Greg said, "but no sign of our people."

"Do you think they were here?" Tam asked.

Greg shrugged. "No way to tell."

"Damn! If Willis and Matt don't find any sign of them, I guess we'll follow the tire tracks and hope it's them." Tam sighed. "And that's another dollar in the jar, too. Working with those two is going to break me."

Willis and Matt appeared a few minutes later, looking sweaty and frustrated.

"We didn't find nothing." Willis cast an angry glance in the direction from which they'd come. "I don't know where those boys got off too."

"We'll have to keep looking." Tam turned toward their vehicle, where Corey sat, pecking away at his laptop. "Any luck tracing their cellphones?"

"No signal out here," Corey said. "You should have issued satellite phones."

Tam bit off her reply as the ground began to tremble.

"What the hell is that?" Willis scanned the horizon. "Somebody drop a bomb?"

A low rumble resounded from somewhere deep beneath the earth, and with it the ground shook even more violently. Tam staggered and grabbed hold of Willis' arm for support.

A column of brilliant, blue light shot up from the ground, consuming the hotel. Tam shielded her eyes from the blinding light. Oddly, it generated no heat, but she felt as if every hair on her body were standing on end. It went on for the span of ten heartbeats, and then stopped without warning.

"What in the name of Jesus?" she muttered, blinking the spots out of her eyes.

"It was like a beam of pure energy." Professor's face was ashen. "It went straight up into space, almost like a…"

"Like what?" Tam asked.

"Like a beacon." He turned his eyes up to the sky. "You know, like the way researchers send messages into space, hoping to make contact with alien life."

Tam's breath caught in her throat. She remembered Tyson's words. "…*prepare for the return.*" Could this be what he meant? Was the so-called Revelation Machine designed to send a message into space? No, she couldn't even contemplate that right now. They still needed to find Maddock and the others.

"Tam, look at this," Greg called.

Where the hotel once stood, a shaft, perfectly round and smooth, plunged deep into the ground. She joined Greg at its edge.

"The stone seems to have melted away, but it's cool to the touch." He ran his fingers along the inside of the shaft to demonstrate.

"Dissolved is more like it," Professor added. "How is that possible?"

"We can figure that out later," Tam said. "Look at what's down there."

Down at the bottom of the shaft, a circle of crystals flickered in the darkness. Tam's sharp eyes could just make out a metallic ring around the crystals. It had to be the Revelation Machine, which meant there was a good chance that was where they'd find Maddock.

Or the Dominion.

Chapter 50

When Bishop Hadel placed the last crystal into place, Maddock closed his eyes and shielded them with his hands. The surprised cries from the Dominion's agents told him he'd guessed correctly.

He spun about and struck at the Dominion agent, who had been rendered temporarily blind by the brilliant light from the Revelation Machine. His fist connected solidly with the man's chin. His legs turned to rubber and Maddock kicked him in the temple on the way down. Beside him, Bones had eliminated his guard with ruthless efficiency, and now closed in on the agent who guarded Jade. She, too had understood Maddock's plan, and now grappled with the man for control of his AK-47.

Maddock turned and made a dash for Robinson, who squinted against the bright light and looked around for a target on which to bring his weapon to bear. He reached Robinson, drove his shoulder into Robinson's chest, and knocked his rifle barrel upward just as the man squeezed the trigger, sending bullets ricocheting through the chamber.

Like a football player hitting the blocking sled, Maddock drove the larger man backward. Surprised, Robinson lost his grip on his rifle, stumbled backward, and hit the rail. For a moment, he struggled to regain his balance, but Maddock drove a sidekick into Robinson's chest, sending him toppling backward.

Robinson's head struck the nearest crystal and a blue aura engulfed him. His body jerked, his mouth twisted in a silent scream of anguish. His hair blackened and crumbled to dust in an instant. Even after the burst of energy ceased, Robinson continued to thrash about like a fish on dry land.

Slowly, the crystals dimmed, flickered, and died. It felt like an eternity, but Maddock knew the phenomenon couldn't have lasted much more than ten seconds. He looked around and saw Bones hauling a whimpering Bishop Hadel to his feet. Jade hurried to him and crushed him in a tight embrace.

"Are you all right?"

"I'm fine." He gently extracted himself from her arms. "You okay, Bones?"

"Hell yes. I almost fell asleep waiting for you to decide what to do."

Maddock recovered their weapons from the fallen Dominion operatives and assessed the situation. The men who had guarded Bones and Jade lay dead, while the man Maddock had taken out wobbled on hands and knees as he slowly regained consciousness. Maddock gave him another kick to the head and then bound him with his own belt.

Still holding on to Hadel, Bones glanced up at the ceiling, where the blast had carved a perfect circle where the apex of the temple had been moments earlier. "I saw you looking up there. What did you see?"

"Orion." Maddock pointed at the remaining crystals. "Most of it's gone, but you can still see his bow. His belt lay centered at the top of the ceiling and the crystals were pointed right at it. It just didn't seem like a weapon to me. With all we've seen, the connections to Orion, I just had a feeling."

"You think Hadel just sent a signal to the aliens?" Bones asked. "I should have thought of that myself."

"I don't know. If we assume the Atlanteans came from a planet orbiting a star in Orion, he picked the wrong time of day. Orion won't be overhead for several hours yet."

"But signals sent into space will diffuse over great distances," Jade said. "They might get the message someday."

Hadel, who stood stock-still next to Bones, his nose still dripping blood, slumped to the ground. "No," he whispered.

"Seriously, dude? You kill thousands of people and don't bat an eye, but make one little call to E.T. and you lose it?"

"You don't understand what will happen if the people find out…"

"Find out what? The truth?" Maddock said. "People are resilient. How about putting a little faith in them instead of in your twisted version of God?"

"People are sheep. They must be shown the way, else they stray into peril."

"After all the people you've killed, you're going to talk about keeping them from peril?" Maddock clenched his fists and, with a supreme effort of will, stopped himself from decking the man.

"Better a temporal death than an eternal one." The madness now receded from Hadel's eyes. Now a crafty grin spread across his face as he rose to his feet. "Besides, I have killed no one."

"Neither did Hitler," Maddock retorted, "but you're responsible for every killing done by your minions. For Sofia Perez, for the people of Norfolk and Key West, and all the others."

"Key West?" Hadel forced a laugh. "A modern day Sodom. I was proud to give the order."

"I'd watch what I say about Sodom," Bones cautioned, "considering where you're headed. We work for the government now, and I can guarantee you our boss will find you an affectionate cellmate to comfort you in your declining years."

Hadel blanched. "You'll never get a conviction. The government can't hope to match the attorneys I have at my disposal."

"Who says you'll be going to trial?"

Maddock turned to see Tam, in rappelling gear, lowering herself to the floor. A few seconds later, Willis and Greg followed.

"Where's Matt?" Maddock asked.

"Watching our backs with Professor. They weren't happy about it but I couldn't trust nerd boy to do it by himself."

"What do you mean I won't be going to trial?" Hadel demanded.

"Shush!" Tam held up a finger, silencing him. She turned in a slow circle, taking in the chamber. "Lord Jesus. So this is it."

"This is just a tiny bit of it," Jade said. "There's a library, a crypt, and all sorts of chambers. Lots of Atlantean instruments and devices, too."

"It would take years, maybe even decades, to glean all the knowledge from this place," Maddock said. "But I don't think that's a good idea."

"We've had this conversation before, Maddock, and my opinion hasn't changed any more than yours has. Technology can be dangerous, but I'd rather have it in our hands than in those of an enemy." Tam paused. "Where's Sofia?"

Maddock tried to answer, but his mouth was sandpaper and emotion held his throat in a chokehold. He felt Jade's hand on his shoulder.

"The Dominion got her." Bones' voice was as tight as his fists, which he clenched so hard that his arms trembled.

"Damn." Tam put her hands on her hips, took a deep breath, and composed herself.

And then she whirled and drove her fist into Hadel's gut. His breath left him in a rush and he slumped over. Tam grabbed a handful of his unkempt hair, kicked his feet out from under him, leaned down, and whispered in his ear. "I'll tell you why you won't be getting a trial any time soon, if ever. First of all, I don't plan on letting anyone know we've got you. We'll let them think you're dead while you rot away in Guantanamo Bay. And then we'll label you an enemy combatant."

"It won't stick." Hadel grunted. "I'm a citizen. I have rights."

"That's okay, sweetie. By then, I'll have taken my pound of flesh and squeezed every last secret out of you. The Dominion will be dead. Broken. Have fun using a public defender to fight charges of high treason, murder, and whatever else we can think of throwing at you."

"You have to let me go. You have no choice."

"I don't think so." Tam yanked Hadel to his feet. "Greg, bind this fool. And don't be gentle."

Greg pulled out a pair of cable ties and grabbed Hadel by the wrist.

"Do you think I would let my plan, my purpose, die without me? If, at any point, twenty-four hours pass without my people hearing from me, or if they learn I have been captured, the failsafe is activated. One city every forty-eight hours. Can you let that happen?" Hadel winced as Greg yanked his arms behind his back and bound his wrists.

"We'll stop you." Only a slight twitch in her cheek belied Tam's resolve.

"How? You don't know where the next attack will be, and the Atlantean weapon can be hidden on any boat. You can't guard every inch of the American coastline. Then again, perhaps your hubris is so great that you believe exactly that."

Maddock thought Tam might punch Hadel again, but she smiled instead. "You're going to tell me where the next attack will take place."

"You *are* an arrogant little girl." Hadel had regained some of his bluster, if not his self-assurance.

"Or you will tell Bonebrake." Tam turned to Bones. "You and Willis take our guest somewhere out of sight of us witnesses and teach him some of your traditional interrogation techniques."

"What?" Hadel gasped.

"Can I just scalp him?" Bones drew his Recon knife and licked the blade.

"If that don't work, I got some tricks I can show you." Willis bared his teeth and mimicked biting Hadel's face.

"I don't care," Tam said. "Just make it slow and make it hurt. For Sofia."

Bones and Greg hauled Hadel, who struggled and hurled racial epithets at them, into one of the passageways leading out of the chamber.

Maddock watched them go, wishing he could feel good about this turn of events, but unable to put Sofia's death out of his mind. "You do realize Bones doesn't know any kind of Indian torture methods, unless you want him to wear Hadel down with juvenile banter."

"I know that and you know that, but Hadel doesn't know that." Tam gave him a wink and then turned to Greg.

"As long as we're waiting, I'd like to check out the alcove back there." Jade pointed to the small room on the far side of the chamber.

In the other Atlantean temples, the small room was the adyton, a place exclusive to priests. Here, it served a very different purpose.

A tall, impossibly thin man with an elongated head lay perfectly preserved in a coffin of blue-tinted crystal. Jade gasped and Greg took a step back, but not Maddock and Tam, who had seen something like this only months before.

"There's another connection," Maddock said.

"I wonder who he was." Jade moved in for a closer look.

Maddock took in the sight. The man had long greenish-brown hair and beard, wore sea green robes and a silver crown inset with mother of pearl and topped by the largest shark's teeth Maddock had ever seen. His long, slender hands gripped a crystal tipped...

...trident.

"Poseidon."

The name hung in the air while the others struggled to reconcile this alien being with the god out of Greek mythology. Tam finally broke the silence.

"You're saying the Greek gods were real? Or, at least, this one was?"

"I'm saying I think this guy was the source of the Poseidon myth. He was important enough that his was the only body they preserved. I'll bet he was the Atlantean ruler, which is why he's represented in their temples, though in a form to which humans could relate. Think about it. The Atlanteans' alien appearance and their advanced technology would have made them seem godlike to primitive humans. I wouldn't be surprised if other Atlantean leaders provided the inspiration for other ancient world myths, legends, and gods."

Tam turned and hurried away. She stopped, dropped to one knee, and rested her hands on the rail that encircled the Revelation Machine. Her shoulders heaved and her head drooped.

"I'd better check on her." Jade took a few steps toward her before Maddock laid a hand on her shoulder.

"No, let me. I've spent more time than you coming to grips with this stuff." He hurried to Tam's side and knelt down beside her. When she didn't tell him to leave, he took her hand and gave it a squeeze. "It's okay."

"How is it okay? Everything I've believed all my life isn't true. Adam and Eve were aliens? All the miracle stories are just advanced technology from another world? What does that mean for the world if there's no more power of God to believe in? If it's all a lie?"

"Never underestimate the power of denial." At Tam's angry frown, he hurried on. "Seriously, though. Some might lose faith, and many didn't believe in the first place, but others will hold on. Heck, in some cases, it might even make their faith stronger. These crystals, they're miracles. The Atlanteans harnessed their power, but where did that power come from? And maybe the Atlanteans did intervene in human history, but that doesn't explain where humans come from or where Atlanteans come from, for that matter."

"It's not enough. An awful lot of people need to believe in the power of God, and in spite of all that we've seen, I need to believe it."

Maddock hesitated. He'd lost his religion when his wife died, but honesty compelled him to go on. "You know Bones and I did some serious damage in Utah a few years back, but do you know what we found down there?"

Tam shook her head.

"It's too long a story to tell you right now, but I promise you, it will restore your faith. Not only did we find treasures from out of the Old Testament, we experienced something that couldn't be explained by crystals or advanced technology. It was miraculous."

"I want to believe you," Tam said.

"Ask Jade and Bones. We all saw it."

"Ask me what?" Bones emerged from the hallway holding a pencil.

"Never you mind." Tam composed herself in an instant and sprang to her feet. "What did you find out?"

"New York City. It's hidden inside an Ellis Island tour boat."

"How can you be sure he's not lying?" Tam asked.

"Because, once he confessed, I cut the tips of his thumbs off just to make sure he kept his story straight."

"You didn't!" Jade gasped.

"Of course not, but he believed I would, so it amounted to the same thing. Besides, I don't think he could have given so many specific details under duress. Willis hung back with him to do some fact checking, but I think we've got what we need to know." He recounted the specifics of the Dominion's plan, and Tam sent Greg back to the surface to report this new information.

"You think they'll believe you this time?" Maddock asked.

"Oh yes. Issuing that public ultimatum had to be the stupidest thing the Dominion has ever done. Hadel must have thought he had the Revelation Machine in the bag. When that announcement came out, a lot of people started taking me seriously. They'll come down on those operatives in New York like a hard rain."

They took a minute to fill Bones in on their final discovery and on Maddock's theory. Having long supported the theory that aliens intervened in the ancient world, Bones agreed with all of Maddock's conclusions and proclaimed himself vindicated.

"From now on, Maddock, no more calling my theories 'crackpot,' okay?"

"No promises, Bones."

"What I want to know," Jade piped up, "is how you got Hadel to confess in the first place."

"Easy. I gave him time to get nervous and then I asked Willis for a pencil, a light, and some flammable liquid. I was just messing with Hadel's head, figuring I'd let his imagination run wild before I tried something less exotic, but Willis actually had a pencil on him. He said he's taken up Sudoku."

"And?" Jade asked.

"I showed Hadel how a pencil can be used to stretch open any orifice." He illustrated by placing the pencil between the corners of his mouth. "And then," he said around the pencil before spitting it out onto the floor, "I pulled out my Zippo, bent Hadel over, and pulled down his…"

"Okay, I get the picture." Jade covered her ears and turned away, but not fast enough to hide her smile.

"What happens now?" Maddock asked Tam.

"We take the bishop and any of the operatives you left alive into custody for enhanced interrogation."

"They can have my pencil if they need it," Bones offered.

Tam rolled her eyes. "Our embassy is already negotiating for us to have unfettered access to this area for research purposes. As soon as Greg reports in, we'll have men on the way to secure the site, just to be safe. That blast will have drawn attention. Right now, I imagine scientists all over the world are trying to figure out what in the hell happened. We need to clean this place out before there's an international incident."

"So there's no way we could keep it a secret even if we wanted to," Maddock said.

Tam shook her head.

"Like it or not, you've changed the world, boys. Let's just hope it's for the better."

Chapter 51

"We're going to need another keg!" Bones proclaimed as he handed Corey a cup of beer. "That's the last of this one."

Corey frowned at the mound of foam in his blue cup. "That's all I get?"

"I'll check the kitchen. Maddock hasn't re-stocked his fridge, but I think Professor brought a cooler. It's probably Bud Light or something else crappy." Bones wobbled back inside and reappeared with a cheap Styrofoam cooler. "Perfect. A cheap cooler for cheap beer."

"I happen to like Bud Light." Professor sat with his feet propped up on the rail, gazing out at the Gulf. "Besides, I'm not a highly-paid government employee like you."

"You will be if you take Tam's offer." Maddock turned a questioning look at Jade, who shrugged.

"I'm thinking about it, but it's been a long time since I've had bullets flying in my direction. I'm not sure I want to go back."

"Hey, if I can handle it, so can you." Kasey had been out of the hospital for one day, and had foregone the beer due to the painkillers she was taking while she recovered from her wounds, but she'd managed to put away more ribs than Maddock would have thought possible for a woman of her size.

Maddock leaned against the rail and bathed in the warmth of the sun and the sounds of revelry. They'd spent the early part of the afternoon filling in Kasey and Avery on all that had transpired since they'd left for Mauritania. Kasey had bemoaned the injuries that put her out of action, while Avery took some consolation in finally having an adventure of her own to share with the others. Tam had already told them about the discovery of the Templar library, but Maddock and the others listened in rapt attention as if the story were brand new to them. By the time Tam arrived with a box of polo-style shirts embroidered with a Spartan helmet and the words "Myrmidon Squad" over the breast, they'd finished swapping stories. They shared a drink in Sofia's memory, and then let the Dos Equis do its work.

Inside, Greg pounded out an Irish drinking song on his portable keyboard, while Willis, Tam, and Avery sang along. Where a kid from inner-city Detroit had learned an Irish song, Maddock had no idea, but the sound washed over him in a pleasant way and he allowed his mind to drift.

It had been a week since they'd uncovered the Atlantean mother city. Tam had shut down the Dominion's plot to attack New York City before it got off the ground, and even managed to get Krueger back in one piece, if a bit worse for the wear. Meanwhile, the U.S. Government had pulled enough strings, or greased enough palms, to buy time for its researchers to go over the complex with a fine-tooth comb. Working around the clock, they'd removed everything they could—even the remains of the Atlanteans. Soon, they'd reveal their discovery to the rest of the world.

For what felt like the thousandth time, Maddock wondered how people would respond. Although most of the trappings of alien technology and all of the alien remains were gone, the star charts and engravings on the walls remained, as did the Revelation Machine. As expected, the world had taken notice of the massive blast of energy shooting up into the heavens, and the absurd claim by the American and Mauritanian governments that it was part of a joint experiment in solar energy, would soon be put to lie.

He supposed it didn't matter. It was out of his hands now.

"I swear, you think longer and harder than any man I've ever known."

Maddock was surprised to discover that he and Tam were now alone on the deck.

"Long and hard. That's me."

"That's unworthy of you, Maddock."

"You spend enough time around Bones, he starts rubbing off on you." Maddock offered her a seat and then sat down next to her.

"I like your place. If we keep our headquarters here, I guess I'll need to invest in some real-estate myself." She smiled as a pair of seagulls drifted past them, floating on an updraft.

"I'm surprised the squad's staying together now that we've shut down the Dominion."

"We've shut down the Kingdom church, but there's plenty still to do. And that's only here in the States. Or have you forgotten your Heilig Herrschaft friends?"

Maddock frowned. He, in fact, hadn't spared a thought for the German branch of the Dominion.

"On top of that," Tam continued, "there are definitely elements in Italy, and we've got hints of them in a dozen other places. I'll be chasing them down until I'm old and gray. Plus, there's the Trident to investigate. Lord only knows what they're about."

"I'm never going to be free of my obligation to you, am I?"

"Baby, you can leave any time your conscience allows it." Tam paused and ran a finger through the condensation on her cup of beer. "That's not fair of me. You've more than repaid me for the help I gave you. If you want to be free, I won't stand in your way." She stood and moved to the rail, where she perched on the corner and turned her gaze on Maddock. "But I wish you'd stay, and that goes for the rest of your crew. Even Bones. We've got a good team here, and I want you to remain part of it. Not just for what you can do, but because you keep me honest. You challenge me without being insubordinate, and you make me think."

"I thought I just pissed you off."

Tam smiled and raised her beer. "Cheers."

Maddock returned the salute. "I'll think about it."

"That's all I ask." Tam slid down off the rail and gave him a quick hug. "I think somebody else wants to talk to you." She glanced to the doorway where Jade waited. "Tag. You're it."

Jade took up the spot Tam had occupied moments before. She sat there, chewing her lip and not quite meeting Maddock's eye, while Maddock finished his beer and tossed the cup in a half-filled garbage bag at his feet.

"I don't know the right way to say this," Jade began, "so I'm going to dive in. Just don't interrupt me, okay?"

Maddock nodded. He knew how Jade felt about being interrupted and it was never pretty.

"You don't want to spend your life fighting the Dominion. You're more than capable, but that's not your passion. You're a treasure hunter at heart. There's nothing in the world you love more than finding a mystery from the past and solving it. And that's what drives me, too. We're perfect for each other. I love to dive and climb and I love archaeology, maybe more than you do. Yes, we drive each other crazy sometimes, and we even fight, but so what? That's because we're passionate. I'll bet you never fight with Angel."

Maddock was about to correct that misconception when he remembered he'd agreed not to interrupt.

"Let's do it, Maddock. Let's spend the rest of our lives solving mysteries and making discoveries. Someone else can dodge bullets. You've done your time." She lapsed into silence, her eyes boring into his. After a suitable pause, he decided it was safe to talk.

"I can't imagine how Bones would react if I broke up with Angel and brought you on to the crew."

"That's not a reason to stay with someone, and you know it. Besides, didn't Bones just dump your sister? It would be awkward, but we'd get through it. It wouldn't be the first time he and I were at loggerheads."

Maddock didn't have an answer. He couldn't remember ever being so confused.

Jade came and knelt before him. She took his head in her hands and drew his face close to hers. The familiar scent of jasmine was strong in his nostrils and her eyes, deep dark pools, filled his vision.

"I know I've said it before," she whispered, "but it's time you started doing what you want instead of what you should."

She kissed him softly and left him alone with his thoughts.

Epilogue

Angel drove her fist into the heavy bag, relishing the solid feel of a blow well struck. She bobbed, doubling her jabs, digging in hooks, and delivering crushing roundhouses and vicious spin kicks. She poured her anger into her workout, attacking as if it, and not Maddock, had wronged her.

Two days! It had been two days since Maddock, Bones, and the others returned from wherever the hell they'd been off to on their latest mission to save the world. Since then, all she'd gotten from Maddock were a couple of lame text messages. She wondered if Jade had been a part of the mission, but when she'd asked, Bones had pushed her off the phone, and Avery wasn't picking up her phone. She'd taken that as a *yes*.

"Argh!" She slammed her elbow into the bag again and again, imagining Jade's face and then Maddock's. Tears welled in her eyes, and she knew she should take a break, but she was out of control. She continued to slam the bag until rough hands pulled her away.

"What the hell are you doing?" Javier, her striking coach, shouted. "What happened to your composure? Your discipline?" Though now in his sixties, Javier retained the strength and fire that fueled a successful boxing career in his younger days. "You are better than this."

"I know." Angel jerked away and headed for the locker room. "I've got a lot on my mind."

"You've got a fight in one week!" Javier shouted. "Do you think you can clear your head by then, or are we wasting our time?"

Angel stripped her gloves off and gave him the finger with both hands. She didn't bother with the doorknob, but kicked the door in instead. It wasn't until she reached the shower that she let the tears flow. How had she messed things up so badly? She'd carried a torch for Maddock for years, and when she finally got him, she let jealousy get in the way. She deserved to lose him.

She turned the hot water all the way up and waited for it to get warm. One at a time, she removed her ankle braces, trunks, and tank top and flung them all against the wall as hard as she could. None was a satisfactory substitute for a heavy bag or someone's face.

"Need somebody to wash your back?"

"Crap!" Though she still wore compression shorts and a sports bra, she snatched a towel and wrapped herself in it before turning back around. "Maddock! What the hell?"

His eyes, so like the sea on a stormy day, captivated her. She took an involuntary step toward him and then froze. There was something about the way he looked at her that didn't seem quite right. His jaw was set, his posture rigid, and she saw a hint of uncertainty in his eyes that was so unlike him. He smiled, but it was a small, sad thing.

She wanted to run to him, to wrap her arms around him and cheer him up like she'd done so many times before, but she held back. "Why are you here?"

"Because I can't get you to talk to me. Texts don't count, especially the ones you've been sending."

"I suppose that's fair. So what do you want to talk about?" She wasn't sure she wanted to know, but she supposed it was better this way. She steeled herself for the worst.

"I couldn't do this over the phone." Maddock took a deep breath. "I've made some big decisions."

~End~

PRIMITIVE

A Bones Bonebrake Adventure

Prologue
1575- Off the Coast of La Florida

The storm raged. The wind shrieked in a banshee wail. Lightning shredded the slate gray blanket of clouds that hung low over the churning sea. The *San Amaro* pitched and rolled, her heavily laden holds causing her to ride low in the water, the icy waves breaking again and again over her decks.

Miguel de Morales squinted against the chill wind and icy rain. The temperature had dropped precipitously since the storm that had been brewing all day finally broke with the fury of a thousand hells. He clutched the ship's wheel, trying to keep her on a southeasterly course that would take them around the tip of La Florida and back out to the Atlantic.

"Captain, do you want me to take the wheel?" Dominic, his first mate, shouted to be heard above the howling wind. Rain streamed down his face like funeral tears and he staggered to maintain his footing on the tilting deck.

Morales shook his head. "The helm is mine until we get out of this storm." He didn't need to add *if we get out at all.*

"Very well." Dominic turned to look out at the roiling waves. "I've never seen anything like this. Not even out in the ocean."

Morales had to agree. This was, without a doubt, the worst storm at sea he'd ever encountered. He'd already ordered the sails be furled to prevent a broken mast or, worse, the ship capsizing. Now they were swept along by the wind and current, struggling to keep some control over the direction of their ship.

"What kind of storm can carry a ship this size along like a bobbing cork?" Dominic shouted.

Morales had no answer. The truth was, he was deathly afraid, but he could not let it show. He was the captain and, as such, must lead both in word and deed. If he feigned confidence, so might his crew.

The faint sound of cries from the foredeck drifted back to his place at the helm. "See what that's about."

Dominic nodded but before he could take a step, a small voice cried out in the darkness.

"Captain, we see land ahead!" A short, slender young man of a dozen years melted out of the darkness. Eugenio was Morales' page and his nephew. The young man had no business being out on the deck in this storm, but the boy was determined to become an apprentice sailor as soon as he was old enough, and insisted on acting as if he were already a full member of the crew. He turned and pointed forward. "There, off the port bow."

Morales strained to see what his nephew had spotted. The *San Amaro* rose on a swell, and in the next flash of lightning he saw the low-slung silhouette of a *cayo*, one of the small islands formed atop a coral reef that lined the south and west coasts of La Florida.

"We are closer to shore than I thought," Dominic said.

Morales didn't answer. He'd performed quick mental calculations and realized they were headed directly toward the southern tip of the *cayo*. What was more, even if he managed to steer *San Amaro* around the *cayo*, another of the low-lying islands lay just to the south. They had only a small gap through which to safely pass. Of course, he didn't know what lay beyond, but that was a problem for later.

"Tell everyone to get down below!" he called to Eugenio. "There is nothing more they can do here." While the possibility of being run aground on the *cayo* was very real, at least in that situation the crew would stand a chance of surviving such a fate. Should a man be swept overboard, death was a virtual certainty. Even those who were capable swimmers could not remain afloat in this churning, black maelstrom.

Eugenio turned and ran for the bow. He'd barely made it ten paces when the wave struck. A massive wall of water like the hand of Satan reaching up from the depths of Hell reared up on the port side. It swept across the deck, scooped the young man up, and carried him over the starboard rail and into the sea.

"Eugenio!" Morales cried. Brief, irrational flickers of thought flashed through his mind like fireflies. *Turn the boat around. Toss the boy a rope. Go in after him.* They were all absurd, of course. The ship was virtually beyond his control and Eugenio would be dead in a matter of seconds, a minute at most.

Perhaps he should shed a tear for his sister's oldest child, but present circumstances were too dire for such sentiments. He would do his best to keep his crew alive, and if he succeeded, mourn Eugenio at his leisure.

"Get below!" he shouted to Dominic.

"No, Captain. I'll be here to take the wheel if something should happen to you."

Morales gave a single nod. The man spoke sense and there was no time for arguing.

The lightning flashed again, silhouetting the dark fingers of the twin *cayos* that seemed to reach out to grab *San Amaro*. Morales leaned on the wheel, trying to gain even a small measure of control against the force of the storm. He gritted his teeth and strained with every muscle, every last drop of energy. His body, soaked with rain, sweat, and sea water, trembled with the effort. He tasted salt in his mouth, felt the shiver of the cold wind, and wondered if these were the last sensations he would ever experience on this earth.

The shadowy form of the *cayo* loomed directly ahead, seemingly coming closer with each flash of lightning. Dominic hit the deck as they surged forward, carried on the crest of a wave.

Down they came, crashing into the angry sea.

And then they were past the island and its sharp coral reef. Dominic clambered to his feet and let out a whoop of delight. But it wasn't over.

The force of the storm, powerful beyond belief, continued to drive them forward as if by a supernatural force. The ship swept through the small bay and directly toward land.

"This cannot be happening," Morales whispered.

"This storm is the devil's work!" Dominic shouted.

Morales couldn't disagree. Helpless, he watched the shore approach, the thick tree line standing dark and sinister in the stormy night. What would happen when they ran aground?

And then he saw it.

"A river!" A dark channel wound back into the mainland and disappeared from sight. Could they make it?

The surge carried *San Amaro* past the shoreline and up the narrow river that fed into the bay. Morales could not help but marvel at the force required to sweep their galleon upstream against the current. But his wonder did not last. They came to a bend in the river and *San Amaro*, despite his best efforts, did not make the turn.

Morales cried out in rage and dove to the deck as their ship smashed into the forest. The masts snapped with ear-splitting cracks. The sound of splitting wood rang in his ears as the heavy galleon ripped limbs from trees and boards split from the force of repeated collisions as they plunged deeper into the forest.

Morales dared to look up, wondering how far they could possibly go before they broke apart or came to a halt. He raised his head just in time to see a section of mast sweeping toward him. He ducked too late. Pain like hot fire erupted in his skull.

And then all was black.

I told you this was the work of the devil." Dominic scowled out the window at the dense foliage of the swamp into which *San Amaro* had come to rest. "This place is nothing but a haven for foul creatures, both great and small. Biting, stinging, and worse."

"We lived through that storm. That is the work of God." Three days later Morales still felt the effects of the blow to the head he had suffered. He'd spent little time outside of his cabin, just enough to remind the crew that he was still alive and in command. Too much exertion made him feel faint, and it would not do to show weakness in front of a crew that stood on the verge of desperation.

He'd managed to keep the men busy with hunting, gathering, and scouting. They couldn't range far. The storm had turned this swamp into one giant pool of quicksand. Already *San Amaro* was sinking into the soft earth. He prayed the ship would hold together, as she provided their sole protection from the elements.

"What are we going to do, Captain?" Dominic's dull voice struck a note of fatalism. "We're trapped in this quagmire."

"The weather is hale. Eventually, the swamp will become passable and we will make our way to shore. From there we will find our way to an outpost. La Florida is filled with game and fruit. We should have no trouble keeping ourselves fed during the journey."

"That is not what I meant." Dominic turned to face him, his face wan. "There is something out there, many somethings if our scouts are correct. The men have never seen the like before."

"Superstitious nonsense." Morales waved his first mate's comment away. "The men had a great fright, and they are temporarily trapped in a forbidding environment. It is only natural that their minds begin to deceive them."

Dominic hesitated. "Manuel is hardly a superstitious man. He is the oldest and most experience of them all and he says he has seen demons in the swamp."

"All sailors are superstitious, and the fact that he claims to have seen demons proves it. Besides, I seem to recall Manuel insisting he once made love to a mermaid." He would have said more, but shouts from the direction of the crew deck drew his attention. "What is going on out there?"

"I'll see." Dominic hurried out of the cabin and returned ten minutes later with a grave look on his face. "You must come and see this."

"What is it?" The look on his mate's face gave Morales an uneasy feeling.

"You have to see it for yourself."

Morales eased himself up off the bed and paused to let the wave of dizziness pass. Slowly, taking great care to stand up straight, he made his way to the crew deck.

The men were huddled around a sand fire pit they'd made in the center of the deck. The scents of acrid smoke, roasting meat, and coppery blood greeted Morales as he approached the excited men. He lacked the strength to force his way through the crowd, so he merely stood there, leaning against the wall in what he hoped was a casual manner, until the men became aware of his presence. Silence rippled through the group as, one by one, the men spotted the captain. Not one man met his gaze.

"We didn't do it, Captain," one of the younger men, Alonso, muttered. "We came back from patrol and found…that." He pointed at the fire pit.

Summoning all his reserves of energy, Morales made his slow way forward. The sailors parted like the Red Sea to Moses as the captain approached the fire pit, until only one man stood in his path.

"We needed meat," Manuel, the veteran sailor said.

"And what sort of meat have you brought us?" Morales stepped around Manuel and froze. Even stripped of skin, he could recognize human arms and legs roasting in the fire. "Cannibalism!" He drew his sword in a flash and pressed the tip to Manuel's throat. "I'll flay you alive for this. Whose body is this? Who have you killed?"

"You misunderstand," Manuel gasped, his eyes locked on the gleaming blade of Morales' sword. "It's one of the creatures we've been seeing. I thought they were demons, but they're actually some sort of ape. One of them attacked me with a stone club and I ran it through."

"An ape? In La Florida?"

"Someone show him." Manuel said.

One of the crewmen picked something up off the deck and held it up for the captain to see. Morales' jaw and sword arm dropped in unison as his eyes fell on the horrific sight.

"What in God's name is it?" That thing, whatever it was, was no ape.

No one had time to answer, because angry howls coming from outside the ship split the air, echoing down into the crew deck. Something heavy thudded against the ship and Morales flinched. What was happening?

"Manuel. Get up on the main deck and see what's happening."

The sailors exchanged dark looks but no one aside from Manuel made a move. They all waited in tense silence until the sailor returned.

"I can't see anything through the trees, but the sounds are coming from all around." He swallowed hard. "I think it's the…apes… or whatever they are. They have us surrounded."

"How many do you think there are?"

"I can't say for certain. Ten? Twenty?" Manuel began to tremble. "I didn't mean to anger them. I was only defending myself."

"If the situation was reversed, and it was one of our own killed by these…apes, would that matter to you?"

Manuel hung his head.

"It doesn't matter," Morales said. "You had no choice. You couldn't let yourself be killed. We need you." He looked around at his men, all wide-eyed and various shades of pale. "We must be prepared to defend ourselves, should it prove necessary. Dominic, set a guard." The mate nodded.

Morales turned his eyes to the fire pit and the disturbingly human-looking meat that cooked there. "You might as well eat. We're going to need our strength."

He headed for his cabin, unable to watch the men devour their unsavory meal.

"Madre de Dios," he whispered. "The monsters are real."

Chapter 1
Miami, Florida

It was a bar like any other. Loud music and even louder conversation competed to drown out the baseball game showing on the televisions hanging from the walls. Bones selected a table in the corner, ordered up hot wings and a bottle of Dos Equis, and sat back to watch the door. This was his kind of place. The only thing missing, he thought, was the stale smell of cigarette smoke, but that had been absent since banning smoking in public places had become a thing. Bones didn't care for cigarettes, but there was something about the musty aroma that made the atmosphere in this sort of place just right.

He didn't have to wait long. He was just digging into his chicken wings when a slender, dark-haired woman came in through the door. She spotted him immediately, smiled, and made her way across the room. As she passed, several sets of eyes followed her progress. Bones couldn't blame them. The woman moved with confidence and grace. Of course, most of the men were probably admiring the way she filled out her form–fitting clothing. She had just the right amount of curves to balance out her athletic build and she tossed her long, brown hair in just the right way. She was a looker, no doubt.

"Mister Bonebrake, she said, reaching out to shake his hand. "I'm Joanna Slater. You can call me Jo or Slater, whichever you prefer."

"You can call me Bones. I don't answer to anything else unless I'm at a family reunion."

"Fair enough." Slater slid gracefully into her seat and signaled for the waiter, who was already on his way over.

"I would've ordered you a round, but I don't know what you like to drink."

"I'll drink just about anything if someone else is buying." She turned to the waiter. "I'll take one of what he's having, and go ahead and bring us another round."

"You're off to a good start," Bones said, nodding in approval. "So, tell me what I can do for you. I assume it has something to do with your television show." Bones knew that Slater hosted *Expedition Adventure,* a cable television show that focused on ancient mysteries and cryptids—mysterious creatures whose existence had not yet been documented by science. "You're in Florida, so what are we talking here? The Fountain of Youth?"

Slater smiled. "So you're already familiar with my show? I'm flattered."

"I never miss an episode. I'm interested in the subject matter, and you're not nearly as full of crap as some of the other hosts of programs like you're. The guy with the wild hair? Total nutbag." Bones said.

Slater laughed. "Let's not name any names, but I know exactly what you mean." Just then, the waiter arrived with their drinks. "Good service here."

"I thing beautiful women get good service here. He wasn't nearly that fast when I did the ordering."

Slater arched an eyebrow. "Do you really think I'm beautiful or are you just hitting on me?"

"A little bit of both, but business before pleasure." He took a long drink, enjoying the rich flavor and the tangy zing of lime.

Slater took a drink, set her bottle down, and then leveled her gaze at Bones. "I'm investigating the skunk ape."

Bones closed his eyes and shook his head. "Seriously? Dude, I can point you to half a dozen legends that are more worthy of investigation than that thing."

Also known as the swamp ape, Florida Bigfoot, and swampsquatch, among other names, the skunk ape was a primate cryptid reputed to reside in the southeastern United States. Though sightings ranged throughout the South, from North Carolina all the way to Arkansas, the creature was most commonly identified with southern Florida, where nearly all the alleged sightings had occurred.

"You don't think there's at least a story worth investigating? You weren't always such a skeptic." Slater opened a portfolio, drew out a sheet of paper, and slid it across the table. She had printed out a screen capture from an Internet forum. Bones recognized it immediately.

"Look at the date on that post. I made it years ago. I didn't know crap back then."

Slater was undeterred. "You believed it at the time. What changed?"

"I did a little investigating. There's no solid evidence, just some crappy video of drunk college kids in monkey suits and a few misidentifications of black bears."

"There's a lot more than that," Slater said. "I've investigated my share of cryptid reports and some of these witnesses seem reliable to me. They describe the way it looked, sounded, even the way it smelled."

"And if any of them had spent much time in the woods they'd have recognized that smell for what it probably was — a bobcat." He held up a hand, forestalling her next argument. "I've also seen the plaster casts of supposed skunk ape tracks. They're all fake. You've done Bigfoot investigations so you know the telltale signs."

Slater sighed. "I can see you're going to be a hard sell. You are correct. I *do* know the telltale signs of falsified primate tracks, which is why I believe these are genuine." She took out a stack of glossy, 8 x 10 photographs and handed them to Bones. "I haven't had the chance to examine them up close yet, but from what I can tell, they look like the real thing."

Bones could see what she meant. Most of the castings that were made of primate footprints, at least of the cryptozoological kind, were too regular, too even. These were different. They were deeper in some places, reflecting the way a primate's weight distribution shifted as it walked and the way it bore more weight on the big toe than on the others. He couldn't deny he was impressed. What's more, he had, in his time, personally confirmed the existence of a few so-called cryptids, though he kept that information to himself.

"Not bad," he admitted, handing the photographs back to Slater. "Where did you get these?"

"From an investigator who lives south of Sarasota. You know, the area where the Myakka photographs were taken?" Slater smiled, her brown eyes twinkling. She seemed to think she had Bones hooked.

"You mean the anonymous photographs of an orangutan? Even if they're legit, all it proves is someone's pet got loose."

"And if that's what the investigation turns up, that's fine by me. The Everglades is home to plenty of non-native species: exotic birds, escaped pet snakes that grow to giant size, and more. I think our viewers would be fascinated by the idea of an orangutan, or even a troop of them, surviving and maybe even thriving in the Florida swamps."

Bones nodded. He couldn't deny the woman was persuasive but he still wasn't completely buying it. "Why did you reach out to me?" he asked, changing the subject.

"We found you through that message board post. My staff tracked you down and vetted you. There's surprisingly little information about you out there."

"No comment." Bones took a long drink and let Slater continue.

"Anyway, we learned enough about you to determine that you have interest in, and knowledge of, cryptids. Also, nothing we found raised any red flags, meaning you're not a total whack job." She hesitated, blushed, and took a drink. "Also, you would look... impressive on camera."

"So my porn career never came up?" Bones laughed as Slater's eyes went wide and her jaw dropped. "Just kidding." He took another drink just to keep her in suspense, and then smiled. "All right, you've piqued my interest. What's the pay?"

Chapter 2
Sarasota, Florida

The offices of the Sarasota Sun stood on the corner of Ringling Boulevard and South Osprey Avenue in the heart of town. Bones squeezed his Dodge Ram pickup truck into a narrow parking space, cranked up some AC/DC on the stereo, and waited for Slater to arrive. He hadn't been there long when a sharp rap on his tailgate startled him. He glanced in the rearview mirror and saw a man in the all-black uniform of the Sarasota County Sheriff's Department beckoning to him.

Bones rolled down his window and stuck his head out. "What can I do for you, officer?"

"It's deputy, and you can start by shutting off that vehicle and getting your narrow behind out here where I can talk to you." Though his ruddy features and sturdy build didn't scream "inbreeder", the man's southern drawl marked him as a likely member of the long-term native families rather than a more recent transplant from somewhere up north. He was probably a redneck. Bones hated rednecks.

Slowly, he cut the engine, opened the door, and slid out into the tight space between his truck and the vehicle alongside him.

"I don't know how they do things down in Munro County," the deputy said, glancing at Bones' license plate, "but around here, when an officer of the law gives you an order you obey it without..." He halted in midsentence as Bones stepped out from between the vehicles. The deputy was not a small man. He was a shade over six feet tall and solidly built, and probably accustomed to physically intimidating most of the people he encountered, but next to the broad shouldered, six foot five Cherokee, he was a bit on the small side.

"Sorry about the delay," Bones lied, trying to make his smile as friendly as possible, "Deputy Logan," he added after a glance at the man's name tag. He said nothing else. He knew he done nothing wrong so he simply waited for the deputy to explain himself.

"You know why I called you out here?" The deputy had regained some of his fire, but his demeanor was decidedly less pugnacious than it had been a moment before.

"If it's to tell me how freaking hot and humid it is in this town, I've noticed."

The deputy didn't crack a smile. "You mind telling me what you doing sitting here?"

"Listening to music. Good old classic rock. You into that stuff?"

"Excuse me?" The deputy shuffled his feet as if debating whether or not to take a step toward Bones.

"Am I free to go?" Bones knew he probably shouldn't mess with the man, but he didn't appreciate being rousted for no particular reason. "Or am I under arrest?"

"I just want to know what you're doing here. You're from down south, which is a pipeline for the drug trade, and you're sitting here in this parking lot doing nothing."

"He's waiting for me." Slater had arrived. She strolled up to the deputy and flashed an apologetic smile. "He and I have an appointment with someone inside." She inclined her head toward the newspaper office. "I'm running late. Please accept my apology."

The deputy looked like he had just sucked a lemon. He looked from Bones to Slater and then nodded. "All right. Just don't loiter in the parking lot when you're done." He didn't wait for a reply but turned and stalked back to his car, climbed in, and drove away.

When the deputy was gone, Slater turned and frowned at Bones. "Do you always treat people like that?"

Bones shook his head. "Nope, but bullies and rednecks get on my nerves."

"I don't know how many of the former we will encounter but we're likely to meet up with plenty of the latter. Do you think you can keep your attitude in check?"

"You're the boss." Bones looked up and squinted at the late morning sun. "What do you say we blow this appointment off and head over to the Siesta Key Oyster Bar? I hear it's a great place to hang out and pound a few brews."

"When this investigation is finished I'll let you buy me a pitcher, but not until the work is done."

"Bummer. I thought you were a party girl."

Slater rolled her eyes and led the way into the office.

The reporter who greeted them was a weedy, bespectacled man with a rat face and a thatch of yellow hair. He barely glanced at Bones, having eyes only for Slater. Bones couldn't blame the man. She was garbed in a tight tank top, snug fitting khaki shorts, and hiking boots. With her brown hair hanging in a braid down the middle of her back, she was giving off a serious Lara Croft vibe. Bones couldn't deny the look worked for her.

"I'm Gage," the reporter said. "Please follow me." He led them to a tiny cubicle in the far corner of the building, and sat down in front of a cluttered desk lined with bobble head dolls of famous baseball players. When bones and Slater had pulled up chairs and sat down, Gage got down to business.

"I understand you are interested in the skunk ape." He kept his voice low, frequently glancing about as if spies lurked in every corner.

"That's right," Slater said. "I host a television show and we're doing a feature on it. I understand you are the man to speak to on the subject."

The compliment did the trick. Gage relaxed and a smile spread across his face. "I'm a local affairs reporter, so the skunk ape is strictly a hobby. I have, however, done extensive research." He took out an overstuffed accordion folder and handed it to Slater. "This is all of the information I've gathered: newspaper clippings, articles from the web, transcripts of eyewitness reports including interviews I personally conducted, research into possible scientific explanations, and a summary of my conclusions in the back."

"This is great," Slater said. "Is there somewhere we can sit and examine it?"

"These are copies," Gage said. "I only ask that you credit me if you use any of the material in your show."

"You've gone to a lot of trouble. Thank you."

"If it will help you prove that the skunk ape is real, or at least its existence is a real possibility, it will have been more than worth the effort." He looked around again. "I don't mind telling you that people around here give me a hard time about my research."

"I know what you mean," Bones said. "I'm into cryptids, alien visitor theories, and all that kind of stuff. Most people don't get it."

Gage nodded. "Yes, but it's not just that. In general, the locals don't like it when anyone talks about the skunk ape. The transplants from other parts of the country are concerned about our community's image. They think treating the legends seriously makes us look like a bunch of hicks. The families who have lived in the community for generations are afraid Sarasota is going to, I don't know, turn into Roswell, New Mexico. You know, drawing in the oddballs and pseudo-scientists. Sorry," he said, blushing, "but you know what I mean."

Bones and Slater nodded in unison.

"I'm just saying," Gage continued, "don't be surprised if you get a lot of push-back. And be careful where you go and who you talk to."

Chapter 3

Gage snapped his head around as a long shadow ran across his keyboard. He looked up to see a tall man in a sheriff's department uniform standing over him, arms folded.

"How can I help you, Deputy Logan?" He couldn't stand the man. He was a scion, if someone who lived in rundown mobile home on the edge of the swamp could properly bear that title, of a long-time local family. As such, the deputy stuck his nose into everyone's business and had an opinion on how just about everything should be done.

"You had some visitors today." It wasn't a question.

Gage gritted his teeth. Damn Logan and his reticence. "Would you care to explain why you're investigating my activities?"

Gage threw back his head and laughed. "Don't get your panties in a bunch,

Gay," he said, using the high school nickname Logan and his football buddies had slapped onto Gage so many years ago. "I happened to be in the office and saw some unfamiliar faces, and I wondered who they were and what they were up to. I mean, why would outsiders need to meet with a local affairs reporter?"

"I'm afraid that's confidential," Gage said through gritted teeth. He felt his cheeks begin to heat. He hated Logan and despised the way the man could get a reaction out of him with such ease. Sometimes it didn't get better after high school.

Logan smiled and sat down on the corner of Gage's desk. "You got this all wrong. I'm just looking out for my town, same as always. I'm not trying to get on your nerves or anything.

"Well, you have. Same as always."

"Look, you know I care about this town and the people who live in it, even the fellows who are still mad about a wedgie twenty years ago." He grinned. "Truth is, there was an incident outside with that big Indian fellow. It didn't amount to nothing, but something ain't right about him. He's from down south and we know what kind of characters come from there. I ran his plate, so I already know his name." He leaned in and laid a heavy hand on Gage's shoulder. "I'm just asking you, as an old high school buddy, to give me an idea of what the man's up to. No details, nothing personal. Just the big picture."

Gage bit his jaw, holding back a profane retort. He knew Logan would keep pestering him until he got what he wanted.

"By the way," Logan said, letting go of Gage's shoulder and sitting back, "we're starting afternoon rush hour patrols on your street. I'll tell the boys to keep an eye out for your car."

The implication was clear. If Gage played ball, the deputies would leave him alone. If not, he doubtless would be pulled over for some nonexistent violation. Besides, given that Gage's interest in the skunk ape was well-known, he figured Logan had already put two and two together. The deputy was a buffoon but he wasn't a complete idiot. Despising himself for giving in so easily, he sat up and looked Logan in the eye.

"It's nothing serious. They're from one of those pseudo-investigative television shows and they're doing an episode about the skunk ape."

Logan guffawed and slapped his thigh. "So that fellow *is* crazy. I knew he wasn't right, but at least it isn't drugs. I should have known, since the skunk ape is sort of your thing. What did you tell him?"

"Just the usual stuff. Nothing they couldn't find on the internet."

"You didn't tell them it's all a big fake?"

Gage scowled. "You know I don't believe that."

Logan slid down off the desk. "No, you don't, do you? All right, Gay, I'll tell the fellows to let the ace reporter in the yellow Volkswagen pass unmolested."

I'll just bet you will, Gage thought as he watched the deputy walk away. He considered calling Slater to warn her about the meddling deputy, but decided he didn't need to be involved any more deeply than he already was. "I've done my part," he mumbled, "and good luck to you."

Chapter 4

Slater had left her car behind and walked from her hotel to the newspaper office, so she rode along with Bones as they headed to their next appointment. He was pleased to find they shared similar taste in music, though she did request the Black Eyed Peas, which he told her in no uncertain terms was not on his phone. "They can't decide if they are rock or rap, and they suck at both," he explained.

"Just when I was starting to respect your opinion," Slater said, shaking her head.

"So, who is this guy we're paying a visit to?" He asked, struggling to keep his eyes trained on the road and not on Slater's legs.

"Nigel Gambles. He's the cryptozoologist who made the plaster castings of the alleged skunk ape tracks. He lives in a cabin near the entrance to the Myakka River State Park. My crew will meet us there."

Slater's crew turned out to be a two-person team: a short, skinny young woman named Carly, and a round-faced, thickset man named Dave. The two hurried over when Bones and Slater got out of the truck.

"I'm the cameraman," Dave said, unnecessarily holding up his camera, "and Carly is the sound engineer."

"I'm Bones. I don't think I have a title."

"Of course you do. You're the resident expert." Carly grinned and gave him a tiny wink which he returned. She was cute—not Slater-level, but not bad.

"I'm not paying any of you to flirt," Slater said. "Let's go. Mister Gambles is expecting us."

Gambles' cabin stood at the end of a long, winding dirt driveway lined by live oaks and draped by low-hanging Spanish moss. The deep shade did little to dull the Florida heat, but any respite was welcome to Bones, who had ditched his trademark leather jacket but kept his jeans. Shorts weren't his thing unless he was going to the gym or for a run.

Gambles was a trim man with close-cropped hair and friendly eyes. He spoke with a slight accent, but Bones wasn't familiar enough with the various regional forms to say from where in Britain the man hailed. London, perhaps? Gambles invited them in and immediately set to talking about his most recent discovery, but Slater gently interrupted him.

"We really want to hear everything you have to say, but let's get it recorded so you don't have to cover anything twice, okay?"

Gambles agreed, and when Dave and Carly had everything in place, he took up a position in front of a bookcase laden with titles relating to cryptozoology. Slater sat down in a chair facing him and began an Oprah-style interview.

"Can you tell us about the skunk ape?"

Gambles nodded. "The skunk ape is a legendary primate that is believed to inhabit the Everglades and outlying areas, though sightings have been reported all around Florida and in other states in the Southeast. It's known for its elusiveness and its distinctive smell."

He went on to discuss the history of skunk ape sightings in the area, beginning with Native American legends and reports from Spanish explorers, including a harrowing tale of a shipwrecked crew, of whom all but one were killed by the legendary beasts. He then moved along to modern sightings, skirting around the obvious fakes, but providing multiple accounts from ostensibly reliable witnesses, and even sharing a few grainy photographs. Bones had seen and heard it all before, but what Gambles said next surprised him.

"Some people believe that the creature is not an ape, but a primitive human."

Bones almost spoke up, but remembered the camera was rolling, and kept his silence. Slater, however, followed up.

"Primitive humans? Is there any evidence to support this theory?"

"In truth, there's not much evidence to support *any* theory, but I have found what I believe are rudimentary tools and stones that show signs of being worked. What's more, I discovered them in the general area where I recently came across the tracks."

Gambles picked up the briefcase sitting beside his chair, opened it, and took out a palm-sized stone. "This looks like a scraping tool." He held it up for the camera and then handed it to Slater, who examined it with polite interest. "And this one," he continued, taking out a triangular stone, "appears to be for cutting. See how the edges have been chipped away? It's not a regular break. Someone or something has worked it."

The man wasn't wrong. Even from where he stood, Bones could tell that someone had scraped and chipped the rock to give it a sharp edge. Slater seemed to agree, nodding slowly as she looked it over. "But how do we know these aren't artifacts from the Native Americans who once lived in this area?"

"Because I have evidence that at least one item was used quite recently." Gambles took out a smooth, round stone about the size of a tennis ball and a Ziploc bag containing small, gray fragments of some unrecognizable material. "It appears this stone was used to break open freshwater clams."

Slater frowned. "Why would someone smash them instead of just prying them open? It ruins the meat."

"Exactly!" Gambles sat up straighter as he spoke, a triumphant smile playing across his face. "You or I would do just that. But what if you did not have a knife or other implement at your disposal? Or what if you didn't know such things existed? Only a true primitive would use a bludgeoning tool for this sort of work."

Slater adopted a properly interested expression, paused for a few moments to let viewers appreciate the implications, and then continued with the questions.

"Tell us about the other evidence you've recently uncovered."

This was clearly the moment Gambles had been waiting for. He leaned forward, his words coming faster. "I was taking a stroll down by the river and the tracks were just there. My first thought was that someone was winding me up."

"Why would you think that?" Slater asked.

"My neighbors know I'm a cryptozoologist. Truth told, they think I'm a bit of a nutter so I thought one of them might be having some fun at my expense. Then I realized that I was well off my usual route. No one would have any reason to believe I'd have gone so deep into the swamp. If someone wanted to play a joke on me, they'd have planted the tracks somewhere I'd be sure to stumble across them."

"Of course, that doesn't mean the tracks aren't fake—only that they probably weren't intended specifically for you," Slater pointed out. Bones was impressed that she didn't merely accept the man's story at face value. "What makes you believe these tracks are genuine?"

"That's a fair question." Gambles once again reached into his briefcase, this time taking out a set of photographs. He passed most of them to Slater, but kept one which he held up for the benefit of the camera. "I immediately took some photographs with my cellphone, just in case someone or something disturbed the tracks before I could return. I then hurried home to retrieve my camera and my footprint kit. These are the high-resolution images I took. You can see they bear some resemblance to ape footprints, but are also reminiscent of very old tracks found in Africa." He handed the last photograph to Slater.

"Finally, there are the castings I made of the prints." He carefully removed two bubble-wrapped objects from the briefcase, closed the case, and set it on the floor. "The prints do not show the telltale signs of fakery." He went on to describe the same details Slater and Bones had discussed at the bar.

When Gambles finished his analysis of the print castings, Slater asked a final question.

"Do you believe the skunk ape is real and lives in this area?"

Gambles looked directly into the camera and gave a firm nod.

"Absolutely."

Chapter 5

They parked in a gravel lot just inside the Myakka River State Park and hiked from there, following a walking trail south along the river bank until it ended. After that, they relied on Gambles' directions and a topographical map he had provided. Bones had plenty of experience with this sort of thing so they had little trouble making their way to the spot the researcher had described — a place where a rutted dirt road, little used, met the river.

Here, the Myakka River made a sharp bend. A sandy shoal protruded out into it, and a mud bank lay on the other side of the water, rising in a gentle slope up to the dense forest beyond. Birdsong and the gentle rush of the river filled Bones' ears. He could almost forget they were only a few miles from civilization.

"Do you think this is the right spot?" Slater asked, looking around.

"This is definitely it." He pointed to the location on the topographical map where the winding blue ribbon of the Myakka formed a loop. "Here's where we are on the map. It matches perfectly."

"In that case, let's get started." Slater took up a position near the water's edge and waited for Dave and Carly to get their equipment ready. Dave had left his large camera locked in the trunk of his car and was now using a small, handheld video recorder, while Carly opted for a portable digital recorder.

When Dave gave Slater the thumbs-up she recorded a brief segment, introducing this as the spot where Gambles had found the skunk ape tracks and describing the setting. Once the recording was finished, they began a search of the area.

While the others scoured the shoals and the bank on their side of the river, Bones waded across to inspect the opposite side. The water was shallow, little more than ankle–deep, and it felt cool and refreshing on his bare feet. When he was halfway across, he turned and called back to Slater.

"What do you say we let those two keep looking around while you and I do a little skinny dipping?"

"Keep dreaming." Slater didn't even look up from her searching.

"Maybe later then." Bones turned around and froze. Even at a distance of twenty feet or more he could clearly make out a set of long-toed footprints on the mud bank. At first glance they appeared to be the twin of those Gambles had found.

"No way. Hey, Slater, get over here!" He turned and beckoned to her.

"Give it a rest. I'm trying to work here and I don't have time to…"

"I found a track."

"Really?" Slater looked in the direction he pointed and her jaw dropped. "Fantastic! Dave, get over…" She paused and cocked her head to the side. "What's that noise?"

From somewhere in the distance came the low rumble of an engine, growing louder as it drew near. Moments later, a monster truck bounded into view, bouncing on its raised suspension as its oversized tires rolled through the ruts of the overgrown dirt road. Dave and Carly leaped to the side as the truck shot down the bank, fishtailed on the sand, and sped into the water. It roared past Bones, drenching him in cold river water.

Bones cursed and sprang back. He shook the water out of his eyes just in time to see the truck rumble of the mud bank, lose traction, and slide backward.

Right over the footprints.

"Are you freaking kidding me?" he yelled. He stomped toward the truck, but the driver threw the vehicle into reverse and back straight at him, forcing Bones to spring out of the way again. The driver did a donut, churning up a wall of water that wash the mud bank clean and sprayed Bones with another cold, wet wave. The truck shot back across the river toward the old dirt road but skidded to a halt in the sand when Slater ran directly into its path.

"What the hell do you idiots think you are doing?" she screamed. "You almost killed three of my people."

The doors opened and two men stepped out of the truck. The driver was bald with a bushy red beard and a bowling ball body. The passenger was a tall, brown-haired man with a rat tail and several gaps in his teeth.

"You got a problem, girl?" Rat Tail folded his sinewy arms and spat a wad of phlegm on the sand.

Slater didn't give an inch. She stood with her hands on her hips and fire in her eyes, staring daggers up at the taller men. "I just told you what my problem is. Are you deaf or just stupid?"

"I didn't expect no sass from a girl as pretty as you," Rat Tail cackled. "Maybe for Miss Short-haired Lesbian over there." He inclined his head toward Carly, who held out her hands, frowned, and mouthed, *I'm not gay.*

Slater trembled with rage. "We're conducting research here and you morons just screwed it up. I've got half a mind to sue you. I hope your mom's double-wide is worth something, or else we'll have to take your neon beer sign and your NASCAR memorabilia."

"This one's got a mouth on her," Bowling Ball observed. "I think somebody should shut it."

"I can't tell you how much I'd love to see you try." Bones said, stepping up behind the men and giving each a shove in the back. He didn't put much force into the effort — just enough to divert their attention from Slater.

The two men rounded on him in unison but hesitated when their eyes fell on him. Bowling Ball was as broad of shoulder as Bones and Rat Tail nearly as tall, but neither had his combination of height and breadth. This, however, did not stymie them in the least. They exchanged grins.

"Well, it looks like it's going to be a good day after all," bowling ball said. "You see, we came here to drink beer and…"

"I know, I know. Drink some beer and kick some ass and you're almost out of beer. Dude, do you know how old that movie is? Come up with some new material or go back to kissing your boyfriend."

The man frowned, trying to process the insult.

"You know, you talk pretty big for a man who's outnumbered two to one, Indian Boy," Rat Tail said.

"I'm surprised you can count that high," Bones said. "I guess that second grade education was good for something after all."

"And it's not two to one. It'll be two on two." Dave handed his camera to Carly and made to join Bones.

"Thanks, Bro, but it's not your fight. How about you get the girls out of here?"

Dave hesitated. Bones could tell the young cameraman was struggling between a sense of duty and the natural aversion to of violence common in most people. Normal people, that was. But Bones was hardly normal.

"Seriously, dude. You don't need to watch this and neither do they."

Bowling Ball chuckled. "You don't want your little girlfriend to see you get your ass kicked?" he taunted as he and Rat Tail advanced shoulder-to-shoulder.

Bones looked the man in the eye and smiled. "Not exactly."

He lashed out with a vicious sidekick that caught Rat Tail in the gut. Taken by surprise, the tall man folded forward and crumbled to his knees. He knelt there, arms pressed to his stomach, struggling to catch his breath.

Bowling Ball's reaction time was better than that of his friend. He swung a wild haymaker at Bones' head. Bones moved back just enough for the blow to miss his chin by half an inch, and then he drove his fist into the exposed temple of his off-balance opponent. Bowling Ball wobbled backward. Bones followed with a knee to the man's groin, a blow which sent him to the ground, and then a roundhouse kick to his head that turned out his lights.

He turned on Rat Tail, who had regained his feet and was charging at Bones. Rat Tail lowered his head and tried a tackle, but he wasn't strong enough to bring the larger man down. Bones flung him to the ground, jumped onto his back, and caught him in a chokehold. Rat Tail struggled and clawed at Bones' forearm, which was locked around his neck in a Python grip, but his efforts were futile and he soon went limp. Bones let the man fall to the ground.

"He's not dead is he?" Carly asked.

Bones shook his head. "Just unconscious." He strode over to the still idling truck, took the keys from the ignition, and pitched them into the river. He then searched the glove compartment and found a 38 revolver. He emptied the cylinder, tossed the bullets into the water, and put the weapon back where he'd found it.

"Come on," he said to the others. "Let's get out of here before these idiots wake up. If I have to deal with them again I might bruise my knuckles."

Dave chuckled. "That was crazy. You took them out in, like, thirty seconds."

"It only took that long because I decided to choke the dude out." He looked down at Dave. "It's not like the movies. A real fight is short and nasty and somebody almost always gets hurt. That's why you should try to stay out of them if at all possible." He turned and walked back out into the river.

"Where are you going?" Slater asked. "They destroyed the prints."

"Were going to do this old-school. Something left those prints and I'm going to track it down."

Chapter 6

Bones was an experienced tracker and he was able to follow the signs left by the passage of whatever had passed this way with little trouble. The ground was thick with undergrowth, but here and there he spotted a partial footprint, broken branch, or a twig or leaf pressed down into the soft earth. The first couple of times he spotted something, Slater had him point it out and explain it for the benefit of the camera, but after that they moved on as quickly as they could.

The path they followed, if it could be called that, plunged deep into the swampy forest, occasionally bending back in the direction of the river, but generally following a southeasterly course. Bones lost the trail a couple of times and was forced to double back again, but always managed to find it. The farther they went, the quieter their surroundings grew. It was hard to believe they were only a handful of miles from a decent-sized city.

Spirits were high during the first hour or so of their trek. The crew was duly impressed by his tracking skills and never voiced any concerns that he might be steering them on the wrong course. By the second hour, though, their enthusiasm began to wane.

"Is it dangerous here?" Dave asked. "I mean, aside from crazy rednecks?"

"It can be if you're not careful. While we're in the woods, you're not likely to run into anything. I guess there's an outside chance we could stumble across a black bear, but the odds of one of them messing with us are pretty slim. They just want to be left alone. If we do see one, just follow my lead and it'll be cool."

"You said 'while we're in the woods.' What about when we get to the swamp?" Dave smiled as he spoke, but Bones could hear a tremble in his voice.

"Snakes and gators, but just keep your eyes open and you should be fine. And try to stay out of the water. I don't want to have to pull you out of quicksand."

"I hear there are giant pythons in the swamp," Carly said. "People buy them as pets and set them free when they grow too big."

Bones donned his most patient smile. "Tell you what. You guys take a break from worrying and stay close to me. It'll be fine."

"How far are we going to go?" Carly asked, glancing back the way they'd come.

"Until we find something, I guess," Bones said. "Or until the boss tells us it's time to knock off for the day."

"It's still early," Slater said. "Plenty of daylight left."

Carly didn't seem pleased. "Are you sure we'll be able to find our way back?"

"I'm sure *I* can get us back. All I have to do is follow the tracks you three have trampled into the ground. Seriously, it's like an elephant walk back there."

"What if we get separated from you?" Dave chimed in, unabashed by Bones' commentary on his woodcraft.

"Don't." Bones turned away and resumed his trek, but Dave wasn't satisfied.

"No, really. What do we do if we get lost?"

Bones stopped and counted to three before replying. "Seriously? The kind of show you do and you've never spent any time out in the woods?"

"Not in such a small group, and not with a guide who can follow invisible trails through the middle of nowhere. Besides, this place is…"

"…creepy," Carly finished.

Bones shrugged out of his backpack, took out a bottle of water, and took a long drink, buying time for his annoyance to subside. "All right. Listen carefully. If one of you wanders off, head east until you hit the river and then turn right. Follow it until you get back to the park. It's really that simple." He supposed he should explain to them how to determine which way was east. "To know which direction is east, you just…"

"It's cool," Dave said. "Our cell phones have compass apps." His countenance suddenly brightened. "Wait a minute!" He took out his phone and tapped it a few times. "I've got a signal. That means I can use GPS to get back. Looks like there was nothing to worry about."

Bones pressed his lips tightly together until he could speak without cursing. "That's just…awesome." Not trusting himself to say more, he turned on his heel and plunged forward, double-time.

Bones continued to follow the signs left by whatever had passed this way. The occasional partial print kept his spirits up. These were no shoe or boot prints. They were tracks left by large, bare feet. He was finally beginning to consider the possibility that the skunk ape was, in fact, a reality and not a mere legend. Of course, he was predisposed to wish that such things were true, but that didn't change what he saw as he moved through the forest. Tracks were immune to personal bias.

"Do you think we might actually find something?" Carly's tone indicated she wasn't exactly thrilled by the possibility.

"I hope so," Bones said, keeping his eyes on the ground in front of him.

"What if we come across an actual skunk ape?" Dave asked.

"No offense, but as clumsy as you white people are out here in the woods, any woodland creature worth its salt is going to hear you coming a mile away and clear the hell out of the area until we're gone."

"Somebody's snippy today," Slater said.

"Sorry. I get that way when I concentrate. It hurts my brain to think too hard." He grinned at his three companions, hoping to break the ice a little.

"We'll try to be quiet, won't we, guys?" Slater glared at her crew, who nodded in unison.

Bones knew it wouldn't do much good. None of them were practiced at woodcraft, but at least they were making an effort. He supposed he might as well give them some pointers.

"A few things to keep in mind. First of all, don't step on anything that will make noise, like twigs, dry leaves, or loose stones. Try to step where I step."

"Because we're all seven feet tall." Slater gave him a wink.

"Just do your best. Also, try not to brush against anything. That makes unnecessary noise. Ideally, the only thing you'll touch out here is soft earth with the balls of your feet. And try not to talk so much. Got it?"

"It ain't going to help." A new voice rang out from somewhere up ahead, amused, with a touch of youthfulness. A young man, freckled and sandy-haired, stepped out from behind a live oak. He wore overalls with no shirt underneath and carried a .22 rifle. Bones put him at about thirteen years old, give or take a year. "Either you're a woodsman or you ain't." The boy cleared his throat and spat on the ground. "You are," he nodded at Bones, "but they ain't."

"They're trying," Bones said. "You live around here?"

The boy shrugged. "Not real close by, but I spend a lot of time out here."

"What's the gun for?"

"Squirrels or whatever else I might feel like having for dinner."

Bones nodded. He enjoyed squirrel meat from time to time, though he had to go home to North Carolina to get any. "You got a name?"

"Yep." The boy's face cracked into a wide smile and his eyes sparkled. He seemed to think he'd made a great joke.

Rednecks, Bones thought. *I can't even stand the juvenile of the species.* "I'm Bones; this is Slater, Carly, and Dave."

"I'm Jack."

"You said you spend a lot of time in these woods?" Bones asked.

The boy raised his eyebrows. "Is Danica Patrick a race car driver?"

"I have no freaking idea."

"She is and she ain't. She drives a race car but she's a woman so she ain't no race car driver." The boy threw back his head and cackled.

"Youthful misogyny," Slater mumbled, "such a sight to behold in its nascence."

"I actually understood that," Bones said. He turned back to Jack. "We're tracking something," he said. "Something that moves on two feet. You haven't seen anything unusual, have you?"

The boy froze, his eyes suddenly hard and his expression blank. "That ain't a good idea. You should just go on back where you came from."

"Can't do it. You got any idea which way we should go? I'm going to find the trail one way or the other, but it would save me some time if you'd point me in the right direction."

"There's twenty bucks in it for you," Slater said.

Jack spat on the ground again. "Thank you, but I shouldn't take your money. If you're hell-bent on this, you need to turn south and head into the swamp. I don't know if you'll find much of a trail once you get there, but that's the place you should look." He paused and looked away. "I don't never go in there. Nobody does."

"Thanks," Bones said.

"You see them two pines that are leaning together?" Jack pointed deeper into the woods. "You want to walk right under them and that'll put you on the game trail that takes you where you need to go."

"Got it." The kid didn't seem the handshaking type, so Bones made a curt nod and turned the group south. He kept his eyes on the ground, watching for signs to confirm they'd been steered in the right direction.

"You think he knows what he's talking about?" Slater asked as soon as they were out of earshot.

"He seems to know his stuff. Worse case, we retrace our steps and find the trail again." He glanced back over his shoulder. Jack was gone. "He can move in the woods, I'll give him that much."

"There's the two pine trees. The game trail should be right through there."

Dave quickened his pace and moved ahead of Bones and Slater just as they passed beneath the pine arch.

Bones smirked at the cameraman and returned his eyes to the path in front of him. Something wasn't right.

"Stop!" He dove forward and grabbed Dave by the belt just as the ground disappeared between the cameraman's feet.

Dave cried out in alarm, his arms pinwheeling as he slid forward, his fall not fully arrested by Bones' strong grasp.

Slater sprang to Bones' side and grabbed hold of one of Dave's flapping arms. "Hold still," she hissed. Together, she and Bones pulled the young man out of the dark hole that gaped beneath him. Once he was free, he lay back, breathing hard.

What... was... that?" he gasped.

"A Burmese tiger pit," Bones said, staring down at the dark hole that had been only partially uncovered by Dave's fall. "You dig a hole, put sharpened stakes at the bottom, and cover it with twigs, leaves, and dirt. Someone comes along and falls right in." He knelt for a closer look. "This one is deep and there are no stakes at the bottom, just a lot of muck since we're so close to the swamp. It's not a killing pit."

"So what is it for?" Carly asked.

"Trapping. Bones and Slater exchanged a dark look.

"So, was the kid trying to trap us?" she asked.

"I don't know. How about I ask him?" Bones made to rise but Slater put a hand on his arm.

"Don't bother. He's got a head start and you said he moves well in the woods."

"You don't think I can catch that little assclown?"

Slater smiled. "I'm sure you can, but it'll be a waste of time. He'll just say he didn't know the pit was there."

Bones gritted his teeth and gave a single nod. She wasn't wrong. "It could be that the pit is just there to make outsiders feel unwelcome." He sighed. "I guess we go back to where we left Jack and try to pick up the trail again."

"Um, isn't that a footprint down there?" Carly pointed down the barely-visible game trail. In the middle of a patch of soft earth lay a single, perfect print.

Chapter 7

They set to work immediately, their spirits buoyed by the discovery. While Dave filmed, Slater took measurements and photographs, all the while discussing her thoughts regarding the print.

"This print is fourteen inches long," she began. "Not as large as most of the alleged Sasquatch tracks, but certainly large enough to be of interest to us. The toes are elongated, with a pronounced big toe. The depth of the toe prints are not uniform, which is consistent with what we would see with genuine footprints. We don't tend to evenly distribute our weight when we walk, and certain toes dig in deeper than others, just like this print."

She looked up and motioned for Dave to move in closer. "You can also see that the extremely moist earth has preserved portions of the foot's dermal ridges. It requires ideal conditions to preserve these ridges, and the fact that we only see bits of a few here actually adds to the possibility that these prints are genuine. With a forgery, you're likely to see full ridges."

She then set about making a plaster cast of the print. She placed a cardboard ring around the print, leaving extra space at the heel and toe. Next, she took out a small bucket, a package of plaster of paris, and a large bottle of water. She mixed the plaster and water and stirred vigorously, explaining to the camera that plaster of paris begins to set the moment it comes into contact with water, therefore speed is of the essence when casting a print.

After banging her mixing bucket on the ground a few times to remove the bubbles, she carefully filled the track, starting with the toes and working her way down. She bit her lip as she concentrated on the task, something Bones found very attractive. When she was finished, she explained that the time required for the plaster to set varied depending on the dryness of the ground and air. In this damp environment, it would take a good hour before they could safely remove the plaster, though the curing process would continue for a few days as moisture leached out of the cast.

They took an early lunch while they waited for the cast to set. Despite Bones' warnings that they should remain quiet, the crew was unable to contain their excitement. They chatted about their television show, wondering if further discoveries would merit a two-part episode. Bones remained silent, chewing on beef jerky and washing it down with tepid bottled water. When Slater finally proclaimed the casting ready, she covered it in bubble wrap, slid it inside her pack, and they headed farther down the game trail.

The air grew cooler and the vegetation thicker as they proceeded into the swamp. The soft earth beneath their feet gave a little with each step, lending to the feeling of heaviness all around them. The humid air seemed to weigh them down, and the moss-draped, leaning trees only added to the sensation as they trudged on through a maze of greens, grays, and browns. Little by little, the shafts of sunlight grew fewer and farther between until it felt like twilight lay upon them, though it was barely midday.

As they moved deeper, the musky, earthy aroma of the swamp gradually gave way to a dank smell. The scent grew stronger and Bones stopped, crinkled his nose, and sniffed the air.

"What is that odor?" Slater's face twisted into a 'Tom Cruise just invited me to church' grimace.

The scent grew stronger, pungent. Bones shook his head.

"I don't know. It's not a... get down!"

Bones dove at the television crew, corralling Slater and Carly in his arms and plowing into Dave. The three fell in a heap to the damp earth as a rock the size of Bones' fist smashed into a pine tree where Slater had stood only moments before.

Something flashed through the undergrowth—a shadow of indiscernible shape, moving from left to right.

"Get behind that log." Bones pointed to the remains of a fallen tree a few yards away. Slater and her team scrambled for cover while Bones rolled to his left as another stone flew. It struck the earth with a wet slap like a fist hitting flesh, bounced once, and splashed into the stagnant pool behind him. What living thing could throw that hard? Either Craig Kimbrel had gotten lost on the way to Spring Training or Bones was up against something entirely new. He drew the Recon knife sheathed at his side and crawled in the direction where he'd seen the shadow moments before.

What a time to leave my Glock in the truck.

A third stone came flying out from the dense foliage. This one smashed into a rotten stump a foot from Bones' outstretched hand and stuck there. Bones snatched it free, rolled to his feet, and hurled it with all his might at the spot from which it had come. He heard a slap as it struck something soft, then a deep, chuffing sound that might have been pain or surprise.

Bones let out a roar of defiance and dashed toward the spot, zigzagging here and there to hopefully avoid getting crushed by another flying projectile. Up ahead, the underbrush rustled, the sound fading away as their assailant fled.

Bones chased it a good fifty yards before slowing to a trot and finally stopping. He hadn't seen a thing. Whatever it was that attacked them had simply melted into the forest. It was gone. He supposed he should go back and check on Slater and the others, and then search for any tracks it might have left behind. He sheathed his knife and mopped his brow.

And cried out in surprise when the earth gave way beneath his feet.

Chapter 8

Bones had only a moment to realize he was falling before his feet hit something solid. Or somewhat solid, because whatever it was his feet struck held for only a moment before it gave way and he plunged deeper into darkness. He landed hard on his feet, pain shooting along his legs. A splintering crack split the air, and for a moment he thought he'd broken a leg, but he realized it was the sound of breaking wood. He rubbed his leg and the pain soon diminished, leaving behind only a dull ache at the base of his spine.

He looked around, the dim light shining through the hole where he'd fallen illuminating a circle about ten feet wide. He stood on a wooden floor, its boards covered in a thin film of dust. Beneath his feet, a series of cracks spread outward, and he took a step back just in case more open space lay beneath him. He took out his Maglite and shone it around.

"No freaking way."

He was inside a ship, probably sixteenth-century by the looks of the cannon his light fell upon. Sweeping his beam back and forth, he saw several more cannons, some still in their tracks, others lying on the floor. This was the gun deck of a large sailing vessel.

He took a cautious step, and then another. The deck supported his weight. Encouraged, he began to explore. The fact that the deck still hadn't given way beneath all these cannons gave him hope that the structure was sturdy enough to bear the weight of one big Cherokee. He supposed he would find out.

At the far end of the deck, a ladder led up to an open trapdoor. He tested the first rung, found it sturdy, and climbed up. He emerged in another sizeable space. All around, the moldering remains of hammocks dangled from the beams that supported the main deck. Lying on the floor amidst the accumulated silt from centuries of leakage lay the skeletal remains of the crew. Some held pitted swords or rusted knives, while others lay curled in fetal balls.

The ceiling up above was blackened with soot. Apparently the crew had made their homes here after being run aground, but how in the hell had a ship gotten this far inland?

"Must have been one hell of a storm," he mumbled.

He shone his beam down to the far end of the deck, where a door hung haphazardly on broken hinges. That would be the officers' quarters. He picked his way across the deck, reluctant to tread on the remains of the deceased. As he skirted the bones of the soldier nearest him, he did a double-take.

The back of the man's skull had been smashed in, leaving a baseball-sized hole.

"What in the..." He knelt for a closer look. The back of the skull had been caved in. Fragments of bone lay inside the hollow of the cranium. Whatever had delivered the fatal blow had compressed the skull. The victim had died lying face-down, and as the soft tissue decayed, the fragments of bone had simply fallen into the hollow space once occupied by the brain.

"Sorry, bro," he said. "That's a nasty way to die."

He stood and resumed his careful trek. It quickly became apparent that every member of the crew had died in the same way—their skulls crushed by a blunt object. He shivered, the fresh memory of flying stones strong in his mind. This ship had been here for a good four hundred years. Could there possibly be a connection? He didn't want to believe it, but he knew better than to dismiss the improbable.

"Bones!" Slater's voice called out from somewhere above. "Where are you?"

"I'm down here!" he called. "But don't come any closer. The ground's not stable."

He moved toward the hole through which he'd initially tumbled, but before he could get there, a pair of hiking boots slid through the opening, followed by trim, deeply tanned legs. Slater!

"Hold on a second. There's a hole right below your feet and you'll fall through if you're not careful. Believe me, I know from experience." He hurried over to her, stumbling over the rib cage of a dead sailor. He reached up, grabbed Slater by the waist, and guided her down to the deck.

Her eyes grew wide as she took in their surroundings. "Where are we?" she marveled.

"Inside an old sailing ship. I'm not sure what kind, exactly."

Slater rounded on him, hands on hips. "A sailing ship? Underground? Are you winding me up?"

"Nope. Check it out." He swept his light across the deck and over the remains of the crew.

"Wow!" Slater gaped, her voice soft and her eyes wide. "How do you think it got here?"

"The only theory I can come up with is one hell of a hurricane carried them inland and they got stuck here when the water receded. It looks like they decided to live inside the ship. You can see they had fires in here." He pointed to the blackened beams up above. "Over time, it sank down into the swamp and the mud preserved it."

"This is amazing. I don't care if it has nothing to do with the skunk ape, it's still going to make for an amazing story." She turned and barked out a sharp command. "Dave! Carly! Get down here. I want this all on video."

"Be careful," Bones called. "Let me help..."

With a hollow crack, the main deck above them gave way again and Dave came crashing down on top of them. Bones managed to wrap his arms around the young cameraman and partially slow his fall, but Dave still landed hard on his backside. Bones froze, wondering if the force of the fall would cause the deck to give way again. This time, it held.

Carly followed, more carefully than her colleague. Bones sat her down lightly on her feet, and she stared in wide-eyed amazement at the macabre scene.

"This is like a haunted house," she breathed.

"More like the Pirates of the Caribbean ride," Dave said, climbing to his feet. "You know, the part where they all turn into skeletons?"

"How about we focus on doing our jobs?" Slater rode over her crew's conversation. "You can talk about amusement parks later."

"Sorry." Dave's gaze dropped to the floor, but he brightened almost immediately. "This is going to be some of the best footage we've ever gotten." He made a slow circuit of the deck, recording every inch of the bizarre scene. He lingered over the fire pit in the center. The crew had piled a thick layer of sand on the deck to prevent the wood from catching fire. Chunks of bone poked out of the silt and ash. When Slater was satisfied that they had enough footage, they moved on to the officers' quarters.

Inside, they found more skeletal remains, all with smashed skulls.

"It's strange," Slater observed, "that some are lying curled up in a ball. Do you think they just curled up and waited to be killed?"

"Possibly," Bones said, "if they were frightened enough. We don't know how long they holed up here. It's possible some of the crew were already dead from malnutrition or disease, and whoever did this to them bashed their heads in just to make sure."

"Scary stuff." Slater led her crew around the cabin, commenting on the few artifacts she found lying about. The officers' personal effects were few, but among them were knives, rings, Spanish coins, and crumbling bibles. "It's clearly a Spanish galleon. And the fact that things like this remain," she held up a fat gold coin, "proves that we are the first to find it. If its presence had been discovered before, it's almost a guaranteed the valuables would be long gone."

They ascended to the captain's cabin, which lay just above the officer's quarters. The door was wedged closed, and Bones finally resorted to main force to smash open the top half of the decaying wood.

"Looks like somebody blocked themselves in," he said, looking down at the footlocker and small chest that pushed up against the base of the door. But that wasn't the only thing that had held the door fast. Here, the intrusion of years of silt was clearly evident, as a thick layer of dried black muck caked the floor. Bones climbed over the remaining portion of the door and then helped the others in.

The captain lay on his bed, his empty eye sockets gazing up at the ceiling. Dave moved in with the camera while Slater resumed her hosting duties.

"At first glance it looks like the captain also had his skull smashed." She pointed his shattered left temple. "But that isn't the case. If you look at the other side of his head, you'll see a smaller hole. And then there's this." She pointed an object half-buried in the muck. "It's a pistol, lying roughly where it would have fallen from limp, dead fingers."

"So he barred himself inside and took his own life." Dave said the words slowly as if trying to convince himself of their veracity.

"Whatever was outside that door was more terrible than the prospect of suicide." Slater turned to Bones. "Can you tell u anything about the gun?"

"It's a matchlock." Bones knelt beside the weapon but left it untouched. "The matchcord, which was just a burning wick, went here," he pointed to the hammer. "It came down and hit the flash pan which ignited the gunpowder. That's about all I can tell you."

"Does the type of gun give us any clue as to the age of the wreck?"

Bones nodded. "By the early 1600s, matchlocks were out and flintlocks were in, so this is probably sixteenth century."

An inspection of the captain's truck revealed little of interest, but the small chest was filled with coins, many of them silver and gold. Bones resisted the urge to pocket a few. Maybe when the camera was no longer rolling.

"Where to next?" Slater asked.

"All the way to the bottom," Bones said.

"What do you expect to find down there?"

He grinned. "The cargo hold."

Chapter 9

Of all the various parts of the galleon, the cargo hold had suffered the most from the intrusion of soil and water. Toward the bow of the ship, where the hull had been split when the ship ran aground, the dark mud lay knee deep, descending to a depth of several inches toward the stern. But it did little to cover the crates that lay all around, scattered and broken by the wreck so many centuries ago.

Carly clapped her hands and Dave let out a whoop of triumph as the beam of Bones' light glinted off blocks of gold and silver bullion and scattered gold chains. Here and there, jewels sparkled like stars in the dark mire. Trying but failing to suppress a grin, Slater discussed the find at length for the benefit of the camera.

"Why so many gold chains?" Dave asked.

Bones knew the answer to this one. "Tax evasion. The Spanish crown placed a tariff on precious metals, but jewelry was exempt. Europeans didn't do much in the way of fine craftsmanship in the New World, but they could make rough chains and rings like what you see here, and that was good enough to get around the law."

"Why not make it all into jewelry?" Carly asked.

"I guess it's one of those things you can only take so far. The crown would look past a certain amount of circumvention as long as it made its share from the transportation of New World treasure, but if it got out of hand, they'd have eliminated the exemption. Nobody wanted to be the one that killed the goose that laid the golden egg."

"Speaking of eggs," Slater said. "Have you seen anything like this before?" She pointed to a small crate filled with dirt, straw, and mud-encrusted egg-shaped objects caked in mud.

"I've never seen one up close, but I've read about them." He knelt beside the crate, took out his recon knife, and scraped away the mud that encased one of the strange objects. "These are bezoars."

"You're kidding," Dave and Carly said in unison.

"What are bezoars?" Slater asked.

"Somebody hasn't read Harry Potter," Dave said.

"A bezoar is a sort of stone formed from material found in the digestive tracts of two-stomached animals. Given that this is a Spanish ship, we're probably looking at stones from a llama or alpaca since those were found in the major Spanish colonies. And, just like in Harry Potter, people believed a bezoar could absorb poison. Somebody rich enough to buy one would dip it in his cup of wine before drinking it, just in case his enemies had tried to poison his cup."

"I take it they were pretty valuable?" Slater asked.

"Very, and not just because of their supposed properties. Being able to afford one was a status symbol. People would have them carved, mounted in a gold setting, and would wear them as jewelry."

"Did they work?" Dave asked. "I mean, do they really absorb poison?"

Bones chuckled. "Tell you what. When we get back to town, we'll put rat poison in a beer, drop one of these in, and you can drink it. Sound good?'"

Dave laughed. "I'll pass." With that pronouncement, he cut the camera. "Does this mean we get, I don't know, salvage rights or whatever?"

They all looked at Bones, the only treasure hunter in the group.

"If we were three leagues out in the gulf waters or three miles off the Atlantic coast, things would be a lot simpler. On land it's a little more complicated."

"But, finders keepers, right?" Carly asked.

"Not necessarily. A lot depends on who owns the property. If we're still inside the state park, Florida treasure trove law says that whatever we find belongs to the state."

"That's not fair," Dave said.

"That's just the way it is. The good news is, the common practice here is for the government to keep everything of historical value and give the finder seventy-five percent of the intrinsic value of the find."

"What if we're on private property?" Carly asked.

"It probably goes to the owner. There would definitely be a legal battle."

"And since we're doing this under the auspices of the television show, there are other ownership angles to consider," Slater said. "This could be a mess."

"So, maybe we're rich and maybe we're not," Dave said. "It's Schrödinger's treasure."

"I'm sure this will sort itself out eventually," Slater said. "But for now, I say we cover up the holes where you two klutzes fell through, and get back to the job at hand."

Bones nodded. "I want to track down whatever it was that attacked us."

"You think it was a 'what' and not a 'who'?" Carly asked.

Bones merely nodded.

They made their way back up to the crew deck and Bones helped Slater and then Carly climb out. Both were light and agile so it required little effort. Getting himself and Dave out would take a little more creativity.

"Let's gather all the boards and crates we can. We'll pile them up and climb out that way. If that doesn't work, we'll have to dig up enough dirt to make a mound that we can get up on, and hope it isn't so heavy that it causes the floor beneath it to collapse."

He waited for Dave to reply, but no response was forthcoming. The young cameraman knelt by the old fire pit, poking at the bones that lay there. "Take a look at this." He held up a thick leg bone—a femur if Bones didn't miss his guess. "It's got cuts all over it—signs that the meat was butchered. We've seen this before on the show. Cannibalism."

Frowning, Bones took the femur from Dave and gave it a close look. "Maybe not cannibalism."

"But the cuts..."

"You're not wrong about the cuts," he said. "But I don't think this is human. At least not human as we know it."

Chapter 10

"Let me get this straight," Slater said. "You think this is a bone from a primitive form of hominid?" Slater asked. She turned it over in her hands, scrutinizing every inch of its length. Nearby, Dave kept the camera rolling.

"That's what it looks like to me. Of course, it's the actual bone, not just a fossil, which means it's not very old."

"About as old as the ship?" Dave offered.

Slater nodded. "Mister Gambles did mention the theory that the skunk ape is, in fact, a form of human ancestor. Between the footprint and this bone, we should be able to put that theory to the test." She looked directly into the camera, her jaw set and her gaze hard. "We now have to consider the possibility that the stranded crew sealed their own fate by killing and eating one of the local population of whatever hominid the skunk ape might be."

Quieted by dark thoughts, the group retraced its steps and waited while Bones searched around until he picked up the trail of the fleeing attacker. He found no clean prints, but more than enough sign to guide them in the proper direction. As they followed the tracks, the dank swamp began to dry up, and eventually gave way to forest.

It was early afternoon when Bones spotted something in the distance. "Somebody lives here."

Up ahead, in a clearing, stood an old mobile home. A sagging, makeshift covered porch sheltered the front door. A rusted out 1968 Camaro stood on blocks amidst a patch of tall weeds. Behind the trailer, a decrepit outbuilding hugged the tree line where the forest resumed. To the south, a rutted dirt road wended its way into the dense foliage and vanished from sight.

"I wonder who lives here," Slater whispered.

"I don't know, but it's a shame they didn't restore that Camaro. What a waste." Bones moved a few steps forward, still scanning the ground. "The tracks end here. Whatever we're chasing, it must have skirted the clearing."

"We'll see if anyone's home," Slater said. "They might have seen something."

"Does anyone have dueling banjos playing in their head right now, or is it just me?" Dave whispered.

Carly giggled. "I'll bet you'd be good at squealing like a pig."

Dave raised his middle finger and kept the camera rolling.

Tension cramped Bones' shoulders as they strode across the intervening space between the tree line and the old mobile home. His eyes flitted about, keeping alert for danger. Slater noticed.

"What's wrong?" she asked. "It's just a house."

"I've got a feeling that, any second now, some dude in a John Deere had is going to jump out of the woods with a shotgun and start blazing away."

Slater chuckled but Dave missed a step and Carly's eyes grew wide.

"I was kidding about the banjos. Do you really think it's dangerous?" Dave asked.

"Probably not. It's just that redneckish places like this put me on edge."

The sagging steps up to the front porch creaked under Bones' weight, but they supported him. Just as he reached the porch, Slater grabbed him by the arm.

"Let me. I don't look as intimidating as you." She winked and slipped past Bones, who backtracked down the steps and moved to stand beside Dave.

Slater knocked, a dull sound in the quiet clearing

No answer.

She knocked again.

"I don't think anyone's home." A note of hopefulness rang in Dave's voice. "Let's just keep following the trail."

"Third time's a charm." Slater raised her fist to knock again, but the door flew open and an angry face poked out.

"This is private property. What are you doing here?" The speaker was a white-haired woman no more than five feet tall. Sharp blue eyes gleamed in the midst of a craggy, sun-weathered face.

Slater introduced herself and explained that they were a television crew investigating local legends. If she thought her fringe Hollywood credentials would earn her any points with this woman she was mistaken.

"I don't know no legends. You need to get on out of here before I call the sheriff."

"I done called him, Granny." A familiar figure appeared in the doorway. "He'll be here any second." Jack froze when his eyes fell on Slater. "What are *you* doing here?"

"You know these people, Jack?" The old lady rounded on her grandson, eyes flashing.

"He tried to kill us," Bones said.

"I didn't!" Jack took a step back, but his grandmother snatched him up by the hair and hauled him out on the porch with surprising strength.

"Were you messing around with that rifle again? I done told you, it's for hunting and nothing else. If you can't be responsible I'm going to take it back from you." She glanced at Bones. "I'm surprised the big fellow didn't take it away from you and whoop your butt with it."

Bones chuckled. He decided he liked this lady.

"Actually, he directed us right into a tiger trap," Slater said.

Jack held up his hands. "I didn't know that pit was there. Ow!"

His grandmother gave his hair a twist and then let him go. "You knew. Now go fetch me a switch." As Jack trudged down the steps and toward the woods, head hung low, she folded her arms and addressed the group. "I hope none of you have any objection to some old-fashioned discipline. The boy ain't got no mama and someone's got to teach him to mind."

"I've lost count of how many times I've been switched in my life," Bones said. "Even now I think my grandfather would whip me if I stepped out of line."

"If you don't mind my asking," Slater began, "have you seen anything unusual here?"

"Unusual?"

"Something attacked us in the woods. We followed its trail which led us here. I'm just wondering if you saw who or what did it."

The old woman shook her head. "Just me and Jack here."

"The pit we fell into, what's it for?" Slater asked.

The sound of a car approaching drew their attention and they turned to see a police cruiser rolling slowly up the driveway.

"You'll have to ask him." That ended the conversation as she stepped back inside and closed the door.

The car rolled to a stop and Deputy Logan stepped out and closed the door behind him. He pocketed his sunglasses and took a seat on the hood of his car.

"You mind telling me what you're doing here?"

"We're doing an investigation," Slater said, coming down off the steps. "Something attacked us in the park. We followed its tracks which led here."

"What do you mean by attacked?" Logan' kept his tone level but something in his eyes suggested alarm, even fear.

"Something was chunking rocks the size of my fist at us," Bones said. "Any one of them could have killed us."

"Don't you mean 'someone'? There's not an animal around here that can throw a rock, unless the gators have figured out how to slap them with their tails."

Slater cocked her head. "Isn't there?"

"What's that supposed to mean?" Logan snapped.

"Deputy," Bones began, "there's not a man alive who could throw a rock that big with the velocity those things were flying at our heads."

"We also found footprints." Dave piped up.

Slater turned a hard eye on her cameraman, whose face reddened.

"I'm going to have to ask you to turn over anything you collected," Logan said. "Video, photographs, cameras, cell phones and especially any castings you made of tracks."

"On whose authority?" Bones resisted the urge to get in the deputy's face.

"The county sheriff's department, that's who." Logan rested his hand on his sidearm. "Don't make me arrest you."

Slater moved between Bones and the deputy. "First of all, you and I both know the law. You don't have probable cause to confiscate our property. Second, everything is already uploaded to the cloud—photos, video, audio, all of it. Taking our belongings would be a waste of your time and ours, and it would make unwanted publicity for your department."

Logan' jaw worked as he stared past Slater at Bones.

"We might as well tell them, Pa." Jack's voice broke the tension as the young man slunk out of the woods, trailing a long, thin stick behind him.

"He's your kid?" Bones asked.

Logan nodded.

"Tell us what?" Slater asked.

"Nothing." Logan said.

"Just go on and tell them." Jack's grandmother called out the front window. "You knew it couldn't last forever."

Logan' shoulders sagged. "I suppose you're going to find out sooner or later.

Turn your camera on and let's get this over with." He flashed a rueful grin at Slater, who stared at him with a bemused expression. "You ain't figured it out yet?"

Slater shook her head.

"The skunk ape is just a myth. We've been faking it."

Chapter 11

Slater appeared poleaxed. After a few seconds of stunned silence, she found her voice.

"Who is *we?*"

"Me and my boy." Logan pointed at Jack. "But before we go any further I have to ask that you don't show my face or give my name. Don't show my house, either. I want that in writing."

Slater sighed. "Fair enough. I'll even change your voice. Hold on a minute." She dug a few papers out of her backpack and she and Logan took a few minutes to complete them. When all was ready, Logan led them to the outbuilding behind the trailer.

"This is where we keep our stuff." He unlocked a metal gun cabinet and took out a pair of false feet. They were made of some sort of rubber, and were intricately detailed. All the lines and creases one would expect to see in an actual foot were carefully rendered. The big toe was angled downward so it would bite deeper into the earth than would the other toes. Velcro straps extended from the rubber on either side. Presumably the wearer could strap them to whatever shoes he had on.

Bones took one and looked it over. It was about the size of the other prints they'd seen. It certainly could have been the source.

"What about weight distribution?" Slater asked. "If someone with an average sized foot wears this, the weight will be too close to the center."

"It's got a metal frame inside. It distributes the weight but still has a little flexibility."

"Where'd you get it?" Slater asked.

"I had it made, but that's all I'll say. I don't want to bring anyone else into this"

Slater nodded. "But why go to all this trouble? What did you hope to gain?"

Logan smiled sheepishly. "I could tell you it was about publicity for the town, or to keep a favorite legend alive, but it wouldn't be true. The fact is, I did it because I thought it was funny. It started out as a way of messing with campers. Rattle the bushes, leave a couple of tracks, and get out of there." He chuckled. "I got bored with it, but then I started hearing about a fellow named Gambles who was taking the skunk ape thing way too seriously, so I decided to mess with him too."

"We met him," Slater said. "He'll be disappointed when he hears."

"Don't bet on it. He's one of them true believers. If he doesn't want to hear it, it'll just bounce right off of him." Logan looked down and scuffed the dirt with his booted toe. "Anyway, I started feeling bad about that, but then Jack got curious, so I let him do it sometimes."

"What about the strong smell?" Carly chimed in.

"Bobcat urine, fox urine, whatever the store's got in stock."

"You can buy that stuff?" Dave asked.

"People use it to keep pests away," Bones said. He handed the false foot to Slater, turned, and took a few steps back to the shed door where he leaned against the frame and gazed out at the late afternoon sun. Jack was approaching, walking gingerly and grimacing. Apparently his grandmother had put the switch to use. The sight of the boy sparked something in his mind.

"So, which one of you attacked us today?"

"It must have been the boy." Logan spat on the ground. "I'm sorry about that. I'm sure he wasn't trying to hurt you; he just has bad aim with that sling of his."

"A slingshot couldn't throw a stone as large as the ones that were hurled at us, much less achieve the velocity," Slater said. "Those things were really flying. It's no exaggeration to say we could have been killed."

"Not a slingshot. A sling. You know, like David and Goliath. They're easy to make."

"I don't see how Jack could have done it," Bone said, turning back to face Logan. "This place is a long way from where we ran into him. How could he have come here, gotten what he needed, and then gotten back in time to attack us?"

"It's not a long way if you know where you're going." Jack had arrived at the shed. "I knew I'd left some prints in the swamp, so I sent you that way and then ran home to get my stuff. I figured I'd track you down and mess with you a little. I flung a few rocks at you and then took the long way home. You were following my trail which is why it took you so long."

"We *did* take a lunch break while you made the casting of the footprint," Bones said to Slater.

"But still..." Slater began.

Bones shook his head. "It doesn't matter. We've solved the mystery. I'm sorry it's not what you hoped it would be but at least you have your answer."

"I'll give you all a ride back to your car," Logan said.

"That won't be necessary." Slater bit off each word. "We can find our way back."

"Please. I've done you wrong. At least let me do this one little thing for you." He grinned at Bones. "I also won't make an issue of the incident that happened at the river." He waited for Bones to fill the silence, but Bones knew that trick and held his tongue. "Two boys said a great big Indian jumped them and stole their truck keys. Had to pay a locksmith to cut a new set."

"It serves them right," Carly said.

Logan laughed. "I'm sure it does. Them two are no good. I've been dealing with them for years. Now, how about that ride?"

Chapter 12

The alarm on his phone vibrated. Bones rolled out of bed and shut it off. Midnight. Time to move.

While the Keurig in his hotel room brewed a cup of strong coffee, he bathed his face in cold water and then trickled a little down the back of his neck for good measure. He'd reluctantly declined Slater's invitation to dinner in favor of an early bedtime, knowing he'd be up in the middle of the night. When his coffee was ready, he grabbed it along with his keys, strapped on his Recon knife, pocketed his

MagLite, and headed out the door.

The soupy Florida air enveloped him in its damp arms the moment he stepped out the door. No matter how long he lived, he doubted he'd ever grow accustomed to the humidity. He spared one longing thought for the lumpy mattress and blasting air conditioning in his room, and then closed the door behind him.

"I knew you didn't buy his story," said a soft voice.

Bones grinned. "I wondered why you gave up so easily." He turned to see Slater sitting on the floor, back against the door of her room. Smiling, she cracked open a can of energy drink.

"I didn't want to pound this baby until I was sure you were coming out."

"Drink it slow. Those things will mess you up." Bones winced at the sound of his words. Caution was Maddock's thing, not his.

"Understood. Help me up?" She reached out a hand and Bones hauled her to her feet. "So, what's the plan?"

"Here, I'll show you." He took out his phone and called up the map he'd studied earlier. "'Logan' house is here, near the bend in the Myakka River. This area here is pure swamp—it's a no-man's land all the way to the spot where I estimate the sunken galleon sits, and well beyond. I think it's worth checking out. We'll park down the road from Logan' house and try and find the trail."

Forty minutes later, Bones pulled his truck off to the side of the rutted dirt road that led to Logan' home. He pulled it into the woods out of sight of the main road and cut the engine.

"Do you want to wait here while I see if I can pick up the trail?" he asked Slater.

"Not a chance. You'll go on without me and I'll be left sitting here looking like an idiot." She reached into her backpack and took out a small handheld video recorder.

"No cameras," Bones said.

"What are you talking about?"

"This isn't for the show. This is about satisfying my own curiosity." He saw the hard look in her eyes. "If you bring a camera, I'll just slip off into the woods and leave you wandering til morning."

Slater looked like she might take that as a challenge, but then her shoulders sagged and she returned the camera to its bag. "You're an ass, you know that?"

"I know. My sister reminds me every chance she gets."

Slater cocked her head. "You have a sister? What's she like?"

"Pretty like you; abrasive personality like me." While Slater chewed on that, he reached into the glove box and took out his Glock. He checked the magazine and then slipped the holster onto his belt.

"You're not thinking about shooting Logan, are you?"

"I'm not thinking of shooting anybody. I just want to have the option in case we're forced to defend ourselves. Come on. We're wasting time."

Using only the moonlight to illuminate his path, he led the way into the woods. A few minutes later, the mobile home loomed in the distance. A single light glowed from somewhere inside, but otherwise all was dark and quiet.

"Do you need my flashlight?" Slater whispered.

"I've got it covered." He took out his MagLite, into which he'd slipped a red lens, and turned it on. "White light would draw too much attention and would screw up my night vision. This way we're unlikely to be spotted."

"You're smarter than you look."

"And you're not," he replied with a wink.

"Point for your side."

Bones carefully searched the area behind the outbuilding where Logan had shown them the false feet earlier that day. Finally, he came across a partial print, and then another.

"We've got a trail," he whispered.

"That took a long time. Think we'll be back in time for breakfast?"

"I always tell a lady to plan on being out all night. This time is no different." He winked, though he was sure she couldn't see it in the dark. "If we're lucky, the tracks follow that trail up ahead." He pointed to a game trail that wound off into the forest.

They hurried along, and Bones was encouraged to find enough tracks and sign to keep them moving at a steady clip. Whatever had passed this way, it had been in a hurry. Here and there he picked up shoe prints the size of a youth or a small man. Jack had been this way.

The path curved around to the southeast, bending back toward the swamp. The air grew dank and the ground sloppy.

"Do you think we're headed back toward the old ship?" Slater asked.

Bones shook his head. "Wrong direction. I think..." He froze. A powerful stench wafted through the night air. "Get down." He put his hand on Slater's shoulder and forced her down into a crouch.

"Do you see something?"

"Not yet. I caught a whiff of something so I'm playing it safe. I don't want any big rocks flying at our heads." He waited, looking and listening, but nothing seemed to be about. "I guess we follow our noses." He turned out his MagLite, drew his Glock, and began to move forward.

"Don't use your gun on them," Slater pleaded.

"Not unless it's in defense of our lives. I generally don't relish killing. There have been a few people I didn't mind taking out, but they all deserved it."

"If you say so."

The trail soon disappeared, giving way to soggy earth that squelched with each step, threatening to suck the boots off of their feet. Slater let out a small gasp of surprise as she suddenly found herself ankle-deep in muck.

"So gross." She grimaced as she slowly worked her foot out of the mire. "We won't be able to go much farther, I don't think."

"Don't be so sure. There are stepping stones up ahead." The faint slivers of moonlight cast a thin, silver glow on a line of flat stones in the midst of the swamp.

"Where do you think it goes?" Slater asked.

Bones took a deep breath. "Only one way to find out."

Chapter 13

Bones took the steps with painstaking care, trying hard to make no sound as he crept forward. The stepping stones led them on a curving path through the black water, bending around ancient oak and cypress and beneath gray curtains of

Spanish moss, until the way suddenly opened up and Bones froze.

Before them lay an island in the middle of the swamp. Dotted with huge oak trees, their overlapping branches forming a roof-like canopy, the place was well hidden, even from above. The odor he now associated with the skunk ape hung heavy in the air.

"Should we go closer?" Slater whispered.

"Let's wait a minute." He turned out his light and allowed his eyes to fully adjust to the darkness.

The largest oak at the center of the island was hollowed out at the base, cave-like. As he watched, he saw something move there. Slater grabbed his wrist and squeezed. She saw it too.

Something emerged from the darkness out into the moonlight. Its shape was vaguely human, with cords of muscles knotting its broad shoulders, short neck, and powerful arms and legs. A thatch of thick hair hung down to its shoulders, but otherwise it had little more body hair than an adult *homo sapiens*. Its brow jutted out in a prominent ridge, shading eyes that were mere pools of black in the dim light.

"Oh my God." Slater's faint voice scarcely reached his ear. "It really is a primitive human. But what kind is it? *Neanderthal? Cro Magnon?* Something else?"

"I don't know. It's not exactly my area of expertise."

Slater continued to grip his wrist. "But humans didn't come to the Americas until late in history. They were Paleo-Indians, not primitive hominids."

"I guess that theory needs revising. Trust me, it's far from the strangest thing I've ever learned."

Bones continued to gaze at the creature, mesmerized by its presence, by its very reality. The thing walked hunched over, sometimes scurrying on all fours, other times loping along on two legs as it moved back and forth along the waterline. Finally it picked up a long, pointed stick, and returned to the edge of the water. A faint sliver of silver light shone on its face, and Bones finally got a good look at it.

"I think it's young. No facial hair, not a lot of body hair either."

It squatted there, its prominent jaw working as it gazed intently at the water. Slowly it raised the sharpened stick.

"What's it doing?" Slater asked.

In a flash, it brought the stick down, and drew it back to reveal a skewered fish flopping at the end.

"Fishing." Bones grinned and turned toward Slater. "What are you doing?"

Slater held her phone up, recording video of the scene.

"I have to." She snatched the phone in close to her body and took a step back. "This is too incredible to just ignore. I can't pretend... whoa!" She stepped backward into the water, her arms flailing as she struggled to regain her balance, and her phone went flying. Bones managed to catch her before she fell. "My phone!" she cried.

Before Bones could tell her to forget the phone, the creature on the island let out a low, guttural cry.

"It heard you. Look out!" They ducked. A moment later, one of the now-familiar stones flew through the air and smacked into a cypress tree.

"Sorry," Slater whispered.

"Let's get out of here. Stay low."

Slater turned but before she could take a step another stone splashed into the water inches from her feet.

Bones drew his Glock. He didn't want to do this, but he was not going to let them die here. He took aim as the creature reached back to throw again. If it forced his hand…

"Bones, wait!" Slater grabbed the barrel of the Glock and tried to force it down. "Look over there." She nodded toward the hollowed-out tree.

Another creature emerged, this one clearly an older female. She held an infant to her breast. She grunted something that must have been language, because the young male dropped the stones he was holding and scurried away.

A few moments later, another creature appeared, this one an older male. He was huge—much broader and more muscular than the young male. The footprints they had found must have been his.

He reached the female's side and put an arm around her. The intimacy…the humanness of the moment took Bones' breath away. He holstered his pistol and rose to his feet. The two creatures met his gaze, and he thought he saw sadness and resignation there.

"Do you think there are any more?" Slater whispered.

"I don't see any." Bones was surprised to hear a catch in his voice. Was this the last, tiny remnant, of a primitive people who'd called this swamp home?

"Let's just leave them alone." Slater said. She took his hand, and they turned and retraced their steps out of the swamp.

Chapter 14

Logan was seated on the tailgate of Bones' truck when they finally reached the dirt road. He was dressed in street clothes and carried no weapon that Bones could see. He and Bones exchanged a long, level stare. Finally, Logan broke the silence.

"How was your hike?"

"A complete waste of time. Nothing but mud out there."

Logan folded his arms and looked up at the sky. "Did you happen to take any pictures or videos of all that nothing?"

Bones shook his head. "Not a thing."

Logan nodded. "How about we quit dancing around each other and just tell the truth?"

"We found them," Slater said, "but we're not going to do anything about it. We don't have any photos or video and we're not going to tell anyone what we saw. As far as we're concerned, the mystery ended when we found out that an unnamed local faked the tracks. That's how the episode of our show is going to play out, anyway."

"Thank you. I mean it." He slid down off the tailgate, walked over, and shook hands with Bones and Slater.

"So, what's the real story?" Bones asked.

"My family's lived on this land for more than a hundred years, and we've known about the skunk apes pretty much the whole time. We've been protecting them, trying to keep people from finding out the real story. It wasn't that hard until Sarasota really started to grow. We still don't get too many folks coming into this neck of the woods, but it happens."

"What's the deal with the fake footprints?" Bones asked. "Seems like that would just draw the kind of attention you don't want."

"We've never made any footprints. Matter of fact, we try to wipe out all we find. That's one of the reasons Jack wanders so far afield. The skunk apes range wide sometimes and we do our best to cover their tracks. The false feet and such, that's stuff I had made in case anyone came snooping around." He flashed them a grin. "If somebody got too close to the truth, I figured I'd tell them me and Jack had faked the whole thing."

"We saw shoeprints leading toward their island," Bones said. "Do you have any interaction with them?"

"Not really. We keep an eye out for them, take them food. Fruit and the like. But we keep our distance."

"Did your family ever consider bringing in someone who could protect them?" Slater asked. "University researchers or a government agency?"

Logan barked a laugh. "Protect? Hell, no. They'd take them away for study. If they really were just a breed of ape that didn't belong here, an exotic species of orangutan or something, that might be one thing, but primitive humans? There's no way the government would pass up a chance to study their genetics and such. They wouldn't leave them out here in the swamp where anyone and anything could get to them."

Bones nodded thoughtfully and scratched his chin. He could think of all kinds of scenarios in which the so-called skunk apes would be in danger if their presence were made known. "You're right. If word got out that they were here, the government would almost have to take them into custody for their own protection. There are too many people who would want to get their hands on them: zoos, private corporations, government groups. Heck, if somebody was violently anti-evolution they might be tempted to come out here and erase the possible evidence."

"I didn't think of any of that," Slater admitted.

"I'm a cynic. I always look on the dark side."

Logan breathed a sigh. "I don't think it's going to matter for much longer. There's only four of them left, and they've been breeding from the same family tree for a couple of generations. The young male had a mate, but a gator got ahold of her. I tried to get to her so I could help her, give her first aid, but they wouldn't let me come close. She bled out." He shook his head slowly, staring at the ground. "I don't know if the baby is male or female. Even if it's a girl and she lives long enough to bear children, it won't matter in the long run. It's almost over for them."

"It's not a breeding population," Slater said. "I understand why you're doing this, but it really seems like a missed opportunity to study a primitive human population."

"We've got years of notes, pictures, and videos our family's taken," Logan said. "We aren't scientists, but somebody will be able to make something of what we've learned when the time comes."

"And when will that be?" Bones asked.

"Whenever the last one dies. Whether it's me, Jack, or Jack's children, the body will go to the Florida Museum of Natural History for study. They can take their DNA and stuff after that. Until then, I say let them be."

Bones and Slater exchanged a long look.

"Agreed," Bones said. "Sorry for trespassing. We just had to know the truth."

"Don't mention it. Sorry you and I got off on the wrong foot."

They bade Logan goodbye and drove back to the hotel in reflective silence. It was a shame, in a way. Mystery solved, and he couldn't tell anyone.

Chapter 15

A gentle breeze blew in off the Gulf of Mexico, carrying with it a hint of salt. Bones squeezed a slice of lime into his bottle of Dos Equis and sat back to watch the traffic moving up and down Ocean Boulevard on Siesta Key. A few stray vehicles cruised the street, slowing to check out the girls in shorts and bikini tops walking along the thoroughfare. Bicycles and a few Segways zipped along. From his perch on the blue painted deck of the Siesta Key Oyster bar, it seemed to him a perfect day at the beach.

"I freaking love Siesta Key," Bones said as he winked at a tall redhead who grinned shyly up at him as he passed. "I might move here some day when I'm too old to handle Key West."

"I just wish it wasn't so hot." Dave frowned up at the yellow Landshark umbrella above their table as if offended by the insufficiency of the shade it provided.

"It's Florida. The beach. If you're hot, take off your shirt," Bones said. "That's how it's done down here."

"Please leave your shirt on," Carly said. She took a sip of her margarita and gazed into the distance.

"What's up with you, chick? Didn't get enough sleep last night?"

"I'm just disappointed. When we talked to Gambles, I let myself get excited. I was so sure we were going to find something definite about the skunk ape. Instead we uncovered a hoax."

Bones nodded but didn't comment. He and Slater had decided not to let the others in on their discovery of the previous night.

"Sometimes that's the way things go," Slater said. "In fact, that's usually how it goes. You should know that by now."

"I do," she said. "I just thought this time would be different."

"It'll still make for an interesting episode." Dave absently ran his finger through the beads of condensation on his bottle of Budweiser. "Usually, shows like ours find a few lame-ass clues, exaggerate them, and end the episode without anything definitive. At least we got to the bottom of the mystery. That's something." He closed his eyes and rubbed the bottle against the back of his neck. "Ah! That feels good."

"Seriously, dude, it's not that hot." Bones shook his head and took another drink.

"And there's the pirate ship," Dave said. "Depending on how much footage we use from it, we could make the episode a two-parter. Heck, we could go back and investigate the ship even more. That would make a great episode."

"Speaking of the ship," Slater said, "I've done some checking. The good news is, it's on public land."

Carly's eyes lit up. "So that means the state might give us a cut?"

"The state might give *the show* a cut." Slater let the statement hang in the humid air while she finished off her IPA and motioned for another one. "I made a few calls this morning. Nothing's final, but everyone I spoke to said the producers claim ownership of all discoveries."

They all fell silent, contemplating this bit of news.

"Damn," Dave finally said. "I was this close to being rich." He held his thumb and forefinger an inch apart.

"I just wanted to get LASIK," Carly said glumly. "I'm sick of these contacts."

Bones decided the time had come to spill the beans.

"I can't make you rich, but I think you'll be able to afford your eye surgery."

Triple frowns bored into him, and he dismissed them with a laugh and a wave. "Check this out." He reached under the table and hefted the backpack he'd worn the previous day. It made a heavy thump when he sat it down, causing the others to flinch. "I don't need to tell you, this is just between us." He unzipped the pack just enough for them to see what lay inside—four gold bars and a handful of Spanish coins.

"You stole that stuff?" Dave's whispered question conveyed a heap of admiration and no criticism.

"I snagged it before we left the cargo hold. The way I see it, it doesn't really belong to anyone. There's still a whole mess of treasure for the government and your producers to fight over, millions upon millions worth, and they'll never know this little bit was gone."

"I have to say I'm surprised and a little uncomfortable," Slater said.

"I get that. I had a misspent youth, and even though I've been straight for a long time, I sometimes stray off the path. You guys can't tell me you couldn't use a little cash."

"I could." Slater spoke deliberately. "But what am I going to do with coins and a gold bar? I can't put them in the bank, or even let anyone know I have them."

"Relax. I've been a treasure hunter since I left the service. I know a guy. Hell, I know several guys."

That broke the tension.

"Cheers!" Dave proclaimed, raising his bottle. They all clinked glasses and laughed.

"Drink up," Bones said. "Next round is on me."

~**End**~

About the Author

David Wood is the author of the Dane Maddock Adventures and several other titles. Under his David Debord pen name he is the author of The Absent Gods fantasy series. When not writing, he co-hosts the Authorcast podcast. He and his family live in Santa Fe, New Mexico. Visit him online at www.davidwoodweb.com.

Made in the USA
Coppell, TX
18 May 2020